Henry M Lyman

Artificial Anaesthesia and Anaesthetics

Henry M Lyman

Artificial Anaesthesia and Anaesthetics

ISBN/EAN: 9783337418939

Printed in Europe, USA, Canada, Australia, Japan

Cover: Foto ©Andreas Hilbeck / pixelio.de

More available books at **www.hansebooks.com**

ARTIFICIAL ANÆSTHESIA

AND

ANÆSTHETICS

BY

HENRY M. LYMAN, A.M., M.D.,

Professor of Physiology and of Diseases of the Nervous System, in Rush Medical College, Chicago, Ill., and
Professor of Theory and Practice of Medicine, in The Woman's Medical College, Chicago, Ill.

NEW YORK
WILLIAM WOOD & COMPANY
27 GREAT JONES STREET
1881

Trow's
Printing and Bookbinding Company
201-213 *East 12th Street*
New York

PREFACE.

Into the following pages I have endeavored to distil all the excellences of the writers who have investigated the subject of Artificial Anæsthesia. The practised expert will, therefore, everywhere recognize the quality of Perrin, of Snow, of Simpson, of Sansom, of Anstie, of Turnbull, of Kappeler, and of Rottenstein. To this fine ethereal essence I would fain have added something of substantial value, but the unyielding limits of the time within which my endeavors were necessarily restricted would permit no such gratification. For the consequent inequality and insufficiency of a work performed without access to any library of importance, I must ask the forbearance of a generous profession.

To my eminent colleague, Moses Gunn, Professor of Surgery in Rush Medical College, to the members of the surgical staff of the Cook County Hospital, and to my laboratory assistant, Mr. Edward P. Davis, my thanks are due for much practical assistance in the prosecution of these studies.

HENRY M. LYMAN.

Chicago, Ill., May 10, 1881.

CONTENTS.

ARTIFICIAL ANÆSTHESIA

AND

ANÆSTHETICS.

HISTORY OF ANÆSTHESIA.

From the earliest ages of antiquity man has continually sought for the means of relief from pain. The most ancient record of the race introduces the hero of the flood plunged in a deep and scandalous sleep, under the influence of wine which he had prepared. At the siege of Troy the Grecian surgeons were skilled in the art of assuaging the pains of injured men by the application of alcohol and carbonic acid to their wounds. Thus the venerable Nestor came to the relief of the wounded Machaon with a medicated poultice composed of cheese, onions, and meal, mixed with the wine of Pramnos. Other agents, still more potent, were known to the wise men and women of Egypt, and by them were transmitted to their friends in other lands. Some preparation of opium or of Indian hemp, it may have been, with which, after the ten years' siege was ended, beautiful Helen, once more in her lawful home, coming "out of the sweet-smelling, lofty-roofed chamber," drove away sad memories from the minds of her husband and his friends, by making them drink of wine into which she cast a drug chosen from the "cunning and excellent" stock presented to her by the Egyptian princess Polydamna. Most potent drug this same nepenthe must have been, for we are told (Odyss., iv. 220 *et seq.*), that it delivered men from grief and wrath, and caused oblivion of every ill.

It is said (Casp. Hoffmann : De Thorace, lib. ii., cap. xxix., Francof., 1627, in fol., p. 77) that among the ancient Assyrians the pain of circumcision was prevented by compression of the veins in the neck during the time of operation. This was doubtless an ancient discovery of the possibility of producing temporary unconsciousness by pressure upon the carotid arteries and pneumogastric nerves, to which attention has been again directed in modern times.

The Chinese, also, in those remote ages, had learned the anæsthetic properties of an urticaceous plant which was probably related to the Indian hemp, if it was not that plant itself. They used the drug for the purpose of blunting the sensibility of patients who were subjected to the operation of acupuncture.

Throughout the East, from time immemorial, the virtues of opium and of Indian hemp have been known. The fertile plains of India then nurtured the soporiferous poppy—perhaps less abundantly than they do under the stimulus of British rule ; and the praises of *bhang* were everywhere whispered among the neophytes in the mystic crew of astrologers, soothsayers, poets, and story-tellers who filled so large a place in oriental life.

Among the Egyptians the stupefying effects of carbonic acid gas were probably known. Pliny and Dioscorides describe a mineral brought from Memphis, which, when pulverized and moistened with sour wine, possessed the power of rendering insensible of pain those wounded parts of the body to which the mixture was applied. Could this have been a calcareous carbonate, some kind of marble, which thus yielded carbonic acid gas when moistened with an acid ?

But, of all the drugs that were known as anæsthetics by the ancients, mandragora seems to have kept the first place. Apuleius and Dioscorides particularly mention its power to produce insensibility and a loss of consciousness lasting for several hours. It was used for this purpose by the surgeons who flourished at the commencement of the Christian era, and its reputation continued until comparatively modern times. For anæsthetic use mandragora was infused in wine, and the liquor thus prepared was known to the Greeks by the name of *morion*. Apuleius states that half an ounce of this preparation would render a person insensible even to the pain of an amputation. Dioscorides taught that the sleep thus produced might continue four hours or more ; hence, no doubt, various legends which were by Shakespeare woven into the network of the story of Juliet. The "wine mingled with myrrh" (Mark xv. 23) which was offered, according to the custom of the kind-hearted Jewish women of that day, to Jesus on the cross, but which he refused to drink, was unquestionably this same mandragora wine ; for it was a common practice with pitying souls to furnish this pain-defying drug to those who were were about to suffer the horrors of crucifixion.

The earliest reference to anæsthesia by inhalation is contained in the works of Herodotus, who relates that the Scythians were accustomed to produce intoxication by inhaling the vapors of a certain kind of hemp. This was probably something closely allied to *bhang* or *hasheesh*. The Scythian practice may have been the origin of the method of anæsthetic inhalation which was in vogue with Theodoric, a celebrated surgeon of the school of Bologna, who was at the height of his reputation when Dante was writing the Inferno. The Italian surgeon taught the ancient art—transmitted from generation to generation, and by him learned from Hugo de Lucca—of preparing a soporific inhalant for the use of patients who were about to undergo operation. The method consisted in causing the patient to breathe the vapors that were given off from a sponge moistened with warm water, after it had been thoroughly steeped in a decoction of opium, deadly nightshade, hyoscyamus, mandragora, hemlock, ivy, and lettuce. Sponges thus medicated were to be dried in the sunshine, and stored for use as occasion might require. After the conclusion of an operation the patient was aroused by inhalations of vinegar applied with a fresh sponge to the nostrils. If this expedient failed, the juices of rue might be poured into the ears of the too somnolent victim. Traces of this last mode of medication may be found in the play of Hamlet.

The heroic use of these powerful narcotics gradually diminished as the superstitions of the middle ages and the arts of the sorcerer fell into disrepute after the days of the Reformation of the Church in Germany. Works on demonomania and the art of magic still recorded the soporific effects of mandragora; and even in the earlier part of the last century, Augustus, king of Poland, so famous for his strength and for his gallantry, underwent amputation while insensible from the use of a narcotic drug; but when Sassard, a Parisian surgeon, wrote, in 1781, recommending the administration of a narcotic before capital operations, he appears to have had in view the diminution of shock, rather than any prospect of abolition of pain.

A curious passage in an old volume on natural magic, composed by Jean-Baptiste Pesta, describes the preparation and administration of certain volatile substances, of which the effects appear to have closely simulated the effects of ether. "These substances," wrote the author, "were converted into an essence which had to be kept in leaden vessels, hermetically sealed, to prevent the escape of its volatile part. Without such precaution the remedy lost all its virtues. When required for use, the cork was removed, and the flask was applied to the nostrils of the patient, who inhaled the volatile essence till his senses became, as it were, locked up in a citadel, and buried in a sleep so profound that only by the greatest violence could he be aroused. After awaking from such sleep there was no uneasiness in the head, nor any recollection of what had taken place." In a little volume by the celebrated Albertus Magnus (Liber de mirabilis mundi, 1555)—the learned professor of philosophy at Cologne, afterward member of the Faculty of the University of Paris, finally archbishop of Ratisbon, and teacher of the famous Thomas d'Aquinas (A.D. 1193—1280)— is given a formula for the preparation of a liquid, which he called *aqua ardens*. This "fire-water" was obtained by distillation from a mixture of red wine, quick-lime, common salt, tartar, and green figs. Such a process would undoubtedly yield a very highly concentrated alcohol, perhaps charged with a certain trace of ether, which, when applied to the nostrils, might have sufficed to produce anæsthesia, very much as it may now be produced by the inhalation of an impure sulphuric ether.

As the knowledge of physicians increased, the hardihood of their experiments with anæsthetic drugs diminished. Probably a certain number of the patients, who are said to have slept three or four days under the effects of narcotics, did actually fail to awaken at the expected time. At any rate, the practice seems to have fallen out of use; and at the close of the eighteenth century we find civilized surgeons limiting their efforts to the moderate use of opiates, with recourse in certain cases to the effects of intoxication with brandy. Refrigeration of the tissues with freezing mixtures, and the phenomena of hypnotism, were occasionally employed for the relief of pain. An English surgeon, named James Moore, published, in 1784, a tract entitled "A Method of Preventing or Diminishing Pain in Several Operations of Surgery." The method consisted in the application of pressure, by means of properly adjusted clamps, to the trunks of the principal nerves leading to the members upon which operation was to be performed. The obvious disadvantages of such a method were, however, so great that, after a number of trials by various surgeons in England and in France, it passed into oblivion.

The very tardy progress thus far noted toward the possession of a really satisfactory method of producing artificial anæsthesia was evidently owing to the rudimentary condition of chemical science. The great advance in this department of knowledge which was effected by the labors of Scheele, Lavoisier, and Priestley, during the latter half of the last century, could not fail to increase the acquaintance of mankind with numerous agents potent to modify the functions of the animal economy. As the properties of newly discovered gases were studied, the hope arose that among them might be found something valuable in the treatment of pulmonary disease. In the year 1798, in the little village of Clifton, near Bristol, in England, was founded a *Pneumatic Institution*, for the treatment of various diseases by inhalation of certain of the newly discovered gases. The originator of this scheme was Dr. Thomas Beddoes, a man of great natural ability and extensive acquirements, who, born in 1760, graduated in medicine at Oxford, studied chemistry with Lavoisier, and then lectured on chemistry at Oxford until the year 1792, when his sympathies with the French revolutionists led to his removal from the university. His attention had been at an early period of his life directed to the treatment of consumption, and he now devoted his leisure to the work of establishing an institution in which this disease might be treated by a *pneumatic method*. Through the liberality of the celebrated potter, Josiah Wedgwood, he was at length enabled to realize his design; but the practical results in the treatment of disease were by no means equal to his sanguine anticipations. But the final outcome of the institution was of the utmost importance to mankind, for it gave to the world nitrous oxide gas and Sir Humphry Davy. Requiring an assistant in the laboratory of his institution, Dr. Beddoes made the acquaintance of a young medical student, who, though only nineteen years old, had already alarmed his friends by the violence of the explosions which he had produced in the garret where he pursued the study of chemistry. Assuming the charge of the new laboratory, young Davy immediately launched out upon that brilliant career which made his name one of the most famous in the annals of science. It was but a few months before he made the discovery of the intoxicating effects of nitrous oxide gas (April 9, 1799). Had his remarkable ability been less, the full knowledge of its anæsthetic properties might possibly have long antedated its final consummation; but in 1801 he was transferred from the humble sphere of a provincial hospital to the vastly wider field of scientific research that was opened by the foundation of the Royal Institution, in London, where his time was henceforth occupied with the work of original discovery, without any special reference to the medical and therapeutical relations of such work. The possibilities of the subject, however, did not escape his notice. He had succeeded by its use in calming the pain that was caused by the eruption of a wisdom tooth, while experimenting at Clifton, and he recorded his opinion in the following words: "As nitrous oxide, in its extensive operation, seems capable of destroying physical pain, it may probably be used with advantage in surgical operations in which no great effusion of blood takes place." The essay which contained this most suggestive sentence was widely read, but no one seemed inclined to pursue the investigation to its legitimate conclusion. His experiments were repeated all over the world, though with varying results, owing to the difficulties which then attended the purification and administration of the gas. The rubber bags which are now so invaluable to the chemist were then unknown, and experimenters were obliged to content themselves with the use of quantities of the gas so insignificant that an exhilarating effect was usually the only result of its inhalation. Sometimes, however, an inordinately susceptible individual would become insensible, or perhaps would be convulsed, during the act of inhalation, so that cautious physicians were not disposed to look with favor upon the use of the gas. As nitrous oxide thus seemed destined to be remembered only as one of the curiosities of the chemist, the properties of sulphuric ether became gradually known in an empirical way among young druggists and medical students. Employed by Dr. Pearson, of Birmingham, in 1785, as a means of relief for spasmodic asthma, it was, no doubt, one of the substances of which the trial had suggested to Dr. Beddoes the idea of the Pneumatic Institution at Clifton. Dr. Warren, of Boston, made use of inhalations of ether, in the treatment of the later stages of consumption, as long ago as the year 1805. In 1818 the *Journal of Science and the Arts*, published at the Royal Institution, in London, contained the following anonymous paragraph—since usually attributed to Faraday: "When the vapor of ether mixed with common air is inhaled, it produces effects very similar to those occasioned by nitrous oxide. . . . It is necessary to use caution in making experiments of this kind. By the imprudent inspiration of ether a gentleman was thrown into a very lethargic state, which continued with occasional periods of intermission for more than thirty hours, and a great depression of spirits; for many days the pulse was so much lowered that considerable fears were entertained for his life." Here, again, certain unfortunate accidents were doubtless the cause of the indifference to the properties of ether which continued to prevail among the members of the surgical profession for still another quarter of a century. The delightful exhilaration produced by inhalation of its vapor led to the increasing use of ether in an unprofessional way by young people, in various parts of the world, when they desired a respirable deliriant without the disreputable associations which attach themselves to the use of alcoholic drinks. The physiologists also learned, by experiments on the lower animals, to know something of the profoundly stupefying energy of ether. Orfila, R. C. Brodie, and Giacomini, had all recorded observations of this character before the year 1839. In the second edition of his work "On Poisons," 1836, p. 804, Christison related the case of a young man who had been rendered completely insensible by the vapors of ether; and there was also a dismal tradition of some drug-clerk or shop-boy who had fallen a victim to the stupefying vapors which escaped from an accidentally broken bottle of the liquid.

Occasional disasters like these, however, did not deter thoughtless young people from exhilarating themselves by inhalation of the seductive vapor. In the year 1839, a party of boys, in Anderson, S. C., were thus amusing themselves, when in their excited mood they seized a negro boy, who was watching the antics of his betters, and by main force compelled him to inhale the ether from a handkerchief which was held over his mouth and nose. At first his struggles only added to the amusement of his captors, but soon they ceased—the boy was unconscious, motionless, stertorous, evidently dying. But after an hour of consternation on the part of the spectators, he revived and was no worse for his alarming experience. Three years after this occurrence one of the actors in this affair, a young man named Wilhite, entered the office of Dr. W. C. Long, a physician who was then practising in the town of Jefferson, Jackson County, Ga. The worthy doctor and his pupils were in the habit of diversifying more serious occupations by the inhalation of ether, and during the course of this amusement he often observed that while thus excited he was quite insensible to the effects of the blows and bruises which were sustained in this condition. Young Wilhite's account of his experience with the negro boy, who had been unconscious for an hour without injury, added courage to his meditations, and in March, 1842, he persuaded a patient, from whose neck he was about to remove a tumor, to inhale ether, of which he had previously become very fond, until quite insensible. The operation was then performed without pain, and recovery followed without any accident. This great event was thus simply recorded by Dr. Long in his ledger:

"James Venable, 1842. Ether and excising tumor, $2.00."

Three months later, another tumor was removed by the doctor, under similar circumstances, from the same patient. Three other patients were operated upon with equal success, during the years 1842 and 1843 ; but, as the region of country in which he lived was then, before the days of railways and telegraphs, so far removed from contact with the great world, the wonderful discovery remained unknown beyond the circle of the immediate neighborhood until long after the properties of ether had been fully investigated elsewhere.

In like manner, during the year 1839, a young student of chemistry, in the city of Rochester, N. Y., William E. Clarke by name, now a veteran physician in Chicago, was in the habit of entertaining his companions with inhalations of ether. Among the participants in these frolics was another young man, named William T. G. Morton, who afterward became a dentist. At the Berkshire Medical College, during the winter of 1841–42, Clarke diligently propagated this convivial method among his fellow-students. Emboldened by these experiences, in January, 1842, having returned to Rochester, he administered ether, from a towel, to a young woman named Hobbie, and one of her teeth was then extracted without pain by a dentist named Elijah Pope.

The next step on the pathway of experiment was taken in Hartford, Conn., in December, 1844. A Dr. Colton, an itinerant lecturer on chemistry, undertook to divert the citizens of that venerable town by an exhibition of the properties of "laughing-gas." An ingenious dentist, named Horace Wells, was present, and made note of the fact that one of the men, who had fallen and had considerably bruised himself while under the influence of the gas, was quite oblivious of the fact of pain during the period of inhalation. Here was the very thing for which he had so often longed—an agent capable of annulling pain during the extraction of teeth. He resolved that the experiment should be tried upon himself, and next morning, after inhaling a quantity of the gas prepared by Colton, one of his largest molars was extracted by his friend, Dr. Riggs. As consciousness returned, he exclaimed : "A new era in tooth-pulling ! It did not hurt me more than the prick of a pin ! It is the greatest discovery ever made ! " Archimedes in his bath could not have been more elated.

The two dentists, Wells and Riggs, immediately employed the new method in their practice, and in a few weeks had, without pain, extracted teeth from a dozen different patients. In only two or three instances was there any failure to produce complete anæsthesia. Wells then visited Boston, for the purpose of introducing his discovery in that city. He proposed to the celebrated surgeon, Dr. Warren, to exhibit his method by extracting a tooth from a patient in the surgical theatre of the Harvard Medical School. The offer was accepted. A large class of students were present as critical spectators of the event. The patient was introduced ; the inhaling-bag was applied to his face ; he seemed insensible, and the tooth was forced from his mouth. Alas ! The volume of gas had been insufficient, and a cry of pain in the arena was followed by a tumultuous storm of hisses upon the benches above. The doom of nitrous oxide gas had been pronounced beyond all manner of doubt.

In the year 1846, an enterprising dentist in the city of Boston, William T. G. Morton by name, was occupying his brain with the idea of painless dentistry. The memory of his experience in the year 1839, and his conversation with apothecaries and chemists—notably with Dr. Charles Jackson, an expert chemist—led him to experiment with ether by inhalation. On the evening of September 30, 1846, he put himself to sleep with ether, and when he recovered consciousness he found that he had been insensible for eight minutes. This was the result for which he had hoped, and the first patient who entered his office, a boy named Eben Frost, was persuaded to undertake a repetition of the experiment. Unconsciousness was again produced, a tooth was extracted without pain, and the original object of his desires had been attained. But the more important question of the applicability of ether to the production of anæsthesia during the capital operations of surgery remained without answer until Morton, like his predecessor Wells, proposed to administer the anæsthetic to a patient selected by the surgeon, Dr. Warren, at the Massachusetts General Hospital. Consent was readily obtained, and on October 17, 1846, the attempt was made in the old surgical theatre of the hospital. A patient with a venous tumor of the jaw was etherized by Dr. Morton. The tumor was removed by Dr. Warren without causing pain, though the patient did not become completely insensible. Next day a woman with a fatty tumor on her arm was subjected to operation while under the influence of ether. This time the anæsthesia was perfect, and after one or two other similar experiments an amputation of the thigh was performed by Dr. Hayward, one of the surgeons of the hospital, upon a woman named Alice Mohan, who was etherized by Dr. Morton in the presence of a large number of spectators. From this date the success of anæsthesia in surgery was placed beyond all doubt.

The great discovery was immediately heralded throughout the civilized world, and was everywhere adopted with the utmost enthusiasm. The news reached England on December 17, 1846. Two days afterward, Mr. Robinson, a dentist in London, introduced the practice of extracting teeth from persons under the influence of ether, and on December 21st the famous surgeon, Mr. Liston, operated upon his hospital patients in the same manner. Malgaigne and Velpeau, in Paris, immediately introduced anæsthesia among their patients, and the method was generalized as fast as the means of communication would permit. Dr. James Y. Simpson, of Edinburgh, at once conceived the idea of mitigating the pains of childbirth by the administration of the vapor of ether, which he did on January 19, 1847, and his practice was everywhere imitated with success. During the same year the eminent physiologist, Flourens, addressed to the Academy of Sciences a paper in which he related his experiments with a hitherto almost unknown substance — chloroform. The success of his attempts to produce anæsthesia with hydrochloric ether had induced him to experiment with chloroform, a substance chemically related to chloric ether. He found that animals subjected to the vapor of chloroform became completely insensible during the most painful physiological experiments upon the naked spinal cord and sensitive nerve-roots. This observation passed without notice outside of a narrow circle; but during the year 1847, Mr. Holmes Coote, who was at that time in the habit of assisting Sir William Lawrence in his surgical operations, was one day, at St. Bartholomew's Hospital, relating the particulars of a recent operation for the removal of a cancerous breast, in the course of which it had been found very difficult to induce anæsthesia on account of an exceedingly harassing cough which was excited by the inhalation of the vapor of ether. A surgical pupil who was present, Michael Cudmore Furnell by name, remarked that he had discovered a milder anæsthetic than ether, and he begged Mr. Coote to make trial of chloroform. The properties of this substance Furnell had accidentally learned while a student under Dr. John Bell.

The anæsthetic properties of ether had just been announced, and this young man had exhibited such a passion for the article that his master, fearing some accident, gave strict orders that he should not be allowed access to the ether-bottle. Hunting through the cellar of the shop, he was fortunate enough to discover a bottle labelled chloric ether—the name by which chloroform was then known. The adventurous student immediately made trial of its contents, and succeeded in procuring an insensibility that was more agreeable than the anæsthesia which had followed the inhalation of ether. This was the discovery which he now announced at St. Bartholomew's. Sir William Lawrence and Mr. Holmes Coote made a number of trials of the new agent during the summer of 1847, and were so much pleased with its effects that they were about to undertake an exhaustive investigation of its properties when Simpson published the remarkable paper which introduced chloroform to the world. A Liverpool druggist, named Waldie, who had learned from Dr. Bell the properties of chloroform, had advised Dr. Simpson to make trial of the article. Simpson was at that time experimenting most enthusiastically with everything that seemed likely to produce anæsthesia, and he soon satisfied himself of the advantages of chloroform. On November 10, 1847, he read before the Medico-Chirurgical Society of Edinburgh a paper in which were detailed the particulars of the successful administration of chloroform in not less than fifty cases of the most varied character. The agreeable qualities and the superior concentration of the new anæsthetic at once recommended it to general favor, and throughout Europe its use soon superseded the employment of ether. Unfortunately, however, this change was quickly followed by the occurrence of death while under the influence of chloroform. The continuous repetition of such accidents stimulated the most extensive research and experimentation with a large number of chemical compounds, of which the history and properties will hereafter be given in detail ; but nothing has yet been found to supplant ether and chloroform in the general estimation of mankind. Of these agents the first is still preferred in the country where its utility was originally made known—the last is more highly valued in England and in Europe ; but the palm of safety must always remain with ether—the simplest, the surest, the safest of all the potent anæsthetic agents that are known among men.

PHENOMENA OF ANÆSTHESIA.

The number of substances capable of producing anæsthesia is quite considerable. Besides nitrous oxide gas, carbonic oxide and carbonic acid gases will cause insensibility if inhaled. The vapor of carbonic disulphide is endowed with analogous properties. But the majority of the volatile anæsthetics are either alcoholic or of alcoholic origin—each one of the alcohols yielding an ether when treated with an acid—so that the number of homologous and collateral compounds is very large. The analogies of their physiological effects are correspondingly close, so that a description of the action of ether or of chloroform conveys in general terms an accurate idea of the characteristic phenomena that are common to all the agents of this class.

The first effect of an anæsthetic vapor of the alcoholic class is an impression upon the olfactory nerves. The sense of taste is also excited by contact of the vaporous particles with the nerves of the tongue and pharynx. Usually there is a sensation of fruity sweetness, due to the characteristic properties which the anæsthetic ether possesses in common with the vegetable ethers which are produced in the process of ripening, and which contribute so largely to the perfection of flavor in well-mellowed fruit. The nerves of common sensation, derived from the fifth pair, also react, and sensations of coolness or of increasing heat may be perceived as a consequence of their disturbance. The action of the salivary glands is increased, and acts of swallowing are repeated. This insalivation is more noticeable during the inhalation of ether than when chloroform is employed. Sometimes the unwonted contact of the vapor causes irritation of the laryngeal terminations of the pneumogastric nerve, and the patient will cough. This occurrence depends largely upon the natural nervous excitability of the individual, but also to a considerable extent upon the degree of abruptness with which a highly concentrated vapor is introduced into the lungs. A feeling of suffocation is sometimes experienced, and the patient starts up in an attitude of resistance, struggling to free himself from the inhaling apparatus. Animals, confined in a retentive apparatus, sometimes attempt to prevent the entrance of the anæsthetic vapor by restricting their movements of respiration within the narrowest possible limits.

This first effect of local contact is soon succeeded by the more extensive results of general saturation of the tissues with the stupefying agent. Penetrating every part of the air-cells of the lungs, it rapidly passes into the blood, and is conveyed to every living element of the body. The initial effect is disturbance of function ; the subsequent effect is paralysis of function. Disturbance usually assumes the form of exaltation ; it is also always marked by perversion of the normal order of physiological sequences. The special senses give evidence of this agitation. There is a humming sound in the ears, and subjective impressions of light flash in varying forms across the visual field. General sensibility is also exalted. The pulsations of the heart can be felt, and the vermicular movements of the intestines can sometimes be perceived. The arteries throb, the brain seethes, waves of heat flush the surface of the body, the skin grows warm, perspiration appears upon the face, and sometimes becomes general ; the pulse rises, respiration becomes accelerated, the pupils contract, the eyes close, reflex irritability is exalted, and the patient resembles in his general appearance a person in the earlier stages of alcoholic intoxication. To this period of excitement succeeds the stage of diminishing function. The sensibility of the surface grows less ; the temperature falls ; the pulse, at first rising in volume and rate of movement, begins to recede toward the normal standard ; the blood-pressure diminishes ; the movements of the respiration follow the same course, and finally become deep and full like those of profound sleep ; voluntary movements cease ; consciousness gradually fails, reflex movements are abolished ; and, after a period characterized, perhaps, by less and less articular attempts at speech, the patient lies insensible and without power of voluntary motion. If the action of the anæsthetic is urged beyond this point, the palatal, buccal, and pharyngeal muscles yield, and respiration becomes stertorous ; the action of the heart is enfeebled ; the countenance grows pallid ; respiration becomes irregular, or ceases altogether, and death may ensue.

The effects of anæsthetic inhalation are to be traced most easily through their disturbance of the processes of sensation, perception, volition, movement, respiration, circulation, secretion, and calorification. It will be convenient to consider each one of these classes by itself.

During the administration of the vapor the eyes are generally closed ; the eyelids often move as if winking. At first the pupils are variable in their diameter, as if oscillating between a condition of contraction and relaxation of the sphincter muscle. When anæsthesia is fully declared, the pupils are contracted; but if the condition of stupefaction is carried to an extreme degree, the pupil dilates, and remains expanded till death occurs. During the period of complete insensibility the eyeballs are often turned upward and inward, sometimes assuming the position of conjugated deviation.

General sensibility is disturbed at a very early stage of the anæsthetic process. After the brief period of initial exaltation is passed, cutaneous sensibility diminishes at a rapid rate. This diminution is first manifested upon the least sensible portions of the surface, such as the back, the posterior surfaces of the limbs, and the scalp. Sensibility persists longer upon the anterior surfaces of the trunk, about the eyes, at the tips of the fingers and toes, and especially in the neighborhood of the anus and the organs of generation. It has been remarked that a larger consumption of the anæsthetic agent is required to produce a degree of insensibility sufficient for the tolerance of incision in those parts of the body than for any other purpose.

The initial effects of inhalation are manifested in the brain by a great exaltation of the power of perception and reasoning. Ideas are quickened in their growth and succession. But, with a diminution of the powers of sensation, the sphere of vivid perception is correspondingly narrowed. Consciousness remains perfect so long as it exists, but its field progressively contracts to a vanishing-point, around which seems to gather an atmosphere of half-formed and ever fainter perceptions. The powers of attention, memory, reasoning, judgment, and volition can be exercised with perfect precision so long as the formation of ideas persists; but the progressive movement toward severance of the brain from all contact with the external world, through the medium of the senses, becomes at length so complete that consciousness can deal only with ideas which originate within the brain itself. In this condition the patient seems to dream, and the memory of these dreams may be preserved after awaking. Sometimes all avenues of communication with the external world may be closed but one—usually the sense of hearing; and the patient experiences a feeling as if separated from his body—as if occupying the position of an impassive spectator of the scene in which his material organization forms a constituent part. In such instances volition has ceased; perception, memory, imagination, and consciousness alone remain. But, as the anæsthetic saturation of the tissues advances, these functions also lapse into the potential state, and the patient passes into a condition of vegetative existence, with no more feeling or intelligence than the trunk of a tree.

When volition ceases, and the power of directing the current of ideas has lapsed, the condition of the anæsthetized person is closely analogous to that of one who dreams. The habitual characteristics of the individual, the automatic activities of the cerebral organs, then manifest themselves, sometimes as a result of subjective incentives, sometimes under the influence of external irritants acting upon a nervous system which has not yet wholly passed beyond the condition of exalted reflex excitability. The sailor will imagine himself upon the deck of his ship, bellowing orders to the top-man in a gale of wind. The ruffian thinks himself in the hands of the police, and he curses and struggles furiously in his efforts to escape. The saintly woman folds her hands, and gently sinks to sleep with a prayer of resignation and faith upon her lips. Action is as varied as the actors, and the scene is never twice alike.

The effects of anæsthetics upon the power of volition and voluntary motion are somewhat variable. Children and adults of an impressible temperament are more easily overcome than patients of a vigorous intellectual character. By an effort of the will the progress of anæsthesia may be delayed, and a mind trained in habits of introspection and analysis will retain consciousness longer than if less happily organized. A similar phenomenon is often remarked during the progress toward alcoholic intoxication, when a sudden and powerful act of volition, exercised, perhaps, as the result of some unexpected stimulus from without, serves to restore the condition of sobriety. By such effort, and even without apparent effort, perfect intelligence may often be maintained for a considerable period after the loss of the power of perceiving painful sensations. The patient may be conscious, intelligent, and capable of conversation, yet almost wholly insensible to pain, and, on recovery, quite oblivious of the passage of time and of the majority of incidents that have transpired. During the initial stage of anæsthesia the power of muscular movement is usually exaggerated. Such voluntary movements as may be put forth are performed with unwonted vigor and celerity. The patient may raise his hand or move his foot without willing the act, yet with perfect knowledge of what is done. The involuntary muscles exhibit the general disturbance with the greatest uniformity. The heart beats more rapidly, and sometimes more violently ; the temples throb, the movements of respiration are accelerated. Sometimes, especially when ether is used, cough will be excited ; the patient vomits ; the bladder and the rectum may be evacuated. Convulsive phenomena sometimes appear ; they may be limited to insignificant fibrillary twitchings of the facial muscles, or the patient may be shaken as if in an ague-fit. Epileptic patients may be roused by the anæsthetic to the manifestation of a complete convulsion, from which they will pass into a condition of the most profound insensibility, which is a combination of coma and anæsthesia. Sometimes the convulsive movement assumes the tonic form. This is said to be more frequently witnessed under the influence of chloroform than when ether is employed. An arm, or a leg, half of the body, or even the entire frame, may become perfectly rigid, as if fixed in a tetanic spasm. Such conditions are not to be regarded with indifference, for they indicate a profound and dangerous implication of the most important nervous centres. This is especially the fact when tonic spasm invades any of the respiratory muscles. These convulsive and spasmodic movements must not be confounded with the simple reflex movements caused by the local irritant action of the anæsthetic vapor when it first enters the respiratory passages ; nor should they be mistaken for the half voluntary struggles with which the patient sometimes strives to avoid inhalation during the period just before the establishment of unconsciousness.

As the process of stupefaction advances, reflex action diminishes, the power of voluntary movement ceases, and the patient enters upon a condition of perfect repose, in which the only movements that persist are those which sustain the functions of respiration, circulation, and unconscious life. By careful graduation of the anæsthetic dose, this condition may be maintained without danger for a considerable period of time.

The function of respiration is very considerably disturbed during the progress of artificial anæsthesia. At first the respiratory movements are accelerated, even before the commencement of inhalation, when the patient is agitated by nervous apprehensions. Anstie furnishes the following tables, which exhibit the movements of the pulse and of the lungs during the time occupied with the production of complete insensibility.

ANÆSTHETIC—ETHER.

	At the commencement of inhalation	At end of first minute.	At end of second minute.	At end of third minute.	At end of fourth minute.	At end of fifth minute.
Average frequency of pulse........	74.5	92.7	109.8	110.2	94.3	69.3
Average frequency of respiration ..	23.	23.	24.7	26.3	18.9	15.67

ANÆSTHETIC—CHLOROFORM.

	Average frequency of respiration at commencement.	Average frequency, end of second minute.	Average frequency, end of fourth minute.	Average frequency, end of sixth minute.	Average frequency, end of tenth minute.
Twenty-four men	20.8	18	16	14.8	14.2
Twenty-six women.............	26.	19	16	15.5	15.5

It thus appears that ether tends to quicken respiration during the early and middle stages of the induction of anæsthesia, and to depress its rate slightly below the normal when the stage of insensibility has been reached. Chloroform tranquillizes the initial agitation at an earlier stage of the process, and produces the same final result during the period of unconsciousness.

The above-quoted tables exhibit the general course of respiratory movement, but they do not represent the variations which are sometimes observed. These variations depend, to a very considerable extent, upon the age, sex, temperament, and previous history of the individual, so that it is almost impossible to include all cases in a general description. In certain instances the respiratory movements succeed each other with the utmost irregularity—now fast, now slow, then ceasing altogether until asphyxia seems imminent. Such patients are said to tolerate the anæsthetic badly, and are more liable than others to pass into a condition bordering on the convulsive state. In other instances there is not the slightest appearance of agitation; the inspirations are purely diaphragmatic, or exceedingly shallow. The patient may be perfectly conscious, and capable of intelligent response when addressed by the surgeon, but he seems to have forgotten to breathe. From this condition of apnœa he may be aroused by the voice of the operator telling him to breathe; or, if intelligence is too far gone for this, the respiratory act may be excited by a pinch or by sudden pressure upon the thorax or abdomen. Fortunately, however, when the condition of general muscular relaxation is reached, the movements of respiration become deep and regular. Though less frequent than during the waking state, they are more profound, so that they obviate all risk of asphyxia if the respiratory passages are not mechanically obstructed. During this stage of artificial anæsthesia the gaseous exchanges of the blood are modified to a certain extent. The exhalation of carbonic acid gas is increased during the period of excitement, and it is diminished in proportion to the approach and maintenance of tranquil anæsthesia. For a considerable time after the removal of the inhaler the expired air is charged with the anæsthetic vapor.

The action of the heart corresponds closely with the conditions of 'respiration. If the patient breathes in an irregular, rapid, and convulsive manner, the movements of the heart will vary accordingly. During the occurrence of tetaniform rigidity the pulse may become almost imperceptible. When respiration is slow and feeble, the heart beats in a faint and sluggish way. Again, it may suddenly start off at a very rapid rate, only to sink suddenly into a condition approaching that of syncope. Such inordinate fluctuations and rapid variations should excite grave apprehensions for the safety of the patient.

The normal course of the heart during the induction of anæsthesia has already been indicated by the observations of Anstie. At first the pulse is small and frequent, increasing its rate as respiration becomes accelerated, until the stage of muscular resolution is approached, when it begins to recede. The greatest average frequency noted in the table is 110.2 pulsations in the minute, but it often largely exceeds this figure. As the stage of insensibility approaches, the arterial coats relax, the pulse grows softer, and may even seem to be quite feeble. When complete unconsciousness supervenes, the volume of the pulse is considerably enlarged, and its rate may fall below the normal standard. In these changes it corresponds with the altered mode of respiration, and during the period of complete anæsthesia a condition of equilibrium is maintained, from which any sudden or considerable departure should be observed with suspicion.

As the pulse falls the general circulation improves. The turgid veins collapse; the cutaneous vessels resume their normal calibre. The face may even become pallid, and the mucous surfaces exchange their lively red for a fainter tinge. These conditions generally persist throughout the entire period of anæsthesia.

The temperature of the body is lowered during the time of anæsthesia. At the commencement of inhalation there is an increase of surface temperature, caused by the increased afflux of blood to the skin ; but, as the process advances, the liberation of heat diminishes, and the temperature of the body manifests a considerable fall. This becomes more notable when chloroform is used than when ether is administered.

The function of secretion is augmented by the first acts of inhalation. The flow of saliva increases, and perspiration may appear upon the forehead. But as the stage of calm is entered, all these functions are diminished. It is only in the stage of extreme resolution that the surface of the body is moistened with a colliquative sweat—the result of paralysis rather than of excitement of the mechanism concerned in the production of perspiration.

The length of the period during which the effects of an anæsthetic may persist after the cessation of inhalation is somewhat variable. It usually continues three or four minutes after ether, and a little longer after chloroform. Recovery is almost immediate after nitrous oxide or ethylic bromide. When a condition of complete anæsthesia has been reached, it is not difficult to maintain its perfection by the continuous administration of relatively small quantities of the anæsthetic. In this way a patient may be kept in a tranquil sleep, during the most serious operation, for an indefinite period of time. Operations continuing for an hour or more may thus be conducted with perfect safety and freedom from all movement and pain. The contrary state, in which the patient continues to moan and cry —perhaps even from time to time resuming a feeble struggle with the attendants—is an evidence that the anæsthetic is either not properly inhaled, or that the individual is in an abnormal condition not wholly free from danger. The exercise of patience and perseverance, on the part of the assistant who has been charged with the administration of the anæsthetic, will usually overcome the difficulty; but there are persons who are especially refractory. Drunkards, by reason of long practice in the use of a potent anæsthetic agent like alcohol, are often extremely difficult to overcome. Their tissues are accustomed to the action of a stupefying substance, and have become tolerant of its effects. Great mental agitation, such as fear or excitement, may produce a temporary tolerance of the vapor. Operations about the anus and genital organs also require a longer time for the induction of a sufficiently profound unconsciousness. Women and children are more speedily rendered insensible; but, as a general rule, with vigorous adult males a period of six to ten minutes is necessary for the production of complete anæsthesia. Chloroform, being a more potent drug than ether, requires a little less time.

The recovery from anæsthesia is usually more rapid than its induction, and the time necessary for the process is largely dependent upon the length of time during which unconsciousness has been maintained. The phenomena of recovery as a general thing consist in a regular inversion of the manifestations which mark the stages of induction. This orderly course may, however, be greatly disturbed by the interference of the surgeon, if the concluding acts of operation, such as ligation of arteries and dressing of the wound, have been deferred till after the removal of the inhaling apparatus. When the patient has been previously exhausted by age, privation, cachexia, hemorrhage, or any cause of depression, the period of recovery may be greatly prolonged, and alarming symptoms of prostration may appear. After long and severe operations it may be very difficult, if not impossible, to decide between the effects of shock and of the anæsthetic agent. In all such cases, no doubt, the condition is the complex result of the coincident effects of the injury and of the protracted use of the drug. Brief operations, on the contrary, seem to produce less depression when the element of pain is abolished.

PHYSIOLOGY OF ANÆSTHESIA.

A considerable number of the earlier authors who interested themselves in the subject of artificial anæsthesia have expressed the opinion that the insensibility produced by etherization is the result of mechanical compression of the brain. The vapors of ether, or chloroform, or any other similar substance, according to their opinions, possess such a degree of "tension" that the blood, charged with them by the act of inhalation, produces actual compression of the brain analogous to the condition which obtains after effusion within the cranial cavity. This hypothesis may be speedily laid aside for numerous sufficient reasons derived from the facts of physics and of physiology. Ether and its congeners do not exist in a vaporous condition within the body. They are dissolved in the blood, and they exercise no more pressure than is exerted by the current of the blood itself. This pressure may even diminish as the phenomena of anæsthesia are intensified.

Other observers have advanced the hypothesis that the anæsthetic state is really a condition of asphyxia. The majority of anæsthetic substances are rich in carbon; and this carbon is supposed to act as a reducing agent upon the blood, depriving it of its oxygen, and thus asphyxiating the nervous tissues. But the chemical composition of the blood is not changed during anæsthesia in any way that is consistent with such a hypothesis.

The blood does not even exhibit the blackness that is so characteristic of asphyxia. Its color is a dark brown; its corpuscles may be slightly contracted and crenelated, or they may present no visible alteration of shape and condition. This will depend largely upon the various physical accidents to which freshly drawn blood may be exposed. In the living channels of circulation it is not probable that any distinct and definite change can be determined. It is well known that ether possesses the power to dissolve fatty substances, and thus to extract them from matters with which they have been incorporated. Accordingly, we find that, after removal from the body, blood surcharged with ethereal vapors exhibits upon its surface a certain appreciable quantity of liquid fat. This may have some definite influence in the production of that molecular paralysis which is the essential physical cause of the phenomena of anæsthesia.

Prof. Walter S. Haines, of Rush Medical College, Chicago, has recently recalled attention to the manner in which various substances, in the state of a gas or vapor, operate by their contact to prevent the ordinary molecular combinations which would normally be effected in their absence. For example, if into a jar filled with seven parts of oxygen and one part of carbonic acid gas, a lighted taper be introduced, the flame will be immediately extinguished, exactly as if the jar had been filled with carbonic acid gas. Now, this extinction of the flame is not due to the absence of oxygen. There is abundant presence of that element. But, in the presence of the carbonic acid gas, the ordinary process of oxidation which is essential to the constant activity of combustion is completely arrested. In like manner, if a drop or two of sulphuric ether be introduced into a retort containing a strong solution of caustic potash and a few fragments of phosphorus, no visible reaction will take place in the atmosphere above the liquid, when heat is applied to the apparatus. If this precaution be neglected, an explosive oxidation of the hydrogen phosphide may be expected as the gas is liberated from the water. The same arrest of oxidation may be effected by the introduction of small quantities of the vapor of naphtha, oil of turpentine, or numerous other kindred substances, into the enclosed space which contains the gaseous hydrogen phosphide. Now, it is not the absence of atmospheric oxygen which prevents the oxidation of phosphorus in this case, for that gas is present in quantities relatively very large when contrasted with the amount of ethereal vapor. Even more conspicuous to the eye is the very common experiment of placing a stick of phosphorus in a jar of atmospheric air in a darkened room. The visible glow of light which illuminates the space, as a consequence of a continuous slow oxidation of the phosphorus, is at once extinguished by the introduction of a drop of ether, or chloroform, or any similar substance, into the luminous jar. There can be no appreciable displacement of oxygen in this experiment, but the capacity of that gas for entering into stable combination with phosphorus seems to undergo a species of paralysis. As the ethereal vapor evaporates, the process of oxidation is renewed, and the phosphorus glows once more as perfectly as at first.

Now, the fact to which attention should be directed in all these phenomena is the circumstance that all the substances which are thus capable of arresting the process of oxidation, without taking the place of oxygen or even excluding its presence in any marked degree, are substances capable of producing anæsthetic effects when brought into contact with living tissues. Carbonic acid gas, carbon disulphide, hydrocyanic acid, oil of turpentine and its congeners, alcohol, ether, chloroform, and the numerous class of kindred compounds, are all capable alike of arresting oxidation outside of the body and of producing anæsthesia within the body.   Claude Bernard relates the details of a group of interesting experiments which serve to exhibit the community of the action of anæsthetics upon the living protoplasm of vegetable tissues as well as animal.   The presence of a minute fungus in fermenting solutions that contain sugar has long been known.   As a concomitant of the process of fermentation, this fungus grows and multiplies, and elaborates an efficient amount of ferment by which the chemical exchanges in the fluid are greatly promoted.   Now, if ether be added to the saccharine solution, all ferment action ceases.   The sugar remains undecomposed ; the fungus no longer proliferates ; ferments are no more elaborated ; the fluid remains as stable as common water.   But this is not the result of death. The fungus is not dead, as would be the case had the liquid been sterilized by the action of an elevated temperature.   The elements are merely asleep in the presence of an anæsthetic substance; and as soon as the ether has been removed by evaporation, or by filtration from the yeast, all the previous phenomena of active life are resumed.

That the phenomena which are most intimately associated with life are more easily modified by anæsthetic agents than the phenomena which are dependent upon simple chemical exchange, is clearly indicated by another observation of Claude Bernard relative to the conversion of cane-sugar into grape-sugar.   This transformation is dependent upon another ferment than that which is peculiar to the yeast-fungus.   When the fungus is put to sleep by the action of ether, the process of alcoholic fermentation ceases because the alcoholic ferment is rendered dormant with the plant that gives it birth.   But the passage of cane-sugar into the form of grape-sugar is effected by the action of a soluble, chemical ferment which is not an organized body like yeast.   Upon this ferment ether seems to exercise very little restraining influence, and the transforming process is continuous during the sleep of the yeast-fungus and the arrest of the alcoholic fermentation. When the anæsthetic has been removed the fermentative change attacks the considerable quantity of grape-sugar now ready for transformation, and the production of alcohol and of carbonic acid gas is resumed exactly as if it had never been interrupted.

The action of vegetable protoplasm upon carbonic acid gas, by virtue of which plants are enabled to absorb carbonic acid and to exhale oxygen, when subjected to the rays of light, is arrested by the presence of anæsthetic substances in the fluids of the plant.   The experiment may be most conveniently performed with an aquatic plant.   If a healthy specimen of one of these be immersed in a watery solution of ether or chloroform, and if a bell-glass be inverted over the vessel in which the whole has been placed, it will soon be found that the absorption of carbonic acid gas and the exhalation of oxygen have ceased.   The plant does not die ; it remains green and healthy.   On removing it from the ethereal solution and placing it in pure water, the natural processes of vegetable respiration are renewed.

The germination of seeds may also be arrested by the action of anæsthetics.   Claude Bernard surrounded with the vapor of ether certain seeds which he had placed in conditions otherwise favorable to speedy germination.   Under the influence of warmth and moisture, supplied in the absence of light, this process ordinarily presents a visible result by the second day ; but during the five or six days of the experiment no signs of change appeared.   At the expiration of this period, when pure air was substituted for the vapor of ether, the vital processes were renewed and the seeds at once began to sprout.

Another experiment exhibited the effects of anæsthetics upon a still more complex organism—the irritable protoplasm found in the cells at the base of the petiole in the leaf of the sensitive plant. Placing a vigorous individual of this species under a bell-glass which also contained a sponge saturated with ether, Claude Bernard found, at the expiration of half an hour, that the plant was no longer irritable. Its healthy, verdant appearance was unchanged, but it no longer absorbed carbonic acid gas, and its leaflets would not shrink when touched. As the effects of the ether passed off, after removal of the sponge, the plant gradually recovered its irritability, and its leaves drooped again whenever touched, exactly as if nothing had happened.

Now, in each one of these experiments the same fact is illustrated, to wit, the tendency to cessation of molecular movement in the presence of the anæsthetic substance. This tendency becomes evident in relation with certain movements rather than in relation with all sorts of motion. It is perhaps too much to say that the most complex forms of molecular change are the first to cease under the influence of an anæsthetic, but it is very evident that there is a difference. Alcoholic fermentation, for example, is arrested by a solution of ether in which the transformation of cane-sugar into grape-sugar is still continued. But the less complicated exchanges of inorganic chemistry, such as the simple oxidation of phosphorus, are also prevented in a similar manner. It is not impossible that this familiar process of oxidation is not so very simple a matter, after all. Our present knowledge, however, will not permit any great degree of dogmatic assurance regarding the ultimate nature of many of the most ordinary processes. The only thing that seems beyond dispute is the fact that anæsthetic substances tend to diminish the ordinary freedom of chemical change in matter. Certain changes may thus be easily and completely arrested, while others are but partially restrained.

This fact is very clearly illustrated by the phenomena of anæsthesia as exhibited in animals whose organization is so much more complicated than the structure of even the most highly organized plant. The animal frame, like that of the plant, is built up with microscopical cellular elements not unlike those which form the tissues of the lower organisms. But in the animal there is a greater degree of differentiation among the individual elements. Certain groups of these elements are modified for the work of secretion. Others are modified in a manner that specially fits them for the manifestation of contractility. Others again are fitted chiefly for the reception of sensitive impressions, while still another group has for its particular function the initiation of motion. Obviously these differences imply very considerable variations of structure. Their relations with external forces must be correspondingly variable. Accordingly, we find that certain portions of animal tissue are much more easily affected by anæsthetic substances than other portions. Certain cell-groups are quickly paralyzed, while others are capable of long resistance. To this fact is due the progressive character of the phenomena of artificial anæsthesia. The more highly differentiated the tissues of an animal, the more evidently successive and complex the phenomena of anæsthesia. For this reason the induction of sleep in a plant is a process that exhibits fewer different phenomena than the induction of sleep by the aid of anæsthetics in a rabbit; and the production of sleep in the case of an infant is an easier and simpler affair than the reduction of a vigorous adult to a condition of anæsthetic insensibility.

The animal tissues which exhibit the highest degree of susceptibility to anæsthetics are the elementary structures of the nervous system. But in the nervous system there is an immense variety of subordinate structures—connective tissues, blood-vessels, lymph-channels, nerve-fibres, motor cells, sensory cells, ganglionic cells, peripheral end-organs, and central recipient mechanisms. It is important to ascertain the manner in which these various structures are affected when invaded by the anæsthetic substance that is circulated with the blood. This we may learn by experiment upon the lower animals. It is convenient to commence with a cold-blooded creature like the frog, which lends itself so readily to the uses of the physiological laboratory. Small fishes may be treated in the same way, but the frog is the most convenient object of experiment. Claude Bernard has pointed out the method of study, and to him we are indebted for the following details. Taking a glass filled with a solution of chloroform in water—one part chloroform in two hundred parts of water—it should be closed with a sheet of india-rubber stretched across its mouth. Through a slit in the rubber diaphragm the body of a frog may be fixed in such a manner that it shall be half immersed in the water within the glass. Two specimens may be thus prepared for experiment—one frog being placed with the head and upper part of the body under water, while the other frog is adjusted in the upright position with only the hind legs and inferior half of the body in contact with the anæsthetic fluid. Notwithstanding this difference, at the end of a few minutes anæsthesia is complete in every portion of the two animals. This is due to cutaneous absorption, succeeded by circulation of the chloroform with the blood, so that the anæsthetic is transported to every part of the body alike. The same result is obtained if only one of the extremities of the frog be immersed in the liquid.

If, now, we take measures to prevent the flow of blood from the heart into a given portion of the animal, the experiment will be varied to a certain extent. Removing the sacrum of the frog, and exposing the great lumbar nerves which are distributed to the inferior extremities, a ligature may be passed beneath their trunks, and drawn tightly around the remaining mass of the body so as to arrest the circulation at that point, and to cut off all communication between the upper and the lower portions of the animal, excepting through the medium of the nerves that have been excluded from the ligature. In a frog thus prepared, it is evident that the circulation of blood between the upper and the lower halves of the body is completely arrested, but the functions of the nerves and of the separated segments of the spinal cord are still persistent. Reflex movements may still be excited in the lower extremities, as well as in the upper, by irritation of the cutaneous nerves.

Two frogs, thus prepared and immersed in chloroformed water, as in the previous experiment, present the following results : the frog which is placed with his head and upper half of the body under water soon becomes insensible not only in the submerged portions, but also in the parts, beyond the ligature, that are situated above the caoutchouc diaphragm. So far as the submerged portion of the animal is concerned, this is perfectly intelligible. But the parts that have been cut off from the general circulation by the ligature are also paralyzed. Obviously this cannot be due to the circulation of chloroformed blood through the lower half of the body. The only means of communication between the portion above the ligature and the portion below the ligature is through the lumbar nerves. These spring from the spinal cord above the ligated portion, where it is freely irrigated with chloroformed blood from the heart. Evidently, therefore, the paralysis of the lower extremities is owing to a loss of capacity for the origination and emission of motor impulses on the part of the apparatus contained in the roots of the lumbar nerves.

In the case of the companion frog, which was at the same time placed with his hind legs and inferior portion of the body in the chloroformed water, the parts that are above the water remain uninfluenced by the chloroform. This fact shows that the anæsthetic has not reached these parts, and the obstacle presented by the ligature to the process of circulation is sufficient to account for this circumstance. The posterior portion of the animal loses its sensibility exactly as if no ligature existed, because the skin absorbs chloroform wherever it is in contact with the anæsthetic liquid. The peripheral sense-organs are completely paralyzed by this local action, but it remains local. The anæsthetic influence cannot ascend the lumbar nerves to their central origin in the spinal cord above the level of the water in the jar; consequently, all parts above the ligature remain in their normal condition of sensibility and motricity.

By these experiments we are taught that the action of anæsthetic substances is local, and is only manifested by those tissues which are directly in contact with the paralyzing agent. When the spinal cord, or the brain, is etherized, the animal ceases to feel, because the central recipient apparatus is paralyzed. When the anæsthetic is excluded from the central organs, but is at the same time freely supplied to the peripheral organs of sensation in the skin, the animal ceases to feel, because the peripheral apparatus for the reception and transmission of sensory impressions is in a condition of paralysis.

It was, just now, intimated that the frog might cease to exhibit sensibility as a consequence of the action of chloroform upon the spinal cord. In order to determine whether the cord can become the seat of changes capable of destroying sensibility, independently of changes in the brain, the following experiment may be performed. Two frogs should be prepared by transversely dividing the spinal cord in the upper dorsal region. This operation will not hinder the circulation of blood, but the power of executing voluntary movements with the hind legs will be lost by the animal, because all nervous communication between the brain and the posterior extremities has been destroyed by the spinal section. The capacity for reflex movements will, however, continue to be exhibited by those extremities—in fact, it will be considerably improved as a consequence of the loss of the inhibitory influences previously derived from the brain. If now the two frogs, thus prepared, be placed as in the preceding experiments, so that the upper half of one and the lower half of the other is in contact with the chloroformed water, they will soon become insensible in every part. The condition of anæsthesia is generalized by the free circulation of the anæsthetic liquid, without regard to the portion of the skin through which it is absorbed. The phenomena of anæsthesia, illustrated by the cessation of reflex action, etc., are exhibited as completely in those portions of the animal which are connected with the brain as in those which are in communication with the posterior segment of the cord alone. This proves not only that the cord is, to a certain extent, an independent nervous centre, but also that the action of the anæsthetic is direct and local in its effect upon the nervous centres. This may be still further illustrated by the experiment of ligating the body of a frog so as to prevent all passage of blood from the heart into the lower half of the animal, and, having divided the spinal cord a short distance below the ligature, placing the head and upper extremities of the animal in chloroformed water. The submerged portion becomes anæsthetized, as in the previous experiments; but, since the chloroform cannot reach the parts beyond the ligature, the posterior extremities continue to execute reflex movements, showing that the lower segment of the cord is still capable of receiving and transmitting sensory impressions.

The effect of anæsthetics upon the nervous centres results in the production of a state that exhibits many points of resemblance to natural sleep. The principal difference consists in the greater profundity of the insensibility that belongs to anæsthesia. During ordinary healthful sleep there is no loss of reflex energy. The spinal cord does not lose its sensibility; it is the brain that lies dormant. But in the sleep of anæsthesia the voluntary muscles become completely relaxed—there is a disappearance of that tonicity which is dependent upon the waking energy of the cord. Let us now investigate the condition of the nerve-centres, first in natural sleep, and then in the sleep of anæsthesia.

Sleep commences in the organs of sensation. The sensory nerve-tissues are evidently composed of matter in a condition of less stability than obtains in the other tissues of the body. If this were not the case, sensation could never precede motion in the nerve-centres. Every impulse that reaches a complex organ like the spinal cord or the brain must necessarily disturb the equilibrium of the more unstable molecules before it disturbs more stable masses. This unstable matter, therefore, constitutes a recipient apparatus for all impulses that move in a centripetal direction—from the surfaces of the body to the central organs in the cerebro-spinal axis. While the constituent matter of the recipient apparatus preserves its condition of instability, it is said to be irritable, and by virtue of that irritability, motion is liberated in its substance—probably through rapidly successive isomeric changes—and is transmitted to the specifically motor centres, or to the apparatus of conscious sensation. But when, as a consequence of repeated changes of this nature, the irritable matter has deteriorated in nutrition, and has become overcharged with the waste products of tissue-change, it is no longer the unstable substance it was at first. It no longer liberates motion under the influence of impulses from abroad. There can be no further distribution of motion through its agency, and the motor ganglia, with the organ of consciousness, can receive no incitements to action through the normal channels. During this condition of the recipient nervous apparatus, the individual must necessarily remain ignorant of all that passes without. He becomes unconscious of the external world—he may even lose all consciousness of self—we say that he is asleep. This condition may be the result of the ordinary tissue-changes that conform to the daily rotation of the earth, and then the sleep is natural. Or it may be a pathological result of morbid conditions of the body, constituting a condition of stupor. Or, finally, it may result from the presence and peculiar energy of certain substances that have been artificially introduced into the blood, producing artificial anæsthesia. The causes differ, but the effect upon consciousness is the same.

The advent of normal sleep is heralded by a gradual failure of the special senses. Usually the eyes are the first to yield. Their lids collapse; the ciliary apparatus ceases to adjust the eye to varying distances; the retina no longer reacts under the waves of light. The general sensibility of the surface of the body becomes diminished, and finally ceases to manifest itself under ordinary impressions. The sense of hearing persists longer than any of the other special senses. It is through the medium of this sense that one can be most easily aroused from sleep; yet it is by an appeal to the ear that sleep may often be induced. Witness the peaceful slumber effected by the monotonous humdrum of a droning preacher. This, however, is the normal consequence of the fatigue induced throughout the nervous apparatus by long-continued repetition of identical impulses. It is an example analogous to the continuous dropping that wears away the hardest rock.

The incidence of sleep upon the locomotive apparatus is first exhibited by the voluntary muscles that belong to the limbs. Then follow the muscles of the trunk. The power of reflex movement is not abolished; respiration and circulation continue, though with a slightly diminished rate.

As sleep invades the brain, perception of the external world is gradually diminished as the wearied senses cease to introduce sensations from without. But this cessation of communication does not at once arrest the development of ideas within the brain. Certain groups of cortical cells may remain active for a considerable time after the establishment of sleep in certain other groups. Deprived of that guidance which is derived from the impressions of sense, the attention of the waking portions of the brain is attracted to such impressions of internal origin as may arise in the territories of the pneumogastric and sympathetic nerves. In other words, these uncompensated connections become more influential. Hence a succession of erratic ideas, attended with varying degrees of consciousness dependent upon the degree of uniformity in the state of the cortical portion of the brain. Or, again, disturbing causes may be originated in the cerebral centres themselves. Groups of cells, which have acquired an excessive or morbid degree of irritability, may still continue to perform a certain amount of functional work as a consequence of previous impressions that have not yet been effaced; and this work will produce results in the field of consciousness, precisely as similar work would result during the waking state. But, through lack of a simultaneous production in consciousness of that vast complex of associated perceptions and conceptions which is occasioned by the co-ordinated activity of all parts of the brain during the waking state, this isolated cell-work excites only imperfect trains of thought, which, for the reasons above indicated, must necessarily progress after a very imperfectly ordered fashion. Such inco-ordinated processes constitute what is called a dream, in which the degree of intensity, coherence, and amplitude of the ideas is dependent upon the variable extent and completeness of the cessation of cell-function throughout the brain. When special cell-function is rapidly, uniformly, and completely arrested, sleep is profound and dreamless. When, on the contrary, the process is conducted in an irregular and imperfect manner, sleep is correspondingly disturbed and unrefreshing.

The act of awaking from sleep is the result of reconstruction of the irritable matter of the nervous tissues. During sleep this process—which is a nutritive process—goes on without interruption until a certain degree of instability—irritability—has been renewed. The ordinary external impressions of light, heat, sound, and touch are then once more sufficient to liberate motion throughout the nervous system, and to excite the formation of ideas which reach the field of conscious perception. The individual is then awake, and will continue to enjoy the waking state until the irritability of the sensory apparatus is again exhausted. Thus, sleep and consciousness succeed each other in an orderly cycle which is curiously related with the diurnal revolution of the earth about its axis.

In the preceding analysis sleep has been made to depend upon the condition of the cells which compose so large a part of the cerebral and nervous substance. This, however, is not the opinion that was formerly entertained by physiologists. In the days that preceded experiment, various hypotheses were constructed to account for the phenomenon of sleep. It was by some considered a function of the immanent vital principle which alternated with other functions of the same principle. Respiration, thought, sleep, all were ascribed alike to the activity of this principle. But this mode of viewing the subject afforded no explanation of the mechanism by which the function was made apparent. Others—and they were the majority—taught that sleep was caused by an afflux of blood into the brain, sufficient to compress the organ in such a manner as to arrest its ordinary functions. Sleep was thus regarded as a sort of physiological coma which never transgressed the limits of safety. The deep sleep that characterizes all diseases attended by a marked determination of blood to the head, the injection of the cornea during natural sleep, the influence of heat and of opiates which were supposed to increase the cerebral circulation, were all accepted as sufficiently convincing proofs of the causal connection between cerebral congestion and sleep.

The last twenty-five years have witnessed a reaction against this hypothesis, and its complete opposite has found many able advocates. Cases have been reported in which accident or disease had caused a loss of portions of the cranium and meninges, so that a certain amount of brain-substance was exposed to view. Caldwell observed, in such a patient, that during sleep there was a subsidence of cerebral pulsation. During the act of dreaming there was an increase of circulation and a degree of turgescence of the brain that was in direct relation with the vividness of the dream. In another patient, under similar conditions, Blumenbach observed a marked diminution of cerebral vascularity during sleep, and a revival of the circulation at the moment of awaking. As long ago as 1854, Wm. A. Hammond—an American army surgeon—observed the same thing in the victim of a railway accident which had caused the loss of the cranial bones over a portion of the skull, measuring six inches in length by three inches in breadth. This extensive wound had cicatrized, without restoration of the osseous substance, so that there existed, as it were, an artificial fontanelle which fluctuated in conformity with the variations of blood-pressure. When the patient was awake, the surface of the cicatrix was neither elevated nor depressed. Any great excitement caused an increased prominence of the part. The concluding phenomena of the epileptic convulsions, to which the patient was liable, were accompanied by extensive bulging of the surface, indicating great turgescence of the vessels below. During sleep, on the contrary, there was a decided depression, from which circumstance was inferred a diminished pressure in the cerebral vessels.

In 1860 an English physician, Dr. Arthur E. Durham, published, in *Guy's Hospital Reports* (3d series, vol. vi., p. 149, 1860), an article entitled "The Physiology of Sleep," in which were detailed the results of experiments performed on dogs, to determine the condition of the cerebral circulation during sleep. Opening the skull with a trephine, the surface of the brain could be observed at all hours. A condition of relative anæmia was thus demonstrated during the period of sleep. Dr. Bedford Brown, an American physician, during the same year, 1860, finding under his care a patient who had sustained a fracture of the skull (*Am. Jour. Med. Sci.*, p. 339, October, 1860), observed the same comparatively anæmic condition of the brain while under the influence of chloroform. The initial stage of its administration was characterized by an increased turgescence of the cerebral vessels, but as the stage of complete anæsthesia was induced the condition of hyperæmia was succeeded by a condition of decided anæmia.

Numerous experimenters have remarked the same thing in animals which have been subjected to the action of opium and other narcotics. Anæmic individuals have been observed to manifest greater intellectual activity while occupying the recumbent position than in the erect—a circumstance which may be urged in favor of the anæmic hypothesis of sleep. Advantage of this fact has been taken in the construction of a rotating table for the induction of sleep in cases of persistent wakefulness that were supposed to be dependent upon cerebral hyperæmia. Placing the patient in the recumbent position upon such a table, with his head nearest to the axis, when the apparatus is rotated, the blood is driven out of the brain by centrifugal repulsion, and is accumulated principally in the lower extremities. Sleep is said to result very promptly as a consequence of the cerebral anæmia thus produced. The somnolence that sometimes accompanies the act of digestion has been ascribed to a diversion of blood from the brain to the gastro-intestinal capillaries. In like manner it has been suggested that the disposition to sleep which is caused by an excessive atmospheric temperature is due to a general dilatation of the capillary net-work in the skin, producing a detention of blood at the periphery, with a corresponding degree of anæmia in the internal organs. The good effects of warming the feet before retiring to bed, and the soporific influences of the traditional dry crust of bread when taken at the same hour, have been thus explained.

It has been urged, on the opposite side, that these hypotheses do not account for the excessive wakefulness which often accompanies the anæmic state. Nor do they seem to be consistent with the explanation ordinarily assigned to the cause of the contracted pupil which is constant during natural sleep. Dilatation of the pupil is the normal condition of that aperture in conditions of general anæmia. It is also a consequence of that irritation of the cervical sympathetic nerve which produces contraction of the arteries of the head, and, presumably, diminishes the amount of blood conveyed to the brain. On the contrary, all those conditions which favor accumulation of blood in the brain, such as exist in asphyxia, or after section of the cervical sympathetic nerves, tend to produce contraction of the pupil. It is evident, therefore, that if contraction of the pupil is to be assumed as a positive indication of intracranial hyperæmia, the brain must be the seat of increased blood-pressure during the time of sleep. But this inference is opposed by the experiments of Durham and others. It would appear, therefore, that we either have not in the eye an unvarying index of the state of the cerebral circulation, or that sleep may be associated with different conditions of blood-supply in the brain.

The highest degree of probability, therefore, belongs to the hypothesis which undertakes to explain the phenomenon of sleep as the consequence of a certain stage of exhaustion of energy in nervous matter. It expresses the wear and tear of the intellectual apparatus. The machine can liberate motion for a certain length of time ; but at last its potential energy, derived from nutritive substances that have been introduced through the blood and have been incorporated by the cells, is entirely exhausted. Cessation of function must necessarily follow at once. Cessation of muscular function, occasioned by such exhaustion of the muscular apparatus, is muscular sleep. Cessation of the functions of the sensitive organs of the body, occasioned in a similar manner, constitutes anæsthesia. Cessation of all the cerebral functions, thus induced, is natural sleep. That exhaustion of the materials furnished to the brain by the processes of nutrition is an important cause of sleep is indicated by the increased power of resistance against soporific tendencies which becomes apparent after eating during a period of enforced wakefulness. But mere reinforcement of the nutritive supply in the blood is not alone sufficient for the restoration of the potential energies of the brain. For this a season of absolute repose is imperative. The same law holds good throughout the physical frame. Continuous exertion —continuous liberation of motion—is impossible. Even the heart must stand still and sleep about seventy times a minute. Perfect rest is one of the conditions essential to perfect nutrition. This period of perfect rest constitutes sleep on the part of the brain. The condition of the cerebral circulation is an entirely secondary affair in comparison with the state of the intracellular molecules of the cerebral substance. Sleep, therefore, may occur in states of hyperæmia as well as in conditions of anæmia. In normal sleep there is no such thing as absolute anæmia. Absolute cessation of the circulation would produce, not sleep, but syncope. During sleep the waking functions of the cerebral cells are suppressed, and can no longer interfere with the active changes of nutrition. The entire work of the cell is concentrated upon the nutritive process. This requires a continuous supply of blood, but it does not necessarily require a supply equal to that demanded by the brain when its cells are engaged in active intellectual function. Consequently, there is a diminution of the circulation of blood in the brain. If slumber is disturbed, or if the individual be aroused to consciousness, the liberation of motion by the cortical cells communicates an impulse to the heart and to the regulative apparatus, which at once admits more blood into the vessels of the brain.

This is the cause of the increased dimension of the blood-vessels at the moment of awaking or during the act of dreaming, as observed by those who have enjoyed the opportunity of inspecting the uncovered surface of the cerebrum in the living individual. The relation between the brain and the blood-current is thus shown to be identical with the relation which exists between that current and any glandular organ or muscular apparatus whose action is rhythmical or intermittent in its character. So delicate and so intimate is the connection between all parts of the animal body, that, whenever motion is liberated in any cell or group of cells, a portion of the impulse is conducted directly to the organs of circulation, and is distributed in such a manner that the resistance between the heart and the point of agitation is reduced to a degree which permits an easier passage of blood to the seat of action. We accordingly find the various glands turgid during their period of functional activity, but they are pale and comparatively bloodless throughout those intervals of repose which in the course of their life occupy the place of sleep in the history of the brain.

Reference has already been made to the observations of Durham, Bedford Brown, and others, upon the cerebral circulation during natural sleep. Similar observations have revealed the circulatory phenomena which result as a consequence of the action of anæsthetics. The immediate consequence of their initial action is a hyperæmic and turgid condition of the brain. This soon subsides, and the completely anæsthetic state is marked by a diminished flow of blood. The brain becomes relatively anæmic, just as in the case of ordinary sleep. When a condition of hyperæmia persists, it is owing to the fact that the anæsthetic process is by some disturbing cause complicated with the symptoms of partial asphyxia. This may not unfrequently result from accidental hinderances to respiration, such as so often manifest themselves during the first stage of artificial anæsthesia.

The conclusion to which the analysis of all these observations leads is identical with the conclusion drawn from the experiments of Bernard regarding the effect of anæsthetics upon the lower forms of organic life. Anæsthesia is the result of the local action of the anæsthetic upon the individual elements of the organism. Ether abolishes the functions of the nerve-cell, in precisely the same way that it abolishes the functions of the plant-cell. This arrest of function is probably due to the same properties by which the anæsthetic substance interferes with the reactions which would otherwise take place between oxygen and phosphorus in the inorganic kingdom. This local action of anæsthetics is further illustrated by an interesting experiment reported by Serres. Having ligated the hind leg of a dog in a manner that effectually prevented the entrance of blood into the limb, he found, on etherizing the animal, that the irritability of the sciatic nerve in the ligated extremity remained intact, notwithstanding the abolition of nervous irritability in every other part.

Experimenting in a similar manner upon frogs, Claude Bernard arrived at the conclusion that loss of excitability in such cases was due to the action of the anæsthetic upon the brain and spinal cord rather than upon the nerves themselves. But this conclusion may be reconciled with his other experiments and with the observations of Serres, Perrin, and others, by recalling to mind the fact that the tissues of the body are exceedingly variable in their tolerance of anæsthetics. The sensory apparatus succumbs to their influence sooner than the motor, for reasons which have been already specified. This fact is well illustrated by an observation of Claude Bernard, who found on irritating the sciatic nerve of a chloroformed frog that the muscles could be aroused to action when no evidence of sensation could be made apparent. Certain portions of the nervous apparatus yield sooner than other portions. Witness the staggering gait of a man partially under the influence of alcohol. The lower animals, also, can move their upper limbs, and can execute well-ordered movements of the head and neck for a considerable time after they have lost all control over the posterior extremities. In fact, it is the rule that the muscular paralysis of anæsthesia advances from below upward, involving the peripheral organs first, and only invading the movements of respiration at the moment when the medullary centres are overwhelmed. In this respect the behavior of anæsthetic substances is not peculiar. Many toxic substances exhibit the same progressive action. This fact need not be referred to any special affinity between the tissues of the inferior part of the spinal cord and the poisonous agent. It is undoubtedly due to the peculiarities of the blood-supply connected with the lower segments of the spinal cord. Sensory impressions which should reach the brain through the medium of the cord are diminished, while the motor impulses which should pass from the higher centres to the lower are also hindered in their course. It is in the medulla oblongata that the power of liberating molecular motion is most completely organized. Consequently, the movements of respiration and the control of the circulation, being directly dependent upon this quality of the nerve-substance in the medulla, persist after the cessation of all other motor functions in other portions of the nervous system. The respiratory centre is the *ultimum moriens* in all cases of death from the administration of anæsthetics. Paralysis of function advances from the cerebral periphery downward, and from the sensory periphery upward, until at length the " vital knot " is loosed and death occurs.

Molecular paralysis, then, is the cause of all the varied phenomena of anæsthesia. Not only the loss of consciousness which marks an advanced stage of the process, but also the initial period of excitement, is the result of the paralyzing energy of the anæsthetic. It is usual to speak of the excitement which is evident at the commencement of etherization as the *primary* effect of the anæsthetic action. This, however, is an error, which has its origin in a confusion of the effects of the anæsthetic upon the vaso-motor nerves with the effects that are produced by the changes thus occasioned in the circulation of the blood among the elements of the nervous tissues. When ether, for example, is inhaled, it passes directly through the walls of the pulmonary capillaries, and is dissolved in the blood within the lungs. Thence it is carried directly to the left side of the heart, and is forced through the coronary arteries into every portion of the organ, simultaneously with its transportation through the medium of the systemic circulation to the most distant parts of the body. The immediate effects of the anæsthetic are, therefore, experienced first by the tissues which constitute the walls of the pulmonary veins and the coats of the coronary arteries. In the coats of these vessels are placed the ganglia of their vaso-motor nerves. Upon these, as well as upon the other constituent tissues of the cardiac blood-vessels, the paralyzing influence of the anæsthetic is directed. The muscular walls of the arterioles, after a brief period of contraction, relax by reason of their diminished tonicity, thus effected. An increased supply of blood is distributed to the muscular substance of the heart and to its intrinsic ganglia. This increased flow of blood serves to increase the function of both nerve and muscle. The heart contracts more vigorously and propels a larger amount of blood to the brain, to the spinal cord, to every portion of the body. This sudden impulse increases the propulsion of blood throughout the arterial channels, and arouses the activity of nervous tissue everywhere. A general, though temporary, increase of function in all kinds of tissue is the result. But the excitement thus produced effects its own arrest. The blood becomes more thoroughly charged with ether, which soon extends its paralyzing influence beyond the walls of the circulatory canals, and invades the higher nervous ganglia. As their functional activity subsides, their accelerating influence upon the circulation is diminished, and the rate of the pulse recedes in the direction of its normal figure. At length, if an equilibrium be established between the introduction and the elimination of the anæsthetic vapor, the anæsthetic process is continuously sustained with a uniform degree of intensity. But, if its introduction be compelled beyond the power of the tissues to free themselves, they become supersaturated with the substance. One after another the nervous elements pass into a condition akin to *rigor mortis*, and systemic death is the final result. This conclusion of the process, must, of course, be more likely to follow the result of an energetic agent, or a substance that is not readily excreted by the tissues. For this reason chloroform is more dangerous than ether.

That a paralyzing agent should as its first effect produce an increased tonicity of the arterial walls, thus raising the blood-pressure for a short time after the introduction of the anæsthetic substance into the current of the blood, may at first sight seem quite paradoxical. In fact, it is customary to speak of such substances as producing an irritant effect before they produce paresis or paralysis. But this is not the only instance of a temporary increase of muscular movement that is directly caused by the abolition of some special source of nervous impulse. Witness the tremendous liberation of muscular motion which follows a paralysis of the influence of the brain by sudden decapitation of a fowl, for example. Witness the pervasive shudder which effects the respiratory muscles when a sudden dash of cold water diminishes the molecular movements of the cutaneous sensitive nerve-endings. This may even result in a succession of general muscular convulsions, producing considerable displacement of the limbs and other levers of the body—shivering and chattering of the teeth. These very considerable liberations of motion are not the consequence of an increase of motion upon the sensitive side of the nervo-muscular arc. On the contrary, they are dependent upon conditions which retard or wholly abolish the transmission of ordinary impulses between the surface and the centre. The liberation of a motor impulse by the cells of a central motor ganglion may, then, be effected by a single disturbance of the ordinarily existing equilibrium between their protoplasm and the protoplasm of the structure by the aid of which such liberation is ordinarily initiated. This disturbance may assume the character of a diminution of the ordinary influx of sensory impulse as well as of an exaltation of the same. A lump of ice in the rectum will thus excite reflex respiratory movement even more efficiently than a red-hot iron in contact with the skin. Cold, which diminishes molecular movements, may thus be as painful as heat, by which they are increased. Now when anæsthetics—and this is more conspicuously evident in the action of the stronger substances, like chloroform—act through the blood upon the nervous apparatus in the walls of the vessels, they tend to paralyze the sensory endings of the nervous fibrils. This means a diminution of the normal impulses which should continually reach the central intraparietal ganglia in order to maintain a perfect nervo-muscular equilibrium between the different structures of the vessel. The motor cells no longer experience the inhibitory influence which they should receive from the periphery of their territory, and a liberation of motor impulse immediately follows the loss of equilibrium thus occasioned. Reaching the muscular fibrils, this motor impulse excites muscular contraction, and we have a vascular spasm, with temporary increase of arterial pressure, produced by the initial stage of that general nervo-muscular paresis which shall shortly involve not only the entire local apparatus, but also the whole mass of the general nervous system.

That anæsthetic agents do really diminish or retard the specific molecular movements of nervous and muscular tissues, is clearly exhibited by the beautiful experiments of the committee of the British Medical Association (*British Medical Journal*, p. 2. January, 1879). "By a refined method of experimenting with Regnault's chronograph, it was ascertained that a few respirations of air containing chloroform or ether produced remarkable retardation in the time of signalling back that a visual impression had been perceived, although the person operated on was quite unconscious of any such delay." Thus it appears that the immediate presence of an anæsthetic agent is always and everywhere followed by a diminution, if not by a complete arrest, of the normal modes of motion in other forms of contiguous matter. It also appears that the temporary increase of motion which may be exhibited by certain kinds of organized matter under the mediate influence of the anæsthetic is not the result of a direct impulse communicated by that agent, but is the consequence of an overthrow of equilibrium in the complex structure of which it forms a part.

The question has often been asked, How do anæsthetics act upon nervous tissues? Reasoning from analogy, it has been suggested that they coagulate protoplasm, somewhat after the manner in which alcohol acts upon albuminous substances outside of the body. But coagulation is not compatible with life, consequently, it is hardly probable that this can be the mode of action. When it is remembered that the effect of an anæsthetic is temporary, and that it leaves the tissues in no way different from their original condition, it seems more probable that in the substance of the protoplasm through which the paralyzing agent is diffused, the anæsthetic operates to arrest those chemical exchanges—chiefly oxidation—that are associated with the normal diffusion of motion throughout the system. It effects no new combinations or decompositions. Among the molecules it merely plays the part of a cloud between the sun and the earth, hindering the energies of the one from acting upon the susceptible matter of the other.

Having thus reviewed the manner in which anæsthetics may be supposed to produce their effects, it becomes comparatively easy to explain the causes of the various phenomena which succeed each other during the induction of anæsthesia. The acceleration of respiration and of circulation are due to the increased flow of blood into the capillaries of the heart and of the nervous apparatus, exciting the reflex functions of the cardiac ganglia, of the spinal cord, and of the medulla oblongata. The same condition exists in the mucous membrane of the nares, mouth, and pharynx—hence, an increase of the local reflexes, marked by an augmented flow of saliva. That this is occasioned chiefly by a local action of the anæsthetic is indicated by the fact that if a dog, for example, be made to inhale chloroform through an opening in the trachea, such copious salivation is avoided. The same condition of local hyperæmia arouses the reflex apparatus of the larynx and of the lungs—often to a degree sufficient to excite a paroxysm of cough. The sensory apparatus of the body is in like manner rendered more efficient, and for a brief period all the sensations and the cerebral perceptions are exalted, by reason of the increased energy of the circulation. Painful sensations are thus intensified by the means that are employed for their abolition. The muscular contractility may also be exaggerated in the same way, producing those annoying phenomena of muscular rigidity sometimes observed during the administration of chloroform. The weaker anæsthetics, like diluted alcohol, or the attenuated vapor of ether, if administered slowly, may sustain this period of intensified activity for an indefinite period; but if the stronger agents, like chloroform, are used, or if the weaker anæsthetic substances are employed in extraordinary quantity, the toxic effect at length invades the less impressible tissues, and the phenomena of complete anæsthesia are made apparent. The differing energy of the various anæsthetic substances is well illustrated by a comparison of the periods of time necessary for the induction of anæsthesia by their use. Dr. Norris, of Birmingham, placed a number of rats under bell-jars filled with different gases and vapors. Noting the time requisite for the production of insensibility in each case, he found that unconsciousness and muscular resolution were apparent in an atmosphere of

	Minutes.	Seconds.
Hydrogen	in 9	0
Air saturated with ether vapor	in 5	0
Air saturated with chloroform vapor	in 1	30
Air saturated with methylene dichloride vapor	in 0	20
Nitrous oxide	in 0	25
Oxygen saturated with ether vapor	in 8	30
Oxygen saturated with chloroform vapor	in 0	25
Oxygen saturated with methylene dichloride vapor	in 1	45
Carbonic anhydride	in 0	8

The insensibility produced by hydrogen is apparently due to the simple exclusion of oxygen—to pure asphyxia. The rapid effects of nitrous oxide and of carbonic anhydride must be attributed to their double energy as anæsthetic and asphyxiant substances.

ADMINISTRATION OF ANÆSTHETICS.

The administration of nitrous oxide gas, and other unusual anæsthetic substances, will be discussed in the chapters which treat particularly of their use. In the present chapter the ordinary employment of ether or chloroform will form the subject for consideration.

A physical examination of the patient should precede the commencement of inhalation. A passing illness, an unusual degree of fatigue, loss of sleep, excessive mental excitement—any and all of the various causes which may intervene to depress the vitality of the patient, should be carefully considered before the final decision in favor of a resort to anæsthesia. Before the days of anæsthesia, it was not uncommon to conceal from the patient the hour of operation, in order to avoid that mental perturbation and depression which might arise from anticipation of the painful event. Now, however, we are fortunately relieved from this necessity ; but still there are many nervous individuals who cannot contemplate the approaching danger of operation without the greatest degree of agitation. Every possible effort should be made to calm such apprehensions. The tact of the surgeon will guide him to the methods best calculated to effect his purpose in this particular. The administration of a few doses of an alcoholic stimulant before inhalation is highly recommended as a means of tranquillizing a timid patient.

The time of operation should be fixed at such a distance from the hour of the last meal as will insure an empty stomach for the patient. This precaution is especially needful when ether is to be administered, since it is liable to excite vomiting if the stomach is distended. Nothing is more disagreeable than a torrent of undigested food pouring from the gullet of a half unconscious and helpless individual. The act of vomiting under such conditions is, moreover, attended with considerable danger. In numerous instances death by suffocation has occurred during the induction of anæsthesia as a consequence of the accidental passage of food from the œsophagus into the trachea in the act of vomiting. Care, however, should be taken to avoid such postponement of the time of operation as will incur the risk of exhaustion from want of food. About three hours after eating is probably the best time for inhalation.

The patient should, for all ordinary operations, be etherized in the recumbent position. The risk of syncope is thus diminished by a position which favors the access of blood to the brain. It is well, in hospitals, to etherize the patient in a room adjacent to the surgical theatre, in order to avoid on the one hand the risks attendant upon transportation in the anæsthetic state through long corridors and over difficult stairways, and on the other hand to avoid the unpleasant incidents which might arise during etherization in the presence of a large crowd of cynical spectators.

Bodily quiet should be secured for the patient by every possible means. His struggles, if he resist inhalation, should be gently but resolutely restrained. Sudden shifting of position should be avoided, especially the change from a recumbent posture to the vertical. An abrupt change of this character might easily occasion syncope. Far less dangerous would be the reverse movement for a person who had been etherized in the sitting posture. In fact, if this position be for any reason desirable, the patient should occupy a chair which has been constructed in such a way that its back can be easily depressed to a level with its seat. If syncope should then seem likely to occur, it may be readily obviated by depressing the head of the patient, while inhalation is suspended.

The administration of the anæsthetic vapor should never be confided, excepting in special emergencies, to unprofessional or unskilful hands. No department of surgery demands more thorough acquaintance with the necessities and the possible dangers of the situation. The assistant to whom the responsibility of etherization is committed, should be specially instructed with regard to all the signs of danger that may appear, and he should also be perfectly familiar with the methods of resuscitation in case of accident. The comparative rarity of accident is the unquestionable cause of the indifference to these matters that is everywhere apparent. But the rarity of accident is no excuse for the absence of precaution. The trusty surgeon will leave nothing to chance when proceeding to operation. He should be as sure of the security of his patient on the side of anæsthesia as he believes him to be in the matter of hemorrhage. How often this is neglected! The administration of even the more dangerous anæsthetics is confided to the junior assistant—perhaps to a student scarcely out of his teens—a youth without experience and without any adequate comprehension of the real nature of the process in which he is engaged. Instead of devoting his attention to the respiration and circulation of the patient, he may be seen craning over the body of his stertorous and semi-asphyxiated victim, striving with childish curiosity to follow the details of an operation for perineal section, or for the relief of a vesico-vaginal fistula. Such misplaced attention is entirely wrong. The assistant who is charged with the responsibility of maintaining the anæsthetic state should entertain no other care. He should devote himself to the most conscientious study of the phenomena which attend that condition, leaving for another occasion the observation and study of the surgical operation for which anæsthesia is induced.

Having prepared the patient by adjustment of the clothing in such a manner that there shall be no compression of the thorax or constriction of the channels of respiration and circulation in the neck, the administration of ether may be commenced. The assistant to whom this process has been confided should stand either at the head of the recumbent patient, or at his right side, where he can conveniently hold the inhaling apparatus with one hand, while with the other he can ascertain the condition of the pulse. The ordinary inhaler is the best—a napkin twisted into a cone, and placed in a conical sheath of paper or of leather. This napkin should not receive more than a drachm of chloroform at once, but it may be saturated with ether. At first it should be approached gradually toward the face, in a manner calculated to avoid giving alarm to the patient. By this method the feeling of suffocation and of instinctive apprehension, which otherwise might lead to furious agitation on the part of the patient, may be in great measure obviated. A few encouraging words at this moment are often needed to reassure the patient, engaging him to inspire deeply, for the purpose of abbreviating the period of excitement. As the respiratory passages become accustomed to the vapor, and as the phenomena of laryngeal irritation disappear, the inhaler may be placed near the face, so as to exclude the greater portion of air unmixed with the anæsthetic vapor. The conical sheath should be supported by resting the little finger of the hand which holds it upon the malar prominence of the face. By this method the apparatus can easily be carried farther from the face if occasion should require the admission of more air. The temporal artery can at the same time be utilized for observation of the condition of the circulation.

The induction of anæsthesia should proceed at a moderate rate. From five to ten minutes are ordinarily required for the complete subjection of an adult male. Children yield more rapidly to the soporific influence. The patient should not be deluged with the vapor, as some surgeons have advised. When ether is employed, the napkin may be saturated, but it should not overflow. A neglect of these precautions may arouse that excitement which is so unfavorable to safety through its tendency to develop the phenomena of syncope, or it may even occasion the addition of asphyxia to anæsthesia. A turgid condition of the veins of the head and neck, associated with a dusky color of the surface, especially if there be muscular rigidity, rapid and irregular pulse, and an excited state of respiration, should always lead to a partial suspension of the anæsthetic. More oxygen is needed by the tissues; and, until these symptoms subside, the inhaler should be raised from the face.

It is desirable, so far as possible, to maintain a uniform rate of inhalation, and a uniform saturation of the air that is passed into the lungs. This, however, can be only approximately maintained. The administrator should test the condition of the napkin by approaching it quickly to his own nostrils. The relative pungency of the emanating vapor will afford the means of deciding the time for adding to the amount of the anæsthetic already poured into the inhaler. The act of replenishment should be performed with the least possible delay, especially when the more volatile substances are employed. When the inhaler is restored to its position before the mouth, it should be rather gradually approached to the face, in order to permit a sufficient degree of dilution of the highly concentrated vapor that is first given off by the newly charged apparatus.

Certain deviations from the quiet progress of anæsthesia are very commonly encountered. The surgeon should understand their significance, and be prepared to act accordingly. Of these irregularities a disposition to cough is usually the first to appear. This is very common at the commencement of inhalation, and is the result of direct irritation of the superior laryngeal nerves. It usually is slight and transitory, requiring no special attention; but if it persists with severity, and, particularly, if it be associated with any appearance of dyspnœa or tendency to asphyxia, the administration of the vapor should be suspended until quiet is restored.

The patient will sometimes offer a violent resistance to the attempt at etherization. This is usually an automatic effort, which originates during the period of semi-consciousness, before the induction of complete anæsthesia. Under such circumstances it is not uncommon to see a half-dozen assistants throwing themselves upon the struggling form of their victim, while several youthful doctors deluge his head and face with a shower of ether—perhaps even chloroform may be discharged upon him with almost equal liberality. Such a course is imprudent, to say the least. Nor is it necessary. With patience and perseverance, employing a little more time than usual, the most intractable individual can ordinarily be subdued without recourse to violence. It should always be kept in mind that these violent cases belong precisely to that class in which the transition from the excitement of delirium to the collapse of syncope is so often sudden and dangerous.

It sometimes happens, during the course of orderly inhalation, that the patient will suddenly grow pale and will attempt to vomit. The stomach does not disgorge its contents, but the chest and the abdomen heave with ineffectual effort.   The pulse will be found rapid and feeble, demanding an immediate suspension of the process of etherization.

That sort of respiratory forgetfulness, of which mention has been made in a previous section, in which the respiratory movements are slow and feeble, with considerable intermissions, calls for stimulation of the function. If the pulse is good, the condition need not excite alarm.   Compression of the abdomen, exposure of the chest to the air, the various methods of exciting reflex action, will suffice to arouse the energy of the respiratory apparatus without suspension of the process of inhalation.   But if the respiratory intermissions are the result of laryngeal spasm, the phenomena of asphyxia appear immediately, and the patient is in danger.   The anæsthetic should be removed until all convulsive symptoms have disappeared, and the circulation and respiration have resumed their normal course.   It sometimes happens that persons of a nervous temperament—especially if they approach the operator with apprehension and alarm—will exhibit their mental perturbation by a sobbing respiration.   This need not excite anxiety on the part of the operator, if the pulse does not give way.   If the circulation becomes enfeebled, or if symptoms of asphyxia are manifested, a brief delay will usually suffice to remove all unpleasant phenomena.   The process of inhalation may then be resumed.

The state of the circulation should receive constant attention.   By many surgeons it has been considered sufficient to watch the respiration, but the condition of the pulse is the best guide to an interpretation of the respiratory symptoms.   It is desirable that the rate and the quality of the pulse should be frequently observed ; in fact, if the more potent anæsthetics, like chloroform, are employed, the finger of the observer should scarcely quit the artery of the patient.

Every sudden modification of the rate or volume of the pulse should place the surgeon on his guard.   It is true that the period of complete anæsthesia is characterized by a diminution of the number of beats ; but this diminution is gradual, and does not occur before the development of unconsciousness.   A small, hard pulse need not cause suspension of the act of inhalation.   The admission of more air will be sufficient.   But if the pulse becomes intermittent and thready, the danger of syncope is immediate.   Etherization should at once be arrested ; the head of the patient should be depressed ; the face and chest may be sprinkled with cold water ; the surface of the body may be rubbed in a manner favorable to the propulsion of the blood through the capillary net-work of the skin. Usually these measures are sufficient ; but if syncope should be fully declared, it will become necessary without delay to have recourse to the more energetic measures to be described in the chapter which treats of the accidents of anæsthesia.   Sometimes these notes of alarm—these precursors of danger—are repeated more than once during the course of an attempt to produce artificial anæsthesia.   The operation should, in such cases, be adjourned, if unfavorable symptoms follow the exhibition of sulphuric ether.   If chloroform or any one of its congeners has been the cause of the difficulty, it should at once be discarded in favor of the milder anæsthetic. In fact, were sulphuric ether the only anæsthetic agent employed by inhalation, the numerous cautions and precautions which are now found needful when speaking in general terms of anæsthesia, would be less needful.

Epileptiform, or even epileptic convulsions, sometimes occur during the administration of anæsthetics.   Such an event need not excite alarm, unless it be the climax of previous excitement in a subject who has never experienced such symptoms of disease in his normal condition.   For all the ordinary forms of convulsive seizure the induction of anæsthesia affords the best means of relief. The occurrence of a convulsion should therefore constitute no reason for the cessation of inhalation.

The condition of complete anæsthesia may be recognized by the moderation of the pulse and the respiration. The patient lies quietly as if in a deep sleep. The movements of respiration are regular, and rather less frequent than the normal rate. Inspiration is deeper, and sometimes accompanied by snoring. The pulse becomes full, soft, and scarcely accelerated—sometimes even slower than at the commencement of inhalation. The expression of the countenance is tranquil, the eyes are closed, the muscular system is relaxed. A favorite method of ascertaining this fact is by raising an arm of the patient and then allowing it to drop by his side. If the stage of complete anæsthesia has been reached, the limb will fall like an inert mass, showing that the muscles no longer present any resistance to the action of gravity. If any degree of rigidity persists—a fact which may be readily ascertained by undertaking to make flexion of the arm at the elbow-joint—the patient is not fully etherized. The cutaneous sensibility may also be tested by pinching the skin sharply between the nails of the finger and thumb. The indications thus obtained are more reliable than the results of touching the conjunctiva of the eye.

When complete insensibility has been thus determined, the anæsthetic state should be carefully maintained by the continual administration of small quantities of the vapor. This method should be preferred to the common practice of intermittent inhalation, during the intervals of which the patient is liable to partial emergence from the condition of unconsciousness, necessitating, perhaps, a suspension of the operation until anæsthesia can be again induced. After the conclusion of the operation, the patient should be allowed to remain in quiet until consciousness is fully restored. The condition of the pulse and of the respiration should still be observed until it is evident that the depressing effects of the anæsthetic have entirely disappeared. Not before that time is it safe to agitate the sufferer by removal from the place of operation. For a considerable time, if there has been any great loss of blood, he should not be allowed to sit up, for fear of dangerous syncope. The diminution of bodily heat, which is one of the direct consequences of anæsthetic interference with the molecular changes within the body, will often require the application of artificial heat. Wine and ammonia should be given if the circulation remain enfeebled after the return of consciousness. If severe pain is likely to continue, or to follow after the operation, it is advisable to administer a hypodermic injection of morphine before the renewal of sensation.

Sometimes the first emergence of the patient from the anæsthetic state is complicated by the occurrence of a severe chill. This, however, is usually of short duration, yielding readily to ordinary restorative measures. But such an occurrence marks a profound disturbance of the ganglia at the base of the brain, and it should serve to render the surgeon doubly attentive to the condition of his charge—for it is sometimes the prelude to a very distressing series of nervous phenomena characteristic of irritable weakness.

A renewal of hemorrhage from the wound is not an infrequent consequence of emergence from artificial anæsthesia. This will usually be found to depend upon an increased vigor of the circulation, by which blood is forced out of the incised extremities of arterial twigs which were collapsed, and thus had escaped notice during the period of anæsthesia. For this reason many surgeons prefer to delay the final dressing of the wound until a certain time has elapsed after the removal of the anæsthetic. Under any cir-cumstances the wound, if involving any considerable vessel, should be kept under observation until the normal circulation has been renewed.

The process of recovery after operation is seldom affected in an unfav-orable manner by the previous induction of anæsthesia. A few surgeons have attributed secondary hemorrhages, prolonged suppuration, and other accidents, to a constitutional condition supposed to be induced by the an-æsthetic. But the opinion of the vast majority of experienced men is un-favorable to this view. It is difficult to comprehend the possibility of such a result from a single brief contact of the tissues with a volatile liquid that does not enter into combination with their substance. In all such unfav-orable cases the difficulty may be with far greater certainty traced to a previous condition of cachexia.

It was the opinion of Sir James Y. Simpson, based upon his compari-son of the statistics of British hospitals, for the times before and after the introduction of artificial anæsthesia into surgical practice, that the mortal-ity after surgical operations was diminished by the use of anæsthetics. But such a question is exceedingly difficult of decision by the statistical method. So many other facts must be taken into consideration, that the influence of etherization really occupies a relatively insignificant space in the list of agents which operate in favor of or against the recovery of the patient. The great improvements in hospital construction and hospital hygiene that were initiated about the time that etherization was intro-duced, have undoubtedly contributed the largest share of the influences that have tended to depress the rate of mortality after surgical operations. But it may be admitted, without fear of contradiction, that any process which diminishes the terrors of operation will be likely to economize the vital powers of the individual, and so far forth to increase his ability to sur-mount the dangers through which he must pass.

METHOD OF PRODUCING ANÆSTHESIA.

The liquid anæsthetics will produce insensibility if swallowed in suffi-cient quantity. But this method of producing anæsthesia is attended with dangers which render it quite inapplicable in practice. For the induction of artificial anæsthesia, it is therefore necessary to introduce the agent, in the form of a gas or vapor, through the medium of the respiratory pas-sages. In this way insensibility may be very easily and quickly effected.

Unfortunately, however, the inhalation of the concentrated vapor of certain anæsthetics is a dangerous proceeding. If the amount of chloro-form vapor exceeds a certain percentage to the air that is inspired, death is the immediate result. According to the experiments of Lallemand, Per-rin, and Duroy, mammals can live in an atmosphere containing four per cent. of the vapor of chloroform ; but if the quantity be increased to eight per cent., they very soon cease to breathe. In Dr. Snow's experiments, warm-blooded animals were killed by an atmosphere containing only 2.3 per cent. of chloroform. Now, it has been ascertained that at the temperature of 15.5° (60° F.) the air will take up twelve per cent. of chloroform vapor ; consequently it is a very easy matter to fill the lungs with a deadly atmos-phere, if special precautions are not taken to prevent the saturation of the air. For this purpose various forms of apparatus have been contrived, having for their common object the sufficient dilution of the anæsthetic vapor. Besides these ordinary inhalers, a special form of apparatus is necessary in order to facilitate the inhalation of nitrous oxide gas—the principal object being the exclusion of atmospheric air and the introduction of the undiluted gas. During the past few years a modification of this apparatus has been devised by Mr. Clover, of London, in order to permit the concurrent inhalation of nitrous oxide gas and ethereal vapors.

Theoretically, many of these complicated contrivances, with their valves, and stop-cocks, and mouth-pieces, and reservoirs, are very perfect; but, practically, the majority of them are quite useless—some of them are positively dangerous. The reason of this lies in the fact that they do not accomplish that for which they have been devised—the uniform and sufficient dilution of the anæsthetic vapor. Besides this difficulty is the equally important fact that a definite dilution of the more powerful anæsthetics is no safeguard against danger in their use. A dose which produces no appreciable harm in thousands of cases will promptly destroy the life of a susceptible patient. It is not so much the excessive percentage of vapor that kills as it is the excess of vapor without regard to percentage. The amount that constitutes an excess varies with the individual. What is excess for one patient is the extreme of moderation for another. The varying conditions of the same patient, as regards his health, or vigor, also exercise a great effect upon the relation between the living tissues and the anæsthetic substance. Consequently a person may succumb to-day in the presence of a dose which he has on previous occasions received without the slightest risk. The rate of inhalation has a very decided influence upon the risks that attend the act. There is, on the part of the living units which compose the animal body, a power of gradual self-adjustment to altered conditions of existence. But, if the process of adjustment is urged too rapidly, that equilibrium of forces by which the continuous manifestation of vital phenomena is maintained is violently overthrown, and vital phenomena can no longer be exhibited by that particular congeries of molecules. It is for this reason that all sudden shocks are so much more dangerous than the gradual application of the same amount of force. It is for this reason that the commencement of etherization should always be slowly and cautiously introduced. It is for this reason that all rapid anæsthesia is more dangerous than that which proceeds by gradual induction. Now, the fault of the majority of the forms of inhaling apparatus consists in the fact that these contrivances either do not sufficiently provide for the gradual increase of the proportion of the anæsthetic vapor that is inhaled, or, if they do profess to accomplish such gradual increase, the profession is more nominal than real. The percentage of vapor will vary with changes in the temperature of the atmosphere to such an extent that, when the administrator supposes his apparatus to be safely evolving three per cent. of chloroform vapor, it may actually be liberating five per cent., or even a larger proportion. The patient will therefore be placed in circumstances of greater danger than if the operator had dispensed with all forms of apparatus. Since the dangers depend so largely upon the internal reactions which take place, it is far more important to watch the condition of the patient than to provide for a uniform dilution of the vapor. The simplest method of dispensing the vapor is, therefore, the best. Vaporization by evaporation from a towel is always practicable, and is a method quite as safe as any that has yet been devised. It has the advantage which attaches to a method that is simple, easy, and as free from danger as anything connected with anæsthesia can be. The napkin can, moreover, always be furnished in a cleanly condition for each patient, which is a great deal more than can be said of the filthy mouth-pieces that are so often seen where inhalers are in fashion. The operator can as readily control the rate of inhalation, when using a napkin, as it is possible for him to do when employing a complicated piece of apparatus by which the face is concealed, and the actual condition of the patient is in too great measure hidden from view. By removing the napkin a little from the face at the commencement of inhalation, and for a few seconds after each reinforcement, the quantity of vapor that is inhaled can be intelligently controlled and regulated by its physiological effects rather than by any arbitrary method of admixture with the air that is breathed. In short, it is by reference to the quantity of the anæsthetic substance in contact with the tissues of the body that the process of inhalation must be regulated. The operator should let nothing intervene between himself and his patient.

For all ordinary inhalations, then, a simple napkin, a bit of lint, a handkerchief—almost any porous substance that can be adapted to the face —is quite sufficient. When chloroform is administered, there should be no restraint placed upon its evaporation and diffusion through the air; but, if sulphuric ether is used, it may be confined by a cone of paper or of

Snow's Inhaler.

leather, open at the apex, and placed outside of the towel. Unless this conical sheath is open at its apex, there may be danger of almost complete exclusion of the air, as the towel becomes wet and heavy enough to collapse upon the face of the patient.

The earliest form of apparatus for inhalation was the glass globe with double tubulation, devised by Morton for his earliest experiments. This, however, was soon discarded. The English physician, Snow, devised an inhaler, which was really only a modification of Morton's original apparatus. The above illustration will exhibit the principle that governs the construction and use of all such articles.

Dr. Sansom undertook the introduction of an inhaler for chloroform, which is represented by the following cut. This piece of apparatus differs principally from Dr. Snow's inhaler by the substitution of a gutta-percha jacket in place of the water-bath which surrounds the chloroform cylinder. The flexible delivery-tube is replaced by a double sheathing tube which is provided with a rotatory joint at its point of junction with the cylinder, so that it can be adapted for convenient use in the sitting posture, as well as in the recumbent attitude. In order to regulate the admission of air for the dilution of the chloroform vapor, the inner and outer casings of the de-

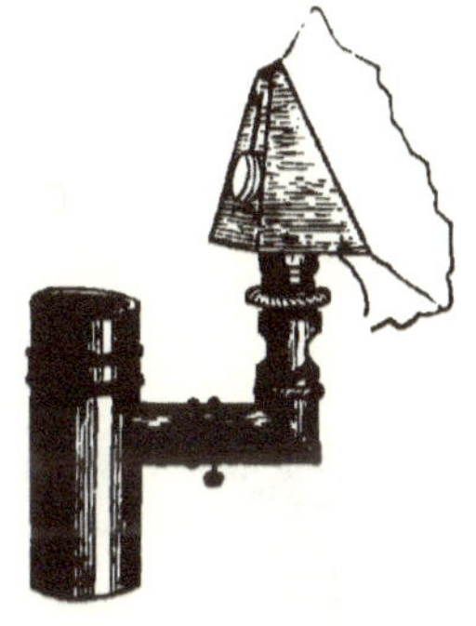 

Sansom's Inhaler.

livery-tube are perforated with holes, which by a rotatory movement of the outer sheath may be made to coincide in a more or less perfect manner. When thus rotated into coincidence, these apertures admit the external air with perfect freedom, and the vapor of chloroform is scarcely perceptible in the mixture. This is the proper arrangement for the commencement of inhalation. As the patient becomes accustomed to the anæsthetic, so that it ceases to irritate the air-passages, the administrator is expected to rotate the external sheath in such a manner that the communications with the external atmosphere shall be gradually closed. The final closure of the aperture in the face-piece reduces the apparatus to a condition virtually identical with the mechanism of Snow's inhaler. It then exhibits substantially the same advantages and disadvantages that exist in connection with that instrument.

Various other forms of inhaling apparatus have been contrived for the purpose of graduating the quantity of chloroform vapor that is furnished to the patient, but not one of them is capable of self-adaptation to the continually varying necessities of each particular case. The operator is compelled at each instant to intervene in order to compel the instrument to accomplish what can be as easily effected without it. Intelligent surgeons have, therefore, generally abandoned the use of complicated apparatus, and now content themselves with a simple napkin, or, at the most, with something which is essentially nothing more than a napkin-holder. This fact is well illustrated by the methods of Billroth (*Chicago Med. Journ.*, p. 617, June, 1880), who uses nothing but a strip of cotton-flannel, stretched over a metallic frame, and held about an inch from the face of the patient. Upon this cloth the anæsthetic is carefully poured, in quantities dictated by the peculiarities of each individual case. A somewhat ambitious form of the same thing is thus described by Dr. L. Turnbull, in his work on "Artificial Anæsthesia" (p. 249), under the name of Skinner's Chloroform Inhaling Apparatus, as a wire frame "in the form of a scoop-net, which, when in use, is covered with a thin flannel or domette drawn tight.   There is an accompanying green glass bottle for the chloroform, with a stopper and cap, and on removal of which a tubular stopper is fitted so as to use it for a dropper. . . .   When soiled, or, indeed, after administering chloroform to any patient, a fresh cover should always be put on. . . ."

The theoretical importance of furnishing for inhalation a vapor of definite and uniform strength led Mr. Clover, the veteran London anæsthe-

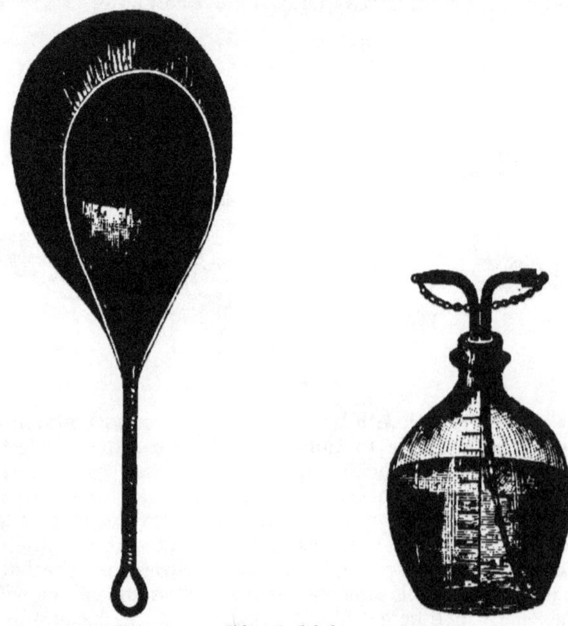

Skinner's Inhaler.

tizer, to devise a method of inhalation that was thus described by Sansom (Op. cit., p. 179): "The apparatus he employs is, first, a bag for containing the anæsthetic mixture; secondly, an arrangement for filling the bag with a certain proportion of chloroform and air.   The bag is of a large size, capable of containing sufficient of the chloroform-atmosphere to serve for several cases of inhalation.   It is lined with a film of a material (such as gold-beater's skin) which is capable of resisting the solvent action of chloroform.   A flexible tube leads from the bag to the mouth-piece, which is of the same conformation as that described as Dr. Sibson's; but Mr. Clover has introduced an improvement, by using for the valves thin plates of ivory, supported by spiral springs.   The india-rubber which is usually employed for the valves is apt to curl up.

"The apparatus for filling the bag with the atmosphere for inhalation consists of a bellows, shaped like a concertina, with a receptacle for a definite amount of chloroform attached to its nozzle.   This receptacle is a metallic box, which is kept warm by an interstratum of hot water, so as to facilitate the evaporation of the chloroform, which is received on blotting-paper in its interior.   The lid of the box contains an aperture for the reception of a graduated syringe, by which the chloroform is supplied.   Opposite that part of the box to which the nozzle of the bellows is attached is an open tube, to which the bag can be adapted. The apparatus being thus connected, air is blown over the chloroform into the bag by means of the bellows. For each thousand cubic inches of air which the bellows throws in, forty minims of chloroform are supplied by means of the syringe. Thus, since forty minims of chloroform produce about forty-five cubic inches of vapor, the atmosphere in the bag contains $4\frac{1}{2}$ per cent. of chloroform vapor. Of course, the percentage is determined at will by the amount of chloroform supplied.

"When sufficient of the atmosphere has been thus prepared, the bag is detached from the metallic box and the mouth-piece applied. It is then suspended in a convenient position from the collar of the administrator's coat. The position of administrator and patient is seen in the engraving."

Mr. Clover's Apparatus.

The advantage of this method of administration consists in the uniform strength of the vapor in the bag. But it has to be further diluted by manipulation of the valve in the mouth-piece as inhalation proceeds, consequently the advantage secured by the reservoir is quite neutralized by the mouth-piece, and the apparent superiority of the method is quite negative in practice.

ETHER-INHALERS.

The practical immunity from danger which attends the inhalation of the vapor of sulphuric ether, renders it almost unnecessary to employ any special precautions against too great concentration of the vapor. The only necessity, therefore, for the use of an inhaling apparatus, arises from considerations of convenience and economy. When ether is poured upon a napkin in hot weather, comparatively little of the resulting vapor can ever be inhaled. The greater portion is dissipated through the air, and is of no use whatever—may even be a source of great annoyance to the surgeon and to his assistants. To obviate this inconvenience, it is customary to surround the towel upon which the anæsthetic is poured with some kind of impervious sheath which shall hinder the general diffusion of ether-vapor. To furnish something more durable and permanent than the newspaper cone ordinarily extemporized for each occasion has been the object kept in view by the numerous

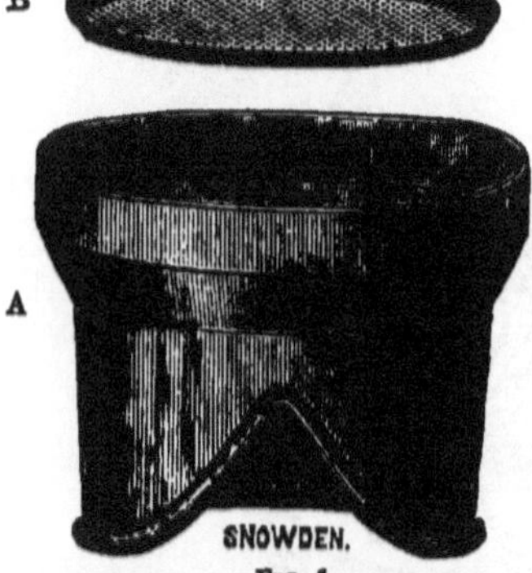

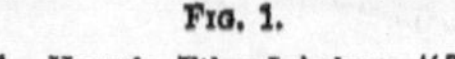

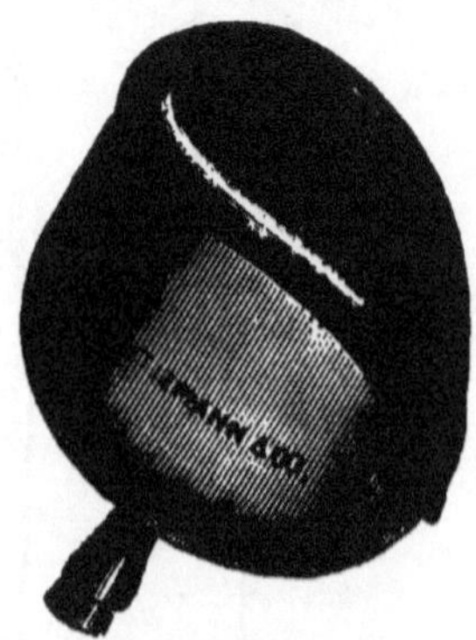

FIG. 1.FIG. 2.

FIG. 1.—Hearn's Ether-Inhaler: "The inhaler has its outer case, A, made of thin sheet-metal, having the lower edge, which comes in contact with the face, covered with rubber. Inside of this case a screen of wire gauze, B, is fitted, which comes opposite the lower joint, as at A. The lint or canton flannel upon which the ether is poured is shown at C, and is held in place between the wire-gauze screen B and the funnel-shaped top D."
FIG. 2.—Lente's Ether-Inhaler.

inventors who have turned their attention to the construction of ether-inhalers. One of the simplest and best of these articles is the inhaler invented by Dr. Lente, of New York.

This consists merely of a modified cone—which may be constructed of metal, wood, gutta-percha, celluloid, or any other convenient material—provided with a cushioned rim, fitted as nearly as possible to the contour of the face. When used, the cone is filled with sheet lint, which should be removed after each inhalation, in order to secure cleanliness. The apex of the cone is closed with a cork, which should be removed if the rim of the mouth-piece fits too closely to the face. Ether may be poured through this apicial opening without removing the inhaler from the face.

Dr. Joseph W. Hearn, of Philadelphia, has introduced an inhaler which differs from Dr. Lente's only in the direction of greater complexity of structure.

It is impossible to describe all the forms of inhaling apparatus which have been recommended, without giving to a scientific treatise the aspect of a surgical-instrument maker's catalogue. Those who are curious in

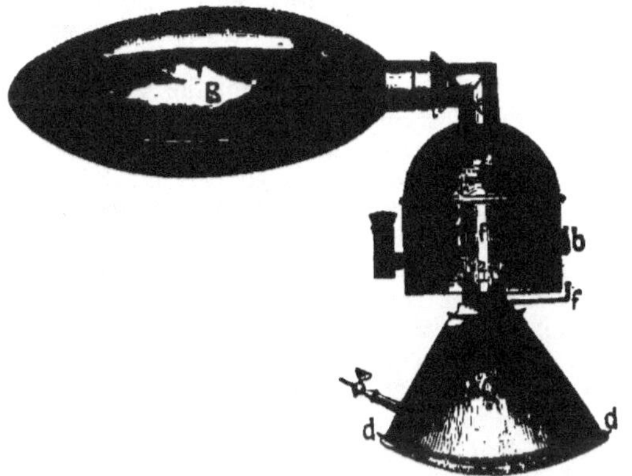

Clover's smaller Apparatus for Inhalation of Ether (Kappeler).

such matters will find abundant stimulus to their inventive faculties upon the pages of any work that treats of surgical anæsthesia. The principle

Clover's Inhaler for Ether and Nitrous Oxide: E, container for ether; F, face-piece; G, caoutchouc bag traversed by a tube, for the direct transmission of ether vapor. By a proper arrangement the vapor can be combined in the bag with nitrous oxide from the receiver R, K. Re, regulator.

which should guide the construction of these varied instruments is the same, to wit: a free admission to the lungs of air that has been as nearly as possible saturated with ether-vapor, while the general diffusion of that vapor outside of the body is hindered in every way consistent with unimpeded respiration on the part of the patient. This matter of unimpeded respiration has not, however, always received the consideration to which it is entitled. Witness the following description of the small clover apparatus :

This consists of a metallic container A, for the reception of liquid ether, which may be introduced through the funnel-mouth a. The ether-vessel is spherical and one-half is surrounded by water, introduced into the chamber c, through the opening at b, to prevent the ether from becoming too cold by rapid evaporation. The container is traversed by a jointed tube, Pf 1, Pf 2, which opens a communication between the rubber bag B and the mouth-piece C. The face-piece is edged with an air-cushion. The ether vessel and water-chamber rotate upon the mouth of the face-piece C. When the instrument is first applied, the stopper at b should stand opposite the forehead of the patient, who then breathes directly in and out of the bag B. As the ether-vessel is turned round, the air is obliged to enter the ether-chamber and pass through it before it reaches the bag ; and when the vessel is turned half round, so that the stopper b is opposite the chin of the patient, all the air going in and out of the bag must pass through the ether-vessel.

The objections to this apparatus are those which lie against all forms of inhaling apparatus. It is heavy, inconvenient, and unclean. By continuous respiration of the contents of the rubber bag B, the phenomena of anæsthesia by carbonic anhydride are added to the effects of ether vapor. As Mr. Clover himself admits, the thing "is rather too complicated for general use."

A method of producing anæsthesia by combined inhalation of nitrous oxide gas and ether vapor is now employed by certain experimenters. It is convenient in this operation to use a form of apparatus that will permit the alternate inhalation of these substances.

NITROUS OXIDE INHALERS.

The great desideratum in the use of nitrous oxide gas is an inhaler which shall not be heavy and clumsy, but which shall at the same time furnish space sufficient for the free passage of gas in and out of the mouth. The older inhalers consisted of little more than a mouth-piece, connected with the gas-tube, or a mouth-piece and gas-tube, which required the use of a clamp to close the nostrils in a manner to prevent the admission of atmospheric air through the nose. Sometimes, in the absence of a clamp, the patient was expected to hold his own nose, or perhaps the operator might volunteer that gentle service.

The sensation of suffocation thus produced was anything but agreeable. Great difficulty has always been experienced in securing a uniform adaptation of the same mouth-piece to different countenances. For obvious reasons, an inflexible inhaler that happened to fit the cheeks of a youthful maiden in her prime, would not be very likely to exclude the external air when pressed against the emaciated features of a bearded invalid. Messrs. Codman & Shurtleff, the ingenious instrument-makers in Boston, have succeeded in producing a piece of apparatus which surmounts all these difficulties in a manner more effectual than the similar attempts of any other instrument of this sort (see Figs. 1, 2, and 3, pp. 43 and 44).

The figure on page 44 represents this inhaler with the ether-reservoir attached in place of the gas-tube leading to the gasometer for nitrous

Early Method of Administering Nitrous Oxide (Rottenstein).

oxide gas. The ether is poured through the opening G, upon a sponge or piece of lint placed in the reservoir F. The simplicity and cleanliness of this apparatus must commend it to all who are obliged to resort to the use

Fig. 1.   Fig. 2.

Codman & Shurtleff's Inhalers for Nitrous Oxide.

Fig. 1.—Inhaler for Nitrous Oxide Gas: A. hard-rubber mouth-piece; B, metallic hood.
Fig. 2.—A, metallic hood; B, flexible rubber hood, projecting from within the metallic face-piece; C, exhaling-valve; D, two-way stop-cock; I, packing, through which a silk cord passes; E, sliding-joint, where J is detached to connect the ether-reservoir; J contains the inhaling-valve.

of nitrous oxide gas. The great secret of comfort in the employment of such an inhaler will be found in the perfection of its valves and in the sufficiency of amplitude in the diameter of its passages.   Their smallest diameter should not be less than the diameter of the glottis.   If this degree of width

FIG. 3.—Codman & Shurtleff's Inhaler for Ether.

is not secured, the respiration of the patient will become labored and distressing, as if actual suffocation were experienced.

ACCIDENTS OF ANÆSTHESIA.

In treating of the fatal results which occasionally follow the employment of an anæsthetic agent, it is not deemed necessary to discuss those cases in which death has occurred with an interval of many hours, or after a number of days have passed, since the inhalation.   Only those cases will be considered in which alarming symptoms or cessation of life have supervened during the administration of the anæsthetic, or before the normal conclusion of the period of anæsthesia.

In certain rare cases death occurs suddenly, without any note of warning.   The process of inhalation has proceeded without disturbance.   The patient has remained quiet, and has seemed perfectly tolerant of the vapor, when all at once respiration ceases and the heart stops.   This accident may occur at any time, before or after the production of complete insensibility, and it is commonly witnessed among patients who have been greatly enfeebled by previous disease or by hemorrhage.   It may be termed the adynamic form of accident.

Death by suffocation may occur during the administration of ether or chloroform, as a consequence of maladjustment of the inhaling apparatus, so that atmospheric air is excluded from the lungs.   This can only occur as the result of great negligence or great ignorance on the part of the operator.   More frequently the phenomena of asphyxia are excited by local irritations produced by the particular agent that is employed.   The vapor of chloroform is very irritating to the oral, pharyngeal, and laryngeal branches of the fifth, ninth, and tenth pairs of cranial nerves ; and the reflex energies of certain patients are greatly excited by local contact of the vapor with the terminal branches of these nerves in the localities indicated.   The patient seems to experience a degree of suffocation as soon as the act of inhalation is commenced.   He coughs convulsively ; the veins of the head and neck become turgid with black blood.   The skin is livid ; perspiration covers the surface.   There is a convulsive effort to escape from the vaporizing apparatus, and after a few brief struggles the unfortunate victim is dead.

Such accidents, happily, are exceedingly rare. More frequently the intervention of danger manifests itself otherwise. The stage of excitement is unusually prolonged; the patient does not yield to the stupefying effects of the vapor, or, if he seems for a moment to become unconscious, the excitement is again and again renewed. The muscles may pass into a condition of rigidity, during which the pulse suddenly disappears, respiration ceases, the face assumes a corpse-like hue, and death occurs.

By whatever antecedents the event is ushered in, the final mode of death is essentially the same—an abrupt cessation of respiration and circulation. It is not the result of obstructed breathing, except in those rare examples of death from actual suffocation, either by mal-adjustment of the inhaling apparatus or through an occlusion of the larynx by intrusion of a morsel of food brought from the stomach by the act of vomiting. Unless thus complicated, death is the direct result of the toxic action of the anæsthetic upon the nerve-centres which preside over the functions of respiration and circulation. A minor degree of asphyxia may accompany this toxic action in the cases where death occurs during the early stage of etherization, characterized by an unusual degree of laryngeal and respiratory spasm; but even then it is the anæsthetic rather than the absence of oxygen which is the principal efficient cause of a fatal result. Post-mortem examination of the body confirms this opinion, for in the vast majority of cases—in all cases which are not confessedly the result of direct suffocation—the blood has not the black and viscous appearance which it displays after death by occlusion of the air-passages. It is uniformly distributed throughout the circulatory channels instead of being accumulated in the large veins and in the right side of the heart. Its color, also, approaches the normal coloration of oxygenated blood—darker than normal blood, but still of a brighter color on the arterial than upon the venous side of the circulatory apparatus. Various local congestions upon the surface of the brain, in the mucous membrane of the bronchi, or in the parenchyma of the lungs, etc., are too variable in their character and presence to be considered among the causes of death. They are, doubtless, more frequently than not the result of the convulsive struggles of the patient during the period of excitement.

The manner of death during anæsthesia is often, in its abruptness and in its essential features, closely related to the occurrence of syncope. In both cases there is often a period of exaggerated excitement, followed by sudden failure of vital phenomena, and, in certain instances, by death itself. But there is between the two conditions the capital difference created by the presence of a toxic agent in one case, and its absence in the other. Death from etherization is the consequence of a genuine toxæmia. Death from syncope is the result of a certain specific disturbance of the nervous equilibrium which should be maintained between the different nervous centres of the body. In many cases syncope is the immediate antecedent of death in the course of anæsthesia; but the final result is the consequence of syncope plus ethereal intoxication.

A consideration of the manner in which the mode of death may be changed by variations in the magnitude of a fatal dose of hydrocyanic acid will serve to explain the different modes of death which occur under the influence of surgical anæsthetics. H. C. Wood ("Therapeutics, Materia Medica, and Toxicology," second edition, p. 173) states that, after the administration of the acid in an amount just sufficient to kill, "no phenomena are offered for some seconds; then the breathing becomes labored, and the pulse slow and full. The animal perhaps cries out, and muscular tremblings invade the whole body, to give place, in a very short time, to clonic and tonic convulsions, which continue at intervals until the third stage, that of collapse, is developed. The convulsions are less violent and less frequent than those of the acute poisoning; all the symptoms noted as occurring during the second stage of rapid cases are present in the corresponding period of the subacute poisoning, although less violent and less intense in their manifestations. When the third stage is developed, the anæsthesia is marked, affecting first the hind leg, but finally spreading to all parts of the body, and even being complete in the widely dilated pupil. Death finally results from failure of respiration."

The parallel between these symptoms, and the phenomena which are observed in the majority of deaths from ether and in many of the deaths from chloroform, is very close.

Wood further describes the symptoms of acute poisoning with large doses of hydrocyanic acid as follows:

"The animal gasps once or twice, and then instantly falls into a tetanic or clonic convulsion, or else drops motionless and powerless upon its side. In either case, at once the signs of asphyxia manifest themselves, and grow more and more intense, until they end in total arrest of respiration. The heart beats irregularly, often at first slowly and strongly, with intervals of suspension of movement, but always becoming weaker and more rapid in its action, until, after the breathing has ceased, its efforts gradually die away. If the dose has been enormous, *the heart and lungs may stop acting at once;* otherwise the cardiac pulsations may continue some minutes after the arrest of respiration. Ordinarily, three distinct stages are apparent; a first, very brief one, of difficult respiration, slow cardiac action, and disturbed cerebration; a second, convulsive stage, with dilated pupils, violent convulsions, unconsciousness, loud cries, vomiting, often spasmodic urination and defecation, erections, etc. ; a third, period of asphyxia, collapse, and paralysis, sometimes interrupted by partial or even general spasms."

The picture thus presented has too often found its exact counterpart in death from chloroform upon the table of the surgeon.

Since the phenomena of anæsthesia are the result of a paralyzing action on the part of the anæsthetic, and since this action extends in greater or less degree to all parts of the nervous system, it follows that every act of anæsthetic inhalation is a step in the direction of respiratory paralysis and death. It is, therefore, impossible to employ any anæsthetic agent without, in some small degree at least, departing from the normal standard of perfect security. All diseases which diminish the energy of the heart and of the lungs tend to increase the dangers of anæsthesia by favoring the production of syncope. Profuse hemorrhage operates in the same way. Intemperance and fatty degeneration are also unfavorable to safety. Cold, hunger, want, misery, mental anxiety, loss of sleep, over-exertion of all kinds, are causes of danger, because they serve to depress the sum of vital energies. Consequently, a person who has often been subjected to anæsthesia with perfect impunity may yet succumb upon another trial.

Repletion of the stomach has been specified as the cause of a fatal accident in a certain number of cases. How far this condition may operate directly is uncertain; but several cases have been recorded in which, after a hearty meal, the administration of an anæsthetic—and ether is more liable than chloroform to provoke such a complication—has induced vomiting, during which, a convulsive inspiration has drawn a bulky morsel of food from the pharynx into the larynx, producing death by suffocation. It is, therefore, prudent to perform all operations requiring the use of ether during the interval in which the stomach may be reasonably supposed to be empty. This, however, should not lead the operator to the other extreme, so as to incur danger from exhaustion through prolonged abstinence from food.

The position of the patient has been assigned as a cause of death in certain instances. Perrin has collected sixty-seven cases in which the position was recorded. Of these, nineteen were etherized in the sitting posture, and forty-eight were recumbent. As a general rule it may be desirable to preserve the recumbent posture in order to guard against the dangers of syncope, which are supposed to be greater in the vertical position.

The mode of inhalation is supposed to constitute a cause that may be capable of effecting a disastrous result. A too hasty administration of the vapor may produce too rapid saturation of the tissues, and consequent death. It should never be forgotten that the primary stage of anæsthesia is a period of excitement. A sudden inhalation may, therefore, operate as a shock to the nervous centres, tending to produce syncope before the fully toxic action has been developed. Convulsions, also, may thus be excited, which may themselves arrest the respiratory function, and thus occasion death ; or they may be the forerunners of fatal syncope. Perrin has collected twenty-eight cases in which this was observed. Turnbull reports, among one hundred and sixty cases of death after chloroform, at least seven cases which may probably be assigned to the same cause. In all cases, irrespective of the danger of creating asphyxia by actual suffocation, a moderate rate of inhalation affords the greatest degree of security, especially during the use of chloroform.

There is a certain amount of danger to the patient from violent nervous reaction if the operative proceedings of the surgeon are commenced before the establishment of complete anæsthesia. Physiologists are well aware of the fact that a sudden excitement of sensitive nerves may seriously disturb the action of the heart—may even be sufficient to arrest its movement. Before the days of artificial anæsthesia, an emotion of alarm at the preliminaries of operation, or the pain experienced at the first instant of incision, has been known to produce a fatal syncope. It is not in the least degree improbable that, when the controlling influence of the brain has been partially abolished by an anæsthetic vapor, such a painful impression, suddenly experienced, might concentrate its effects upon the reflex apparatus of the heart, and thus occasion an abrupt inhibitory arrest of its movements. This hypothesis has been subjected to the crucial test of experiment upon the lower animals by Romain Vigoureux, who found that the nerves of sensation may continue to influence the apparatus of circulation during the period of anæsthesia, even to the degree of stopping the movements of the heart. Obviously, however, this could only be true in cases of incomplete loss of sensibility. When the reflex apparatus is completely overwhelmed, no such communication between a peripheral nerve and the cardiac ganglia can be possible. The comparatively frequent connection between anæsthesia and insignificant and yet suddenly painful operations, such as the extraction of a tooth or the evulsion of a toe-nail, renders this explanation highly probable. Under such circumstances the operator is tempted to act before the complete establishment of insensibility, and a mortal accident may be the result. Out of sixty-five fatal cases reviewed by Perrin, death occurred during the course of the operation in eighteen instances; but the degree of anæsthesia was incomplete in only ten of the eighteen, so that operation during imperfect insensibility is not necessarily fatal.

It is, however, fatal in a number of cases sufficiently large to condemn the practice. Etherization should always be carried to the abolition of the cutaneous reflex manifestations, in order to avoid this very considerable danger. It is true that we may thus occasionally incur the risk of developing the toxic effects of the anæsthetic; but this—especially if ether be the agent employed—is by far the lesser risk of the two.

The practice of using powerful anæsthetic vapors during the operations of minor surgery should always be discouraged. Of one hundred and sixty cases of death from chloroform reported by Turnbull, but forty-two of the cases deserved to rank above the minor operations of surgery. Of seventy-seven fatal cases, collected by Perrin, in which chloroform was used, no less than eighteen were operations of a trifling character, such as the extraction of a tooth, the opening of an abscess, and the evulsion of a nail. If patients about to undergo an insignificant operation insist upon insensibility to pain, it should be procured by local anæsthetics, or by the inhalation of sulphuric ether, which still remains beyond all question the safest of all anæsthetic agents.

Various conditions, which may be considered accidental or peculiar to the individual, are capable of modifying the effects of anæsthesia. Such are the varieties produced by differences of age, sex, temperament, constitution, health or disease. Children support anæsthesia with remarkable tolerance. They yield promptly to the anæsthetic influence, and their sleep is peaceful and profound. A fatal result is among these little patients exceedingly rare. Turnbull reports a case of death during the administration of chloroform to a child of three years: but it was remarked that the child was always weakly, and its "lungs had never been inflated." This remarkable susceptibility to anæsthetics, combined with a corresponding tolerance of their toxic possibilities, is due to the preponderance of the vegetative functions in the organization of the infant. The rapidity of circulation and respiration, and the larger relative surface of the body, provide for a speedy elimination of the drug, so that "cumulative effects" are almost impossible. The rudimentary development of the higher cerebral centres of the nervous system also diminishes the danger of agitation and disturbance of the lower ganglia through the agency of perturbation descending from the brain.

Old people tolerate anæsthesia to such a degree, that it has been claimed that after the age of sixty-five years it was devoid of danger. Reference to the statistical table hereafter will show this to be incorrect. It should be remembered that the number of aged people who are obliged to resort to anæsthesia is not large in comparison with the great multitude in middle and early life who are the subjects of surgical operation. Anæsthetics should be administered to the aged with more than ordinary care, for with them the phenomena of etherism are liable to assume an adynamic character. The pulse sinks rapidly into a condition of great weakness, respiration becomes slow, feeble, and obstructed by mucus, the countenance becomes corpse-like, and the general muscular relaxation is more complete than with subjects in middle life. For this reason the administration of an anæsthetic to an elderly person should always be conducted with great deliberation. Aside from the liabilities thus particularized, there seems to be no special danger from anæsthesia at an advanced period of life.

The influence of sex is quite apparent among the phenomena of anæsthesia. Women pass more readily than men into the stage of insensibility, and the anæsthetic sleep is more profound. As a consequence of this fact, syncope is less frequently observed among them than among men. They resemble children in this particular. The mortality of the male sex is accordingly greater than that of the female. This may be partly owing to the greater frequency of surgical operations among males ; but, as an offset to this fact, the female sex enjoys an absolute monopoly of obstetrical anæsthesia. The menstrual period would seem to expose the female to greater risks of nervous disturbance, and to the unfavorable consequences of a suppression of the monthly flow ; so that, unless absolutely necessary, the employment of anæsthesia should be deferred till the monthly interval is established. Still, it must be confessed that there is very little experience of actual harm from etherization during the period. The same remarks apply to the condition of pregnancy. Aside from the risk of injury through violent efforts during the stage of excitement, there seems to be no reason why anæsthesia should not be tolerated during the time of gestation. Lactation constitutes no contraindication to the use of anæsthetics.

Peculiarities of temperament and constitution appear to exercise no appreciable effect upon the course of anæsthesia. Unless there exists an individual predisposition to syncope, it is a matter of very little consequence whether the patient is gifted with a bilious temperament rather than a sanguine. Such predisposition may be permanent or it may be temporary. It may be the result of disease or of exhaustion. Numerous causes may operate singly, or may combine to produce this element of weakness. If it is known to exist, it should contraindicate the use of anything more powerful than sulphuric ether, and even that benign compound should be administered with caution.

The various diseases of the brain and spinal cord should cause hesitation in the use of anæsthetics. All diseases which encroach upon the regions adjacent to the medulla oblongata increase the danger of accidents during anæsthesia. Epileptic patients are extremely liable to experience an epileptic convulsion during the stage of excitement, but the speedy resolution which so quickly supervenes is highly favorable, and is sufficiently advantageous to warrant the inhalation, if the occasion requires. The same thing is true in cases of hystero-epilepsy—the most violent contortions need not intimidate the attendants. Alcoholic intoxication, and a condition characterized by *delirium tremens*, should, on the contrary, prohibit the use of anæsthetics. The employment of chloroform for the purpose of inducing sleep has too often caused a sudden termination of life in cases of *asthenia e potu*. In all such cases there is extreme cardiac debility, and death is liable to occur as a result of profound syncope induced by the toxic effects of the agent operating upon vital centres which have already lost the greater part of their energy. For the same reason anæsthesia should be avoided during the period of shock after severe injuries. The respiratory centres in the medulla oblongata may have been damaged by the violence of concussion, so that they are no longer in a condition to tolerate the additional effects of artificial toxæmia. Hence the wisdom of the surgical rule to defer operation until the establishment of reaction. Gunshot wounds upon the field of battle, however, seem to form an exception to this rule. The exception is, nevertheless, more apparent than real, for a gunshot wound which does not directly involve the brain or the spinal cord seldom disturbs the integrity of tissue in those organs in any way that can be compared with the actual solutions of continuity which are caused by ordinary concussions of the brain or spinal cord. The experience of military sur-

4

geons is unanimously in favor of the almost unrestricted use of anæsthetics in the surgery of the battle-field.

Diseases of the lungs do unquestionably add to the risks of anæsthesia,
not so much by any danger of asphyxia as by reason of the increased liability to syncope which is produced by every condition that is competent
to hinder the free passage of blood from the pulmonary artery into the
pulmonary veins. Caseous or tubercular deposits, cancerous growths,
pleural adhesions, pleuritic effusions, pericardial adhesions or effusions,
enlargement of the bronchial glands, dilatation of the bronchi, stenosis of
the trachea, and the accidental presence of foreign bodies in the respiratory passages, should all be counted among the causes of possible syncope
and its consequent perils.

For the same reason, organic diseases of the heart or of the larger
blood-vessels should preclude the use of chloroform. Obesity is so often
accompanied by an overloading of the cardiac walls with fat that it should
suggest caution at least. Fatty degeneration of the muscular structure
of the heart is a far more dangerous condition ; but, unfortunately, it does
not reveal its presence during life by any positive group of symptoms. A
slow, irregular and feeble pulse, associated with precordial pain, difficult
respiration, general lassitude, and evidences of degeneration in tissues ac-
cessible to observation, should excite suspicion of this form of degeneration. The violent palpitations which sometimes disturb the anæmic or
chlorotic patient should exclude the more potent anæsthetics. In all cases
which present any notable departure from the normal type the mildest
agents alone should ever be employed.

The emotions of the patient should always be observed before commencing the act of etherization. Excitement and fear may overpower the
heart to a degree that shall constitute all the difference between safety and
danger. A few words of encouragement will often serve to tranquillize the
circulation, and to invigorate the action of the heart. In many instances
it is desirable to educate the courage of the patient by previous conversation about the operation ; and in all cases it is important to avoid everything like sudden and unexpected intrusion with the anæsthetic. Even
with children there should be a certain amount of explanation and persua-
sion, sufficient to obviate the shock which would result from abrupt and
seemingly violent measures. These little patients, fortunately, are so tolerant of anæsthesia that their fears and their struggles are less dangerous
than would be a similar degree of agitation in adult life.

The cautions which have been thus detailed are principally important
during the use of chloroform and its powerful congeners. When sulphuric ether is employed, the risks attending its use are so insignificant that
they may be almost entirely neglected. But it must be ever kept in mind
that the inhalation of ether is not wholly void of danger. Alarming
symptoms have been not so very infrequently observed during its administration, and death does occur while under its influence. The fact should
be always borne in mind that no anæsthetic agent can be used without in-
curring the risk of a certain amount of danger—very slight it may be, but
still an appreciable quantity. Every patient should, therefore, be made
an object of careful study before the act of inhalation is commenced, and
all possible contraindications should be scrupulously noted. There can
be no doubt that, if such cautious methods had always obtained, artificial
anæsthesia might never have been discovered, and, during the experimental period which followed the introduction of the discovery, a considerable degree of latitude was excusable. But the age of experiment has

long been passed. The verdict of experience is decisive, and the dangers of anæsthesia are known with a degree of precision sufficient to render the administrator responsible for all accidents which may be foreseen as a possible, if not probable, consequence of the physical condition of the patient, and of the nature of the agent selected for the production of insensibility.

TREATMENT OF THE ACCIDENTS OF ANÆSTHESIA.

The dangers of anæsthesia group themselves under two principal heads: cessation of respiration, and cessation of circulation. It is extremely important that the operator should be fully awake to the character of the risks to which his patient is exposed, in order that he may be prepared to act with celerity and decision in case of accident. Too often has the history of such cases disclosed a scene of panic and bewilderment in which the most various expedients have been employed without appearance of method or comprehension of the real condition of the sufferer. The single object of the attendant should be the renewal of respiration on the part of his patient, and, in order to secure success in this attempt, the efforts should be prompt, energetic, and long-continued.

The first expedient, in case of anæsthetic syncope, is inversion of the patient. The head should be lowered as far as possible, to permit the distention of the intracranial vessels by gravitation. This is a frequent experiment in the physiological laboratory: when animals have ceased to breathe in consequence of excessive loss of blood, they may be revived by hanging them by the hind legs. Piorry, Nélaton, and Holmes of Chicago, were the first to employ this method for the resuscitation of patients who had passed into a condition of mortal syncope. In this position the blood finds its way again to the respiratory centres in the medulla oblongata, and arouses them once more to their normal function. The adjustment of the position of the patient forms, therefore, one of the accessories of the process of artificial respiration.

In a valuable paper on this subject, read before the Illinois State Medical Society, by Edward L. Holmes, M.D., Professor of Ophthalmology in Rush Medical College, Chicago ("Transactions of the Illinois State Medical Society," p. 81, 1868), the doctor says: "Every surgeon has, not infrequently, observed that chloroform produces considerable pallor, prostration in the action of the heart, arteries, and lungs, apparently without any imminent danger. In all such cases the danger seems to depend entirely upon syncope. I have never witnessed a case in which there was turgidity and redness of the face, in which there was not also a regular pulse, and a regular, though often stertorous respiration, causing, perhaps, a peculiar, heaving motion of the head. On several occasions, as I observed this tendency to syncope, although I saw no reason for alarm, I directed, experimentally, my assistants to raise the foot of the table sufficiently high to place the patient with the head downward on an inclined plane of at least 40°. I found, invariably, that the pulse at once became fuller and more frequent, and that the color returned to the face.

"Subsequently, in administering chloroform to a patient at the Chicago Charitable Eye and Ear Infirmary, the breathing and pulse, almost without warning, suddenly ceased. Although the pulse and respiration had been quite good, there still had begun to be a peculiar, cold perspiration upon the brow, and a cold, moist condition of the hands, which I attributed to the depressing influence of fear under which the patient was laboring.

I was watching the patient most carefully, thinking in this condition he should receive no more chloroform, when he ceased to breathe. His aspect was most appalling ; the face and hands were cold and wet, the features pinched, muscles of the face relaxed, lids half opened, and the cornea turned upward. The foot of the table had not been raised fifteen seconds, the tongue having at once been withdrawn, before the pulse reappeared at the wrist, and the respiration was re-established. Upon restoring the patient to the horizontal position, the pulse and respiration again ceased. The elevation of the foot of the table, however, again re-established the action of the heart and lungs.

"Some time after this occurrence, precisely the same symptoms appeared during the inhalation of chloroform. The patient was a young, strong man. In this case the pulse for a few minutes was growing less frequent, although the breathing continued quite strong and regular, till without further warning, the pulse and breathing suddenly ceased. The appearance of this patient was as frightful as in the case of the other just described. A similar mode of treatment restored at once the action of the heart, some seconds passing before the respiration was fully re-established.

"I have had an opportunity, at the Infirmary, of demonstrating experimentally to the students and physicians more than thirty times, in cases where there was no apparent danger, and yet where there was a tendency to pallor and weakness of the pulse, that, in the position I have described, the cheeks become instantly flushed, and the pulse stronger. . . . . I watched, with great care, the condition of the pulse and respiration ; and yet it is sometimes somewhat difficult to distinguish the difference between the effects of fear and those of the chloroform."

Animals which have been killed with alcohol or with other kindred poisons may be restored by artificial respiration. If they can be made to breathe, the blood will circulate, and the natural processes of elimination thus sustained will at length relieve the system of the toxic agent. The treatment of opium-poisoning presents a familiar illustration of the method, and of the success which attends its use. Its failure is due either to a tardy commencement of the process, or to an inefficient mode of carrying it into effect. Sometimes we read of cases in which artificial respiration had been undertaken as a last resort after the failure of other expedients. Sometimes the patient is said to have gasped a few times with the result of causing a cessation of the artificial movements, and an immediate collapse of the nascent energies of the medulla oblongata. Long and patient effort is the price of success in these unfortunate conditions.

The most simple method of effecting artificial respiration consists, as recommended by Dr. Sylvester, in the production of a rhythmic movement of the walls of the chest, by alternately pressing the abdomen or the chest-wall so as to expel the air in the lungs, and then drawing the arms upward and outward in such a way as to elevate the ribs and expand the cavity of the thorax. The method advocated by Marshall Hall differs from this in the production of expiration and inspiration by rolling the body, first upon its face during compression of the walls of the thorax, and then upon its back during the withdrawal of pressure. This process, which was supposed to prevent obstruction of the pharynx through falling back of the tongue, is not so satisfactory as the method previously described.

Great importance is usually attached to the expedient of drawing forward the tongue whenever respiration is arrested in the anæsthetic state. The recent investigations made by Dr. Benjamin Howard, of London (*Lancet*, May 22, 1880, p. 796), indicate, however, that this operation is of no more value than any other peripheral irritation of the superficial nerves of the body. By a series of careful experiments upon the dead body, Dr. Howard ascertained that the epiglottis, when relaxed and collapsed, cannot

Fig. 1.—Pressing and draining water from the lungs and stomach.

be raised from the glottis by the act of drawing forward the tongue. If the epiglottis could thus be raised, that act alone would accomplish no good result for the patient. The chest must be compelled to expand, in order to effect the introduction of air through the most patulous glottis. This

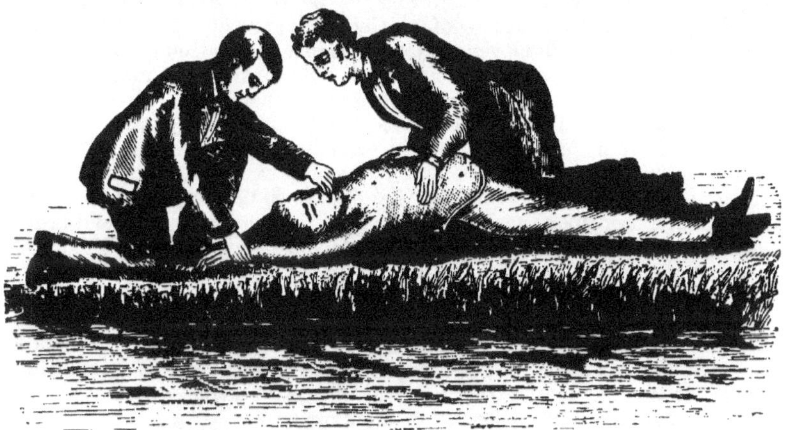

Fig. 2.—Bellows-blowing movement for drawing air into the lungs.

movement of expansion may possibly be excited by any reflex irritation of the nervous system, but it is most likely to be effected by placing the patient with his head lower than his feet, and by artificial respiration.

Dr. Howard has also suggested a mode of artificial respiration (*Lancet*, May 25, 1878) which is a decided improvement upon the method of Marshall Hall and of Sylvester. It was originally devised for the restoration of persons who had been drowned, but the second stage of the process is equally applicable to cases of respiration arrested by anæsthetic vapors.

"Turn the patient downward, with a large firm roll of clothing under the stomach and chest.

"Press with all your weight two or three times, for four or five seconds each time, upon the patient's back, so that the water is pressed out of the lungs and stomach, and drains freely downward out of the mouth. Then :

"Turn the patient face upward, the roll of clothing put under his back just below the shoulder-blades, the head hanging back as low as possible. Place the patient's hands together above his head. Kneel with the patient's hips between your knees. Fix your elbows against your hips. Now, grasping the lower part of the patient's chest, squeeze the two sides together, pressing gradually forward with all your weight for about three seconds, until your mouth is nearly over the mouth of the patient ; then, with a push, suddenly jerk yourself back. Rest about three seconds, then begin again. Repeat these movements about eight or ten times a minute."

Faradization of the phrenic nerves has been advocated as a means of resuscitation. Theoretically the method is good, since it proposes to excite the movements of the diaphragm, and thus to inflate the lungs more effectually than is possible by elevation of the ribs alone. Its use should be combined with the attempt to fill the lungs by Howard's method. One electrode of the faradic apparatus should be firmly pressed over the right phrenic nerve, just outside of the carotid artery in the neck, while the other electrode should be placed in contact with the wall of the thorax, over the sixth intercostal space on the right side of the body. The right side should be preferred to the left, in order to avoid the risk of producing arrest of the movements of the heart. Richardson has shown by actual experiment upon animals that, during the period of anæsthesia with impending syncope, the passage of an electrical current through the heart will at once arrest all movement, and produce an inevitably fatal result. The electrical circuit should be completed only during the elevation of the arms, and should be at once broken at the commencement of the depression of the ribs. These applications should be renewed about twenty times in a minute. By this method of procedure the diaphragm is brought into a condition of contraction and depression at the same time that the ribs are elevated. The capacity of the thorax is thus enlarged to its utmost, and a corresponding volume of air will enter the trachea and bronchi. As it passes over their mucous surfaces, the current thus produced arouses the reflex activities of the various branches of the par vagum ; and, if coagulation of the protoplasm of the nervous ganglia has not previously reached the point of final stasis, the heart will begin once more to move. The electrical current should never be very energetic. It should never be strong enough to tetanize the diaphragm, for fear of occasioning retraction and depression of the lower ribs, with a consequent dyspnœic attitude and imperfect distention of the lungs.

General electrization of the surface of the body is worse than useless, since it diverts attention from the great object of every effort—a renewal of respiration and circulation, and because of the danger of tetanizing the heart while it is feebly beating. Such a result has been shown, by actual experiment on the lower animals, to be inevitably fatal. The same thing is true of electro-puncture of the heart.

Besides the methods above indicated, we should have recourse to pulmonary insufflation. It has been objected to this very efficient method that the integrity of the pulmonary tissues might be very easily compromised by violent inflation of the air-cells. This accident is not likely to occur under any ordinary circumstances, as the experiences of the physiological laboratory abundantly show. Air is every day forcibly introduced into the lungs of curarized animals by the use of various kinds of insufflating apparatus, and this without much regard to the amount of surplus energy that may be called into action. But it is a rare thing, at the autopsy of a dog or a rabbit that has thus been treated, to find even a rupture of an air-cell. In operating upon the human subject, however, it is desirable to imitate the normal pressure in the lungs as closely as possible.

The methods of insufflation which may be employed are various. A vulgar method consists in the application of the mouth of the operator to the mouth of the patient, at the same time closing his nostrils with the finger and thumb, and blowing forcibly into the lungs. This process has been pronounced efficacious in the restoration of asphyxiated infants, and has, accordingly, been recommended in the treatment of anæsthetic syncope. But, unless the air is thus impelled with force sufficient to expand the walls of the chest, it can in no possible manner find admission to the lungs—a current cannot be produced. If great force is employed in the act of insufflation, the air will at once follow the path of least resistance, and will enter the œsophagus, passing into the stomach, and causing distention of the abdominal walls. The patient may thus be made to appear as if he had executed a movement of inspiration, but he does not supplement it by an act of expiration. The thorax does not subside as it would do after the lungs had been filled, and the manœuvre fails of any useful result. The same objection lies against the attempt to fill the lungs by carrying a tube through the mouth into the pharynx, so as to direct a blast of air upon the chink of the glottis. Instead of passing into the trachea, the air distends the pharynx, and finds its way into the stomach. If, however, a flexible tube, like a gum catheter of large size, be passed through the larynx into the trachea, the lungs may then be inflated with ease. The only difficulty consists in the introduction of the tube. If this occasion any delay, the trachea should be opened in the neck, an operation which need not create any appreciable delay. If the ordinary methods of arousing artificial respiration fail, and if an electrical apparatus is not at hand, this operation of tracheotomy and tracheal insufflation should be performed at once. Let it never be forgotten that success depends upon the prompt celerity with which everything is done. There is no time for consultation, for the collection of apparatus, for meditation upon the condition of the patient, when asphyxia is imminent, or has already been declared. If one cannot always administer chloroform with an electrical apparatus at his elbow, he can at least provide himself with an elastic catheter of large size, and a scalpel which can be trusted to enter the trachea.

We may, therefore, sum up the rules that should govern the situation as follows :

In every instance of syncope, threatened or actual, the head should be depressed to the utmost limit of bodily inversion.

Artificial respiration, preferably by the aid of rhythmical pressure upon the chest and abdomen, should be commenced at once, and should be continued, deliberately and persistently, until the patient is either out of danger or is unquestionably beyond all hope of recovery. While these artificial movements are effected by the operator, an assistant should attempt the introduction of the laryngeal sound, in order to supplement the thoracic movements by laryngeal insufflation. Failing in this endeavor, tracheotomy should be performed, and the sound should be introduced into the windpipe through the wound in the neck.

A clear comprehension of the object toward which all these efforts should be directed will relieve the surgeon of all embarrassment and hesitation with regard to the proper course of action. Many a life, no doubt, might have been saved, which was lost in consequence of delay on the part of attendants who knew not what to do in the hour of danger. Unfortunately, however, the energy of certain anæsthetic substances is so great that no vigilance can obviate danger, nor can the most scientifically devised methods of relief always effect a restoration when the patient has ceased to breathe. The only real safety, the only irreproachable course of action, lies in complete abstinence from these potent drugs.

The subjoined group of cases will serve to illustrate the different methods of resuscitation which have been successfully employed after apparent death from inhalation of chloroform.

Apparent death from chloroform averted by cold affusion upon the chest.—Male, about fifty years, intoxicated; dislocation of the head of the femur. After becoming somewhat sobered, chloroform was inhaled from a handkerchief. About five minutes after the commencement of inhalation the breathing suddenly became stertorous, slow, and labored, with corresponding flagging in frequency and force of pulse and lividity of the skin. The dislocation was promptly reduced, but respiration became less and less frequent, until he ceased to breathe entirely. The pulse also stopped, and no sound could be heard at the heart. The face was black and distorted; the eyes were bloodshot. An assistant was sent for a pail of water, while the surgeon stripped his patient entirely, and slapped his chest and buttocks with both hands. After some delay the assistant—all others having fled in dismay—arrived with a *pint cup* full of water. This was dashed upon the naked chest, and more water was sought. A pail had to be hunted up—and then water was brought from a neighboring pump. The cold water was then poured in a slow and steady stream, from an elevation as high as one could reach, directly on the centre of the chest, while the slapping process was faithfully continued. After three or four minutes a deep inspiration was drawn. By gently pressing the chest, the air was expelled, and in a few seconds there was another inspiration, followed by external pressure, the stream of cold water being maintained without intermission. Five or six deep inspirations per minute were thus secured at first, when the lividity of the face began to clear up, the heart to act feebly, and the pulse to be felt at the wrist. In less than half an hour the patient was able to converse.—*Am. Med. Times*, p. 143, August 25, 1860.

Apparent death from chloroform—Insufflation and artificial respiration—Recovery.—Male, twenty-two years; scrofulous disease of elbow-joint, requiring partial excision of the joint. The operation was nearly completed, when the patient suddenly became pale and cold, with intermittent pulse, and convulsive breathing. Bathing the face with cold water, and fresh air, did no good; inspiration grew more feeble, and the pulse ceased to beat at the wrist. He was instantly laid on the floor, and the feeble action of the chest was aided by the hands; but, in about a minute after the first seizure, he ceased to breathe, and the lower jaw fell Immediately, one of the surgeons, closing the mouth, inflated the lungs by the nose, which was first covered with a handkerchief, while another with a hand on each side of the chest gently emptied them. This process was continued for four minutes without any apparent result, when a gentleman who held the wrist exclaimed, "There is a beat!" and after the lapse of a few seconds, "There is another!" Then a third. Now it began to beat violently, and the chest to heave deeply, but with a short period between each action. Presently the pulse beat more slowly, quietly, and regularly, but more feebly, and the chest acted spontaneously. After the lapse of a few minutes, the man opened his eyes and smiled. Brandy, blankets, and hot-water bottles, soon completed his restoration, and shortly afterward he was able to sit up and be sent home in a carriage.—*Med. Times and Gaz.*, p. 174, August 13, 1853. Reported by E. W. Lowe, M.R.C.S.E.

Apparent death from chloroform—Patient restored by drawing forward the tongue.—Removal of a tumor from a female.—After a few inhalations of chloroform the pulse stopped suddenly. Cold affusion, and friction all over the body, excited a few feeble pulsations, which soon ceased. No respiration. The surgeon then passed his finger into the pharynx, raised the epiglottis, and drew forward the tongue. This excited an inspiration. As soon as the tongue was released it fell back, and respiration stopped again. The same traction was now repeated, and the tongue was held out of the mouth ; respiration then began again, and the patient quickly recovered.—*Abeille Médicale*, November 3, 1851.

Apparent death from chloroform averted by the injection of brandy and water into the rectum.—" On one occasion, while I was removing a scirrhous tumor, the patient, who was rather advanced in life, got an overdose of chloroform, ... and I do believe that her recovery was owing entirely to injecting a glass of brandy and water into the rectum. The accident happened owing to the gentleman who had charge of the chloroform getting so interested in the dissection that he forgot to raise the towel off her face till respiration had become imperceptible."—*Med. Times and Gaz.*, p. 652, December 27, 1856.

Apparent death from chloroform—Restoration by Marshall Hall's " ready method."—Chloroform was administered to a young man during an amputation of the thigh. Just as the last artery was tied, the patient ceased breathing, the pulse could not be felt, the jaw dropped, and he seemed really dead. The usual means of restoration having failed, a vigorous application of the *ready method* was undertaken. About every five seconds the air was forced from the lungs by grasping the thorax upon both sides and depressing the ribs. In addition to this, the patient was turned suddenly upon his side and partly upon his face, and almost immediately back again, about three times in a minute. These procedures were continued for more than half an hour before it became certain that any sign of life was manifest. It was indeed forty-five minutes before the patient was able to speak. The restoration was, however, at last complete.—*Med. Times and Gaz.*, p. 416, April 7, 1858.

Apparent death from chloroform—Resuscitation by the aid of electricity.—Male, fourteen years, chloroformed for the removal of a sequestrum from the tibia. In the midst of the operation he began to struggle, and this was followed by stertorous breathing : the heart's action ceased, respiration became imperceptible, the lips blanched, and the limbs flaccid. Recourse was immediately had to artificial respiration by Sylvester's method, and the face and chest were slapped with a wet towel. After the lapse of two or three minutes he gasped faintly. Electricity was then applied, one pole to the back of the neck, the other to the epigastrium. The heart's action was instantly excited, and the boy gradually recovered.—*Med. Times and Gaz.*, p. 540, November 23, 1861.

Apparent death from chloroform averted by electro-puncture.—A lady, during a plastic operation in the perineal region, inhaled badly, but became finally insensible. The operation was about half finished when the pulse suddenly stopped. Cold affusion and continual fanning restored it again, but with a slow and uncertain beat, and at length it ceased for the second time. Friction, drawing the tongue forward, and Sylvesterism failed; ten minutes had passed, when Dr. Kidd brought his portable electric battery, and, pulling a pin out of his necktie, stuck it into the region of the phrenic nerve as it lies in the sterno-mastoid, another pin into the diaphragm, and quickly applying the wetted sponges of the faradic current, the effect astonished every one present; where a quarter of a minute before there was to all intent a body all but stone-dead, now the chest heaved and fell with each interruption of the electric circuit; the sterno-mastoid was thrown into strong contractions; there was a moan, a sigh, followed by natural breathing, and a gradual flicker of the restored pulse—*Med. Times and Gaz.*, p. 333, March 28, 1863.

Apparent death from chloroform—Resuscitation by inversion.—The discovery of the power of inversion to revive patients apparently killed by chloroform is due to an accidental observation in the laboratory of the famous Nélaton. His son was one day experimenting with rats—making them insensible with the vapor of chloroform. A number of the animals were thus treated until their life seemed to have departed. The boy then picked them up by their tails, carrying them away for final disposal, when to his surprise, they began to give evidence of returning animation, and soon recovered. This observation was not lost upon the boy's father, who soon found occasion to repeat the experiment upon the human subject with the most convincing success. The following interesting narrative, from the experience of Dr. J. Marion Sims, forms a part of a paper read by himself before the British Medical Association, at Norwich, August, 1874. The patient was a beautiful woman, young and titled, upon whom an operation for the cure of a vesico-vaginal fistula was to be performed. This was done November 3, 1861, at St. Germain, a few miles from Paris. The operation was to be performed by Dr. Sims, assisted by Drs. Nélaton, Beylard, and Johnston. The administration of chloroform was intrusted to the celebrated obstetrician, Charles James Campbell. "Many years ago," writes Dr. Sims, "I imbibed the convictions of my countrymen against chloroform in general surgery, and have always used ether in preference, never feeling the least dread of danger from it under any circumstances. It is otherwise with chloroform, and in this particular case I felt the greatest anxiety, frequently stopping during the operation to ask Dr. Campbell if all was going on well with the patient. At the end of forty minutes the sutures (twelve or thirteen) were all placed, and ready to be secured, and I was secretly congratulating myself that the operation would be finished in a few minutes more, when all at once I discovered a bluish livid appearance of the vagina, as if the blood was stagnant, and I called Dr. Johnston's attention to it. As this lividity seemed to increase, I felt rather uneasy about it, and I asked Dr. Campbell if all was right with the pulse. He replied, 'All right, go on.' Scarcely were these words uttered, when he suddenly cried out, 'Stop! stop! No pulse, no breathing;' and looking to M. Nélaton, he said, 'Tête en bas, n'est-ce pas?' Nélaton replied, 'Certainly; there is nothing else to do.' Immediately the body was inverted, the head hanging down, while the heels were raised high in the air by Dr.

Johnston, the legs resting one on each of his shoulders. Dr. Campbell supported the thorax. Mr. Herbert was sent to an adjoining room for a spoon, with the handle of which the jaws were held open, and I handed M. Nélaton a tenaculum, which he hooked into the tongue and gave in charge to Mr. Herbert; while to Dr. Beylard was assigned the duty of making efforts at artificial respiration, by pressure alternately on the thorax and abdomen. M. Nélaton ordered and overlooked every movement, while I stood aloof and watched the proceedings, with, of course, the most intense anxiety. They held the patient in this inverted position for a long time before there was any manifestation of returning life. Dr. Campbell, in his report, says it was fifteen minutes, and that it seemed an age. My notes of the case, written a few hours afterward, make it twenty minutes. Be this as it may, the time was so long that I thought it useless to make any further efforts, and said, 'Gentlemen, she is certainly dead, and you might as well let her alone.' But the great and good Nélaton never lost hope, and by his quiet, cool, brave manner, he seemed to infuse his spirit into his aids. At last there was a feeble inspiration, and after a long time another, and by and by another; and then the breathing became pretty regular, and Dr. Campbell said, 'The pulse returns, thank God! she will soon be all right again.'

"Dr. Beylard, who always sees the cheerful side of everything in life, was disposed to laugh at the fear I manifested for the safety of our patient. I must confess that never before or since have I felt such a grave responsibility. When the pulse and respiration were re-established, M. Nélaton ordered the patient to be laid on the table. This was done gently; but what was our horror, when, at the moment the body was placed horizontally, the pulse and breathing instantly ceased. Quick as thought the body was again inverted—the head downward and the feet over Dr. Johnston's shoulders—and the same manœuvres as before were put into execution. Dr. Campbell thinks it did not take such a long time to re-establish the action of the lungs and heart as in the first instance. It may have lacked a few seconds of the time, but it seemed to me to be quite as long, for the same tedious, painful, protracted and anxious efforts were made as before; but, thanks to the brave men who had her in charge, feeble signs of returning life eventually made their appearance. Respiration was at first irregular and at long intervals; soon it became more regular, and the pulse could then be counted, but it was very feeble, and would intermit. I began again to be hopeful, and even dared to think that at last there was an end of this dreadful suspense, when they laid her horizontally on the table again, saying, 'She is all right this time.' To witness such painful scenes of danger to a young and valuable life, and to experience such agony of anxiety, produced a tension of heart and mind and soul that cannot be imagined. What, then, must have been our dismay, our feeling of despair, when, incredible as it may seem, the moment the body was laid in the horizontal position again, the respiration ceased a third time, the pulse was gone, and she looked the perfect picture of death. Then I gave up all for lost, for I thought that the blood was so poisoned, so charged with chloroform, that it was no longer able to sustain life. But Nélaton, and Campbell, and Johnston, and Beylard, and Herbert, by a consentaneous effort, quickly inverted the body a third time, thus throwing all the blood possible to the brain, and again they began their efforts at artificial respiration. It seemed to me that she would never breathe again; but at last there was a spasmodic gasp, and after a long while there was another effort at inspiration, and, after another long interval, there was a third—they were far between; then we watched, and waited, and wondered if there would be a fourth ; at length it came, and more profoundly, and there was a long yawn, and the respiration became tolerably regular. Soon Dr. Beylard says, 'I feel the pulse again, but it is very weak.' Nélaton, after some moments, ejaculates, 'The color of the tongue and lips is more natural.' Campbell says, 'The vomiting is favorable ; see, she moves her hands, she is pushing against me.' But I was by no means sure that these movements were not merely signs of the last death-struggle, and so I expressed myself. Presently Dr. Johnston said, 'See here, doctor, see how she kicks ; she is coming round again ;' and very soon they all said, 'She is safe at last.' I replied, 'For heaven's sake, keep her safe ; I beg you not to put her on the table again until she is conscious.' This was the first and only suggestion I made during all these anxious moments, and it was acted upon ; for she was held in the vertical position till she, in a manner, recovered semi-consciousness, opened her eyes, looked wildly around, and asked what was the matter. She was then, and not till then, laid on the table, and all present felt quite as solemn and thankful as I did ; and we all in turn grasped Nélaton's hand, and thanked him for having saved the life of this lovely woman.

"In a few minutes more the operation was finished, but, of course, without chloroform. The sutures were quickly assorted and separately twisted, and the patient put to bed ; and on the eighth day thereafter I had the happiness to remove the sutures in the presence of M. Nélaton, and show him the success of the operation."

Apparent death from chloroform—Resuscitation of the patient by tracheotomy.—Male, thirty-six years, ruptured his urethra by falling astride of the edge of an iron box. Four years afterward, September 27, 1878, he entered Guy's Hospital with retention of urine. On October 18th he was chloroformed, and during an attempt at catheterism he suddenly stopped breathing. Sylvesterism failed to give relief, as no air entered the chest. Drawing the tongue forward did no good. The patient's face and neck became deeply congested. Tracheotomy was immediately performed. With the first incision into the trachea, air began to pass through the wound, and artificial respiration was immediately recommenced. Considerable blood found its way into the trachea before the canula was introduced, and this had to be coughed up. Gradually the face returned to its normal appearance, the hemorrhage ceased, and the spasm of the glottis— for such it seemed to be—disappeared. The patient made a good recovery. On a subsequent occasion, when made to inhale ether, a similar spasm occurred during the stage of excitement, but without paralysis of the respiratory muscle, so that no harm followed.—*Brit. Med. Jour.*, October 26, 1878.

In this case it is probable that the advantage to the patient was not so much owing to the mere opening of the trachea as to the reflex excitement caused by the incision. It is no uncommon thing in the physiological laboratory to witness the resumption of breathing by an asphyxiated animal when the first incision through its skin is made.

Death from chloroform averted by the inhalation of amylic nitrite.—Female, forty-nine years, married, thin and nervous, but otherwise in good health. A fatty tumor in the left lumbar region requiring removal, she received two teaspoonfuls of undiluted brandy, followed after a few minutes by the inhalation of chloroform. A drachm was poured on lint, and inhaled slowly. This produced no apparent effect. A second drachm caused excitement, talking, and struggling. This gradually subsided, and she was becoming insensible, when she made an abortive effort to vomit, and raised her head from the pillow. As she did so, the pulse flickered and stopped altogether; she gasped; foam gathered on her lips; her jaws became rigid—she seemed to be dead. Cold water affusion, pulling the tongue, and artificial respiration after the manner of Marshall Hall, utterly failed. Nitrite of amyl was then poured on lint, and held to her nostrils. In about ten seconds there was flushing of the face, the pulse was again felt, respiration was resumed, and all went well to the conclusion of the operation.—*Brit. Med. Jour.*, August 18, 1877.

ANÆSTHETIC MIXTURES.

The dangers which soon became conspicuous from the use of chloroform have suggested the use of various mixtures with the hope of diminishing the perils of anæsthesia from that agent. A mixture of three parts of ether with one part of chloroform has been used more than eight thousand times in Vienna without an unfavorable result. Linhart has recommended the use of a mixture containing alcohol one part and chloroform four parts. Billroth constantly uses a mixture containing three parts of chloroform and one part each of sulphuric ether and alcohol. Sansom found that alcohol "had the greatest effect in sustaining the heart's action during the influence of chloroform." He found it impossible to kill with chloroform a frog which had previously inhaled the vapor of alcohol. In his opinion, if chloroform is to be used without an inhaling apparatus, to insure a supposed uniformity of strength of vapor it should be mixed with alcohol, or with alcohol and ether. James Townley ("Parturition without Pain or Loss of Consciousness." London, 1863) advised the use of an anodyne mixture composed of "alcohol, two ounces; one drachm of aromatic tincture; with sufficient chloroform added short of the production of a turbid state of the fluid." The formula for the aromatic tincture is: "One drachm of nutmegs; two drachms of cloves; pterocarp chips, a drachm and a half; water, four ounces; alcohol, five ounces." This agreeable mixture was successfully employed by Dr. Townley in obstetrical practice, for the purpose of blunting the sensibility to pain without abolishing consciousness.

The Committee of the London Medical and Chirurgical Society recommended (Med.-Chir. Trans., vol. xlvii., 1864) three different mixtures:

Mixture A.—Alcohol .... 1 part.
                Chloroform.......................... 2 parts.
                Ether............................... 3 parts.

Mixture B.—Chloroform......................... 1 part.
                Ether............................... 4 parts.

Mixture C.—Chloroform......................... 1 part.
                Ether............................... 2 parts.

The committee stated that:

"It was found that the physiological effects of the Mixture B were very similar to that of simple ether; an animal might inhale it for forty or fifty minutes, even in a tolerably strong form (15 per cent.), without destroying life.

"The mixtures A and C were very similar to each other in their action.

This quite accorded with the fact that the proportion of chloroform was the same in both. The mode of their action, moreover, was intermediate between that of ether and that of chloroform.

"These mixtures exercised a much less depressing effect upon the action of the heart than chloroform alone. In this respect, again, the mixtures appeared to combine the qualities both of ether and of chloroform; it being clear that, at the same degree of insensibility, the depression of the heart's action was less with either mixture (A or C) than with chloroform.

"These considerations tend to establish the fact that a mixture of ether and chloroform (such as A or C) is as effective as pure chloroform, and a safer agent when deep and prolonged anæsthesia is to be induced, while at the same time it is sufficiently rapid in its operation to be convenient for general use.

"Of the two mixtures, preference is, in the opinion of the committee, due to A, on account of the uniform blending of the ether and chloroform when combined with alcohol, and probably the more equable escape of the constituents in vapor. The alcohol which it contains probably stimulates and sustains the action of the heart."

The advantages connected with the use of these alcoholic and ethereal dilutions of chloroform consist in a more perfectly sustained action of the heart and of the respiratory centre. The disadvantages consist in an irregular rate of evaporation, and in a consequent variability of the nature of the anæsthetic substance. The committee above quoted found that, by saturating a cloth with a certain quantity of the ether and chloroform mixture, and exposing it to the air, the percentage of loss after three minutes amounted to eighty-nine parts of ether and seventy-five parts of chloroform. After evaporation for fifteen minutes the loss was ninety-three parts of ether and eighty-five parts of chloroform.

Ellis ("Anæsthesia with Mixed Vapors." London, 1866) found that, when the Mixture A was evaporated, during the six or seven minutes required for the evaporation of half a drachm (two grammes) of the liquid, the vapor of ether, almost exclusively, was given off during the first minute, the vapor of chloroform predominated during the next three minutes, and the evaporation of the alcohol occupied the last three minutes. The commencement of inhalation with this mixture would, therefore, place the patient chiefly under the influence of ether, while the condition of anæsthesia, at the most dangerous stage of the process, would be established by the vapor of chloroform, leaving the confirmation of insensibility to the moderately efficacious alcohol. This would be true if only a measured quantity of the mixture were introduced into an inhaling apparatus; but, when administered by repeated affusion upon a napkin, this objection loses much of its force. The occurrence of several fatal cases under the use of these mixtures is a sufficient demonstration that they are not devoid of danger.

Death from inhaling a mixture of chloroform and alcohol.—Male, twenty-three years, dragoon, very intemperate. Examination of an injured elbow. Two or three drachms of a mixture, composed of one part chloroform to two parts alcohol, were given on a sponge in a tubulated bell-glass. Having breathed this for five minutes without effect, a towel was substituted for the inhaling apparatus. Some excitement was soon manifested, but neither the respiration nor the pulse were affected at first. Suddenly, however, the eyes were turned upward, the face became turgid, the muscles relaxed, and the patient vomited. The pulse, which had been beating at the rate of 100, stopped instantly. It was thought that vomited matters were obstructing the glottis, and in fact a large piece of cabbage was removed with the finger from the pharynx. The patient breathed two or three times after vomiting, but the heart did not move again. Artificial respiration did no good. *Autopsy.*—The stomach contained unmasticated food; the lungs were full of blood; the heart was covered with fat; it weighed fourteen ounces, and its muscular structure had undergone fatty degeneration.—W. A. HAMMOND, U.S.A. ; *Am. Jour. Med. Sci.*, p. 41, July, 1858.

Death from inhaling a mixture of chloroform, ether, and alcohol.—Male, thirty-five years ; had previously undergone amputation of the leg for a railway injury of the ankle. Necrosis of the end of the tibia required a second operation. A mixture, containing alcohol one part, chloroform two parts, ether three parts, was used. Before anæsthesia could be induced the patient became convulsed and died. At the previous operation he had inhaled pure ether alone, without any accident.—MORTON and HEWSON, Pennsylvania Hospital, May 4, 1865 ; *Am. Jour. Med. Sci.*, p. 415, October, 1876.

In order to obviate the difficulties arising from the different rates of evaporation of alcohol, chloroform, and ether, Ellis (loc. cit.) conceived the idea of mixing their vapors instead of the liquid substances. For this purpose he constructed a very ingenious, expensive, and complicated apparatus, consisting of an elaborate mouth-piece and mask for the face, to which was attached, by an appropriate complication of tubing, a container provided with not less than three chambers, that could, by a skilfully adjusted system of valves, be separated from or made to communicate with a common apartment, into which opened the tube from the mouth-piece. In one of the many chambers, chloroform, in measured quantity, was carefully evaporated ; in another, ether ; in another, alcohol was encouraged to change its state. From these evaporating-rooms the vapors were conducted at will, by opening the proper valves, into the receiving-room where they were thoroughly mixed in the desired proportions, and whence the compound was drawn through the mouth-piece into the lungs by ordinary inspiration. It is not recorded that this valuable apparatus was ever duplicated, but it will long continue to occupy a high position among the tangible evidences of surgical ingenuity.

The mixture of amylic nitrite with chloroform has been employed by several American physicians (see article on Amylic Nitrite). For brief operations it has given good satisfaction, but it is doubtful whether its prolonged administration may not be attended with danger.

During the last few years the production of *anæsthesia by the successive inhalation of nitrous oxide gas and ether vapor* has been practised in England under the auspices of Mr. Clover. He commences the inhalation with nitrous oxide and completes it with ether, or ethidene dichloride, or whatever other anæsthetic vapor may be desired. By this means it is thought to avoid the initial excitement which sometimes follows the commencement of ether-inhalation. The time necessary for the production of anæsthesia is thus considerably shortened, especially when the patient is made to reinhale his own breath, and the quantity of ether that is needful is thus greatly diminished. The complexity and bulk of the necessary apparatus will, however, always tend to restrict its use within comparatively narrow limits. The explosive character of the mixture of nitrous oxide with ether vapor should not be forgotten.

Death during inhalation of nitrous oxide and ether.—1. Male, thin and pale, about to undergo a partial removal of the tongue. Partial anæsthesia was induced by the inhalation of nitrous oxide gas, which was then followed by the administration of ether in a cone of lint covered with oiled silk. The patient made very little resistance, and was soon fully etherized. The operation was in progress, with very little loss of blood, when, about five minutes after its commencement, the face became purple. The pulse was good, but respiration was superficial and gurgling. Artificial respiration was commenced, but natural breathing soon ceased, though the pulse continued to beat for some time longer. Electricity and inversion were tried without effect. *Autopsy.*—The usual evidences of asphyxia were present, and in the trachea was a large blood-clot, occluding the passage.—BAILEY, Cancer Hospital, London ; *Lancet,* July, 1875.

2. Female, fifty-five years ; femoral hernia, which had been strangulated for over forty-eight hours. She was much exhausted by frequent vomiting. Nitrous oxide gas and ether were successively given by means of Clover's inhaler. In about four minutes she was well under the influence of the anæsthetic, without any previous excitement. Taxis was then attempted, when almost immediately the patient became pale, and recommenced vomiting stercoraceous matter. At the same time the respiration became weak, and the pulse was imperceptible. Artifical respiration was employed for a few minutes without effect. An enema, containing three ounces of brandy, was then administered. Ammonia was held under the nose, and was also injected into the right median basilic vein, but without result. The patient died within about ten minutes after the appearance of alarming symptoms. *Autopsy.*—Stercoraceous matter in the trachea and right bronchus ; right side of the heart and the large veins were full of dark fluid blood ; ventricular walls thin and flabby, the cavities slightly dilated, left ventricle empty ; numerous patches of atheroma in the arch of the aorta.—University College Hospital, London ; *Medical Times and Gaz.,* March 17, 1877.

The use of opiates in connection with the operations of surgery has been practised from remote antiquity, but their employment for the purpose of modifying and perfecting the anæsthetic process is of more recent origin. Pitha relates (*Wiener Wochenschr.,* 25, 26, 1861) that, having unsuccessfully attempted for two hours to anæsthetize a patient, first with a mixture of ether and chloroform, and then with chloroform alone, he finally injected into the rectum a solution of the extract of belladonna. This overcame the difficulty, and the patient passed into a condition of anæsthesia that persisted for twelve hours. He then awoke, with no other disagreeable consequence besides the ordinary disturbances of accommodation. In 1863 Nussbaum discovered that, by the hypodermic injection of morphine at the commencement of inhalation, the anæsthesia produced by chloroform could be prolonged for several hours. A few years afterward a German surgeon named Uterhart (*Berlin. klin. Wochenschr.,* Nr. 32, 1868) attempted to reduce a dislocation of the shoulder which had occurred in the person of a drunkard under his care. For this purpose he had attempted to relax the patient by a hypodermic injection of morphine ; but, failing in this endeavor, he resorted to the use of chloroform. To his surprise, he found that an unusually small quantity of the anæsthetic was required to produce the desired effect. Pursuing the subject experimentally, he came to the conclusion that the injection should procede the commencement of inhalation by at least ten minutes. In the meantime the subject had been carefully examined by Claude Bernard, whose attention had been arrested, in the year 1864, by the following incident: while experimenting with the alkaloids of opium, he injected under the skin of a dog, which had so far recovered from chloroform that the conjunctiva again manifested sensibility, five centigrammes (about three-quarters of a grain) of hydrochlorate of morphia; the animal was speedily narcotized by this dose; but this was not all—the insensibility due to chloroform reappeared. This was the same phenomenon which, during the same week, had been observed by Nussbaum in the case of a woman whom he had kept under the influence of chloroform for an hour, until, through fear of danger from so long an inhalation, he had withdrawn the anæsthetic, and had sought to replace its influence by a hypodermic injection of morphine. Reversing the experiment, Bernard found that the injection of morphine rendered animals more sensitive, or, rather, more excitable than is natural. The inhalation of chloroform vapor abolished this excitability as well as the normal sensibility of the animal. Less chloroform was needed to produce anæsthesia than without morphine, and the anæsthetic state persisted for a long time after the withdrawal of chloroform. In this condition the animal remained perfectly passive, relaxed, and insensible—a condition extremely favorable to the performance of difficult vivisections, such as section of the lingual nerve in the pharnyx at its point of emergence, an operation which is almost impossible under the influence of chloroform alone. This combination of effects, and especially the reappearance of insensibility after the addition of morphine to chloroform, as in the case of Nussbaum, and in the dog observed by Claude Bernard, is due to the fact that the two substances tend to depress nervous sensibility. They supplement each other, so that with morphine a smaller amount of chloroform in the blood is sufficient to render the nerves insensible. The nervous excitability above mentioned is not an indication of increased nervous vigor, but implies quite the reverse. In the lower animals, in which it is so conspicuous, it is one of the direct effects of the depressing action of opiates, and is coincident with an actual diminution of sensibility. This is proved by immersing in acidulated water the paw of a frog which has received an opiate sufficient to render the creature excessively excitable. The animal remains insensible to the action of an acid liquid that would excite a lively manifestation of pain on the part of a frog which had received no opium.

Extending these observations to the respiratory organs and to the heart, it appears that morphine deadens the sensibility of the respiratory passages to such a degree that the inhalation of chloroform vapor produces less reflex disturbance of the respiration and circulation. The pressure of the blood is also better sustained in the arterial system by the stimulating effect of morphine upon the contractility of the arterial coats and upon the motor ganglia of the heart.

Claude Bernard has collected ("Leçons sur les Anæsthésiques," Paris, 1875) a large number of cases contributed by his pupils, illustrating the advantages which are connected with the combined administration of opiates and chloroform. Quite insignificant quantities of morphine injected hypodermically, half or three-quarters of an hour before inhalation, rendered the induction of anæsthesia less difficult and attended with less than ordinary excitement. Guibert found that, after only one or two centigrammes of morphine had thus been injected, the inhalation of a very small quantity of chloroform was sufficient to alleviate the sufferings of parturition, and to render tolerable many of the minor operations of surgery without abolishing the consciousness of the patient. Dr. Grosjean (loc. cit.), concluded

5

from the experience of MM. Rigaud and Sarazin, in the hospitals of Strasburg, that small doses of morphine (less than one centigramme) gave the best results by injection about forty minutes before operation. If the injection was made immediately before the commencement of inhalation, the period of excitement was augmented. If a large dose was used, there was danger of death by asphyxia—an opinion shared by Demarquay, who had met with serious consequences following mixed anæsthesia. All observers agree that the after-effects of this method are exceedingly gratifying. Drunkards, and other individuals who tolerate chloroform with difficulty on account of the degree of excitement produced by its inhalation, are rendered quite tranquil by preliminary injection of morphine. If used with caution the dangers of this form of mixed anæsthesia are probably on a par with the dangers from the use of chloroform alone.

As a result of his experiments in treating the same patients, sometimes with chloroform alone, and sometimes with chloroform and morphine, making an injection about twenty minutes or half an hour before the operation, Kappeler concludes ("Anæsthetica," p. 209) that the course of the resulting anæsthesia does not materially vary under either set of conditions. He, however, believes that the character of the anæsthesia is more tranquil, and that the patient passes more rapidly, and with less excitement, into the stage of insensibility. Abusers of alcohol are often found as exceptions to this rule. The depressing effects of chloroform upon the heart are generally diminished by the addition of morphine; but the same reduction of the frequency of the pulse is observed, and sometimes a very alarming irregularity and weakness of the pulse necessitates an interruption of the inhalation. The temperature of the body is reduced with and without the use of morphine. Irregular respiration, dilatation of the pupils, and muscular rigidity at the commencement of inhalation, are diminished by the combination of chloroform with morphine. Vomiting occurs more frequently with than without morphine. By reducing the necessity for large doses of chloroform to produce the desired degree of anæsthesia, Kappeler thinks that the dangers of chloroform are somewhat diminished. This will, of course, depend upon the quantity that is used, and upon the individual susceptibilities of the patient. The doses recommended—0.015 (about one-fifth of a grain) for adults—are probably within the limits of safety.

All physicians, however, are not convinced of the advantages of this combination of morphine and chloroform. M. Demarquay observed that the temperature of animals subjected to this treatment often sank from two to four degrees of the centigrade scale. His conclusion was unfavorable to the employment of this species of anæsthesia. During the siege of Strasburg, in the last Franco-German war, Dr. Poncet, one of the principal surgeons, employed this method for a time in the treatment of the wounded upon whom he was obliged to operate. He soon abandoned the practice, on account of the dangerous stupor which followed the combination of the two drugs. While not disposed to condemn the method when applied to the treatment of minor injuries, it was his opinion that the severe operations and accidents encountered in military surgery could not tolerate the prolonged anæsthesia that is produced by the concurrent action of morphine and chloroform.

Similar opinions have been declared by M. Chauvel, of Val-de-Grace; by Pietri; and, in a qualified manner, by Professor Koenig, who has analyzed not less than seven thousand cases treated in this way. According to his experience, the hypodermic injection of morphine before inhalation of chloroform is useful in the case of professional drunkards and chronic tipplers. By this introduction the period of excitement under chloroform is considerably nullified. He also recommends this combined anæsthesia in protracted operations which render the continuous inhalation of chloroform inexpedient. Among the more than seven thousand cases collected by Koenig, not a single death was reported—a fact which seems to indicate that this kind of anæsthesia is less dangerous in civil than in military life.

Chloral and chloroform.—Forné makes the statement that the administration of chloral hydrate in connection with the inhalation of chloroform produces an effect upon the patient that very closely resembles the effects produced by the combined use of morphine and chloroform. In a discussion of this affirmation before the Chirurgical Society of Paris, Dolbeau and Demarquay insisted upon the dangers attending such a combination. M. Dolbeau related the case of a patient who had unintentionally taken a dose containing ten grammes (nearly eight scruples) of chloral previous to an inhalation of chloroform. Other surgeons have spoken, some in favor, and some against this association of therapeutical agents.

Morphine and ether.—Claude Bernard observed that, when dogs were hypodermically injected with morphine before the inhalation of ether, the period of excitement was prolonged and rendered more tempestuous. Eulenburg also came to the same conclusion. Kappeler experimented upon twenty-five patients, injecting one and one-half centigramme (one-fifth of a grain) about twenty or thirty minutes before the commencement of etherization. The results were very unpleasant. Subsequent headache and nausea were greatly aggravated by this mode of treatment. In only nine of the twenty-five cases was there anything like success. Five cases yielded partial results, and twelve cases failed completely. Vomiting occurred nine times, either during or after the period of anæsthesia.

Chloral and ether.—Kappeler has also made trial of the association of chloral hydrate with ether. His experiments were extended to seventy cases. Thirty or forty minutes before the administration of ether he gave, to adult patients, two grammes and a half (forty grains) of chloral hydrate. Children received half of this amount. The character of the anæsthesia produced by ether under these conditions was not' materially altered. The principal difference consisted in the longer duration of insensibility, and the more lingering recovery of consciousness. Vomiting occurred in twenty-nine of the seventy cases. The degree of prostration and the duration of headache, etc., seemed to be greater than when ether alone had been employed. On the whole, though rather less disagreeable than the association of morphine with ether, there is very little to recommend this mode of inducing anæsthesia.

Death from the effects of chloral and ether.—Male, thirty-five years ; necrosis, following a gunshot fracture of the femur. The patient was reduced by a copious discharge of pus from numerous sinuses, and amputation was decided upon. Just before the administration of ether, twenty grains of chloral were given. After the anæsthesia had become complete, he was kept under the influence of ether for a little while, during transportation into the operating-room, before the commencement of the operation. Just as the surgeon was about to perform the amputation, collapse occurred, and death followed at once.—MORTON and LEVIS, Pennsylvania Hospital, 1872 ; *Am. Jour. Med. Sci.*, p. 415, October, 1876.

Death while inhaling a mixture of ether and amylic hydride.—Male, sixteen years, a delicate boy, about to be operated upon for the removal of diseased bone from the hand.   About an ounce of a mixture of ether and amylic hydride was given, the two fluids being mixed in such proportions as to give a specific gravity of 0.650.   This was inhaled from a piece of lint, with very little disturbance, and at the end of four minutes the patient was quite insensible.   Suddenly the respiration ceased, the face grew pale, and the pupils were widely dilated.   The pulse also stopped at about the same time.   Cold affusion, inversion of the body, artificial respiration, and electrization of the phrenic nerves, did no good.   *Autopsy*, negative.—HARDIE, Manchester ; *Lancet*, April, 1875.

Death while inhaling a mixture of sulphuric ether and bichloride of methylene.—Female, sixty-two years, about to be operated upon for an ovarian tumor.   After inhaling about five drachms of the mixture she became unconscious, but suddenly appearing to revive, opened her eyes and passed urine ; the pupils were largely dilated, and the pulse could not be felt. Artificial respiration, etc., did no good.   *Autopsy*, negative.—*Brit. Med. Jour.*, p. 290, March 2, 1878.

ARTIFICIAL ANÆSTHESIA IN OBSTETRICAL PRACTICE.

The employment of ether in the production of artificial anæsthesia had no sooner been introduced to the medical profession, than the idea was conceived of annulling the pain of childbirth by its aid.   Sir James Y. Simpson became at once the most enthusiastic champion of the new method, and it was soon, largely through his efforts, naturalized throughout the greater part of the civilized world.   A certain amount of opposition to the new practice was experienced at first, on the ground that the pain of childbirth being a constituent part of a natural process, there could be no real advantage in its abolition.   This objection was based upon a dim perception of a great fact which was overlooked by the first advocates of obstetrical anæsthesia, but which in a scientific form has now been adopted by all intelligent obstetricians.   This was the fact that really normal labor is not a painful process.   It is sometimes a difficult and tiresome effort, but not necessarily a painful effort.   The use of anæsthetics in such labor can afford no advantage—may even work an injury to the patient.   But in civilized society the majority of mankind are living under quite abnormal conditions.   As a consequence of this, the reproductive functions suffer disturbance in a manner that becomes more conspicuous than the minor affections of the other bodily functions.   Woman, being more sensitively organized than man, exhibits these reproductive derangements in their highest degree.   Hence, in civilized society it is the rule, rather than the exception, to find parturition attended with a high degree of suffering.   Such suffering, it is true, may be occasionally remarked among savage races of people who are quite in harmony with their environment, just as it may sometimes be discovered among the lower animals ; but such examples are the exception, and not the rule, as in civilized society.   As soon as these abnormalities intervene, we no longer have to deal with natural labor, in which the employment of artificial anæsthesia is superfluous, but we are placed under artificial conditions, in which artificial adjuvants may be as serviceable as in any other departure from nature.

The use of anæsthetics is, therefore, perfectly justifiable in all cases of painful obstetrical function, on precisely the same ground that the use of anodynes in painful menstruation is defensible.

In all cases of normal parturition, the employment of anæsthetics is as undesirable as would be the practice of using opiates during the period of normal menstruation.

Parturition may be considered as consisting of three stages: 1, the stage of dilatation; 2, the stage of expulsion; 3, the stage of delivery. The first of these stages is of exceedingly variable quality and duration. It may be quite free from pain, or it may become the most unendurable of all the stages of parturition. Nervous and irritable women often suffer exquisitely during the process of dilatation, but are comparatively quite comfortable when once the lancinating pains of this period have been transformed into the steady, expulsive efforts of the second stage.

The questions which arise in the mind of the obstetrician, when called to a case of painful labor, are: When to give an anæsthetic? What to give? and, How to give it?

Some authors have refused to sanction the use of anæsthetics during the first stage of labor, reserving it as a means of solace during the second stage. But when we see patients suffering more severely during the first stage than during the second, this seems like an unnecessary refinement. Each case should be estimated by itself, and pain should be alleviated without regard to the time of its occurrence. This decision—to *alleviate* pain —will be found a very different thing from a determination to abolish pain altogether. The unfavorable results which have been ascribed to anæsthesia during an early period of labor have been due to an excessive use of the anæsthetic rather than to its use at all.

The use of anæsthetics having been decided upon, the choice of an agent comes next in order. Chloroform is the obstetrical anæsthetic *par excellence*. Its convenience, the agreeable effects of its inhalation, and the very trifling degree of changes which accompanies its use, all unite in maintaining for this elegant preparation the first place among anæsthetic agents preferred by the obstetrician. This, however, should be true only of its use as an anodyne. When complete anæsthesia is required for the graver operations of midwifery, sulphuric ether should be preferred to all other articles.

The question, How to use anæsthetics in midwifery? can best be answered by a reference to their physiological action upon the nervo-muscular apparatus. The primary effects of moderate etherization are apparent in an increase of functional power throughout the body. The secondary effects are manifested in a progressive paresis, invading the lower extremity of the spinal cord with its dependencies, and extending upward until the respiratory centres in the medulla oblongata are reached. Therefore, when the object of inhalation is merely to deaden pain, it may be carried to an extent sufficient to effect this single purpose. During the first stage of labor, then, chloroform may be used with comparative freedom, if the pain is sufficient to require its use. An opiate, or a dose of chloral, may often be sufficient for the purpose; but distressing cases will occasionally present themselves, in which nothing less than the more potent anæsthetics will suffice.

Continual attention to the general state of the patient should accompany the use of the anæsthetic, and the vapor should be furnished as economically as possible. It is never necessary to reduce the patient to silent insensibility. It should be remembered that there is a point in the process of anæsthesia where consciousness of suffering is abolished, though the patient is still able to talk—to cry out, even, as if in considerable pain. Beyond this point it is undesirable to push the induction of anæsthesia. It is no unusual event to hear a woman declare, at the close of a tedious labor, during which her complaints have been most volubly uttered, despite constant inhalations of chloroform, that the whole period had not seemed longer than fifteen minutes. "It takes off the edge of the pain," is another very common expression. Surely, an agent which can be used in this way must be of the greatest advantage to suffering humanity.

During the second stage of labor, the administration of chloroform must be modified to correspond with the change in the character of the pain. The suffering, which was previously almost constant, now becomes more intermittent, and the intervals are more sharply defined by their greater contrast with the successive periods of effort. The administration of the anæsthetic should be correspondingly intermittent. It is advisable to withhold the vapor during the interval, and to renew the inhalation at the commencement of each pain. By this method the stimulating effects as well as the anodyne effects of the drug will be sustained. This will obviate the most serious objection that has been urged against the employment of chloroform during the stage of labor. It is a matter of daily observation that, if complete anæsthesia be induced, the contractions of the abdominal muscles are weakened or completely annulled, and the uterine contractions occur less frequently than in the normal condition. This is the natural consequence of the sleep of the spinal cord which results from the saturation of its tissues with an anæsthetic. The voluntary muscles are the first to yield; then follow the muscles which are used in semivoluntary expulsive acts; finally, the non-striated and purely involuntary muscles, like those of the uterus, bladder, and intestines. Accordingly, if the patient be placed in a condition of profound anæsthesia, the diminished reflex excitability of the cord is indicated by the lengthening intervals between the pains, or even by an almost complete cessation of the abdominal contractions. The uterus will ordinarily continue to contract, even though death itself should be imminent; but its efforts become infrequent and devoid of their normal energy.

For these reasons, it is undesirable that the condition of complete anæsthesia should ever be established in a parturient woman, unless for the avowed purpose of diminishing and retarding uterine contraction. This can only be desirable when some obstetrical operation is to be undertaken. During the normal progress of ordinary labor, the anodyne and stimulant effects of anæsthetics should be the only object for which inhalation is undertaken. Especially should this be true of the use of anæsthetics at the climax of labor. During the last supreme efforts the patient should have the aid of her senses, to supplement the involuntary uterine contractions with those powerful voluntary exertions which can be intelligently and efficiently directed only in a condition of conscious sensation. From this rule we should not depart, except in cases where the expulsive efforts are inordinately violent, and are accompanied by a condition of frenzy which renders the sufferer temporarily incapable of controlling her actions. Inasmuch as this frenzied state may in certain women be induced as a result of the combined action of pain and of partial anæsthesia, it will be found advantageous, in cases where there is evident lack of energy, to suspend the administration of chloroform long enough beforehand to secure a complete restoration of intelligence at the moment of delivery. When the suffering is continuous, and when the pains are at the same time abundantly energetic, it is better to procure complete anæsthesia at the instant of delivery rather than to run the risk of being called upon, at that critical moment, to deal with an uncontrollable maniac.

With the birth of the infant the anæsthetic should be withdrawn, un-

less some surgical operation, such as placing a stitch in a lacerated perineum, should require its continued use. As a remedy for after-pains
chloroform can hardly be required. Opiates and chloral hydrate are usually
sufficiently efficacious without recourse to more potent anodynes. The
possibility of hemorrhage as a consequence of too abundant or long-continued use of chloroform should not be overlooked. This could only occur
in cases of great exhaustion, associated with anæsthesia carried to its last
degree, producing a temporary paralysis of the uterine muscular fibre.
Whenever a necessity may arise for the induction of profound anæsthesia
at the conclusion of labor, it should be preceded by a trustworthy dose of
ergot, so timed that its contractile effect may immediately succeed the relaxing effects of the chloroform. That it may interfere with the desired
relaxation need not be feared, for the experiments of Claude Bernard have
demonstrated the almost total arrest of the action which takes place when
various drugs are exhibited in connection with chloroform. The retarded
actions of strychnia and of curare are familiar examples of the inhibitory
action of anæsthetics upon other powerful neurotic drugs.

The possible effects of chloroform upon the fœtus must not be neglected. When administered in small and stimulating doses during the
pains alone, the new-born infant rarely exhibits any symptoms that can be
certainly referred to the anæsthetic ; but an excessive saturation of the
blood may prove dangerous to the child. Inasmuch as such cases are generally associated with tedious and difficult labor, it is not an easy matter
to decide, when a dead child has been delivered with the aid of forceps,
whether death was caused by long-continued pressure or by chloroform.
Turnbull relates a case in which a woman received three pints of chloroform during a protracted labor, and was finally delivered with forceps of
a child which was so completely narcotized that every effort for its resuscitation failed. When one reflects upon the fact that three or four ounces
of chloroform furnish an abundant supply for the conduct of any ordinary
case of labor, the occurrence of danger from such an extraordinary use of
the anæsthetic seems quite within the range of probability. The peculiarities of the fetal circulation are such, however, as to prevent any rapid transmission of chloroform from the blood of the mother to the blood of the
child ; consequently, the chances of death from asphyxia produced by compression during the delays of a lingering labor are much greater than the
possibilities of anæsthesia, even after three pints of chloroform have been
expended upon the mother.

Puerperal convulsions require the employment of anæsthesia in connection with other methods of treatment addressed to the particular condition
of the patient. For the relief of the convulsions it is necessary to produce
complete anæsthesia. This should be effected by inhalation of ether.
The same objections that are raised against the use of chloroform in general surgery can be urged against its use in all obstetrical contingencies
which render necessary the induction of profound insensibility. For the
same reason ether should be invariably preferred to chloroform in all the
capital operations of midwifery, such as the application of the forceps,
turning, destruction of the fœtus, etc.

The use of anæsthetics in midwifery practice is justly deemed the least
dangerous occasion for their employment. This has been supposed to depend upon some increased power of resistance to the paralyzing effects of
anæsthetic substances developed by the existence of pain. But this is not
in accordance with observed facts. The parturient woman is, apparently,
as promptly overpowered by chloroform or ether as the non-parturient.

The greater immunity of these patients is probably due to the fact that they are selected patients, as it were. Young women in the prime of life, at an epoch when all the nutritive functions of the body are at their highest degree of activity, must necessarily present the best possible cases for tolerance of anæsthesia. Such patients are in a very different condition from that in which we find the victim of disease, or of shock, upon whom the surgeon is called to operate. The partial degree of anæsthesia, to which alone the majority of parturient women are subjected, is far less dangerous than the condition of absolute anæsthesia which must be the rule in all cases of surgical operation. The conjectural pressure of blood into the brain during the expulsive act is also supposed to protect against the danger of syncope. This, however, is questionable.

The contraindications to the use of anæsthetics in obstetrical practice are the same as those which have been specified in a previous chapter. Cardiac and respiratory paresis are positively prohibitory under all circumstances. Retardation and diminution of the pains are also reasons for withdrawing the anæsthetic. There is always danger, in such cases, if the wishes of the patient are gratified to their full extent, that the use of forceps will become necessary in order to complete the labor.

ANÆSTHESIA IN DENTISTRY.

The excruciating pain caused by the extraction of a tooth, though brief in its duration, probably is excelled in severity by no other form of suffering. To discover some means of escape from such agony had long been the aim of the dental profession, when Horace Wells, of Hartford, adopted the suggestion derived from an exhibition of "laughing gas" by an itinerant lecturer. It was the same desire that prompted the restless energies of Morton in the city of Boston. He knew that if the pain of extraction could only be abolished, he might have all the work he could desire in the manufacture of artificial sets of teeth for people who were deterred from patronizing the dentist through fear of the pain that his forceps would produce. It was for the relief of such patients that he experimented with ether. The extraction of a tooth was the first operation ever performed with the aid of ether in London after the announcement of the discovery of the anæsthetic effects of that agent. Since that date it is probably no exaggeration to say that the members of the dental profession have been, in proportion to their number, the principal practitioners of anæsthesia.

Nitrous oxide gas was the first article essayed by the dentists—Horace Wells and his friends. This was superseded by the introduction of sulphuric ether, which in its turn was supplanted by chloroform. But the too frequent occurrence of death in the dentist's chair soon effected a reaction against so dangerous a substance. The disagreeable effects of etherization, the magnitude of the contrast between ether and chloroform—so well calculated to impress the members of a profession whose taste for convenience and elegance in their appliances is notable—and, withal, the possible dangers that might attach themselves to ether, notwithstanding its reputation for safety—all these considerations operated to stimulate a revival of interest in nitrous oxide gas. The statistics of the Colton Dental Association served to exhibit the almost absolute safety with which this gas could be employed; while the ingenuity of the manufacturer of dental goods, the late S. S. White, of Philadelphia, left nothing to be desired in the way of convenience in the preparation and administration of the substance.

By the Colton Dental Association, in New York, nitrous oxide had been administered to one hundred and twenty-one thousand seven hundred and nine persons, without a single death, previous to March 14, 1881. The Drs. Thomas, in Philadelphia, previous to the year 1879, had also administered the gas to fifty-eight thousand four hundred patients with an equal immunity from harm.

These statistics alone are sufficient to indicate the high degree of safety that attends the use of nitrous oxide in dentistry. Contrasted with the mortality occasioned by chloroform—estimated by Richardson at one in two thousand, or, at his lowest calculation, one in three thousand five hundred cases—there can be no comparison between the two substances. Chloroform should never be used in dentistry.

The cumbrous character of the apparatus employed for the liberation of nitrous oxide gas, and the difficulty sometimes attendant upon the effort to secure a supply of the liquefied gas in distant parts of the country, will always compel the dentist to have something convenient and safe upon which he can rely when nitrous oxide cannot be used. Various experiments with the different anæsthetics have been made. Chloroform is still too often used ; but nothing has yet been found to equal the safety of sulphuric ether. For the dentist the choice should lie between nitrous oxide gas and the vapor of ether alone.

The special precautions necessary in the administration of these substances will be considered in connection with each one separately. In general terms it may be well to urge the importance of an empty stomach when ether is used. The patient should occupy the semi-recumbent position, and all the precautions usual in surgical anæsthesia should be enforced. The dental operator should not administer the anæsthetic without the presence of a third party as an assistant and witness of the proceedings. Unless he is himself an educated surgeon, administration of the ether should be confided to a well-trained physician. In view of the fact that death has been known to occur during the use of nitrous oxide gas, the prudent operator will desire the presence of a physician whenever he resorts to the induction of anæsthesia. Many dentists habitually advise the attendance of the family physician of their patient under such circumstances. Certainly, no conscientious man will undertake an operation which may in the least imperil the life of another without first learning all the dangers that may attend the process, and then making full preparation to combat them with intelligent energy as they appear.

Another reason for the presence of a competent assistant whenever anæsthesia is introduced into the practice of dentistry, grows out of the risks to which the reputation of the operator may be exposed in case he has no witness to vouch for the perfect propriety of his conduct during the etherization of female patients. Excited by the anæsthetic vapor, the patient dreams. Her dreams may assume the form of hallucination, and may persist as the most extravagant delusions. Numbers of unfortunate and innocent men have found themselves, in the earlier days of anæsthesia, deprived of reputation and of fortune through ignorance and neglect of this precaution. This subject will be fully treated in the chapter on the medico-legal relations of anæsthesia.

The use of anæsthetics in dentistry is confined, almost exclusively, to the operation of tooth-extraction. When only a single tooth is to be drawn, if ether is employed, it is unnecessary to proceed to the stage of complete unconsciousness. If dealing with an intelligent adult, the patient may sometimes be trusted to give a signal, such as the dropping of a handkerchief, when the sensibility to pain has been sufficiently blunted. But if the patient be a child, or an adult from whose mouth at least two entire rows of rotten snags must be forcibly removed, it is desirable that complete anæsthesia should be induced. By this means the patient is rendered more easily manageable, and the shock of severe pain is avoided. When nitrous oxide gas is employed, the rapidity with which the patient is rendered insensible, and the transitory effects of the gas, make it difficult and unnecessary to stop short of complete unconsciousness.

It has been thought safer, when using chloroform, to carry the patient as far as the stage of complete anæsthesia before attempting to extract the tooth, for fear of dangerous results from the sudden shock of pain which might be experienced in a semi-conscious condition. There can be no doubt that, if the heart were beating feebly, such a shock might be reflected from the cerebro-spinal centres with dangerous energy, just as the same thing may occur when no anæsthetic is used. Anæsthetic substances diminish the facility of transmission of such inhibitory influences through the nervous system, so that, if they did not also enfeeble the locomotive apparatus of the heart, they would constitute an invaluable shield against the effects of sudden shock. But chloroform is conspicuous for its depressing effects upon the heart. When this depression outstrips the rate of depression in the reflex centres, any sudden painful impression, though retarded in its transit by the condition of partial anæsthesia, may trangress the barriers that have been only partially established in the centres of reflex action, and may fall with overwhelming force upon the enfeebled apparatus connected with the heart. Syncope is the inevitable consequence of such a process. For this reason, complete anæsthesia will secure for the patient a greater degree of safety during the use of chloroform. Even then, however, in seeking to avoid Scylla one may thus fall upon Charybdis, for the complete anæsthesia produced by chloroform has its peculiar dangers, due to the directly poisonous action of this potent drug when carried in excess to the molecules of the nervous system. Chloroform should be discarded from use in dentistry. The same thing may be justly said of all the other numerous candidates for favor as agents for the production of anæsthesia. Nitrous oxide gas should be preferred before all others, while sulphuric ether stands second and final in the list of articles warranted and approved for use in the ordinary operations of dentistry.

LOCAL ANÆSTHESIA.

The anæsthetic effects of cold have always been known throughout those portions of the world in which the atmospheric temperature sinks below the freezing-point of water. The application of snow or pounded ice as a means of benumbing the sensibility of the skin has been practised from time immemorial. Of more recent date is the knowledge of the various freezing mixtures that have been introduced by chemists. So effectual is the local result of their action that, were they sufficiently easy of application, their use might be urged in a large number of the operations of surgery. But the difficulty that attends the effort to limit exactly the sphere of action of a refrigerant application, while at the same time endeavoring to produce a complete abolition of sensibility throughout the part, is so great, that the utility of the method is very considerably restricted. For minor operations upon the extremities, such as the removal of a nail or the incision of a felon, or the amputation of a finger, local anæsthesia may afford very satisfactory results.   But, in all cases that require deep and extensive incisions, the method is far inferior to the production of general anæsthesia.   Notwithstanding the disadvantages which limit its use, local anæsthesia is a valuable addition to the resources of the surgeon. The experiments of Richardson have illustrated its utility even in cases as serious as the amputation of a breast.   Whenever any of the graver contra-indications to the employment of general anæsthesia exist, the possibility of gaining the desired relief through the aid of local anæsthesia should therefore be thoroughly discussed.

Freezing mixtures.—The action of freezing mixtures depends upon the fact that the liquefaction of a solid body causes a disappearance of heat in the newly formed liquid.   The heat thus employed in the maintenance of the fluid state is derived from adjacent bodies.   They lose heat and their temperature falls.   The following list of freezing mixtures may be found in Miller's "Chemical Physics," fifth edition, p. 339:

"One hundred grammes (about 4 ounces) of nitre and 100 of sal-ammo-niac, each in fine powder, when mixed with 200 grammes of water, reduce the thermometer from 50° to 10° (10 to −12° C.).   Equal parts of ammonium nitrate and water reduce the temperature from 50° to 4° (10° to −16° C.). So, likewise, equal parts of water, of powdered crystallized ammonium ni-trate, and of sodic carbonate, also crystallized and in powder, effect a re-duction from 50° to −7° (10° to −22° C.).   In like manner, the solution of crystallized sodic sulphate in commercial hydrochloric acid, is attended with a rapid reduction of temperature; this mixture is employed in the common refrigerators, 5 parts of the acid being poured upon 8 parts of the salt reduced to powder: the temperature may thus be reduced from 50° to 0° (10 to −18° C.).

"The most convenient mixture, however, when procurable, consists of 2 parts of pounded ice (or, better still, of fresh snow) and 1 part of com-mon salt.   A steady temperature of −4° (−20° C.) can by its means be maintained for many hours.   Again, a mixture of 3 parts of crystallized calcic chloride and 2 of snow will produce a cold sufficient to freeze mer-cury; if, before making the mixture, both the vessel in which the experi-ment is to be performed and the chloride be cooled to 32°, such a mixture will cause a thermometer, when plunged into it, to fall to −50° (−45° C.)."

The mixture of salt and snow was highly recommended by Dr. James Arnott.   In the arts it is daily employed for the preparation of ice-cream. For its successful use as an anæsthetic, the mixture should be enclosed in a piece of gauze, and care should be exercised to effect the rapid removal of the resulting liquid as fast as it is formed.   At the best, however, the method is troublesome in practice.   The application is quite painful, and the revival of the part after refrigeration is even more distressing.   The fingers of the surgeon, also, are liable to more or less suffering during the application.   But, for minor operations attended with great pain, such as the incision of a felon or an abscess, the absolute absence of risk that characterizes the method renders it an invaluable resource.   Were it not for the immense convenience which attends the use of ether, local anæsthesia by refrigeration would be more frequently employed than it is. In all cases of debility, characterized by a weak and intermittent pulse, and in cases of cardiac disease, or in an advanced stage of pulmonary dis-ease, it should be decidedly preferred to general anæsthesia.

Local anæsthesia by means of general anæsthetics.—Immediately after the in-troduction of etherization, Simpson, Nunnely, and others, conceived the idea of producing local anæsthesia by the external use of ether.   Experiments on the lower animals seemed to hold out a prospect of success, but upon the human subject the results were not as encouraging. The effects of ether were too superficial, and its application was often attended with great pain.

A French surgeon, named Roux, undertook about this time to treat cases of amputation, in which he feared the supervention of tetanus, by keeping the stump of the limb in an atmosphere of anæsthetic vapor. This success was so purely negative that the method soon passed out of use. Another Frenchman, named Aran, advocated the use of local etherization as a means of relief for the painful effects of disease; but it was a Dublin gynecologist—Dr. Hardy—who first attracted much attention to this method. He recommended the use of chloroform vapor, introduced into the vagina, as a means of relieving the atrocious pain of uterine cancer. His observation excited great interest and became the point of departure for an immense amount of experiment. In some cases there was a considerable degree of success, not only in relieving painful disease, but also in producing local insensibility to the operations of surgery. As a general rule, however, the degree of success was very limited. The applications of ether and chloroform are found, in many instances, especially when applied to the mucous surface and delicate integuments about the orifices of the body, to produce an intolerable amount of suffering.

The subject of local anæsthesia remained in this condition until the year 1866, when Dr. B. W. Richardson published in *The Medical Times and Gazette* (February 3, 1866) an account of the production of local anæsthesia by the concentration of an ethereal spray upon the part to be deprived of sensibility. The apparatus necessary for this operation is exceedingly simple, being, in fact, nothing more than a reinforcement of the common hand-ball perfume atomizer with an additional elastic bulb to serve as a reservoir of compressed air, by which a uniform current of mingled ether-spray and atmospheric air can be maintained.

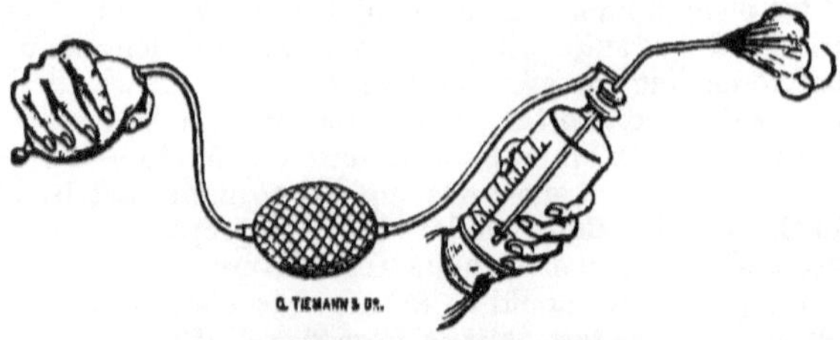

Dr. Richardson's Hand-ball Perfume Atomizer.

By means of this apparatus a continuous jet of pulverized ether can be directed upon any portion of the surface of the body. As the ether evaporates it abstracts heat from the skin until its temperature is depressed even below the freezing-point of water. The skin becomes bloodless, white and tallow-like, precisely as if it had been acted on by frost or by a freezing mixture. In this condition it is of course quite insensible, and may be incised without pain. For the rapid and perfect production of this state, it is necessary to employ the more volatile species of ether. Richardson himself made use of a mixture of anhydrous ether, having a specific gravity of 0.720, with hydride of amyl. Dr. Henry J. Bigelow, the well-known Boston surgeon, made an improvement upon this mixture by the introduction of rhigolene, one of the products resulting from the distillation of petroléum. This is probably the most volatile liquid in existence.

Its specific gravity is only 0.625, and it will boil in the palm of the hand. With this liquid it is very easy to refrigerate the tissues sufficiently to deprive them of life and color.

The disadvantages attendant upon this method consist in the irregular congelation of the tissues—in certain places too great, in others insufficient for the purpose desired. The difficulty of cutting through frozen flesh is not inconsiderable—indeed, it is so great that Dr. Richardson found it necessary to discard the knife and to supply its place with strong, curved scissors. It is not always easy to secure the blood-vessels during the time of congelation, and to search for them after the passage of the anæsthetic state is invariably painful. The return of sensibility in the frozen parts is often attended with pain. There is also a certain degree of risk that the tissues may become too deeply frozen, so that their vitality shall be compromised, with sloughing of the part as a result. These facts must always serve as limitations to the usefulness of this mode of producing local anæsthesia. Within certain narrow limits its utility is indisputable, but for all the graver operations of surgery, general anæsthesia must be preferred.

Carbon disulphide has been occasionally used as a local anæsthetic. Its action is prompt and energetic. If used with a spray it causes congelation of the watery vapor associated with the jet. The frost thus formed gives up so much heat that congelation of the tissues is prevented, but they become insensible, notwithstanding this fact. The vascularity of the part is not diminished, and the flow of blood under the knife is as great as if the anæsthetic were not employed. In order to avoid the practical difficulty which attends the use of this substance in a pulverizing apparatus, it has been allowed to fall, drop by drop, upon the skin while an assistant hastened the process of vaporization by directing upon the surface a current of air from the nozzle of a pair of bellows. The very offensive odor of the compound, and its positively poisonous qualities if inhaled in any quantity, will not hasten its general adoption in surgery.

Carbonic acid gas has been used from time immemorial as a local anodyne. The stone of Memphis, used by the ancient Egyptians, owed its virtues to the carbonic acid gas that was liberated by its solution in vinegar. Yeast poultices are familiar examples of the survival of a similar method of securing relief from pain. The good effects of aërated waters and of kumyss, in irritable conditions of the gastric mucous membrane, are doubtless to be ascribed to the carbonic acid that they contain. The benefits derived from the treatment of chronic alcoholic gastritis with the fermented *poi* which forms so large a portion of the diet of the Pacific Islanders are in like manner due to the abundance of carbonic acid gas in the pasty substance. The pains of uterine cancer have been alleviated in some instances by injections of water charged with the gas. Relief is experienced for an hour, or even more, but then the pain returns without any change for the better. For the production of any substantial effect, or as an agent sufficiently potent to annul the suffering incident to a surgical operation, the gas is quite useless.

Professor Brown-Séquard (*Gaz. Hebdom.*, November 10, 1880; *Med. Times and Gaz.*, November 27, 1880; *Med. News and Abstract*, January, 1881) has recently observed a very remarkable result from the local application of chloroform to the skin of the guinea-pig, the cat, and the dog. If chloroform is poured rapidly upon the shoulder of a guinea-pig, a reflex contraction of the platysma myoides and subjacent muscles immediately follows. In a short time respiration diminishes, the temperature falls, the animal staggers and becomes torpid.   It allows itself to be placed on the side or the back, without attempting to resume its natural position ; and then it falls suddenly into a state of anæsthesia which may last for several hours, during which sensibility may disappear absolutely, the animal remaining in a state of the most complete resolution, resembling that of anæsthetic sleep.   A young kitten, thus treated, will pass into a condition resembling shock, or the state of syncope following severe injuries or profound drunkenness, which may persist for several hours, occasioning complete insensibility to the most vigorous pinching.   Recovery of consciousness is ushered in by muscular tremors, and the animal gradually acquires the power of raising itself upon its feet.   Sometimes there is an appearance of delirium, or the skin may exhibit a condition of hyperæsthesia with more or less tendency to inflammation.   The experiment may prove fatal.   Death may either supervene suddenly, or it may occur after convulsions, epilepsy, diminution of the reflex faculty on the side to which chloroform had been applied, pupillary contraction in the cat, or considerable dilatation in the dog.   Respiration then becomes slow and shallow ; the diaphragm seems paralyzed ; the temperature falls ; and, finally, the animal dies suddenly, generally without convulsions.   Inspection of the internal organs discovers general, brightly colored vascular turgescence ; the aorta contains blood ; both ventricles are gorged with blood, and the blood in the vena cava is less dark than usual.   The excitability of the nerves is also greatly increased, and is much more persistent than in animals which have not been subjected to chloroform.   But the phrenic nerve and the diaphragm, upon the side opposite to the point of local application of chloroform, exhibit a great diminution, or even abolition, of galvanic irritability.

These phenomena are by M. Brown-Séquard attributed to a process of inhibition.   A remote action takes place in the skin, but its effects extend to the nervous centres, and their functions are temporarily modified. Such inhibition may go on to simple syncope, to syncope with asphyxia, or finally to syncope with arrest of the exchanges of motion and nutrition. That these phenomena cannot be referred to inhalation of the vapor of the chloroform which is used, is proved by covering the mouth and nose with a muzzle connected with a caoutchouc tube sufficiently long to prevent the respiration of the vapor.   A chloroform enema, moreover, produced in a dog no analogous phenomena ; yet they were afterward manifested by the same dog as a consequence of the application of chloroform to the skin.   The close relation between these phenomena and the manifestations of hypnotism in animals is quite remarkable.

MORTALITY OF ARTIFICIAL ANÆSTHESIA.

It is impossible to form even an approximate notion regarding the number of cases in which surgical anæsthesia has been produced since the year 1846.   Nor is there any means of reaching an accurate conclusion regarding the number of fatal cases which have occurred during that interval of time.   Both terms of the comparison being thus defective, the conclusion must be correspondingly inaccurate.

By collecting the experience of hospitals and armies for given periods of time, certain conclusions may be formulated which will serve to guide future explorers in this territory.   The first attempt of this kind, on any considerable scale, was made by Andrews of Chicago (*Chicago Med. Ex-*

aminer, May, 1870). He collected statistics of 92,815 cases of etherization, including 4 deaths, 1 : 23,204 ; 117,078 cases of chloroform anæsthesia, with 43 deaths, 1 : 2,723 ; 11,176 cases of anæsthesia with mixtures of chloroform and ether, with 2 deaths, 1 : 5,588 ; and 7,000 cases of the use of bichloride of methylene, with 1 death, 1 : 7,000. Dr. Coles of Virginia carried this research a little farther, giving 152,620 cases of chloroform inhalation, with 53 deaths, 1 : 2,873 ; and 10,000 cases of bichloride of methylene, with 2 deaths, 1 : 5,000.

The inquiries of Richardson among the provincial hospitals of England exhibited a high rate of mortality from chloroform, and also illustrated the irregular incidence of death from that cause. In eight hospitals (Norwich, Lynn, Stafford, Wolverhampton, Newcastle-under-Lyme, Brighton, Birmingham General and Queen's Hospital) there were, during the interval from 1848 to 1864 inclusive, 17,000 cases of anæsthesia from chloroform, with one fatal case. In the same hospitals, from 1865 to 1869 inclusive, 7,500 cases of chloroform-inhalation yielded six fatal cases. In six other hospitals (Lincoln, Bath, Cambridge, Oxford, Reading, and Nottingham) the same periods gave 7,900 cases with three deaths, and 2,765 cases with one death. Sum total, 35,165 cases of anæsthesia from chloroform, with 11 deaths, 1 : 3,196.

Ker (Chisholm : " What Anæsthetic shall we Use ? ") states that, during the twenty-eight years from the time of the introduction of chloroform, there were only two deaths caused by its use in the Royal Infirmary at Edinburgh. During the last ten years of that period, he estimates that there were 36,500 cases of chloroform anæsthesia, with only one death, 1 : 36,500. Elser, of Strasburg, had used chloroform 16,000 times, without a fatal case. Kidd, of London, had seen it administered upward of 10,000 times, and had seen no fatal case. Richardson had seen it used in the London hospitals 15,000 times before he met the first fatal case. Clover has recorded 3,000 administrations without a single death. Billroth, of Vienna, had given chloroform 12,500 times before he met with his first accident. McGuire, surgeon to Jackson's corps, in the Confederate Army, reported 18,000 administrations without one death. Chisholm himself used chloroform 6,000 times without a death. His estimate of the mortality from the use of chloroform was 1 : 20,000.

During the Crimean war, chloroform was given in the French army 30,000 times, with at least two deaths (*Med. Times and Gaz.*, p. 485, May 7, 1859). In the English army, Macleod heard of one fatal case (*Med. Times and Gaz.*, p. 40, July 10, 1858). The whole number of administrations was 12,000.

During the war of the rebellion, in America, 1861–65 (Circular No. 6, p. 87), chloroform was given in 80,000 cases, with seven deaths, 1 : 11,448.

Among German surgeons (Kappeler : " Anæsthetica," p. 124), Nussbaum reports 15,000 inhalations of chloroform, Koenig about 7,000 without accident, while Kappeler, had one death among 5,000 cases. Bardeleben (*Med. Times and Gaz.*, August 2, 1879) witnessed more than 30,000 cases of chloroform-inhalations, prior to the year 1876, without a single death ; but, during the year 1876, among 1,200 inhalations there were four fatal cases. Up to 1879 this gave a mortality of four in about 84,000 cases.

In St. Bartholomew's Hospital, during the years 1875–80 (*Brit. Med. Journ.*, p. 103, January 15, 1881), chloroform was administered 4,810 times, with two deaths, and ether was administered 6,440 times, with two deaths. Among these cases of ether-inhalation, however, were reckoned 1,304 inhalations of ether preceded by nitrous oxide.

Summing up these figures, we find the following ratios, which, however, are very little better than mere guess-work :

Ether, 99,255 inhalations, 6 deaths—1 : 16,542.
Chloroform, 492,235 inhalations, 84 deaths—1 : 5,860.

With the exception of nitrous oxide gas, other anæsthetic substances have not yet been sufficiently used to form any very accurate idea of their relative fatality.   Amylene, for example, was used by Snow until two deaths occurring in about two hundred and forty administrations, compelled its abandonment.   The one hundred and forty-fourth inhalation was the first fatal case ; it was then administered upward of ninety times before the second accident gave the coup de grace.

Nitrous oxide gas has been used with the greatest immunity from accident, owing to the brevity of the operations during which it is employed. Rottenstein believes that it has been inhaled more than one million times since its reintroduction in the year 1863.   Not more than eight or ten cases have resulted fatally during that period ; and, in a majority of that number, the gas can only indirectly be charged with the result.

MEDICO-LEGAL RELATIONS OF ANÆSTHESIA.

The introduction of anæsthesia has given occasion for an entirely new class of medico-legal inquiries.   Death sometimes occurs during the use of an anæsthetic.   If inhaled by the decedent in private, and of his own motion, was it a case of suicide, or was it an accidental death ?   If administered by the hand of another, it may be important to ascertain whether or no it was given by a person skilled in the theory and practice of etherization, or by an individual destitute of these qualifications.   The object for which anæsthesia was attempted may also become a subject of legal investigation.   It may have been innocently given for the purpose of annulling the pain of disease, or of an operation, or it may have been used for the purposes of murder or assault, to facilitate a robbery, or to conceal the occurrence of childbirth.

All these, and even other inquiries, may demand the attention of a court of justice ; hence, the medico-legal relations of anæsthesia are usually of the most important and absorbing character.

The question of medical responsibility for the fatal results of anæsthesia during the ordinary course of medical and surgical practice is of the first importance.   An inquiry of this nature resolves itself into two questions :   Are all anæsthetics possessed of properties which may render them dangerous to life ?   And are these dangers so far inevitable that in no individual case can they be foreseen and in some measure avoided ? Clear and decisive answers to these questions are demanded by that public which is so profoundly agitated by the occurrence of death during anæsthesia.   Certainly, nothing can more powerfully address the imagination and excite the sympathies than a sudden decease under such circumstances. A young and beautiful woman, the mother of an interesting family, the pride and joy of an extensive circle of relatives and friends, enters the office of a dentist, it may be for a brief and trifling operation.   She inhales the pleasing vapor, with scarcely a thought of anything but the delightful relief from pain thus easily procured.   A few hurried inspirations, and then no more—life is extinct.

Our analysis of the physiological action of anæsthetics shows that anæsthesia is produced by forces which are antagonistic to those processes upon which all vital phenomena depend. Consequently, all anæsthetics act by the development of a tendency to death. Exhibited in sufficient quantity, for a sufficient time, any one of them must inevitably destroy life. This, however, does not preclude their use, for the same thing is true of the majority of substances that can be introduced into the current of the circulation. But experience shows that anæsthetics differ among themselves in the degree of their energy. During the earlier years of anæsthetic practice, that is, during the period necessarily abandoned to experiment, the surgeon was fully excusable for the unfortunate consequences of a comparatively untried remedy, especially if it had been sufficiently tested upon the lower animals, and had received the sanction of men eminent in the profession. But, for a large number of anæsthetic substances, the age of experiment has passed. Their qualities have been thoroughly ascertained by innumerable trials. To continue, then, to employ certain articles without restriction can only be deemed unjustifiable and culpable. If, having employed an anæsthetic that is duly accredited by the weight of authority, accident follow its use, the surgeon must still be able to show that it was administered in accordance with the rules of his art. Was it a case in which no contraindications to anæsthesia could be discovered? Was the proposed operation characterized by gravity sufficient to warrant the induction of insensibility? If these inquiries can be answered in the affirmative, it only remains to investigate the history of the individual case. Were all precautions against asphyxia regarded? Was the condition of the pulse and of the respiration carefully noted? Had complete anæsthesia supervened? Had the operation been commenced? Might not the fatal result have been the result of hemorrhage or exhaustion rather than due to the ânæsthetic? Were all proper measures for resuscitation of the patient employed? Such are some of the questions which suggest themselves as indicative of the proper course for a judicial investigation.

It is not sufficient for the exoneration of a surgeon to show that there was on his part no criminal intent to cause the death of his patient. Homicide may, indeed, be involuntary; but, in order to exculpate its agent, he must show that there was on his part no lack of attention, no imprudence, no carelessness, nor any failure to observe all the rules of procedure in such emergencies.

In case of the death of a patient under the influence of a new and comparatively untried anæsthetic, the surgeon who has observed all the rules of anæsthetic practice could only be censured for temerity in the use of a substance of which the properties were not yet fully known. He then must be able to urge in his defence that the article belongs to a class of substances whose general properties are well ascertained, and are not esteemed dangerous to life. He must also be fortified with evidence to show that it has been often administered to numerous animals of various species, especially of those species which most resemble man in their physiological reactions. He must, if possible, show that it has been often administered to individuals of the human species; that its peculiar properties are such as to excite the belief that its use will be attended with less danger and with a greater degree of comfort than is characteristic of the best anæsthetics already in use; that it was not employed without sufficient consultation with well-informed surgeons who were qualified to express an intelligent judgment in such cases; and finally, that it had been administered with the full knowledge and consent of the patient, after he had been informed of the nature and possible consequences of the experiment. It

6

is to be feared that in certain cases, heretofore, these rules have not been conscientiously regarded. There was a time when temerity like that which characterized the attempts of Morton and of Simpson was deserving of the highest admiration, but the world has outlived the necessities of that period. The great increase of knowledge that has followed the efforts of those early experimenters has terminated forever the need and the propriety of such exhibitions of courage. Future researches, to lie beyond the possibility of reproach, must be conducted in a spirit of caution which we may well be thankful that our predecessors did not display.

The same tendency to an increase of the degree in which an operator is held responsible for the consequences of ordinary artificial anæsthesia, will manifest itself in proportion to the progress of knowledge toward the exactness of science. As we increase our acquaintance with the behavior of therapeutical agents, we equally increase our responsibility for their proper use. It can no longer be urged in defence of the surgeon whose patient has been chloroformed out of existence, as it was successfully argued in behalf of the young Parisian surgeon who, in the year 1853, had been imprisoned for the death of a patient under the influence of chloroform, upon whom he was operating without assistance, that "there are no fixed rules for the administration of chloroform." There were none then, it is true; and every case was in a certain sense a physiological experiment for the purpose of discovering some fixed principles of conduct in such matters. This condition of uncertainty can no longer be claimed to exist. Our knowledge of anæsthesia, and of its risks, is sufficiently complete for all practical purposes, and it admits of formulation in the shape of definite rules of action.

In every judicial investigation of death ascribed to the use of anæsthetics, two principal lines of inquiry must be traversed. In the first place, it must be ascertained whether death was caused by the action of an anæsthetic. In the second place the responsibility of the surgeon, or other administrator, must be defined. When doubt arises regarding the use of an anæsthetic, in the absence of testimony, recourse must be had to the expedients of toxicological analysis. The possibility of a coincidence of other causes of death must be excluded by the results of autopsy. Sudden deaths, unconnected with surgical intervention, have occurred at the time of operation before the days of anæsthesia. The rupture of an aneurism, a cerebral hemorrhage—even an emotion of terror, may have been the cause of death irrespective of all anæsthetic influence. Death occurs less frequently now as the direct result of an operation than during the period before the introduction of anæsthesia. This fortunate result is due to the prevention of shock through pain. As for such accidents as the entrance of air into the veins, or the aspiration of blood into the air-cells of the lungs, during operations about the oral or naso-pharyngo-tracheal passages, anæsthesia affords no immunity. The possibility of death through obstruction of the larynx with an extracted tooth should not be lost sight of when inquiring for the causes of death during the operation of dentistry. In short, no decision regarding the cause of death during anæsthesia should be announced without a careful *post-mortem* examination of the entire body.

Having determined it as a fact that death was caused by the action of the anæsthetic, the question of the purity of the article should be investigated. The trade-mark of the most reputable manufacturer is not always sufficient to insure the perfection of the article. Accidents may have occurred to vitiate the process of manufacture; or an inferior article, designed for external use, may have been carelessly substituted for the purified drug. A few years ago the surgeons connected with one of the most celebrated hospitals in the United States were greatly perplexed by a series of cases which presented symptoms of distressing laryngeal irritation, and, in one instance, alarming syncope, while inhaling what had been furnished as the very best quality of sulphuric ether. The lot was returned to the manufacturer, who readily admitted the presence of impurities in the ether, but was not so lucid as might have been desired in his explanation of their occurrence. Chloroform sometimes contains alcohol. It then is tardy in its action, and the unpleasant after-effects are very slowly dissipated. Methylic and amylic alcohols, and various essential oils or ethers, are sometimes present in chloroform, and are the cause of obstinate gastric and nervous derangements. A case is related by Wald, in which chloroform containing hydrochloric acid and chlorine produced great irritation of the air-passages and inflammation of the bronchi. Such cases, however, cannot be very common.

It may become necessary to investigate the quantity of the anæsthetic that was administered. The dose of course varies with the nature of the anæsthetic substance, so that the inquiry regarding the proper amount for inhalation might be most fittingly considered in connection with each article. In general terms it must be admitted that there is no universal law that governs the safe administration of anæsthetics, so far as quantity is concerned. As in the case of alcohol, so it is with ether and chloroform and their congeners—they may be administered in almost indefinite quantities. Some persons can drink, and drink, and drink again, without becoming intoxicated, while others are inebriated by the smallest amount. When sulphuric ether is used for the production of insensibility during an ordinary surgical operation, it is no uncommon thing to vaporize from two to eight ounces (70 to 250 grammes). Patients have been kept for many hours under its continual influence, at an expense of many pints of the liquid, in order to effect euthanasia. Of chloroform, one ounce (30 c.c.) is ordinarily sufficient for the purposes of the surgeon; but Turnbull relates a case in which three pints (1,500 c.c.) were employed during the course of a difficult labor. Christison administered eight ounces (240 c.c.) during a period of thirteen hours. Jackson gave sixteen ounces (500 c.c.) to a man eighty-three years of age. Hergott used over two pints (1,000 c.c.) for the maintenance of anæsthesia during a period of eighteen hours. Exceedingly small quantities, on the other hand, have been known to destroy life. Taylor quotes, from Dr. Warren's "Table of Fatal Cases," an instance in which only fifteen or twenty drops caused death. In another instance only thirty drops had been vaporized when the patient expired. In such cases, however, some means of estimating the actual quantity more reliable than the mere assertion of the administrator should be sought. Without intending any deception, the mental agitation produced by the terrible event of sudden death must inevitably impel the majority of men to minimize their share in the causation of the disaster.

It has been ascertained by experiment that for inhalation the vapor should not exceed three or three and one-half per cent. of the air that is breathed. If the amount of the vapor exceed five per cent., danger exists. But experience shows that it is impossible thus to graduate the quantity of vapor that is mixed with the air; consequently, danger may obtrude itself every time that a fresh charge of chloroform is placed upon the napkin.

The great difference in the quantities which may be tolerated by different individuals has led to a belief in the existence of idiosyncrasies by virtue of which certain persons are intolerant of anæsthetics. This can with difficulty be admitted to be true. But, as in the analogous case of alcohol, it is undoubtedly true that certain patients are, more easily than others, affected by these substances. Children yield to their effects in less time than is necessary to overcome an adult. Women are more susceptible than men. The present condition of the patient, doubtless, has more influence over the course and results of anæsthesia than any original peculiarity of constitution or diathesis. Individuals have been chloroformed many times without accident, and then have perished under its influence at last.

The investigation of the cause of death after anæsthetic inhalation should take under consideration the mode of its production. Of forty-eight cases collected by Sabarth (*Das Chloroform : Eine Zusammensetzung der wichtigsten Erfahrungen und Beobachtungen*, 1866), thirty-six deaths were caused by asphyxia, eleven by syncope, and one by spinal hemorrhage. This indicates for chloroform a directly poisonous character. It tends strongly to prevent the access of oxygen to the tissues, and operates in this way more frequently than by direct paralysis of the heart. Thus it happens that death by asphyxia may follow the use of a powerful substance like chloroform, without any fault of the physician. The asphyxia in such a case is the direct consequence of the presence of chloroform in the blood and in the tissues.

The exact time of death relative to the stage of anæsthesia should, if possible, be ascertained. According to Sabarth's tables of death by chloroform, of one hundred and twenty-one cases, fifty-four expired before the operation ; forty-two during the operation ; and twenty-five after its conclusion. Dr. Snow states that, among forty-six cases, death occurred before the operation in eighteen instances ; during the operation in twenty-two ; and shortly after the operation in six. Scoutteten gives, for the corresponding figures, twenty-two, six, and twelve. Kidd gives fourteen, fourteen, and seven. The Report of the Committee of the Medical and Chirurgical Society of London gives eighty-eight deaths before and during operation—of which fifty appear to have preceded operation—fourteen after the completion of the operation and seven at a period not recorded.

The following tabular exhibition of these figures will be convenient for reference :

	Sabarth.	Snow.	Scoutteten.	Committee.
Death before operation	54	18	22	50
Death during operation	42	22	6	38
Death after operation	25	6	12	14
Deaths not classified	—	—	—	7
Total	121	46	40	109

For additional information, see the article on Chloroform.

When the patient ceases to breathe during the administration of anæsthetics—other complicating or possible causes of death being excluded—it is easy to assign the cause of the unfortunate result. But when the patient survives for a time—for a number of hours—after the conclusion of etherization, it may not be very easy to determine the exact relation of anæsthesia to the act of dissolution. As a general rule, if consciousness is recovered during life, it is presumptive evidence that the anæsthetic had very little, if any, direct relation with the disease. It is, nevertheless, true that in certain instances the exciting or stupefying effects of the drug are seen to persist until the time of death. Even then, however, if life be prolonged beyond three or four hours after the operation, it is probable that the consequences of the operation were the chief agents in the termination of existence, for the experiments of Tourdes indicate that chloroform, at least, is entirely eliminated from the system in less than three hours after inhalation. In one experiment, after inhaling chloroform for twenty minutes, the breath of a woman, examined one hour and a half after the cessation of the inhalation, still contained chloroform. In another case, examined three hours after an inhalation that had continued half an hour, the breath contained no trace of chloroform.

The length of time during which it is proper to maintain a continuous condition of anæsthesia does not admit of precise limitation. Sir James Y. Simpson treated a case of puerperal convulsions by continued inhalation of chloroform for twenty-four hours. Christison administered the same anæsthetic for thirteen hours. Hergott continued the process during eighteen hours. When insensibility has once been reached, it is easy and safe to maintain the anæsthetic influence by continuous inhalation of small quantities of the vapor. The period of greatest danger is usually confined to the early stages of anæsthesia, so that, after the induction of tranquil sleep has been effected, the risks of continued cautious inhalation are greatly reduced.

After having traversed the entire range of such an investigation, if the operator can show that he was aware of all that has been repeated above, and was on his guard against danger, and did actually employ the varied measures recommended for the resuscitation of patients who have succumbed during anæsthesia, he must be regarded as blameless and free from all responsibility for the unfortunate occurrence. But how often it has happened that the surgeon could not be thus completely acquitted. It has been well remarked that "the mistakes and blunders which the most famous men have committed are innumerable ; the most fortunate is he who errs the least." If it can be shown that the fatal result was the consequence of ignorance and neglect, the administrator must be held accountable for the consequences of his imprudence. If, on the contrary, it appears that he was ordinarily well acquainted with the duties and responsibilities of his profession, and had exercised all ordinary precaution, he cannot be adjudged guilty of malpractice, even though there may have been omissions in his method.

In the course of a medico-legal investigation it may become necessary to determine the fact of previous anæsthesia. This may require examination of a living person, in case of alleged anæsthesia without fatal result, or it may be necessary to examine the dead with a view to ascertain the cause of death. For the rules which should govern such an inquiry we are largely indebted to Casper and to Tourdes, whom we shall closely follow.

To determine the cause of death in a case of suspected anæsthesia, three kinds of proofs are necessary—the results of chemical analysis, the symptoms exhibited by the patient, and the anatomical changes revealed by *post-mortem* section.

Chemical analysis.—It is necessary to proceed as in other cases of poisoning : the poison must be recovered from the tissues, or the effects of its presence must be demonstrated in an unequivocal manner.

If the patient is alive, oral testimony is usually sufficient for the discovery of truth. But this is not always enough. A young woman may protest that she has been chloroformed and violated. It is important to ascertain whether she has been actually submitted to the action of an anæsthetic.

The *ethereal odor* is quite transient. An hour is usually sufficient for its disappearance from the clothing. Fifty c.c. (nearly two ounces) of chloroform, poured upon a piece of cloth about ninety centimetres (three feet) long and sixty centimetres (about two feet) wide, exposed to the open air at a temperature of $6.8°$ C. ($44°$ F.), had entirely evaporated at the expiration of an hour, without any trace of odor left behind. The evapoation of ether is still more rapid. If these substances contain alcohol or other impurities, their evaporation is considerably retarded.

The examination of the breath should be made as early as possible, for the odor of the anæsthetic soon ceases to be noticeable in the expired air ; in from one to three hours it may be no longer perceptible. Individuals who have been etherized sometimes profess to be able to taste the anæsthetic for hours, or even for one or two days after the inhalation, but this is supposed to be a reminiscence rather than an actual sensation. In order to recover the substance from the breath, it is necessary to examine a quantity of the air that has been expired from the lungs. This may be done by causing the patient to expire into a rubber bag until ten litres of air have been secured. This air should then be passed through a red-hot porcelain tube, and conveyed by aspiration into a solution of nitrate of silver. The carbonic acid of the breath forms carbonate of silver, which dissolves readily on the addition of nitric acid. If chloroform is present, the chlorine that was liberated in the tube combines with the silver to form chloride of silver, which remains as a precipitate. Tested by this method, the breath of one patient, a woman who had inhaled chloroform for half an hour, gave no trace of the substance at the end of three hours, while, in another case, the breath of a woman who had taken chloroform-inhalations for twenty minutes, gave an abundant reaction with nitrate of silver at the end of an hour and a half.

Chloroform soon disappears from the blood. The experiments of Duroy have shown that the blood of animals to whom chloroform had been given contained not a trace of the substance when drawn at an interval of twenty or thirty minutes after the restoration of the animal to a condition of sensibility. The rate of elimination depends largely upon the volatility of the anæsthetic. If mixed with alcohol it lingers longer in the blood.

The presence of sugar in the urine has been considered as indicative of the action of chloroform, but this is not a sign upon which much reliance can be placed.

If the dead body is to be examined, toxicological analysis may give decisive results. But a negative result might not be a proof that anæsthetics had not been administered. If life were sufficiently prolonged for the elimination of the substance, of course no trace of its presence could be detected. In such a case it would be permissible to suspend judgment regarding the immediate cause of death.

For the discovery of alcohol and the ethers it is necessary to resort to the process of distillation. Chloroform may be detected by the nitrate of silver process. These anæsthetic substances pass with great rapidity into the current of the blood. A few inspirations of the vapor are sufficient to charge the blood with a quantity that admits of easy discovery by ordinary chemical tests. It is most easily discovered in the lungs and in the nervous tissues. According to the analyses of MM. Perrin, Duroy, and Lallemand, when the blood contained one part of the anæsthetic, the tissues of the brain contained respectively two and six-tenths parts of amylene, three and twenty-five hundredths of ether, and three and ninety-two hundredths of chloroform. The tissues do not ordinarily exhale any odor of the anæsthetic ; or, if noticeable at the time of death, it soon disappears.

A source of error exists in the ordinary test for chloroform. If the distillation is conducted at a high temperature, the chlorides contained in the blood may pass through the heated porcelain tube and produce a reaction with the solution of nitrate of silver. Traces of chlorine may thus be discovered in the fluids of an animal which had not been chloroformed. This difficulty may be obviated by the introduction of a flask containing a solution of nitrate of silver, between the retort and the porcelain tube. The normal chlorides will thus be arrested, while the chloroform vapor will pass on, to be decomposed in the heated tube. By this process the presence of chloroform is indirectly demonstrated. If the chloride of silver is not formed, chloroform is certainly absent. If a chloride is precipitated, it becomes necessary to investigate its source. It may have been derived from some medicinal chloride or chlorate which the patient had taken. It will then be necessary to institute a search for the metal with which the chlorine may have been combined. In this way, operating by exclusion, a high degree of probability may be reached by the analyst. Traces of chloroform may thus be detected for a long time after death. After four days of putrefaction in a warm place, it may still be demonstrated in the tissues of rabbits. Duroy claims that its presence may be revealed by analysis after the lapse of many months.

It sometimes happens that the physician is called upon to examine a person still living, who is supposed to have been the victim of anæsthesia, either voluntarily or involuntarily. He should search for the container and for the residue, if there be any, of the anæsthetic. He should take notice of the air of the room, whether it seems to contain any vapors that can be recognized by the sense of smell. He should carefully observe the patient, taking note of appearances indicative of intoxication—such as heaviness of sleep, stupor, dulness, and confusion of ideas as consciousness returns. The eyes, the nose, and the lips are often reddened, and their mucous surfaces may even be excoriated by contact with an impure article of chloroform. Usually consciousness is rapidly recovered. This is especially true of children. Sometimes sleep is considerably prolonged, especially if chloroform has been swallowed with suicidal intent. As a general rule, however, the effects of the drug disappear entirely after the lapse of a few hours.

As for the *post-mortem* appearances revealed by autopsy, Casper and others have been inclined to the opinion that they present nothing in any way specially characteristic. According to Taylor, " congestion of the vessels of the brain and its membranes have been met with, but not uniformly ; the lungs congested, or in an apoplectic condition ; the heart flaccid, and the cavities frequently empty, or containing but little blood ; in some cases the right cavities have been found greatly distended ; the blood generally dark in color, and very fluid, sometimes mixed with air-bubbles." In twenty-seven out of thirty-four examinations recorded by Dr. Snow (*Med.*

Times and Gazette, October 23, 1858), "there is engorgement of the lungs, or of the right side of the heart—in the majority both these conditions were met with." Woodman and Tidy remark ("Forensic Medicine and Toxicology," p. 458) that generally, after death from chloroform, "all the cavities of the heart are distended, while exceptionally the left side is empty. The countenance is livid and pale, and putrefaction is usually somewhat slow." In the record of cases which these authors have given, it is stated that after death from chloroform, the brain or its membranes are congested.

The following are the principal appearances noted after death by chloroform, as given by Tourdes ("Dict. Encyc. des Sci. Méd.," t. iv., p. 505).

"There is paleness of the face ; the expression of the countenance is tranquil ; the pupils are dilated ; upon the limbs are visible rose-colored spots ; there is very little appearance of cyanosis ; at its base the tongue is sometimes injected ; the retraction of that organ is the physical consequence of the attitude of the corpse when muscular contractility has ceased.

"The lungs are congested, and present a rose-colored tint, or even a decided red coloration. This congestion may, in the lower animals, become a disseminated lobular engorgement. In forty-eight cases of autopsy, pulmonary congestion has been noted thirty-six times. Sometimes there is serous infiltration of the lung. Great importance has been assigned to the pulmonary emphysema encountered in many cases : this is almost always observed in the lower animals, even if the sudden and convulsive forms of asphyxia have been avoided. Redness of the mucous surfaces of the trachea and bronchi have often been remarked. A certain amount of froth may be found in the air-passages : the degree of their injection will be more intense if, in a case of homicide or suicide, a few drops of chloroform have found their way into the respiratory tract—an accident which rapidly produces injurious results. It should be remembered that certain authors, among whom Casper may be found, have mentioned a anæmic condition of the lungs.

"A flaccid condition of the heart has been observed (sixteen times in twenty cases). This phenomenon, however, is principally dependent upon the time of the examination. The same remark is applicable to the condition of its cavities (fourteen times out of twenty cases). The muscular fibres of the heart have been found paler than usual. The heart may be filled with blood—especially on the right side. The great veins may be distended with blood, and there is often a sufficiently notable quantity of this fluid in the principal arteries. The blood is liquid, brownish, or of a deep red color. This condition is rarely absent–Berend having remarked its presence fifteen times in twenty examinations. This fluidity of the blood is coincident with the rapidity of death. Sometimes we have noticed a few clots mingled with the fluid blood ; in one case the blood in the left side of the heart had a very deep red tint, indicative of sudden syncope. Very little importance should be attached to the presence of free gases in the blood, as this is a consequence of putrefaction which may be very rapidly evolved. A chemical analysis would be necessary in order to determine the character of the gas. In twenty autopsies the presence of these gases was noted seven times. Putrefaction was progressing in three of these seven cases ; in three cases the mode of death doubtful ; and in only one case could any [illegible] attached to the [illegible]tion. (Berend.)

"The pia mater [illegible] cerebral parench[yma] [illegible] moderately injected. Congestion is the [illegible], occurring only f[illegible] in forty-eight (Sabarth), and it is [illegible] considered a cause of d[eath] [illegible] anæmic co[ndition] of the cerebral organ [illegible] been remarked. [illegible] connected with putrfactive changes. We have noted a trifling amount of ventricular fluid. he liver is often congested. This organ is variously affected by the actia of deleterious vapors and gases. Injection of the kidneys has been olerved."

It is worthy of nte, that in the above summary the appearances arc principally those wlch are to be found after death from asphyxia and syncope. There aronany points of resemblance with the appearances discovered after deathby drowning. It will therefore be necessary, in a doubtful case, to bæ the opinion regarding the cause of death not upon the *post-mortem* appurances alone, but upon a review of the history of the case in connection vth the external appearances and surroundings of the corpse, and the resits, it may be, of a toxicological analysis. Of course, it will be necessary ɔ search all parts of the cadaver for the lesions of dis- · ease or injury, and ɔ assign to such, if discovered, their proper value as possible causes of th death of the individual.

Recognition of snulated diseases.—Certain alleged deformities, contractures, paralyses, leafness, aphemia, etc., may sometimes be unmasked by the employment of artificial anæsthesia. *In vino veritas* is a maxim that is equally applable to the condition induced by anæsthetics. The three stages of anæhesia—the initial period of excitement, the period of unconsciousness, an the period of recovery, may each and all furnish valuable information iususpected cases.

The question at nce arises: Is it right to employ this method of investigation? The aswer to this will depend upon the condition in which the subject for invetigation is placed. If the individual has voluntarily, or in obedience to rbitrary law, abdicated his position as a free agent, it may be legally righfor his superior to subject him to anæsthetic examination. A soldier, oa sailor in the navy, or a conscript, may thus be etherized, for the purpœ of investigating his alleged simulation of disease. But no free man mæ thus be examined without his full and free consent. If a person be charpd with simulation for criminal purposes, it is neither legally nor morally ght to subject him to this method of examination, for it would be a violatm of the personal liberties of an individual who in the sight of the law is iuocent until he has been convicted of crime. It would also involve an infiction of the great principle that no accused person shall be compelled ɔ incriminate himself. It would be as proper to use the rack, as was anently done, for this purpose, as to compel a prisoner to undergo anæsthæia with the design of thus securing his own evidence against him. In lik manner, no convicted criminal, undergoing imprisonment, can be subjectd against his will to the action of anæsthetics, because that cannot have foned a part of his original sentence. To subject him to additional indignitiæ would be illegal and cruel.

It may be laid dwn as a general proposition, that, in all cases where an investigation for th detection of simulation is to be made by the aid of anæsthetics, only th safest methods should be employed. In the present state of our knowlege this proposition practically limits the inquisitor to the use of sulphuriether.

The induction ɑ anæsthesia will always enable the surgeon to estimate at its true value evry case of alleged ankylosis in which the diagnosis is rendered doubtful uring the state of voluntary consciousness. Baudens ʼ *Gazette Méd. de Iris*, p. 209, 1847) was the first to put on record the ʼccessful investigaon of a fraud of this description. A patient under his ɹe claimed to be eformed by disease and ankylosis of the spinal articulations, producing angular curvature of the spine. Under the influence of ether the joints of the backbone were perfectly movable, and all deformity disappeared. The patient afterward confessed himself a malingerer. In military hospitals it is not an uncommon thing to see patients who claim to be suffering with various forms of contracture. The persistence with which this condition may be simulated is sometimes remarkable. It may be carried to such a degree of perfection that it has been said to be maintained even during the hours of sleep. Under the influence of ether, the contracture will disappear if it be simulated. There is, however, a source of difficulty in the diagnosis of these cases, for the reason that contractures of a purely irritative character—such as may be observed in certain cases of hysteria—are reproduced immediately after the withdrawal of the anæsthetic.   Bayard (*Ann. d'Hygiène et de Médecine Légale*, t. xlii. p. 201, 1849) relates a case in which a chronic retraction of the foot, though accompanied by disease of the bones themselves, disappeared during anæsthesia, and was reproduced again on the recovery of consciousness. Tourdes ("Dic. Encyc. des Sci. Méd." 1ʳᵉ série, t. iv., p. 516) relates the case of one of his own patients, a young girl, ten years of age, who suffered a contracture of the muscles of the right leg and thigh, causing her to limp at first, and then to resort to crutches. Suspected of deception, she was subjected to examination during anæsthesia. While relaxed by the anæsthetic the limb was perfectly movable, and the joint seemed to be thoroughly serviceable; but the contracture was reproduced with the recovery of consciousness, and after a time the symptoms of coxalgia became clearly evident.

During the period of excitement which ushers in the condition of anæsthesia, and during the time of recovery from the unconsciousness that it has produced, various forms of alleged disorder of the nervous system have been unmasked. In this condition, patients who have feigned deafness, or idiocy, or speechlessness, have been found capable of hearing and speaking, and of comprehending with perfect ease what they had claimed to be incapable of doing when thoroughly conscious. Genuine stammering or stuttering is increased while under the partial influence of anæsthetics. The pretended disorder is completely relieved during the inhalation. Sédillot experimented upon the possibility of self-restraint at the moment of awaking from the sleep of anæsthesia. He found that, no matter how forcibly he had charged his patients to keep silent, when interrogated at that moment they all forgot his commands, and answered his questions in spite of themselves. His conclusion was to the effect that it would be impossible, under such circumstances, to simulate the aphasic or aphemic condition.

Induction of anæsthesia during sleep.—Dr. W. R. Cluness reported (*Pacific Med. and Surg. Journ.*, June, 1874) two cases in which he had succeeded in chloroforming two children during sleep. One of them was a girl, aged eight years, suffering with purulent inflammation of the mastoid cells. No difficulty was experienced in the production of insensibility to pain by inhalation without awaking. The abscess was opened and dressed, and when the child recovered consciousness she was not aware that anything unusual had occurred. The other case was also a little girl, two and a half years old, who was in like manner chloroformed during sleep, for the removal of a supernumerary toe.

In the January number of the *Annales d'Hygiène* (1874) is a report by Professor Dolbeau on the "Employment of Chloroform in Relation to the Perpetration of Crime." The professor instituted a series of experiments for the purpose of ascertaining whether a person can be subjected to anæsthesia while he is asleep.

He found that sleeping animals were promptly awakened by small quantities of the vapor of chloroform in the air about them. He then extended his experiments to human beings. In three cases the sleepers were easily aroused by evaporating a little chloroform at a short distance from their nostrils. "In a second series of experiments, made on seven patients, ten drops of chloroform were poured on a napkin folded in four, which was gradually brought to the vicinity of the air-passages, so that all air inspired had traversed it. In all these cases the patients were suddenly aroused from their sleep—some immediately, and one only after the eleventh inspiration.

"A third group of cases, consisting of twenty-nine patients, was next experimented upon." The professor found that as his experience increased there was a corresponding increase of dexterity on his part, so that of these twenty-nine subjects he was able to induce complete anæsthesia in ten without disturbing their sleep. He found that the presence of impurities in the chloroform increased its irritating qualities, and diminished the probability of inducing anæsthesia without awaking the patient. Children were less difficult than adults to manage. The conclusion arrived at was to the effect that chloroform may be administered during sleep in such a way as to facilitate the commission of crime, but that this result is not likely to happen in ordinary unskilled use of the anæsthetic.

At the annual meeting of the American Medical Association, in 1880, Dr. J. V. Quimby, of Jersey City, presented a history of three cases in which persons had been successfully chloroformed during sleep.

The following abstract of his paper is given in the *Boston Medical and Surgical Journal*, p. 592, June 17, 1880. His attention was directed to this subject "by the noted case of the murder of policeman Richard Smith, of Jersey City. This occurred while Smith and his wife were together in bed, and for this reason the latter was arrested as being *particeps criminis*. She held that she had been chloroformed during sleep, but the State contended that this was impossible, because the fumes of the chloroform would have awakened her from her natural sleep. Here, then, was a nice and very important medico-legal question : If chloroform be properly given, will it awaken a person, or will the person pass from a natural to an artificial or chloroform-sleep without being awakened? This was asked of Dr. Quimby at the trial, by Mrs. Smith's counsel, and he replied that he had never attempted the administration of chloroform to an individual during natural sleep, and that the books, so far as he knew, were silent on the subject. He then made three experiments with a view of determining this point. He first made arrangements with a gentleman of his acquaintance to enter his room while he was asleep, and give him chloroform by inhalation. This he did with entire success, easily transferring him from natural to artificial sleep without arousing him. He used for the purpose about three drachms of Squibb's chloroform, and occupied seven minutes in the experiment. The second case was that of a boy, thirteen years of age, who had refused to take ether for a minor operation. By Dr. Quimby's advice his mother gave him a light supper and put him to bed. When he was asleep the doctor administered chloroform, and performed the operation without awaking him. The third case was similar, the patient being a boy of ten, who was suffering from an abscess which it was necessary to open, and the same course was pursued here with equal success. Two inferences might be drawn from these cases, the writer said : 1st, minor surgical operations could thus be done with perfect safety, and much more agreeably than in the ordinary way ; and 2d, an individual somewhat skilled in the use of chloroform might enter a sleeping-apartment and administer chloroform, with evil intentions, to a person while asleep."

The possibility of inducing anæsthesia for criminal purposes, upon waking persons, has been extensively discussed. When the use of anæsthetics was first introduced, much alarm was experienced in certain quarters lest the new agents should be employed for the purpose of overpowering individuals, in order to facilitate the commission of robbery or rape. It has comparatively often been alleged that in this way a custodian has been overpowered by an inspiration of chloroform, causing immediate insensibility. But we know that this is impossible. Anæsthesia cannot be induced upon a waking individual without either his own consent or an exhibition of constraining force that would render its induction unnecessary. So long ago as 1850 (*Lond. Med. Gaz.*) Dr. Snow remarked : "The public have been greatly and unnecessarily alarmed about the employment of chloroform by thieves ; what they really have to dread is that robbers will still resort to the old means of the bludgeon, the pistol, and the knife, and not to one which, like chloroform, allows the victim so good an opportunity of escape, and themselves so great a chance of detection." There is no doubt, however, that thieves have attempted the use of chloroform with the hope of facilitating their schemes. Lord Campbell, in a speech before the House of Lords, in favor of a bill to make the unlawful administration of chloroform and other stupefying agents felonious, made the statement (Wharton and Stillé's "Medical Jurisprudence," Book v., § 595) that : "It stood, indeed, on record, that since the discovery of chloroform, persons had been convicted before the competent courts of using that article for the purpose of robbery." In the same work (*loc. cit.*) the following narrative is quoted from the *Medical Gazette* for November, 1850 : "A gentleman named Mackintosh had retired to bed at a hotel in Kendal. He was awakened about twelve by a man attempting to suffocate him by means of a rag steeped in chloroform. Mr. Mackintosh, who is an elderly man, struggled desperately with his assailant ; but, whether from the fumes of the chloroform or the disadvantage at which he was taken by his midnight assailant, he felt himself fast fainting, when his cries of 'Help! murder!' roused the house. When the landlord made his way into the room, Mr. Mackintosh was almost powerless, and his assassin or robber was lying upon the bedding, which had fallen upon the floor in the scuffle, apparently sound asleep. On being roughly shaken, the latter professed that he had long been a sleep-walker, and appeared to be astonished to find himself where he was. A policeman was sent for, and the man taken into custody. A strong smell of chloroform was perceived by the parties who entered the room upon the alarm being given, and a bottle containing chloroform was found under Mr. Mackintosh's bed, and a similar bottle in the carpet-bag of the prisoner, who had been at the hotel several days. The probability was that the ruffian was secreted under the bed when Mr. M—— retired to sleep, as the latter had placed a chair previously against the door to prevent intrusion, there being no lock upon the door. This criminal escaped with eighteen months' imprisonment, the offence not being a felony at that time, since there was no intent to commit murder shown."

In a trial for an attempt at robbery by the use of chloroform, at New Bloomfield, Perry County, Pa., January 18, 1871, the possibility of anæsthetizing a sleeping person was discussed in court by Dr. F. F. Maury and B. Howard Rand, M.D., Professor of Chemistry and Lecturer on Medical Jurisprudence in Jefferson Medical College. Dr. Maury stated (Wharton and Stillé, *loc. cit.*) that he had "experimented with chloroform on six sleeping persons. Out of that number all resisted, more or less. Two men woke up immediately, and one remarked ' You are trying to give me something.' . . . I administered it to a child four days old : it offered resistance. With my experience I could not administer chloroform to four persons."

The use of anæsthetics had scarcely been introduced, when an alarming form of accusation appeared in the criminal courts of the world. In the year 1847, a dentist in Paris was condemned to punishment on the accusation of a young lady to whom he had administered ether. On recovering her consciousness she found herself in a condition of disorder which, in connection with an alleged recollection of what had transpired during etherization, led her to charge the dentist with a violation of her chastity. A few years later a similar case occurred in Philadelphia. This has become one of the celebrated cases in Medical Jurisprudence. It was carefully reviewed by Dr. Hartshorne, in the Philadelphia *Medical Examiner*, December, 1854, and is quoted in full by Wharton and Stillé, vol. ii., pp. 201–208.

The young lady was accompanied to the dentist's door by her accepted lover. She therefore entered the office in a condition of more than ordinary amatory exaltation, which was undoubtedly augmented by the local spinal and uterine hyperæmia, naturally coincident with the approaching menstrual *nisus*, due on that very day. In this extraordinarily elevated state of nervous excitability she was closeted with an agreeable gentleman who had not long previously, perhaps jestingly, talked of making her his wife. She inhaled ether, and, of course, passed through a stage of additional erethism which—according to the remark of the dentist, to a lady who came in after the operation, that ether had not much effect on her —was not fully merged in complete anæsthesia. While in this condition of exalted sensibility, the contact of a finger with the wrist was magnified into a voluptuous sensation ascending the arm and invading the breasts. The sharp pain, caused by thrusting a probe into the cavity of a decayed tooth, like painful excitations under other circumstances of obtunded or perverted sensibility occasioned by abnormal states of the nervous system, is referred, not to its real point of origin, but to some other distant portion of the body. By such irradiation the pain in the dental pulp was referred to a portion of the body that happened just then to be unusually irritable —the sexual centres in the pelvis. As a consequence of the incompleteness of the anæsthesia, the patient was in a dreaming state. The half-formed perceptions were not controlled by the external senses, and the ideas thus originated followed one another in the most extravagant and improbable manner. But, as a consequence of the hyperæmic state of the cerebral tissues, the functions of the waking portions of the brain gave to the nascent ideas a degree of vividness and a persistence in memory that did not belong to the ordinary processes of thought. When full consciousness was restored, these illusions and hallucinations persisted under the form of delusions. It may then be with perfect assurance of the truth of her belief that the patient asserted her ruin, and her perfect knowledge of what she declared herself to have been powerless to resist.

The utter ignorance of all logical connection between the actual impressions made upon the patient during the stage of ethereal exaltation, and his perception and recollection of the same, is well illustrated by numerous examples. I have seen a patient—an officer in the army—who declared that his sensations during an examination of his wounded arm while under the influence of ether, were of the most delightful character. He fancied himself borne upon a roseate cloud, rushing through space on his way to plunge into the sun. Wharton and Stillé (*loc. cit.*) have collected a number of illustrative cases. "A patient of Prof. Pitha, being put under the influence of chloroform, at once fancied himself in his beloved Italy, and gave full vent to his expressions of delight; he raised himself up during the operation for the liberation of a hernia, and watched it with great interest, answering to the question whether he felt any pain, *Si, io sento l'incisione, ma no sento dolori.* . . . During an extremely painful operation by Velpeau upon a young girl, she raised herself into a sitting position as if to observe it. She said afterward that she supposed herself seated at a dinner-table." Dr. J. F. B. Flagg, a surgeon-dentist in Philadelphia, collected several similar cases, published in his work on Ether and Chloroform. "After an operation," writes Dr. F——, "performed on the forehead of Mr. T——, a dentist of this city, he said that, although his eyes were shut, *he saw every cut of the knife.* He saw the shape of the wound upon the forehead, and, what was better than all, this cutting appeared to him to be done upon somebody else." In this case we have an example of irradiation of sensations during the hypersensitive condition induced by the anæsthetic. Impressions made with the knife upon the sensory nerves of the skin do not stop in the appropriate centres for the perception of such sensations; they leap over the limits of these cortical recipient areas, and invade the territory set apart for the perception of impressions coming through the retina. The patient sees without opening his eyes. This false judgment is not corrected by the sensation that originated the process, because the anæsthetic effect of the ether in this case has sufficiently progressed to blunt the fine edge of common cutaneous sensibility, while at the same time exalting the receptivity of particular cortical portions of the brain.

"Another young lady mentioned by Dr. Flagg, when the forceps was placed upon the tooth cried out, 'Stop pulling! stop pulling!' The tooth was nevertheless extracted. 'She *rose* from the chair in much excitement, and would have fallen to the floor, but I caught and sustained her for a moment, when the ether instantly passed off.' This young lady dreamed that she was in danger of shipwreck, and, seeing the rocks and breakers ahead, cried out to the man at the wheel, with all her strength, to *stop pulling.* In another instance, a lady, while under the influence of ether, resisted the attempt to extract her tooth. She *got up* from the chair, seeming much offended, and took her seat in another part of the room. When the effect of the ether passed off, which was in about a minute, she was much astonished at finding herself so remote from the position she occupied when she fell asleep."

The following example of delusion produced by ether is quoted by Wharton and Stillé from the *Union Médicale*, September, 1857: "A young man, having been sufficiently etherized, the dentist prepared to extract a tooth. In a moment he dashed the instrument from his mouth, *left the chair*, and, striding about the room, demanded what they meant to do with him. In a few moments the effect of the ether passed off. Being again put under its influence, the same scene was enacted, with even greater violence, and he endeavored to jump out of the window. When he regained his memory, he related that he imagined himself surrounded by a great number of enemies, one of whom endeavored to drive a nail into his mouth, and, being unable to struggle with them, he had sought safety in flight." Such illusions are not uncommon consequences of the dreamy state that precedes the advent of complete unconsciousness. The external senses are closed, but the *internal senses* may be, for a time, more active than during the waking state of the individual. As we have seen, when considering the physiology of sleep, the sequence of ideas in these dreams is largely—sometimes wholly—determined by internal impulses proceeding from the different internal organs of the body. It may be an agitation of the peripheral extremities of the pneumogastric nerve in the stomach or in the lungs. It may be an irritation arising within certain portions of the brain itself. It may be a commotion springing from the genito-urinary organs. Whatever portion of the body may chance to be a point of unusual excitement, from that proceeds the impulse which causes the dream and gives direction to its course. The extraordinary variety that characterizes erotic dreams in natural sleep is sufficient to suggest the possibilities of such dreams when occurring under the stimulation of alcohol or of ether. Dr. N. L. Folsom, of Portsmouth, N. H., has recorded the following case (*Med. and Surg. Rep.*, January 12, 1877), illustrative of this phenomenon :

"In 1854 a clergyman's sister came to my office for the purpose of taking ether and having a tooth extracted, and brought her brother's wife with her. I began to administer the ether to the patient, and whilst renewing it she got away from me, and seemed alarmed and offended. I did not attempt to compel her to breathe any more ether, but urged her to take it, and so also did her brother's wife, but she would take no more. She had the impression, so her brother told me, that I attempted to violate her, and that his wife assisted me. It was a long time afterward before she would fully give up that she was mistaken in the matter." The Boston *Med. and Surg. Jour.*, p. 287, November, 1858, gives an account of a case in Montreal, in which a dentist was tried for an alleged attempt to commit rape upon one of his patients to whom he had given chloroform. One of the witnesses for the defence testified that his own wife was fully impressed with the belief that she too had been violated by the prisoner under the influence of chloroform, and she persisted in this delusion, notwithstanding the fact that her husband was present during the whole period of anæsthesia. In spite of this and other testimony, the jury brought in a verdict of *guilty of an attempt to commit rape*, though they had the grace to join with it a *recommendation to mercy.* "Siebold relates the case of a woman whom he rendered insensible by ether. Upon regaining her consciousness she appeared to be in a highly excited state, and was loud in her praises of the delightful condition in which she had been ; her eyes sparkled, and a certain erotic excitation was very observable ('Ueber die Anwendung der Schwefel-Æther-Dämpfe in der Geburtshülfe.' Göttingen, 1847). Pitha observed excitement of the sexual feeling in two cases, one of a woman, and the other of a man, upon whom he operated (*Prager Viertaljahrschrift*, Bd. 3, 1847). In one of these cases, observed by M. Dubois, the woman drew an attendant toward her to kiss, as she was lapsing into insensibility, and this woman afterward confessed of dreaming of coitus with her husband while she lay etherized. In ungravid women, rendered insensible for the performance of surgical operations, erotic gesticulations have occasionally been observed ; and in one case, in which enlarged nymphæ were removed, the woman went unconsciously through the movements attendant on the sexual orgasm, in the presence of numerous bystanders " (Wharton and Stillé, *loc. cit.*).

The following case, derived from English sources, is contained in the *Philadelphia Medical Times*, December 22, 1877 : "A case of the utmost importance to the whole profession, not in Great Britain only, but everywhere, was tried before Mr. Justice Hawkins, at the assizes at Northampton, on the 9th of November. It was a charge against a surgeon's assistant of criminal assault—of rape upon a patient when under the influence of chloroform. If there is a dastardly crime, it is to take advantage of a woman's helpless unconsciousness to violate her person. And so the magistrate thought who sent the accused to jail on the 14th of September, declining to hear anything in his favor, and resolutely refusing to accept bail. The charge was that a married woman, named Child, went to the surgery of her family medical attendant to have her teeth operated upon. She had been there a day or two before, but the attempt to put her under chloroform then failed. A second attempt was rather more successful. She evidently had some peculiarities or idiosyncrasies in relation to chloroform, for he gave it for an hour and yet she was never sufficiently under its influence to admit of the operation being performed. She was accompanied by a friend—a Miss Fellows. At the end of the hour Miss Fellows went out of the room and saw Mr. Child. In a quarter of an hour Miss Fellows returned. The prosecutor maintained that on Miss Fellows' return she was quite conscious, but was unable to speak. Finding it impossible to perform the operation, the accused accompanied the prosecutrix and her friend home. So far Mrs. Child had been unable to speak, but shortly after the accused left the house she complained to her husband that he had taken advantage of the absence of Miss Fellows to assault her criminally. Next day, when the accused called, he was told about what she had said, and he replied that she was laboring under a delusion. Under cross-examination, Mrs. Child said that she told the accused that if he would admit the offence and quit the town (Birmingham) she would forgive him. This the accused declined to do, denying that he had committed any offence. He was then given in custody. The prosecutrix stated that the offence was perpetrated immediately after Miss Fellows left the room ; that the prisoner went upon his knees and then assaulted her. Miss Fellows stated that on her return she found Mrs. Child in precisely the same position in the chair which she occupied when she went out of the room. Such were the facts of the case. It was quite clear that there had been either an assault committed, or that the woman was under the influence of a very pronounced delusion. The whole of the accused's conduct was in favor of the latter hypothesis. But, in such a matter, where no third person was present, the statement of one of the two parties concerned must be taken. When a woman whose character was apparently without blemish (for in cross-examination no attempt was made to call her reputation in question) makes a definite charge against a man of assaulting her under circumstances which permitted of such an assault, the law could only send the case to a jury. In the meantime the unfortunate surgeon's assistant was sent to prison.

"When the case came to be tried, a large number of medical men of repute came forward voluntarily to aid the accused's defence, and did this quite gratuitously. The chief witness for the defence was Dr. B. W. Richardson, F.R.S., whose celebrity is world-wide. As is well known, Dr. Richardson has studied anæsthetics very carefully and for many years. He stated that there were four stages or degrees in which chloroform operated. The first stage was that in which consciousness was not lost ; there was resistance and a desire for air. In the second, consciousness is lost, but the operation is impossible, the patient screaming, often without provocation. The third stage is that of complete unconsciousness, and where all rigidity is lost. This is the stage which permits of operation. In his opinion the patient was in the second stage; the third never having been reached. He stated that in his own experience he had known persons in this second stage to have delusions as to what had taken place during that time. He related a number of cases, and stated that the fact of such delusions being induced by chloroform was one of the earliest objections raised to its adoption. He related one case where the patient, a female, was being operated upon by a dentist, and alleged that the dentist criminally assaulted her. And this she persisted in, though her father, her mother, Dr. Richardson, and the dentist's assistant were all present throughout the whole time. She persisted in her conviction long after the effects of the chloroform had passed away; and Dr. Richardson said she was probably of that belief still. This evidence of Dr. Richardson's was corroborated by the experience of Dr. Hawksby, of London, and by Dr. Saundby and Mr. J. F. West, of Birmingham. The judge asked the jury if it was necessary to sum up, and they replied it was unnecessary—they were already agreed upon a verdict of acquittal. Mr. Justice Hawkins pointed out that such a verdict would not be the slightest imputation upon the absolute sincerity of the prosecutrix, who, no doubt, firmly believed every word of what she had said. He then congratulated the accused upon having had an opportunity of fully vindicating himself upon the charge preferred, and said that the verdict of acquittal did not mean that there was insufficient evidence, but that the accused was entirely cleared of any imputation in respect to the charge preferred against him. There could be no doubt the prosecutrix labored under a delusion. The accused was then discharged from custody, having been in prison two months for no offence."

In this connection, the remark may be added that such cases of delusion should be carefully investigated with reference to their possible connection with an "insane temperament." Inquiry should be made regarding the family history of the individual. The fact of consanguineous insanity is often successfully concealed by the apparently healthy relatives and members of a family in which these morbid predispositions may nevertheless exist. It often requires, as alienist physicians very well know, an immense amount of tact and perseverance to elicit such facts, but the effort should always be made. The strong excitement that so often attends the early stage of anæsthesia may indeed, in certain instances, be the exciting cause of illusions and delusions which would never have existed but for the insane background, now for the first time discovered, upon which they are projected. It is, at least, probable, that in all such cases the existence and presence of an extraordinarily excitable nervous temperament may be detected. It is not an uncommon incident in the experience of feeble "nervous" persons to have any powerful mental or emotional excitement culminate in a sexual orgasm. Let such an individual be subjected to the depressing influence of pain and the agitation of preparation for an operation, so complete a condition of nervous erethism may be engendered that the additional irritation caused by inhalation of the anæsthetic vapor will be sufficient to liberate a sexual convulsion. The phenomenon finds its parallel in the epileptic convulsions which may be in like manner aroused in epileptic patients who are made to inhale ether or chloroform. The sensations thus produced are conveyed to the brain, where they are received without modification and correction by comparison with sensations derived from the external sense organs, because those organs, under the benumbing influence of the anæsthetic, have more or less completely ceased to perform their appropriate functions. The patient is actually dreaming, and the results of her dreams, though vividly impressed upon the memory, as any dream may always be, have no more necessary connection with external facts than ordinary dreams can have.

While we may thus interpret the vast majority of the phenomena which have originated such accusations against doctors and dentists who have thus innocently administered chloroform, to their sorrow, we may not lose sight of the fact that anæsthetics may be, and probably have been, used to facilitate the violation of women. The now well-established possibility of success in the induction of anæsthesia during sleep, points in this direction. But, before conviction in such cases of alleged violation, the fact of intercourse should be established by evidence more satisfactory than the mere assertion of a woman who at the time of the alleged assault must necessarily have been engaged in the act of dreaming. Evidence of actual defloration, such as rupture of the hymen, if a virgin, or stains upon the clothing or person, should be insisted on. No evidence whatever relating to these particulars was adduced, or, apparently, even asked for in the trial of the unfortunate Beale. In the case of Dr. Davis Green (Wharton and Stillé's "Medical Jurisprudence," vol. ii., § 267), the evidence regarding the alleged administration of chloroform was of the most unsatistory character, and yet the defendant was convicted. The principal evidence against the doctor consisted in the fact of his having occupied a room adjoining the apartment in which the prosecutrix had slept. She became pregnant, and was delivered of a child.

The possibility of the successful commission of rape upon a woman while sleeping under the influence of ordinary alcoholic beverages, is beyond all question. This sleep is a modification of the sleep of ordinary artificial anæsthesia—it is, in short, alcoholic anæsthesia. This may result from the ingestion of very moderate quantities of alcohol—an amount quite insufficient to produce intoxication. Dr. Hartshorne relates such a case, on the authority of Dr. D. F. Lewis, then of Philadelphia, in a note to the American edition of Taylor's "Medical Jurisprudence." In London, in the year 1853, Dr. Lewis "was called to attend a young woman previously well known to him as of excellent character, and found her in a violent hysterical paroxysm, brought on by the discovery that she had been violated, during sleep, by her accepted admirer. She had returned to her mother's home with him, from a long walk, very much fatigued ; and, after having drank a glass of ale, had sunk into a profound slumber, during which the act had been perpetrated without the slightest evidence of consciousness on her part. This was admitted by her companion ; and her prompt discovery of her wrong, and immediate alarm and agitation, as well as her known liability to unusually heavy sleep, fully established the truth of her assertion. The usual physical signs of recent defloration were presented on her person."

ANÆSTHETIC SUBSTANCES.

In the following list of anæsthetic substances, the classification employed in Miller's "Elements of Chemistry," fifth edition, has been adopted.

ORGANIC COMPOUNDS.

METHANE ; CH_4 ; *Methylic hydride ; Formene ; Marsh-gas ; Light carburetted hydrogen, or Subcarburetted hydrogen.* One of the principal constituents of coal-gas, giving to that substance very decided anæsthetic properties.

MONOCHLOROMETHANE; CH_3Cl; METHYLIC CHLORIDE; *Methyl chloride; Methyl hydrochloric ether; Hydrochlorate of methylene; Chlorure de méthyle; Methylchlorür.*

DICHLOROMETHANE; CH_2Cl_2; METHYLENE BICHLORIDE; *Methylene dichloride; Bichloride of methylene; Methyleni bichloridum; Chlorure de méthyle monochloré; Éther chlorhydrique monochloruré de l'esprit de bois; Methylen bichlorid; Chloromethyl; Chloromethylchlorür.*

TRICHLOROMETHANE; $CHCl_3$; CHLOROFORM; *Chloroformum; Chloroforme; Trichlorate of formyl.*

TETRACHLOROMETHANE; CCl_4; CARBONIC TETRACHLORIDE; *Tetrachloride of carbon; Chlorocarbon; Carbonii tetrachloridum; Bichlorure de carbone; Formène perchloré; Vierfachchlorkohlenstoff; Tetrachlormethan; Carbon tetrachlorür.*

TRIBROMETHANE; $CHBr_3$; BROMOFORM; *Bromoformum; Bromoforme.*

IODOMETHANE; CH_3I; METHYLIC IODIDE; *Methyli iodidum; Iodide of methyl; Iodure de méthyle; Jodmethyl.*

TRIIODOMETHANE; CHI_3; IODOFORM; *Iodoformum; Iodoforme; Jodform.*

MONOCHLORETHANE; C_2H_5Cl; ETHYLIC CHLORIDE; *Hydrochloric ether; Éther chlorhydrique; Aethylchlorür.*

α—DICHLORETHANE; $CH_2Cl.CH_2Cl$; ETHYLENIC CHLORIDE; *Ethylene bichloride; Ethylene dichloride; Dutch liquid; Ethene chloride; Æthylenum bichloridum; Æthylenum chloratum; Liqueur Hollandais; Huile du gaz oléfiant; Aethylenchlorid; Elaylchlorür; Oel der holländischen Chemiker.*

β—DICHLORETHANE; $CH_3.CHCl_2$; ETHIDENE DICHLORIDE; *Ethylidenic chloride; Ethylidene chloride; Æthylidenum chloratum; Aethylidenchlorid.*

α—TRICHLORETHANE; $CH_2Cl.CHCl_2$; MONOCHLORETHYLENCHLORIDE.

β—TRICHLORETHANE; CH_3CCl_3; METHYLCHLOROFORM; *Monochlor-ethylidenchloride.*

MONOBROMETHANE; C_2H_5Br; ETHYLIC BROMIDE; *Bromide of ethyl; Ethyl bromide; Æther hydrobromicus; Hydrobromic ether; Éther hydrobromique; Bromure d'éthyle; Bromwasserstoffäther; Aethylbromür.*

IODETHANE; C_2H_5I; ETHYLIC IODIDE; *Iodide of ethyl; Hydriodic ether; Æther hydriodicus; Iodure d'éthyle; Jodwasserstoffäther; Jodäthyl.*

α—TETRANECHLORIDE; C_4H_9Cl; BUTYLIC CHLORIDE.

β—TETRANECHLORIDE; $CH(CH_3)_2CH_2Cl$; ISOBUTYLIC CHLORIDE.

PENTENE; C_5H_{10}; AMYLENE; *Pentylene.*

PENTANE; C_5H_{12}; AMYLIC HYDRIDE.

MONOCHLOROPENTANE; $C_5H_{11}Cl$; AMYLIC CHLORIDE; *Chloride of amyl.*

MONOIODOPENTANE; $C_5H_{11}I$; AMYLIC IODIDE; *Iodide of amyl.*

OCTANE; C_8H_{18}; CAPRYLIC HYDRIDE; *Octylic hydride.*

KEROSELENE, a mixture of various hydrocarbons distilled from coal-tar.

OIL OF TURPENTINE; $C_{10}H_{16}$.

BENZENE; C_6H_6.

PYRROL; C_4H_5N.

ETHYLIC ALCOHOL; C_2H_6O; ALCOHOL: *Alcool; Alkohol; Weingeist.*

PHENOL; $C_6H_5.OH$; CARBOLIC ACID; *Oxybenzene; Phenic acid; Phenylic alcohol; Acidum carbolicum; Acidum phenicum crystallizatum; Acide phénique; Acide carbolique; Hydrate de phényle; Carbolsäure; Phenylsäure; Phenylalkohol.*

TRICHLORETHALDEHYDROL; $CCl_3.CH(OH)_2$; CHLORAL HYDRATE; *Hydrate of chloral; Chloral hydras; Hydrate de chloral; Chloralhydrat.*

TRICHLOROBUTALDEHYDROL; $C_3H_4Cl_3CH(OH)_2$; BUTYL CHLORAL HYDRATE; *Chloral butylicum; Hydrate de chloral butylique; Butylchloralhydrat.*

METHYLIC OXIDE; $CH_3.O.CH_3$; METHYLIC ETHER; *Methylene hydrate; Éther méthylique; Oxide de méthyle; Methyläther; Holzäther; Formäther.*

ETHYLIC OXIDE; $C_2H_5.O.C_2H_5$; ETHER; *Ethylic ether; Sulphuric ether; Éther vinique; Schwefeläther.*

METHYLAL; $CH_2(OCH_3)_2$; *Methylene dimethyl ether; Formal.*

ETHALDEHYDE; $CH_3.COH$; ALDEHYDE; *Acetic or Ethylic aldehyde.*

DIMETHYL KETONE; $CH_3.CO.CH_3$; ACETONE.

ETHYLIC FORMATE; $C_2H_5.CHO_2$; FORMIC ETHER; *Æther formicus; Éther formique; Ameisenäther.*

ETHYLIC ACETATE; $C_2H_5.C_2H_3O_2$; ACETIC ETHER; *Æther aceticus; Ethyl acetate; Éther acetique; Essigäther.*

ETHYLIC NITRITE; $C_2H_5.NO_2$; NITROUS ETHER; *Éther nitrique; Salpeteräther.*

ETHYLIC NITRATE; $C_2H_5.NO_3$; NITRIC ETHER; *Éther azotique; Aethylnitrat.*

AMYLIC NITRITE; $C_5H_{11}.NO_2$; *Nitrite of amyl; Amylo-nitrous-ether; Amylum nitrosum; Azotite d'amyle; Amylnitrit.*

INORGANIC SUBSTANCES.

NITROGEN; N; *Nitrogenum; Azote; Stickstoff.*

NITROUS OXIDE; N_2O; *Laughing gas; Protoxide of nitrogen; Nitrogen monoxide; Protoxyde d'azote; Stickstoff oxydul.*

CARBONIC OXIDE; CO; *Carbonei oxidum; Oxyde de carbone; Kohlenoxyd.*

CARBONIC ANHYDRIDE; CO_2; CARBONIC ACID GAS; *Acidum carbonicum; Acide carbonique; Kohlensaüre.*

CARBONIC DISULPHIDE; CS_2; *Sulphocarbonic acid; Bisulphide of carbon; Carbonei bisulphidum; Sulfure de carbone; Schwefelkohlenstoff.*

MISCELLANEOUS.

PUFF-BALL; *Lycoperdon proteus.*
ANÆSTHESIA BY RAPID RESPIRATION.
ANÆSTHESIA BY ELECTRICITY.

METHYLIC CHLORIDE—CH_3Cl.

Methyl-hydrochloric ether; Hydrochlorate of methylene; Methylchlorür, G.

Specific gravity, 1·736.
Boiling-point, $-22°$ ($-7.6°$ F.).

Methylic chloride was discovered by Dumas and Peligot in the year 1835. It is a colorless gas, characterized by an ethereal odor and a saccharine taste. Water dissolves 2.8 times its volume of the gas at 16° C. (60.8° F.).

Methylic chloride burns with a white flame, green at the edges, producing water, hydrochloric acid, and carbonic anhydride (Watts).

Hermann and Richardson have found the solution of this gas in ether a very efficient and agreeable anæsthetic. According to the Committee of the British Medical Association (*Brit. Med. Jour.*, January 4, 1879), the gas itself, liberated from its alcoholic solution, is not very potent. A rabbit was subjected to its inhalation, but "after somewhat prolonged use there was not any abolition of reflex action, and the animal almost immediately recovered. The only effect was slight drowsiness."

METHYLENE BICHLORIDE—CH_2Cl_2.

Dichloromethane—Methylene dichloride—Bichloride of methylene, E. ; *Methyleni bichloridum*, L. ; *Chlorure de méthyle monochloré—Ether chlorhydrique monochloruré de l'esprit de bois*, Fr. ; *Methylenbichlorid—Chloromethyl—Chlormethylchlorür*, G.

Specific gravity, 1.344 at 18° (64.4° F.) ; 1.36 at 0° (32° F.).
Boiling-point, 30.5° (87° F.) ; 40°—42° (104—107.6° F.)—(Miller).
Vapor density, 3.012.

Methylene bichloride was discovered by Regnault in the year 1840. It is a colorless liquid, with an odor resembling that of chloroform. It is neutral in its reaction with test-paper, and is soluble in alcohol and ether. Its vapor burns with a brilliant flame. It is prepared by passing gaseous methyl chloride through water into a glass globe into which chlorine gas is conducted at the same time. From this globe the mixture is conveyed through a series of Woulfe's bottles, cooled with ice, which condense and detain the chloroform that is produced. The residuum, which condenses in a cooled receiver at the end of the series, is pure methylene bichloride.

The blood of animals to which methylene bichloride has been administered is of a bright red color. It clots readily, even after removal of its fibrin. The effect upon respiration and circulation is very similar to the effect produced by chloroform, though the movements of the heart and lungs are somewhat more accelerated than after chloroform. It soon paralyzes the heart of the frog. Richardson found blood in both sides of the heart of a rabbit which had been killed by the vapor of methylene bichloride. The Committee of the British Medical Association saw the right ventricle become enormously distended with blood when the heart was exposed during inhalation. The lungs were not congested. Owing to the low temperature at which the liquid boils, it cannot conveniently be employed during warm weather. For the same reason its vapor escapes more rapidly from the blood, so that recovery from anæsthesia produced by its inhalation is more rapid than after chloroform. Its effects are, therefore, speedy, but not persistent. Four cubic centimetres (one drachm) are sufficient to produce insensibility. There is no disagreeable sensation aroused by the act of inhalation, and there are no unpleasant feelings in the head on awaking. Richardson describes his experience with the anæsthesia induced by methylene as having given him the impression that he had merely closed his eyes and had immediately opened them again. In many cases muscular disturbances have preceded the occurrence of insensibility. Tourdes and Hepp observed the immediate production of rigidity by injection of the muscular arteries with methylene bichloride. The pupils are always contracted for a short time during anæsthesia induced by its use. Vomiting occurs very frequently, though not quite so often as after chloroform or ether. This symptom was observed by Miall in forty-two out of one hundred cases.

Spencer Wells, in England, has been one of the most enthusiastic advocates of this anæsthetic. In 1877 he declared that, after ten years' experience of its use in more than one thousand cases of ovariotomy, he believed it "to be, without a single exception, applicable to every patient, perfectly certain to produce complete anæsthesia, relieving the surgeon from all alarm and even anxiety; and its use has never been followed by any dangerous symptoms which could be fairly attributed to it." Turnbull states that this anæsthetic was tested by the late Washington Atlee, who was not so well satisfied with it as with a mixture of ether and chloroform. It has been suggested that the substance used by Mr. Wells was really a mixture of chloroform and methylic alcohol or ether—in fact Mr. Wells admits that such may have been the case. Mr. Morgan states that he has used the substance one thousand eight hundred times without a single accident (*Brit. Med. Jour.*, January 4, 1879). Professor Kocher, of Bern, expressed to Kappeler the opinion that the favorable results which had followed his administration of methylene bichloride, in about thirty cases of ovariotomy, were due to careful preparation of the patient, and to economy of blood during the operation, rather than to any special superiority of the anæsthetic.

Other surgeons have been less fortunate with methylene. Kappeler has collected from the medical periodicals of Great Britain alone a list of nine deaths occasioned by this anæsthetic between the years 1869 and 1875. To this list might be added at least one more death (*Lancet*, July 5, 1873), which occurred in the Birmingham Hospital. Besides these cases, several others have been reported in which methylene bichloride had been administered in alternation with some other anæsthetic. A number of cases have also been reported in which alarming symptoms made their appearance either during or after the inhalation of the substance, rendering necessary the most energetic treatment for the restoration of·the patient.

Taking, therefore, into consideration the physical properties of the liquid, the inflammability of its vapor, its considerable expense, and the absence of any special advantages over chloroform, together with the high rate of mortality that has attended its use, it is impossible to recommend the further employment of methylene bichloride.

The first case of death from the inhalation of bichloride of methylene occurred in Charing Cross Hospital, London, October, 1869. It is reported as follows:

1. Male, thirty-nine years, pale and broken in health. Malignant tumor in the left antrum of Highmore. Frequent bleeding from this had considerably exhausted the patient. Pulse was of ordinary force and frequence. Anæsthetic taken in the sitting postion; at first four and afterward two grammes were given. The pupils were slightly dilated. While inhaling the second dose the head of the patient suddenly fell backward, the pulse weakened, and then became imperceptible. There was no stertor, no lividity of the face. The usual restoratives all failed.—Marshall: *Brit. Med. Journ.*, October 23, 1869.

2. Male, forty years, healthy. Iridectomy in both eyes. One drachm of methylene. Great excitement, struggling to get free, and appearance of cyanosis. Becoming quiet, at length, the anæsthetic was removed, and the operation was performed. Signs of pain were apparent during the second iridectomy. About three minutes after the eyes had been bandaged, respiration became shallow and gasping, and the pulse ceased. The patient was laid upen the left side, but death occurred after a few gasps. Electricity, and artificial respiration for an hour, were of no avail. *Au-*

topsy.—Blood dark and fluid; small specks of ecchymosis over the left ventricle; left side of the heart empty and contracted, liquid blood in the right cavities; lungs hyperæmic.—Burroughs, Guy's Hospital; *Brit. Med. Journ.*, May 7, 1870.

3. Amputation of the finger. The operation did not occupy more than a minute. After the finger had been removed, the head of the patient fell on one side, the eyes rolled out, respiration and pulsation ceased. *Autopsy.*—Negative.—Canton, Charing Cross Hospital; *Brit. Med. Journ.*, April 29, 1871.

4. Female, forty-four years. Removal of a cancerous breast. The anæsthetic, in very small quantity, was given on a flannel-cloth. The patient gave two or three convulsive gasps, and ceased to breathe.—Radcliffe Infirmary, Oxford; *Brit. Med. Journ.*, September 16, 1871.

5. Male, fifty-one years. Dislocation of the shoulder. Became insensible in two or three minutes. Soon after this his countenance became livid, and respiration ceased; the pulse stopped at the same time. Tongue forward; ammonia to the nose; electricity for three-fourths of an hour. *Autopsy.*—Heart large and flaccid, but otherwise exhibiting no signs of disease. This was the first death in two hundred and fifty administrations of methylene in this hospital.—United Hospital, Bath; *Brit. Med. Journ.*, August 31, 1872.

6. Male, forty-eight years, apparently healthy. Fistula in ano. Two drachms produced insensibility, and the anæsthetic had been withdrawn for a minute, when, just as the operation was about to be commenced, the patient became livid and ceased to breathe. Sylvesterism excited one or two gasps. Electricity failed. *Autopsy.*—A large and flabby heart was the only discovery.—Middlesex Hospital; *Brit. Med. Journ.*, October 12, 1872.

7. Male. Two drachms inhaled from a conical inhaler of leather. Great excitement, general muscular rigidity, opisthotonus. The process of inhalation was continued, and at the expiration of two minutes more, insensibility was perfect, and the inhaler was removed. As the patient was placed upon his left side, he suddenly became livid; respiration ceased, and the pulse disappeared. He was rolled over upon his back, and the attempt was made to bring back life with artificial respiration, electricity, brandy clysters, etc. At the outset of dangerous symptoms the pupils were narrow, but they soon became widely dilated, and so remained. *Autopsy.*—Body livid; brain and lungs engorged with blood; ecchymoses in the trachea and bronchi; heart, large, flabby, empty, and covered with fat, but the microscope revealed no fatty degeneration; blood, liquid and very dark.—*Brit. Med. Journ.*, October 19, 1873.

8. Female, twenty-five years, had already been once anæsthetized with methylene bichloride. An operation on the lachrymal apparatus being required, she inhaled three drachms from flannel placed in a cone of leather. Two minutes after the commencement of inhalation the breathing became noisy and stertorous. The inhaler was then removed, and the operation was commenced. The lips and face soon lost their natural color, and respiration was deep and snoring. A few seconds later the pulse weakened and ceased suddenly, while respiration continued for a little longer. Sylvesterism, inversion, ammonia, brandy clysters, slapping, dragging the tongue, gave no relief; after a few sighing inspirations the patient was dead.—Royal Ophthalmic Hospital, London; *Lancet*, December 1874.

9. Male, twenty-seven years, healthy-looking sailor. Iridectomy. Previous to inhalation, physical examination detected nothing abnormal. The

patient seemed to feel no anxiety. Half a drachm, at first, followed by a full drachm, of the anæsthetic was inhaled from a leather cone. The patient struggled considerably, but soon became quiet, breathing easily. Four or five minutes after the commencement of anæsthesia, it was observed that the face of the patient was reddened and somewhat livid, the breathing slow and stertorous, and the pulse scarcely perceptible. In spite of artificial respiration and electricity, the breathing became irregular, and the face quite livid. *Autopsy.*—Negative. The heart was healthy and nearly empty; the blood was very dark and liquid; everything else seemed healthy.—Central London Ophthalmic Hospital; *Brit. Med. Journ.*, July 24, 1875.

10. A young man. Amputation of the leg for disease of the bones of the foot. Bichloride of methylene was given on lint. After the operation, before the dressing of the stump was complete, the patient became pulseless, and respiration ceased. Artificial respiration, etc., failed to revive him.—Radcliffe Infirmary, Oxford; *Med. Times and Gaz.*, September 22, 1877.

11. Male, fifty-six years, suffering with caries of the tibia, inhaled bichloride of methylene for an operation. As the patient did not readily succumb, methylated ether was substituted. He soon became unconscious; but, quickly recovering, the bichloride of methylene was resumed. Great struggling and peculiar epileptiform convulsions ensued, followed by tonic spasm; this spasm relaxed; the breathing became stertorous; the pulse failed; and death supervened. There was no autopsy.—East Suffolk Hospital; *Med. Times and Gaz.*, June 23, 1877; *Brit. Med. Journ.*, March 2, 1878.

METHYLENE ETHER.

A mixture of ether and methylene bichloride was first employed as an anæsthetic by Richardson in the year 1859. The exact composition and chemical nature of the substance are difficult to determine, though Robbins and Archbold are of the opinion that it is a genuine compound rather than a mixture.

According to Richardson four to eight cubic centimetres (one or two drachms) of the liquid are sufficient to produce anæsthesia in from one minute and a half to two minutes. Sleep is tranquil and seldom disturbed by convulsive movements. In a condition of profound anæsthesia the pupil frequently appears less contracted than would be the case after chloroform. Vomiting also occurs less frequently than it does when chloroform or ether are inhaled. Unfortunately for the reputation of this anæsthetic a death soon occurred, during its administration by Lawson Tait, and its use was speedily abandoned.

Death from Methylene Ether.—Female, sixty-two years, suffering with a large multilocular ovarian tumor. She was placed readily and quietly under the influence of methylene ether. After five drachms had been administered, she seemed so perfectly insensible that in a few seconds the operation would have been commenced. Suddenly she moved herself, as if recovering consciousness; she voided her urine; her eyes opened; the pupils dilated; and the pulse stopped. After a few efforts at respiration, and a spasmodic retching as if about to vomit, the patient ceased to breathe. Sylvesterism, strong ammonia to the nostrils, a stimulant enema, cold affusion upon the chest, friction with a brush, etc., were tried without effect. *Autopsy*, twenty-four hours after death.—Nothing could be discovered to account for death.—Lawson Tait, Hospital for Women ; *Med. Times and Gaz.*, July 5, 1873.

CHLOROFORM—$CHCl_3$.

Chloroformum, L. ; *Chloroforme*, Fr. ; *Chloroform*, G.

Chloroform was almost simultaneously discovered in the year 1831 by the French chemist, Soubeiran, and by the German professor, Justus Liebig. It is a colorless, volatile, highly refractive liquid, possessed of an agreeable, aromatic odor, and a sweetish, pungent taste. Its specific gravity is 1.502 at 15° (60° F.), and 1.4936 at 20° (68° F.). Under an atmospheric pressure equal to 760 millimetres of mercury it boils at 60.8° (141.44° F.). Alcohol and ether dissolve it in every proportion, but water at 15° dissolves only about one part in one hundred by weight. It is burned with difficulty, yielding a reddish flame according to Regnauld, or greenish bordered according to other chemists. As it burns it disengages a black, sooty smoke, and abundant vapors of hydrochloric acid, carbonic anhydride, and water.

A number of elementary bodies, for example, sulphur, phosphorus, and iodine, are readily dissolved in chloroform. Among organic substances it dissolves fats, resins, gutta percha, caoutchouc, many vegetable alkaloids, cantharidine, digitaline, etc. Its solution of iodine is characterized by the extraordinary beauty of its violet-purple color.

Chloroform may be produced by a variety of reactions. If chlorine is made to act upon methyl chloride, chloroform will be produced :

$$\underbrace{CH_3Cl}_{\text{Methyl chloride.}} + 2Cl_2 = 2HCl + \underbrace{CHCl_3}_{\text{Chloroform.}}$$

If four measures of chlorine be mixed with one measure of marsh-gas, diluted with an equal volume of carbonic anhydride, to prevent explosion, chloroform and carbon tetrachloride will be slowly formed under the influence of diffused sunlight. The reaction may be thus represented :

$$\underbrace{2CH_4}_{\text{Marsh-gas.}} + 7Cl_2 = CCl_4 + 7HCl + \underbrace{CHCl_3}_{\text{Chloroform.}}$$

Chloroform may also be produced during the reaction between an alkaline hydrate and a trichloracetate :

$$\underbrace{KC_2Cl_3O_2}_{\text{Pot. trichloracetate.}} + \underbrace{KHO}_{\text{Pot. hydrate.}} = \underbrace{K_2CO_3}_{\text{Pot. carbonate.}} + \underbrace{CHCl_3}_{\text{Chloroform.}}.$$

It may also in like manner be produced by the action of an alkaline hydrate, or the hydrate of an alkaline earth, upon chloral :

$$\underbrace{2C_2HCl_3O}_{\text{Chloral.}} + \underbrace{CaH_2O_2}_{\text{Calcium hydrate.}} = \underbrace{Ca2CHO_2}_{\text{Calcium formiate.}} + \underbrace{2CHCl_3}_{\text{Chloroform.}}.$$

Chloroform may contain impurities that are present in consequence of neglect during the processes of manufacture, or they may be the result of intentional adulteration, or they may have been produced by the action of light upon an originally perfect article.   The following tests of its quality have been recommended by Regnauld ("Dict. Encyc. des. Sci. Méd.," t. xvi., p. 649) ; and by Kappeler (*Deutsche Chirugerie*, Lieferung 20).

The specific gravity of the liquid should be 1.48 at a temperature of 18° (64.4° F).   If the specific gravity falls below this figure, the specimen is probably adulterated with alcohol. This may be determined by the following reactions :

A mixture of equal parts of chloroform and almond oil will become turbid if alcohol be present.

A solution of acid potassium chromate (1.10) mixed with an equal quantity of concentrated sulphuric acid, and well shaken with an alcoholic specimen of chloroform, will assume a green color through the reduction of chromic acid to chromic oxide.

If a drop of pure chloroform be added to fresh egg-albumen, no change will take place ; but if alcohol be present, the albumen will be coagulated.

If pure chloroform be allowed to fall, drop by drop, into distilled water there will be no disturbance of the transparency of the water ; but if alcohol is present, the water assumes an opalescent or milky appearance.

The presence of ether as an impurity may be detected by the following tests :

If chloroform changes to a dusky red the color of an aqueous solution of iodine, ether is present.   Pure chloroform should give to the solution an amethyst color, and should not disturb its transparency.

Crystallized nitro-sodic sulphide of iron remains unchanged in pure chloroform ; in the presence of ether or alcohol it is dissolved.

A fragment of sodium will remain without change in pure chloroform ; the presence of acid substances will occasion the evolution of gas.

Contamination with methylic compounds is indicated by the blackening of the liquid on addition of concentrated sulphuric acid.

Agitated with zinc chloride, the presence of a methylic compound is also indicated by the production of a dark oily film.

If well shaken with a small quantity of di-nitro-sulphide of iron, chloroform that contains methylic impurities is colored brown.   The same color is produced by the presence of aldehyd ether, ethyl- or amyl-alcohol.

Chloroform that is exposed for any length of time to daylight is liable to alteration.   Such specimens of the drug exhale a chlorine-smelling vapor, which may be sufficiently acid to corrode the corks of the bottles in which they are contained.   The nature of this change has been carefully investigated by M. Personne.   This analysis of the vapors yielded by chloroform that has thus been exposed to light, indicates that they owe their properties to the presence of chloroxycarbonic acid gas—$COCl_2$,—which is derived from chloral hydrate, present as an impurity in the chloroform.   The chloral, thus mixed with the chloroform, is an unreduced remnant of the chloral that is produced by the action of calcium hypochlorite upon alcohol during the process of manufacture.   This chloral continually exhales chloroxycarbonic acid gas—hence the peculiar quality of such chloroform. By long agitation of chloroform with a solution of caustic soda, before the final process of rectification, the last trace of chloral may be removed, and the distillate then remains without subsequent change.   Chloroform which has been thus treated has been exposed to daylight for a year without deterioration.

The following tests will be found useful:

The absence of acids may be determined by the use of blue litmus-paper. If the test-paper is bleached by immersion in chloroform, either free chlorine or euchlorine is present.

Starched-paper imbued with iodide of potassium is colored by immersion in chloroform that contains free chlorine.

Hydrochloric acid gives a precipitate of silver chloride when a watery solution of the acid containing chloroform is treated with nitrate of silver.

The presence of aldehyd is indicated by the formation of a silvery film upon the sides of the test-tube when the impure chloroform is heated with a solution of nitrate of silver.

Ethylene chloride is present if the addition of caustic potash liberates a disagreeable odor of chloracetyl, with an evolution of gas and an elevation of temperature.

The addition of a solution of chloride of iron causes a precipitate, changing from blood-red to a yellowish red color, when formic and acetic acids are present.

A very delicate test for the demonstration of the existence of chloroform in suspected liquids has been devised by A. W. Hoffmann. By distilling the liquid with alcohol at a temperature of about 65° (149° F.), the chloroform is obtained in the distillate. To this should be added an alcoholic solution of sodium or potassium hydrate with a drop of anilin. On the application of a moderate degree of heat the disagreeable odor of isobenzonitrile is evolved. So delicate is this test, that one part of chloroform in five thousand, or even in six thousand, parts of alcohol may thus be discovered.

By the passage of vapors containing chloroform through a red-hot glass tube, the substance is decomposed into carbonic anhydride, hydrochloric acid, and chlorine. The presence of chlorine can be demonstrated by its characteristic reaction with the potassic-iodide of starch, while the hydrochloric acid may be recognized by the production of a precipitate of silver chloride from a solution of nitrate of silver.

It was but a few months after the discovery of chloroform by Soubeiran, in the year 1831, when Dr. Ives, of New Haven, undertook the treatment of pulmonary diseases by inhalations of chloroform vapor. Neither he nor Dr. Formby, who, in 1838, prescribed its use in the management of hysteria, nor Dr. Tuson, who, in London, in 1844, employed it for the relief of neuralgia and pain of cancerous growths, nor Dr. Guillot, who, in Paris, in the same year, recommended its use as a remedy for asthma, had suspected the possibility of procuring complete anæsthesia by continued inhalation of its vapor. By Dr. Guillot its solution in water was administered internally, and by him it was highly esteemed as a sedative and antispasmodic agent, but the new remedy attracted very little attention. On the 8th of March, 1847, Flourens laid before the French Academy of Sciences a report of his experiments on animals with certain new anæsthetics. Having obtained successful results with hydrochloric ether, he had been led to substitute the analogous substance, chloroform. He had found that animals which had been compelled to inhale the vapor of this little-known compound were speedily rendered insensible. While in this condition the spinal cord had been exposed without pain, and the complete abolition of its excito-motor functions had been recognized. These remarkable observations of the celebrated physiologist yielded no practical result—in Paris, at least; nor is it certain that any knowledge of them had found its way as far as Scotland, when Dr. Waldie, of Liverpool, finding Dr. Simpson enthusiastically occupied with experiments in anæsthesia, advised him to make trial of chloroform. Dr. Jacob Bell had been previously experimenting in the Middlesex Hospital with hydrochloric ether, and with a solution of chloroform in alcohol. Dr. Lawrence had also used "chloric ether" instead of ordinary ether, in St. Bartholomew's Hospital, and it was a knowledge of these facts, apparently, that caused Waldie to suggest to Simpson an investigation of the anæsthetic properties of chloroform. Accordingly, on the evening of Nov. 4, 1847, Drs. Simpson, Keith, and Duncan sat down together, to inhale the vapor of chloroform for the first time. Each one was provided with a tumbler, in which was placed a napkin moistened with chloroform. The reputation of chloroform was in a few minutes established to the satisfaction of the trio; and on the 10th of November, 1847, Simpson read before the Medico-Chirugical Society of Edinburgh an account of the new anæsthetic, with a detailed history of its administration in not less than eighty cases. Intelligence of this discovery was received with an enthusiasm which can only be compared with the interest awakened by the introduction of ether one year earlier. The convenience and the comfort which attend the administration of chloroform served to recommend it everywhere; and the use of ether was almost immediately abandoned throughout the continent of Europe.

If a drop of chloroform be allowed to fall upon the skin, it evaporates quickly, and produces only a trifling sensation of cold. But if a thimble be inverted over the spot, so that evaporation cannot take place, there is presently felt a lively sensation of heat, which soon becomes positively painful, as if a blister were in the act of evolution. The skin becomes reddened; the epidermis softens, and may even exfoliate; its sensibility is obtunded to a degree that will admit of its puncture without pain. Pure chloroform thus maintained in contact with the skin for a brief period rarely causes anything more than redness and smarting pain—actual vesication is rare. The vapor of chloroform is not particularly irritating to the external surfaces of the body. It may produce redness, if highly concentrated, and a certain degree of cutaneous insensibility, which soon disappears after removal of the cause. Simpson remarked that the effects of the vapor were inversely proportionate to the thickness of the skin, and that its action was greatly intensified by previous cleansing of the surface with warm water. He was not encouraged by his experiments to believe that by the external application of chloroform vapor a degree of local anæsthesia could be induced sufficient to allow the painless performance of surgical incisions of the skin. In this respect he disagreed with Nunnely, of Leeds, who claimed that by exposure to the vapor of chloroform he had succeeded in rendering a finger and an eye sufficiently insensible for the performance of a surgical operation.

Upon the lower animals, the observations of the distinguished Scotch physician demonstrated the local effects of chloroform vapor in a very notable manner. If the vapor is brought in contact with a portion of the body of a leech, an earthworm, or a millepede, that portion is rendered completely insensible. Immersed in an atmosphere of chloroform, the tail of a salamander, the limb of a frog, and the hind-leg of a guinea-pig, or even of a rabbit, become so profoundly anæsthetized that the power of motion is temporarily abolished, and the member may be amputated without pain. In the same way Simpson, and, after him, Claude Bernard, have shown that the sensitive-plant loses its irritability, and its leaves remain without motion in an atmosphere charged with chloroform. The same effect is exhibited by the stamens of certain species of *Mahonia*. Endowed with the power of movement in their natural condition, under the influence of chloroform they cease to move.

Upon the mucous surfaces of the body, the local effect of liquid chloroform is quite severe. The epithelium is soon destroyed, and great pain is excited. If chemically pure, the vapor is very slightly irritant; but if it contains impurities, such as absolute alcohol, it is quite insupportable, and may be the cause of distressing phenomena—cough, suffocative symptoms, and arrest of the heart. By the inhalation of chloroform the vibratory filaments of the ciliary epithelium cells lose their power of movement. The mucous glands and adjacent organs, like the salivary glands, are considerably excited. Tears begin to flow, the mouth and fauces fill with saliva, the bronchial tubes become partially obstructed with mucus, the gastric juices overflow, and there may even be a diarrhœa as a result of the local action of chloroform vapor upon the gastro-intestinal surfaces.

Various explanations have been advanced to account for the local effects of chloroform. Some have considered it an astringent ; others have referred its results to certain modifications in the local circulation; while others have acknowledged a directly anæsthetic effect upon the histological elements of the tissues. No doubt the delicate structure of an organized cell may be destroyed—coagulated, adstringed—if treated with an overwhelming quantity of the liquid. Undoubtedly in moderate doses it affects the local circulation very much as that is affected by alcohol. In the smaller quantity that is furnished by contact with the vapor alone, the vitality of the tissues is not destroyed—it is simply degraded. All these effects may concurrently appear in succession, or in different parts of the anæsthetic field, when a limited portion of the surface is subjected to the action of the liquid anæsthetic. Its caustic and disorganizing energy is not manifested by the vapor, which is really a dilution—an attenuation of the active agent.

The directly paralyzing effect of chloroform upon the tissues is well illustrated by an experiment performed for the first time by Coze, in 1849 ("Dict. Encyc. des Sci. Med.," t. xvi., p. 654). Having exposed the heart of an animal, he injected liquid chloroform, through an opening in the trachea, into the lungs. Immediately the left side of the heart ceased to beat ; the chloroform had been conveyed in the blood from the lungs to the left auricle and ventricle. If the injection was thrown into the jugular veins, the right side of the heart was paralyzed in like manner, while the left side continued its pulsations. Whether produced by an effect upon the muscular fibres, or by paralysis of the nerves that are connected with those fibres, need not now be discussed. The effect is certainly local and direct. It is a purely paralyzing effect, quite different from the permanent rigidity of the arterial coats which may be produced by the injection of liquid chloroform into the arteries. In this experiment, chloroform produces a purely physical result which is identical with the effects that are produced by all agents capable of coagulating albumen. Muscular rigidity may thus be readily produced in small animals by injecting liquid chloroform under the skin or into a blood-vessel. Such rigidity can only be produced upon the living animal, or before the death of the muscular fibres. After the disappearance of cadaveric rigidity, chloroform cannot restore it. The coagulable elements of the muscles have disappeared in the process of decomposition. The only effect of chloroform, then, is the retardation of putrefaction. It operates like alcohol to prevent the decomposition of organic substances. The close relationship between anæsthetic action and antiseptic action is thus indicated. It is probable that these two modes of action differ in degree rather than in kind.

When chloroform is introduced into the lungs in the form of vapor, it passes readily into the general circulation, and the whole body becomes saturated with the substance. But when the liquid is introduced into the stomach, it is absorbed and conveyed through the portal vein and the vena cava ascendens to the right side of the heart. From the right ventricle it passes with the blood into the vast capillary network that is spread out in the walls of the air-cells. Here it is rapidly discharged, like carbonic acid gas, with the expired air. Consequently, the blood that reaches the left side of the heart carries very little, comparatively, of the anæsthetic into the general circulation. For this reason the induction of anæsthesia by this method is slow and uncertain, unless a large quantity of the drug has been taken into the stomach. The phenomena of poisoning may then be produced with a fatal result, like that so often observed after excessive draughts of concentrated alcoholic liquor. Taylor, in his work on Poisons, relates the following cases :

"A man swallowed four ounces of chloroform. He was able to walk for a considerable distance after taking this dose, but he subsequently fell into a state of coma ; the pupils were dilated, the breathing stertorous, the skin cold, the pulse imperceptible, and there were general convulsions. He recovered in five days. . . . . A private, in a cavalry regiment in the United States, swallowed nearly two ounces of chloroform. He was seen ten or fifteen minutes afterward ; he had already vomited, and was found insensible, with stertorous breathing, and a pulse of about 60. The stomach-pump was employed, and some spirits of ammonia injected. The pulse became more feeble, the breathing slower, and the pupils were insensible to light. The surface became cold, and for a time he continued to get worse, the face becoming purple, while the pulse was intermittent, and hardly discernible. Two hours and a half after taking the poison, however, a gradual improvement commenced, but sensibility did not return until four hours later. For several days he continued to suffer from great irritability of the stomach, and eventually he had an attack of jaundice. . . . . In March, 1857, a lady swallowed half an ounce of pure chloroform. In five minutes she was quite insensible, generally convulsed, the jaws clenched, the face slightly flushed, the pulse full and rather oppressed, and she foamed at the mouth. She vomited, and in twenty minutes the convulsions had left her ; soon afterward she had a relapse, and did not recover for twenty-four hours. . . . . A boy, aged four, was brought to him (Mr. Thursefield) by his father in a state of total insensibility. It appears that he had swallowed a drachm of chloroform, and soon afterward laid his head on his mother's lap and lost all consciousness. Mr. Thursefield saw him about twenty minutes afterward. He was then insensible, cold, and pulseless. Mustard plasters were applied to the legs ; they acted well, but produced no impression on the sensibility. His breathing varied : it was sometimes natural, at other times stertorous. He became warmer, his pulse full and regular ; and he continued three hours in this state, when he died quite calmly, without a struggle, in spite of every effort made for his recovery."

It is evident that the essential phenomena after chloroform is taken into the stomach, are identical with those which are manifested after inhalation of the vapor. There is the same initial exhilaration, followed by excitement, lapsing into loss of intelligence and of the power of sensation. The patient becomes unconscious, the muscles relax, the heart beats less rapidly, the respiration falls, the general temperature is lowered, and death results either through syncope or asphyxia.

The appearances after death are those commonly discovered after death from inhalation of chloroform vapor, with the addition of changes due to the local effect of the liquid upon the coats of the stomach. The cavities of the heart are usually filled with blood; consequently, the cerebral vessels are generally engorged. Sometimes the left side of the heart is found empty. The stomach is usually congested in some portion of its surface, apparently where the chloroform was chiefly applied to the mucous membrane. The remainder of the surface may even be paler than natural. In short, the local effects of chloroform upon the mucous surface of the stomach are not unlike the effects produced by swallowing a large dose of strong alcohol.

When chloroform is swallowed in small doses, well diluted, the phenomena which follow are similar, though in much less degree, to the phenomena which are produced by large doses. There is first a sensation of coolness and sweetness in the mouth, succeeded by an unpleasant degree of heat. These are symptoms of excitement of the oral, buccal, and pharyngeal nerves. In the stomach is presently experienced a sensation of weight, with which are joined certain symptoms of agitation which may culminate in painful eructations of the vapor, if not in actual vomiting. The salivary secretion is considerably increased, and the intestinal discharges may be enlarged.

Upon the general nervous system such moderate doses produce an agreeably tranquillizing effect. The muscular apparatus is placed at rest, if previously irritated; the temperature of the body is lowered, and respiratory excitement is diminished. These are the secondary effects of the drug. Its primary action is stimulant, since it produces at first an acceleration of the circulation, with all the consequent liberation of motion throughout the entire economy.

Analysis of the blood after the introduction of chloroform, either through the stomach or by inhalation, indicates its presence in the circulating fluid, but connected with the different elements of the blood in unequal proportions. Schmeideberg ("Ueber die quantitative Bestimmung des Chloroforms in Blute, etc.," Archiv. für physiol. Heilk., viii., 1867) has shown that the fluid portions of the blood contain very little chloroform, while the red blood-corpuscles yield, on analysis, a much greater amount of chlorine than is present in their normal state. Distillation extracts very little chloroform from the clot in which these corpuscles are included, hence, it is inferred that the substance has entered into a chemical combination with some constituent of the corpuscles. When chloroform is shaken with fresh blood, the mixture assumes a brilliant scarlet color. This is supposed to be the result of a physical change in the corpuscles, since everything that renders them less convex brightens the color of the mass, while an increase of their convexity darkens the blood. These changes are observed in blood that has been withdrawn from the body. While circulating in the vessels, no change can be detected by the eye viewing the current through their walls, though the fluid as it escapes from a wounded vessel often appears brighter colored than usual. After death from chloroform, the blood is always dark and fluid. This, however, may be the result of other causes than the presence of the poison.

If blood be treated with a small quantity of chloroform outside of the body—a drop of blood upon the glass slide of a microscope, for example—the corpuscles will be dissolved, and the coloring matter will crystallize upon the glass. This result is more notable in the case of blood from the lower animals than from the human subject. The red corpuscles of human blood are simply dissolved. Certain observers have believed that the poisonous effects of chloroform might, in part, at least, be due to the solvent effect of the substance upon the corpuscles; but the only fact which seems to justify such an opinion is the occasional appearance of icterus after dangerous doses of chloroform. Still, it must be confessed that this occurrence is not sufficiently frequent to serve as a basis for the belief that the corpuscles are thus destroyed by any such quantity of chloroform as can circulate with the blood in a living animal. It is rather to be ascribed to secondary disturbances of the spleen and liver than to any direct action upon the corpuscles.

Like other anæsthetic substances of the same class, chloroform retards the movement of oxygen in the blood. Reducing agents deprive the hæmoglobin of its oxygen with much greater difficulty after the addition of chloroform.

As for the changes that may be produced in the tissues themselves by the action of chloroform transported to them through the medium of the blood in the living animal, our knowledge is purely hypothetical. That it must be an evanescent effect is proved by the brief and transitory character of the symptoms. The patient soon recovers after inhalation, and all his organs once more perform their functions as if nothing had interfered with their continual activity. This fact is certainly inconsistent with any permanent modification of the structure of the elements of the body. It is a change quite analogous in its rapidity, and in its respect for the integrity of the cell-constituents, to the changes which take place in the corpuscles of the blood during the act of respiration. As a consequence of this, the postmortem appearances which are revealed by an autopsy after death from inhalation of the vapor of chloroform, are chiefly related to the location of the blood in its vessels. It is true that many different organic lesions have been discovered and described after death from chloroform, but they were due to pre-existing disease of a chronic character, such as the degenerations of the liver and kidneys which are so often encountered among the patients in a general hospital.

Sometimes the results of examination after death are purely negative. The brain is sometimes charged with blood, and, again, it may be quite free from unusual congestion. These differences depend upon the mode of death. If preceded by asphyxia, there is great distention of the cerebral vessels with black blood, and the ventricles of the brain are filled with a serous fluid; but if death has been caused by syncope, everything is reversed, and the brain is quite comparatively bloodless and pale.

The condition of the heart and of the lungs in like manner varies in accordance with the mode of death. The lungs may be full of blood and infiltrated with serum, presenting all the appearances detailed in the above-quoted record of autopsy; or the organ may be pale, bloodless, and normally crepitant, while the heart is relaxed and filled throughout with dark, clotted blood. Sometimes the bronchi and the trachea are filled up with thick, bloody mucus, and the mucous membranes are red and congested. This condition is not uniformly discovered, and it may be in part occasioned by local irritation resulting from the use of impure chloroform.

When the lower animals are poisoned with chloroform, the heart is generally arrested in diastole, but sometimes it is found contracted firmly upon its coagulated contents. The lungs are sometimes bloodless, while the right side of the heart is distended with blood. This is the consequence of a spasmodic rigidity of the contractured walls of the branches of the pulmonary artery, analogous to the rigidity of the voluntary muscles that is often witnessed during the inhalation of chloroform. It is usually the result of a sudden and rapid introduction of the anæsthetic, producing effects similar to the consequence of an intra-cardiac injection of the substance. When the substance is gradually introduced, the muscular tissues are paralyzed, rather than tetanized, before death, and the heart is then found relaxed in diastole.

Various degrees of vascular distention are found in the abdominal organs. The hyperæmia is usually passive in its character, and is the result of the general arrest of the circulation.

Chloroform remains in combination with the tissues for a considerable time after death. It retards their putrefaction, and by reason of its permanence may be recovered from the tissues after a number of days. Snow was able to detect its presence six days after death. Prolonged cooking does not entirely expel it from the flesh. Labbée states that a rabbit which he had killed with chloroform was eaten by a hospital nurse, who complained of the disagreeable flavor of chloroform that persisted in the meat in spite of careful cooking.

It is, in the present state of science, useless to discuss the nature of the process by which chloroform and other anæsthetic substances act upon the molecular constitution of the cellular elements of the nervous tissues. We can only say that it does in some way temporarily modify that constitution in such a manner that certain alterations of function become apparent. These changes, as Flourens and his contemporaries have long since pointed out, become conspicuous through the medium of the nervous system in a regularly progressive order. First, the cerebrum exhibits signs of intellectual disturbance, characterized by excitement merged in final paralysis; then the cerebellum and other centres of motor energy and coordination are in like manner overpowered. The posterior half of the spinal cord, with its sensory nerve-roots, yields next in order; then the anterior or motor tract of the cord; and finally the medulla oblongata, with its dependent functions of respiration and circulation. Upon all these organs, after the first outbreak of excitement, produced by the increased influx of blood that follows the initial stimulation of the circulation through the action of the anæsthetic upon the circulatory apparatus, the effect of the drug is of a paralyzing character. Consequently, the respiration becomes retarded, the blood-pressure sinks, and the pulsation of the heart loses energy and rapidity of motion. The gradual subsidence of these functions is due to the directly poisonous effect of chloroform upon the mechanism of the heart. Scheinesson, and many others, have proved this by division of the pneumogastric nerves in the neck of an animal before the administration of chloroform. By this operation the possibility of arrest of the heart by any inhibitory impulse from the medulla oblongata is precluded. Krishaber defends the opinion that under such conditions the occurrence of death is delayed, but it takes place in spite of the severance of all connection between the heart and the medulla. The anæsthetic agent causes death of the heart in this case by its poisonous energy alone. The arrest of the heart is delayed by section of the pneumogastric nerves, because the intra-medullary agitations which accompany the dissolution of that centre can no longer be transmitted as excitants to the heart. Under ordinary circumstances, with pneumogastric nerves intact, the death of the medulla is attended with a certain liberation of molecular motion which may be sufficiently exciting to maintain a feeble pulsation after the cessation of respiratory movements.

8

Sudden death in the early stages of chloroform inhalation cannot be thus explained. In such cases the medulla oblongata, and the pneumogastric nerves intervene in their ordinary manner. The strong excitement of the sensory terminations of the pneumogastrics in the respiratory passages, produces a violent disturbance in the molecular structure of their medullary nuclei. This disturbance may be reflected over the appropriate conductors upon the heart, producing its inhibitory arrest in diastole. Or, as A. W. Smith (*Am. Journ. Med. Sci.*, 1871) has remarked, the anæsthetic may, by its local effect upon the sensory endings of the pneumogastric nerves in the air-passages, produce a paralysis of those nerves, so that the reflex respiratory movements shall cease, as if the patient had forgotten to breathe. If this be accompanied by a concurrent paralysis of the medulla oblongata, death follows at once. It is thus evident that the paralyzing influence of chloroform may at several different points break the nervous circle upon the integrity of which depend the normal performance of the acts of circulation and respiration.

Chloroform is eliminated from the body through the lungs, the skin, and the kidneys. It may also be eliminated through the mammary glands of nursing women, as seems to be proved by the stupefaction of infants who are suckled after the use of chloroform by the mother. The familiar odor of the drug may always be recognized in the breath for a considerable period of time after the cessation of the act of inhalation. If the air that is expired is passed through a red-hot porcelain tube, the presence of chloroform vapor will be indicated by the formation of a precipitate of silver chloride in a solution of nitrate of silver. The actual presence of chloroform in the perspiration has not been demonstrated, but every analogy indicates the probability of its elimination by this method. It cannot easily be directly recovered from the urine ; but if air be drawn through a quantity of urine, shortly after the use of chloroform, and if it then be carried through a heated tube into a solution of nitrate of silver, the presence of a chlorinated substance may be demonstrated. The application of the copper test to such urine indicates the presence of a reducing substance, exactly as if glycosuria existed, or as if chloroform instead of urine had been employed in the experiment ("Dict. Encyc. des Sci. Méd." t. xvi., p. 664). This test, however, is not decisive, for the reason that the alkaline formiates also reduce the cupro-potassic solution. A certain amount of chloroform seems to be decomposed in the body by the action of oxygen, yielding formic acid and hydrochloric acid, which are eliminated in the state of chlorides and formiates. Of course, it is impossible to say that such are the actual changes that take place in the laboratory of the cell where the oxidations of the body are principally performed. It is not improbable that still more complete dissociations and more complex reconstructions are effected.

Before passing to the consideration of the surgical use of chloroform by inhalation of its vapor, we may profitably review its uses as an ordinary therapeutic agent.

Previous to the introduction of chloral hydrate, chloroform was considerably employed as a remedy for sleeplessness. Its solution in water may be given, as a hypnotic, with great advantage. Hartshorne showed by his experiments, in 1854, that four cubic centimetres (one drachm) of chloroform, administered internally, produce no more effect than thirty or thirty-five drops of laudanum. Since the discovery of the hypnotic properties of chloral hydrate, this use of chloroform has been almost entirely abandoned. It has been occasionally administered by hypodermic injection. From ten to twenty minims may thus be placed beneath the skin. The injection is at first productive of pain, but this is soon succeeded by a local anæsthesia and by a feeling of numbness which may for a number of days affect the nervous territory connected with the site of the injection. Swelling, induration, and sometimes the formation of abscess, or even of a sloughing ulcer at the point of injection, are among the disadvantages to which this method of administering chloroform is liable.

Under all ordinary circumstances, therefore, the administration of the liquid by the mouth, or by inhalation of its vapor, is to be preferred. The effect of the drug is thus more rapidly secured. The caustic and astringent properties of chloroform occasion such a coagulation of the surrounding tissues when the liquid is injected under the skin, that its absorption and diffusion throughout the body are very gradually performed. Sleep comes on very slowly, but it is continuous, and may persist for several hours—in fact, until the exhaustion of the hypodermic reservoir.

As a therapeutic agent for the prompt and effectual suppression of the symptom pain, chloroform has no superior. In the essential neuralgias it is invaluable, and oftentimes absolutely curative ; but in cases where the pain is only a symptom of grave organic change, the drug is merely palliative. The evanescent character of its effects unfits it for constant use. But in the terrific pain which is caused by parturition or by the passage of gall-stones or renal calculi, it is almost the only remedy that can give relief. During the passage of a calculus the pain is often so excruciating that opiates are powerless to relieve, unless given in absolutely poisonous doses. Under the tranquillizing influence of chloroform an ordinary dose of morphine becomes sufficient without endangering the life of the patient. The fact that the cholesterine which enters so largely into the composition of gall-stones is soluble in chloroform, has suggested to many physicians the idea that the pain of hepatic colic was relieved, and the disintegration of the calculus was effected, by the directly solvent action of the remedy. But there is no more reason to believe that relief is thus produced than to believe that the agony of childbirth is abolished by solution of the child's head in the chloroform that has been inhaled by the parturient female. The quantity of the drug that can by any possibility reach a gall-stone in the cystic duct is too infinitesimally small to exert any solvent power upon the obstructing mass. Relief is the result of relaxation of the walls of the duct. It is the consequence of paralysis of the sensory nerves of the part, by which the reflex spasm that hinders the progress of the calculus toward the intestine is overcome. In the same way, when the delivery of a woman in labor is retarded by spasmodic and consequently ineffectual pains, the administration of chloroform soon causes a subsidence of these exaggerated reflex actions, and the pains assume their regularly expulsive character.

Puerperal convulsions may in like manner be arrested by the active employment of chloroform. Without undertaking to discuss the nature of eclampsia and its relations to supposed renal lesions, it is sufficient to know that the symptom *convulsion* is due to an over-excitable condition of the convulsive centres in the upper portion of the medulla oblongata and in the protuberance. This inordinate irritability is promptly subdued by chloroform, and the exhaustion of the nervous system which so often proves fatal may thus be obviated. To accomplish this end, the anæsthetic must be inhaled not merely during the paroxysm, but in such a manner that continuous anæsthesia may be maintained. Other remedies, appropriate to the condition of the patient, must not be neglected, but the constant repose of the nervous system must be secured until the exciting causes of convulsion can be removed.

The eclamptic convulsions of children are very easily controlled by chloroform. Anstie directed attention to the fact that they might be arrested by the administration of alcohol; but, when violent and frequently repeated, it is usually necessary to reduce the agitation of the patient by the use of chloroform. Alcohol may then be administered. Chloral has generally taken the place of alcohol in such cases at the present time. As a rule chloroform is very well tolerated by young children. Sir J. Y. Simpson, who first employed chloroform in the treatment of infantile convulsions, administered its vapor to a child only thirteen days old. The result was favorable, and the patient quickly recovered. To another infant, thirty days old, he gave, in the course of twenty-four hours, not less than three hundred cubic centimetres (about nine ounces) by inhalation.

For the relief of convulsions which are the result of epilepsy, or hysteria, or metallic-poisoning, or disease of the kidneys, chloroform may be used as a palliative, but it can in no way be regarded as a curative agent. The convulsions which sometimes precede and accompany the death-agony may thus be treated.

Chloroform has been recommended for the treatment of chorea. After inhalation of its vapor the spasmodic movements of the patient cease for a time, and sleep may be thus procured. But the usual self-limitation of the disease, and the readiness with which its graver symptoms may be controlled by the exhibition of alcohol or chloral hydrate, render it unnecessary to resort to so powerful an agent as chloroform, excepting in certain rare cases where milder remedies have failed.

Labbée records the fact ("Dict. Encyc. des Sci. Méd.," t. xvi., p. 672), that on November 24, 1847, the very next day after the first inhalation of chloroform in France for the production of surgical anæsthesia, its vapor was administered by Escallier, one of Velpeau's hospital internes, to a patient who was suffering with traumatic tetanus. To the great delight of all, the tetanic spasm was at once relieved; but, unfortunately, the disease progressed, and the patient finally expired in a convulsive paroxysm. Since then, chloroform has been frequently employed with variable degrees of success in the treatment of this formidable disease. Against the spasmodic symptoms it is a most potent remedy, but essential changes in the central nervous system remain uninfluenced by its action. It, therefore, serves only as a palliative resource. In the acute forms of tetanus it may sometimes be suspected even of working injury to the patient by favoring the occurrence of asphyxia during the paroxysms. Its effects are most salutary in the subacute and chronic forms of tetanus. It may be given by inhalation, or by suspension in a liquid vehicle. The external application of liquid chloroform is of very little value in such cases. The introduction of chloral hydrate has, however, almost entirely superseded the use of chloroform as an antispasmodic remedy in tetanus. The more potent drug may, therefore, be reserved for those patients who require speedy relief, or who cannot be made to swallow a solution of chloral.

As a means of overcoming all kinds of accidental or local muscular spasms and contractures, chloroform has been used with success. The superior safety that attends the employment of other anæsthetic substances should, however, limit and greatly restrict the number of cases in which chloroform may be used for this purpose.

Attempts have been made to relieve the sufferings of the victims of hydrophobia, but with nothing better than temporary success. Lailler

("Dict. Encyc. des Sci. Méd.," t. xvi., p. 676) kept a patient for thirty-six hours under the influence of the anæsthetic, using for this purpose somewhere between four hundred and five hundred cubic centimetres (twelve to sixteen ounces), but without any success beyond a partial abatement of the convulsive paroxysms.

Chloroform has been suggested as an antidote to strychnia. It, however, is not precisely such. The exaltation of the cord may be abated by inhalation of the vapor of the anæsthetic, and the energies of the patient may thus be economized during the elimination of the poison. But, if a certain limit of magnitude has been passed by the dose of strychnia, the result will be fatal in spite of chloroform. The convulsive phenomena may be abolished, but death will follow notwithstanding the relief thus procured. Labbée states that frogs which had been poisoned with strychnia died more quickly with chloroform than when left to the action of one poison alone. It follows that the employment of chloroform in cases of strychnia-poisoning should be undertaken with great caution.

Whooping-cough has been successfully modified by the action of chloroform. The employment of ether in spasmodic coughs and in irritable conditions of the air-passages had long been practised before the discovery of its special anæsthetic properties ; consequently, the introduction of chloroform was soon followed by its adoption into the voluminous list of remedies for whooping-cough. By its inhalation the severity and the frequency of the paroxysms are reduced, and the duration of the disease may sometimes be shortened. It is said that by carrying its effects to the extent of complete muscular resolution, the course of the disease may be arrested by a sort of artificial crisis. However this may be, chloroform should not be used for such a purpose ; sulphuric ether should be preferred for such an experiment. Since the establishment of the reputation of chloral hydrate, the use of chloroform in whooping-cough has been almost entirely abandoned.

The paroxysms of asthma may, like the paroxysms of all other spasmodic diseases, be arrested by chloroform. But, though generally successful at the outset of its employment, the respiratory passages soon accommodate themselves to its influence, and it ceases to control the disease. As an occasional resource it may be very highly esteemed, but as a constant remedy it cannot be recommended.

Spasm of the glottis and angina pectoris may sometimes be relieved by inhalation of chloroform. But its use in such cases is not without danger. If the laryngeal spasm is severe, there is a probability of increasing its intensity during the first moments of inhalation, thus adding to the dangers of asphyxia. On account of this local effect of chloroform, it is safer in such a paroxysm to administer the drug by injection into the rectum. If time will permit, the administration of chloral hydrate is to be preferred.

Previous to the introduction of chloral, it was not an unusual thing to employ chloroform for the purpose of quieting the maniacal excitement of the insane. At the present time it is seldom used for this purpose, unless a very speedy effect is desired. The same remark may be applied to its use in the treatment of delirium tremens. Its administration in the form of vapor to the victims of chronic alcoholism is always attended with danger. Sudden death has too often followed its use under such circumstances. If, for any sufficient reason, it must be employed in a case of this description, it should be given internally in the liquid form, rather than by inhalation.

Extravagant expectations regarding the efficacy of chloroform in the treatment of cholera were entertained at the epoch of its introduction into therapeutics. It has certainly proved itself a valuable remedy for the relief of the algid and spasmodic phenomena of the disease. The vascular spasm which marks the earlier stages of the attack may often be arrested by the administration of the liquid, or by inhalation of its vapor if the stomach cannot retain the fluid form of the drug. In this respect its action is identical with that of the other diffusible stimulants of alcoholic origin. Its only superiority consists in the possibility of its use as a vapor, when liquids cannot be tolerated by the stomach.

Chloroform has been recommended in obstinate intermittents, as a substitute for quinine. As a remedy for the fever it must be ranked far below the alkaloids of Peruvian bark ; but, as a means of shortening, or of completely arresting the initial chill of an intermittent paroxysm, it is certainly very useful. For this purpose it has been swallowed in doses of four cubic centimetres (one drachm) at the commencement of the chill; but it is better to divide this quantity, giving one-half the amount at intervals of ten minutes, until reaction takes place.

In the various inflammatory conditions of the bronchi and of the lungs, including pulmonary consumption, chloroform has been praised as an efficient anodyne. The local effect of the vapor, as it enters and leaves the blood through the walls of the pulmonary air-cells, is exceedingly tranquillizing. It should always be preferred to opiates when there is any impediment to the sufficient aëration of the blood, as indicated by a dusky color of the lips and face. For internal administration, however, the use of chloral hydrate is more convenient.

The pain of dysmenorrhœa may be allayed by the insufflation of chloroform vapor into the vagina. Trousseau advised a vaginal injection of oil in which five to ten per cent. of chloroform had been dissolved. Notwithstanding the attempt to retain the injection by plugging the vulva with lint, the obvious inconveniences of the method soon led to its abandonment. Hardy, of Dublin, and Heurteloup each contrived an insufflation apparatus by which the vapor of chloroform could be propelled in unlimited quantity against the neck of the womb. By this means Hardy was enabled to relieve the pain of non-ulcerated cancer of the womb. After the occurrence of ulceration the remedy was of no avail. The same method has been employed with similar results in the treatment of cancer of the rectum.

The local application of liquid chloroform has been undertaken with success in the treatment of fissures of the anus. But the pain that follows the application is very severe, and the results are by Trousseau pronounced to be inferior to the effects of lunar caustic or tincture of iodine.

Lotions and unguents containing chloroform are useful to allay the irritation produced by lichen, prurigo, and various forms of pruritus. In other skin diseases it is inferior to other standard remedies. By its use the parasite of scabies may be exterminated, but other remedies which are less irritant to the skin are to be preferred. The poisonous qualities of chloroform are not limited in their application to the itch-parasite. Other human parasites may be in like manner destroyed. Intestinal worms may be dislodged by its internal exhibition. The larvæ of flies which sometimes infest neglected wounds, or even invade the nasal cavities, may be instantly killed by exposure to the vapor of chloroform.

In general surgical practice, chloroform has scarcely been used except as an anæsthetic by inhalation. It has been occasionally applied in solution or as a glycerole to the surface of painful wounds. But its volatility and the pain which often attends its application to a denuded surface have served to limit its use. Its antiseptic properties give it rank with alcohol, chloral hydrate, and carbolic acid, so that its solutions cannot fail to be of service. Langenbeck is said to have used it instead of tincture of iodine as an injection for the radical cure of hydrocele. The painful swelling of orchitis and the suppurative tendencies of inguinal bubo have been arrested by continual application of the anæsthetic liquid. An incipient paronychia may be aborted by constant irrigation of the finger with chloroform for six or seven hours. Its mode of action seems in these respects to resemble and exceed that of alcohol.

The employment of chloroform for the induction of artificial anæsthesia by inhalation has already been mentioned. It will now be interesting to examine in detail the symptoms which follow its use for this purpose.

The first impression produced by the inhalation of chloroform vapor is a cooling sensation of pungent sweetness in the mouth and fauces. A feeling of partial suffocation generally follows the first acts of inspiration of the vapor. This is soon succeeded by a general sensation of warmth throughout the body. The senses of sight and hearing become partially obscured. There is a buzzing sound in the ears, and the voices of the bystanders seem to proceed from an increasing distance, while a vaporous film clouds the field of vision. Perception of unwonted internal sensations is greatly exalted ; the beating of the heart, the movement of the blood in the larger arteries of the head and neck, and the vermicular movements of the intestines, may all be felt by individuals gifted with a highly sensitive nervous temperament. A feeling of numbness gradually creeps over the frame. The limbs seem as if glued down to the couch upon which they have been placed—a sensation which usually excites an irresistible desire to break loose and to get up. A feeling of levitation, as if one were sailing through space, is not unfrequently experienced just before complete loss of consciousness. If addressed by any one, the patient replies vaguely and indistinctly, showing a diminution of the powers of utterance and articulation. Sometimes he passes into a condition of joyous exhilaration, laughing and gurgling in the most gleeful manner ; or he may exhibit the opposite mood, sobbing and crying, swearing, and complaining bitterly of his fate. Sensations of dizziness are usually experienced. The sense of sight fails before the sense of hearing. The intellectual functions become more and more restricted and perverted ; various forms of hallucination consequently occupy the mind. The face flushes, the conjunctivæ become injected, the eyes weep tears, the pupils dilate and contract, sluggishly responding to the influence of the light. The pulse becomes frequent and full ; the movements of respiration are accelerated ; and the various forms of sensibility are diminished to a degree that may permit the performance of minor operations without any considerable suffering.

Kappeler, in his treatise on anæsthetics ("Deutsche Chirurgie," Lief. 20), recognizes three different varieties of behavior under the influence of chloroform. In the first class inhalation proceeds quietly, without any excitement or muscular disturbance, until the patient is merged in a tranquil sleep. This agreeable course is usually exhibited among children or very young persons.

In another class of cases, complete unconsciousness is preceded by symptoms of muscular irritability, or brief tonic cramps affecting individual groups of muscles. These phenomena are often associated with irregularity of the respiration and with the utterance of various guttural sounds.

The third class comprises all those cases in which anæsthesia is preceded by great muscular commotion, wild delirium, and a condition of general excitement. This manifests itself by convulsive movements of the extremities, contraction of the facial muscles, and the appearance of trismus or even of cataleptic phenomena, so that the limbs may for a considerable time retain the position in which they have been placed. These convulsive movements extend from one group of muscles to another; the patient brandishes his legs and arms in the air; gets up on his couch; bends backward as if suffering an attack of opisthotonus, and can scarcely breathe because of a tonic persistence of the chest-walls in the position of expiration. Similar compression of the abdominal contents may, at the same time, expel the contents of the bladder and rectum. Sometimes the degree of excitement arrives at such a pitch that the patient leaps like a madman from the table, and clears a space for himself with his fists and his feet. Other patients exhibit a minor degree of excitement, pushing away their attendants and striving to free themselves from the inhaling apparatus. Others cling convulsively to the bed-clothes, or to the hand of an attendant. Along with these muscular disturbances are manifested the evidences of cerebral excitement and disorder. The patient laughs, screams, cries, or groans, in a more or less inarticulate manner. His mind is occupied with his disease, or with the impending operation, or it may wander away from its present surroundings. Sometimes an ugly temper, released from all restraint, pours forth a torrent of abuse upon the surgeon and upon his attendants, and the hurricane of yells and screams rises higher, and rages more furiously until the advent of anæsthesia once more brings back a period of calm. This generally concludes the exhibition, but in certain cases the period of awakening is occupied by a similar outbreak. In Germany, we are told that sometimes the patient occupies the earlier portion of inhalation with a lachrymose narrative of the sudden death under chloroform of some acquaintance, and finally sinks to sleep with the ejaculation, "That's just my luck too." In countries where the milder anæsthetics are employed, the remarks of the patient are generally uttered in a more cheerful strain, and may even rise to the harmony of a song which can be continued without interruption by any conscious perception of the pain of an operation. Long prayers, or attempts at a foreign language, may sometimes occur to diversify the scene. Kappeler has rarely observed a complete dissociation between the mental operations of the patient and his immediate surroundings and condition.

Perfect tranquillity in these cases is reached at a rather later period than in the other two classes of individuals. But at length the contracted muscles are gradually relaxed, the limbs collapse; finally, even the masseter muscles yield, and the jaws fall apart. The countenance loses its rigidity and its color; the contracted pupils no longer respond to the light, nor to any kind of irritation of the sensory nerves. The eyeballs move unsymmetrically; the circulation is retarded; the movements of respiration become regular, but are not as deep as usual in the natural condition, being often scarcely perceptible. Gradually, also, the temperature of the body begins to fall. In this stage of the anæsthetic process the severest surgical operations can be performed without pain and without any recollection of the event after awakening. Emergence from anæsthesia is usually preceded by a sudden dilatation of the pupils. A disposition to sleep is frequently remarked after this awakening, especially among children, who will again fall asleep after the conclusion of the operation. Women, and other patients who are delicately organized, often begin to sob and to weep as they awaken. In many instances the patient experiences headache, dizziness, uneasiness, nausea, and vomiting, during this period. Recovery is generally very prompt, but occasionally these disagreeable phenomena may continue for many hours. Sometimes the recovery of consciousness is succeeded by a series of disturbances of locomotion and of cerebral function similar to the consequences of alcoholic excess.

Kappeler records the statement (*loc. cit.*) that the majority of surgeons undertake to divide the anæsthetic process into four stages or periods: 1st, the period of excitement; 2d, the period of sleep or toleration of pain; 3d, the period of muscular paralysis or collapse; 4th, the period of awakening. Nussbaum makes three stages: 1st, voluntary activity; 2d, exaltation of functions, and 3d, insensibility. Sansom ("Chloroform: its Action and Administration," p. 57) also divides the process into three stages: "First, perversion of consciousness; second, abolition of consciousness; third, muscular relaxation. The only difficulty is in the division of the first stage from the second. I have said that the sign afforded by touching the eyeball is fallacious. My own opinion is that the muscular tremor is the best sign. Just after it has subsided there is complete insensibility."

Kappeler recognizes only two stages: a stage during which consciousness persists, and a stage in which consciousness is abolished. The first of the periods is characterized by aberrations of special sense, intellectual disturbances; diminution of general sensibility and of the susceptibility to painful impressions; dilatation of the pupils; acceleration of the heart; and irregularity of the respiratory movement. The second stage is frequently, though not always, introduced by the occurrence of delirium and by an agitation of the voluntary muscles, which may vary from a slight shivering or tension of single muscles or muscular groups to the severest tonic and clonic convulsions invading almost every muscle in the body, and accompanied by continued dilatation of the pupils, anæsthesia, persistent reflex irritability, acceleration of the action of the heart, with irregular and generally accelerated movements of respiration. These phenomena are succeeded, or sometimes superseded, by muscular relaxation; diminution of reflex irritability, attended by progressive contraction of the pupils; with final loss of reflex power, marked by contracted and immovable pupils, irregular movements of the eyeballs, retardation of the circulation and respiration, and depression of the temperature of the body. Skilful administration of chloroform consists chiefly in retaining the patient in the condition characterized by these symptoms, and in quickly bringing him back to it from every excursion into that dangerous stage of final paralysis of the nervous centres that maintain the functions of circulation and respiration—a paralysis which is ushered in by a wide dilatation of the pupils of the eyes.

The effect of chloroform upon the circulatory apparatus is best illustrated by the tracings of the sphygmograph. By the aid of this instrument, the smallest variations of arterial pressure and rate of pulsation are immediately noted by the eye. The changes, which may be recognized by ordinary methods, consist during the early stages of anæsthesia in an increase of the rapidity and a decrease of the force with which the heart performs its functions. The pulse ordinarily executes from ten to twenty beats per minute more than before the commencement of disturbance. It is not often that the degree of acceleration reaches thirty or forty beats, or falls below ten beats per minute. When the stage of muscular relaxation has been attained, the frequence of the pulse recedes, and often falls below the rate which preceded the commencement of inhalation. The changes that are effected in the quality of the pulse are exhibited by the following tracings.

Experiment I.—A full-grown rat, weighing 130 grammes (four ounces).

Animal secured upon a board.   After quiet had been established, the sphygmograph was applied to the wall of the chest, immediately over the heart.

No. 1.—Normal movement of the heart.

No. 2.—After inhalation of five drops of chloroform.

No. 3.—After ten drops.

No. 4.—Fifteen drops have been inhaled.   Complete anæsthesia.

EXPERIMENT II.—A full-grown rat, weighing 130 grammes (four ounces), treated in like manner with the first.

No. 1.—Before inhalation.   Animal frightened and struggling.

No. 2.—Animal quiet.   Inhalation not yet commenced.

No. 3.—Same condition.

No. 4.—After inhalation of ten minims of chloroform. Respiratory movements well marked.

No. 5.—Three minutes later. No more chloroform since the last tracing. Death immediately after this tracing. Suspension by the tail, administration of amyl nitrite and of ammonium hydrate were essayed without success. The thorax was then opened, and the lungs were seen to be congested. The heart was contracting feebly, and by the aid of artificial respiration it continued to pulsate for twenty-three minutes longer. On opening the heart, its four cavities contained black clotted blood. The kidneys were intensely congested.

EXPERIMENT III.—A kitten, two-thirds grown, was made to inhale sulphuric ether until insensible. The common carotid artery was then exposed in the neck, and the sphygmograph was applied to the vessel with the following result:

The animal was then allowed to become conscious, when ten minims of chloroform were given by inhalation, producing partial insensibility, and the following effect upon the circulation :

Ten minims more were then administered ;

this produced complete anæsthesia, with the following pulse :

The animal now passed suddenly into a state of syncope, from which it was with difficulty resuscitated, and the experiment was discontinued.

EXPERIMENT IV.—A medium-sized dog was placed under the influence of chloroform, August 6, 1880. The carotid artery was exposed in the neck, and the subjoined sphygmogram was obtained during complete anæsthesia :

No. 1.—This tracing exhibits the sluggish commencement of contraction of the arterial walls, and the abolition of the secondary elevations of pressure during the period of contraction. The influence of the vaso-motor nervous system is greatly reduced. The administration of chloroform having been discontinued, the next tracing was taken :

No. 2.—Anæsthesia passing off. Pulse-curves resuming their normal contour.

No. 3.—Still improving.

No. 4.—Animal quite conscious.   Pulse nearly natural.

Chloroform vapor was now administered in as concentrated a form as possible, for the purpose of killing the animal.   The following effect upon the circulation was immediately manifested—probably due in great measure to reflex action through the medium of the trigeminal and pneumogastric nerves, as well as to an immediate action upon the heart itself:

No. 5.—Cardiac paresis.

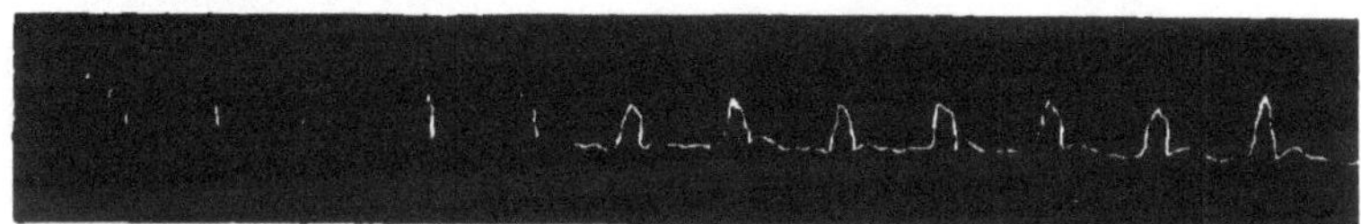

No. 6.—Snoring.

No. 7.—One minute later.   Snoring.

No. 8.—One minute later.   Respiration becoming irregular.

No. 9.—Circulation improving.   Chloroform increased.

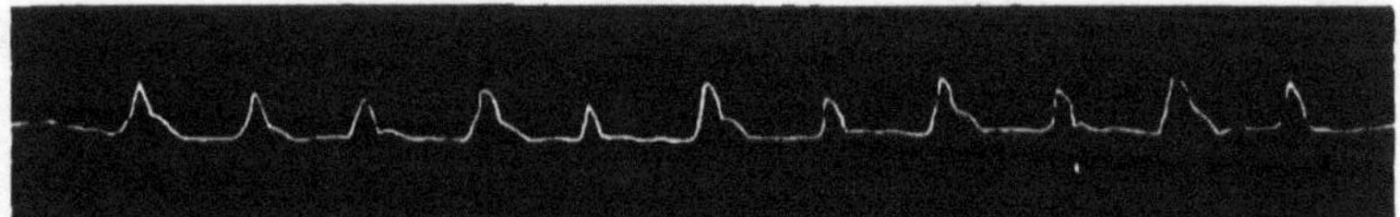

No. 10.—One minute later.

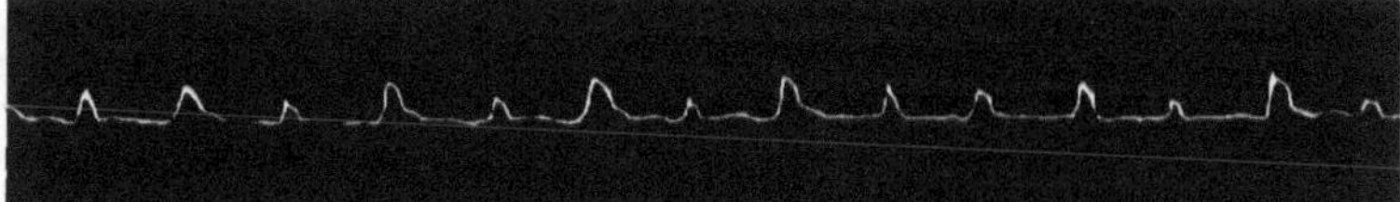

No. 11.—One minute later.

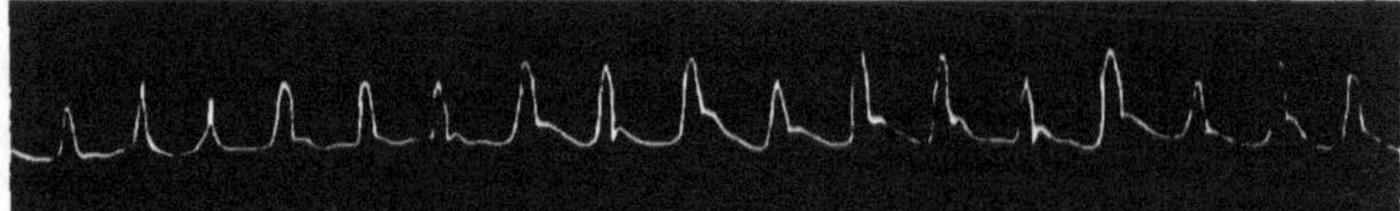

No. 12.—One minute later.   Great muscular relaxation.

No. 13.—One minute later.   Syncope.

No. 14.—One minute later.

No. 15.—One minute later.

No. 16.—Respiration imperceptible.   Death followed immediately after
the completion of this tracing.   It would probably have occurred earlier, if

the administration of the anæsthetic vapor had not been necessarily relaxed a little during the inscription of each tracing.

Observations upon the human subject.—As a standard of comparison, the following tracing was taken from a man in perfect health, whose pulse had not been disturbed by emotion or by any material agent.

The instrument with which the tracing was made is one of Pond's improved sphygmographs.

With the above may be contrasted the following:
A. B., male, aged twenty-three years, anæmic, suffering with iritis, for which an iridectomy was proposed. Nervous and apprehensive, pulse feeble. Chloroform administered July 6, 1880.

No. 1.—Immediately before inhalation.

No. 2.—Commencement of inhalation.

No. 3.—One minute later.

No 4.—One minute later. Operation begun. Anæsthesia.

No. 5.—One minute later.   Operation in progress.   Anæsthesia.

No. 6.—One minute later. Operation concluded. Inhalation suspended.

The above series exhibit several of the effects of chloroform in a very convincing manner.   In the first place it should be remarked that the induction of anæsthesia occupied an unusually brief period.   Two minutes only were necessary to prepare the patient for the operation.   The excessive brevity of the operation, moreover, afforded scarcely time enough for the evolution of the phenomena of profound anæsthesia ; consequently the depressing effects of chloroform are not made conspicuous.   The first tracing, before the commencement of inhalation, serves very well to illustrate the depressing effects of emotion.   It is the work of a feeble heart operating through a relaxed and imperfectly distended artery.   The next tracing shows that the artery is filling more completely at each contraction of the heart.   The emotional impedient is being withdrawn under the stimulating effect of chloroform.   One minute later—the third tracing exhibits this stimulus at its height.   Already the upward stroke of the lever is more than normally inclined from the perpendicular, showing a more gradual impulse on the part of the heart.   The apex of the graphic cone is losing its sharpness, indicating a more deliberate commencement of contraction on the part of the arterial muscular coats.   These changes are rendered still more apparent by numbers four and five, which also exhibit the almost complete abolition of the second wave that is propagated through the blood-column by the closing of the aortic valves in the normal condition of the circulation.   All these changes exhibit a progressive modification for the better in the last tracing, after the suspension of the anæsthetic.   The pulse, also, now beats more rapidly than at any previous period since the commencement of inhalation, probably because the irritation of the inhibitory branches of the pneumogastric nerve had not previously been fully withdrawn.   The indications of the sphygmogram, therefore, all unite in pointing to a diminished innervation of the blood-vessels, and to a diminution of the blood-pressure, by reason of which the walls of the artery contract under the influence of their own elasticity rather than because of any active participation in the movement by their muscular coat—in other words, we have evidence of the existence of a certain amount of vaso-motor paresis under the influence of chloroform.

The following sphygmographic series was taken from a boy aged twelve years, weight about eighty-five pounds, in good health, to whom chloroform was given to facilitate an operation for the relief of double strabismus.

Owing to a delay in the adjustment of the apparatus, the patient was quite insensible before the first tracing was taken. The sphygmograms followed each other at intervals of about thirty seconds, without interruption by the progress of the operation :

No. 1.—Patient is becoming insensible.

No. 2.—Condition of anæsthesia.

No. 3.—Patient snoring. Chloroform withdrawn.

No. 4.—Operation commenced.

No. 5.—Operation in progress.

No. 6.—Operation still continued.

No. 7.—Patient remains perfectly motionless.

No. 8.—Patient begins to move.

No. 9.—Signs of returning sensibility appear.

No. 10.—Renewed administration of chloroform becomes necessary.

No. 11.—Inhalation in progress.

No. 12.—Patient again insensible.   Pulse accelerated.

No. 13.—Inhalation suspended.   Operation resumed.

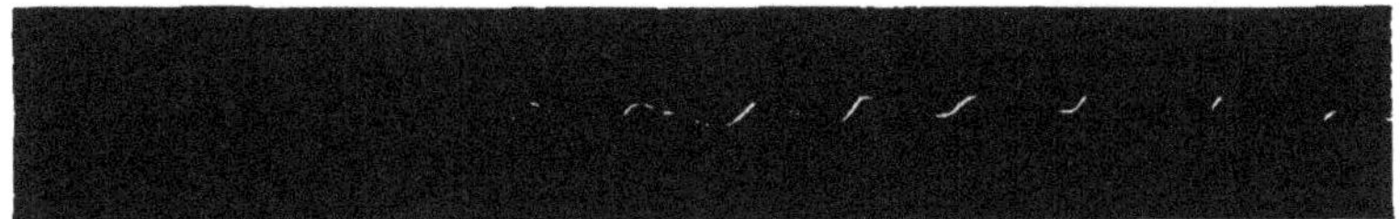

No. 14.—Complete anæsthesia.

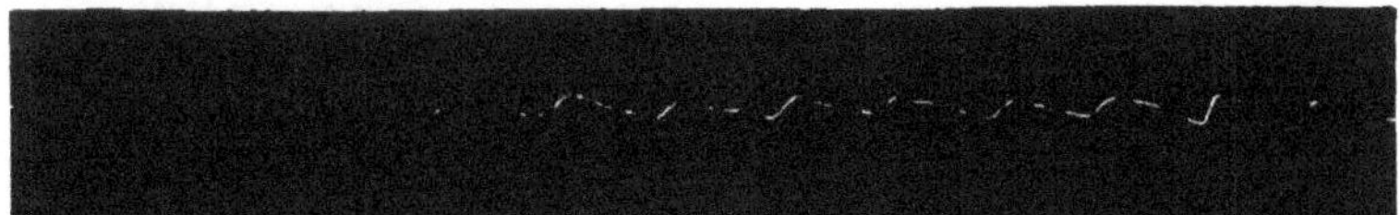

No. 15.—Still insensible.

No. 16.—Operation completed.   Consciousness returning.

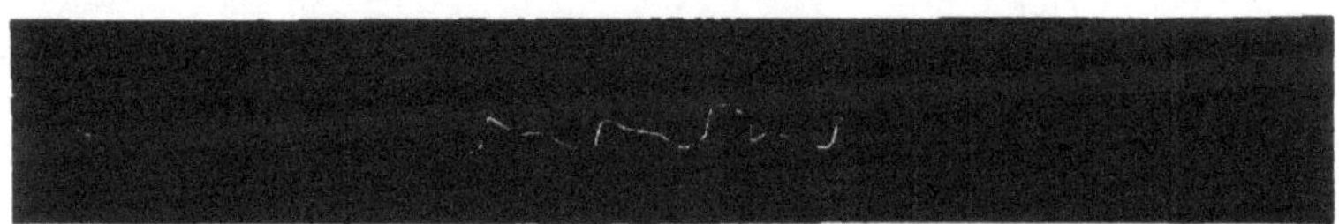

No. 17.—Twenty-four hours after the operation.   Patient fully recovered from the effects of the chloroform.

It was observed by the London Chloroform Committee that when the hæmatodynamometer was adjusted to the femoral artery of an animal, there was a notable elevation of the column of mercury for nearly, if not quite a minute.   This took place without reference to the condition of respiration, whether stormy or quiet.   But very soon, as the anæsthetic effect of the chloroform began to appear, the mercury began to sink.   The rate and the degree of its subsidence were directly proportioned to the rate and to the degree of the anæsthetic process.   If inhalation was suspended, the mercury rose in its tube, and sank again when the inhalation was resumed.

In the similar experiments of Scheinesson upon cats and dogs, no initial increase of blood-pressure was remarked.   The intra-arterial pressure fell to about twenty-seven to thirty-eight per cent. of the amount before inhalation was commenced.   These observations indicate either a paresis of the vaso-motor nerves, or a decrease of cardiac energy, or a combination of both conditions.   Observation of the dilatation of the blood-vessels of the ear, in animals under the influence of chloroform, led Scheinesson to believe that its effect upon the vaso-motor nervous system is very similar to the effect of section of the cervical sympathetic nerves.   Since, however, the degree of vascular injection is proportioned to the degree of anæsthesia, and since an irritation of the upper extremity of the divided sympathetic nerve will produce a prompt constriction of the dilated auricular arteries, even during complete anæsthesia, he concluded that the paralyzing effect of chloroform is, so far as the vascular innervation is concerned, chiefly concentrated upon the vaso-motor centre in the medulla oblongata. This conclusion receives additional confirmation from the fact that a dilatation of other small arteries may be observed in other parts of the body. Sansom and Harley remarked a contraction of the vessels at the commencement of inhalation, and this was succeeded by their general relaxation, especially if chloroform was given in the form of a highly concentrated vapor. Additional proof of the participation of the vaso-motor centre in the effect of chloroform is furnished by an observation of Koch. He found that when a manometer had been adjusted to one of the large arteries of an animal which was profoundly under the influence of chloroform, if the spinal cord was divided in the neck, the blood-pressure was diminished by only one-sixth or one-eighth part—a result inconsistent with the hypothesis of central immunity from the action of the anæsthetic. Other experiments performed by Bowditch and Minot, and by Scheinesson himself, all tend to confirm the same result.

Upon the action of the heart, chloroform exercises a decidedly depressing effect. The velocity of the blood-current is consequently diminished. According to Lenz, this diminution amounts to one-seventh of the normal rate.

The respiratory function exhibits a greater degree of variable and irregular disturbance than any other series of vital phenomena under the influence of chloroform. The movements of respiration are generally increased in number at the commencement of inhalation, and may become irregular, jerky, and sighing. Sometimes they become exceedingly restricted and almost imperceptible. An extreme rigidity of the abdominal muscles may limit the excursions of the diaphragm. The act of inspiration may be shortened while the act of expiration is prolonged ; and then the proportion may be completely reversed. All the symptoms of laryngeal stenosis, with inspiratory depression of the infra-clavicular spaces and of the inferior portion of the thorax, may be sometimes observed. Complete arrest of respiration may take place at any time during the course of inhalation, but is more likely to happen at an early period. Occasionally —and this is almost exclusively observed among youthful individuals—no disturbance of the respiration is observed, and the patient sinks into a quiet sleep, in which he breathes rather more slowly than during natural slumber. Generally the period of complete anæsthesia is marked by noisy, snoring respiration, occasioned by insensibility of the air-passages, by a paretic condition of the palatal muscles, and by accumulation of mucus in the fauces. A disposition to cough is often noticed at the commencement of inhalation, and it may persist to the extent of considerable interference with the anæsthetic process.

According to the report of the Committee of the Medical and Chirurgical Society, it appears that, under the influence of chloroform, "the depth of the respiration became less and less, and after the stage of perfect insensibility was reached, the amount of air entering the chest was exceedingly small." The same report states that if animals are made to inhale a 40 per cent. vapor of chloroform, the pulse ceases in eighty seconds, and the respiration stops after one hundred and five seconds, though the heart continues to beat from three to five minutes longer. If the concentrated vapor is conveyed to the lungs through an opening in the trachea instead of traversing the mouth and nose, the heart will be arrested before the respiration. This result agrees with what is observed when chloroform is injected into the jugular vein—immediate paralysis of the heart. If the chloroform vapor be largely diluted with air, it makes very little difference how the anæsthetic may enter the lungs; respiration will generally cease before the stoppage of the heart, and the pulse also disappears before the heart is arrested. Respiration is frequently checked for a brief period by the inspiration of a highly concentrated vapor, and then is again resumed as the proportion of chloroform in the air sinks to the proper standard, below 6 per cent. An increased rate of respiration at the commencement of inhalation under these different conditions is followed by a gradually diminishing rate. With dilute vapor the respiration may fall to nothing, and then, after twenty seconds or longer, it may be renewed, to be again arrested by each new reinforcement of the vapor.

Division of the pneumogastric nerves during inhalation of chloroform produces very little effect upon the movements of respiration. The beating of the heart, though somewhat accelerated, is not so rapid as when the operation is performed without chloroform. If performed before the administration of the anæsthetic, the subsequent respiration during anæsthesia is less frequent and less difficult, so that all the consequences of the nerve-section are rendered much more tolerable. (Kappeler: "Anæsthetica," p. 55.)

The principal changes in the state of the pupils during inhalation of chloroform consist, first, in a retardation of the reactions of the iris under the influence of light. The iris then becomes almost insensible to light, and finally, with the advent of anæsthesia, the pupils gradually assume the appearance characteristic of myosis. The reflex dilatation of the pupils, which follows any impression upon a sensitive nerve during the persistence of consciousness, may be remarked in the earlier stages of inhalation, but it disappears with the progress of anæsthesia.

The cause of the above specified changes in the state of the pupils, must be referred to the relations of the iris to the double set of nerves which it receives. By the action of the oculo-motor nerve-filaments the pupil is contracted, while, on the contrary, it is dilated by the intervention of the sympathetic nerve. Whenever an impression is made upon a sensitive nerve, as Bernard and Schiff remarked long ago, the centripetal impulse is reflected over the cervical sympathetic to the eye, and the pupil is dilated. When a psychical impression in like manner is made upon the cortex of the brain, the impulse thus received is propagated to the medulla, and passes over the sympathetic filaments that are connected with the cord, until the iris is reached. The pupil then dilates. Rachlmann and Witkowsky (Kappeler: "Anæsthetica," p. 60) have employed these facts to construct a theory of the changes noted in the condition of the pupil while under the influence of chloroform. The dilatation ordinarily apparent during the early stage of inhalation, is due either to the influence of irritation of the sensitive nerves in the naso-laryngeal passages, or to emotional disturbances of the brain, which leave the central axis and reach the pupil through the sympathetic channel. With the suppression of the functions of the brain, due to the arrest of sensation as inhalation progresses, the sympathetic nerves no longer receive those impulses which provoke pupillary expansion, and the influence of the oculo-motor nerves acts without opposition. The pupil thus becomes contracted, just as it does in natural sleep. The dilatation that occurs just before complete awakening is due to the resumption of sensation, and the renewed influx of sensory impressions, extending even to the iris. The dilatation that is observed when death is imminent under chloroform, is caused by the arrest of oculo-motor influence, leaving the iris to the uncounteracted impression still received, through the medium of the sympathetic nerves, from the medulla oblongata.

The same explanation will apply to the dilatation of the pupils which accompanies muscular disturbances during the period of inhalation. Rough handling and violent exertion on the part of the patient are accompanied by those sensory and psychical irritations which react upon the iris. Nausea and vomiting may also be included among the causes of pupillary dilatation during anæsthesia.

At the commencement of anæsthesia the eyeballs are generally directed upward, so that the pupils are concealed behind the upper lids, and exhibit a slight divergence, such as may be observed in natural sleep. Oscillations like those observed in nystagmus are sometimes remarked. After the complete evolution of anæsthesia, during the condition of profound insensibility, the axis of the eye commonly re-enters the horizontal plane. Mercier and Warner have called attention (Kappeler) to the fact, that during this period it may be sometimes observed that while one eyeball is directed straight forward and remains stationary, the other moves slowly inward, upward, or outward. Sometimes the two eyeballs move in different directions, or with unequal pace in the same direction. These phenomena all point toward the loss of co-ordinative power in the region of the corpora quadrigemina.

The careful experiments of Scheinesson, Bärensprung, Mendel, and others, indicate that the diminution of temperature which accompanies and follows the inhalation of chloroform, is caused by a diminished production of heat within the tissues, owing to the retardation of tissue-change in the presence of chloroform.

The fall of temperature in the human subject under chloroform has been very carefully observed by Kappeler, who has registered the temperature of thirty patients, with the thermometer in the rectum. Care was taken to retain the individual in the same position, and unruly cases were excluded, together with all cases in which a considerable loss of blood might vitiate the result. The operations were performed between the hours of eleven and twelve in the morning. A light breakfast of coffee and milk, or of broth and egg, was allowed three or four hours before inhalation, so that the stomach was nearly, if not quite empty at the time of observation. No diminution of temperature was indicated by the mercurial column until a considerable time after the commencement of inhalation, "ten minutes in four cases, fifteen to nineteen minutes in eleven cases, twenty to twenty-four minutes in eight cases, twenty-five to thirty minutes in five cases, once after thirty minutes, and once after sixty minutes. In the great majority of cases the lowest temperatures followed the latest commencements of subsidence, and the time of the greatest depression did not correspond to the highest grade of anæsthesia. On the contrary, the minimum temperature was usually noted long after the cessation of the phenomena of the anæsthetic state. The depression of temperature, however, goes hand in hand with the other effects of chloroform to such a degree, that ordinarily a condition of profound narcosis predicates a greater diminution of temperature than may be expected after a lesser grade of anæsthesia. Like all other effects of chloroform, so also varies the depression of temperature. But as this subsidence requires for its complete evolution a longer time than any other symptom, so also the equalization of this disturbance demands a correspondingly long period, which, according to my observations, varies between twenty minutes and five hours, seldom occupying less than one hour." (Kappeler: "Anæsthetica," p. 37.)

Occasionally (in five cases) during the initial stage of excitement, there was a slight elevation of temperature—amounting in four instances to about 0.2°, and in one to about 0.3°. This was soon followed by a fall of temperature, which varied between 0.2° and 1.1° with an average of 0.59°. Previous elevation of the temperature by fever did not prevent the manifestation of this effect of chloroform.

Vomiting is the principal evidence of gastric disturbance that may occur during the action of chloroform. It may happen at any stage of anæsthesia. The exact method of its causation is not clearly understood, but it is doubtless connected with the effect of the anæsthetic upon the medulla oblongata, perhaps in a manner analogous to the way in which anæsthetic substances sometimes produce convulsions. Kappeler noted in 14 per cent. of two hundred cases, specially observed for this symptom, vomiting during anæsthesia, and in 4 per cent. after recovery from insensibility. Ridgen (*Lancet*, p. 620, October 31, 1874) observed nausea and vomiting in 32.86 per cent. of five hundred and sixty-nine patients.

The secretion of mucus and of saliva is not exaggerated to the degree which is reached during the inhalation of ether. It is dependent upon the local action of chloroform vapor, and does not appear when the vapor is introduced through a canula into the trachea. In the same way the increased secretion of tears may be referred to a local irritation.

The passage of chloroform into the milk that is secreted in the breast has been inferred, rather than proved, by observation of children who are suckled after inhalation by their mothers. In like manner the anæsthetic is supposed to pass from the maternal blood into the circulation of the foetus.

Nadler examined the urine of twenty-five of Kappeler's patients after inhalation of chloroform, without discovering any trace of bile-pigment in a single instance. By the same analyst was ascertained the diminished production of urea in the majority of cases after inhalation of chloroform. The results are exhibited as follows:

Case.	Before Inhalation.	After Inhalation.	Case.	Before Inhalation.	After Inhalation.
1	1.36 per cent.	1.26 per cent.	11	1.25 per cent.	1.18 per cent.
2	1.36 "	1.17 "	12	1.43 "	1.30 "
3	1.62 "	1.02 "	13	0.75 "	0.82 "
4	2.27 "	1.87 "	14	1.27 "	1.20 "
5	0.42 "	0.32 "	15	1.42 "	1.59 "
6	0.52 "	0.39 "	16	0.85 "	1.17 "
7	1.08 "	0.60 "	17	2.00 "	1.83 "
8	0.99 "	0.97 "	18	1.69 "	2.25 "
9	0.89 "	0.59 "	19	1.36 "	1.84 "
10	2.03 "	1.07 "	20	2.97 "	2.17 "

According to Zuelzer the quantity of phosphoric acid is increased relatively to the nitrogen in the urine voided after chloroform.

Kappeler withdrew the urine from twenty patients immediately after chloroformic anæsthesia, but only once did he discover a trace of albumen, or of a reduction of the cupric oxide solution.

CASES OF SUDDEN DEATH DURING THE INHALATION OF CHLORO-FORM.

The first victim of chloroform was a beautiful young girl, just fifteen years old, in the English village of Wincanton. Her sad fate is thus recorded :

1. Hannah Greener, fifteen years ; had long suffered with an ingrowth of the great toe-nails. For the removal of the right toe-nail she had undergone an operation while under the influence of ether. The vapor of this substance had caused such severe headache, and so much irritation of the throat, that she was unwilling to inhale it again. Her surgeon, therefore, promised to make use of the new anæsthetic, chloroform, when the left toe-nail should be removed, confidently asserting that she would thus avoid all the disagreeable effects of ether. She was not, however, at all encouraged by such assurances. Bathed in a flood of tears, she was brought into the presence of the surgeon on the appointed day, January 28, 1848, crying and declaring that she would prefer to die rather than submit to the operation. The chair upon which she sat was shaken by her sobbing ; but the surgeon cheerfully poured a drachm of chloroform upon a handkerchief, and held it before her face. Two inspirations, and she pushed away the handkerchief ; but presently placed her hands in her lap in obedience to the instructions of the operator. After half a minute of quiet inhalation in this position, the muscles of the arm became rigid and resistant when the surgeon attempted to raise her hand. Thinking that anæsthesia must now be sufficiently advanced, an incision was quickly made around the root of the nail, when the patient moved as if about to start from the chair. A little more chloroform was, therefore, sprinkled upon the handkerchief, when her face and lips grew pale, foam issued from her mouth, and her eyes remained open and staring. Cold water dashed upon her face did no good. A little brandy poured into her mouth seemed to be swallowed, but with difficulty. They laid her upon the floor, and opened a vein, first in the arm, then the jugular itself, but without result—the blood would not flow. In less than a minute she had ceased to breathe—she was dead. An autopsy was made with curious care, twenty-seven hours after death : its results were negative. The brain, lungs, liver, kidneys, and spleen were engorged with dark and fluid blood ; the stomach was full of food ; the heart and large vessels were healthy ; dark blood, without clots, was found in all the cavities of the heart, especially upon its right side.—Snow, p. 123 ; *Am. Jour. Med. Sci.*, p. 558, April, 1848.

2. Female, thirty-five years, married, mother of six children ; generally in good health. Tooth extraction, February 23, 1848. Shortly after dinner she repaired to the office of her dentist, where she inhaled chloroform from a sponge in a glass globe. After a few inspirations her face became pale ; at the end of a minute four old roots were removed, during which operation the patient groaned, but gave no other sign of sensibility. About two minutes after the commencement of inhalation, her head turned on one side, her arms stiffened, her head was drawn a little backward, and she seemed about to slip out of the chair. Just then her pulse grew weak, and almost immediately it ceased to beat ; respiration stopped at about the same time. The paleness of her countenance was succeeded by a livid hue ; the lower jaw fell ; the tongue was slightly protruded ; her arms sank by her side—she was dead. Ammonia, cold water, and brandy were tried

without effect.   Half an hour later a physician arrived with an electrical machine, but neither this nor artificial respiration did any good.   *Autopsy, twenty-six hours after death.*—Brain healthy, its membrane filled with blood ; lungs healthy, but hyperæmic ; six ounces of sanguinolent serum in the pericardium ; heart flaccid and empty ; the stomach contained about a pint of partly digested food, and, like the intestines, was distended with gas ; liver pale ; kidneys engorged with blood ; all the other viscera were normal ; blood everywhere fluid and dark, its corpuscles irregular in shape and more distended than usual ; the sympathetic nerve was healthy.— *Western Lancet,* Cincinnati, March, 1848 ; *Am. Jour. Med. Sci.,* April, 1848.

3. Male.   March, 1848.   Fistula in ano.   Had previously inhaled chloroform without accident.   Thirty drops of chloroform were given, when the patient was placed on his side for the operation.   He seemed to experience pain, putting his hand upon the part.   About one minute after the commencement of inhalation the pulse ceased.   *Autopsy.* —Brain and membranes healthy ; heart dilated, pale, and soft ; two or three ounces of fluid in · the pericardium ; lungs filled with tubercles, and exhibiting cavities on both sides ; pleuræ everywhere adherent ; stomach, softening of the mucous membrane, and turgescence of its veins.—John C. Warren, Boston : Snow, p. 130.

4. Female, adult, Hyderabad, India.   Disease of the distal phalanx of the middle finger, requiring amputation.   A drachm of chloroform was given on a handkerchief.   She coughed a little, and gave a few convulsive movements.   When these subsided, the amputation was performed.   It was then found that the patient was dead.   Artificial respiration was continued for five hours, but she never breathed again.—*Am. Jour. Med. Sci.,* October, 1848, p. 505 ; Snow, p. 135.

5. Male, nineteen years, druggist's apprentice.   Inhaled chloroform February 8, 1848, as he had been frequently accustomed to do, for pleasure, and was found dead in the shop, leaning over the counter with several folds of cloth applied to his nostrils.   A short time previously he had been observed weighing out chloroform for a customer, and holding his handkerchief to his mouth.—*London Med. Gaz.,* February 26, 1848 ; *Am. Jour. Med. Sci.,* p. 560, April, 1848.

6. Male, twenty-two years.   Scrofulous disease of the left hand, requiring cauterization.   Chloroform was given with an inhaler.   Inhalation continued five minutes, and the patient died at the commencement of the operation.—Hôtel-Dieu, Lyons ; Perrin et Lallemand : "Traité d'Anæsthésie," p. 256.

7. A young man, recently returned to England from Australia, was chloroformed for an operation on his great toe, December, 1848.   Death occurred almost instantaneously after the commencement of inhalation.— Snow, p. 136.

8. A young woman.   Amputation of the left middle finger.   One drachm of chloroform was given on a handkerchief.   The patient coughed, and made several convulsive movements.   The finger was quickly removed, when it was noticed that blood did not flow from the wound.   The woman was dead, and could not be revived, though artificial respiration was maintained for five hours.—Snow, p. 135.

9. Male, twenty-three years, generally in good health, though often complaining of palpitation of the heart.   Tooth extraction, June 30, 1848. Inhaled chloroform for one minute, when he spoke, saying it was not enough. The dentist then left him for three-quarters of a minute, searching for the

chloroform bottle. On returning, he found his patient dead. A physician was summoned, who attempted bleeding, but could only obtain half a spoonful of black blood. Artificial respiration and other measures were essayed for half an hour without success. *Autopsy*, seventeen hours after death.—Membranes of the brain slightly congested ; lungs crowded upward, to the space between the third and fourth ribs, by the liver, which weighed eight pounds ; heart, pale, thin walls, with interstitial fat, which at the apex of the left ventricle replaced the muscular tissue. The substance of the ventricular walls was scarcely one line in thickness where it should have been five or six lines. The valves of the heart were diseased. —Snow, p 201 ; *Am. Jour. Med. Sci.*, October, 1848.

10. Female, thirty years, in fair health, but had suffered with anæmic palpitation of the heart a few months previously. An injury to her thigh had caused an abscess, which did not heal. Incision of its track was deemed necessary, and she inhaled fifteen or twenty drops of chloroform from a handkerchief. After a few inspirations she cried out that she was choking, and clutched at the handkerchief. Her face grew pale, respiration became labored, and foam appeared upon her lips. The anæsthetic was removed, and the surgeon proceeded to lay open the sinus, at the bottom of which appeared a sliver of wood that had been forced into the flesh at the time of the original accident. This done, it was evident that the patient was in a most alarming condition. Every effort was employed to restore her, but in vain. *Autopsy*, twenty-seven hours after death.—Brain healthy, its vessels containing blood and air ; lungs filled with air and blood ; right lung adherent to the cortical pleura, and crowded upward by an enlarged liver ; heart remarkably flaccid and enlarged, its cavities empty, a little bloody foam in the auricular orifice of the ascending vena cava, the pulmonary veins contained blood and air, right ventricle dilated, thin, and pale, left ventricle contracted, muscular substance of the heart easily torn ; incision of the liver permitted the escape of black fluid, and aërated blood ; the stomach contained half digested food, and great quantities of fœtid gas. The length of time after death detracts from the value of this examination.—*Am. Jour. Med. Sci.*, October, 1848 ; Perrin : "Traité d'Anæsthésie," p. 257.

11. Male, twenty-four years, lymphatic and corpulent. Gunshot fracture of the femur. Amputation at the hip-joint. Chloroform was inhaled through the mouth—the nose being held by an assistant—from a flask containing a cloth saturated with the anæsthetic, and provided with a face-piece. After three or four minutes the usual agitation was observed, and this was followed by complete muscular resolution. The patient moved during the operation, and a little more chloroform was administered, but in about fifteen seconds the breathing became stertorous, and the anæsthetic was removed. The face of the patient had now become pale, the lips blue, the pupils dilated, and the eyeballs turned upward. The pulse could no longer be felt, and the respiration was sighing and infrequent. The operation was discontinued ; artificial respiration, etc., were vigorously employed for three-quarters of an hour, but without success.—Hôpital Beaujon, June 25, 1848 ; Perrin, *ibid.*, p. 261.

12. Male, thirty-one years, sailor. Chronic diarrhœa and hemorrhoids, chancres, and phimosis. Had inhaled chloroform, December 26, 1848, during an examination of the rectum. January 19, 1849, Dr. Gurdon Buck proposed an operation for the removal of the hemorrhoids, and also circumcision. Chloroform was given on a napkin. Great excitement followed, but after a few minutes the patient became insensible. The cloth was re-

moved, he was placed on his side, and the hemorrhoids were quickly excised.
Just as he was being replaced upon his back, for circumcision, it was remarked that his face was livid and the pulse had disappeared. After two
or three widely separated inspirations, respiration also ceased. Between
five and ten minutes only had elapsed since the beginning of inhalation.
Autopsy, twenty-four hours after death.—Brain and membranes slightly
congested ; lungs engorged with blood ; heart large, flaccid, and quite
empty, left ventricle a little softer than usual ; blood everywhere liquid ; no
congestion of the abdominal viscera.   Analysis of the chloroform indicated
9 per cent. alcohol.—*London Med. Gaz.*, vol. xli., p. 255 ; Perrin, *ibid.*, p. 264.

13. Male, seventeen years ; lymphatic temperament, in fair health. Necrosis of the bones of the right middle finger, requiring amputation, January 31, 1849. Chloroform given drop by drop upon a towel. After inhaling for five minutes, the patient spoke and seemed to be somewhat agitated.
About eight grammes of chloroform had then been used. Suddenly the
patient started up, and endeavored to escape from the attendants ; then
fell back pulseless.   The towel was removed, revealing a livid countenance.   The heart had stopped, though respiration continued irregularly
and feebly for half a minute longer.   Cutaneous irritation with ammonia
and mustard produced, after two or three minutes, a partial resumption of
respiration, but the heart would not move again.   Air was blown into the
mouth, but it passed into the stomach, and an insufflation tube was therefore passed into the larynx.   The actual cautery was applied to the precordial, epigastric, and prelaryngeal regions, but without result. *Autopsy*,
sixty-two hours after death.—Heart normal, empty, a fibrinous clot, weighing four or five grammes, adhered to the Eustachian valve ; the blood was
dark and fluid ; lungs healthy ; brain and other viscera also healthy.—Hôtel-
Dieu, Lyons ; *L'Union Médicale*, p. 69, 1849 ; Perrin, *ibid.*, p. 265.

14. Male, thirty-six years, mason. Gangrenous wound of the great toe,
necessitating amputation, February 17, 1849. Chloroform, on a handkerchief. Great excitement, and failure to produce anæsthesia. The supply
of chloroform being exhausted, a delay of two hours occurred, during
which the patient recovered himself completely. A fresh supply of the anæsthetic having been obtained, half an ounce was poured upon the cloth ;
which was laid upon the face. Excitement continued for three minutes,
when the patient became insensible and stertorous, with dilated pupils,
and a pulse of seventy beats. The toe was now amputated, but no blood
flowed. The respiration grew tardy, the skin became pale and covered with
cold sweat, the pulse soon ceased. Respiration persisted for a few seconds
after the disappearance of the pulse, but it stopped entirely within ten minutes after the commencement of inhalation. Pulmonary insufflation and
all other measures failed to revive the patient. *Autopsy* negative. About
an ounce of dark blood in each ventricle.—*Lancet*, February 24, 1849 ;
Perrin, *ibid.*, p. 267.

15. Female, thirty-three years, married ; full of life, but of a very nervous temperament ; had previously been anæsthetized for tooth extraction,
without any unpleasant result. For the removal of another tooth, the physician who administered the anæsthetic for the dentist was reluctant to
incur its risks, and resolved to produce only partial anæsthesia, hoping thus
to avoid all danger. Less than a gramme of chloroform was given on a
handkerchief, held at a distance from the face. In eight or ten seconds the
dentist undertook to commence operations, but the patient pushed him
away, and, approaching the handkerchief to her nostrils, drew four or five
deep and rapid inspirations. The physician immediately removed the hand-

kerchief, and placed it upon a table near by. Instantly her face became pale, her lips blue, her eyes turned up, with the pupils frightfully dilated, her teeth were set firmly together, her head was drawn backward, the pulse had vanished, her limbs were relaxed, and a few inspirations, at long intervals, constituted the only remaining sign of life. Ammonia, friction, insufflation, artificial respiration, the actual cautery over the precordial region, galvanism. *Autopsy*, thirty-eight hours after death.—Engorgement of the cerebral vessels; bubbles of air mixed with the dark, fluid blood; heart flaccid, containing black, aërated blood, no clots; lungs healthy.—Langres, France; *L'Union Méd.*, p. 494, 1849; Perrin, *ibid.*, p. 268.

16. Male, forty-eight years, intemperate, but usually in good health. Removal of the nail of the left great toe, October 10, 1849. One drachm of chloroform was given on a sponge. For two minutes no appreciable effect, then excitement began. Ten drops of chloroform were then poured upon the sponge; this produced insensibility. The sponge was laid aside, and the nail was removed. As he did not revive after the operation, but became purple, and lay with a small, frequent, but regular pulse, and with laborious respiration, cold affusion was made upon the chest, and ammonia was applied to his nose. For a minute the pulse fluttered, then ceased, and breathing stopped two seconds later. Artificial respiration, insufflation, distention of the lungs with oxygen, galvanism of the heart and diaphragm. After fifteen minutes the effort to bring back life was abandoned.—St. Thomas's Hospital, London; *Med. Gaz.*, vol. xliv., p. 757; Snow, p. 143; Perrin, *ibid.*, p. 270.

17. Female, single. Removal of the eye. Chloroform was given on a sponge, and the operation was commenced before the establishment of complete anæsthesia. This necessitated more chloroform, which was then given in considerable quantity for several seconds. The operation was then recommenced, when the patient uttered an indescribable sound, some unintelligible Welsh phrases, and immediately expired.—Shrewsbury, England; *Jour. of Provincial Med. Surg. Assoc.*, 1849, p. 698; Snow, p. 145; Perrin, *ibid.*, p. 271.

18. Male, forty years; intemperate, worn and emaciated. An injury to the knee, badly treated by a quack, necessitated amputation of the thigh. One or two drachms of chloroform were given on a silk handkerchief. After inhaling for a minute, his breathing became labored and the pulse began to fail. No more chloroform was administered. A swallow of brandy improved the pulse, but the patient continued stertorous and his face was purple. The amputation was, however, performed, and the stump dressed, the patient still insensible and snoring, with a purple face, and a feeble, frequent pulse. He was placed in bed, and an attempt was made to arouse him, but without success. Death occurred about twenty-five minutes from the commencement of inhalation. The face was purple to the last.—Avery, South Otselic, 1850; *Buffalo Med. Jour.*, March, 1859.

19. Male, age and operation not stated. Had previously undergone amputation, without chloroform, for a cancer of the penis. Chloroform was given, January 29, 1850, on a handkerchief. The patient breathed badly, struggled, and pushed away the sponge; it was reapplied, but in a few seconds respiration became stertorous. Inspiration at long intervals, finally ceasing altogether. *Autopsy.*—General engorgement of the cerebral and pulmonary vessels; black blood in the right cavities of the heart; disease of the aortic valves, and a certain amount of fatty degeneration of the heart.—Public Hospital, Kingston, Jamaica; *Edin. Monthly Jour.*, p. 377; April, 1850; Perrin, *ibid.*, p. 272.

20. Male, thirty years. Hydrocele. It was proposed to operate by incision, so as to remove the testicle if that should appear to be diseased. Chloroform on a compress. After two or three minutes, more chloroform. The patient was much excited, and the anæsthetic was removed until he became quiet. It was then renewed, as the patient was not completely insensible, but after a few inhalations the pulse suddenly stopped. The skin grew pale, the eyes were turned up and down, breathing became slow, but continued full and deep, with increasing intervals between the inspirations, until at length they ceased altogether. The operation had not been commenced when death occurred, five minutes after the beginning of inhalation. Among other restorative measures, cold water was poured in a slow stream upon the epigastrium. This excited movements of respiration, but did not arouse the heart. *Autopsy*, thirty-two hours after death.—Dura mater congested, considerable serous effusion into the meninges of the brain, osseous deposits under the dura mater, and arachnoidal adhesions, indicating chronic meningitis; heart normal, but flaccid, left ventricle empty, but the auricles and large vessels were distended with uncoagulated blood, a small soft clot in the right ventricle; lungs engorged with blood.—Seraphin Hospital, Stockholm; Snow, p. 148; Perrin, *ibid.*, p. 273.

21.—Male, seven or eight years; in bad health for several years, caused by a stone in the bladder. Chloroform was given on lint; after a few minutes a sound was introduced into the bladder, though the child still moaned so loud that it was difficult to hear the sound clicking against the stone. As the surgeon withdrew the instrument, the patient became livid, and his heart stopped. After one long, deep inspiration, the respiration also ceased. From the distended jugular vein several ounces of blood were immediately drawn; but neither this, nor artificial respiration, nor electricity, did any good.—Glasgow Infirmary; Snow, p. 150; Perrin, *ibid.*, p. 273.

22. Male, twenty-four years, on board ship. February, 1850. Death from chloroform.—Mauritius; Snow, p. 147.

23. Male, thirty-four years, policeman, healthy. Amputation of a portion of the right hand. Chloroform given on a handkerchief, twisted into a cone. During the operation, which had occupied a minute and a half, the wound ceased to bleed, and the patient suddenly expired. *Autopsy.*—Hyperæmia of the brain and lungs; heart flaccid, containing a little blood on both sides.—Guy's Hospital; *London Med. Gaz.*, vol. xlvi., p. 39; Perrin, *ibid.*, p. 274.

24. Male, twenty-four; greatly reduced in strength by scrofulous disease of the ankle-joint. Amputation of the leg was proposed. A drachm of chloroform was given on lint, in a hollow sponge, covered with a napkin. Thirty drops more were soon given. The patient had not made over fifteen inspirations when it was discovered that he was dead. No autopsy.—Cavan Infirmary, Ireland; Snow, p. 152; Perrin, *ibid.*, p. 275.

25. Female, twenty years, in good health. Tooth extraction. Took chloroform at nine A.M., and, after three unsuccessful attempts at extraction, the completion of the operation was postponed till afternoon. Fifteen or sixteen drops of chloroform were then given on a sponge in a handkerchief. In a few minutes she became unconscious, but the jaws remained firmly closed. The effort to separate them awakened the patient. About twenty drops of the anæsthetic were then administered, while a piece of wood was held between the teeth. After a few inspirations, tracheal rattles were audible, the face became livid, froth issued from the mouth, and

she was dead. *Autopsy* negative.—Casper's *Wochenschrift*, January 12, 1850 ; Perrin, *ibid.*, p. 277.

26. Male. Operation upon the penis, April, 1851. Half a drachm was given without effect. Another half drachm was therefore given, when the patient expired. Stepney Work-house ; *Med. Times and Gaz.*, p. 577, May 24, 1851 ; Snow, p. 153.

27. Male, forty-five years, light mulatto, large and powerful frame. Abscess of left testicle, requiring castration, July 8, 1851. Chloroform on a handkerchief—ten to twenty minims at a time. Inhalation preceded by a glass of wine, as was usual in that hospital. Chest had been previously examined and pronounced healthy. Patient was somewhat excited, but became insensible after about seven minutes. Condition good, pulse 70. At the first incision the pulse stopped, and the wound ceased to bleed. Not more than two inspirations followed. Artificial respiration, tracheotomy, and cold affusion, did no good, though continued for an hour. *Autopsy.*—Brain and lungs hyperæmic ; heart covered with fat, large, weighing $12\frac{1}{2}$ ounces, flabby and soft, containing a little dark blood, a white clot in the pulmonary artery, right ventricular wall thin, and some of the muscular fibres were granular ; liver 5 lbs. 13 oz., puckered, containing numerous encysted masses, apparently the remains of old abscesses ; spleen large and soft ; kidneys weighed fourteen ounces, hyperæmic, but otherwise healthy.—Seamen's Hospital, London ; *Med. Times and Gaz.*, p. 98, July 26, 1851.

28. Female, thirty-seven years ; much exhausted by uterine cancer. Had inhaled chloroform several times for the removal of impacted fæces from the rectum. On the final occasion she inhaled for about nine minutes, using ten drachms and a half, in half-drachm doses. After removing the impacted masses, the surgeon found that his patient was dead.—Chipping Norton, England ; *Med. Times and Gaz.*, p. 620, December 13, 1851.

29. Male, twenty-three years. Had suffered since four years of age with aneurism by anastomosis, occupying the whole of the right ear and its vicinity. February 14, 1852, he was chloroformed for half an hour, while the temporal artery was ligated. From this he recovered without harm. It was decided that another large artery behind the ramus of the jaw should also be ligated, and chloroform was administered for that purpose, March 17th. The patient struggled considerably, but, after inhalation between five and ten minutes, he became insensible. At the first incision through the skin his pulse stopped, and a few seconds afterward his respiration also ceased. Artificial respiration seemed to produce a partial revival, but it was only temporary. Renewed efforts, aided by a galvanic apparatus, again restored the movements of the heart and lungs for a few seconds, only to be followed by another relapse. The turgid jugular vein was then opened, tracheotomy was performed, the lungs were inflated, and the patient was placed in a warm bath at 104° F., but every effort, though prolonged for an hour, failed to effect the slightest improvement. *Autopsy.*— Right side of the heart and the veins distended with dark fluid blood ; left ventricle contracted and nearly empty ; heart and valves quite healthy ; apices of both lungs adherent, but the lungs were healthy : brain healthy, but its membranes showed slight evidences of long antecedent inflammation ; kidneys congested ; other organs healthy.—St. Bartholomew's Hospital ; *Med. Times and Gaz.*, March 20, 1852.

30. A lady was chloroformed by a dentist, for the purpose of painless extraction of teeth. About four scruples of chloroform were placed on a handkerchief, and held close to the nose for a minute. This dose proved

instantaneously fatal. Traces of chloroform were found in the lungs, spleen and blood.—Strasburg ; *Med. Times and Gaz.*, April 3, 1852.

31. Male, adult, addicted to drink. Fistula. Chloroform, given on a handkerchief, shortly produced twitchings of the muscles. The surgeon went to the door to call for assistance in holding the patient ; then poured a little more chloroform on the handkerchief, and applied it to the face of the patient, who spluttered at the mouth, and suddenly expired. Death occurred not more than one minute after the first inhalation. About one drachm had been used. *Autopsy.*—Heart dilated, and flabby ; considerable serous effusion in the pericardium ; lungs healthy ; " slight appearance of disease about the liver, such as is observed in persons addicted to intemperance."—Melbourne, Australia ; *Med. Times and Gaz.*, p. 531, November 20, 1852.

32. Male, adult, cattle-dealer ; inhaled chloroform for the application of caustic potash to some ulcers of the leg. The inhalation produced great excitement. The caustic was partially applied before the patient was fully insensible, so more chloroform was given. During the second application of the caustic the patient sobbed and died.—Earlstoun, near Melrose, Scotland ; *Monthly Journ. of Med.*, vol. xv., p. 377 ; *Med. Times and Gaz.*, p. 402, October 16, 1852.

33. Male, seventy-three years ; had been chloroformed five or six times between May, 1850, and May, 1851, and again four times in December, 1851, for the operation of lithotrity. He had manifested alarming symptoms of syncope during at least two of these occasions. The patient was tall and stout, had an intermitting pulse, and well-marked arcus senilis. Nevertheless, Dr. Snow succeeded in chloroforming him twice without any unpleasant symptoms. It became necessary to repeat the lithotrity operation, and for this purpose Dr. Snow again gave chloroform with his own inhaling apparatus. The patient became insensible, without excitement or struggling, in the course of three or four minutes. A little chloroform was administered two or three times during the operation. After a few minutes, the anæsthetic having been withdrawn for two minutes, his face and lips turned pale, and then grew red, and he made straining efforts with the muscles of respiration, as if sensibility to pain were returning. A little more chloroform was then given, but he only took three inspirations when his breathing ceased, and the temporal artery could no longer be felt, nor could any sound be heard over the heart. After a few seconds there was a deep inspiration, and it was thought that the heart could be heard beating very feebly and frequently, but after one or two more very feeble inspirations, at intervals of about fifteen seconds, there were no more signs of life. *Autopsy*, fifty-two hours after death.—Heart larger than natural, and overlaid with fat, the right side contained aërated blood, the product of decomposition, right ventricle dilated and very thin, left ventricle also dilated, muscular substance soft and friable, a calcareous incrustation on one of the aortic valves ; kidneys highly congested, one of them slightly granular. Microscopical examination indicated fatty degeneration of the muscular substance of the heart.—John Snow : *Med. Times and Gaz.*, October 9, 1852.

34. Female, thirty-six years ; married, generally had good health, but latterly somewhat exhausted by severe toothache and the dread of extraction. Chloroform given on a handkerchief, and inhaled in the sitting posture. Three teeth were extracted before she was fairly insensible, and death took place suddenly during the operation. About a drachm of chloroform had been used. *Autopsy*, sixty-two hours after death, June 13th, was of little value, owing to the advanced state of decomposition of

the body ; the internal vital organs all appeared to have been in a healthy condition.—*Union Médicale*, p. 54, 1852 ; Perrin, *ibid.*, p. 282.

35. Female, thirty-two years, in good health. Tooth extraction. Chloroform given, twenty or twenty-five drops, on a sponge wrapped in a handkerchief. After four or five inhalations, the doctor asked if she heard any buzzing in her ears. With a trembling, raucous voice she answered in the affirmative, then stiffened her limbs, while her face turned blue, and her head sank down—she was dead. *Autopsy*, twenty-five hours after death.—Blood aërated ; brain and lungs filled with blood ; heart healthy ; liver and kidneys filled with frothy blood ; other organs healthy.—Ulm, Germany ; Snow, p. 161 ; Perrin, *ibid.*, 285.

36. Male, twenty-five years, soldier. Removal of a cystic tumor in the cheek, December 20, 1852. Fifteen minims of chloroform given on a hollow sponge. This excited no disturbance, and was followed, after a minute, by the addition of a drachm of the anæsthetic. In the course of four minutes the patient became insensible, without the slightest preliminary excitement, and the operation was commenced. Scarcely had the necessary incision been made when the face turned pale, the breathing stopped, and the pulse became exceedingly weak. Aspersion of cold water, insufflation by mouth to mouth, pulmonary inflation with a tube after tracheotomy, etc., only excited a few occasional inspirations. Electro-puncture in the region of the heart also failed. *Autopsy.*—Brain negative ; lungs engorged with blood ; heart larger than natural, excessively flaccid, left side empty, right side containing clots ; liver, spleen, and kidneys full of dark blood.—Hôtel-Dieu, Lyons ; Snow, p. 165 ; Perrin, *ibid.*, p. 286.

37. Male, adult. Tumor, probably cancerous, upon the right thigh, to be removed December 24, 1852. Chloroform given, in drachm doses, with an inhaling apparatus. Patient greatly excited, but became quiet at the expiration of about seven minutes. As the surgeon made his incision through the skin, it was remarked that the face was turgid with blood, the pupils were immovable, respiration was excessively slow, but not stertorous. An attempt was made to arouse the patient, but in vain. Anæsthesia was incomplete at the commencement of the operation, for the patient complained, after the first incision, that a cat was biting his thigh.—Royal Infirmary, Manchester ; *Lancet*, 1853, vol. i., p. 21; Perrin, *ibid.*, p. 288.

38. Female, thirteen years ; to be operated upon for the removal of a large lipomatous tumor from the back. A drachm of chloroform was given. When insensibility had been reached, the operation was commenced ; but scarcely had the surgeon divided the skin, when the head of the patient sank down and she was dead.—Neustadt, Germany ; Perrin, *ibid.*, p. 281.

39. Female, twenty-eight years, prostitute. Application of nitric acid to a gangrenous ulcer of the vulva and vagina. One drachm of chloroform given on folded lint. Patient was much excited, but soon became insensible and died at once. *Autopsy.*—Microscopical examination indicated fatty degeneration of the heart.—University College Hospital ; *Lancet*, vol. i., p. 307, 1853.

40. Male, adult, Frenchman. Chloroform was given for some purpose not stated. Ten or twelve drops were administered upon cloth. After five or six inspirations the patient laughed, spit into the towel, pressed the hand of the operator, drew a long breath, followed by a convulsive movement of the muscles of the face and hand, and immediately expired.—*Moniteur des Hôpitaux*, p. 480, 1853 ; Perrin, *ibid.*, p. 291.

41. Male, forty-three years, intemperate. Stricture of the urethra, for

which Syme's operation was to be performed, 1853.   About one ounce of chloroform was used, in divided doses, on a handkerchief.   At first the patient was attacked with epileptiform convulsions.   These were followed by insensibility and stertorous breathing, and the inhalation was suspended.   As the surgeon was about to make his first incision, the pulse weakened, and ceased entirely a few seconds later.   Respiration stopped at the same time, or afterward.   Artificial respiration excited five natural inspirations at long intervals, but the pulse did not reappear.   Tracheotomy, bleeding, and galvanism of the diaphragm, all failed, though employed for an hour.   *Autopsy.*—All the organs were healthy.—Royal Infirmary, Edinburgh; Perrin, *ibid.*, p. 292.

42.   Male, nineteen years, idiotic and an onanist.   Chloroformed for forcible extension of an anchylosed knee-joint.   Two drachms on a sponge.   Inhalation had proceeded for thirty seconds when the pulse became feeble and fluttering ; the jaws were set ; respiration was irregular ; the countenance became purple, and foam escaped from the lips.   Insufflation, cold aspersion, artificial respiration, friction, ammonia, and bleeding from the jugular vein to the extent of eight ounces, were all employed in vain.   *Autopsy* negative.—Prof. Dumreicher, Vienna ; *Gaz. des Hôpitaux*, p. 372, 1854 ; Perrin, *ibid.*, p. 306.

43.   Female, forty years, intemperate.   Strangulated femoral hernia had existed for two days and a half.   Operation for reduction was necessary, October 5, 1853.   One drachm of chloroform was given on lint, and at the end of three or four minutes forty minims more were added.   A minute later the patient began to struggle violently, but at the end of a minute became stertorous.   The anæsthetic was withdrawn, but the pulse could not be felt.   Cold water was dashed on the face.   Two or three short, stertorous inspirations, then two or three long ones, and breathing ceased.   Artificial respiration, and, within a minute, electricity to neck and diaphragm.   This was followed by tracheotomy.   These efforts were continued for three-quarters of an hour. *Autopsy*, thirteen hours after death.—Abdomen very tympanitic ; anterior surface of the heart covered with fat, heart-valves healthy, ventricular walls thin and flabby, fatty degeneration of their muscular fibre ; lungs healthy, but adherent ; brain healthy, but the arachnoid exhibited chronic thickening and opacity ; liver, kidneys, and spleen normal ; intestines distended and inflamed.—University College Hospital ; *Med. Times and Gaz.*, p. 422, October 22, 1853.

44.   Female, twenty-two years, prostitute.   Cauterization of a chancroid ulcer of the vagina.   Chloroform with an inhaler, a padded metal cup supplied with valves.   Two drachms and a half were given in divided doses.   Some excitement, but after inhaling for about five minutes she became insensible, the inhaler was removed, and the position was adjusted for the operation, when the pulse fluttered, the countenance became congested, and the respiration was interrupted and feeble.   Cold affusion, insufflation through the nose, with compression of the chest, were performed for ten minutes.   Tracheotomy was then performed, and electricity was employed.   After three-quarters of an hour it was evident that death had occurred. *Autopsy*, twenty-two hours after death.—Lungs healthy ; heart also healthy ; all other internal organs were sound ; blood everywhere liquid.—St. Bartholomew's Hospital ; *Med. Times and Gaz.*, October 29, 1853.

45.   Male, thirteen years.   Cleft palate.   Staphylorraphy.   Chloroform given, a few drops on a compress.   Patient sitting.   He had been much alarmed about the operation, and now struggled violently.   After three or

four minutes the operation was commenced, but very soon the heart ceased to beat. Insufflation, friction, and cauterization of the precordial region were practised for half an hour. Two or three raucous inspirations alone rewarded these efforts. *Autopsy* completely negative.—Hôtel-Dieu, Lyons ; Perrin, *ibid.*, p. 295.

46. Male, adult, suffering with aneurism of the aorta. For a painful hemorrhoidal tumor he desired chloroform, which was given, though its danger was fully recognized. After inhaling for two minutes and a half, anæsthesia was reached, and the chloroform was withdrawn. Respiration became slightly stertorous and embarrassed, the jaws were set, and the heart stopped. Insufflation and electricity excited movements of respiration for twenty minutes, but the heart did not beat again.—Hôpital la Pitié ; Perrin, *ibid.*, p. 297.

47. Female, forty-five years, in feeble health. Cancer of the breast, for which amputation was to be performed, February, 1853. Chloroform was inhaled from a sponge for the space of twenty minutes without effect. Another bottle was then brought, and in twenty minutes time the pulse fell from 136 to 104, and the patient appeared to become insensible. Just as the surgeon was about to commence the operation, the countenance of the patient changed, and the pulse disappeared. The efforts at resuscitation were continued for an hour and a half. *Autopsy.*—Heart and lungs healthy ; lungs engorged with blood ; kidneys degenerated ; commencing cancer in the neck of the womb ; half an ounce of blood in the spinal canal.—Sheffield, England ; Perrin, *ibid.*, p. 299.

48. Male, eighteen years, dissolute, pale and cachectic. Phymosis and chancres, requiring circumcision, May 3, 1854. Two drachms of chloroform in an inhaler. After inhaling for about six minutes, insensibility was nearly complete, when the pulse suddenly failed, and the face became livid. Artificial respiration, slapping the chest with a wet towel, and ammonia, restored the patient after about four minutes. For ten minutes longer he continued to breathe, and the pulse beat at the rate of 40–50 per minute. At the end of that time the pulse and respiration stopped together, and could not again be restored. *Autopsy.*—Brain and lungs both engorged ; heart slightly enlarged, with thin walls and fatty degeneration ; blood everywhere dark and liquid.—Lock Hospital, London ; *Med. Times and Gaz.*, June 3, 1854.

49. Female, forty years ; enfeebled by uterine hemorrhages, caused by a polypus of the uterus. Removal under chloroform was attempted, 1854. Chloroform was given on a compress. This produced great excitement, which ceased under the influence of a fresh dose, two minutes after the first inhalation. The operation was then commenced, and was in progress when the pulse stopped, though the respiration continued slowly. The head was lowered and the legs were raised without effect. During the next two minutes the body was slapped, and artificial respiration was attempted ; then the trachea was opened, and air was blown into the lungs. Acupuncture needles were thrust into the precordial region, and the heart was electrified, but in vain. *Autopsy* negative.—Hôpital St. Antoine, Paris ; Snow, p. 176 ; Perrin, *ibid.*, p. 300.

50. Female, thirty-seven years, pale and delicate. Removal of a mammary glandular tumor, May 11, 1854. Very anxious. One drachm of chloroform in Snow's inhaler. Inhalation was performed badly, with irregular and spasmodic inspirations. After inhaling for a minute and a half, she suddenly stopped breathing, and became very pale. No pulse. Cold affusion, artificial respiration, and galvanism, failed. Two distant

and gasping inspirations, within a minute after the appearance of danger, were the only signs of life perceived. *Autopsy.*—General venous engorgement; heart small, overlaid with fat, right ventricle thin, and its muscular wall had undergone slight fatty degeneration.—St. George's Hospital; *Med. Times and Gaz.*, May 20, 1854.

51. Female, fifty-nine years; good health. Reduction of a forward dislocation of the left forearm, January 19, 1854. Chloroform, one drachm, on a sponge. At the end of five minutes of quiet inhalation, another drachm. Respiration became almost immediately stertorous; the pulse disappeared, and then breathing stopped. The tongue was drawn forward; cold affusion; insufflation through the nose, and then, after tracheotomy, through the windpipe; galvanism. These efforts produced a few convulsive inspirations, and then all was still, though the surgeons continued their endeavors for an hour. *Autopsy.*—Extensive pleural adhesions on the right side; lungs healthy, but full of dark blood; left side of the heart normal, right side flabby, valves healthy; a little dark blood in all the cavities of the organ; two or three little atheromatous patches on the mitral valve; coronary arteries atheromatous; commencement of fatty degeneration of the walls of the right ventricle.—Bristol Infirmary, England; Perrin, *ibid.*, p. 303.

52. Male, adult. Dislocation of the hip. Unsuccessful attempt at reduction. Next day, June 1, 1854, he was bled, and, after a short time, chloroform was given with an inhaler. After a few minutes, insensibility was complete, and the luxation was reduced. Immediately the pulse stopped, but respiration continued feebly and irregularly. Cold affusion, friction, and ammonia produced a partial revival, but he soon relapsed, and could not be again aroused, though every effort was continued for an hour. Electro-puncture of the heart was performed in this case. *Autopsy.*—Heart large and flabby; everything else normal—Hospital at Pisa, Italy; Perrin, *ibid.* p. 304.

53. Male, sixty-five years; stout, muscular, and florid. Removal of malignant tumor from inner side of left femur, July 13, 1854. Two drachms of chloroform in Snow's inhaler. Eight minutes later another drachm was added. Ten minutes after commencing to inhale, violent spasm was induced, which continued for about three minutes. The pulse then fell from 120 to 70, full and steady. Pupils had been much dilated, but now lessened their width. Respiration free and deep. At this moment, between thirteen and fourteen minutes after the commencement of inhalation, the pulse gave a few rapid and irregular beats, and then ceased. Respiration ceased simultaneously. Cold affusion, mouth to mouth insufflation. After a few inflations, there was a slight effort at inspiration. Electricity was tried within two minutes after cessation of the pulse. A canula for artificial respiration was introduced through the crico-thyroid membrane, and was used for forty minutes. *Autopsy,* forty-eight hours after death.—Brain hyperæmic, but healthy; heart large and loaded with fat, especially the right side; its muscular tissue in a state of extreme fatty degeneration; blood in the cavities of the heart was firmly coagulated and fibrinous, extending down the aorta,—Middlesex Hospital; *Med. Times and Gaz.*, p. 86, July 22, 1854.

54. Male, middle-aged. Stricture of the urethra; retention of urine. Chloroform on lint, October 11, 1854, for catheterism. After inhalation, between four and five minutes, patient became insensible, and the operation was commenced. Partial return of sensibility required the administration of more chloroform. Two minutes later the patient began to snore

loudly, and the face flushed. The anæsthetic was withdrawn, and cold water was dashed upon the face. In about one minute it was evident that respiration was ceasing altogether. The tongue was then pulled forward, and mouth to mouth insufflation was attempted, but was soon exchanged for ordinary artificial respiration. The pulse had continued to beat feebly, and, after about four minutes, the patient began to breathe again; but this soon ceased once more. Electricity was then tried, without success. At the end of forty minutes all further effort was abandoned. *Autopsy*, seventy hours after death.—Lungs healthy; heart flabby and soft, weighing twelve ounces, its muscular substance in a state of advanced fatty degeneration; liver and kidneys more fatty than usual.—University College Hospital; *Med. Times and Gaz.*, p. 390, October 14, 1864.

55. Female, fifty-six years, but looking ten years older. Malignant ulcer on left leg, requiring amputation, December 5, 1854. One drachm of chloroform on lint covered with oiled silk. After about two minutes, another drachm. Considerable excitement followed this. The patient then became insensible, and the surgeon was commencing his operation, when the pulse suddenly ceased. Almost immediately there was a deep sighing inspiration. For two or three breaths the cheeks puffed out during expiration, and then the breathing ceased. Drawing forward the tongue, and artificial respiration, excited a few slight inspirations, but no other sign of vitality was ever exhibited. Cold affusion, electricity, and artificial respiration for half an hour. *Autopsy.*—Lungs gorged with blood; heart normal, left side nearly empty, right side distended with fluid blood, its walls very thin; liver cirrhosed; kidneys cystic; brain pale; general atheroma of the arterial walls; blood dark and fluid.—Guy's Hospital; *Med. Times and Gaz.*, p. 591, December 9, 1854.

56. Male, eighteen years, of ruddy complexion, inhaled chloroform in one of the provincial hospitals of England, one day during the quarter ending October, 1854, for the removal of an encysted tumor from under the left eyebrow. The breathing became stertorous, and the inhaler was removed for a time. On a second application, after about half a minute's inhalation, a convulsive attack resembling epilepsy occurred, the man became purple in the face, and almost immediately died. All attempts to restore animation failed. *Autopsy,*—Great congestion of the brain; the left ventricle of the heart was tightly contracted.—*Med. Times and Gaz.*, January 13, 1855.

57. A lady, during the early stage of labor, in the care of a nurse, her physician being absent, inhaled about five drachms of chloroform from a handkerchief, went to sleep, and was found dead and cold when the nurse, who had also fallen asleep, awoke.—*Med. Times and Gaz.*, p. 361, April 14, 1855.

58. Male, forty years, healthy-looking and temperate. Injury of the left eyeball, necessitating its removal for protection to the other. Chloroform was given from Snow's inhaler. During the first four minutes no unusual effect. Suddenly symptoms of excitement appeared, with general muscular rigidity. The anæsthetic was removed, and cold water was poured over the chest. Mouth to mouth insufflation for the space of five to eight minutes. This produced slight sighing efforts at voluntary inspiration, but they finally ceased. The pulse had stopped at the first appearance of dangerous symptoms. *Autopsy*, forty-eight hours after death.—Brain hyperæmic; heart healthy, except some slight deposits on the curtains of the mitral valve, its muscular substance was easily lacerable. The right ventricle contained considerable fluid blood, the left was nearly empty; lungs engorged

with blood ; some pleuritic adhesions ; blood everywhere fluid.—Royal Ophthalmic Hospital, London ; *Med. Times and Gaz.*, p. 353, April 14, 1855.

59. Lady, thirty-six years, married ; had previously taken chloroform four times during the space of a year. Tooth extraction. Chloroform, to the amount of one drachm, was given on a handkerchief. At the end of a minute she spoke intelligibly, but immediately passed into a state of convulsive rigidity, and fell upon the floor with her eyes staring and her mouth open. Dr. J. Y. Simpson reached the patient in five minutes, and commenced artificial respiration and the use of electricity. At times there were feeble appearances of spontaneous respiration, and it was even thought that the pulse returned to the wrist, but everything finally failed. *Autopsy.*—Right cavities of the heart gorged with blood, the muscular wall of the right ventricle was thinner than usual, and had undergone a certain amount of fatty degeneration.—*Edinburgh Med. Times and Gaz.*, p. 552, December 1, 1855 ; Perrin, *ibid.*, p. 309.

60. Female, twenty-nine years, wife of a physician, undertook the self-administration of chloroform, September 8, 1855. Not obtaining the desired effect, ten minims more chloroform were put into the inhaler, and the patient, being seated on a sofa, began to inhale very eagerly, but had no sooner commenced than she gave a sudden start, and died immediately.—Snow, p. 188.

61. January 14, 1856. Death after chloroform given to a patient for amputation of the leg.—Kelso, England ; *Med. Times and Gaz.*, January 26, 1856, p. 103.

62. Male, thirty years, sailor ; intemperate ; delirium tremens two weeks previously. Necrosis of one of the digital phalanges, requiring amputation, October, 1856. One drachm of chloroform was poured on a sponge folded in lint, and given to the patient sitting in a chair. After a little he began to raise his hands, and trembled. He kept spitting into the lint, and appeared as if about to vomit. Suddenly he was violently convulsed. The anæsthetic was removed, and the patient was laid in a semi-recumbent position. The convulsion lasted for only a few seconds, and the breathing was irregular, labored, and puffing. The pulse was intermittent and almost imperceptible. Artificial respiration, pulling the tongue, cold affusion, and ammonia, restored the patient in about a minute, so far that he could breathe without assistance, but in a few seconds he relapsed, and could not be recovered, though electricity and insufflation of oxygen were employed. *Autopsy.*—Brain was pale and its membranes were thickened ; fatty degeneration of the heart, liver, and spleen.—St. Thomas's Hospital ; *Med. Times and Gaz.*, p. 442, November 2, 1856.

63. Male, adult, stage-driver. Fistula in ano. About one drachm on a towel. Four or five inspirations only had been taken, when the countenance changed, the pulse ceased, and the patient was dead. Tongue drawn out ; cold affusions ; artificial respiration ; electricity. *Autopsy*—Fatty degeneration of the heart ; other organs healthy.—Sacramento, Cal., 1856 ; Gibbons : *Pacific Med. and Surg. Jour.*, June, 1869.

64. Male, adult, Chinaman. Compound fracture of the leg, requiring amputation. Chloroform was given in large quantity and rather carelessly. Death before the commencement of the operation.—Columbia, Cal. ; Gibbons : *Pacific Med. and Surg. Jour.*, June, 1869.

65. Male, adult, Chinaman. Removal of a large tumor. Death immediately after operation.—San Francisco ; Gibbons : *Pacific Med. and Surg. Jour.*, June, 1869.

66. Male, fourteen or fifteen years ; inhaled chloroform in the sitting

position, and died suddenly.—"Report of the London Chloroform Committee," Case No. 109.

67. Male, nine years, delicate, nervous, and timid, but without organic disease, except a tumor of the scapula, for which the greater part of that bone was to be removed, February 28, 1857. Patient became insensible in about three minutes. During the removal of the patient to the operating-room he became partially sensible, spoke aloud, and vomited froth. More chloroform was given, in two doses. After a little time the patient made one long inspiration, breathed with stertor a few times, and seemed to pass at once into deep sleep; but suddenly the pulse began to beat very quickly, then ceased for two or three seconds; then it beat rapidly several times with a flickering movement, and then it ceased to be perceptible. Cold sprinkling of the face, and cold air blown upon the face and throat for about two minutes, revived the patient so that he again breathed deeply and freely, about twelve times in the minute. This continued for three minutes, and color returned to the face, and the sounds of the heart could be heard, though the pulse did not return to the wrist. Wine and brandy were poured into the mouth, but in less than two minutes respiration again ceased. Artificial respiration, after the manner of Marshall Hall, was thought beneficial, but soon all signs of life disappeared. At the end of five minutes there was a discharge of fæces, and the patient was dead.—James Paget, notes from private practice: *Med. Times and Gaz.*, March 7, 1857, p. 236.

68. Female, adult; intemperate; during a paroxysm of drunkenness had sustained a compound fracture of the knee. M. Masson, intending to operate at once, administered chloroform; but the patient, once plunged into the anæsthetic sleep, could never, in spite of every effort, be roused again. M. Nélaton believed that the coincidence of alcoholic intoxication in this case determined the fatal result, for he had observed that when dogs were made previously drunk with alcohol, chloroform acted both more promptly and more fatally.—Nélaton: *Med. Times and Gaz.*, p. 149, August, 8, 1857.

69. Male, thirty-five years, had been previously chloroformed six times, and on one of these occasions the femoral artery had been ligated for a popliteal aneurism. This had caused gangrene, necessitating amputation of the thigh, April, 5, 1857. Half a drachm of chloroform was given on lint, soon followed by additional small doses. The patient became insensible, but, just before the commencement of the operation it was found that the pulse had stopped, the pupils were dilated, and respiration had nearly ceased. The head was lowered, the legs were raised, cold affusion upon the face and slapping of the belly were practised. The patient began to breathe again, and at the end of two minutes the pulse could be felt at the wrist. This improvement continued during two or three minutes, and then alarming symptoms again appeared. The pulse stopped once more, and in less than two minutes there was no more breathing. As the heart ceased to beat, the muscles of the leg contracted spasmodically, and a viscous perspiration covered the skin. After practising artificial respiration for half an hour, electricity was tried, but in vain. *Autopsy.*—Brain and lungs healthy; right cavities of the heart contained a little blood mixed with small clots. The blood was liquid, but coagulated slightly when exposed to the air. The muscular tissue of the heart tore easily, but the microscope detected no evidence of fatty degeneration.—Liverpool Infirmary; *Lancet*, p. 429, 1857. Perrin, *ibid.*, p. 313.

70. Female, seventeen years, had twice been chloroformed without accident. Syphilitic warts and mucous tubercles, requiring cauterization with nitric acid, August 7, 1857. One drachm of chloroform was given with

Snow's inhaler.   As soon as the patient became insensible, the inhaling apparatus was removed, and the acid was applied.   In a few minutes, during the stage of recovery, she became pulseless and cold, though she had previously moved her legs, and had urinated in bed.   Artificial respiration and electricity failed to revive her.   *Autopsy.*—Great thickening of mitral valves, and organized lymph in the pericardium, and attached to the surface of the heart; other organs healthy.—King's College Hospital; *Med. Times and Gaz.*, p. 171, August 15, 1857.

71. Male, adult. Died in a dentist's chair, February 1, 1858, after inhaling chloroform for the purpose of having teeth extracted.—Toronto, Canada, *Med. Times and Gaz.*, p. 415, April 17, 1858.

72. Male, forty-nine years; disease of elbow-joint, requiring excision. Chloroform administered on a sponge, to the amount of one drachm. After inhaling for about two minutes, he began to gasp, his limbs moved slowly and irregularly in the death-struggle, and his pulse stopped. Electricity, tracheotomy, and artificial respiration for half an hour. A warm, saline solution was also injected into the cephalic vein, but all without effect. *Autopsy.*—Mitral valve somewhat atheromatous; heart overlaid with fat; right ventricle contained dark, frothy blood; considerable coagulated and fluid blood in the abdominal cavity, probably consequent upon the violence of the artificial respiratory efforts.—Bristol Infirmary, February 12, 1858; *Brit. Med. Journ.*, March 13, 1858.

73. Male, twenty-three years; student, strong and healthy, but much given to beer. A cicatrix on the forehead, requiring an operation. Chloroform, to the amount of six drachms, was given. Great excitement, the patient starting up and tossing his arms about; complete collapse, however, rapidly supervening—all this happening within ten or twelve seconds. Cold affusion, finger in the pharynx, brushing the soles of the feet, and artificial respiration for an hour. Melted sealing-wax was dropped on the chest, and electricity was used, but in vain. *Autopsy.*—Cerebral vessels engorged with blood containing air-bubbles of decomposition; heart relaxed, pale, and empty, its valves and substance healthy; abundant coagula in both venæ cavæ.—Binz, Bonn; *Med. Times and Gaz.*, p. 457, May 1, 1858.

74. Male, thirty years; a French professor of natural history, and healthy. Toothache for several days, for which he had recourse to inhalations of chloroform. He went to bed one evening, suffering great pain. In the morning he was found lying on his side, dead in bed, having in his hands a handkerchief held at a little distance from his mouth. On a table, at the bedside, was a bottle holding chloroform.—*Med. Times and Gaz.*, May 22, 1858.

75. Male, forty-five years; soldier. A tuberculous testicle, requiring castration. Chloroform was given on charpie in a compress, twisted into a cone. After two or three minutes of quiet inhalation, at the first touch of the bistoury the patient suddenly sat upright, with haggard eyes, pupils widely dilated, and his arms stretched out. He then fell back, heaved a sigh, and was dead. Revulsives, tickling the pharynx, præcordial friction, burning coals upon the thorax, artificial respiration, mouth to mouth insufflation, all failed. *Autopsy.*—Brain healthy, and not hyperæmic; lungs full of blood, and loaded, especially the right lung, with miliary tubercles; a large cavity in the apex of the right lung.—Hôpital du Gros-Caillou; *Gaz. des Hôpitaux*, p. 272, 1858; Perrin, *ibid.*, p. 316.

76. Female, a girl. Tooth extraction, August 27, 1858. Chloroform on a napkin was given by a dentist. Death almost immediately after the

extraction.   Epsom, England ; *Med. Times and Gaz.*, p. 248, September 4, 1858.

77. Male, eleven years ; injury of the great toe, necessitating an examination, August 27, 1858.   Chloroform was given on a handkerchief, about fifteen mimims at a dose.   After the patient had apparently become insensible, he made two short, stertorous inspirations.   The anæsthetic was discontinued, but the pulse weakened, and after a few feeble beats ceased to be perceptible, the lips and surface became livid, and a small quantity of frothy mucus ran from the mouth.   Cold affusion, rolling the body over, hot flannels to the epigastrium, failed ; the patient ceased to breathe in about ten minutes.   Ordinary artificial respiration was continued for several minutes longer.—Towcester, England ; *Med. Times and Gaz.*, p. 282, September 11, 1858.

78. Male, eight years.   Double internal strabismus, necessitating operation, October 1, 1858.   Chloroform was given on lint.   The child struggled and cried.   When inhalation had lasted about four minutes, the operation was commenced on the right eye ; but, as he flinched, a fresh dose of chloroform, about half a drachm, was given.   Immediately the face grew pale, and the pulse stopped.   The tongue was drawn forward, and artificial respiration was maintained for three-fourths of an hour, by pressure of the hands on the thorax and abdomen.   During the first twenty minutes the boy gasped several times.   *Autopsy.*—The membranes were congested and adherent to the brain ; lungs, liver, and kidneys intensely congested ; heart healthy.   It was thought that the boy had suffered from meningitis in early infancy.—London Ophthalmic Hospital ; *Med. Times and Gaz.*, p. 374, October 9, 1858.

79. Female, married ; six times pregnant ; had taken chloroform at each confinement.   September 20, 1858, her pains commenced at two A.M.   No one but a nurse was in attendance.   About twenty minutes, to eight A.M., expulsive pains came on, when she called for chloroform.   After breathing it a few times from a handkerchief, she threw herself violently back, gave a gasp or two, a slight gurgle was heard in her throat, and respiration and the pulse instantly ceased.   Her physician arrived on the spot ten minutes later, and found her dead.   The quantity used did not exceed two drachms.—Ayrshire, Scotland ; *Med. Times and Gaz.*, p. 465, November 6, 1858.

80. In a letter, dated November 15, 1858, Dr. Duncan states that he was called to a case of confinement, in which, on arrival, he found that the patient had died suddenly while inhaling a small quantity of chloroform during the pains of labor.—Matthews Duncan, Edinburgh : *Med. Times and Gaz.*, p. 534, November 20, 1858.

81. Male, forty-three years, mechanic.   Dislocation of the left shoulder.   A few drops of chloroform were given on linen, January 16, 1859.   About five drachms were thus given in divided doses.   The patient was considerably excited.   From three to five minutes after the commencement of inhalation the muscles became relaxed, and the dislocation was easily reduced.   It was then found that the pulse had ceased at the wrist, and, though respiration continued calm and deep, the heart had also stopped.   Suddenly, after five or six rapid and deep inspirations, respiration ceased abruptly.   Artificial respiration was continued for more than half an hour, but the only effect was three full inspirations at intervals of several seconds.   *Autopsy* negative.   The heart was flaccid and easily torn.—Hôpital St. Louis ; Perrin, *ibid.*, p. 318.

82. Female, seven and a half years, suspected of onanism.   Coxalgia,

for which forcible extension of the limb was to be performed, February 3, 1859. Chloroform was given, a few drops at a time, on a sponge. Inhalation proceeded quietly to apparent anæsthesia. The surgeon then attempted to extend the thigh, but the child cried out, and made resistance. More chloroform. Apparent resolution. Renewed opposition to forcible movement, when suddenly all outcry and resistance ceased. The countenance had changed, the heart had stopped, and, after three or four feeble inspirations, the breathing ceased also. The head was dropped, and the feet were raised ; the tongue was drawn out, and mouth to mouth insufflation attempted ; but the air merely passed into the stomach, and consequently a sound was introduced through the larynx for further insufflation. Electricity was tried in vain. After three-fourths of an hour all efforts were abandoned. *Autopsy.*—Lungs adherent, cretaceous masses in the apices of both lungs ; cavities of the heart were distended with dark, fluid blood ; brain hyperæmic.—Hôpital Ste. Eugénie ; *Gaz. des Hôpitaux,* p. 71, 1859 ; Perrin, *ibid.,* p. 322.

83. Female, fifteen years, healthy. Strabismus. Chloroform was given on linen cloth. She inhaled the anæsthetic without any unusual symptoms until nearly insensible, when she uttered a sudden and very peculiar shriek. After this she soon became insensible. Soon after the first snip with the scissors her countenance became livid and the pulse disappeared. Artificial respiration aroused slight gasping efforts at inspiration, which recurred at intervals for some time. Movement of the nostrils, as if in the attempt to inspire, were apparent at least half an hour after the pulse had ceased. A brandy enema was given very early in the treatment, at which time the sphincter ani was found quite relaxed. Artificial respiration was maintained for an hour. *Autopsy,* next day.—Left side of the heart empty, the right side contained a small quantity of spumous and fluid blood, with probably not less than two ounces of pus. No organic disease in the body. Numerous spots of extravasation in the lungs, probably caused by the effort at artificial respiration.—Royal Ophthalmic Hospital, London ; *Med. Times and Gaz.,* p. 581, June 4, 1859.

84. Male, sixty years ; suffering from dislocation of the hip. Chloroform was administered, but without the induction of complete anæsthesia. The efforts at reduction of the dislocation were very violent. Twenty minutes after the removal of the anæsthetic, "symptoms of cerebral congestion supervened, which in due course terminated in death." M. Maisonneuve, the operator in the case, exonerated the anæsthetic from all blame in this instance, ascribing death to the severity of the operation.—Hôpital La Pitié, Paris ; *Med. Times and Gaz.,* April 9, 1859.

85.—Male, forty-five years ; requiring incision of the penis and scrotum, on account of extravasation of urine. One drachm and a half of chloroform was given, in two doses, with an inhaler. The anæsthetic was withdrawn as soon as the patient became insensible. The operation occupied about one minute. As it was completed, the pulse fluttered, and ceased. Respiration continued for a minute or two longer ; as soon as it stopped, the trachea was opened, and artificial respiration, with Marcet's apparatus, was kept up for more than half an hour. Electricity and all other restoratives failed. *Autopsy.*—Body very fat ; blood everywhere fluid ; lungs healthy, slightly emphysematous, had not been gorged at death ; heart contained blood in all its cavities, but was not distended ; its walls were thin and very soft. The muscular substance of the heart was in a high degree of fatty degeneration. Kidneys fatty ; brain healthy.—Westminster Hospital ; *Medical Times and Gaz.,* p. 81, July 23, 1859.

86. Male, twenty-eight years; irritable temperament, and intemperate. Dislocation of the ankle-joint, followed by erysipelas, necessitating amputation of the leg, August 8, 1859, nearly two months after the original accident. The patient drank stout and brandy a short time before the operation. Chloroform was given—one drachm—with an inhaler. About half of it had been inhaled when the pulse weakened. The anæsthetic was withdrawn, but the face of the patient became pale, he gasped a few times, emptied his bladder, and died. Brandy enema; electricity; artificial respiration for half an hour. *Autopsy.*—Heart and lungs healthy; liver slightly enlarged, but healthy; spleen very soft; kidneys healthy, though the left was twice the size of the right; on the under surface of the anterior portion of the right middle lobe of the brain were the remains of an old clot; there was a similar condition of the under surface of the anterior lobe of the same side, the olfactory bulb being destroyed. No other deviation from healthy structure.—St. Thomas's Hospital; *Med. Times and Gaz.*, p. 194, August 20, 1859.

87. Male, adult; application of nitric acid to syphilitic sores, October 22, 1859. Two drachms and a half of chloroform were given, in divided doses, on lint. The acid was applied before the induction of complete anæsthesia. The patient resisted; struggled to get free; then turned pale, and died. Pulse and respiration ceased at once.—Dreadnought Hospital Ship; "Report of the Chloroform Committee," Case No. 73.

88. Male, fifty-seven years; waiter at a low public-house; very intemperate. Fracture of the tibia and fibula, extending into the knee-joint. Delirium tremens set in next day. On the following morning, November 7, 1859, chloroform, half a drachm on lint, was given to quiet his raving. After three inspirations the man writhed, and fell back dead. *Autopsy.*—No disease anywhere, except slight deposits on the tricuspid and mitral valves. —London Hospital; *Med. Times and Gaz.*, p. 503, November 19, 1859.

89. Female, fifty years; domestic. Dislocation of the right shoulder. Chloroform was given, November 21, 1859, with a view to reduction of the dislocation. The operation was easily performed, and the surgeon had left the patient, when an assistant observed that the patient scarcely breathed. The usual attempts to resuscitate the body were made, and a few inspirations followed, but the heart remained motionless. *Autopsy.*—The right lung was contused, and there was pleural adhesion; concentric hypertrophy of the heart, without valvular disease; brain hyperæmic, but healthy; the other organs were healthy.—Hôpital la Charité, Paris; *Gaz. des Hôpitaux*, p. 550, 1859; Perrin, *ibid.*, p. 333.

90. Male, twenty-six years; physician. Ingrowing toe-nail, for which the nail was to be removed January 1, 1860. Chloroform was inhaled from a towel which the patient held in his own hands. After the operation, which did not occupy more than two minutes, had been finished, he did not awaken. Cold affusion produced no effect. After a few minutes the breathing became less frequent and more labored; his countenance began to change, and the pulse became imperceptible. Artificial respiration was continued for half an hour, but all in vain.—Alloa, Scotland; *Med. Times and Gaz.*, p. 26, January 7, 1860.

91. Male, twenty-nine years; of lymphatic temperament. Removal of a small cystic tumor from the external angle of the right upper eyelid, January 14, 1860. Chloroform was given slowly on cloth. Strong muscular contractions, especially of the sterno-cleido-mastoid muscles, soon occurred, with frequent pulse, and lively injection of the face. The anæsthetic was withdrawn, but the patient passed at once into collapse. He fell back, and

made three deep inspirations, followed by the discharge of mucus from the mouth and nose.   The heart stopped beating, and, after a few distant inspirations, breathing also ceased.   The face grew pale, the eyeballs were turned upward, and the extremities became cold.   All this took place within two minutes.   Only two drachms of chloroform had been used.   *Autopsy.* —Extensive pleuritic adhesions and ecchymoses ; lungs hyperæmic, vesicular dilatation at their apices ; veins turgid ; two small clots in the right ventricle, dilatation of the auriculo-ventricular orifices ; brain hyperæmic. —San José Hospital, Lisbon ; Perrin, *ibid.*, p. 335.

92. Female, adult ; in the habit of frequently inhaling large quantities of chloroform.   June 9, 1860, she inhaled chloroform from a napkin held by her little daughter, a girl ten years old, until death occurred ; she had twice previously, on the same day, made herself insensible with the same anæsthetic.—Doncaster, England ; "Report of the Chloroform Committee," Case No. 77.

93. An old woman, insane, and violent.   The governor of the institution, a non-medical man, undertook to quiet her with chloroform, administered on lint.   The patient struggled violently, and knocked the lint out of the administrator's hand.   It was reapplied to her face, and after about a minute she became insensible, and in the course of about ten minutes it was discovered that she was dead.   *Autopsy.*—"Congestion of the lungs" was assigned as the cause of death.—Liverpool Workhouse ; *Med. Times and Gaz.*, July 28, 1860.

94. Male, forty years ; chancre under the prepuce, requiring circumcision.   Chloroform, to the amount of an ounce and a half, was given in divided doses upon a napkin.   After four or five minutes the patient gave a sudden, stertorous inspiration.   The napkin was removed, and, after noisy breathing for about a minute, respiration ceased.   Artificial respiration excited a few inspiratory efforts, but they soon ceased.   The pulse had also disappeared, and the sounds of the heart could not be heard.   Electricity, insufflation with a tracheal tube and bellows, and a brandy enema, failed ; and at the end of an hour and ten minutes the case was abandoned.   *Autopsy.*—Small patches of old lymph on both hemispheres, brain otherwise healthy ; lungs collapsed, but healthy ; heart soft and flabby, its muscular tissue had undergone fatty degeneration, one or two atheromatous patches on the curtains of the mitral valve ; other organs apparently healthy, but hyperæmic.—Bellevue Hospital, New York ; *Am. Med. Times*, p. 99, August 11, 1860.

95. Male, forty-two years ; intemperate.   Tumor upon the back.   Chloroform was given on a handkerchief.   Its effects were soon visible upon the patient, who became insensible without any unusual phenomena.   On turning him over, to reach his back, it was observed that his countenance was much changed.   Artificial respiration was employed in vain for an hour.   *Autopsy.*—Great hyperæmia of the brain, heart and lungs.—Northampton Infirmary ; *Med. Times and Gaz.*, p. 319, September 29, 1860.

96. Male, fifty-five years ; very intemperate.—King's College Hospital ; "Report of the Chloroform Committee," Case No. 82.

97. Male, twenty-six years. Ingrowing toe-nail, for which removal was proposed. Chloroform was given on charpie in a paper cone, applied to the nose, leaving the mouth free. At the end of two minutes no effect had been produced, and a few drops were added. Soon he became restless, tossing his limbs about, sitting up, and repeating unconnected words. More chloroform. The agitation soon disappeared, and complete resolution followed. The anæsthetic was then withdrawn, and the operation was

quickly performed. As this was finished, a moan was heard, and the patient became pale and pulseless. Cold affusion and artificial respiration produced several respiratory movements, but the pulse did not return. Tickling the pharynx, and mouth to mouth insufflation did no good. *Autopsy.*— Old pleuritic adhesions and pulmonary apoplexy.—Dr. Fano, Paris; *Gaz. des Hôpitaux*, No. 142, 1860 ; Perrin, *ibid.*, p 338.

98. Male, forty years, healthy and strong ; crushed his leg by a fall from his horse, and fainted at the moment of the accident. Six or eight hours afterward, being in a state of great fear and agitation, he insisted upon having chloroform before undergoing the amputation of the leg which was deemed necessary. The surgeons, dreading the use of chloroform under such circumstances, determined to make only a pretence of giving the anæsthetic, and accordingly placed it at a long distance from his face. Scarcely, however, had he drawn four inspirations when respiration and circulation suddenly ceased, in spite of every effort for their restoration.—Bordeaux ; *Gaz. des Hôpitaux*, p. 8, 1861 ; Perrin, *ibid.*, p. 338.

99. Male, thirty-one years, compositor, intemperate. Delirium tremens. Chloroform, between one and two drachms, given on a handkerchief, to procure sleep. For two or three minutes the patient inhaled quietly. He then became violently excited, struggling to escape from a spectral figure which seemed to be trying to take away his boots. Excitement continuing for about two minutes, another half-drachm was added. After several inspirations he fell back, and breathed with difficulty. Artificial respiration caused three sighing respirations, growing fainter, and at longer intervals, and then all was still.—Robert Dobbie, London ; *Med. Times and Gaz.*, p. 683, June 29, 1861.

100. Male, adult, in the prime of life ; an eminent physician. Toothache. Going to a dentist, he insisted upon chloroforming himself, April 6, 1861. Extraction was quickly effected, when a movement of the head seemed to indicate pain. Convulsive movements of the face and limbs immediately followed, and the face became purple. In spite of every effort, the convulsions increased in severity, and the patient expired about five minutes after the extraction of the tooth.—Island of Mauritius ; *Union Médicale*, p. 580, 1861 ; Perrin, *ibid.*, p. 336.

101. Male, thirty-two years ; scrofulous disease of the left knee-joint, requiring amputation of the thigh, September 3, 1861. Patient was very anxious, and took brandy prior to inhalation. Two drachms of chloroform were used on cloth. No excitement. The tourniquet was being adjusted, when a sudden relaxation of the sphincters took place, the pupils dilated, the pulse ceased, and respiration continued but a few seconds longer. Electricity, artificial respiration, and other means availed nought. *Autopsy.* —Right side of the heart gorged with blood ; no other abnormal appearances.—Newcastle-on-Tyne Infirmary ; *Med. Times and Gaz.*, p. 321, September 28, 1861.

102. Male, thirty-five years ; carpenter. Stricture of the urethra and retention of urine, requiring catheterization, September 5, 1861. Two drachms of chloroform were given on lint. Anæsthesia was reached without unusual symptoms. The lint was then removed, and the operation was commenced. After about two minutes the lips became livid, the eyelids were half open, and the pupils dilated. The patient then drew a deep inspiration, and the pulse ceased almost immediately. Electricity and artificial respiration, for twenty minutes, produced no more than three or four spasmodic efforts at inspiration. *Autopsy.*—Slight hyperæmia of heart, lungs and liver ; blood everywhere fluid ; the whole structure of the

left kidney was converted into ten abscess-cavities, varying in size from a hazel-nut to a pigeon's egg, and filled with a mixture of pus and a thinner, clear fluid ; left ureter much thickened, and filled with thick pus ; right kidney weighed six ounces and a half, but was healthy ; coats of the bladder thickened.—Cumberland Infirmary ; *Med. Times and Gaz.*, p. 321, September 28, 1861.

103. Male, fifty years ; large and muscular.   Removal of internal piles. Chloroform on a sponge, two drachms at first, followed by forty or fifty minims.   Great excitement, struggling and shouting.   While this yet continued, some stertor appeared, and the sponge was removed.   The face was livid, the pulse ceased, and the respiration was becoming visibly slower.   Slapping the chest with a wet towel, and artificial respiration, excited a few gasping inspirations. . Blood was taken from the turgid jugular vein, and electricity was tried.   At the end of an hour it was clear that the patient was dead.   *Autopsy.*—Heart was loaded with fat, its walls thin and weak, the muscular substance of its right side had undergone fatty degeneration ; the right cavities were gorged with blood ; all other organs were healthy.—W. E. C. Nourse, Brighton, England : *Med. Times and Gaz.*, p. 490, November 9, 1861.

104. Male, eight years ; had suffered deformity caused by a burn in the chin, turning the lower lip inside out.   A plastic operation was to be performed.   Chloroform was given for ten minutes before insensibility was complete.   Just before the conclusion of the operation, the patient died instantly.   Artificial respiration for half an hour.   He was then put in a warm bath, and electricity was used for an hour and a half without success.   *Autopsy.*—Not a trace of disease anywhere.—St. Mary's Hospital ; *Med. Times and Gaz.*, p. 519, November 16, 1861.

105. Male, nineteen years ; medical student.   Was in the habit of sniffing chloroform.   After dinner he went to his bed-room as usual, and locked the door.   Some hours later, making no reply to knocks and calls, the door was broken open, when he was found lying on the bed, dressed, with a cap and pocket-handkerchief over his face.   The handkerchief was inside the cap, and appeared to have been saturated with chloroform. There was a bottle of chloroform near, from which about four drachms had been taken.   *Autopsy* negative.—Notting Hill Dispensary ; *Med. Times and Gaz.*, p. 625, December 14, 1861.

106. Male, sailor.   Extirpation of an enlarged gland.   Before insensibility was fully induced, the pulse weakened and gradually failed, though respiration continued with great regularity.   At the end of twenty minutes the heart ceased to beat.   *Autopsy.*—Lungs, liver, and kidneys engorged with blood ; heart small, soft, and loaded with external fat.—Hobart Town, Tasmania ; *Brit. Med. Jour.*, May, 1862.

107. Male, intoxicated.   Chloroform was given to facilitate the reduction of a fractured ankle.   No particulars.—University College Hospital ; " Report of the Chloroform Committee," Case No. 89.

108. Male, above the middle period of life.   Cancer of the penis, for which amputation was to be performed.   The gentleman in charge of the chloroform, considering the momentary nature of the operation, purposely abstained from giving it as fully as usual, and had removed the cloth containing it from the face before the operation was commenced.   The surgeon now placed his finger on the patient's wrist, and, having ascertained that the pulse was good, at once effected the amputation almost instantaneously.   The passage of the knife through the member was accompanied by a start of the patient's body ; the bandage used to control the bleeding was

then removed, but no blood flowed from the arteries ; he was found to have no pulse at the wrist ; in short, he was dead.—J. Lister : Holmes' "System of Surgery," vol. v., p. 483.

109. Female, adult. Chloroform given for painless examination of an injured shoulder-joint. She was not completely insensible, and died suddenly during the examination.—Bellevue Hospital, New York ; *Boston Med. and Surg. Journ.*, March 20, 1862.

110. Male, thirty-three years ; healthy-looking. Cauterization of a sloughing sore on the penis. One drachm of chloroform was given in an inhaler. Very restless, resisting the vapor. Another drachm was given, when he struggled violently. Suddenly he sank back, with dilated pupils, and pulseless at the wrist. The inhaler was removed, and he gasped for breath at intervals during half a minute. Cold affusion, artificial respiration, brandy enema, ammonia, pressure over the cardiac region, etc., produced no effect, though efforts at resuscitation were continued for more than an hour. *Autopsy* negative.—Devon and Exeter Hospital, 1862 ; *Med. Times and Gaz.*, p. 21, January 7, 1865.

111. Male, thirty-six years. Chloroform was given with an inhaler. One drachm being insufficient, half a drachm more was added, and, after a few inhalations the muscles became rigid and he tried to raise himself in bed, when he suddenly fell back, the pulse stopped, and he was dead.—St. Mary's Hospital, January 12, 1862 ; "Report of the Chloroform Committee," Case No. 92.

112. Female, thirty-eight years ; weak and irritable. Vesico-vaginal fistula. Chloroform given with an inhaler, to the amount of two and a half to three drachms. Six or seven minutes after the commencement of inhalation the muscles became rigid, producing complete opisthotonus and suspension of respiration. The whole surface was pale, lips somewhat livid ; pulse imperceptible, though the heart continued to act feebly for some minutes after. Artificial respiration for an hour and a quarter ; electricity ; cold affusion, etc., all failed. *Autopsy.*—Heart flabby and undergoing fatty degeneration, both sides containing dark blood ; liver and lungs normal, but much engorged ; brain and membrane healthy.—Guy's Hospital, April 11, 1862 ; *Med. Times and Gaz.*, p. 669, June 28, 1862.

113. Female, forty years ; removal of a tumor on the lower jaw. Two drachms of chloroform were given, in two doses, on a napkin. Insensibility was reached at the end of six minutes. The tumor was then laid bare, occupying four minutes. The patient seemed to be growing sensible, and another drachm was poured upon the napkin. She took one inspiration, when the pulse stopped. The napkin was then removed ; she made three or four gasping inspirations, and in half a minute was dead. *Autopsy.* —Fatty degeneration of the heart.—United Hospital, Bath, June 21, 1862 ; *Med. Times and Gaz.*, p. 676, June 28, 1862.

114. Male, a soldier ; robust and healthy. After the battle of Hanover Court House, May 29, 1862, underwent amputation of the thigh. Operation in the open air. He inhaled chloroform very freely, and expired just as the operation was completed. He had lost but little blood.—"Circular No. 6, Surgeon-General's Office, U.S.A.," p. 87.

115. Male, soldier, a prisoner ; had a gunshot flesh wound of the hip. A slight incision for the extraction of the ball was made, October 19, 1862, at Hospital No. 5, Frederick, Maryland. The patient expired suddenly. *Autopsy* negative.—"Circular No. 6, Surgeon-General's Office, U.S.A." p. 87.

116. Male, soldier ; chloroformed October 12, 1862, to undergo amputa-

tion of the right middle and index fingers.   He died in the midst of the operation.   *Autopsy.*—Slight calcareous deposits about the valves of the heart.—"Circular No. 6, Surgeon-General's Office, U.S.A.," p. 87.

117. Female, seventeen years; very nervous, suffering from an offensive, mortifying wound, caused by a fall against an iron railing. Death was produced shortly after the chloroform was administered. *Autopsy.*—A feeble, flabby heart.—King's College Hospital, August 8, 1862 ; *Med. Times and Gaz.*, p. 186, August 23, 1862.

118. Male, sixteen years ; suffering with a diseased condition of the great toe, necessitating amputation.   Chloroform was administered without an inhaler.   Death occurred five minutes after the commencement of inhalation.—Norwich, England ;. *Am. Med. Times*, p. 106, from *The Lancet*, August 23, 1862.

119. Male, thirty-three years ; the subject of a fistula.   His physician had examined the head and heart prior to causing chloroform to be administered, and found nothing to create doubt.   Chloroform was administered without an inhaling apparatus.   Mr. Gant, of the Royal Free Hospital, found the heart and lungs extensively diseased.—*Am. Med. Times*, p. 106, from *The Lancet*, August 23, 1862.

120. Male, twenty-three years ; chimney-sweep.   Abscess in and about the knee-joint, necessitating amputation of the thigh.   Examination indicated healthy lungs and heart.   Chloroform was given with Snow's inhaler. There was a little excitement in the first stage, but this soon subsided, and the patient passed into a tranquil sleep.   Just as the surgeon was preparing to commence the operation, the patient made a noise as if about to vomit, and immediately ceased to breathe.   The sounds of the heart could not be heard.   Tracheotomy at once, and inflation of the lungs with a flexible tube introduced through the opening,   Stimulants, ammonia, cold affusion, artificial respiration, and electricity, all failed.   *Autopsy*, three hours and three-quarters after death.—All the internal organs were in a state of almost typical health.—Hospital at Stroud, England, October 23, 1862 ; *Med. Times and Gaz.*, p. 482, November 1, 1862.

121. Male, twenty-three years ; wasted and debilitated.   A considerable quantity of chloroform was given on lint.   The man moved the limb slightly, and more chloroform was applied, when he suddenly became deathly pale, and his pulse ceased.—London Hospital, October, 1862 ; *Report of the Chloroform Committee*, Case No. 99.

122. Female, twenty-nine years ; about to have a small tumor of the gum (epulis?) removed.   About one drachm of chloroform was used. Death occurred suddenly in less than four minutes from the commencement of inhalation.—London, April 1, 1863 ; *Report of the Chloroform Committee*, Case No. 102 ; *Med. Times and Gaz.*, p. 441, April 25, 1863.

123. Male.   Put under chloroform for the reduction of a dislocation ; he bore the anæsthetic one day very well, but the reduction was not effected.   The next day, when he was only half way under chloroform, his death occurred instantaneously.—Guy's Hospital ; *Med. Times and Gaz.*, p. 446, April 25, 1863.

124. Male, twenty-eight years ; intemperate, and in poor health.   Had taken chloroform without accident four months before. On the present occasion the anæsthetic was given with an inhaler.   The patient had a sort of tetanic spasm, with opisthotonus, and the pulse ceased almost immediately.— King's College Hospital ; *Report of the Chloroform Committee*, Case No. 107.

125. Male, thirty-one years ; physician.   Self-administration of chloroform.—London ; *Med. Times and Gaz.*, June 6, 1863.

126. Female. Put under the influence of chloroform for the removal of a tumor from the back of the neck. The operation was skilfully performed, but the insensibility of the patient was so prolonged as to cause serious uneasiness. At the end of half an hour a spasmodic action of the limbs seemed to indicate that she was about to be aroused, but this was in fact only a convulsion terminating in death.—Lyons, France ; *Med. Times and Gaz.*, p. 237, August 29, 1863.

127. Male, forty-two years. Two drachms of chloroform were given on lint. About one minute after the second drachm was applied, the man struggled and tried to raise himself ; the pulse suddenly failed, and death took place immediately.—London Hospital, September 23, 1863 ; *Report of the Chloroform Committee*, Case No. 103.

128. Female, sixteen. Died from the effects of chloroform when about to undergo a surgical operation.—Finsbury Place, London ; *Med. Times and Gaz.*, p. 471, October 31, 1863.

129. Male, thirty years. Chloroform was given with an inhaler.—St. George's Hospital, September 24, 1863 ; *Report of the Chloroform Committee,* Case No. 104.

130. Female, sixteen years. Took chloroform while sitting on a chair. About four drachms and a half were given on a handkerchief.—Salisbury, England, November 7, 1863 ; *Report of the Chloroform Committee*, Case No. 105.

131. Male, active, prisoner. Death occurred during the passage of a catheter while under the influence of chloroform. Half an ounce of chloroform had been given. Death was said to have been caused by syncope. Twenty ounces of blood were drawn, without effect.—Pentridge, Australia ; *Med. Times and Gaz.*, p. 382, April 2, 1864.

132. Male. Had been bathing a limb with a liniment containing chloroform. His wife found him lying dead on the floor, with the bottle and a handkerchief saturated with the fluid, by his side. *Autopsy.*—The lungs were very much congested from the effects of the inhalation of the chloroform.—Syracuse, N. Y., February, 1864 ; *Amer. Med. Times ; Med. Times and Gaz.*, p. 382, April 2, 1864.

133. Female, twenty-nine years ; married. Removal of a tumor from the urethra. Had taken chloroform safely for a similar purpose two years previously.—King's College Hospital, June 24, 1864 ; *Med. Times and Gaz.*, p. 9, July 2, 1864.

134. Female, of a very nervous temperament, placed in a dentist's chair to have a tooth extracted. While much excited by fear, she inhaled chloroform from a napkin. After a short time, she declared she could not take it, and snatched the napkin from her face. Without further administration the tooth was easily extracted ; but the jaws were immediately clenched, and the head was drawn backward. Respiration was arrested, the face grew livid, and death rapidly ensued, apparently from asphyxia due to spasmodic closure of the glottis. The tonic spasm of the muscles continued until after death.—San Francisco, Cal.; *Boston Med. and Surg. Jour.*, May 19, 1864.

135. Male, eight years. "Great-toe case." Sudden death.—St. Mary's Hospital ; *Med. Times and Gaz.*, August 6, 1864.

136. Male, soldier. Necrosis of carpal bones. Chloroform was inhaled for an operation, September 3, 1864. Sudden death ensued. *Autopsy.*— Fibrinous coagula in the auricles.—"Circular No. 6, Surgeon-General's Office, U.S.A.," p. 87.

137. Male, colonel. Excision of a phalanx of the left index finger.

Sudden death before the commencement of the operation. *Autopsy* negative.—"Circular No. 6, Surgeon-General's Office, U.S.A.," p. 87.

138. Male, soldier. Removal of a ball, by incision, from the calf of the right leg, November 29, 1864. Sudden death.—"Circular No. 6, Surgeon-General's Office, U.S.A.," p. 87.

139. Male, fifteen years. Amputation of leg. Everything went on well till the completion of the operation, when it was found that the circulation had ceased.—United Hospital, Bath, October, 1864 ; *Med. Times and Gaz.*, p. 402, October 8, 1864.

140. Male, twenty-four years ; healthy. Compound fracture of the metatarsal bone of the great toe, necessitating removal of a portion of the bone. Forty mimims of chloroform were given with Snow's inhaler. Inhalation proceeded well for two or three minutes, when the pulse suddenly became imperceptible, and the anæsthetic was withdrawn. After a few seconds the respiration became deep and sobbing, and the tongue was protruded between the teeth. After the cessation of the pulse, respiration continued for a full minute, and not until still later did the face become congested, or the pupils dilated. Brandy enema, ammonia to the nostrils, electricity to the cardiac region, and Sylvesterism for half an hour. *Autopsy*, six hours after death.—Right pleural surfaces everywhere adherent ; both lungs healthy ; both ventricles contracted and empty ; some blood in the auricles, especially in the right, valves healthy, no degeneration of the heart-substance. Liver and kidneys hyperæmic ; brain and membranes healthy.—Devon and Exeter Hospital, November 1, 1864 ; *Med. Times and Gaz.*, p. 20, January 7, 1865.

141. Male, private soldier. Gunshot wound of the leg, for which amputation had been performed, September 28, 1864, under chloroform. Sloughing of the flap necessitated reamputation. Patient was nervous from dread of the operation. Half an ounce of chloroform was given on a sponge. The patient began to sink about fifteen minutes after the commencement of inhalation, and at the end of five minutes death took place. *Autopsy*.—The heart and lungs were found quite healthy.—Beverly Hospital, U.S.A., November 15, 1864 ; *Am. Jour. Med. Sci.*, January, 1865.

142. Male, private soldier, expired suddenly, May 13, 1865, while inhaling chloroform preparatory to a surgical operation.—"Circular No. 6, Surgeon-General's Office."

143. Male, fifteen years, a twin. Chloroform was given on a napkin, to the amount of about three drachms. After inhaling quietly for about twelve minutes, the patient seemed to be insensible, and the operation was commenced. Simultaneously with the entrance of the knife, the boy screamed and made two convulsive movements. The heart ceased to beat almost at the instant of the second spasm. Two or three convulsive respirations followed the attempts at resuscitation, and then life was extinct. *Autopsy* negative.—Bath United Hospital, 1864 ; *Med. Times and Gaz.*, p. 289, March 18, 1865.

144. Male. Dislocation of the shoulder, reduced during complete anæsthesia. The patient was dead on the completion of the operation.—Jarjaway, Hôpital Beaujon ; *Lancet*, June 24, 1865 ; Kappeler : Case No. 1.

145. Child two years. Thirty drops of chloroform were given on lint, for the removal of a fungus. Death occurred five minutes after the commencement of inhalation.—Ophthalmic Hospital ; *Brit. Med. Jour.*, p. 647, June 24, 1865 ; Kappeler : Case No. 2.

146. Female, adult. Accustomed to inhale chloroform for the relief of pain. Feeling indisposed, she retired about eight o'clock in the evening.

11

At six o'clock the next morning she was found dead in her bed, with a handkerchief containing chloroform upon her face.—Anstruther, Scotland ; *Med. Times and Gaz.*, p. 240, August 26, 1865.

147. Male, four and one-half years ; pale and sickly, having suffered with nephritis and dropsy. Chloroform was given on a cloth, for the painless introduction of a catheter. The child cried, but soon became insensible. The anæsthetic was then withdrawn, and the catheter was introduced. After this operation the child began to breathe badly, the lips became blue, and the jugular veins were distended. The respiration now ceased, and the pulse stopped. Tickling the pharynx excited a deep inspiration, and tracheotomy was followed by another. Artificial respiration and galvano-puncture of the heart did no good.—Hüter : *Berliner klin. Wochenschr.*, December 3, 1865 ; Kappeler : Case No. 3.

148. Female, seventeen years. Had frequently taken chloroform for the painless extraction of teeth. Twenty-five minims were now given on a napkin. After a few inhalations the patient became very violent, but she at length seemed to be insensible. The dentist then attempted to extract the tooth, but found the jaws clenched. He forced them open and drew the tooth. He then went for a glass of water, and, on returning, was alarmed by one or two long, yawning respirations. The pupils were dilated, the pulse disappeared, and she was dead. *Autopsy.*—Left side of the heart contracted and empty. Other organs healthy.—Gillespie : *Edinburgh Med. Jour.*, January 1866 ; Kappeler : Case No. 6.

149. Death from chloroform given for the removal of an ingrowing toe-nail.—St. Mary's Hospital, London ; *Med. Times and Gaz.*, p. 107, January 27, 1866.

150. Male, fifty-one years, aural surgeon. Had been experimenting with chloroform, with a view to the passing of the vapor through the Eustachian tubes into the tympanum. Was found dead upon his sofa with a layer of cotton-wool over his face. Before him lay memoranda of the previous experiments, and of that which he was then conducting.—London, July 7, 1866 ; *Med. Times and Gaz.*, p. 46, July 14, 1866.

151. Female, adult. Tooth-extraction. Sudden death, after a few inspirations of the vapor.—Philadelphia ; *L'Union*, June 1, 1866 ; Kappeler : Case No. 4.

152. Male, twenty-seven years ; laborer, strong and healthy. Chloroform was given on a handkerchief for an operation upon a crushed finger. Soon after the induction of complete anæsthesia, the patient snored, and the pulse disappeared. Artificial respiration revived the pulse and respiration, but suddenly they again ceased, and could not be re-excited, though every expedient, including electro-puncture of the heart, was attempted.—Hüter : *Berliner klin. Wochenschr.*, p. 303, 1866 ; Kappeler : Case No. 5.

153. Male, a boy. Lithotomy. Death before the commencement of the operation. The heart and lungs stopped almost simultaneously.—Birkenhead, England ; *Med. Times and Gaz.*, p. 560, November 24, 1866.

154. Male, laborer ; much reduced by hemorrhage and septic fever. Amputation of thigh. After a few inspirations, before operation could be commenced, he became wildly delirious, and died almost immediately. Electricity, artificial respiration, etc., were ineffectual.—Lingen : *Petersb. med. Zeitschrift*, xii., Hft. 2 u. 3, 1867 ; Köhler, *Schmid's Jahrb.*, Bd. 145 ; Kappeler : Case No. 7.

155. Male, thirty-five years. Removal of a ligature from spermatic cord. Had been twice previously chloroformed—the first time with about two ounces, the second time with half an ounce. At the present time

about one ounce was given.   Inhalation proceeded quietly until the patient seemed about to become insensible, when he suddenly began to struggle violently, and became stertorous.   Convulsive movements, opisthotonus, etc., endured for about half a minute, when the pulse stopped.   Electricity, artificial respiration, etc.   Left heart contracted and empty.   Right heart full of blood.   No fatty degeneration.   Aorta dilated.   Considerable increase of cerebro-spinal fluid, and serous effusion into the arachnoid space. —Dubois, New York: *Med. Record*, vol. ii., No. 41; *Schmid's Jahrb.*, Bd. 145, 1870.

156. Male, forty-five years.   For reduction of a dislocated thumb.   The pulse stopped suddenly after inhaling for three minutes the vapor of one drachm from Clover's inhaler.   *Autopsy* gave no information.—*Brit. Med. Jour.*, March 2, 1867; Kappeler: Case No. 9.

157. Male.   At first was made to inhale a mixture of chloroform and ether, 1:2.   Respiration was interrupted, necessitating recourse to Marshall Hall's method of artificial respiration.   Thus restored he was made to inhale pure chloroform from a cloth in a paper cone, which finished him at once.—Cutter, New York: *Med. Record*, vol. xxx., p. 138, 1867; *Schmid's Jahrb.*, Bd. 145, 1870.

158. J. B., male, aged sixteen.   Sebaceous cystic tumor of the neck, adhering to the thyroid membrane.   Habits intemperate.   Subject to fainting-fits, of which one had occurred ten days before the operation.   During the course of the operation the patient began to struggle and to vociferate violently.   Operation completed amidst great struggling and resistance on the part of the patient.   Hemorrhage thus caused could not be arrested until chloroform was again given.   Several minutes after the completion of the operation and the withdrawal of the chloroform, the pulse suddenly ceased to beat.   "Respiration still continued, but in a few instants it became slower and then stopped."   Electricity excited a few inspirations, but they soon ceased.   *Autopsy* showed that no air had entered the veins.   No coagula in any of the cardiac cavities.   Mitral valve somewhat thickened.—Broca: *Gaz. des Hôpitaux*, 125, 1867; Kappeler: Case No. 11.

159. Female, twenty-one years; strong constitution.   Chloroformed, July 24, for excision of condylomata of the vulva.   August 14th, again chloroformed in horizontal position for the same purpose.   A few drops were placed on a cloth at a distance of three centimetres from the patient's face. She had inhaled for less than a minute and a half, when she began to struggle and to breathe badly.   The chloroform was suspended, though pulse and respiration still continued.   Suddenly she voided her urine, became red in the face, and ceased to breathe.   The head was depressed, tongue drawn forward, artificial respiration, etc., continued for half an hour in vain.   *Autopsy* revealed hyperæmia of brain and lungs; enlargement of three bronchial glands, compressing the pneumogastric nerve; enlargement of the spleen, with increase of the number of white corpuscles in the blood; and fatty degeneration of the heart.—Desprès; *Bull. de Thér.*, lxxiii., December 30, 1867; Kappeler: Case No. 12.

160. Girl, nine years. Strabismus. Chloroform carefully given till one drachm and a half had been administered, when the pupils suddenly dilated, and respiration ceased.   Notwithstanding artificial respiration, death was complete about two hours later.—University College Hospital; *Lancet*, June 1, 1867; Kappeler: Case No. 13.

161. Boy, fifteen years.   Operation on the knee-joint.   All went well till the end of the operation, when the pulse suddenly stopped.   Artificial

respiration was maintained for an hour, but without success.—Southern Hospital, Liverpool; *Lancet*, September 21, 1867; Kappeler: Case No. 14.

162. A lady, twenty years; in apparent good health. Extraction of teeth. Three days previously had taken chloroform, and had six molar teeth drawn, without any bad effect. On the present occasion she inhaled the vapor of about one drachm of chloroform for a similar purpose, but suddenly she expired.—Dr. C. R. Parke, Bloomington, Illinois: *Chicago Med. Exam.*, January, 1867.

163. Male. Ligation of external iliac artery.—Hospital at Toronto, Canada; *Med. News and Library*, p. 59, April, 1867.

164. Boy, fifteen years. Removal of necrosed bone from the stump of an amputated thigh. Between two and three drachms of chloroform were used. Autopsy revealed great hyperæmia of the lungs and the right side of the heart.—North Staffordshire Infirmary, March 2, 1867; *Lancet*, April 6, 1867.

165. Woman, twenty-one years. In the habit of inhaling chloroform for the relief of headache. "She locked herself in her room and was found some hours after, dead, with her head resting upon her hands, which retained a folded cloth and a sponge in contact with the nostrils and mouth. She had been dead some hours, and the rigor mortis was marked. . . . A half-ounce vial, containing a little chloroform, was found in her bosom." —Dr. B. E. Cotting: *Boston Med. and Surg. Journ.*, July 18, 1867.

166. George Gillard. Death from syncope while inhaling chloroform. —Taunton Hospital; *Lancet*, May 11, 1867.

167. John Arnold, eight years. Operation for strabismus under chloroform. "About two hours afterward he expired."—Eye Hospital, Manchester, England; *Brit. Med. Journ.*, July 13, 1867.

168. C. R., male, forty-six years. Mate of the ship Countess of Sefton. Being unwell, chloroform was administered in quantity less than usual, as the doctor had examined the patient and suspected a fatty heart. As soon as the patient became insensible his breathing stopped. Autopsy indicated death from syncope.—Northern Hospital, Liverpool; *Brit. Med. Journ.*, May 9, 1868; Kappeler: Case No. 15.

169. Girl, twelve years. In fair health. Caries about the ankle-joint. After inhalation, from a folded napkin, for three or four minutes, the patient seemed to be quite insensible. The surgeon began to explore the fistula with his finger, when she awoke and cried out grievously. Respiration and circulation were regular and vigorous. The napkin was again applied to her face. After a few minutes the pulse suddenly fell about fifteen beats and became very weak. The patient again cried out and became pale, the eyes rolled up, the pupils dilated. Respiration was stertorous, then sighing, finally ceased. *Autopsy.*—Brain and its membranes free from congestion. Lungs, especially the right lung, full of dark blood. Pericardium loaded with fat. Heart normal, both sides containing liquid blood, small clots on right side; right ventricle thin and flaccid; left ventricle contracted and nearly empty; valves healthy; large fibrin-clots entangled behind the mitral valve and the right auriculo-ventricular opening. Patient had been successfully anæsthetized four days previously, using two ounces of chloroform.—Cowling, Philadelphia: *Med. and Surg. Rep.*, vol. xviii., 6, p. 113, 1868; Kappeler: Case No. 16.

170. Male. Iridectomy. Had inhaled the vapor of an ounce. Stage of excitement was passed, but the patient was restless, rendering the conclusion of the operation difficult. Suddenly he became pale and pulseless, and died. *Autopsy.*—Complete adhesion of the pleural surfaces on the

right side. Lungs and air-passages engorged with blood. Heart large, flaccid, not fatty, containing considerable liquid, dark red blood.—C. Krüger : *Der Chloroformtod*, Dissert. Berlin, 1868 ; Kappeler : Case No. 17.

171. Male, twenty-six years, laborer. Anæmic from loss of blood ; probably intemperate. Had wounded the palm of his left hand, cutting an artery with a fragment of broken pottery. Chloroform given with Esmarch's inhaler. Five minutes after commencement of anæsthesia, patient experienced convulsive twitchings throughout the whole body. Inhalation was intermitted for a moment, and then resumed for the purpose of effecting complete muscular resolution. This soon followed, and on examination of the wound it was discovered that hemorrhage had ceased, though compression of the arteries had been discontinued. The patient, who was in a semi-recumbent position with his head drawn backward, exhibited pallor of the countenance, blueness of the lips, and feeble respiration. The mouth was forced open and the tongue drawn forward. Although the pulse was scarcely perceptible, the respiratory movements were distinct, though irregular and weak. The heart ceased to beat in spite of tracheotomy and artificial respiration for half an hour. *Autopsy.*—Very anæmic. Heart contracted. Meningeal œdema. Ossification of larynx, and contraction of vocal cords. Cheesy tubercle in both lung-apices, and in one a small cavern. Right kidney contracted.—Billroth : *Wiener mediz. Wochenschr.*, No. 46, 1868 ; Kappeler : Case No. 18.

172. Male, twenty-eight years. Amputation of finger for a recent injury. One drachm inhaled from a cloth. Patient became violently convulsed, and the heart ceased to beat. Tubercle at the base of the brain. Heart fatty and flaccid. Liver heavy and soft.—Essex Lunatic Asylum, Warley ; *Brit. Med. Jour.*, July 25, 1868 ; Kappeler : Case No. 19.

173. Female, thirty-five years ; healthy, mother of three children. Had inhaled chloroform six months previously for tooth-extraction, and now desired to repeat the inhalation for the same reason. "The dentist poured about two drachms on a sponge, and held it a short distance from her face. After she had made three or four inspirations her respiration ceased, and she became pulseless." Artificial respiration and stimulation of the cutaneous surfaces produced no effect whatever.—Dr. B. F. Brown, Oneida, Knox. Co., Ill. : *Chicago Med. Examiner*, June, 1868.

174. Charles S., thirty-one years. Prolapsus of the rectum and hemorrhoids. Chloroform given, one drachm on a napkin, to facilitate the replacement of the tumor. Patient appeared to be in good health, heart and lungs sound. After inhaling for two minutes, as the parts were still painful, another drachm was given. "Very soon the patient had the usual spasm, and in about thirty seconds the muscles began to relax" and the chloroform was discontinued. Pulse normal, breathing slightly noisy, face livid. Patient was turned upon his right side to facilitate the operation, but in one minute he had ceased to breathe, and the pulse had stopped, while the veins were distended, and the face was of a dark, livid color. Efforts for his resuscitation caused three or four long, full inspirations, but the heart remained motionless. *Autopsy.*—Serous exudation beneath the arachnoid ; venous hyperæmia of the brain and choroid plexuses ; ventricles empty. Heart empty and its structure normal. Lungs healthy, and exhibiting a certain amount of hypostatic congestion.—Dr. E. A. Clark, St. Louis Hospital ; *Humboldt Med. Archives*, November, 1868.

175. Male ; asthmatic. In the habit of inhaling chloroform for the relief of asthma, was found dead in his bed, with a vial of chloroform beside him,

He had apparently taken a little over an ounce.—Dr. W. B. Slayter: *Provincial Med. Jour.*, November, 1868.

176. Male, forty years. Amputation of thigh for inflammation of knee-joint. Inhalation from a towel. Amputation successfully performed, and the anæsthetic was discontinued, patient breathing well, and his pulse good. Three or four minutes later the jaws were firmly clenched, the respiration became stertorous and gasping, pulse very small, skin covered with clammy perspiration. The jaws were forced open, tongue drawn forward, artificial respiration performed, but all in vain. Death occurred about ten minutes after the first alarming symptoms. *Autopsy*, thirty hours after death.—Heart-substance, valves, and aorta were healthy, cavities empty. The lungs, stomach, spleen, intestines, and kidneys were all healthy, but pale. The brain was pale, and its blood-vessels were empty. —Dr. W. B. Slayter, *loc. cit.*

177. A death occurred at Wrexham, from chloroform inhaled "for an operation for fistula."—*Med. Press and Circular*, November 11, 1868.

178. Mrs. Adams, thirty-three years. Tooth-extraction. Every precaution had been taken, "her own attendant and another medical man being present."—*Med. Press and Circular*, November 11, 1868.

179. A druggist, who was in the habit of taking chloroform to relieve pain in his face, was found dead in the evening, with a handkerchief in his right hand, and an empty chloroform phial.—London ; *Brit. Med. Jour.*, December 19, 1868.

180. Male, fifty years ; had been discharged from an insane asylum after treatment for a year, though still complaining of headache and buzzing in the ears. Twenty drops of chloroform were given on cloth. Operation, castration. Having inhaled that amount, while a second dose was being poured out the pulse suddenly failed and the man was dead. Artificial respiration by Sylvester's method, and electricity, employed for an hour, produced no effect. A vein was opened, but only an ounce of dark red blood could be forcibly pressed out of the vessel. *Autopsy.*—The vessels of the brain and of its membranes were charged with liquid blood. Meninges thickened and adherent ; effusion into the cavity of the arachnoid. The heart was dilated, flaccid, fatter than normal, its walls dark red, and its cavities filled with blood of a similar color. The pleural membranes were also in an unhealthy condition.—J. Alexander Ross: *Med. Times and Gaz.*, No. 27, p. 624 ; *Lancet*, p. 506, October, 1869 ; Kappeler : Case No. 20.

181. Male. Lithotomy. After the expiration of eighteen minutes, while the operator was preparing to close the incision, the pulse suddenly weakened, the respiration grew feeble, the jaw fell, and the countenance indicated collapse. In spite of every effort, circulation and respiration ceased about one minute later. Faradization of the phrenic nerve produced no effect.—Jacobson: *Ugerkrift for Laeger*, R. 3, Bd. 8, S. 305 ; Canstatt's Jahresbericht pro 1869 ; Kappeler : Case No. 21.

182. Female, thirty-nine years ; anæmic. Skinner's inhaler was used. Extirpation of malignant tumor of the lower jaw by galvano-cautery. Thirteen minutes after the commencement of inhalation, during the final application of the cautery, she suddenly died. Electricity, mouth to mouth insufflation, Sylvesterism, were all without effect. *Autopsy.*—A large tumor existed ; larynx and upper part of trachea were filled with bloody mucus ; heart empty ; lungs pale and emphysematous.—Monckton : *Brit. Med. Jour.*, December 11, 1869 ; Kappeler : Case No. 22.

183. Female. Tooth-extraction. Three teeth were removed while

under the influence of chloroform. On awakening she insisted on being again chloroformed for the removal of three remaining stumps. This done, and the operation being completed, it was remarked that respiration had almost ceased. The head was bent forward, to permit the escape of blood from the mouth, and artificial respiration was undertaken, but in vain.—Cotton : *Boston Med. and Surg. Jour.*, September 23, 1869 ; *Gaz. hebd.*, September, 1870 ; Kappeler : Case No. 23.

184. Boy, twelve years. Reduction of a dislocation of the hip-joint. Two drachms on cloth. After anæsthesia had continued for twenty minutes, while the surgeon was endeavoring to effect reduction, the pulse weakened, and the patient died immediately.—Devenall-Davies : *Brit. Med. Journ.*, October 16, 1869 ; *Gaz. hebd.*, September, 1870 ; Kappeler : Case No. 24.

185. Male, twenty-five years. Amputation of finger. Small quantity of chloroform. Sudden death. *Autopsy.*—Fatty degeneration of the heart ; rupture of the spleen ; considerable blood in the peritoneal cavity.—*Austral. Med. Gaz. ; Med. Times and Gaz.*, September 18, 1869 ; *Gaz. hebd.*, September, 1870 ; Kappeler : Case No. 25.

186. Male, a chemist. Removal of diseased bone from leg. Very timorous, yet desirous to inhale chloroform. Heart and lungs were examined, and pronounced healthy before inhalation. A small quantity only was given. Three minutes after commencement of inhalation, the patient died. *Autopsy.*—Paralysis of the heart.—*Brit. Med. Journ.*, February 20, 1869 ; *Med. Press and Circular*, February 24, 1869; Kappeler : Case No. 26.

187. Female, married, fifty-two years. Inflamed bursæ patellæ. One of these was ruptured by a blow, causing the loss of a large quantity of blood. The parts sloughed. September 12th, slight return of hemorrhage. It was determined September 15th, to cauterize the wound with nitric acid. Skinner's inhaler was used, with about two drachms of chloroform. After inhaling for three or four minutes, the stage of excitement commenced, lasting three minutes longer. The patient then died instantaneously. Artificial respiration by the methods of Marshall Hall and Sylvester were tried without success. The patient inspired only twice. Electricity was also used without effect. No autopsy.—Johnson : *Brit. Med. Journ.*, October 2, 1869 ; Kappeler : Case No. 27.

188. A death from chloroform.—Hanley Infirmary ; *Med. Times and Gaz.*, September 18, 1869.

189. A lady, mother of eight children. Epithelioma of the tongue. Chloroform inhaled from a pint bottle containing two ounces of the anæsthetic, in which was immersed a coil of paper. Patient was quickly exhilarated. Anæsthesia being imperfect, chloroform was poured upon a napkin held before her face. This speedily produced profound anæsthesia. Chloroform was then withdrawn, and the operation was commenced. After a long and difficult operation, just as the surgeon was about to stitch the wound, the patient "suddenly fainted," and never breathed again.— Squibb : New York Pathological Society ; *Med. Record*, May 1, 1869 ; Kappeler : Case No. 40.

190. Girl, six years. Strabismus. Chloroform was given at the New York Eye and Ear Infirmary ; at first, one drachm on a napkin. A second drachm was also given in like manner. The internal rectus muscle was divided before the patient was fully anæsthetized. Chloroform was then withdrawn. The child had been quite restless during the operation, and ceased to breathe a few moments after its conclusion, fifteen minutes after the commencement of inhalation. *Autopsy*, eight hours after death.—Right side of

the heart filled with dark fluid blood. Kidneys and spleen enlarged. Ovaries were "respectively the size of a kidney bean." Lungs collapsed and comparatively anæmic.—Finnell: *New York Med. Record*, May 1, 1869; Kappeler: Case No 41.

191. John Gray, forty-seven years; drunkard. Chloroformed, July 1, 1868, by Dr. F. Hillar, Virginia City, Nevada. Fracture of the head and neck of the humerus six days before. "Nearly ten drachms of chloroform were given in as many minutes, when the pulse failed and respiration ceased. Water was dashed in the face, artificial respiration instituted, and the patient bled," but in vain. The veins of the head and neck were greatly distended. *Autopsy.*—Brain healthy.—Henry Gibbons, Jr.: *Pacific Med. and Surg. Journ.*, June, 1869.

192. A lady, San Francisco, 1868. Death before or during the operation.—Henry Gibbons Jr.: *Pacific Med. and Surg. Journ.*, June, 1869.

193. A robust soldier. Amputation of a portion of one hand for a gunshot wound received before Atlanta, Ga., 1863. After about six inspirations of chloroform vapor, his breathing became labored and stertorous, the pulse ceased, and in a few moments he was dead. *Autopsy* revealed nothing.—A. T. Hudson: *Pacific Med. and Surg. Journ.*, July, 1869.

194. A vigorous male, forty years; somewhat addicted to liquor. Fell, while intoxicated, and dislocated his shoulder, 1855. Three days later, having become quite sober, chloroform was administered on a sponge. Anæsthesia supervened after a few inhalations, and the head of the humerus was readily replaced in its socket. The face immediately became livid, and death followed at once.—A. T. Hudson: *loc. cit.*

195. Male, middle-aged; anæmic. Preparing for amputation of the leg on account of caries of the ankle-joint. Chloroform inhaled from a towel. After one minute the extremities were convulsed. His condition now became so alarming that the inhalation was suspended, and his head was lowered. The face became livid, the pupils dilated, the lower jaw fell, and, after four or five convulsive inspirations at long intervals, he ceased to breathe. The action of the heart "was maintained for forty minutes."—Cook County Hospital, Chicago; *Chicago Med. Journ.*, August, 1869.

196. A lady died in New York, December 3, 1869, from the inhalation of chloroform, which she was in the habit of taking for the relief of headache.—*Boston Med. and Surg. Journ.*, December 9, 1869.

197.—Female. Prolapsus uteri. Death from chloroform during the operation. *Autopsy* negative.—Lying-in Hospital, London; *Brit. Med. Journ.*, November 25, 1869.

198. Male, forty-two years. Fracture of both bones of left leg, January 19, 1869. Six days later, tetanus. Next day chloroform was given to relieve the tetanic spasm. After a few inspirations the pulse stopped, and the patient seemed to be dead. Artificial respiration and drawing out the tongue resuscitated the patient, who was then transferred to his bed. But a moment afterward he suddenly ceased to breathe, and could not be again revived.—S. Labbé: *Journ. hebdom.*, April 30, 1869.

199. A young man. Necrosis of femur. Had taken chloroform a month previously without unpleasant effects. He died on the operating table while inhaling chloroform preparatory to an operation. *Autopsy*, twenty-four hours after death.—General visceral hyperæmia. Rigor mortis very slight. Recent endocarditis had roughened the mitral and aortic valves, and had thickened the chordæ tendinæ. Extensive granular degeneration of the muscular substance of the left ventricle.—Middlesex

Hospital ; *Med. Times and Gaz.*, January 1, 1870 ; *Brit. Med. Journ.*, January 8, 1870 ; Kappeler : Case No. 39.

200. Boy, fourteen years. Necrosis of the tibia. Had safely inhaled chloroform on a former occasion. Chloroform was administered December 23, 1869, for the purpose of an operation. During the operation patient began to vomit, became livid, and after one or two minutes his respiration ceased, and his pulse stopped. *Autopsy* exhibited nothing, except an enlargement of the liver.—Lincoln County Hospital ; *Brit. Med. Journ.*, January 8, 1870 ; Kappeler : Case No. 38.

201. Male, forty-two years ; careworn appearance. Stricture and stone in the bladder for five years. Chloroform was given with Clover's inhaler, for an exploratory operation. The vapor of thirty minims was mixed with each thousand cubic inches of air. After breathing for five or six minutes, the patient became insensible and stertorous. Pulse at first 84, then 92. During the introduction of the sound, breathing suddenly ceased in inspiration, and the pulse at the same moment became imperceptible. Sylvesterism for twenty minutes, and faradization of the phrenic nerves, accomplished nothing. *Autopsy.*—The right side of the heart was filled with dark blood ; left side nearly empty. The walls of the heart were loaded with fat, and there was considerable interstitial fat. The valves were healthy, but the aorta was atheromatous. Lungs healthy. In the bladder a calculus.—Marshall : *Brit. Med. Journ.*, p. 493, May 14, 1870 ; Kappeler : Case No. 28.

202. Female-servant, twenty-four years. Had been successfully chloroformed four months previously. Anchylosis of knee-joint, requiring forcible extension. Esmarch's inhaler. Patient was lying on her back, and quietly inhaled the anæsthetic until insensible. The operation was then commenced, but was scarcely half completed when the respiration became irregular. Artificial respiration and catheterization of the larynx restored the patient for one minute, and Billroth was about to resume his operation, when respiration again became irregular. Tracheotomy and electro-puncture excited occasional respiratory efforts for about twenty minutes. Venesection was also tried, but without good result. *Autopsy.* —Vegetations upon the mitral valves. Muscular substance of the heart yellowish and soft.—Billroth : *Wiener med. Wochenschr.*, November 16, 1870 ; *Brit. Med. Journ.*, March 12, 1870 ; Kappeler : Case No. 29.

203. Female, married, twenty-two years ; emaciated. Ovarian tumor, carcinoma, large as the pregnant uterus at the sixth or seventh month. Chloroform given on a towel. As the operator introduced his hand into the peritoneal cavity, the patient suddenly vomited, the pupils dilated, the countenance grew pale, and the respiration, which had been quiet and natural, now ceased. Partial restoration followed the attempt at artificial respiration and traction of the tongue, but patient soon passed into collapse, and died. *Autopsy* negative.—Sir J. Y. Simpson, Edinburgh : *Brit. Med. Journ.*, February 26, 1870 ; *Lancet*, same date ; Kappeler : Case No. 30.

204. Female, thirty-one years. Amputation of the foot by Syme's operation, on account of fungus hæmatodes. Less than two drachms of chloroform were used. The foot had been removed, and the stump was being dressed, when the patient, who had exhibited no disturbance of circulation or respiration during inhalation, suddenly ceased to breathe. Electricity, etc., were employed without result. *Autopsy.*—Slight fatty degeneration of the heart.—Dawson, Cincinnati Hospital : *Cincinnati Med. Repertory*, November, 1870 ; *Philadelphia Med. and Surg. Rep.*, p. 474, December 10, 1870 ; Kappeler : Case No. 31.

205. Male, elderly, had been previously chloroformed without harm.

Inhaled a very small quantity with an inhaler. Great excitement followed and the pulse suddenly ceased, though respiration continued for some time longer. *Autopsy.*—Heart, empty, thin, and flaccid; had undergone·fatty degeneration.—Ophthalmic Hospital, Moorfields; *Brit. Med. Journ.*, p. 441, April 30, 1870; Kappeler: Case No. 32.

206. Male, farmer, sixty-eight years. Chloroformed January 11, 1870, for partial amputation of the foot, on account of disease of the bones. After inhaling about one drachm, the patient became rigid, and the heart stopped. Artificial respiration for three-quarters of an hour availed nought. —New York County Hospital; *Brit. Med. Journ.*, January 22, 1870; Kappeler: Case No. 33.

207. A boy, scrofulous and anæmic. Chloroformed with Clover's inhaler, for amputation of the thigh. Two minutes after the completion of the operation and the removal of the inhaler, the patient suddenly became pale, and the heart ceased to beat. Death was attributed to shock rather than to chloroform.—University College Hospital; *Lancet*, April 23, 1870; Kappeler: Case No. 34.

208. Boy, eleven years. Operation for a traumatic cataract. Anæsthesia did not reach the stage of complete muscular resolution, though two drachms were given. The operation, however, was successfully completed, but about ten minutes after its commencement, respiration became disordered, the pupil of the sound eye dilated, and the pulse was lost. Artificial respiration was for a time successful in exciting imperfect attempts at respiration, and the heart again began to beat, but the patient once more passed into a state of collapse and died, notwithstanding the attempt at resuscitation was prolonged for three-quarters of an hour. *Autopsy.*— Meninges bloodless; cerebral substance charged with blood; trachea contained frothy mucus, and the mucous membrane was reddened. Upper lobes of lungs of a clear vermilion color; lower lobes œdematous, engorged with blood. In the large vessels throughout the body the blood was dark and fluid. Left ventricle contracted; right, flaccid; liquid blood in both. Microscopic examination of the blood, negative.—Blodig: *Wiener med. Wochenschr.*, No. 60, 1870; Kappeler: Case No. 35.

209. Male, twenty-eight years, robust. Fistula in ano. Patient inhaled the anæsthetic, lying on his left side. The pulse was good. After the operation, which had not required more than three minutes, he was placed upon his back, when he ceased to breathe, and his face became livid. The heart continued to beat feebly but regularly. After artificial respiration he breathed naturally for a few seconds, then both respiration and pulsation ceased together. Artificial respiration was continued forty minutes longer. *Autopsy.*—The heart weighed fourteen ounces. The left ventricle was full of dark, fluid blood; its walls were pale and flabby; the heart-substance was fatty. The lungs were hyperæmic and œdematous. Blood everywhere liquid. Pulmonary artery distended with blood. Spleen large and soft. Other organs healthy.—London Hospital; *Lancet*, December 24, 1870; Kappeler: Case No. 36.

210. A student, nineteen years. Inhaled two drachms from a towel, for a slight but painful operation. The patient passed quickly into a state of violent excitement, requiring restraint. Half a minute afterward he became insensible, and the operation was performed. The pulse suddenly weakened, and death followed. *Autopsy.*—Dilatation of the heart, and great thinness of its walls.—Hitchings: *New York Med. Journ.*, February, 1870; Kappeler: Case No. 37.

· 211. Male, forty years, laborer. Amputation of fore-arm. Chloroform given on a handkerchief, drop by drop.   After a few minutes the patient became talkative, then violent, requiring restraint.   This was followed by general muscular rigidity and retraction of the head.   The anæsthetic was discontinued, but the pulse began to fail, became imperceptible, and after one or two inspirations the patient was dead.   *Autopsy*, five hours after death.—Lungs healthy.   Yellow serum in pericardial sac.   Right side of the heart greatly distended with dark, liquid blood.   Base of the heart loaded with fat.   Left side of the heart empty.   Valves normal.   Heart-substance normal to the eye, but soft and yielding like tallow under the finger.   The microscope revealed extensive fatty degeneration of the walls of both ventricles.—Miner: *Buffalo Med. Journ.*, and *New York Med. Journ.*, April, 1870 ; Kappeler : Case No. 42.

212. Female.   Ovariotomy.   *Autopsy*, negative.—Alloa : *Brit. Med. Journ.*, pp. 164 and 199, 1870.

213. Boy, eight years, May 31, 1871, dressing a burn.   During the operation was lying on his belly.   Respiration ceased one minute after the cessation of inhalation.   Artificial respiration for three-quarters of an hour. Faradization of the phrenic nerve.   *Autopsy*.—Brain healthy ; lateral ventricles distended with liquid.   Blood fluid.   Left ventricle contracted. Collapse and emphysema of lower lobes of lungs ; pleural surfaces adherent over upper lobes.   Hyperæmia of tracheal mucous membrane ; rusty-colored froth in smaller bronchi.—Watson, Great Northern Hospital ; *Brit. Med. Journ.*, p. 616, June 10, 1870, and p. 641, June 17 ; Kappeler : Case No. 43.

214. Young woman.   Extraction of teeth, March 19, 1870.   Had taken chloroform one week previously, but without effect.   On the present occasion, after extraction of three teeth, it was discovered that she was dying, and she soon expired.—Miller, Accrington : *Brit. Med. Journ.*, April 2, 1870.

215. Female, married, thirty-six years ; Great Barrington, Mass.   Wished to take chloroform for the extraction of twelve teeth.   The anæsthetic was inhaled from a napkin.   The first four teeth were extracted before the patient was completely insensible.   A little more chloroform was then given, and all the teeth were removed.   There were no unfavorable symptoms until after the operation had been concluded.   She then vomited, seemed to suffocate, and died immediately.   Her medical attendant, who had given the anæsthetic, was supporting her head, with his finger upon the temporal artery, and remarked no symptom of danger until the artery ceased to pulsate.   A moment later she ceased to breathe.   Artificial respiration for three-quarters of an hour did no good.—*Dental Cosmos*, April, 1870.

216. Male, sixty-five years.   Died "during inhalation of chloroform at Deer Island."—*Boston Med. and Surg. Journ.*, April 14, 1870.

217. Male, forcible extension of the knee-joint.   One month previously had inhaled chloroform almost every day.   He now inhaled one drachm and a half, and died in three-quarters of an hour.—*Brit. Med. Journ.*, p. 426, April 26, 1871 ; Kappeler : Case No. 44.

218. J. C., male, forty-two years.   Vesical calculus.   Clover's inhaler. Pulse and respiration stopped together.   *Autopsy*.—Heart relaxed, but not distended ; valves normal ; fatty degeneration.—University College Hospital ; *Brit. Med. Journ.*, p. 493, May 14, 1870.

219. Male, elderly, April 12, 1870.   Pulse ceased several seconds before death.   *Autopsy*.—Heart thin, empty and flaccid on left side ; loaded with fat ; walls in a state of fatty degeneration.—Moorfields Hospital ; *Brit. Med. Journ.*, p. 441, April 30, 1870.

220. Male, thirty-four years. Amputation of finger. Chloroform given on lint.—*Brit. Med. Journ.*, p. 338, September, 1870.

221. Male, young merchant. Removal of a cystic tumor over the left eye. Operation nearly completed, when patient threw back his head, his neck became stiff, and he gasped. In half an hour he was dead. *Verdict.*—Paralysis of heart.—Chicago ; *Boston Med. and Surg. Journ.*, September 8, 1870, from *Boston Daily Transcript.*

222. Boy. Amputation of thigh. Syncope.—University College Hospital; *Lancet*, 1870.

223. Male, forty-two years. Disease of the right foot. Chloroform was being administered, when he sank and died in a few minutes. *Autopsy.*—Diseased heart and kidneys.—Royal Infirmary, Liverpool ; *Med. Times and Gaz.*, August 20, 1870.

224. Young lady. Tooth extraction.—Hughes-Bennett, Edinburgh : *Brit. Med. Journ.*, October 1, 1870.

225. Male, forty years. Inhalation of chloroform preparatory to an examination by one of the ablest surgeons of Boston.—*Boston Med. and Surg. Journ.*, December 15, 1870.

226. Dislocation of the shoulder-joint. Death.—Yokohama, Japan ; *Med. Times and Gaz.*, October 8, 1870.

227. Dislocation of the shoulder. No organic lesion discoverable after death. The patient died during the attempt at reduction.—Edinburgh Royal Infirmary ; *Brit. Med. Journ.*, pp. 259, 289, March, 1881.

228. Male, fifty-two years, healthy. Iridectomy. One drachm and a half of chloroform given on a flannel cone. After the operation was ended, the breathing became suddenly stertorous ; countenance livid, and sterno-cleido-mastoid muscles rigid. Sylvesterism at first seemed to give relief, but all the previous symptoms were soon renewed, and death occurred.—Westminster Ophthalmic Hospital ; *Lancet*, January 28, 1871 ; Kappeler : Case No. 46.

229. Male, forty-seven years ; reduced in vigor by a compound fracture of the leg three weeks previously. Three drachms were given on cloth, preparatory to amputation. This produced great excitement, with a weak and rapid pulse, almost imperceptible at the wrist. Respiration ceased while the heart was yet beating. Artificial respiration and electricity restored the patient so that he could swallow a spoonful of brandy, and reply to a question. He speedily relapsed, however, and soon died.—Sylvester : *Brit. Med. Journ.*, p. 426 ; Kappeler : Case No. 45.

230. Iron-merchant, fifty-three years ; healthy, but accustomed to drink. The fall of a piece of iron fractured the first and second toes, necessitating amputation. Had been previously chloroformed with success. Chloroform was given on a cloth, at first without effect, but after five minutes he became excited. This condition lasted two minutes. He then became quiet. At the commencement of the operation there was a convulsive movement. The pulse then suddenly stopped, and not more than one inspiration followed. Artificial respiration and electricity for twenty minutes did no good. *Autopsy.*—Great hyperæmia of the lungs and respiratory passages. Left ventricle flaccid and somewhat dilated, its muscular substance softened and somewhat degenerated. Right ventricle distended with blood. Liver, fatty. Kidneys, hyperæmic. Mucous surface of the stomach somewhat ecchymosed.—London Hospital ; *Brit. Med. Journ.*, December 2, 1871 ; Kappeler : Case No. 47.

231. Male, thirty-seven years ; tolerably vigorous. Radical cure for hernia. Chloroform given on a towel. Patient had been somewhat ad-

dicted to drink, and was very anxious, but passed into a condition of normal anæsthesia.   The heart and lungs stopped simultaneously at the first incision.   Sylvesterism and electricity were tried for half an hour without effect.   The jugular vein was also opened.   *Autopsy.*—Chronic inflammation of the dura mater.   Fatty degeneration of left ventricle and septum cordis ; walls of right ventricle thin.   Kidneys, fatty.   Lungs, hyperæmic. Liquid blood in both sides of the heart.   Chemical analysis failed to discover chloroform either in the blood or in the liver.—Pirie, Aberdeen Royal Infirmary ; *Brit. Med. Journ.*, July 29, 1871 ; Kappeler : Case No. 48.

232. Female, forty-eight years.   Operation on the knee.   Less than a drachm had been given when death occurred.—*Australian Med. Gaz.*, July, 1871.

233. Male, very robust.   Inhaled chloroform for the reduction of an old dislocation of the shoulder.   During the stage of excitement death occurred.   Artificial respiration, electricity, etc., produced three or four inspirations, but the heart remained motionless.   *Autopsy.*—Dilatation and fatty degeneration of both sides of the heart.—Gillespie : *Brit. Med. Journ.*, March 18, 1871 ; Kappeler : Case No. 49.

234. Male.   Fistula in ano.   About half a drachm of chloroform was given on a cone of lint.   This was repeated till he had taken three or four drachms without producing complete insensibility.   Chloroform was then withdrawn, and the patient was laid upon his side for the operation, when respiration and the pulse immediately stopped.   Extraction of the tongue, artificial respiration, cold sprinkling, ammonia, etc., seemed to renew the respiratory movements for a very short time, and then death occurred. *Autopsy.*—All the internal organs were healthy, but greatly loaded with fat.—Withers, Salop Infirmary ; *Brit. Med. Journ.*, March 26, 1871 ; Kappeler : Case No. 50.

235. Lieut.-Col. Rogers, R.A., fifty years ; a vigorous man.   Compound fracture of leg, and dislocation of ankle.   The bones had been set, but it was decided to give chloroform, and to readjust the fractured limb.   A drachm and a half was inhaled from a handkerchief.   Four minutes after the beginning of inhalation excitement had ceased, and the operation was commenced when alarming symptoms appeared.   The tongue was with some difficulty drawn out between the clenched jaws, and after forty minutes of effort at restoration the action of the heart and lungs were established.   But suddenly they ceased to move, and the patient could not be again revived.—Miles : *Lancet*, May 20, 1871 ; *Brit. Med. Journ.*, p. 538, May 20, 1871 ; Kappeler : Case No. 51.

236. Female, forty-eight years.   Long time suffering with syphilitic ulceration of the leg. April 26, 1871, she had taken chloroform for a preliminary operation.   This had been followed by vomiting for three days.   Had two rigors, and a high temperature ; took scarcely any food, and was supported by nutritious enemata.   May 3d, chloroform again administered.   Before insensibility was reached, she made a convulsive movement, and turned suddenly livid.   At this moment her pulse beat very rapidly, and then ceased altogether.   Artificial respiration, cold sprinkling, and bleeding from the jugular vein only excited one or two gasping respirations.   Examination of the eyes with the ophthalmoscope after death, showed great distention of the retinal veins.   *Autopsy.*—Lungs dark red, and diminished in weight.   The venous system was much engorged.   Right side of the heart normal, and emptied by the venesection ; left ventricle contracted, soft and empty.   The microscope exhibited fatty degeneration of the mus-

cular fibres of the heart. Other organs were healthy.—London Hospital ; *Brit. Med. Journ.*, May 27, 1871 ; Kappeler : Case No. 53.

237. Boy, fifteen years. Operation for strabismus. After the operation had been completed, the patient made attempts to vomit. While so doing a deep inspiration drew the vomited matter back into the larynx and trachea, causing death by asphyxia.—London Hospital ; *Brit. Med. Journ.* and *Lancet*, September 30, 1871 ; Kappeler : Case No. 52.

238. Male, drayman, thirty-four years, very strong. Fracture of the leg. On account of the pain attending the effort to set the bones, chloroform was given on a cloth. The patient did not become insensible, but the efforts to reduce the fracture were proceeding, when the pulse suddenly ceased to beat. *Autopsy.*—Brain softened ; heart flabby and dilated ; liver and kidneys fatty.—Manchester Royal Infirmary ; *Brit. Med. Journ.*, October 7, 1871 ; Kappeler : Case No. 54.

239. Dissection of the scalp. Two drachms of Squibb's chloroform were given on a towel. Death during the operation.—W. T. Briggs : *Nashville Journ. Med. and Surg.*, February, 1871.

240. Old dislocation of the elbow. Full anæsthesia, five minutes after the commencement of inhalation. Chloroform was then withdrawn. Suddenly the pulse began to fail, the extremities grew cold, respiration gasping and soon ceased. Artificial respiration and acupuncture of the heart did no good.—Muscroft, Cincinnati ; *The Clinic*, October 28, 1871.

241. Soldier, fifty years, large and strong. Old dislocation of the shoulder. During the stage of excitement the patient suddenly ceased to breathe. Artificial respiration revived him for a little, but presently respiratory movements ceased again, the pulse grew weak, the countenance changed, and death was soon complete. *Autopsy.*—Lungs emphysematous, lower lobes hyperæmic ; bronchial mucous membranes catarrhal ; heart somewhat enlarged, flaccid ; right ventricle dilated ; both ventricles empty ; muscular substance of the heart pale, in some places yellow ; fatty degeneration of the intima of the aorta ; a rupture in the liver, measuring 8 centimetres long and 4 centimetres deep ; two to three hundred grammes of dark, fluid blood in the peritoneal sac ; both kidneys engorged with venous blood. It was concluded that the liver had been ruptured by the violent attempts to produce artificial respiration, and that death was the result of the consequent shock.—Facilides : *Archiv der Heilkunde von Wagner*, 1872, 1 Heft ; Kappeler : Case No. 55.

242. Female, forty-six years. Ovariotomy. As the patient was passing into the stage of insensibility, her respiration became laborious, her countenance livid, pulse weak, and all the symptoms of suffocation appeared. She coughed up bloody mucus, and died. The tongue was pulled forward, and with the finger a metallic plate of artificial teeth was drawn out of the pharynx. Artificial respiration was continued for forty minutes, but without avail. *Autopsy.*—Heart thin and flaccid, but not degenerated ; right ventricle dilated and containing a small quantity of fluid blood ; valves healthy ; lungs normal ; carcinoma of the peritoneum and ovaries. Death from suffocation.—Chaffers : *Brit. Med. Journ.*, p. 419, April 20, 1872 ; Kappeler : Case No. 56.

243. Male. Amputation of the leg for a severe compound fracture, with copious hemorrhage, caused by a shell wound. Two minutes after the beginning of inhalation, before the attainment of complete anæsthesia, the heart suddenly ceased to beat, though several respirations occurred after this event.—Cabasse : *Lyon Medic.*, 12, p. 166 ; Kappeler : Case 67.

244. Male, stout. Compound comminuted fracture of left leg, necessi-

tating amputation. Considerable, but not excessive, loss of blood; no shock. Three drachms were given with an inhaler. Patient vomited twice, but seemed otherwise in good condition, till, during the operation, the countenance suddenly became livid, and respiration ceased, with the tongue thrust between the teeth. On replacing the tongue, respiration was resumed, and he became partly conscious. A little more chloroform was then given. Ten minutes later the respirations became feeble and superficial. In a very short time the countenance again became livid, teeth firmly fixed, and respiration ceased entirely. Artificial respiration and electricity for thirty-five minutes did no good. *Autopsy.*—Heart pale and empty, slight thickening of mitral valve, atheroma of the aorta, no fatty degeneration discovered with the microscope; liver fatty. The stomach was half full of partially digested food, some of which was also found in the pharynx.—Marshall, Nottingham General Hospital; *Brit. Med. Journ.*, October 12, 1872; Kappeler: Case No. 58.

245. Female, fifty-seven years, strong and industrious. Amputation of the breast. Inhaled one half drachm from a sponge. Patient became much excited and noisy. About one minute after the second half drachm had been poured upon the sponge, the already feeble pulse became extinct, cessation of breathing followed, the face became livid, and the pupils widely dilated, Sylvesterism, and other measures were of no avail.—Bird, York: *Brit. Med. Journ.*, p. 42, October 12, 1872; Kappeler: Case No. 59.

246. Male, thirty-five years. Necrosis of the bones of the leg. Inhaled chloroform for five minutes, then for two minutes exhibited great excitement. At the end of this time the heart suddenly stopped, there was a gasping for breath, and the patient was dead. Artificial respiration for ten minutes, then associated with electricity for ten minutes longer.—King's College Hospital; *Brit. Med. Journ.*, p. 717, December 28, 1872; Kappeler: Case No. 60.

247. Male, twenty-six years, laborer, intemperate. Iridectomy. Three drachms of chloroform given with a tin inhaler. Patient was quiet during the first minute, then greatly excited. Inhalation was therefore interrupted for one quarter of a minute, after which a second period of excitement was introduced. The pulse was accelerated and suddenly ceased; the face became livid; respiration became weaker, and ceased one and a half minute later. Sylvesterism, electricity, acupuncture of the heart. *Autopsy.*—Surface of the heart overlaid with fat; muscular substance thin and fatty; left ventricle empty, right side of the heart and the lungs full of blood.—Smith: *Brit. Med. Journ.*, April 6, 1872; Kappeler: Case No. 61.

248. Male, forty-eight years; corpulent. Extraction of both lenses for cataract. Chloroform inhaled from a towel. After taking a drachm in this way, a small quantity was again poured out. After breathing quietly for about fifteen minutes, the patient began to breathe irregularly and endeavored to free himself from the towel. There was then great rigidity of the muscles of the back and neck, making it difficult to hold him. Replaced in proper position, it was discovered that the heart and lungs had ceased to move; the conjunctiva had continued sensitive throughout. Sylvesterism and electricity were employed for half an hour, producing only a few feeble inspirations. *Autopsy.*—Heart considerably hypertrophied and fatty; right side of the heart filled with blood; no valvular disease; lungs slightly emphysematous. The patient had taken chloroform without unusual appearances only six weeks previously.—Glascott; Royal Eye Hospital, Manchester; *Brit. Med. Journ.*, May 4, 1872; Kappeler: Case No. 62.

249. Young man. Phagædenic ulcer. After a few minutes, before the

occurrence of complete anæsthesia, the pulse ceased. Artificial respiration and electricity for an hour failed to revive the patient.—St. Bartholomew's Hospital ; *Brit. Med. Journ.*, May 4, 1872 ; Kappeler : Case No. 63.

250. Girl, sixteen years. Some operation (what ?) on the eye. A short time after the commencement of inhalation the patient appeared to be insensible, and the inhaler was removed. Exhibiting signs of returning sensibility, the inhalation was renewed. Suddenly, at the commencement of the operation, the heart stopped. Five years previously she had once taken chloroform.—South London Ophthalmic Hospital ; *Brit. Med. Journ.*, September 28, 1872 ; Kappeler : Case No. 64.

251. Male, thirty-four years ; publican. Had a chronic inflammation of the foot and leg, with a fistulous opening supposed to communicate with diseased bone. Very little excitement followed inhalation, and the conjunctivæ continued sensitive. After three drachms had been given, the patient was not fully insensible, but was deemed sufficiently so to permit the operation to proceed. The anæsthetic was discontinued, and was not resumed. About nine minutes after this the pulse suddenly ceased under the finger of the attendant. A few seconds later the patient began to sigh, and the face became pale and somewhat livid. Sylvesterism, electricity, friction, brandy clysters, were all tried for three-quarters of an hour. *Autopsy.*—There was rigor mortis ; brain, lungs, and pleura were healthy ; bloody mucus in the bronchial tubes. Heart weighed eleven and three-fourths ounces ; the microscope showed slight fatty degeneration ; valves healthy ; the left ventricle contained a little fluid blood. Liver fatty.— Mackenzie ; London Hospital ; *Brit. Med. Journ.*, October 5, 1872 ; Kappeler : Case No. 65.

252. Hostler, forty-nine years ; intemperate. Fractured leg and dislocated ankle-joint. The previously existing muscular spasms subsided under the influence of the anæsthetic, and the patient breathed quietly and regularly ; but before the commencement of the attempt to reduce the fracture and dislocation, the heart suddenly stopped. *Autopsy.*—Diseased heart and lungs—no statement of the nature of the disease.—Bristol Infirmary ; *Brit. Med. Journ.*, November 30, 1872 ; Kappeler : Case No. 66.

253. Male, twenty-eight years ; laborer. Amputation of a crushed thumb. Chloroform given on a napkin.—Barrow, England ; *Brit. Med. Journ.*, December 14, 1872.

254. Female, seventy years. Fell down-stairs, fracturing her leg into the knee-joint. Chloroform given to facilitate reduction. Death occurred after very brief inhalation.—Brighton, England ; *Brit. Med. Journ.*, October 5, 1872.

255. Male, twenty-two years ; medical student. In the habit of inhaling chloroform to allay pain. Went to bed apparently well, and was found dead in the morning, with a handkerchief applied to his mouth.—West Middlesex ; *Brit. Med. Journ.*, March 9, 1872.

256. "Death from *coma* due to chloroform is rare ; still, the only case with which I have been personally connected was due to this cause. The patient was suffering from chronic Bright's disease, and had slight symptoms of uræmia. The administration of chloroform had not proceeded far when convulsions occurred, followed by coma and death in about an hour. In this case, at all events, the mode of death was evidently predisposed to by the poisoned state of the blood."—J. Eric Erichsen : *Brit. Med. Journ.*, June 8, 1872.

257. Male, thirty-six years ; engine-driver. Disease of the jaw, necessitating an operation. Two minutes after commencement of inhalation he

died. Verdict : paralysis of the heart.—King's College Hospital ; *Brit. Med. Journ.*, June 15, 1872.

258. Male. "Disarticulation at the hip-joint was being performed, May 27th, on account of osteo-myelitis.   The femoral artery had been tied, and Billroth was about to apply the galvano-caustic wire in order to divide the soft parts after enucleation of the head of the bone, when the patient's breathing became stertorous, and he died."   Tracheotomy and all other measures were tried, without success.—Billroth : *Brit. Med. Journ.*, June 15, 1872.

259. Male, fifty-three years. About to undergo an operation for stone in the bladder.—Great Northern Hospital ; *Brit. Med. Journ.*, August 24, 1872.

260. Male, about sixty years, living in Butler Co., Ohio. Caries of the tibia. One drachm of chloroform was inhaled, when the leg was drawn up, and the body was suddenly raised into a sitting posture by spasmodic contraction of the muscles. As their rigidity passed off, pulsation ceased, and the patient died.—W. W. Dawson, Cincinnati ; *The Clinic*, October 26, 1872.

261. At the London Hospital, 1871, a male, eighty-three years, died of syncope during inhalation of chloroform for amputation of a toe.—*Brit. Med. Journ.*, December 18, 1880.

262. Male, injury to a foot. Died under the influence of chloroform, while undergoing amputation.—Sir Patrick Dun's Hospital, Dublin ; *Lancet*, February 22, 1873.

263. Female, forty-five years. Fatty tumor on the back. Chloroform given on lint. Heart stopped before the commencement of operation. *Autopsy.*—Ventricles dilated ; valves atheromatous, but competent.—Wyman ; West London Hospital ; *Brit. Med. Journ.*, February 22, 1873.

264. Male, fifty-one years ; laborer ; intemperate. Dressing of a fractured leg. One drachm and a half given on a sponge. One-third of a grain of morphine had been hypodermically injected thirty-five minutes before the commencement of inhalation. The patient made violent resistance at first during the inhalation of one drachm. At the end of two minutes an additional half-drachm was given, and he became quiet, with regular pulse and respiration. After the dressing had been applied, it was discovered that, though respiration persisted, the heart had stopped and the pupils were dilated. The breathing became deep and infrequent, and soon ceased. Artificial respiration, electricity, galvano-puncture of the heart, venesection of the jugular. *Autopsy.*—Left ventricle contracted and empty ; the whole right side of the heart was filled with dark fluid blood ; ventricular wall thin ; atheroma of the coronary arteries ; liver and heart slightly fatty ; lungs adherent and slightly emphysematous.—Prichard : Bristol Royal Infirmary ; *Brit. Med. Journ.*, p. 194, February 22, 1873 ; Kappeler : Case No. 67.

265. Male, forty years ; in apparent good health. Fissure of the anus, requiring forcible dilatation. The patient came rather slowly under the influence of chloroform, the stage of excitement being somewhat prolonged. He at length fell into a quiet sleep, during which the operation was performed. A few seconds after the completion of the operation the patient suddenly became stertorous, cyanosed, pulseless, and expired. Sylvesterism and electricity. *Autopsy.*—Two small cavities in the lungs ; heart filled with blood. Malformation of the larynx, with narrowing of the glottis.—Léon Lefort : *Gaz. des hôpitaux* ; *Brit. Med. Journ.*, May 17, 1873 ; Kappeler : Case No. 68.

266. Male, forty-five years; intemperate. Dislocation of the shoulder. Inhalation had not reached the stage of muscular relaxation when the patient, who was lying with his mouth open, began to breathe irregularly. The anæsthetic was removed, but one minute later respiration ceased. Artificial respiration and electricity for three-quarters of an hour. *Autopsy.*—Hyperæmia of the brain and its coverings; atheroma of arteries; fatty liver; blood liquid; left ventricle contracted, right flaccid.—Dandridge: *Philadelphia Med. and Surg. Rep.*, p. 349, November 15; Kappeler: Case No. 69.

267. Girl, twelve years; supposed to be suffering with some slight cardiac ailment. Tooth-extraction. Chloroform on a cloth. Immediately after the extraction the pulse began to flutter, and the face grew pale and expressionless. The head was depressed, tongue drawn forward, ammonia, cold douche, and artificial respiration were tried, with the result of exciting ten or eleven deep inspirations, after which she ceased to breathe. The heart did not beat again.—Dr. Gall, Louisville; *Brit. Med. Journ.*, June 28, 1873; Kappeler: Case No. 70.

268. Male, twenty-eight years. Chloroformed for dilatation of the sphincter ani, on account of anal fissure. After inhaling for five to seven minutes, a tendency to opisthotonos was manifested, though without change of pulse or breathing. The chloroform was discontinued. Immediately after the operation the patient became cyanosed, and respiration ceased. Death quickly followed. Examination of the chloroform discovered the presence of a small quantity of allylic chloride.—G. Berghmann: *Hygiea Förh.*, S. 205, 1872; Kappeler: Case No. 71.

269. Male, thirty-nine years. Dislocation of the forearm. Inhaled 22 grammes of chloroform. Ten days previously had inhaled it with impunity. Now, after a period of muscular rigidity and excitement lasting for six or seven minutes after the commencement of inhalation, the patient suddenly passed into a state of collapse, and died two hours afterward, in spite of artificial respiration.—Ijör: *Norsk Magazin* f. Lägeridensk., R. 3, Bd. 2; Förh., S. 209; Kappeler: Case No. 72.

270. Male, sixty years; insane. Fistulous perineum, requiring introduction of a catheter. Chloroform with Clover's inhaler. Inhalation proceeded normally, and the patient became insensible. Passage of the catheter caused struggling, and the inhaler was again employed. Seven minutes afterward the pulse flagged and stopped. *Autopsy.*—Right side of the heart flaccid and full of liquid blood, left side empty and contracted. Arteries generally atheromatous. Examination of the inhaling apparatus discovered *that the machine was out of order, permitting the inhalation of a much more highly concentrated vapor than was intended.*—Broadmoor Asylum; *Lancet* and *Brit. Med. Journ.*, May 24, 1873; Kappeler: Case No. 73.

271. Female. Tooth-extraction by a dentist. Chloroform given on a sponge. Patient had often taken chloroform previously. Had eaten nothing on that day, but drank a glass of sherry immediately before the operation. Inhaled while sitting upright in the chair. Very little excitement, but the jaws had to be forcibly separated. The pulse stopped as soon as the tooth came out. Artificial respiration and electricity. *Autopsy.*—Fatty degeneration of the heart.—Blaker, Brighton; *Brit. Med. Journ.*, August 23, 1873; *Lancet*, September 6, 1873; Kappeler: Case, No. 74.

272. Male; soldier. Removal of diseased tibia, caused by a compound fracture. Chloroform had not been inhaled more than a minute when the heart stopped. *Autopsy.*—Hypertrophy and fatty degeneration of the

heart.—J. L. Erskine, Royal Engineers; *Brit. Med. Journ.*, August 23, 1873.

273. Boy, fifteen years. Spontaneous fracture of the humerus. Inhaled about two drachms to allow examination of the injured bone. Death from syncope during his recovery from the anæsthetic. *Autopsy.*—Viscera all healthy.—St. Thomas's Hospital, London ; *Brit. Med. Journ.*, March 22, 1873.

274. Boy, twelve years. Tooth-extraction. Vomited during inhalation. After the subsidence of nausea, was again partially anæsthetized. Complaining of pain during extraction of one of the roots of the tooth, which had been broken, more chloroform was given. Extraction of the remaining root was immediately followed by failure of the pulse, sudden paleness of the face, and death. About half an ounce of chlorofom had been used. —*Am. Practitioner*, June, 1873.

275. At Lille, France, a death from chloroform at the hands of a dentist. For this he was condemned to imprisonment for one month, and was fined twelve shillings and about twenty pounds damages.—*Lancet*, May 17, 1873.

276. Male, young, healthy ; machinist. Dressing of several fingers, injured by machinery. Before complete anæsthesia had been reached, the patient was seized with convulsive tremors, and died immediately.—W. H. Mussey, Cincinnati ; *The Clinic*, August 9, 1873.

277. At Stoke-Clymesland, December, 1869, a patient died during administration of chloroform for amputation of the thigh. The pulse suddenly stopped.—*Brit. Med. Journ.*, July 19, 1873.

278. Male, thirty-seven years. Exploration of enlarged liver by puncture. Pulse and respiration good until the close of the stage of excitement, when the pulse failed, the patient became cyanosed, and gasped. Artificial respiration and electricity for nearly an hour. *Autopsy.*—Heart apparently healthy ; liver enlarged, lardaceous, adherent to the diaphragm, and containing numerous gummatous masses.—Guy's Hospital; *Brit. Med. Journ.*, September 13, 1873.

279. Female, forty-five years. Had sustained a fracture of the right arm, June 3, 1873. Inhaled chloroform from a handkerchief, June 28th, for the purpose of painless dressing of the arm. At first one drachm was given, but without producing anæsthesia. After about two minutes a second drachm was given, and two minutes later she ceased to struggle, the pulse remaining good. The anæsthetic was then removed, and an attempt was made to reduce the dislocation of the radius. It was then noticed that the pupils were dilated, the face livid, and both pulse and respiration had stopped.—*Med. Times and Gaz.*, July 12, 1873.

280. Male, about forty-five years ; physician. Had for several years been in the habit of occasionally breathing chloroform when fatigued or otherwise suffering. Shortly after dinner, September 9, 1873, he had retired to his room, and was found, next morning, lying in his ordinary dress across the bed, with his face plunged in a mass of undigested food, by which he had been suffocated. A two-ounce vial, still containing two drachms of chloroform, was found by his side. Rigor mortis had supervened, and it was concluded that he had been dead at least twelve hours. —*Brit. Med. Journ.*, September 27, 1873.

281. Male, forty-four years ; German. Dislocation of the shoulder. Chloroform on a towel. The breathing becoming irregular, the anæsthetic was discontinued until it became again natural. The pulse continued good. Chloroform was again given, but was once more removed before the mus-

cles were completely relaxed. Half a minute later, at the moment of reduction, respiration ceased, and could not be renewed. *Autopsy.*—Blood fluid ; left ventricle contracted ; right flaccid and empty ; valves healthy.— Cincinnati Hospital ; *The Clinic,* October 11, 1873.

282. A young man inhaled chloroform for an operation for the removal of a scrofulous tumor in the groin. Pulse and respiration suddenly ceased, and artificial respiration, prolonged for three-quarters of an hour, availed nothing for his relief.—Dawson and Connor ; Good Samaritan Hospital, Cincinnati ; *The Clinic,* May 23, 1874 ; *Brit. Med. Journ.,* June 27, 1874 ; Kappeler : Case No. 76.

283. Male ; intemperate. Old dislocation of the shoulder-joint. Death from the inhalation of chloroform. Among other restorative measures, intravenous injection of ammonia was performed without any result.— *Australian Med. Journ.,* August, 1873 ; *Brit. Med. Journ.,* November 15, 1873.

284. Male. Epithelial cancer of the lip.—Provincial Hospital, New Zealand ; *Brit. Med. Journ.,* January 31, 1874.

285. Female. Cancer of the breast. Death from chloroform during an operation for removal of the tumor.—Dunedin Hospital, New Zealand ; *Brit. Med. Journ.,* January 31, 1874.

286. Male, thirty years ; mason. Stricture of the urethra. Auscultation detecting nothing wrong with the heart, chloroform was given for the purpose of introducing a sound. Chloroform was given, to the amount of two drachms, on a sponge. The patient had eaten nothing for four hours before operation ; he was very nervous, and shivered as he was placed upon the table. After inhaling two drachms a period of violent excitement commenced. The muscles were rigid, and the arms were brandished wildly ; he held his breath, and struggled furiously. His face became cyanosed ; so the chloroform was withdrawn, but no change in his condition followed. Slapping with a wet cloth did no good, for his face grew darker, and the struggling became more feeble till it finally ceased. Sylvesterism brought back a feeble pulse at the wrist, but, in spite of galvanization of the phrenic, death occurred through paralysis of the heart. *Autopsy.*—Heart normal, but its right side was filled with black blood. The lungs were hyperæmic. —Bristol Royal Infirmary ; *Lancet,* January 17, 1874 ; Kappeler : Case No. 77.

287. Male, forty-eight years. Dislocation of the left shoulder. May 18, 1874, one drachm " of Squibb's chloroform was administered on a napkin, and the operation was begun. In ten' minutes a violent spasm came on, the patient's face became red, his eyes fixed, his lips were drawn up, respiration and pulse stopped. The spasm lasted but a short time, and then the patient died."—Butler, Baltimore ; *Med. News and Library,* July, 1874.

288. Male, thirty years ; intemperate. Deep submental abscess, for which aspiration was proposed. Three drachms of chloroform were given. The patient was at first greatly excited, but finally became quiet, if not fully insensible. The needle of the aspirator was then plunged into the abscess, but before the drainage of pus was finished it became necessary to renew the administration of the anæsthetic. The patient then grew suddenly pale, and the pulse became imperceptible. *Autopsy.*—The lungs were emphysematous ; the heart was healthy ; the left side empty ; the right side contained a large quantity of black fluid blood mixed with small clots.— University College Hospital ; *Lancet,* April 11, 1874 ; Kappeler : Case No. 78.

289. Female, fifty years ; married. Iridectomy. Had taken chloroform

one week previously.   Chloroform given with an inhaler.   At first the patient was timid and agitated, and would not breathe.   By cheering her, and by wary administration of the vapor, she was made to breathe more easily.   Soon, however, the head was drawn backward, and the whole body stiffened.   Respiration became stertorous, hurried, and irregular.   The inhaler was then removed, but the patient drew a deep inspiration and ceased to breathe.   The pulse failed at the same time.   *Autopsy.*—Fatty deposit upon the heart, but no degeneration of its substance ; right side of the heart filled with fluid blood ; aorta atheromatous.—Keene : *Lancet*, May 16, 1874 ; Kappeler : Case No. 79.

290. Male, forty-eight years ; sailor.   Fistula in ano.   Twice previously had been chloroformed.   One drachm was given on a cloth.   There was very little resistance, and insensibility supervened at the usual time, without any unfavorable symptoms ; but, just as the operation was to be commenced, the surgeon discovered that the pulse had ceased.   The tongue was drawn forward, artificial respiration was instituted, the chest was slapped with a wet towel, and ammonia was held to the nose.   The patient breathed feebly for two minutes, then gasped, and was dead.   The heart had ceased to beat when the pulse disappeared.—Allingham, St. Mark's Hospital ; *Brit. Med. Journ.*, April 18, 1874 ; Kappeler : Case No. 80.

291. Male, adult.   Tumor in the posterior nares.   Chloroform was given with Clover's apparatus to the patient, as he sat erect upon a chair with a piece of caoutchouc between his teeth.   He inhaled well, but kept swallowing.   At the end of five minutes he vomited three or four ounces of a yellowish liquid.   He then spoke, leaned back, and again inhaled quietly for three or four minutes.   An attempt at examination of the tumor was now followed by nausea ; so the chloroform was pushed to the extent of producing insensibility of the cornea and contraction of the pupils. Pulse regular, but rather weak.   Fifteen minutes having passed since the commencement of inhalation, the surgeon attempted to pass a ligature through the nose into the pharynx.   In consequence of the partial withdrawal of the anæsthetic during this effort, the patient came partly to himself, and the chloroform was renewed.   This occasioned a repetition of the phenomena of nausea, and the pulse grew feeble.   The inhaler was now removed and the patient was placed in a horizontal position, his pupils being dilated and his face very pale.   Respiration becoming more and more feeble, Sylvesterism was undertaken for his relief.   The tampon between the teeth favored the free and noiseless passage of air into the lungs. He groaned three or four times, but the pupils remained dilated and motionless.   Every effort at resuscitation failed.   It seemed probable that the inhaling apparatus had furnished a too highly concentrated vapor.— Clover, London ; *Brit. Med. Journ.*, June 20, 1874 ; Kappeler : Case No. 81.

292. Male, forty-seven years ; intemperate ; feeble heart.   Dislocation of the shoulder.   A very small quantity of chloroform speedily produced such excitement that inhalation was much interrupted.   After this stage had been passed, alarming symptoms appeared, necessitating artificial respiration, electricity, etc., for an hour, but without result.   *Autopsy.*—Nothing abnormal.—Addenbrooke's Hospital ; *Lancet*, July 25, 1874 ; *Brit. Med. Journ.*,, p. 113, July 24, 1875 ; Kappeler : Case No. 82.

293. Male, forty-eight years ; joiner ; strong and healthy.   Amputation of the middle finger.   Two drachms given on a cloth.   The patient was more than ordinarily excitable, but had been fully anæsthetized, so that the operation was about to commence, when he snorted two or three times, grew suddenly black in the face, and ceased to breathe, while the pulse

became very feeble. The sounds of the heart continued audible for twenty minutes after spontaneous respiration had ceased. Sylvesterism, cold affusion, electricity, and ammonia, all failed. *Autopsy.*—Slight hyperæmia of the lungs. Heart weak and somewhat dilated, both ventricles containing a small quantity of liquid blood.—Jessop, General Infirmary, Leeds; *Lancet*, August 1, 1874; *Brit. Med. Journ.*, August 1, 1874; Kappeler: Case No. 83.

294. Boy, fourteen years. Dislocation of the hip. Inhaled sixty drops of chloroform. At the end of two minutes, in a state of semi-consciousness, he suddenly passed into a condition of syncope, and died in spite of Sylvesterism and electricity. *Autopsy.*—Every organ was healthy.—Gant, Royal Free Hospital; *Brit. Med. Journ.*, December 19, 1874; Kappeler: Case No. 84.

295. Female, eighteen years. Took chloroform for the removal of a pin in her hand, and died, 1874.—Woolwich Workhouse; *Brit. Med. Journ.*, p. 999, December 18, 1880.

296. Male. Dislocation of the shoulder. Death from syncope after the operation.—Leeds Infirmary; *Brit. Med. Journ.*, p. 999, December 18, 1880.

297. Female, adult; died, May 6, 1874, from the effects of chloroform inhaled from a handkerchief.—Carlisle: *Brit. Med. Journ.*, p. 654, May 16, 1874.

298. Female, thirty-four years; bar-maid. Suffered with lupus upon the face and neck since her twelfth year. Patient had been operated on, under chloroform, six times in the year 1874—July 17th, August 7th, 17th, and 29th, and September 10th. Each time the period of excitement was long, but otherwise nothing unfavorable occurred. On June 30, 1875, the patient was again chloroformed for removal of recurrent growth over the angle of the jaw, on the right side of the face. Chloroform was given with Esmarch's inhaler, after the most approved scientific method. The patient inhaled with perfect tranquillity; woke once during the operation, so that inhalation was renewed until the cornea became insensible. Pulse and respiration continued good for two minutes after the conclusion of the operation and the withdrawal of the anæsthetic. At this moment the patient suddenly turned pale, opened her eyes with their pupils widely dilated. About the same time the pulse failed at the wrist, and the respiratory movements became slow and feeble, ceasing altogether after a few seconds. Sylvesterism, irritation of the pharynx, cold affusion, tracheotomy, and faradization of the phrenic nerves, all utterly failed, and at the end of three-quarters of an hour the suspicion gradually deepened into a certainty that the surgeon had before him a genuine corpse. *Autopsy negative.*—Left lung adherent posteriorly to the pleural surfaces of the chest-wall; lungs œdematous, at points ecchymosed, and emphysematous—probably from artificial respiration. Right heart contained liquid blood mixed with small clots; left ventricle flaccid and empty; valves very slightly thickened.—Kappeler: *Anæsthetica*, pp. 65, 90.

299. Male, adult; healthy and strong. Tooth-extraction. Died under the influence of chloroform, in the office of a Boston dentist. *Autopsy negative.*—Heart healthy; blood everywhere fluid.—*Boston Med. and Surg. Journ.*, October 1 and 8, 1874.

300. Female, adult. Tooth-extraction, Kingston, Canada. Death from chloroform.—*Canada Med. Record*, November, 1874.

301. Male, forty-five years; strong and healthy. Amputation of the little finger. Chloroform given on a cloth. For two minutes the inhalation

proceeded in a satisfactory manner; the patient then became rigid, and struggled violently. The face and body were everywhere cyanosed. Inhalation was therefore discontinued. As the patient grew quiet it was noticed that he was pulseless, and had ceased to breathe. Artificial respiration, electricity, and inversion of the body, were tried for three-quarters of an hour, but without result. *Autopsy.*—Both lungs hyperæmic. Right heart filled with black, fluid blood; a black clot in the left auricle; valves healthy. Liver, spleen, and kidneys, hyperæmic. Brain, anæmic.—*Australian Med. Journ.; Brit. Med. Journ.*, July 17, 1875; Kappeler: Case No. 85.

302. Male, fifty-six years; healthy heart and lungs. Extirpation of the tongue for carcinoma. Three drachms given on lint. Shortly after the commencement of inhalation the pulse was intermittent, but soon became regular. The patient was restless, but at the end of ten minutes was sufficiently insensible to allow the operation to proceed. A needle had been thrust through the tongue, when suddenly the pulse weakened, and the respiration became irregular and ceased altogether. The pupils were greatly dilated. The heart continued to beat for a short time after the cessation of breathing. Artificial respiration, electricity, etc. *Autopsy.*— Brain healthy. Heart healthy, left ventricle contracted. Blood liquid throughout the body. Lungs healthy and hyperæmic. Pleura thickened on both sides.—Jackson, Sheffield Public Hospital; *Brit. Med. Journ.*, February 27, 1875; Kappeler: Case No. 86.

303. Female, forty-five years. Enucleation of the eye-ball. Chloroform given with Skinner's inhaler, to the amount of one drachm. The patient became excited, and the inhalation was discontinued. Excitement persisted, and suddenly the heart stopped, though the patient still continued to breathe for a short time. Every expedient, including inversion, failed to restore the patient. *Autopsy.*—Everything healthy except the heart— in the anterior wall of the right ventricle were found a number of cancerous nodules.—Wherry, Addenbrooke's Hospital, Cambridge; *Brit. Med. Journ.*, p. 113, July 24, 1875; Kappeler: Case No. 87.

304. Male, nineteen years; bombardier; strong and healthy. Exarticulation of the third toe. Chloroform given on lint. Three drachms produced insensibility without excitement. A fourth drachm was then given, but only partly inhaled, as the patient was sufficiently anæsthetized. Four minutes after, just as the operation was ended, the pulse suddenly failed, and the face became pale and livid. Cold affusion, and depression of the head failed to give relief, and the respiration became first stertorous, then sighing, and gradually ceased altogether. Artificial respiration did no good, and the body was inverted. Galvanism was also tried. These efforts were continued for over an hour in vain.—Smith: *Lancet*, February 13, 1875; Kappeler: Case No. 88.

305. Male, forty-nine years. Had sustained a dislocation of the shoulder. Owing to a displacement of the bandages, the luxation had been reproduced, and the patient requested chloroform, which he had previously inhaled, to facilitate the reduction. Two drachms were given on lint. The patient did not seem to be completely anæsthetized, and, at the instant of reduction, he gave a convulsive shudder, and died. Inversion was here employed without success. *Autopsy.*—Organs universally healthy.—Hardy and Jones, St. Thomas's Hospital; *Brit. Med. Journ.*, October 9, 1875: *Lancet*, same date; Kappeler: Case No. 89.

306. Male, fifty-two years; coal-heaver, strong and muscular, though recently recovered from an attack of bronchitis. Having a necrosis of bone, it was decided to give chloroform for the purpose of painless operation.

An ounce was given. At first, pulse and respiration were normal. The stage of excitement continued for two minutes, during which the patient was red in the face, and shouted aloud, brandishing his fists in the air. After two or three minutes he grew quiet and made two snoring inspirations. Chloroform was immediately withdrawn, but at the same instant the face became livid, pulse imperceptible, and respiration at a standstill. Efforts at resuscitation caused two sighing inspirations, and then no more. Cold air, water-sprinkling, drawing out the tongue, lowering of the head, artificial respiration, application of a hot iron to the epigastrium and to the soles of the feet, did no good. *Autopsy.*—Brain normal. Lungs healthy, full of air and blood. Slight thickening of the pleural and pericardial membranes; blood dark and liquid. Heart flaccid, its muscular substance healthy, and the valves normal.—Helwig, Odense, Dünemark; *Ugeskrift for Laeger; Brit. Med. Journ.*, October 9, 1875; Kappeler: Case No. 90.

307. Male, fifty-six years; sailor, strong and muscular, but anxious regarding the operation. Arcus senilis visible. Sequestrotomy for necrosis of the femur. One drachm given with an inhaler. Great excitement during the first five minutes of inhalation. Esmarch's elastic bandage was then applied. The face soon became livid, and the respiration irregular and noisy; but, laying the patient upon his left side, and drawing his tongue forward, these symptoms were relieved. No more chloroform was given, and the operation was commenced. This was nearly completed, and the patient was returning to consciousness, when the same alarming phenomena reappeared, and after a few seconds the patient was dead. Besides artificial respiration, galvanism, etc., the intravenous injection of ammonia was tried, but without effect. *Autopsy.*—Body very fat. Lungs hyperæmic, but healthy. Heart well covered with fat, but not in a state of degeneration; plenty of liquid blood in all its cavities; valves healthy. Aorta atheromatous. Syphiloma of the liver. Kidneys granular. Cerebral arteries rigid. Arachnoid thickened.—Johnson Smith: *Brit. Med. Journ.*, October 16, 1875; Kappeler: Case, No. 91.

308. Male, forty-two years; gardener; received a gunshot wound in the right eye, November 16, 1875. Enucleation of the eyeball was recommended, to protect the other eye. One hundred drops of chloroform were given on a towel. Half of this was given at first, and the patient seemed to become at once semi-conscious. The operation was then commenced, but it was found necessary to give more chloroform. The pulse immediately grew so weak that the patient was inverted, and artificial respiration was undertaken. The patient, nevertheless, died in half an hour from the commencement of inhalation. *Autopsy* negative.—Chesshire; *Brit. Med. Journ.*, December 11, 1875; *Lancet*, December 11, 1875; Kappeler: Case No. 92.

309. Male, sixteen years. Tooth-extraction in the office of a dentist. Half an ounce of chloroform was used, and in five minutes the patient was dead.—*Dental Cosmos,* May, 1875.

310. Male, forty-two years; feeble; no disease of either heart or lungs. Galvano-cautery for a chancroid of the penis. Chloroform given on a cone of lint. Three or four drachms had thus been administered when the patient became pale, the pulse stopped, and respiration ceased.—*Gazette Méd. de Bordeaux*, November 5, 1875.

311. Male, eleven years; healthy. Reduction of paraphimosis. Two drachms of chloroform given on a napkin, upon which the same quantity was twice again poured out in the course of three or four minutes. The patient then appeared to be unconscious, but an effort to reduce the fore-

skin caused him to sit up and to manifest signs of returning consciousness. Two drachms more were then given, when the reduction was promptly effected.   It was then discovered that respiration had stopped and the pulse had ceased.   The tongue was drawn forward, and the body was inverted. This caused six or eight gasping and irregular respirations, but the pulse did not return.   Death occurred about six or eight minutes after the beginning of inhalation.—J. Buist: *Nashville Journ. of Med. and Surgery*, June, 1875.

312. Male, twenty-seven years; sailor.   Enucleation of the right eyeball, which had been injured in a shipwreck, on a voyage to China.   After inhalation for three minutes, the face became purple and the pulse ceased. Artificial respiration did no good.   Death was attributed to syncope. *Autopsy* negative.—Wilkinson, Ophthalmic Hospital, Gray's Inn Road; *Med. Times and Gaz.*, July 24, 1875.

313. Female, twenty-one years.   Abscess in the abdomen.   Chloroform was given for puncture of the abscess.   *Autopsy.*—Purulent effusion in the peritoneal cavity, abscess in the liver, pus in the pleural cavity.— Ker, Quarrybank; *Lancet*, July 31, 1875.

314. Female.   Mrs. C. inhaled chloroform, administered by herself, and was found dead.   The high social position of the patient precluded the publication of any detailed account of the medical features of the case.— *Brit. Med. Journ.*, December 4, 1875.

315. A patient in Glasgow inhaled chloroform for amputation of a finger, and died.—*Brit. Med. Journ.*, p. 761, December 18, 1875.

316. Male, thirty-four years; soldier, at the Artillery Hospital.   Amputation of the leg.   Died of syncope under the influence of chloroform. —*Brit. Med. Journ.*, p. 999, December 18, 1880; from *Lancet*, 1875.

317. Male, about twenty-three years of age.   Venereal warts and chronic phimosis, necessitating circumcision.   Heart-sounds normal. Two and a half drachms were given.   The radial and temporal pulses were both satisfactory, and chloroform had been withdrawn for a minute, when suddenly, during the operation, the countenance became livid, and the circulation ceased.   Artificial respiration, electricity, etc., availed nothing.— Steeven's Hospital, Dublin; *Brit. Med. Journ.*, January 29, 1876; Kappeler: Case No. 93.

318. Male, laborer, adult.   Amputation of the arm.   Stethoscope indicated no heart disease.   Three drachms were given, and the patient died suddenly during the act of inhalation.   *Autopsy.*—The heart was dilated, and the body is said to have exhibited other evidences of disease.   (What?) Death was attributed to paralysis of the heart.—Reid, Stafford Infirmary; *Brit. Med. Journ.*, February 5, 1876; Kappeler: Case No. 94.

319. Female. Tooth-extraction by a dentist.   Heart and pulse seemed healthy.   Chloroform was inhaled slowly in the sitting posture.   After extraction of three roots, the countenance of the patient suddenly changed color.   As her respiration grew weaker, he commenced the employment of restoratives, but she ceased to breathe.   Sylvesterism restored the breathing for about two minutes, when it ceased altogether, in spite of the use of electricity.   *Autopsy.*—"Heart disease" was reported.—Evan Abraham Morgan, Liverpool; *Brit. Med. Journ.*, April 1, 1876; Kappeler: Case No. 95.

320. Male, fifty-four years; strong and healthy.   Amputation of finger.   Heart-sounds normal.   About one drachm and a half of chloroform given.   Two minutes after the commencement of inhalation the patient became very unruly, and so continued for about two minutes.   He

was then completely insensible, face slightly bluish, respiration regular. Breathing grew stertorous, with increase of lividity ; so he was placed upon his left side, when suddenly pulse and respiration ceased. Artificial respiration and drawing out the tongue produced a deep inspiration after about two minutes, but this was the last, though every effort—inversion, electricity, Sylvesterism, etc., was employed for the space of half an hour. It was found that ejaculation of semen had taken place in the death-agony.— J. W. Hunt, Leicester ; *Brit. Med. Journ.*, April 8, 1876 ; Kappeler : Case No. 96.

321. Male, forty-five years ; laborer ; vigorous. Extirpation of a fibroid tumor from the hard palate. Three or four drachms of chloroform given on a flannel cone. The patient took his last meal six hours before the operation, and had a dose of brandy half an hour before inhalation. He was chloroformed in a semi-recumbent position. Great excitement for two or three minutes, until he was laid flat, when he became more quiet. Suddenly respiration ceased, and the face was cyanosed. The condition of the pulse could not be ascertained. Every effort—dragging the tongue, depression of the head, laying the body on its left side, Sylvesterism, electricity, etc., was tried for half an hour, but only a few gasping respirations rewarded the attempt. *Autopsy* negative.—Heart flaccid. Lungs and brain full of blood.—Norton and Juler, St. Mary's Hospital, London ; *Brit. Med. Journ.*, July 29, 1876 ; Kappeler : Case No. 97.

322. Male, sixty years ; vigorous. Dislocation of the humerus. Chloroform given from a metallic inhaling apparatus. The patient was considerably excited, and the anæsthetic was given slowly in consequence. About two minutes after the commencement of inhalation the heart stopped suddenly, and soon afterward respiration ceased also. Electricity and artificial respiration failed to do any good. *Autopsy.*—Heavy deposit of fat upon the pericardium. Fatty infiltration of both ventricles, especially the right ; both cavities dilated and empty ; valves healthy. Kidneys large and granular ; cortical portion atrophied.—J. C. Ferrier, Leicester Infirmary ; *Brit. Med. Journ.*, July 29, 1876 ; Kappeler : Case No. 98.

323. Male, forty-five years ; apparently healthy. Opening sinuses connecting with the right trochanter. Chloroform given on lint. The patient struggled violently, and the pulse weakened, necessitating intermission of inhalation. Respiration became very irregular, and ceased about six minutes after the commencement of inhalation, *Autopsy.*—Fatty degeneration of the heart. The other organs were healthy.—St. Thomas's Hospital ; *Brit. Med. Journ.*, September 16, 1876 ; Kappeler : Case No. 99.

324. Boy, eight years. Tenotomy, and forcible extension of the knee. Two drachms on lint. Just after the completion of the operation the pulse suddenly stopped. The patient was inverted ; artificial respiration was continued for an hour and a half ; he was slapped with a wet towel, and hot sponges were applied over the heart ; ammonia and amyl nitrite were held to the nose, but all to no purpose.—Walter, Long Eaton : *Brit. Med. Journ.*, November, 11, 1876 ; Kappeler : Case No. 100.

325. Male, thirty-three years, publican. Reduction of an inguinal hernia. Examination of the heart before operation indicated nothing wrong. Chloroform was given on lint, half a drachm at a time. Four or five minutes after the commencement of inhalation, while the fifth half-drachm was being given, without any previous excitement the face became livid, the pulse grew weak, and respiration was slightly stertorous. Death occurred three or four minutes later, in spite of depression of the head, dragging of the tongue, slapping of the chest, Sylvesterism, electri-

city, injection of two ounces of brandy with hot water into the rectum, etc. *Autopsy.*—Lungs and brain engorged with blood. Heart large and its right side full of black blood ; muscular substance of the right ventricle thinner than natural, and infiltrated with fat, but microscopic examination indicated no fatty degeneration.—Charing Cross Hospital ; *Brit.* *Med. Journ.*, December 23, 1876.

326. Male, forty-three years. Inhaled chloroform December 15, 1876, for an amputation of a forefinger. Anæsthetic given on lint folded once. Respiration ceased first. *Autopsy.*—Fatty degeneration of the muscular tissue of the heart.—Wolverhampton Hospital ; *Brit. Med. Journ.*, January 13 and 27, 1877.

327. Female, twenty-five years ; multipara. Entered the Maternité at Lyons, March 23, 1876. Labor-pains continued during the evening and night. The next morning, at seven o'clock, the membranes ruptured ; shoulder-presentation. To facilitate version, chloroform was given by the nurse, without calling upon the attending physicians. The patient did not arouse after the operation. The house physician was then called, who found the pulse very small, the face cyanotic, the inspirations short and frequent. In spite of efforts to the contrary, the patient died in ten minutes.—*L'Union Méd.*, April 13, 1876 ; *Med. News and Library*, June, 1876.

328. Female, twenty-two years ; primipara. The head of the child was at the point of birth, when a slight convulsion occurred. Chloroform was given, and the patient was kept under its influence. After the delivery of the head, while the uterus was contracting, the patient shuddered, and her pulse ceased—she was dead.—Cotting : *Boston Med. and Surg. Journ.*, January 11, 1877.

329. Female, thirty years. Died during inhalation of chloroform for the extraction of a tooth.—*Ohio Med. Recorder*, October, 1876.

330. Male. Died from chloroform inhaled for the extraction of a thorn from his foot.—*Pacific Med. and Surg. Journ.*, October, 1876.

331. Dr. Gustav Judell, Erlangen, October 26, 1876, was found dead in his bed. He had been accustomed to inhale chloroform as a remedy for sleeplessness, by which he was much troubled, and a bottle of the liquid was found near him. The anæsthetic had excited vomiting, and a portion of the food had remained in the œsophagus, causing death by suffocation. (By compression of the trachea ?)—*Med. News and Library*, January, 1877.

332. Male, fourteen years. Inhaled chloroform from a napkin, January 5, 1877, for the extraction of a tooth. Immediately after the tooth had been drawn there was a gasp for breath, a deep sigh, and the head of the boy rolled to one side—he was dead.—Rahway, N. J. : *Med. News and Library*, February, 1877.

333. Male. Carious bone in the stump of an arm. Pulse and respiration ceased nearly together. *Autopsy.*—Marked degeneration of the heart.—University College Hospital ; *Brit. Med. Journ.*, January 20, 1877.

334. Male, fifty-two years. Suffering from strangulated inguinal hernia. Chloroform inhaled from a handkerchief to the amount of two drachms. The pulse suddenly stopped, while the respiration became shallow and soon ceased.—Peterborough Infirmary ; *Brit. Med. Journ.*, p. 120, January 27, 1877.

335. Female, about to undergo operation for the removal of a tumor from the throat.—Staleybridge, England ; *Brit. Med. Journ.*, p. 120, January 27, 1877.

336. Female, forty-three years. About to undergo ligation of the carotid. In the course of the operation, blood entered the trachea during in-

spiration, causing death by asphyxia.—University College Hospital; *Brit. Med. Journ.*, p. 210, February 17, 1877.

337. Male, fifty-six years. About to be operated on for fistula in ano and hemorrhoids. Inhaled about three drachms from a cone of lint. Patient struggled violently during the stage of excitement; the respiration became irregular, and the pulse stopped. *Autopsy* negative.—No organic disease. —Derby Infirmary, *Brit. Med. Journ.*, March 17, 1877.

338. Male, twenty-seven years. Cautery to the knee. Chloroform inhaled from Skinner's inhaler. The pulse became very weak, and then stopped. *Autopsy.*—Old pericardial adhesions. Advanced fatty degeneration of the heart.—Mercer's Hospital, Dublin; *Brit. Med. Journ.*, June 30, 1877.

339. Male, physician. Inhalation of chloroform prior to extirpation of his eye.—*Am. Journ. of Dental Science*, May, 1877.

340. Male. Perineal fistula. Death from chloroform before operation. —Blackburn Infirmary; *Lancet*, June 9, 1877.

341. Female, twenty-three years. Strabismus. Examined before inhalation, and considered a fit subject for chloroform. About four drachms were given during the operation. The patient vomited. After emergence from anæsthesia the patient spoke to the surgeon, and "appeared perfectly right." Between nine and ten o'clock she was visited by the surgeon, who found her asleep, with a quiet and regular pulse. At half-past eleven o'clock she was found dead—in the same place. *Autopsy.*—Brain was softer than natural, and there was "coagulated blood in several places." Other organs were healthy. Chronic "disease of the brain" was considered the cause of death. What particular disease was not stated.—Cann, Dawlish, England: *Brit. Med. Journ.*, August 4, 1877.

342. Female, twenty-five years; had previously inhaled chloroform without harm. She was now about to be operated upon for "some uterine trouble," and died very suddenly after having inhaled only a few drops of chloroform. *Autopsy.*—Fatty degeneration of the right ventricle of the heart.—Toronto General Hospital; *Canadian Journ. of Med. Sciences*, August, 1877.

343. Boy, twelve years. Died from the effects of chloroform, while undergoing an operation for talipes.—Homœopathic Hospital, Toledo, O. *Toledo Med. and Surg. Journ.*, August, 1877.

344. Male, thirty-eight years, suffering for three days with paraphimosis. The pain being very severe, "a small dose" of chloroform was given on lint. The patient immediately began to struggle. In two or three minutes was quiet, and the operation was commenced, when his respiration suddenly stopped, his face became cyanosed, and the pulse failed. Sylvesterism and slapping with a wet towel partially restored respiration after five minutes, but the heart remained motionless. Half a drachm of brandy hypodermically, faradization, and artificial respiration of three-quarters of an hour, did no good. *Autopsy.*—Heart dilated, flaccid, fatty; no valvular disease. Lungs and other internal organs engorged with blood.—London Hospital; *Brit. Med. Journ.*, August 18, 1877.

345. Female, elderly. Tumor in the axilla. Death during inhalation, prior to operation. *Autopsy.*—Fatty degeneration of the heart.—*Canada Lancet*, January, 1878.

346. Death from inhalation of chloroform, at Llanelly, preparatory to an operation for fistula.—*Lancet*, December 8, 1877; *Brit. Med. Journ.*, December 18, 1880.

347. Male, eighteen years; healthy. Circumcision. One drachm given

on a mask. Heart-sounds normal when examined before inhalation. Nothing unfavorable occurred during the first two or three minutes. The patient then became rigid, his countenance grew livid, and the pupils were dilated. Cold affusion and artificial respiration availed nothing.—H. Gordon Cumming, Devon and Exeter Hospital ; *Brit. Med. Journ.*, February 2, 1878.

348. Female, a young lady residing on Staten Island. Had five teeth extracted by a dentist, while under the influence of chloroform. Showing signs of recovery from anæsthesia, more chloroform was given. She was "taken with a spasm," and died. *Autopsy.*—All the internal organs were healthy.—*Med. News and Library*, March, 1878.

349. Male, adult ; sailor. Extirpation of an eye. Three drachms of chloroform given with Skinner's inhaler. Patient much excited. Death just at the commencement of the operation. *Autopsy.*—Fatty degeneration of the heart ; blood in the cavities of the organ. Atheroma of the aorta. Œdema and emphysema of both lungs. Liver much congested, but healthy. Kidneys slightly granular, much congested. Considerable increase of subarachnoid fluid ; cerebral veins gorged with blood.—Liverpool Northern Hospital ; *Brit. Med. Journ.*, February 16 and March 2, 1878.

350. Female, ten years. Extraction of teeth. Sudden failure of the heart, followed by death.—London ; *Brit. Med. Journ.*, May 18, 1878.

351. Female, thirty-four years ; very intemperate. Fistula in ano. Very timorous, and insisted upon chloroform. Three drachms were given, half a drachm at a time, on lint. Pulse feeble and quick. Became much excited, and struggled. As soon as the patient became insensible the anæsthetic was withdrawn, and she was laid upon her left side. Breathing was rapid, but fair ; pulse about the same as at first. Just as the fistula was divided, about two minutes after the cessation of inhalation, the patient screamed, and passed urine ; her pupils dilated, and her face became pale, the heart had ceased to beat. Respiration also ceased after a few moments. Artificial respiration by Howard's method, electricity, injection of brandy into the rectum, and venesection, all failed, though tried for an hour. *Autopsy.*—Heart collapsed, pale, covered with fat ; its weight was nine ounces and three-quarters ; its walls were very thin, and under the microscope showed fatty degeneration. Atheroma on the mitral valve and aorta. The other organs were full of blood, but healthy.—East Suffolk Hospital ; *Brit. Med. Journ.*, May 25, 1878.

352. Male. Amputation of the leg. Had inhaled chloroform until insensible, when, just before the commencement of the operation, alarming symptoms appeared, and death took place at once.—Edinburgh Royal Infirmary ; *Brit. Med. Journ.*, June 1, 1878.

353. Another case, almost identical with the last, is said to have occurred in the same hospital. Particulars not given.—Edinburgh Royal Infirmary ; *loc. cit.*

354. Male, a young man. Iridectomy. Had inhaled two drachms the day before, without accident. Patient was not fully anæsthetized during the operation, which lasted about five minutes. The heart suddenly stopped, two or three gasps for breath followed, and the patient was dead. —J. G. Brooks, Paducah, Ky. : *Am. Med. Bi-weekly ; Brit. Med. Journ.*, October 12, 1878.

355. Male, forty-four years ; laborer, tall and well-developed. Fistula in ano. Heart-sounds healthy. Patient very anxious and excited. Chloroform given from a drop-bottle on lint. Inhaled two drachms very quietly for about five minutes, when he suddenly struggled violently, his pupils

became widely dilated, and his pulse stopped. Electricity was immediately applied over the heart; the chest was severely slapped with a wet towel, and brandy was injected into the rectum. Respiration was gasping, so the patient was inverted for a few seconds, and for a few minutes he breathed more regularly, though the heart could not be felt. Another inversion was then performed, but without effect, and about five minutes from the time he commenced struggling he ceased to breathe. Artificial respiration and electricity were continued about twenty minutes. *Autopsy*, twenty-one hours after death.—Rigor mortis; lungs hyperæmic; heart covered with fat, flabby, its walls pale and thin, the cavities dilated, valves healthy; liver, spleen, and kidneys hyperæmic; brain healthy, but slightly hyperæmic; microscopic examination of the heart showed fatty degeneration.—Sheffield Infirmary; *Brit. Med. Journ.*, October 12, 1878.

356.—Female, thirty-eight years. Dislocation of the elbow. Death during inhalation.—Drumcondra; *Brit. Med. Journ.*, October 19, 1878.

357. Male, fifteen years; clerk, in good health. Reamputation of an ulcerated stump of an amputated humerus. Two and a half drachms of chloroform were given on lint. Immediately after the close of the brief operation—which lasted only one minute—respiration stopped. The tongue was drawn forward, and breathing began again. The wound ceased to bleed, though exhibiting signs of sensibility, and the pulse was gone. The usual endeavors to restore life were continued for an hour. *Autopsy*. —Lungs healthy, the right apex slightly adherent; heart healthy, right side distended with dark fluid blood, left side contracted. The stomach was distended with air. Other organs healthy.—Newcastle-on-Tyne Infirmary; *Brit. Med. Journ.*, October 26, 1878.

358. Male, three years. About to be operated upon for some *malformation*—nature not stated. Twenty minims of chloroform were given with an inhaler when the pulse suddenly stopped, and the apparatus was removed. The child soon recovered, and was then again made to inhale. The pulse again stopped, and this time respiration also ceased. Artificial respiration could not bring back life. *Autopsy*.—The deceased was a weakly child, and the lungs had never been properly inflated, a defect which had not been noticed prior to the operation.—Charing Cross Hospital; *Brit. Med. Journ.*, November 9, 1878.

359. Female, married; in delicate health. Tooth extraction. Half an ounce of chloroform on a napkin. Death during operation.—*Evening Telegraph*, Philadelphia, March 22, 1878.

360. Male, forty-one years; in feeble health. External perineal urethrotomy. An ounce of chloroform was used. Death during the operation. Among other restoratives amyl nitrite was used without effect.—McGuire: *Virginia Med. Monthly*, May, 1878.

361. Male. Hydrocele. Sudden death after inhalation of about half an ounce (15—20 grammes) of chloroform. Tracheotomy and every other method of relief was tried without effect.—*Autopsy* negative.—Dumreicher, Vienna: *Allg. Wien Med. Zeit.*, December 24, 1878; *Med. Times and Gaz.*, January 25, 1879.

362. Male, eight years; healthy. Extraction of a needle from the knee. Four drachms of chloroform were used. The operation was ended, and the anæsthetic had been withdrawn for about five minutes, when the countenance became livid. Artificial respiration and electricity for nearly three-quarters of an hour. *Autopsy* negative.—Rainham: *Brit. Med. Journ.*, March 8, 1879.

363. Dislocation of the ankle-joint, and fracture of the lower end of the

tibia.   During the adjustment of the parts the breathing became stertor-
ous, and almost immediately ceased. *Autopsy* negative.—Toronto ; *Canada Lancet*, June, 1879.

364. Female, fourteen years. Inflammation in the elbow-joint. Abscesses formed in the arm, and had been twice opened under chloroform
without accident.   On the third occasion chloroform was at first inhaled
very easily and quietly, but the breathing soon became noisy and embarrassed, and the face began to grow livid. The usual restoratives were
employed without effect. Death was attributed to asphyxia.—St. Leon-
ard's Cottage Hospital, Mildenhall ; *Brit. Med. Journ.*, p. 97, July 19, 1879.

365. The patient was suffering from an injury of the foot, and was the
subject of *delirium tremens*.   Chloroform was given to procure sleep.
Death instead.—Middlesex Hospital ; *Brit. Med. Journ.*, p. 509, September 27, 1879.

366. Female, adult ; single. Tumor of the breast. Chloroform. The
pulse soon began to fail, and she died in spite of every effort.—Guide
Bridge ; *Brit. Med. Journ.*, p. 666, October 25, 1879.

367. Male, seven years. Had been two years under treatment for contraction of the sinews of the legs and arms. Tenotomy was performed
under bichloride of methylene, and next day he inhaled chloroform for
the purpose of having the limbs placed in splints. At first he was excited, but as he became more quiet, the surgeon began to apply the splints
when it was found that the child was not sufficiently insensible. Just as
more chloroform was about to be given, respiration ceased. Artificial
respiration failed to revive the patient.—University College Hospital ; *Brit.
Med. Journ.*, p. 627, October 18, 1879.

368. Male, adult ; vigorous laborer. Enucleation of the eyeball for
an old injury. Chloroform given on a towel. Patient was quickly anæsthetized without a struggle. Operation was completed in less than five
minutes. Three or four minutes after withdrawing the anæsthetic, when
about to dress the wound, respiration suddenly ceased, and the face became livid. Tongue to the front, electricity, amyl nitrite, but without success. *Autopsy.*—Intense congestion of the kidneys. Heart and lungs apparently healthy.—General Infirmary, Hull ; *Brit. Med. Journ.*, p. 871,
November 29, 1879.

369. Orbital tumor. The patient died from chloroform. No particulars.—Edinburgh Royal Infirmary ; *Brit. Med. Journ.*, p. 949, December
13, 1879.

370. Male, adult. Necrosis of bones of the leg. Death from chloroform during operation. Had previously inhaled chloroform.—Liverpool
Royal Infirmary ; *Brit. Med. Journ.*, p. 1043, December 27, 1879.

371. Male, forty-two years ; surgeon. Had been in the habit of inhaling chloroform from time to time, for nine years previous, to induce
sleep. He had retired to rest apparently in good health, and was found in
the morning lying upon his bed, partially undressed, and evidently dead
for some hours, with a piece of lint, nine or ten inches square, lying upon
his face.—Brampton ; *Brit. Med. Journ.*, p. 176, January 31, 1880.

372. Removal of a projecting phalanx from an injured finger. Death
occurred before any operative interference. *Autopsy.*—Fatty liver ; other
organs healthy.—Edinburgh Royal Infirmary ; *Brit. Med. Journ.*, p. 178,
January 31, 1880.

373. Male, fifty-six years ; had twice taken chloroform without accident. While inhaling the vapor for the third time, he suddenly became
livid, and it was found that his heart had ceased to beat. Artificial respi-

ration and the usual restoratives did no good.—South Infirmary, Cork ; *Brit. Med. Journ.*, p. 372, March 6, 1880.

374. Death from chloroform, inhaled for an operation for the relief of strabismus.—Moorfields Ophthalmic Hospital, 1879 ; *Brit. Med. Journ.*, p. 999, December 18, 1880.

375. Male, adult ; waiter. Dislocation of the shoulder. The patient died during or immediately after the reduction. He breathed the anæsthetic easily. The pulse stopped first, and was soon followed by cessation of respiration. *Autopsy.*—Heart large, with much fat in its substance ; lungs emphysematous ; liver fatty.—Radcliffe Infirmary ; *Brit. Med. Journ.*, p. 900, June 12, 1880.

376. Male, adult ; a tramp. Had been half starved for nine days. "Complaining of severe pain in the lower part of the body, he was sent to the infirmary. An operation being necessary, he was put under chloroform, but died from syncope of the heart."—Blackburn Infirmary ; *Brit. Med. Journ.*, p. 101, July 17, 1880. This is entered as a case of hernia. —*Brit. Med. Journ.*, December 18, 1880.

377. Female, thirty-five years ; married. Died in the office of a dentist, where she was inhaling chloroform for the extraction of a tooth.—Liverpool ; *Brit. Med. Journ.*, p. 352, August 28, 1880.

378. Male, fifty years ; plumber. Compound fracture of the left tibia and fibula, and a simple fracture of the left femur, opening into the knee-joint, necessitating amputation. Had twice before taken chloroform without accident. Two drachms of chloroform were given with Skinner's inhaler. Inhalation went on quietly for four or five minutes, when the patient attempted to rise, and spat a little mucus. Half a minute later, while inhaling, the lower jaw fell, and the face turned blue. The tongue was drawn out, and artificial respiration commenced. After five minutes the patient began to breathe spontaneously, and the pulse returned at the wrist. Very soon, however, the pulse fluttered, became intermittent, and stopped altogether, respiration failing at the same time. *Autopsy.*— Fatty heart ; œdematous lungs ; granular kidneys.—London Hospital ; *Brit. Med. Journ.*, p. 529, September 25, 1880.

379. Male, forty-two years. Epulis of the upper jaw. Two drachms of chloroform. The patient had just come under the influence of the anæsthetic when the heart suddenly stopped. Artificial respiration for an hour, electricity, atropine hypodermically. *Autopsy.*—Fatty degeneration of the heart.—West London Hospital ; *Brit. Med. Journ.*, p. 559, October 2, 1880.

380. Male, fifty-nine years ; foreman. Lithotrity. Had been operated upon under chloroform about ten days previously, and a portion of the stone was then removed. At the second operation about two and a half drachms were given, a few drops at a time, on a piece of flannel stretched over a wire-frame. The stone was crushed twice, and the operator was about to crush it a third time, when the patient turned very pale. The instrument was withdrawn, and the patient was inverted and slapped on the chest with a wet towel, but although breathing continued for about half an hour, the heart did not move again. *Autopsy.*—Heart weak and flabby, especially the right ventricle ; lungs healthy, with the exception of one little patch.—Hull ; *Brit. Med. Journ.*, p. 599, October 9, 1880.

381. Female, eighteen years. Death under chloroform. Electricity and other restoratives failed.—Royal Albert Hospital, Devonport ; *Brit. Med. Journ.*, p. 749, November 6, 1880.

382. Male, forty-three years ; had inhaled chloroform about one month

previously, without accident. Erysipelas of the arm and hand necessitated the amputation of a gangrenous finger. Chloroform was given on flannel stretched over a wire-frame. Some struggling took place. Immediately after the induction of anæsthesia the patient ceased to breathe, and the pulse stopped. He drew a few breaths after this, but in spite of artificial respiration and tracheotomy he never rallied.—Guy's Hospital ; *Brit. Med. Journ.*, p. 935, December 11, 1880.

383. Male, thirty-five years, six feet seven inches high, and weighed two hundred and thirteen pounds. Removal of a wen upon the neck. Death was ascribed to "heart-disease."—*Louisville Med. News*, November 2, 1880.

384. A patient died under chloroform, given for an operation upon a necrosed tibia. *Autopsy* showed an adherent pericardium.—Liverpool Infirmary ; *Brit. Med. Journ.*, p. 999, December 18, 1880.

385. Death from chloroform, caused by syncope. *Autopsy* negative. Organs healthy.—West Norfolk Hospital ; *Brit. Med. Journ.*, p. 999, December 18, 1880.

386. Death from syncope, during an operation for the relief of strabismus.—Cirencester Cottage Hospital ; *Brit. Med. Journ.*, December 18, 1880.

387. Male, twelve years ; scrofulous. Tenotomy and extension of the leg, on account of white-swelling of the knee, with contraction at an acute angle. Chloroform was given, with Esmarch's inhaler, to the amount of twenty-two grammes. The patient resisted at first, but soon became quiet. The operation was then performed. After the operation the patient screamed, and showed signs of pain. Before a fresh dose of chloroform could be given, to facilitate the application of a gypsum bandage, the heart ceased to beat. Respiration ceased a few seconds later. Tongue drawn forward, and electricity to the phrenic nerves, revived the patient, and he again cried out, but the pulse and respiration soon ceased again for good. *Autopsy*—Internal organs all healthy ; blood dark and fluid ; venous system everywhere distended ; left ventricle alone contracted.—Prof. Dr. Bardeleleben, Berlin Charité ; *Deutsche med. Woch.*, June 7, 1879 ; *Med. Times and Gaz.*, Aug. 2, 1879.

388. Male, twenty-one years. Tooth-extraction. Died in a dentist's chair under the influence of chloroform.—St. Johnsbury, Vt. ; *The Med. Record*, January 10, 1880.

389. Male, five years. Removal of a piece of glass from the foot. During the operation the father, who was holding the boy, fainted, and both fell from the chair to the floor. The boy expired almost immediately afterward. Death was due to paralysis of the heart.—Somerville, N. J.; *The Med. Record*, p. 135, January 31, 1880.

390. Male, eighteen years. Injury of the left foot. Three drachms of chloroform. *Autopsy.*—Hepatization of the lower lobe of the left lung, and congestion of the remainder of the lung. The left side of the heart was empty ; the right distended with blood.—St. John, New Brunswick ; *The Med. Record.*, p. 191, February 14, 1880.

391. Male ; robust young farmer, very nervous. Necrosis of the tibia. Before he was fully anæsthetized, respiration stopped, and could not be renewed. *Autopsy* negative.—Bennett College Clinic, Chicago, January 3, 1880 ; *The Med. Record*, p. 581, May 22, 1880.

392. Male, thirty years ; irregular habits, but very muscular. Tumor on the forehead. Had inhaled chloroform when ten years of age, and was made ill by it. Before inhalation the pulse was good. Chloroform given on a towel. The first dose was two drachms. After a minute or two a

13

third drachm was added. The patient then struggled very violently, and his face became livid. The anæsthetic was then withdrawn. Breathing became very slow and gasping. Tongue forward ; artificial respiration. A galvanic battery was sent for, and brought from the infirmary. Efforts at restoration were continued for an hour. Death occurred about four minutes after the administration of chloroform. *Autopsy* negative.—Doncaster, England ; *Brit. Med. Journ.*, p. 62, January 8, 1881.

393. Female, thirty-six years ; primipara. In good health, weighing 145 pounds. Had been unusually well during pregnancy ; kidneys healthy, urinary secretion normal. Had been in natural labor for eight hours. The os uteri was fully dilated, and the head was descending. The severity of the suffering caused her to insist upon chloroform, and finally the physician allowed her to inhale, intermittently, a few drops at a time from a handkerchief. She did not become unconscious, and at the end of ten minutes began to complain of a sense of thoracic oppression and dyspnœa, desiring to be raised into the sitting position. She was thus raised up, and immediately the neck and face became livid. The patient was at once placed in the horizontal position, but had already become unconscious. She frothed slightly at the mouth ; the cheeks were blown out in expiration, and, after half a dozen sighing respirations at increasing intervals, she ceased to breathe. The condition of the pulse was not observed. Hypodermic injection of atropine ($\frac{1}{80}$ gr.), followed by half a drachm of ergotine, was immediately performed. Artificial respiration was continued for an hour. Friction of the surface, affusions upon the chest, and inversion of the body were employed, but all in vain—there was no sign of life after the cessation of respiration. The child was left undelivered. No autopsy.—Wallace K. Harrison, Chicago, March, 1881.

Of the preceding cases, in which the sex of the patient was recorded, 262 were males, and 108 were females.

The ages of such patients as were known are recorded as follows :

From 2— 5 years	*4	From 41—45 years	30
From 6—10 years	15	From 46—50 years	22
From 11—15 years	25	From 51—60 years	23
From 16—20 years	23	From 61—70 years	4
From 21—25 years	25	From 71—80 years	1
From 26—30 years	26	From 81—90 years	†1
From 31—35 years	29		
From 36—40 years	27		255

Death occurred :

At the commencement of inhalation	15
Before complete insensibility	99
During the period of insensibility	70
After completion of operation	35
	219

---

* Aged, respectively, 2, 3, 4½, and 5 years.   † Aged, 83 years.

In one instance death took place several hours after inhalation, and was directly caused by cerebral hemorrhage occurring upon a brain which had been previously injured by old inflammatory lesions. Chloroform in this case was not the immediate cause of death.

The cases in which was recorded the time that intervened between the commencement of inhalation and the occurrence of death, were as follows :

```
Less than 1 minute ....................................   4
From  1— 2 minutes ..............................  11
From  3— 4 minutes ..............................   7
From  5— 6 minutes ..............................  11
From  7— 8 minutes ..............................   4
From  9—10 minutes ..............................   7
From 11—12 minutes ..............................   1
From 13—15 minutes ..............................   3
From 16—20 minutes ..............................   3
25 minutes........................................   1
                                                    —
                                                    52
```

Death occurred :

```
Immediately after addition of more chloroform to the
     inhaler or napkin ................................  13
Immediately after the first incision, or extraction.......  15
Immediately after sudden displacement of the body.....   9
```

Death was caused in four cases by obstruction of the respiratory passages ; in one instance by vomited matters passing into the trachea ; vomited matters in the œsophagus pressing against the trachea ; in one by in one by the passage of blood into the trachea ; and in one by a metallic plate, with artificial teeth, getting itself displaced into the pharynx.

The anæsthetic was administered with some form of inhaling apparatus in 46 cases. It was simply vaporized upon a napkin, towel, sponge, lint, charpie, or an ordinary pocket-handkerchief in 139 cases. Not specified, 207 cases. It was self-administered in 20 instances.

Death was caused on six occasions by the inhalation of chloroform during the pains of natural labor.

Sudden death occurred in three cases of delirium tremens, and in one case of insanity, where chloroform was administered to quiet the ravings of the patient.

In one case it was fatal to a patient suffering with tetanus.

The following table indicates the different surgical operations for which chloroform was administered with fatal effect. The first column contains the operations actually performed or commenced ; the second column specifies the operations proposed but not performed ; the third column enumerates the cases in which the record does not give any information regarding the performance or non-performance of the operation.

Dislocations — Shoulder	10	5	2
Elbow		2	2
Thumb		1	
Hip	3	1	
Nature not specified		1	
Amputations—Fingers or toes	6	9	7
Fore-arm		1	
Arm			1
Foot	1	1	
Leg	3	9	1
Thigh	4	6	2
Hip-joint	2		
Reamputations	2		
Dressing of fractures, or severe injuries	7	3	1
Operations for caries or necrosis of bones	4	7	4
Operations on joints, and forcible extension of joints	5	4	2
Ligation of an artery	2		1
Exploration of the liver by puncture	1		
Opening abscesses or incision of sinuses	3	2	2
Incision of a cicatrix for deformity after a burn, etc.	1	1	
Dressing a burn	1		
Cauterization of ulcers, usually upon the genital organs	4	5	
Operations upon the male sexual organs	16	10	
Operations upon the female sexual organs	2	4	1
Lithotomy or lithotrity	3	2	1
Ovariotomy	1	1	1
Operations on the anus or rectum	6	11	2
Operations for the relief of strangulated hernia	1	2	2
Removal of tumors, including cancerous breasts and tongues	15	15	5
Extraction of a needle from the knee	1		
Minor surgery of the foot	5	3	5
Minor surgery of the hand	1	5	1
Staphylorraphy	1		
Extraction of teeth	16	8	11
Operations on the eye	16	8	1
Total	143	127	55
Sum total			325

A perusal of the history of these cases is sufficient to produce the conviction that comparatively few of the cases of death from chloroform have been acknowledged and published. The vast majority of the cases thus far reported have occurred in the hospitals of Great Britain. A death from the use of chloroform in private practice is seldom announced, unless it may chance to have happened in the office of an unlucky dentist. Then, of course, there is great publicity, and the event is carefully chronicled. Occasionally some elderly physician alludes in a cautious manner to a case of which he was cognizant, long years ago, in a remote quarter of the earth. In some such way it has been published (*The Clinic*, p. 150, March 31, 1877) that in Cincinnati and its adjacent territory not less than twenty-five deaths from chloroform had occurred since the introduction of that anæsthetic. Several of these cases may be found among the preceding histories, but the majority of them are too imperfectly reported to possess any value.

In addition to the cases previously recorded, may be presented the following examples of death from the use of chloroform, either in combination with ether, or given alternately with that anæsthetic.

1. Female, eighteen years of age. Albany, 1854. A tumor removed from the neck, under the influence of successive inhalation of ether

and chloroform. Death took place two hours after the conclusion of the operation, and was probably due to shock and loss of blood.—Report of the Committee of the Boston Society for Medical Improvement; *Boston Med. and Surg. Journ.*, October 24, 1861.

2. A patient in the city of Lyons, France, 1858, died suddenly during the inhalation of chloroform given subsequently to the administration of ether.—*Loc. cit.*

3. Male, five years of age. Virginia, 1857. Inhaled a mixture of ether and chloroform, for the removal of a tumor from the back. The incisions were nine inches long; six arteries required ligation; about six ounces of blood was lost; vomiting took place, and death followed. In this case the anæsthetic probably was not the principal cause of death.—*Am. Journ. Med. Sci.*, July, 1857.

4. Female, forty years. Bleeding from a punctured wound on the outer side of the right fore-arm, close to the bend of the elbow. Had lost a large amount of blood, evidently from the radial artery. It was decided to ligate the artery. One drachm of a mixture (chloroform and ether, 1 : 2) was given on a sponge. This was followed by a second drachm, and as the patient still struggled, a third drachm was poured upon the sponge, but, before it could be administered, the pulse suddenly stopped. Respiration also ceased almost immediately, and could not be revived. Electricity, brandy enemata, and artificial respiration for more than an hour, were useless. *Autopsy.*—Extensive bronchitis. Fatty degeneration of the heart. Liver large, fatty, and soft. Kidneys soft.—"Ludlow, Bristol Royal Infirmary ;" *Med. Times and Gaz.*, p. 378, October 6, 1866.

5. Female, forty-five years. Fatty tumor of the back. Chloroform was given on lint, but the pulse became irregular, and ether was substituted. The pulse then improved, but suddenly stopped, the face being dusky red. Ether was given on a sponge in a felt cone. About one ounce was used. *Autopsy* negative.—Both lungs were gorged with blood.—West London Hospital, February 18, 1873; *Brit. Med. Journ.*, p. 290, March 2, 1878.

6. Female, middle-aged ; Irish ; robust. Rhinoplastic operation. A preliminary operation had been successfully performed. Chloroform was first administered, then ether. Insensibility not being thus satisfactorily induced, chloroform was again given with the desired result, and anæsthesia was from that time maintained with ether. As the surgeon was about to commence his incisions, the patient suddenly grew pale and the pulse ceased. Artificial respiration, electricity, laryngotomy, and all the other methods of resuscitation, were of no avail.—Prof. Frank Hamilton, Bellevue Hospital, New York ; *Med. Record*, p. 24, March 1, 1867.

7. Female, adult. Extraction of a tooth. Inhalation of a mixture of chloroform and ether. Sudden death.—*Boston Med. and Surg. Journ.*, November 20–27, 1873.

8. Male, twenty-eight years. Amputation of the thigh. Chloroform was first given, but, owing to the dangerous prostration produced by it, ether was substituted for it. Vomiting occurred, and the patient died of asphyxia, caused by the lodgment of a piece of meat in the trachea.—Guy's Hospital ; *Brit. Med. Journ.*, p. 381, September 16, 1876.

9. Male, thirteen years. Tenotomy. Chloroform and ether were given alternately until the patient died.—Tipperary Hospital ; *Brit. Med. Journ.*, p. 788, December 16, 1876.

10. Female, twenty-one years. Amputation of the leg. Two drachms of chloroform on lint quietly anæsthetized the patient ; two ounces of ether were then given from a felt cone. While the surgeon was applying

Esmarch's bandage, the face became blue and the pulse stopped. *Autopsy.*—Friction-patches on the heart, but no pericarditis; wall of right ventricle very thin, left side thicker than usual, pale, but not soft; mitral valves much thickened, chordæ tendineæ thickened, papillary muscles hypertrophied; an irregular ulcer, as large as a silver sixpence, at the junction of the anterior curtain of the mitral valve with the wall of the ventricle; aortic valves thickened, but not insufficient; two large decolorized clots in the left ventricle.—Westminster Hospital; *Brit. Med. Journ.*, p. 396, March 31, 1877.

11. Female, forty-six years; extremely fat and hebetated. Operation for senile cataract. Chloroform was given with Clover's inhaler, for three or four minutes. From the first respiration was shallow, and the pulse was feeble, but not intermittent. The face became slightly livid, and ether was given for two or three minutes longer, when the patient expired. *Autopsy.*—Heart flaccid and empty; mitral valve contracted, aortic valves insufficient. Kidneys fatty and granular.—Ophthalmic Hospital, Moorfields; *Brit. Med. Journ.*, p. 266, August 25, 1877.

12. Female, thirty-two years: married. Fistula in ano. November 22, 1877, inhaled a mixture of equal parts of ether and chloroform without accident. Eight days afterward the wound needed examination, and she inhaled from a napkin a mixture of ether and chloroform (2 : 1). A few inhalations produced violent excitement and shouting. Her face became turgid, the whole body rigid, and in a few seconds the patient was dead. No autopsy. This person had been an opium-eater for many years, and at the time of her death was accustomed to take two or three grains of morphia at a dose.—Henry Van Buren, Chicago; *Chicago Med. Journ. and Ex.*, p. 268, 1878.

13. Female, twenty-eight years; accidentally got a pin into her throat. It could not be removed, and an abscess formed about it. After nearly a month she inhaled ether for an operation for its removal, but, as it did not act favorably, the operation was postponed for an hour. Ether was then given, and also some chloroform, but after about a minute the patient began to breathe badly, and the anæsthetic was removed. Artificial respiration revived the patient, but she died the next day. The cause of death was said to be inflammation of the lungs.—Guy's Hospital; *Brit. Med. Journ.*, p. 490, March 29, 1879.

14. Female, eight years; strabismus. Inhaled a mixture of ether and chloroform. After the operation, passed into a state of collapse, and died seven hours after the inhalation.—Ophthalmic Hospital, Moorfields; *Brit. Med. Journ.*, p. 562, April 12, 1879.

15. Male, fourteen years; very anæmic. Spontaneous luxation of the hip-joint after osteo-myelitis in the right lower extremity. Inhalation of a mixture of chloroform, ether, and alcohol (10 : 3 : 3). The patient died suddenly during profound anæsthesia.—Billroth's Klinik, Vienna; *Allg. Wien. med. Zeit.*, No. 48, 1880.

16. Male, under middle age, weakly, having been an invalid for several years. Amputation of a crushed thumb. Ether was first given, but, not being readily anæsthetized, chloroform was substituted. After a few inspirations the patient died. *Autopsy.*—Heart fatty; valves diseased.—Chicago; *The Med. Record*, p. 581, May 22, 1880.

17. Male, thirty-three years, robust and intemperate. Gangrene of the right middle finger, necessitating amputation. Two ounces of whiskey were taken ten minutes before the commencement of inhalation. The anæsthetic was a mixture of equal parts of ether and chloroform, given on

a piece of lint covered with a towel.   About two drachms were poured on the cloth, without apparent effect.   Shortly after, about the same quantity was poured on the cloth.   This produced no effect, and about three or four drachms more were added.   The patient then began to laugh, to gesticulate, and to utter semi-articulate sounds.   He soon became unconscious, and the pulse ceased to beat.   The anæsthetic was at once removed, and cold water was dashed upon the face ; but, in spite of every possible effort, the patient could not be revived.—Cleary, Assistant Surgeon, U.S.A., *Philadelphia Med. Times*, March 15, 1879.

A review of the manner in which death takes place under the influences of chloroform indicates at least two principal classes of characteristic phenomena.   Death occurs either as a result of over-excitement of the nervous apparatus, or as a result of its paralysis.   To the first class must be assigned those cases which take place instantaneously, almost at the commencement of inhalation, and those cases in which death suddenly terminates a scene of violent muscular excitement.   To the same class may be assigned the cases in which death follows the first incision.   Simpson has recorded a number of examples of sudden death without chloroform, in which the first touch of the surgeon's knife was the immediate cause of dissolution.   Though it is true that the benumbing effect of anæsthetic vapor tends to diminish the danger from this source, it still remains possible for an enfeebled and irritable nervous apparatus, which has not been fully overwhelmed by chloroform, to succumb under the shock of such a contact.   The comparatively large number of deaths which have instantaneously followed the reduction of a dislocation involving an important joint, like the hip or the shoulder, all point to the same cause.   It is hardly possible that a fatal result should in any other way be connected with the first few whiffs of the vapor which have sometimes occasioned sudden death.   It is during the initial stage of nerve-excitement that such deaths have occurred, before the blood and the tissues could be saturated with the anæsthetic.   The peripheral excitement of the fifth pair, and the respiratory filaments of the pneumogastric nerve by chloroform may be sufficient to inhibit the respiratory centres in the medulla oblongata, thus producing respiratory and cardiac arrest, just as a powerful mental emotion or a painful peripheral impression may effect the same result.

Somewhat different is the mode of death when a period of violent excitement and muscular rigidity is fatally terminated.   The phenomena are then the result of asphyxia and anæsthesia preceded by the symptoms of nervous excitement.   Spasm of the muscles of the glottis, and rigidity of the respiratory muscles, the result of peripheral irritation, may induce a condition of genuine asphyxia.   But the typical forms of simple suffocation, such as are presented when the trachea of a healthy animal is suddenly occluded, cannot be produced under chloroform.   The action of the anæsthetic must necessarily modify and mask many of the movements which would otherwise take place.

Undoubtedly the occurrence of asphyxia as a cause of death under chloroform would be more frequently recognized, were it not for this inhibition of some of its most conspicuous phenomena.   The researches of Paul Bert (*Comptes Rendus, Soc. de Biologie*, Séance du 26 fév., 1881) indicate that, whenever a certain relative quantity of any anæsthetic has been introduced into the blood, asphyxia will inevitably occur.   Lesser degrees of impregnation produce the phenomena of anæsthesia alone ; but, as soon as a certain degree of saturation is reached, asphyxia appears.   Experimenting upon the dog, the animal must breathe an atmosphere charged with the vapor of ether in the proportion of 37 grammes of ether to 100 litres of air, in order to produce anæsthesia. If the quantity of ether be doubled, so that 74 grammes of ether are mixed with 100 litres of air, the animal will at once die asphyxiated. For each anæsthetic substance the absolute quantity differs, but in every instance the relation between the amount necessary for the production of simple anæsthesia and the quantity which will cause asphyxia and death is nearly the same—1 : 2. One hundred litres of air must contain the vapor of 15 grammes of chloroform in order to produce anæsthesia, and of 30 grammes to occasion death by asphyxia. For amylene, the quantities are 30 grammes and 55 grammes; for ethyl bromide, 22 grammes and 45 grammes; for methyl chloride, 21 and 42 c.c. of the gas to every 100 c.c. of air. A knowledge of these facts renders it easy to comprehend the manner in which death has been so often observed as the immediate consequence of a fresh charge of chloroform upon the inhaler. If the patient has been breathing air charged with chloroform in the proportion of 25 grammes to 100 litres, a small addition only will be necessary in order to reach the asphyxiating point; and death may occur suddenly without accompanying symptoms of excitement, because all power of muscular movement has been effectually abolished by the previously established condition of profound anæsthesia. Asphyxia thus produced may very properly be termed *paralytic asphyxia*, when contrasted with the results of convulsive rigidity of the respiratory muscles under the influence of a powerful excitant. It is highly probable that to this form of asphyxia may be assigned the majority of those cases in which death is said to have been the result of syncope. It has, indeed, been experimentally proved that an overdose of chloroform conveyed directly through the jugular vein or the pulmonary artery may cause immediate death through paralysis of the heart. This would constitute genuine death from syncope—from failure of the heart. But this does not agree with the results of physiological experiment under the conditions of ordinary inhalation. It has been shown that death, under such circumstances, begins at the respiratory centres, while the heart continues to beat for an appreciable time after the cessation of respiration. Against this result of exact experimental observation cannot be arrayed the necessarily imperfect impressions which originate during the confusion attendant upon an anxious effort to resuscitate a moribund patient. It is true that in the greater number of histories it is recorded that the pulse stopped first, and, after a few seconds, respiration also ceased. But the reverse has also been distinctly noted in a number of instances. The stoppage of the arterial pulse does not necessarily imply a complete cardiac arrest—it merely indicates cardiac insufficiency. It is very easy to recognize a cessation of respiratory movement, but it is by no means easy to detect, especially through the clothing, the feeble pulsations of the heart in a condition of syncope. Were it a fact that in the majority of instances danger approaches through the heart, it would be impossible to account for the frequent success which has attended artificial respiration, inversion of the body, and faradization of the respiratory muscles, in cases of suspended animation from chloroform. Electro-puncture of the heart, which always fails to do good, should, according to such a hypothesis, be the most effectual means of revival.

After all, the great fact remains that, in a very large proportion of cases, death from chloroform, as from other anæsthetics, is the result of a general paralysis of the nervous centres. The functions of respiration and of circulation are so closely connected that the failure of one necessarily causes the failure of the other. So closely related are the medullary centres which preside over these functions, and so wide is the diffusion of the anæsthetic process, that a degree of tissue-poisoning sufficient to paralyze one centre cannot fail to overwhelm the other. Paralysis of the respiratory centre signifies absolute repose of the muscles of respiration. Paralysis of the circulatory centre merely liberates the heart from all central control. If its own intrinsic motor apparatus be not simultaneously overwhelmed, it may continue for some time to beat, though in a feeble and ineffectual way.

Thus considered, it becomes evident that the actual structural condition of the heart must necessarily occupy a very much less important position among the causes of death under chloroform than was once supposed. Fatty degeneration of the heart was formerly ranked as one of the most formidable causes of a fatal result ; but the progress of pathological anatomy has shown that this is a condition so frequently encountered after death from the most varied causes that it can no longer be considered as possessing any great importance among the predisposing causes of death. Like all other degenerations, it betrays a condition of corresponding weakness, but this loss of resistance is as general as it is local.

CARBONIC TETRACHLORIDE—CCl_4.

Tetrachloride of carbon, Chlorocarbon, E.; Carbonii tetrachloridum, L.; Bichlorure de carbone, Formène perchloré, F.; Vierfach-Chlorkohlenstoff, Tetrachlormethan, Carbon-tetrachlorür, G.

Specific gravity, 1.599.
Boiling-point, 78° (172.4° F.).
Vapor density, 5.24—5.33.

Carbon tetrachloride is a thin, transparent, colorless oil, with a pungent, aromatic odor. Insoluble in water, it dissolves in alcohol and in ether. It was discovered by Regnault in the year 1839. Various methods of preparing it have been described. It may be formed directly from marsh-gas by replacement of the hydrogen with chlorine. It may also be prepared by the action of chlorine upon chloroform : $CHCl_3 + Cl = HCl + CCl_4$.

The greater molecular weight and the inferior volatility of carbon tetrachloride, as compared with chloroform, point to a more active power of disturbance and a greater persistence of phenomena after its use. When administered to animals it uniformly produces great muscular inco-ordination, disturbance, and rigidity. During the period of anæsthesia, respiration is jerky, frequently intermittent, and sometimes actually dyspnœic. The action of the heart becomes accelerated and irregular. In the frog a contraction of the smaller arteries was observed by Sansom and Harley. The increased blood-pressure thus produced is finally diminished almost to nothing ; the pupils dilate, and the movements of respiration and circulation are brought to a complete standstill.

Nunnely ascertained by personal experience that the inhalation of the vapor of carbon tetrachloride was at first rather irritating to the air-passages. This soon disappeared, and was succeeded by a sensation of heat diffused throughout the body. The temporal arteries throbbed ; there was a feeling of great muscular weakness with labored breathing, and a disposition to sleep. After the cessation of inhalation there was a persistent feeling of heat, and a great indisposition to mental or physical exertion. This was followed by general weariness, cardiac debility, and uneasiness. During the night after the experiment, sleep was restless and disturbed by frightful dreams. Similar disagreeable results were observed by Simpson, Protheroe Smith, and others who attempted to use the drug as a substitute for chloroform in childbirth and in dental surgery. Several deaths are said to have been caused by its use—a fact which need surprise no one, for its chemical constitution and its physiological action indicate that it is an agent more powerful and more dangerous than chloroform.

Dangerous effects of carbon tetrachloride.—Male; anæmic and exhausted. Resection of the hip-joint, Carbon tetrachloride was administered. After a few minutes the pulse suddenly increased in frequency till it could no longer be counted. At the same time the patient complained of a violent pain, or cramp in the vicinity of the heart. Almost immediately after this the pulse and respiration both suddenly ceased. The head of the patient was spasmodically drawn backward; the countenance looked pale and deathly; the pupils were widely dilated. Artificial respiration and aqua ammoniæ revived the patient, and the operation was completed under the influence of sulphuric ether without any further accident.—E. Andrews : *Chicago Med. Examiner*, December, 1867.

BROMOFORM—$CHBr_3$.

Tribromomethane, Bromoformum, L.; *Bromoforme,* Fr.

Specific gravity, 2.9.
Boiling-point, 150° (305.6° F.).
Vapor density, 8.632.

This substance is a clear, heavy liquid, having an agreeable odor. It may be obtained by the action of an alkali upon bromal ($CBr_3.COH$), or by heating bromomethane (CH_3Br) with the requisite quantity of bromine at 250° (482° F.) ; and on distilling alcohol with bromide of lime (Miller). At its boiling-point it is partially decomposed.

The anæsthetic properties of bromoform closely resemble those of chloroform. Inhalation of its vapor causes excitement, followed by deep sleep, muscular relaxation, and dilatation of the pupils. Recovery from its anæsthetic effect, according to Rabuteau, takes place rapidly, even though inhalation may have been prolonged for half an hour.

METHYLIC IODIDE—CH_3I.

Iodomethane, Methyli iodidum, L.; *Iodide of methyl,* E. ; *Iodure de méthyle,* Fr.; *Jodmethyl,* G.

Specific gravity, 2.199 at 0° (32° F.).
Boiling-point, 43.8° (111° F.).
Vapor density, 4.833.

Methylic iodide is a colorless liquid, with an ethereal odor. It burns with difficulty in a flame, giving off violet-colored vapors of iodine. It was discovered by Dumas and Peligot, in 1835, and may be prepared, according to Wanklyn's process, by mixing equivalent proportions of potassium iodide and anhydrous methylic alcohol in a retort. Dry hydrochloric acid gas is passed into the mixture, and the iodide of methyl is separated by distillation. The distillate is mixed with water, to separate the iodide of methyl, and the product is rectified in the water-bath over calcium chloride and lead oxide (Watts).

Methylic iodide is another of the methylic compounds with which Richardson and Simpson have experimented. They ascertained that in a state of chemical purity its vapor could be respired, even to the induction of anæsthesia. It was very liable, however, to decomposition, with great irritation of the various glandular organs connected with the oculo-respiratory passages, through the liberation of iodine. Upon animals it produced fatal engorgement of the bronchial membranes. Sir James Y. Simpson found it a powerful and dangerous anæsthetic. He recorded his experience as follows : " After inhaling a very small quantity for two or three minutes, I remained for some seconds without feeling much effect ; but objects immediately began to multiply before my eyes, and I fell down in a state of insensibility, which continued for upward of an hour. I did not completely recover from the effects of it for some days."

IODOFORM—CHI₃.

Triiodomethane, Iodoformum, L. ; *Iodoforme,* Fr. ; *Jodoform,* G.

Melting-point, 120° (248° F.).

Iodoform is a solid body, occurring in the form of lemon-yellow, pearly, six-sided, scale-like crystals, with a peculiar odor and a sweetish taste. It is a product of the action of iodine in presence of potassic or sodic hydrate or carbonate on ethylic alcohol, aldehyde, acetone, and many other substances. It is not perceptibly soluble in water, but dissolves readily in alcohol and ether (Miller). Its peculiar odor may be disguised in mixtures and ointments by the addition of five drops of oil of peppermint to each ounce of the mass.

The physiological action of iodoform closely resembles the action of other kindred anæsthetics. In the lower animals it produces muscular rigidity, anæsthesia, sleep, muscular relaxation, and, in sufficient doses, death. Two grammes (half a drachm) are sufficient to kill a guinea-pig ; and four grammes (one drachm) have proved fatal to an ordinary dog. According to Binz, the reflex excitability of animals thus poisoned does not wholly disappear during anæsthetic sleep unless a fatal result is imminent. The temperature exhibits a marked decline as death approaches. After death from iodoform, the heart, liver, kidneys, and muscles exhibit fatty degeneration. Placed in contact with the living tissues, it is decomposed, giving up iodine, which combines with albumen and is absorbed as an albuminate. The iodine thus conveyed into the body is finally excreted, chiefly in the form of alkaline iodides, through the medium of the kidneys. In small doses, therefore, it operates as an alterative medicine. Administered to man in doses of half a gramme (seven or eight grains) it may produce a diminution of eight or ten pulse-beats per minute.

It produces no caustic effect, but operates as an anodyne and anæsthetic when applied to painful and ulcerated surfaces. Introduced into the rectum, it may thus render the anus quite insensible to the process of defecation.

ETHYLIC CHLORIDE—C_2H_5Cl

Éther chlorhydrique, Fr.; *Aethylchlorür*, G.; *Hydrochloric ether*, E.

Specific gravity, 0.920 at 0° (32° F.).
Boiling-point, 11° (51.8° F.).
Vapor density, 2.219.

Ethylic chloride is a thin, colorless liquid, having a pungent, ethereal odor, and a sweetish aromatic taste, with somewhat alliaceous after-taste. It is very inflammable, and burns with a green-edged flame, evolving hydrochloric acid. It dissolves sparingly in water, but mixes in all proportions with alcohol and ether. It dissolves sulphur, phosphorus, fats, volatile oils, many resins and coloring matters. The easiest method of preparing this substance consists in the passage of hydrochloric acid gas into a boiling solution of zinc chloride in one and one-half time its weight of 95 per cent. alcohol, contained in a flask connected with an inverted condenser and a wash-bottle containing water. Nearly the whole of the alcohol is thus converted into ethyl chloride (Watts).

The excessive volatility and inflammability of ethylic chloride virtually excludes this substance from practice. Its general effects clearly resemble those of sulphuric ether. Heyfelder employed it with success in a number of surgical operations (Kappeler). Its anæsthetic effects are very transient, and are not liable to be followed by nausea or vomiting. The experience of the Committee of the British Medical Association, however, is not favorable to its use, for they found that when administered to rabbits, though it produced rapid anæsthesia, yet in one case respiration soon ceased, and in another instance the more abundant admission of air was followed by general convulsions.

ANÆSTHETIC ETHER, OR ARAN'S ETHER.

Aran's ether is a mixture of different compounds of chlorine and ethylic chloride, of which the principal element is tetrachlorinated ethyl chloride, C_2HCl_5. It is a clear, colorless liquid, with an odor resembling that of chloroform. Its specific gravity varies with its compositions, from 1.55 to 1.60. Its boiling-point is about 130° (266° F.); and the vapor density of its principal ingredient is 6.975. Mialhe was the first one to propose the use of this preparation, and it has been employed by Aran, Schott, and Heyfelder ; but, on account of its variable composition and the readiness with which it is decomposed, its use for the production of surgical anæsthesia has been completely abandoned.

ETHYLENIC CHLORIDE—$C_2H_4Cl_2$.

a-Dichlorethane, Ethylene bichloride, Ethylene dichloride, Dutch liquid, Ethene chloride, E. ; *Æthylenum bichloridum, Æthylenum chloratum,* L.; *Liqueur hollandais, Huile du gas oléfiant,* Fr.; *Aethylenchloride, Elaylchlorür, Oel der holländischen Chemiker,* G.

Specific gravity, 1.256 at 12° (53.6° F.).
Boiling-point, 82.5° (180.5° F.), under a pressure of 765 mm.
Vapor density, 3.4434.

Ethylene bichloride is a colorless, neutral, oily liquid, having a fragrant, ethereal odor, and a sweetish, aromatic taste. It is imflammable, and burns with a green, very smoky flame, giving off vapors of hydrochloric acid. It is nearly insoluble in water, to which, however, it imparts its odor, but is soluble in alcohol and ether. This compound was discovered in 1795 by the Dutch chemists. It is formed by conducting ethylene gas, which has been produced by heating a mixture of alcohol and sulphuric acid, through a wash-bottle containing potash to free it from sulphurous acid ; through a second containing alcohol, which removes vapor of ether ; and sometimes through a third, containing water to free it from alcohol vapor. It then passes into a large glass globe having a long neck, which descends into a bottle closed with a cork. After the stream of gas has been continued long enough to expel the air, moist chlorine from another flask is also admitted into the globe. The two gases then unite, forming an oily liquid, which runs down into the receiver (Watts).

This substance was fully tested in 1848 and 1849, by Simpson, Snow, and Nunnely, by whom its anæsthetic properties were determined. Its vapor is, however, irritating to the air-passages, and sometimes causes vomiting. Administered to rabbits by the Committee of the British Medical Association, it produced convulsive movements of the extremities, continuing till death. There was no anæsthesia preceding the convulsions. This substance certainly possesses no advantage over chloroform.

ETHIDENE DICHLORIDE—$C_2H_4Cl_2 = CH_3.CHCl_2$.

β-Dichlorethane, Ethylidenic chloride, Ethylidene chloride, E. ; *Æthylidenum chloratum,* L. ; *Aethylidenchlorid,* G.

Specific gravity, 1.189 at 4.3°.
Boiling-point, 60° (140° F.).
Vapor density, 4.954.

Ethidene dichloride is obtained from the by-products of the manufacture of chloral. At Schering's factory, in Berlin, these by-products are collected by causing the vapors which issue from the alcohol retort, together with hydrochloric acid and excess of chlorine, to pass first through water, then through a series of condensers. After a preliminary distillation to separate the ethyl chloride present, the residue is submitted to fractional distillation, and the separate fractions are examined, either by further fractionation, or by first treating them with alcoholic potash, and again separating them by distillation. Ethylidene chloride is a transparent, colorless, oily liquid, resembling chloroform in taste and odor. It is isomeric with ethylenic chloride but differs from it in specific gravity and in boiling-point (Watts). It is insoluble in water, but mixes in all proportions with ether, alcohol, chloroform, and the oils. It is less inflammable than alcohol.

Ethylidene chloride was first introduced to the medical profession in 1852 by Dr. Snow. Professor O. Liebreich, von Langenbeck, Steffen, and others, have also employed this agent, and have been pleased with its effects. It is very rapid in its action, producing anæsthesia in one minute —seldom requiring to be inhaled as long as three minutes. The time of emergence is also proportionately brief, and it is seldom that disagreeable after-effects are experienced. Mr. Clover (*Brit. Med. Jour.*, p. 797, May 29, 1880), states that he has administered its vapor in 1,877 cases; of these, 287 were major operations, and the remaining 1,565 cases were of minor surgery and the extraction of teeth. Vomiting occurred in about one-third of the cases of major surgery, but in only about one-twentieth of the minor cases. The vomiting was always less persistent than after chloroform. In one case, a child nine years old was kept asleep for an hour and a half during a difficult operation on the mouth. In another case, anæsthesia was maintained for the same length of time during an operation for the removal of a malignant tumor of the palate and indurated glands in the neck. "The patient awoke in capital spirits, and made a rapid recovery."

Mr. Clover has been in the habit of first rendering his patients almost unconscious with nitrous oxide, and then gradually substituting the ethylidene for the production of complete insensibility. According to his experience, "the patient falls asleep without moving a limb; a little convulsive twitching is seen, and then stertorous breathing; the pupils at first dilate, about the same time that stertor commences; a very little air is now given at every third or fourth respiration, and the pupil contracts." The pulse is usually much less affected than when the same degree of anæsthesia is produced by chloroform. The patient awakens almost as if from a natural sleep, and within two minutes after the most profound anæsthesia will get up and walk about.

The Committee of the British Medical Association experimented with ethylidene chloride upon frogs, rabbits, and dogs. (*Brit. Med. Journ.*, January 4, 1879.) A frog was rendered insensible by confinement four or five minutes in a glass jar filled with the vapor. The heart was then exposed, so that its pulsations were visible. They continued slowly but regularly, in one case for twenty minutes, in another for twenty-six minutes. Rabbits were anæsthetized in four minutes by inhaling the vapor from a cloth. In one case respiration ceased, but soon began again. When the thorax was laid open, and artificial respiration was employed, the cardiac movements continued with vigor for the space of forty minutes. Dogs were anæsthetized in the same way within two or three minutes. One young puppy seemed to experience sufficient excitement to necessitate "squeaking." A large dog was kept under the influence of the vapor, given very liberally, for half an hour without the slightest manifestation of failing energy either of the heart or of respiration. The animal recovered rapidly without any unfavorable conditions. In two instances the thorax was laid open, and artificial respiration was maintained. The heart exhibited no depression of vigor. When chloroform was substituted, "the right side of the heart began almost immediately to become distended and to be dark in color, and the activity of the heart rapidly failed. The contrast between the effects of the two substances on the heart was most striking. Practically, a dog will live for a lengthened period in a state of complete anæsthesia under the influence of ethidene dichloride, whilst it will die in a short time when chloroform is used." The effect of ethidene upon the respiration and circulation of animals was carefully noted by the same committee, and compared with the effects produced by chloroform. They found that, while chloroform reduced the blood-pressure rapidly and by sudden descents, occurring sometimes even after the cessation of inhalation, ethidene reduces the blood-pressure slowly and by regular gradations. Usually, after such a reduction of pressure, the continued inhalation of the vapor was accompanied by a partial recovery of pressure, as if the heart had commenced to accommodate itself to the anæsthetic. In no case of experiment upon animals did the heart's action or the respiratory movements absolutely cease, though they were sometimes very much reduced. It was evident that, while ethidene does depress the action of the heart, it is much less to be feared in this respect than chloroform. Given to human subjects, it produced anæsthesia as rapidly as chloroform, and with less excitement and disagreeable sensation. It, however, produced vomiting, probably about as often as would have happened with chloroform. Altogether, this substance appears to possess decided advantages over chloroform. Its use is not without danger, however, for Mr. Clover himself has on three occasions been compelled to lower the patient's head and to practise artificial respiration, in order to obviate the manifest tendency to death while under the influence of ethidene. Finally, one of his patients (*Brit. Med. Journ.*, May 29, 1880) did actually expire while under the influence of this anæsthetic during the period of inhalation before operation. The cause of death was cardiac syncope—respiration continuing for several seconds after the cessation of the pulse. In spite of inversion and artificial respiration through a canula inserted in the trachea, the patient could not be resuscitated. After death it was discovered that the muscular tissue of the heart was in a state of fatty degeneration. Another case of death with diseased heart while under the influence of this anæsthetic has been reported from Berlin, so that ethidene dichloride cannot take high rank as a safe anæsthetic.

DEATH FROM INHALATION OF ETHIDENE DICHLORIDE.

1. Male, adult. About to have an operation performed for hæmorrhoids. Anæmic from loss of blood, which had been going on for six months. Was a liquor dealer, and recently had a carbuncle. The heart-sounds were normal. Had eaten nothing since the previous evening. Nitrous oxide had been inhaled for tooth-extraction on a former occasion, but it caused struggling, and did not wholly abolish pain.

Being placed on his right side, with the knees drawn up, ethidene dichloride was administered with the gas- and ether-inhaler. He did not respire regularly at first; but he never coughed, and was not observed to swallow. After twelve or fourteen respirations, he talked, and commenced to struggle. The face-piece was then removed for a little distance from the face to allow inhalation of fresh air. When his struggles ceased there was hardly any pulse, and it soon disappeared; but he continued to breathe ten or twelve times in a satisfactory manner, and then a pause was noticed between the respirations. His head was lowered, the feet were raised, the tongue was drawn forward, and artificial respiration was commenced. In about a minute he tried to speak, but not distinctly; the pulse returned to the wrist, and he was again placed in the position for operation. In doing this he raised his head, as if voluntarily, and the pulse again began to fail.   Artificial respiration was renewed, and, during the first three minutes there were several gasping inspirations, but the pulse was never felt again.   Laryngotomy was then performed, and air was blown through the laryngeal tube during artificial inspirations for three-quarters of an hour, without any good result.   *Autopsy.*—Lungs slightly emphysematous, and congested posteriorly, but crepitant.   Spleen friable.   Liver rather large. Heart large and flabby, pale and overlaid at the apex with fat.   Microscopical examination of the muscular substance of the ventricles exhibited extensive fatty degeneration.—J. T. Clover : *Brit. Med. Journ.*, p. 797, May 29, 1880.

2. Male, forty-five years, suffering from purulent effusion in the right pleural cavity.   Incision and drainage of the chest was proposed, and ethidene was selected as the safest anæsthetic.   During the administration the patient frequently struggled ; but nothing alarming occurred until he was insensible, when it became necessary to turn him on the left side to make the incision.   He had not been in that position more than two seconds when the pulse and respiration began to fail and the pupils dilated widely.   He was at once replaced upon his back, artificial respiration was commenced, the precordial region was slapped with the hand, and, finally, the heart was excited by electro-puncture.   The only result was one long inspiration.   *Autopsy*, two days after death.—The chest contained seventy-two ounces of pus.   The right lung was adherent to the ribs in front ; the pleura was thickened and covered with lymph ; the lungs were engorged with blood ; an abscess occupied a portion of the lung, and was surrounded by a zone of pneumonia.   The right side of the heart was filled with dark fluid blood ; the left ventricle was empty ; microscopical examination of the heart showed no fatty degeneration.   There was a small periosteal abscess upon the frontal bone.—Mouillot, Gen. Hospital, Birmingham, Feb. 24, 1881 ; *Brit. Med. Journ.*, p. 385, March 12, 1881.

MONOCHLORETHYLENCHLORIDE—$CH_2Cl.CHCl_2$.

a-Trichlorethane.

Specific gravity, 1.422 at 17° C.
Boiling-point, 115° (239° F.).

This substance, discovered in 1838 by Regnault, is one of two isomeric compounds formed by the action of chlorine on dichlorethane.   It is a colorless, mobile liquid, with an agreeable odor like that of chloroform.   It may be formed by the action of chlorine upon dichlorethane (ethylene dichloride), $CH_2Cl.CH_2Cl + Cl_2 = CH_2Cl.CHCl_2 + HCl$, or by the action of chlorvinyl (C_2H_3Cl) on the perchloride of antimony.   By the action of alcoholic potash it is readily decomposed into potassic chloride and β-dichlorethylene :

$$CH_2Cl.CHCl_2 + KHO = CH_2.CCl_2 + KCl + H_2O.$$

Dichlorethylene is a colorless liquid, boiling at 37° (98.6° F.), which is the normal temperature of the blood.   The readiness with which it is formed by the action of potash upon trichlorethane has suggested the hypothesis that the anæsthetic effects of this last are really owing to the liberation of dichlorethylene in the blood.   This hypothesis has been advanced by **Dr. Edward Tauber**, Privat-Docent in the University of Jena, who has recently experimented with the isomeric trichlorethanes for the purpose of determining their anæsthetic value. His observations were made upon frogs, pigeons, guinea-pigs, rabbits, and dogs. A few drops were sufficient to produce complete anæsthesia in the smaller animals. For dogs weighing four and one-half to six and one-third kilogrammes (10–14 lbs.), doses of three to five grammes (30–50 drops) were needful. Inhalation of the vapor of these quantities produced complete insensibility in the space of from three to seven minutes. The duration of anæsthesia was from eleven to nineteen minutes. Respiration was very slightly affected, and in the smaller animals the frequency of the pulse was scarcely reduced. Observation of dogs showed in one instance a considerable increase in the rate of the pulse; in three others a slight increase. Diminution of its rate did not occur. The blood-pressure, also, exhibited no diminution when tested by the kymographion upon a large dog weighing not less than twenty-two kilogrammes (fifty pounds).

METHYLCHLOROFORM—$CH_3.CCl_3$.

β-Trichlorethane—Mono-chlor-ethylidenchloride.

Specific gravity, 1.372 at 0° C.
Boiling-point, 75° (167° F.).

Discovered in 1838–40 by Regnault, methylchloroform is the second product of the action of chlorine upon monochlorethane :

$$CH_3.CH_2Cl + Cl = CH_3.CHCl_2.$$
$$CH_3.CHCl_2 + Cl = CH_3.CCl_3.$$

It is a colorless liquid, closely resembling chloroform in appearance and odor. By the action of potassic hydrate at a high temperature, it may with considerable difficulty be decomposed into potassic acetate and potassic chloride :

$$CH_3.CCl_3 + 4KHO = KC_2H_3O_2 + 3KCl + 2H_2O.$$

Since these substances possess no anæsthetic properties, the effects produced by inhalation of the vapor of methylchloroform cannot be due to any action of its components. It operates as its own prime factor in the production of anæsthesia.

In common with its isomer, mono-chlor-ethylenchloride, or a—trichlorethane, this substance has recently been made the subject of experiment by Dr. Tauber, of the University of Jena. Administered in the form of vapor to frogs and rabbits, it produced satisfactory anæsthesia, without any marked effect upon respiration or circulation. The administration of the vapor of four or five grammes (40–50 drops) to a dog weighing about five kilogrammes (10–12 lbs.) produced a condition of insensibility, which endured for nineteen minutes. Respiration during the period of most profound anæsthesia was somewhat accelerated, but the pulse was very slightly affected. Upon himself Tauber experimented by inhaling the vapor of about twenty grammes (200 drops), under the supervision of Dr. von Langenbeck. There was no stage of excitement preceding anæsthesia;

14

respiration remained undisturbed ; the pulse did not exceed eighty-four beats per minute ; it was regular, and exhibited no evidence of diminishing blood-pressure.   Complete anæsthesia was reached in five and a half minutes, and it continued for ten minutes longer.   The prick of a pin was not felt, and evulsion of the hairs of the beard excited no reflex movement. Vomiting occurred soon after the recovery of consciousness, breakfast having been eaten about two hours before the experiment.   A feeling of general discomfort persisted for about an hour.   It then disappeared, leaving no unpleasant effects behind.

ETHYLIC BROMIDE—C_2H_5Br.

Æther hydrobromicus, L. ; *Hydrobromic ether, Bromide of ethyl, Ethyl bromide*, E.; *Éther hydrobromique, Bromure d'éthyle*, Fr.; *Bromwasserstoffäther, Aethylbromür*, G.

> Specific gravity, 1.4733 at 0° (32° F.).
> Boiling-point, 40.7° (105.26° F.) at 757 mm.
> Vapor density, 3.754.

Ethylic bromide is a transparent, colorless, neutral liquid, with a strong, ethereal odor, and a disagreeably sweetish taste with a somewhat burning after-taste.   It is sparingly soluble in water, but mixes in all proportions with alcohol and ether.   It burns with difficulty, giving a beautiful green flame, which does not smoke, but which evolves a strong odor of hydrobromic acid.

Ethylic bromide may be produced by the action of bromine, hydrobromic acid, or bromide of phosphorus, on alcohol.   According to De Vrij, it is easily prepared by distilling four parts of pulverized bromide of potassium with five parts of a mixture of two parts of strong sulphuric acid and one part of alcohol of 96 per cent. (Watts).

Ethylic bromide was discovered in the year 1827, by the chemist Serullas.   Nunnely experimented with it in the year 1849.   He succeeded in producing anæsthesia by administering its vapor in a considerable number of instances, but was obliged to discontinue his experiments on account of the expense attending the use of the ether.   In the year 1876, Rabuteau, of Paris, employed it in certain experiments on plants and animals.   In 1878, Dr. Lawrence Turnbull, of Philadelphia, who had called attention to the utility of ethylic bromide in certain cases of tinnitus aurium, and in painful affections of the ear, administered it with success to a number of patients suffering with minor surgical affections.   Stimulated by his example and counsel, Dr. R. J. Levis, of the same city, commenced its use in the surgical wards of the Pennsylvania Hospital, in April, 1879.   Since then, it has been extensively tried in America and in Europe.

The physiological action of ethylic bromide has been observed by numerous experiments.   Rabuteau (*Le Progrès Médical*, June 12, 1880) found that this substance has no effect upon non-germinating seeds; but plants, which have been placed in an atmosphere saturated with its vapor die in two hours.   Their leaves turn black, and the flowers preserve their colors. A similar plant, exposed under identical conditions to the vapor of sulphuric ether, is not harmed.   From this fact, as well as from others of a similar character, Rabuteau draws the inference that the dangerous properties of an anæsthetic substance have a certain definite relation to its molecular weight.

Frogs, placed in a watery solution of ethylic bromide, become as completely anæsthetized as if they were immersed in an aqueous solution of chloroform. Rabbits do not easily tolerate ethylic bromide. Berger stated to the Paris Société de Chirurgie (*Le Progrès Médical*) that he had been impressed by the rapidity with which these animals succumbed to its vapor. According to his experience, "it was more disagreeable to dogs than chloroform." He had found it difficult to obtain muscular relaxation by its use. The experience of Terrillon was more favorable. When administered to rabbits from a cloth, instead of placing them in a receiver filled with the vapor, they seemed to tolerate its influence. He had given it to eighteen dogs without accident to any one of them. In twelve cases there had been muscular relaxation, and in only five or six was there any period of agitation. In order to produce anæsthesia it was advisable to administer the ether very freely at the outset, on account of its volatility. By this method of proceeding, anæsthesia may be produced in less than a minute, without irritation or suffocation or convulsive phenomena. Muscular relaxation occurred, in his experience, when given to human beings, in two or three minutes. There was great congestion of the face, neck, and upper part of the chest. The pupils did not contract, but were dilated. The pulse was always quickened, and every fresh dose of ether caused fresh acceleration. Respiration was also hastened, and was liable to be hindered by the accumulation of mucus in the fauces. So great was the hypersecretion of the buccal and pharyngeal glands that it was sometimes necessary to wipe out the fauces with a probang during the process of inhalation. Sensibility and consciousness returned with great rapidity, as might be expected in consequence of the great volatility of the liquid. Vomiting was not uncommon —sometimes during the period of insensibility, and sometimes continuing for several hours after awaking.

M. Verneuil, at the same meeting of the society, called attention to the great rapidity with which anæsthesia might sometimes be produced by ethylic bromide. One patient, a woman, to whom he had given it, was "asleep in an instant."

M. Nicaise had frequently employed ethylic bromide when making application of the actual cautery. Its comparatively slight inflammability, and the fact that it was not easily decomposed by the heat of the cautery instruments, rendered it valuable in such operations.

Dr. H. C. Wood, of Philadelphia, found by experiment upon animals that, if given with moderation, anæsthesia might be produced without notable reduction of the blood-pressure ; but, if given freely, it proved itself a very powerful agent for the depression of the force of the circulation. Drs. Wolff and Lee, of Philadelphia, observed that, if rabbits were killed with ethylic bromide, the immediate cause of death was a gradual paralysis of the cardiac inhibitory motor centres, producing rapid cardiac movements, finally ceasing altogether. Dr. Isaac Ott, however, announces the following conclusions from his careful experiments :

1. "Bromide of ethyl, by either inhalation or subcutaneous use, kills by a toxic action on the centre of respiration.

2. "That the decrease of force and frequency of the heart contribute to the paralysis of the respiratory centres.

3. "That injection of ethyl into the jugular toward the heart kills by cardiac arrest, probably due to an action on the cardiac muscle.

4. "Bromide of ethyl in toxic doses depresses momentarily the fre-

quency of the heart, followed by a subsequent permanent rise to normal rate.

5. "Bromide of ethyl in toxic doses depresses the actual tension steadily, due in major part to the depressant action of the drug upon the heart, and in minor part to a partial loss of tone of either the spinal vaso-motor centres, or the peripheral vaso-motor system.

6. "The inhibitory power of the pneumogastric is not paralyzed."

In more moderate doses, Dr. Ott concludes that ethylic bromide increases the pulse by direct stimulation of the heart, and that it increases blood-pressure by direct stimulation of the vaso-motor nervous apparatus, while its tendency to depress respiratory movements is due to its effect upon the nervous centres. In all these particulars the action of this substance, though differing somewhat in degree, is precisely similar in kind to the action of all other ethereal anæsthetics.

My own experiments have been limited to the observation of the effect of the drug upon the cardiac movements. The following sphygmographic tracings, taken in the Physiological Laboratory of Rush Medical College, will illustrate the manner in which the heart and the pulse behave under the influence of ethylic bromide. The first tracing was taken from a healthy, full-grown male rat of medium size. The animal was confined in a gutter, upon his back, and the sphygmograph was placed in contact with the wall of the chest immediately over the heart.

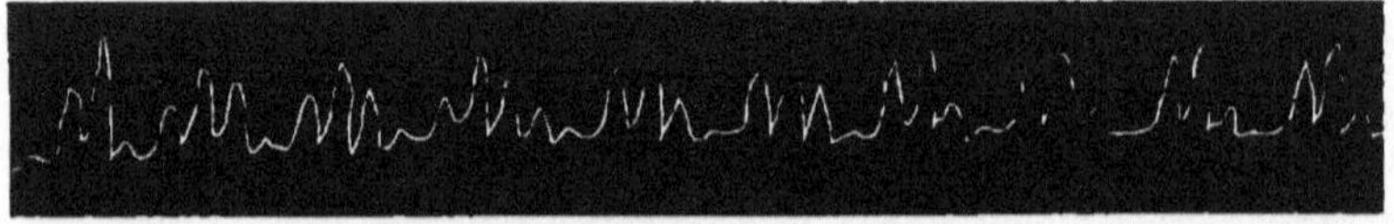

EXPERIMENT I.—No. 1. Immediately before inhalation. Ten minims of ethyl bromide were then administered from a cloth, and tracing No. 2 was taken.

No. 2—After ten minims.

No. 3—After ten minims more. The animal was still struggling, so the amount of ethyl was increased. After the vapor of twenty minims had been consumed, the following result was given.

No. 4—Complete anæsthesia.

No. 5.—Effect of the anæsthetic is passing off. This tracing having been taken, the animal seemed to have again become sensitive to pain. Ten minims were therefore administered, with the following result:

No. 6.—It was decided to kill the animal; ten minims more were administered as rapidly as possible. The following tracing was then taken:

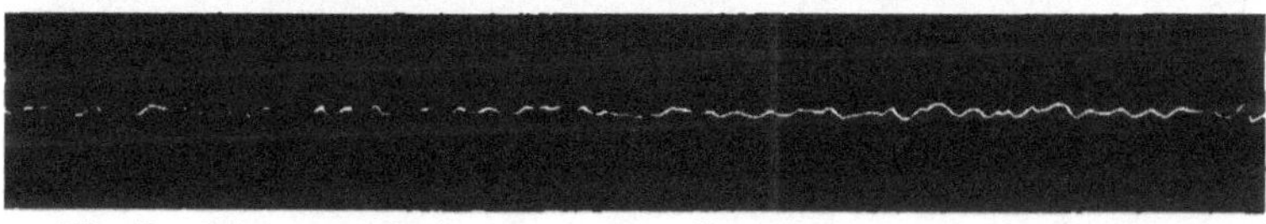

No. 7.—Five seconds before death. Respiration and the movement of the heart seemed to stop at the same time. Result of autopsy negative.

EXPERIMENT II.—Another rat, almost exactly similar to the subject of the preceding experiment, was treated in the same manner.

No. 1.—Before ether. Normal cardiac and respiratory movements.

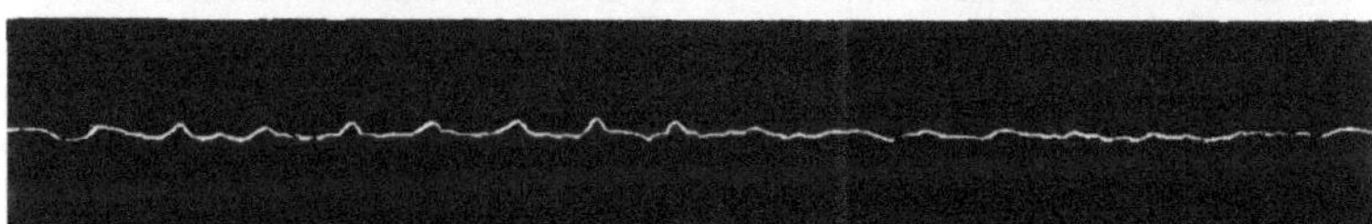

No. 2.—After inhaling vapor of twenty minims. Complete anæsthesia. Almost complete cessation of respiration and circulation. The inhaler was removed, and air re-entered the lungs with an immediate revival of the circulation.

No. 3.—Inhalation discontinued. Animal reviving. Ten minims of ethyl bromide were now administered.

No. 4.—Anæsthesia.

No. 5.—Continued anæsthesia. Twenty minims were now administered.

No. 6.—Profound anæsthesia.

No. 7.—Anæsthesia passing off.

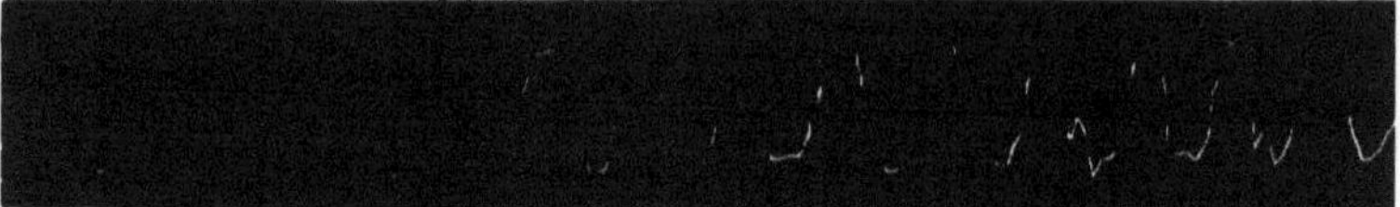

No. 8.—Animal shows signs of consciousness and excitement.

No. 9.—No anæsthesia. Animal quiet.

No. 10.—Effect nearly gone. Animal excited. Thirty minims were
now administered, and the following tracing was taken.

No. 11.—Heart shows signs of failure ; inhalation discontinued.

No. 12.—**Animal again reviving.   Fifty minims were now administered** as rapidly as possible.

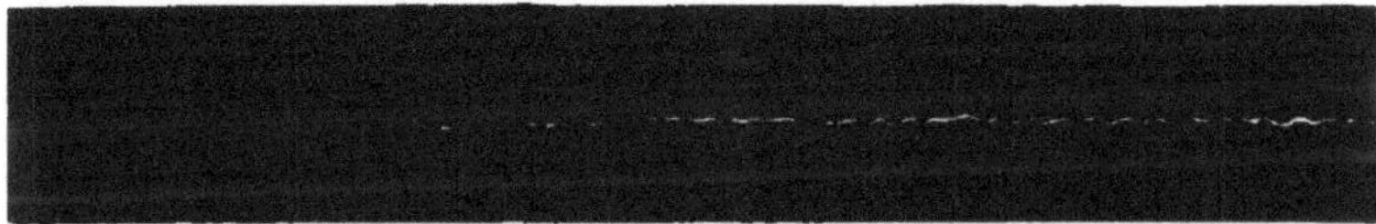

No. 13.—Profound resolution.   Respiration almost imperceptible.

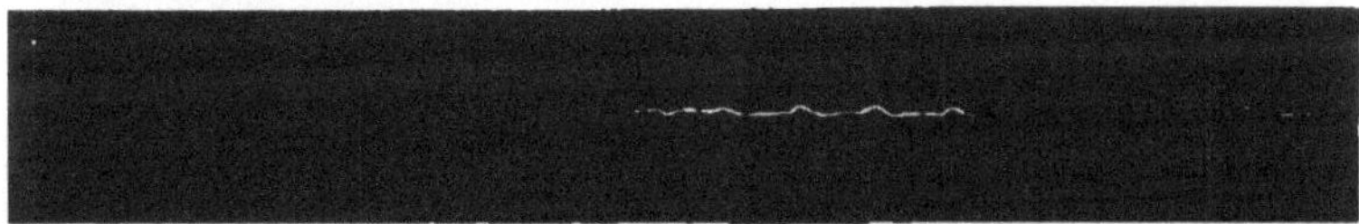

No. 14.—Twenty seconds before death.

Experiment III.—A medium-sized dog was rendered insensible by inhaling the vapor of sulphuric ether.   The common carotid artery was then exposed in the neck, and the sphygmograph was adjusted to the vessel. The following tracing exhibits the effect of ether upon the carotid pulse during complete anæsthesia.

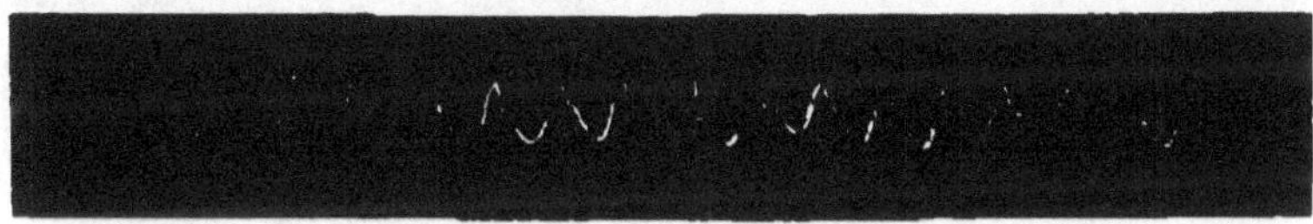

No. 1.—Anæsthesia from sulphuric ether.   The effect of this anæsthetic was allowed to pass off, and the animal was then placed fully under the influence of ethylic bromide.

No. 2.—Anæsthesia from hydrobromic ether.

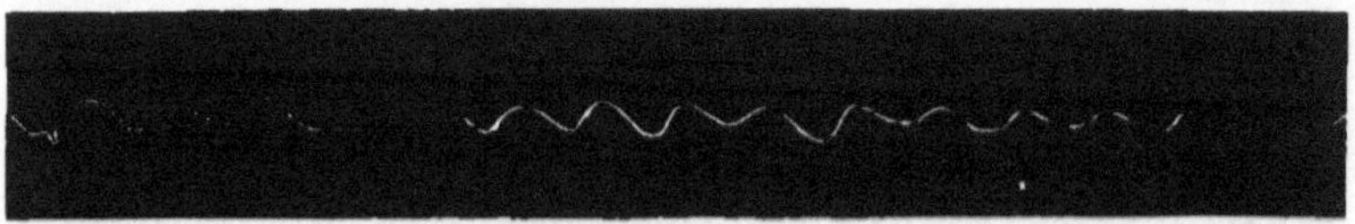

No. 3.—Continued anæsthesia from hydrobromic ether. Chloroform was now substituted for the ether, when the pulse-curve immediately experienced the following change :

No. 4.—Anæsthesia from inhalation of chloroform.

No. 5.—Continued anæsthesia.

The evidences of syncope were now so apparent that it became necessary to suspend the administration at once in order to save the life of the animal. The experiment was therefore discontinued. The contrasts presented by these tracings need no comment, so well do they illustrate the different grades of cardiac depression which may be produced by different anæsthetics.

The next experiment was performed upon the human subject. Through the kindness of Dr. C. Fenger, one of the surgeons to the Cook County Hospital, the administration of hydrobromic ether was undertaken upon an adult male, Swede, who was to be subjected to the operation of opening the knee-joint, July 18, 1880. Half an hour previous to the operation his pulse-rate was eighty-four per minute, and his radial artery yielded the subjoined sphygmogram.

No. 1.—Half an hour before operation. This tracing indicates low blood-pressure and an enfeebled condition of the vascular nervous apparatus.

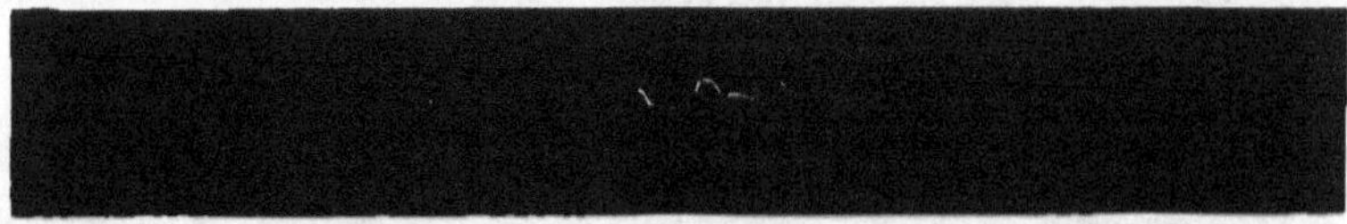

No. 2.—One minute after the commencement of inhalation. Pulse, 146 per minute, tending to anacrotism, but on the whole giving evidence of stimulation.

No. 3.—Two minutes later. Pulse, 200. Consciousness only partially overwhelmed.

No. 4.—Pulse, 200 ; respiration, 48 ; pupils dilated ; general muscular rigidity ; body strongly arched forward. The patient seemed to be unconscious, but not insensible, in spite of free administration of the hydrobromic ether. After having inhaled the vapor of one hundred and fifty cubic centimetres (nearly five ounces) of the ether, during a period of thirteen minutes and a half, the patient, though unconscious, was in such a condition of muscular spasm that nothing better than the following sphygmogram could be obtained :

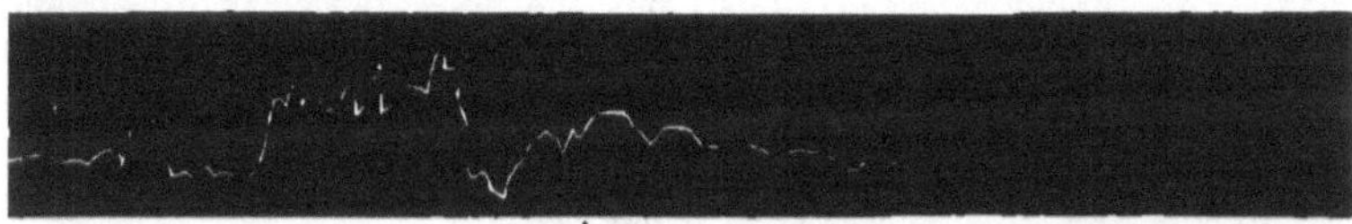

No. 5.—Thirteen minutes and a half after the commencement of inhalation. Sulphuric ether was now substituted for the hydrobromic. The pulse immediately fell to 148 beats per minute, muscular relaxation took place, and the operation was commenced.

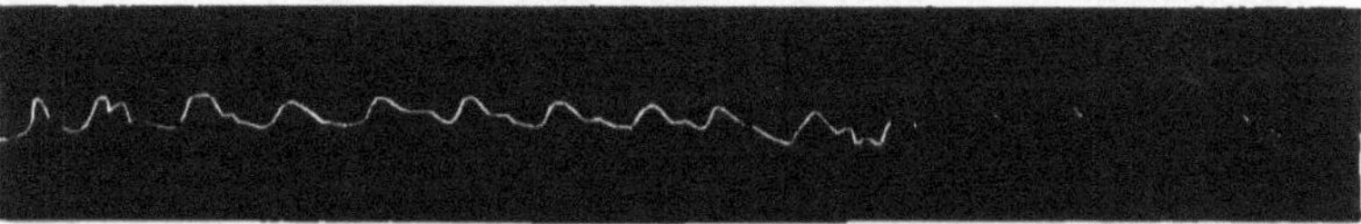

No. 6.—One minute after substitution of sulphuric ether.

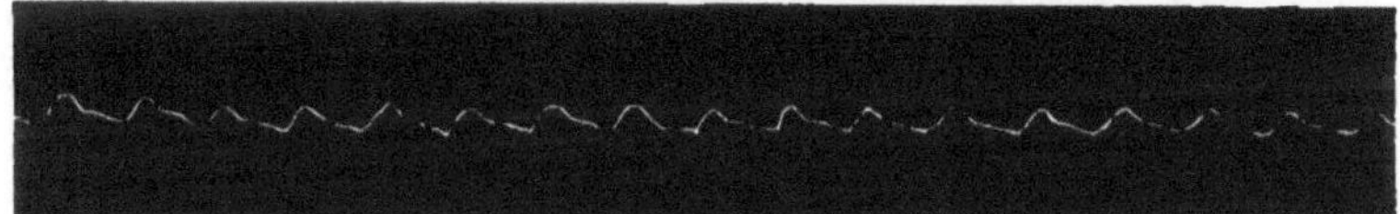

No. 7.—Continued anæsthesia. Pulse, 148.

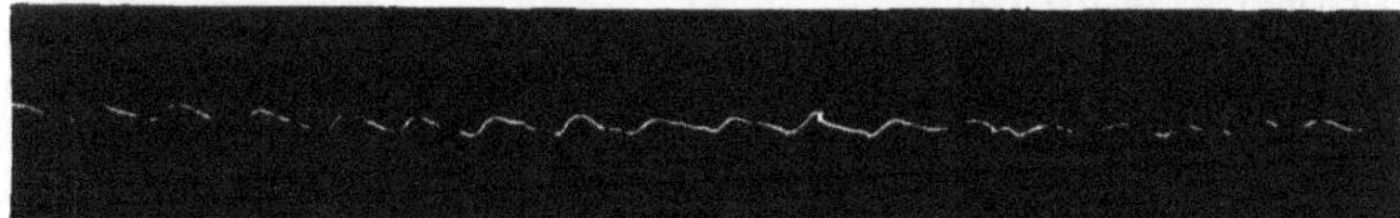

No. 8.—Stertorous breathing. Pulse, 170.

No. 9.—One minute later. The operation was now concluded, and inhalation was terminated.

No. 10.—Consciousness returning. Pulse, 154.

This peculiar experience put an end to my opportunities for experiment with ethylic bromide upon the human subject.

In the Buffalo General Hospital, N. Y., Dr. Charles C. F. Gay reports (*The Med. Record*, July 17, 1880) the use of the "*new anæsthetic.*" It required eleven minutes to bring the patient under its influence, and nine drachms were used. Its odor was very disagreeable, its effect was evanescent. Two drachms had previously put the house physician asleep, and during its administration to the patient, the doctor—who appears to be unusually susceptible to the effects of anæsthetics—came near falling asleep. Another patient, a very strong man, just as he was coming under the influence of the same anæsthetic, became excited, violent, and unmanageable, sprang from the table, and escaped to his bed.

Dr. C. H. Wilkinson, surgeon in charge of St. Mary's Hospital, Galveston, Texas, reports a case (*The Med. Record*, May 15, 1880) of Chopart's amputation, on a male, forty-one years of age, in which ethylic bromide was administered. The patient had, three months previously, been chloroformed without the slightest unfavorable symptoms. On this occasion he received four cubic centimetres (one drachm) of the ethylic bromide from a towel. A speedy and pleasant intoxication was developed in about one minute. Four grammes additional were now poured upon the towel. This caused muscular excitement, lasting for a minute, and requiring some degree of restraint. Pulse and respiration were greatly accelerated. Complete anæsthesia supervened within three minutes from the commencement of inhalation. The operation was now begun, but it was immediately remarked that the pulse had stopped; his face was blanched, and "almost simultaneously his breathing stopped short." Inversion, artificial respiration, and nitrite of amyl revived the patient, who recovered the power of speaking within a minute after the renewal of circulation. The ethylic bromide was then resumed in moderation, so as to produce semi-anæsthesia, in which condition the patient continued during the operation, which lasted forty-five minutes, without consciousness of pain. Vomiting followed, and persisted about five hours.

Dr. J. C. Moore reports (*Chicago Med. Journ.*, August, 1880) two cases of the use of ethylic bromide. The article was obtained from Wyeth & Bro., of Philadelphia, and was supposed to be pure. "The first patient, after twenty minutes' inhalation, exhibited bad symptoms, and retained partial consciousness, so that the ethyl was abandoned for ether, which acted promptly and efficiently." The second patient was a woman, thirty-four years of age, to be operated on by Dr. A. Reeves Jackson, for a uterine disorder. Great care was devoted to the administration of the anæsthetic ; but, at the end of thirty-five minutes of great excitement, with intense and persistent retching and vomiting, though the patient had eaten nothing that day, it became necessary to abandon the ethyl, and to employ ordinary ether, which produced complete anæsthesia without any delay. During the inhalation of ethyl there was excessive venous engorgement, injection of the conjunctivæ, lividity of the countenance, laborious respiration, and acceleration of the pulse to one hundred and twenty beats per minute. Each act of vomiting was attended by complete recovery of consciousness, so evanescent were the effects of the anæsthetic, necessitating an entire repetition of the whole process of inhalation. A few weeks after this experience, the same patient, having occasion to undergo a second operation, was subjected to the vapor of sulphuric ether, " and in thirteen minutes from the commencement, without a single alarming symptom, without excitement, and without nausea, she was completely anæsthetized."

It may be safely assumed that a certain portion of the excitement remarked in these cases was occasioned by a faulty method of administration of the vapor. It is necessary to apply the napkin, upon which four to eight cubic centimetres (one or two drachms) of the liquid have been poured, very closely to the face, in such a manner that air shall be almost entirely excluded. In this particular the rules for the inhalation of nitrous oxide gas are almost literally applicable. Thus administered, the patient becomes very speedily anæsthetized. Recovery takes place with almost equal rapidity. If this were all that is needed to obviate the objections to the use of ethylic bromide, it would speedily become a very popular anæsthetic; but, unfortunately, there are more serious difficulties in the way of its general adoption. The liquid is not a thoroughly stable compound, and unless great care is observed during the process of its distillation, certain residual impurities may pass over and contaminate the ethereal product. Dr. Lawrence Wolff, of Philadelphia (*Am Journ. of Pharmacy*, May, 1880) has shown that this residue is a brown, acrid liquid, having an unpleasant and pungent odor. Twenty drops of this liquid, given to a rabbit which had previously taken two grammes (thirty grains) of pure ethylic bromide without the slightest ill effect, produced irritation of the gastro-intestinal tract, followed by death in eighteen hours. That the specimens of ethylic bromide which have been furnished to the medical profession have frequently been contaminated with these impurities is proved by the analyses of Dr. Carl Jungk (*The Med. Record*, p. 84, July 17, 1880), who has demonstrated their presence in many samples of the drug —notably in two cases where a fatal result followed its use. These impurities consist of carbon bromide (C_2Br_4) and free bromide (Watts). The ordinary process of rectification is insufficient to yield an ether pure enough for inhalation. It therefore becomes necessary to subject the ordinary ethylic bromide to the following additional process : the liquid yielded by the usual method of rectification with water, potash, and calcium chloride, should be mixed with five per cent. of olive oil, and should be agitated with it from time to time for twenty-four hours. The flask should then be placed upon a water-bath, and the process of distillation should be conducted at a heat which will not permit the temperature of the vapor in the space above the liquid to rise above 40° (104° F.). The product thus obtained will be pure ethyl bromide (*Le Progrès Médical*, Aug. 28, 1880).

The importance of using only the purest specimens of ethylic bromide is illustrated by an unfortunate case, reported by J. Marion Sims, M.D., in *The Medical Record*, April 3, 1880. The patient was a single lady, twenty-five years old, subject to epileptic fits recurring after each menstrual epoch. She was placed under the influence of ethyl for an hour and a half, during the performance of Battey's operation for the removal of the ovaries. Complete insensibility was effected at the expiration of five minutes. Respiration was then performed at the rate of sixty per minute. At the end of twenty minutes she vomited, and again at the end of forty minutes. In all about one hundred and forty-five to one hundred and sixty grammes (four and a half to five ounces) of ethylic bromide were used. Consciousness returned quickly after the completion of the operation, but retching and vomiting, with pain in the head, continued most persistently. The urine became greatly reduced in quantity, and a violent, tenesmic diarrhœa set in. The breath and all the discharges were impregnated with the odor of the anæsthetic. The patient finally became restless, frantic, and convulsed. Death occurred about twenty-one hours after the operation. After death the only morbid appearances noted were in the lower portion of the ileum and in the colon, which were darkly congested. The kidneys appeared healthy to the eye, but the microscope indicated the existence of slight cirrhosis and of acute catarrhal nephritis. All parts of the body exhaled the odor of ethylic bromide, even for a considerable time after removal from the cadaver.

A specimen of the anæsthetic used in this case was afterward examined, and its impurity was demonstrated by Dr. Carl Jungk. It seems hardly possible to doubt that in this case death was caused by an irritant poison. Many of the phenomena were identical with those which are produced by poisonous doses of bromine. The long-continued administration of the anæsthetic—itself a source of great danger when the more powerful agents are employed—occasioned the most complete saturation of the entire system with highly irritating impurities, among which bromine and carbon bromide exist; consequently, it is not strange that alarming symptoms and a fatal result concluded the scene.

Another fatal case occurred in the practice of Dr. Levis, of Philadelphia, May 26, 1880. The patient was a debilitated young man who entered the Jefferson Hospital for the removal of a vesical calculus. After the administration of " a stimulant" and one gramme (fifteen grains) of quinine, eight cubic centimetres (two fluid drachms) of ethylic bromide were given on a cloth. The patient struggled, and a second dose of four grammes was given. Four cubic centimetres more were given before the complete induction of anæsthesia. The operation had just been commenced, when respiration ceased. Amylic nitrite, electricity, and artificial respiration, were employed for an hour, without success. Post-mortem examination revealed a hyperæmic condition of the scalp and of the meninges of the brain. The apex of the left lung was adherent to the thoracic walls. The upper lobe of the lung was partially consolidated. There were several cavities, and caseous and purulent deposits. The right lung presented similar appearances. The right side of the heart was dilated, and contained clotted blood in both cavities. There was concentric hypertrophy of the left ventricle, which was contracted, and contained a very small blood-clot. The liver and intestines were healthy. There was concentric hypertrophy of the bladder, which contained at its neck two encysted calculi. The kidneys were enlarged, and exhibited pelvic inflammation.

All experience shows that the administration of anæsthetics to such patients is attended with danger. Even sulphuric ether may prove fatal if the kidneys are seriously damaged, and pulmonary disorganization is a well-known source of danger during the inhalation of anæsthetic vapor. The administration of chloroform to such a patient would have been a very hazardous undertaking. The fatal result in this case cannot be so much charged against the particular anæsthetic that was employed as against the exhibition of any anæsthetic agent whatever. If under such circumstances a surgeon feels obliged to undertake a capital operation, only the safest and best known substances should be used for the production of anæsthesia.

That ethylic bromide may be employed with ease and success has been abundantly proved by the experience of many observers. M. Bourneville (*Le Progrès Médical*, August 7, 1880) has recently administered it to large numbers of the patients in the Salpêtrière Hospital, for the arrest of paroxysms of hysteria and of epilepsy. He has also administered it, by daily inhalation for fifteen or twenty minutes, to a number of epileptic patients, with the fortunate result of considerably diminishing the frequence of the convulsive paroxysms. In several of these cases the temperature was depressed about half a degree centigrade during the act of inhalation. Immediately after the withdrawal of the anæsthetic, the normal degree was recovered, and sometimes even surpassed. The pulse, in about five hundred administrations, was somewhat accelerated during the period of inhalation. In six instances only was a slight retardation observed. Respiration, in like manner, was almost always accelerated. A copious overflow of tears was nearly always remarked. The urine never contained either albumen or sugar, and the quantity of the liquid was not affected. Rigidity of the limbs, and tremor involving the upper extremities, were occasionally noted. Daily inhalations for a period of two months exercised no unfavorable influence over the general process of nutrition; five patients found their weight increased during this period.

It is at present impossible to estimate the ratio of danger from ethylic bromide as compared with other anæsthetics. It must, however, be admitted that its use is not devoid of danger. At least two deaths have occurred as a consequence of its exhibition, and in numerous instances alarming symptoms have appeared during the act of inhalation. The experiments of Rabuteau indicate for ethylic bromide the existence of a greater degree of antagonism to the life of plants than is manifested by ordinary ether. The pulse-curves above given exhibit far greater cardiac depression under its influence than is produced by ether. The pulse-curve, in fact, closely resembles that of chloroform. The sudden occurrence of syncope during inhalation is very suggestive of the manner in which chloroform may paralyze the heart. The great molecular weight of ethylic bromide also brings it into close relations with chloroform. The bromic impurities with which it is liable to be contaminated are even more dangerous than the impurities which may exist in chloroform. Altogether, it must be admitted that ethylic bromide is to be ranked with chloroform as one of the most potent and most dangerous of anæsthetic substances.

ETHYLIC IODIDE—C_2H_5I.

Æther hydriodicus, L.; *Iodide of ethyl—Hydriodic ether*, E.; *Iodure d'éthyle*,
Fr.; *Jodwasserstoffäther, Jodäthyl*, G.

Specific gravity, 1.97546 at 0° (32° F.).
Boiling-point, 70° (158° F.) at 751 mm.
Vapor density, 5.475.

Ethylic iodide is a colorless liquid, having a strong, peculiar, ethereal odor. It was discovered by Gay Lussac, in the year 1815. Slightly soluble in water, it mixes readily with alcohol and ether. When exposed to light, it turns red or brown, from separation of the iodine and ethyl. The decomposition takes place slowly in diffused daylight, quickly in sunshine. It is but slightly inflammable ; when dropped on red-hot coals, it gives off violet vapors without taking fire (Watts).

Ethylic iodide is easily prepared, according to the method of Rieth and Beilstein, by introducing into a flask ten parts of amorphous phosphorus, fifty parts of alcohol of ninety per cent., and one hundred parts of iodine, leaving the mixture to itself for twenty-four hours, and then distilling (Watts).

Ethylic iodide has been used as a remedy for chronic bronchitis, by inhalation of the vapor of ten or fifteen drops from a handkerchief several times a day. Prof. D. R. Brower, of the Woman's Medical College, Chicago, has recently (*Chicago Med. Journ.*, July, 1880) called attention to its value as an agent for the relief of asthma. It possesses anæsthetic properties, and has occasionally been used for the induction of surgical anæsthesia, but its unstable character disqualifies it for such a purpose. It cannot be employed in connection with the actual cautery, on account of its decomposition and the liberation of free iodine when its vapors are brought in contact with the heated instrument.

BUTYLIC CHLORIDE—C_4H_9Cl.

Tetrane monochloride.

Specific gravity, 0.88.
Boiling-point, about 70° (158° F.).

Butylic chloride is a liquid lighter than water, and having an ethereal odor recalling also that of chlorine. It may be obtained by distilling amylic alcohol with calcium hypochlorite. The oily distillate, treated with oil of vitriol, and afterward with potash, to remove chloroform, yields pure butyl chloride (Watts).

The Committee of the British Medical Association state that when this substance was administered to rabbits it affected respiration, but not very rapidly. When the thorax was laid open so as to expose the heart during the experiment, it was seen that the cardiac pulsations became weaker, and after a time ceased altogether. In one instance it was observed that, almost immediately after the induction of complete anæsthesia, the respiration became shallow and soon stopped.

ISOBUTYLIC CHLORIDE—$C_4H_9Cl = CH(CH_3)_2CH_2Cl.$

Specific gravity, 0.8953 at 0° (32° F.).
Boiling-point, 60° (140° F.).

Isobutylic chloride, prepared by saturating isobutyl alcohol with hydrogen chloride, or treating it with phosphorus pentachloride, is a limpid liquid, having a pleasant, ethereal, but slightly alliaceous odor (Watts). It is isomeric with butylic chloride, but its anæsthetic properties are considerably different. The Committee of the British Medical Association state in their report (*Brit. Med. Jour.*, January 4, 1879) that "when it was administered (to frogs) under a glass jar, complete anæsthesia occurred in about five minutes. The heart was then exposed, and it was observed for thirty-five minutes, during which period its contractions were perfectly vigorous. When it was administered with a cloth (to rabbits), anæsthesia was produced in three to five minutes. It was continued after anæsthesia for nearly half an hour without any interference with respiration. It was administered on cloth (to dogs) ; anæsthesia was produced in four minutes. It was continued for half an hour, and respiration was unaffected, except slight occasional stertor."

AMYLENE—$C_5H_{10}.$

Specific gravity, 0.6549 at 10° (50° F.), (Maisch).
Boiling-point, 39°—42° (102.2°—107.6° F.), (Watts).
Vapor density (calculated), 2.4265.

Amylene is a transparent, colorless, very thin liquid, with an offensive, cabbage-like odor. It burns with a luminous flame, is almost insoluble in water, but mixes in all proportions with alcohol or ether.

Amylene was discovered in the year 1844, by Balard. It may be prepared by heating to 130° (266° F.) a mixture of the concentrated aqueous solution of zinc chloride with an equal volume of amylic alcohol. The product is distilled from a water-bath over caustic potash, and should be repeatedly rectified.

This substance was employed as an anæsthetic by Dr. Snow, in the year 1856. He administered its vapor in more than one hundred cases, until the occurrence of two deaths under its influence caused him to abandon its use. Numerous other experimenters have observed its effects upon animals and upon the human subject. The condition of insensibility produced by its inhalation is not' so persistent as after chloroform. Tonic and clonic muscular spasms occur with greater regularity and vigor than when chloroform or ether are exhibited. Respiration becomes irregular and is arrested before the heart ceases to beat in fatal cases. The *post-mortem* appearances in animals which have been killed with amylene are purely negative.

Anæsthesia is produced by inhalation of the vapor of amylene in four or five minutes' time. Vomiting is very seldom observed, and the return to consciousness is usually more rapid than after chloroform or ether. By the Committee of the British Medical Association amylene was administered to rabbits, both by inhalation and by hypodermic injection, without any anæsthetic effects.

DEATHS CAUSED BY INHALATION OF AMYLENE.

1. Male, thirty-three years; in good health, though a free liver. Operation for fistula in ano, April 7, 1857. Six drachms of amylene were administered with an inhaler, by Snow himself. The patient appeared to become quietly unconscious in about two minutes. Pulse good. The operation was commenced about two minutes and three-quarters after the beginning of inhalation. The patient did not flinch, but held his limbs tense, without moving them. Immediately after the conclusion of the brief operation the pulse stopped in the left wrist, and was almost imperceptible in the right. His breathing was, however, good—indeed, quite natural, and he moved his face and limbs as if about to awake. In two or three minutes, however, he seemed to be getting more insensible; he did not wink when the edge of the eyelid was touched, and the breathing grew slower and deeper. Cold affusion did no good. The countenance became livid, and respiration was gasping. It soon began to intermit with deep, distant inspirations. Artificial respiration—method of Marshall Hall—was then tried. Gasping inspirations continued fully ten minutes after the failure of the pulse, and a slight movement of the heart was doubtfully detected at the moment when breathing finally ceased. The patient had drank a pint of ale shortly before the operation. *Autopsy*, forty-eight hours after death.—All the organs were healthy. Blood dark and fluid. Left ventricle contracted; the right was dilated and full of blood.—Snow: *Med. Times and Gaz.*, p. 381, April 18, 1857.

2. Male, twenty-four years; muscular. Removal of a small epithelial tumor from the back. Less than one ounce of amylene was poured into the inhaler (Snow's). In about two minutes the patient appeared to be unconscious; at the end of another minute the sensibility of the margin of the eyelids was diminished. He was then turned upon his face, when he became much excited, and was with difficulty held on the table. This condition lasted about a minute, when he inhaled a little more of the amylene. The operation was then performed, occupying about two minutes, during which time the patient was not completely insensible, but muttered incoherently, and moved himself a little. Inhalation was continued at intervals during the operation. Just as it was completed the limbs became relaxed, and respiration assumed a noisy, snoring character. The pulse was found to be almost imperceptible; the face was livid, and his breathing was of a gasping nature. Mouth to mouth insufflation improved the color of the lips and face, and there were spontaneous inspirations between the insufflations, but the pulse could not be felt. After two or three minutes, artificial respiration by the method of Marshall Hall was commenced, and was continued for an hour and a half. During three-quarters of an hour there were spontaneous inspirations. Twenty minutes after the accident, Dr. Snow thought he could hear the heart beating regularly, but very feebly, and the air seemed to enter the lungs by the patient's own breathing almost as freely as in health. At the end of three-quarters of an hour electro-puncture of the heart was performed. The needles were introduced to the depth of about an inch and a half between the cartilages of the ribs, just to the left of the sternum, and on a level with the nipple. They were afterward found to have penetrated the walls of the left ventricle, near the septum, but without reaching the cavity. This finished him, and there were no further efforts at inspiration after this time. *Autopsy* negative.—The lungs contained several small epithelial tumors similar to those removed

from the back. There was a large cyst in one kidney, but, with these exceptions, the organs were healthy.—Snow, St. George's Hospital, July 30, 1857 ; *Med. Times and Gaz.*, p. 133, August 8, 1857.

AMYLIC HYDRIDE—C_5H_{12}.

Specific gravity, 0.638 at 14° (57.2° F.).
Boiling-point, 30° (86° F.).
Vapor density, 2.382 (Watts).

Amylic hydride is a colorless, transparent liquid, with a very slight, but agreeable odor. It is contained in the more volatile portions of American petroleum, from which it can be separated by fractional distillation. Its density is less than that of any other known liquid (Miller) ; it remains unfrozen at —24° (—11.2° F.). Its vapor burns with a brilliant white flame, without smoke.

Richardson found that inhalation of the vapor of amylic hydride produced insensibility in about two minutes. This was preceded by muscular movements, and sometimes by retraction of the head. There was no irritation of the air-passages, nor any symptom of dyspnoea. Anæsthetic sleep thus procured was quiet, and associated with speedy and complete muscular relaxation, without notable diminution of bodily heat. Upon the smaller mammals anæsthesia was rapidly induced without symptoms of agitation or danger. Recovery was rapid. When given in quantity sufficient to produce death, there was observed a diminution of temperature, with dilatation of the pupils and a simultaneous arrest of circulation and respiration. Post-mortem appearances were negative.

AMYLIC CHLORIDE—$C_5H_{11}Cl$.

Specific gravity, 0.699.
Boiling-point, 101° (213.8° F.).
Vapor density, 3.8 (Watts).

Amylic chloride, or chloramyl, is a colorless, transparent, neutral liquid, with an agreeable odor—to some persons faintly suggestive of garlic. It burns with a luminous flame bordered with green. It may be prepared from amylic alcohol, by passing a rapid current of hydrochloric acid into the alcohol heated in a retort to 110° (230° F.). Chloride of amyl is formed and distils over. When the retort is nearly empty, the distillate is poured back, and the same process is repeated. The product is then shaken with strong hydrochloric acid, in which amylic alcohol is soluble—chloride of amyl being insoluble—then with water (Watts).

According to Snow and Richardson, amylic chloride produces a slowly developed and long-continuing anæsthesia. Dr. Snow inhaled the vapor of four cubic centimetres (one drachm) of the liquid without any specially disagreeable consequences, and by Dr. Richardson it was successfully employed to prevent the pain of tooth-extraction in fourteen cases.

15

AMYLIC IODIDE—$C_5H_{11}I$.

Specific gravity, 1.511 at 11° (51.8° F.).
Boiling-point, 146° (294.8° F.).
Vapor density, 6.675.

Iodide of amyl is a colorless, transparent liquid, of faint odor and pungent taste. It turns brown on exposure to light. For its preparation four parts of iodine are placed in one flask, and an excess of phosphorus in another. Seven parts of amylic alcohol are poured upon the iodine, and the liquid is shaken till opacity is produced, then poured upon the phosphorus and digested till the color is removed—again poured upon the iodine, and so on, till all the iodine is exhausted. The nearly colorless product so obtained is washed with slightly alkaline water, dried over chloride of calcium, and rectified. The latter portions are the purest (Watts).

This is another of the rarer anæsthetic compounds with which Richardson experimented.

CAPRYLIC HYDRIDE—C_8H_{18}.

Specific gravity, 0.728 at 0° (32° F.).
Boiling-point, 115°—119° (239°—246.2° F.).
Vapor density, 4.01°.

Caprylic hydride, octane, or octylic hydride, is one of the constituents of American petroleum ; also found among the light oils obtained by distilling Wigan cannel coal at a low temperature. It is a colorless liquid, having a faint, ethereal odor (Watts).

According to the experiments of Richardson upon animals, this substance produces a long period of preliminary excitement, accompanied by vomiting. Anæsthesia thus induced is very evanescent.

KEROSELENE.

Keroselene is a colorless, inflammable liquid, with an odor somewhat suggestive of chloroform. It is derived by distillation from American petroleum, and is a complex mixture of numerous hydrides of carbon, such as amylic, caprylic, œnanthylic, laurylic, myristylic, and palmitylic hydrides. These compounds may be to some extent separated by fractional distillation. Their mixture boils at a temperature that varies between 50° and 60° (122° and 140° F.). That portion which distils over at a temperature below 50° (122° F.) is called naphtha, and consists chiefly of amylene and amylic hydride. If the vapors are well refrigerated, the product also contains butylic hydride (C_4H_{10}), and constitutes the liquid known as *rhigolene* (Maisch). Butylic hydride boils at 1° (33.8° F.), and for that reason cannot be easily preserved at ordinary temperatures. The liquid which has been employed, under the name of rhigolene, for the production of local anæsthesia, is a mixture of butylic hydride and naphtha, substances which belong to the paraffin series of petroleum derivatives.

Keroselene was experimentally investigated by Henry J. Bigelow, of Boston (*Boston Med. and Surg. Journ.*, July, 1861). It produced, in every instance of its employment, disagreeable and alarming symptoms, such as irritation of the air-passages, lividity of the surface, muscular disturbance, and intermission of the pulse.

OIL OF TURPENTINE—$C_{10}H_{16}$.

Specific gravity, 0.86—0.89.
Boiling-point, about 160° (320° F.).

Oil of turpentine is a volatile oil contained in the wood, bark, leaves and other parts of pines, firs, and other trees belonging to the coniferous order, and separable therefrom by distillation with water. It is usually prepared by distilling crude turpentine, either alone or with water. Turpentine oils obtained from different sources exhibit considerable diversity in their specific gravity, boiling-point, and optical rotatory power. The several varieties, when purified by repeated rectification with water, are colorless, mobile liquids, having a peculiar aromatic, but disagreeable odor. They are insoluble in water, slightly soluble in aqueous alcohol, miscible in all proportions with absolute alcohol, ether, and carbon bisulphide (Watts).

Kappeler has recorded a tradition that once, on shipboard, in the absence of chloroform, a sailor was anæsthetized with the vapor of oil of turpentine. Richardson employed it in his experiments upon animals, and found it a rather tedious, though effectual anæsthetic. The peculiarly irritating effects upon the kidneys which are produced by oil of turpentine would be likely to manifest themselves if its vapor were often inhaled. I have known one instance in which general muscular debility, continuing for several days, was produced by inhaling the vapor. This occurred in a person who had experienced a convulsion after swallowing a grain of camphor, and who was almost completely paralyzed by the use of copaiva.

BENZENE—C_6H_6.

Specific gravity, 0.8991 at 0° (32° F.).
Boiling-point, 80.4° (176.8° F.) ; melts at 5.5° (41.9° F.).
Vapor density, 2.77.

The term benzene is restricted by Watts to the pure hydrocarbon, C_6H_6. Benzol is the name given to the complex commercial substance from which numerous different bodies may be separated.

Benzene is, at ordinary temperatures, a limpid, colorless, strongly refracting oil. When cooled it solidifies into fern-like tufts, or into hard masses like camphor. It has a pleasant smell. It is scarcely soluble in water, but imparts a strong odor to it. In alcohol, ether, wood-spirit, and acetone, it is readily soluble. It is very inflammable, and burns with a bright, smoky flame. The most abundant source of benzene is coal-tar ; but the product obtained from this source is very impure, containing several higher hydrocarbons, volatile alkaloids, and other substances (Watts).

The experiments of Simpson, Snow, and Richardson indicate that benzene possesses undoubted anæsthetic properties, but it produces unpleasant sensations in the head, and a decided tendency to the development of convulsive movements, if administered in quantity sufficient to produce complete anæsthesia. The Committee of the British Medical Association experimented with it on frogs. It was nearly as slow as ether in its action, and it excited struggling on the part of the animal. The action of the heart was also enfeebled, though less than when chloroform was employed.

PYRROL—C_4H_5N.

Specific gravity, 1.077.
Boiling-point, 133° (271.4° F.).
Vapor density, 2.40.

Pyrrol is a colorless, transparent liquid of delightfully fragrant odor, resembling chloroform, but softer and less pungent. It has a hot and pungent taste. Is sparingly soluble in water, but is readily soluble in alcohol, ether, and oils. It is insoluble in alkaline solutions, but dissolves, though not readily, in acids (Watts).

Pyrrol appears to be produced in almost every instance where animal or vegetable matter containing nitrogen is subjected to destructive distillation (Watts).

This is one of the substances with which the Committee of the British Medical Association has recently experimented. In the frog it produced anæsthesia with considerably less rapidity than chloroform, and great excitement and muscular spasms preceded complete anæsthesia. Its hypodermic administration to three young rabbits produced spasmodic movements, principally involving the jaws and fore-paws. These rabbits were not decidedly anæsthetized.

ALCOHOL—C_2H_6O.

Alkohol, Weingeist, G. ; *Alcool* Fr. ; *Aqua ardens, Spiritus vini rectificatissi-mus, Alcohol vini,* L.

The word alcohol is derived from the Arabic words *al* and *kohol,* signifying the impalpable powder of antimonic sulphide with which the oriental women were accustomed to darken their eyebrows. The primitive signification of the word *kohol* is *anything that is burnt* or *that burns.* This probably refers us back to the most ancient times, when ashes were applied to the face, just as the Hindoo women now mark their foreheads with charcoal or ashes. How the term came to be applied by the alchemists of the middle ages to the newly discovered product of distillation is unknown.

Alcohol, except as it exists in the fermented juices of fruits, was unknown to the ancient Greeks and Romans. It has been claimed as one of the products of Chinese industry centuries before it was introduced to the other races of Asia. Albucasis, the Arabian chemist, living in the twelfth century, has been credited with the discovery of brandy ; but it is scarcely probable that such a substance should have escaped the attention of one so well acquainted with the art of distillation as the famous Geber.

From these sources the knowledge of alcohol and its properties was conveyed to European channels through the efforts of Arnauld de Villeneuve. This illustrious physician, born in the south of Europe, about the year 1250, was one of the most learned men of his time. A profound student of alchemy, a successful practitioner of medicine, an ardent debater in philosophy and theology, he became a professor in the rising medical school at Montpellier. At this time the fame of the Moorish schools in Spain was at its height, and the French professor betook himself thither, in order to exhaust their knowledge at its source. It was there, no doubt, that he learned to prize the virtues of that brandy which he praises in his work, *De conservanda juventute et retardanda senectute.* For a long time this liquor was prepared and sold only as a medicine by the apothecaries. Considered at first a poison, then regarded as a valuable remedy, the sixteenth century witnessed its adoption by the European nations as a sovereign remedy for nearly all the ills to which flesh is heir. In the year 1514, Louis XII. of France granted the monopoly of distilling spirits to the newly founded corporation of vinegar-makers. Before many years the work of distillation constituted a separate branch of industry, and the consumption of spirits as an article of common beverage became widely diffused. It was not, however, before the year 1678 that liquors were to be purchased in Paris elsewhere than at the dispensaries of the druggists. From that date their sale has been practically without restriction. Previous to the great European campaigns under Marlborough and Prince Eugene, at the commencement of the eighteenth century, the national beverage of the English was beer. In 1581, Camden tells us, the English soldiers in the Low Countries, during the terrible conflict between the Dutch and the Spaniards, first became acquainted with the use of spirits. But the number of the troops furnished by Elizabeth, though too small to make any serious impression upon the enemy abroad, was sufficient to work great injury upon the nation at home. The magnificent scale upon which the wars of Queen Anne were conducted could not fail to effect consequences of the gravest character. "The habit of gin-drinking (*England in the Eighteenth Century*, Lecky, vol i., p. 516)—the mastercurse of English life, to which most of the crime and an immense proportion of the misery of the nation may be ascribed—if it did not absolutely originate, at least became for the first time a national vice, in the early Hanoverian period. Drunkenness, it is true, had long been common, though Camden maintained that in his day it was still a recent vice, that there had been a time when the English were 'of all the Northern nations the most commended for their sobriety,' and that 'they first learned in their wars in the Netherlands to drown themselves with immoderate drinking.' The Dutch and German origin of many drinking terms lends some color to this assertion, and it is corroborated by other evidence. 'Superfluity of drink,' wrote Tom Nash in the reign of Elizabeth, 'is a sin that, ever since we have mixed ourselves with the Low Countries, is counted honorable; but, before we knew their lingering wars, was held in the highest degree of hatred that might be.' 'As the English,' said Chamberlayne, 'returning from the wars in the Holy Land, brought home the foul disease of leprosy, so in our fathers' days the English returning from the service in the Netherlands brought with them the foul vice of drunkenness.' But the evil, if it was not indigenous in England, at least spread very rapidly and very widely. 'In England,' said Iago ("Othello," Act II., Scene 3), 'they are most potent in potting. Your Dane, your German, and your swag-bellied Hollander are nothing to your English.' 'We seem,' wrote a somewhat rhetorical writer in 1657, 'to be steeped in liquors, or to be the dizzy island. We drink as if we were nothing but sponges, or had tunnels in our mouths. We are the grape-suckers of the earth.' . . . Among the poor, however, in the beginning of the eighteenth century, the popular beverage was still beer or ale. . . . It was computed in 1688 that no less than twelve million four hundred thousand barrels were brewed in England in a single year, though the entire population probably little exceeded five millions. . . . It was not till about 1724 that the passion for gin-drinking appears to have infected the masses of the population, and it spread with the rapidity and the violence of an epidemic. . . . . Retailers of gin were accustomed to hang out painted boards announcing that their customers could be made drunk for a penny, and dead-drunk for two pence, and should have straw for nothing ; and cellars strewn with straw were accordingly provided, into which those who had become insensible were dragged, and where they remained till they had sufficiently recovered to renew their orgies." Very similar was the condition of affairs throughout the north of Europe during the eighteenth century. In America the war of the rebellion against England was the period during which the ancient temperate usages of the inhabitants of the colonies were overthrown. The distribution of a daily ration of spirits—West India rum—among the soldiers was the means of diffusing throughout the community a taste for strong drink which has persisted ever since the close of that war. Could old Raymond Lully have looked forward from the fourteenth century into the nineteenth, he would not have written with such enthusiasm about this "admirable essence of wine, an emanation of the Divinity, an element newly revealed to man, but hid from antiquity, because the human race were then too young to need this beverage, destined to revive the energies of modern decrepitude." More reasonable was his fancy, though in a sense very different from that imagined by him, "that the discovery of this *aqua vitæ*, as it was called, indicated the approaching consummation of all things—the end of this world."

CHEMISTRY OF ALCOHOL.

Alcohol is obtained on a large scale by distilling from fermented saccharine liquids the spirit that has been produced from the sugar by the process of fermentation. Any saccharine liquid may thus be made to yield alcohol, and, in tropical countries, it is usually prepared from solutions of cane-sugar or molasses. In temperate climates it is necessary to procure the needful sugar by transformation of starch into grape-sugar. This is effected by subjecting starch-containing grains, like the cereals, or roots that are richly stored with starch, such as the potato, to the process of mashing. This process consists in digesting the *mash*, as the moistened grain is called, in moderately warm water for a number of hours. The starch is converted into sugar by the action of a ferment, called *diastase*, which is yielded by the nitrogenous portion of the grain during its decomposition. Diastase is always present in germinating seeds, and by its active presence the non-nutritive starch in the cotyledons of the seed is transformed into sugar, which is the normal nutriment of the embryonic plant. In malt, diastase is present to the amount of $\frac{1}{500}$ part by weight. One part of diastase is sufficient to effect the saccharification of two thousand parts of starch. According to Miller, the temperature of 65° (149° F.) is most favorable to this transformation. The sugar thus formed is called *inverted sugar*, from the fact that its solution rotates, or *inverts*, the ray of polarized light which may be transmitted through its medium. As a matter of fact, the sugar is a mixture of lævulose and dextrose—forms of sugar which are so called by reason of their influence upon polarized light.

When the process of *mashing* is complete, the temperature of the mash is reduced to about 22° or 23° (72° F.). Yeast is then added, and the process of *fermentation* commences. This consists in the breaking up of the saccharine molecule into carbonic acid gas and alcohol:

$$\underset{\text{Fruit-sugar.}}{C_6H_{12}O_6} \text{ gives } \underset{\text{Carbonic acid gas.}}{2CO_2} + \underset{\text{Alcohol.}}{2C_2H_6O.}$$

If grape-sugar or dextrose undergoes fermentation, the reaction may be thus represented:

$$\underset{\text{Grape-sugar.}}{C_6H_{14}O_7} \text{ gives } \underset{\text{Carbonic acid gas.}}{2CO_2} + \underset{\text{Water.}}{H_2O} + \underset{\text{Alcohol.}}{2C_2H_6O.}$$

When cane-sugar is fermented, each molecule first assimilates a molecule of water, becoming fruit-sugar. The above-described transformation into carbonic anhydride and alcohol then takes place:

$$\underset{\text{Cane-sugar.}}{C_{12}H_{22}O_{11}} + \underset{\text{Water.}}{H_2O} = \underset{\text{Fruit-sugar.}}{2C_6H_{12}O_6}; \text{ and}$$

$$2C_6H_{12}O_6 = 4CO_2 + 4C_2H_6O.$$

The above formulas illustrate the manner in which alcohol is separated from the molecule of sugar. The process of fermentation, however, is not as simple as they would indicate. The greater part of the sugar is thus transformed into alcohol and carbonic acid gas, but a certain quantity escapes this change, and is converted into other products. According to Pasteur, 100 parts of cane-sugar by fermentation constitute 105.4 parts of glucose (fruit-sugar), and these yield:

Alcohol	51.1
Carbonic acid gas	49.4
Succinic acid	0.7
Glycerine	3.2
Matter passing to the yeast	1.0
Sum	105.4

The above statement, however, is only approximately correct. A small portion of the sugar is transformed into the higher alcohols and ether.

The process of fermentation requires for its initiation the presence of a ferment. Ferments are nitrogenous substances of unstable constitution, which have the power of transferring motion to the molecules of certain bodies with which they are brought in contact. The explanation of this process is largely hypothetical, but it seems quite certain that it is not a process of combination or of double decomposition. Ferments like diastase are yielded by decomposing nitrogenous matter. Animal ferments like ptyalin, pepsin, trypsin, etc., are thrown off among the products of organized animal cells. The ferment of yeast is ordinarily described as a vegetable cell; but, strictly speaking, this is not correct. Yeast-ferment is the product of the cells of the *sugar fungus*—is an excrement, so to speak—

but is not the cell itself. The formation of the ferment is a physiological process; the action of the ferment is a physical process.

The action of the ferment upon sugar is quite the reverse of the action of alcohol upon the same kind of molecules. Under the influence of the ferment, the motion of the atoms of sugar is increased. They rearrange themselves into new groups, with results that are almost suggestive of life. But, as the alcohol thus separated increases in the saccharine solution, the activity of the process diminishes. Alcohol by its presence acts the reverse part to a ferment: it hinders molecular motion. In sufficient quantity it completely arrests certain kinds of molecular motion. If present to the amount of twenty per cent. or more, in the fermenting liquid, it completely neutralizes the energy of the ferment, and puts an end to the process. By virtue of this peculiar property of alcohol it operates upon sensitive living tissues to produce anæsthesia, upon contractile living tissues to produce paralysis, and upon non-living organic matter to produce antisepsis.

Since the fermenting liquid cannot contain more than twenty per cent. of alcohol, in order to procure a stronger alcoholic fluid it is necessary to resort to the process of distillation. The success of this method is based upon the differing degrees of volatility of alcohol and of water. Alcohol boils at 78.4° (173° F.), and may, consequently, be transferred from a retort to a cooled receiver more rapidly than the water with which it is mixed. But a complete separation of the two liquids cannot thus be completely effected, because a certain amount of watery vapor is formed, and passes into the receiver along with the alcoholic vapor. By repeated distillation the strength of the distillate may be progressively increased until it contains ninety-two per cent. by weight of alcohol, and exhibits a specific gravity of 0.817. The remaining eight per cent. of water can be removed only by distilling the liquid from a retort which contains a substance having an affinity for water sufficiently powerful to retain the whole of it. Raymond Lully employed potassic carbonate for this purpose. Quick-lime, chloride of calcium, anhydrous sulphate of copper, and other deliquescent salts, have been used to effect the same result.

Pure alcohol, thus rendered anhydrous, is called absolute alcohol. It is a colorless, spirituous liquid, with a decidedly characteristic odor. At 0° (32° F.) its specific gravity is 0.8095; it is 0.7939 at 15.5° (60° F.); 0.792 at 20° (68° F.). Under an atmospheric pressure equivalent to 760 millimetres of mercury, it boils at 78.4 (172.7° F.). It never freezes, but at a temperature of −100° (−148° F.) it assumes an oleaginous consistence. Alcohol may be mixed with water in any proportion. This, however, is not exactly in all respects a simple mixture, but is rather a species of hydration analogous to the hydration of sulphuric acid. As in the case of the addition of water to the acid, so the addition of water to absolute alcohol causes contraction of volume and liberation of heat. According to Wurtz, 52.3 volumes of alcohol and 47.7 volumes of water produce only 96.35 volumes of hydrated alcohol.

Alcohol is highly inflammable, burning with a lambent, pale blue flame, and with great liberation of heat. If the vapor of alcohol is subjected to a high temperature by passage through a porcelain tube at a red heat, it is decomposed (dissociated) into water, hydrogen, marsh-gas, and olefiant gas. Free carbon is also liberated, and small quantities of benzene, naphthaline, and phenyl hydrate are formed.

Alcohol dissolves many substances, not only gases, but liquids and solids. It dissolves iodine, bromine, some phosphorus and sulphur, the alkalies, and alkaline earths, the chlorides, iodides, and nitrates of many metals, many organic acids, and nearly all alkaloids, resins, volatile oils, camphor, and fixed oils (Maisch).

Physiological action of alcohol.—Alcohol coagulates living animal protoplasm. If highly concentrated, it acts upon mucous surfaces, and upon the cutaneous surfaces near the orifices of the body, as a powerful irritant. Applied to a raw surface, it produces great pain and rapid coagulation of the albuminous fluids which cover the wound. If injected into the veins, in a sufficiently concentrated state, it coagulates the blood. Taken into the stomach in considerable quantity without dilution, it causes inflammation of that viscus. In small quantities, largely diluted, it produces only an agreeable sensation of warmth referred to the stomach, and it stimulates the secretion of the digestive fluids. In large quantities, especially if highly concentrated, it is a powerful irritant poison, producing delirant, anæsthetic, and asphyxic effects. Absolute alcohol is dangerous in almost any dose, by reason of its powerful affinity for water, which it at once abstracts from the tissues to their detriment or destruction.

Alcohol passes readily through the mucous surfaces of the stomach and intestines, thus finding its way into the circulation. From the cavity of the mouth it may also, if well diluted, be absorbed to a certain extent. It is said that it is also absorbed by the skin, but this cannot be true of any considerable quantity of the liquid. Patients with open stumps, or other raw surfaces which are continually bathed with alcohol, are sometimes considerably inebriated by the liquid that is thus taken into the circulation. The vapor of alcohol is readily absorbed through the surfaces of the pulmonary air-cells, as persons who are engaged in certain processes of rectification very well know from their own experience.

The effects of alcohol after it has been introduced into the blood are dependent upon the amount that has found its way into the current of the circulation. It is necessary, therefore, to consider the effects of alcohol in varying doses, as well as its general effect upon the functions of the living tissues of the body. Before passing to a consideration of the perturbations thus occasioned, it is proper to review the course and destination of alcohol as it traverses the body. Mingled with blood in the arteries and veins, it remains unchanged—it is merely diluted by the water of the blood. Perrin states ("Dict. Encyc. des Sci. Méd.," t. II.) that, having drawn from the carotid arteries of two dogs seven hundred grammes of blood, one hour and a half after a quantity of alcohol sufficient to produce intoxication had been administered, he was able by distillation to recover five grammes of the alcohol. Examining by the same method the blood of other animals after all signs of intoxication had disappeared, nine and sixteen hours after taking alcohol, the substance could still be detected. The analysis of human blood, during and immediately after intoxication with brandy, gave the same results. Alcohol, therefore, may circulate without change.

It has been asserted that a certain proportion of alcohol is oxidized in the blood, becoming transformed into aldehyd and acetic acid. Perrin examined the blood of dogs which had been rendered insensible with alcohol, but he was not able to discover any trace of aldehyd or of acetic acid, either free or in combination. Bouchardat and Sandras were of the opinion that acetic acid does exist in the blood of animals under the influence of alcohol, but it was by its odor and by a slightly acid reaction alone that they identified the substance. This is not very convincing, especially since various observers have detected, as they supposed, acetic acid and acetate of sodium in the saliva, blood, muscles and spleens of animals in their normal condition. It is, moreover, now well known that substances are not to any considerable extent oxidized in the blood. The oxidations of the body are for the most part effected in the tissues outside of the blood. In the blood, therefore, must alcohol exist in a state of nature, or else the blood must exhibit an increase of oxidation products derived from the ac-tive processes that take place within the tissue-cells under the influence of alcohol, if it is there oxidized. From the fact that after taking alcohol there is a diminution in the amount of carbonic acid gas exhaled from the lungs, it has been inferred that alcohol is not transformed into water and carbonic anhydride in the tissues. It may be detected in the urine, in the sweat, and to a certain limited amount in the breath ; consequently, it has been concluded that alcohol acts simply by its presence, and that as it passes through the body it modifies, catalytically, the functions of the tis-sues without being itself broken up by oxidation into carbonic anhydride and water. The experiments of Schulinus, Dupré, Anstie, and others, in-dicate, however, that this opinion is too sweeping. Nothwithstanding the fact that alcohol can be recovered from the breath, from the blood, urine, and tissues of any animal to which it has been administered, no one has yet been able to account for anything like the whole amount that has been ingested. It seems reasonable, therefore, to believe that, while the excess of alcohol, over and above the capacity of the tissues, is eliminated through the various emunctory channels, a certain quantity is taken up by the tis-sues and is by them transformed for purposes of nutrition. Whatever amount is not thus disposed of acts, in some manner not yet understood, to retard the various vital processes, so that the liberation of heat, and the formation of water, carbonic anhydride, urea, etc., are actually diminished. At the same time all other vital movements are retarded and diminished to a degree which may produce all the phenomena of paralysis of sensibility and of motion.

It has been claimed that the action of alcohol upon the tissues is at-tributable to its affinity for the water which they contain. But this can hardly be the only cause, for it is not necessary to desiccate animal matters with alcohol in order to prevent their putrefaction. Twenty per cent. of alcohol in a fermenting liquid is sufficient to arrest the process of fermen-tation, though eighty per cent. of water be present. As Binz has remarked (*Real-Encyc. Gesam. Heilkunde*, B. I., p. 181), the removal by evaporation of twenty per cent. of the water from a given quantity of urine will not prevent its putrefaction, while the presence of twenty per cent. of alcohol will prevent all such changes. It is not the absence of water, but it is the active presence of alcohol, that effects the result.

Some have ascribed the effects of alcohol to an abstraction of fat from the cells of the tissues under its influence. Perrin, Lallemand and Duroy remarked that, after the impregnation of the blood with alcohol or with any other anæsthetic, a definite quantity of fatty matter could be discovered upon the surface of blood that had been withdrawn from the veins. It is not probable, however, that this can be the cause of the effects which are noticed after the use of anæsthetics, for their effects are too transitory to be connected with so considerable a modification of structure as this would imply. Nor can we thus account for the effect of these substances upon plants in which no such abstraction of fat has been remarked. The hypo-thesis of Bernard, who attributed the effects of anæsthetics to a brief and partial coagulation of the protoplasmic elements of the tissues, is probably nearer to an expression of the facts. The truth of the matter, however, lies deeper than this. The cause of anæsthesia is to be sought among the modifications to which the movements of the molecules of protoplasm are subjected when exposed to the influences contributed by the heterogeneous movements of the molecules which compose the anæsthetic substance. In their normal condition the vital phenomena of living protoplasm are dependent upon the permanence of a certain "moving equilibrium" in which all its constituent molecules take part. If this equilibrium be disturbed by the removal or suppression of certain of its factors, a lower degree of complexity in the movements of the molecular congeries, is the consequence. This implies a lower grade of vital manifestation. This takes place during starvation, a process which is characterized by insufficiently compensated removal of factors from the molecular congeries. It may be the result of imperfect "defecation" of the tissues—a condition in which the products of interstitial oxidation are not extruded from the congeries, but remain as constituent factors of the moving equilibrium of atomic forces. These oxidation products, being all of them composed of molecules in which the atoms occupy a relative position of greater stability than the position which they held before contact with oxygen from the blood, must necessarily diminish the complexity of the motions exhibited by the constituents of the cells of which they form a part. This diminution of complexity of motion implies a lower degree of vital manifestation. This is what may be often observed during certain processes of disease. It is the cause of that general torpor which may often be so happily relieved by the action of eliminant remedies. Again, the equilibrium of the living molecular congeries may be disturbed by the introduction of matter from without. Every such introduction implies a necessary readjustment of the equilibrium which must be maintained within the organized tissues, if their living identity is to be sustained. Certain substances, oxygen for example, cannot thus be adjusted—cannot harmoniously unite with the factors of living tissue—and are, therefore, poisons to the protoplasm. Other substances can be thus adjusted without difficulty, and serve, by their addition to existing protoplasm, to increase its complexity, or at least to increase the multiplicity of the movements of its factors. Such substances are nutritious to the protoplasm. Carbon, hydrogen, phosphorus, sulphur, iron, and certain other metals belong to this class. But, since the exhibition of vital phenomena by protoplasm depends upon a certain approximation to a particular ratio between the atomic elements of the protoplasm, it follows that any special excess of one or more of its constituents must interfere with the character of the equilibrium into which this excess has been intruded. Plethora may produce results analogous to starvation. Now, this seems to be the condition of things after the ingestion of alcohol and other hydrocarbonaceous substances. They are composed for the most part of two elements, carbon and hydrogen, which are perfectly compatible with the constituent elements of living protoplasm. If introduced with sufficient moderation, they can enter without difficulty into the pre-existent moving equilibrium. They are then highly serviceable as nutritious substances. But, if presented in excess to the tissues, by virtue of their high degree of diffusibility they pervade the living mass without fairly entering the molecular congeries which constitutes the organized protoplasm; in other words, they are absorbed, but not assimilated, and their excessive presence mechanically hinders the access of oxygen to the living matter. Ordinarily, this mechanical hinderance to the respiration of the tissues is not sufficient to arrest the process. The organized cell is in a condition analogous to that in a house which is full of smoke. Breathing is difficult under such circumstances, and it may even be arrested if the quantity of smoke exceed a certain amount. In like manner, alcohol and its related anæsthetics may overwhelm the protoplasm of the tissues, and may actually produce their death by a mechanical effect analogous to overcrowding. If the anæsthetic contains a constituent element which cannot under any circumstances enter into a *moving* equilibrium with the other elements of living matter, but which can only be associated with them in a *stable* equilibrium, then we find added to the dangers arising from overcrowding—the *mechanical* dangers—a new form of danger arising from incompatibility. Such substances tend to destroy the equilibrium of forces which alone admits of the exhibition of vital phenomena, breaking it up and forming with its constituents new arrangements of force which are incapable of exhibiting any kind of vital phenomena. Such a substance is oxygen. By its excessive action all vitality may be extinguished. Such a substance is chlorine, or bromine, or iodine, or hydrocyanic acid. Such substances are not merely mechanical obstacles to the perfection of vital function; they are active opponents to the existence of vital organization—they are chemical poisons.

Here we find the key to the action of anæsthetics, and we also discover a reason for the difference that exists between them in the matter of danger. Alcohol and ether kill by producing a mechanical surfeit of the living mass. Chloroform, the chlorine, bromine, and iodine series of anæsthetics, kill mechanically and chemically also. They are doubly dangerous.

Another source of danger, according to Rabuteau, is connected with the chemical affinities of these substances. There is a certain ratio existing between their molecular weights and their lethal energy. According to this doctrine, the heavier the molecule the greater the danger which is connected with its use. The molecule of ethylic alcohol contains twenty-four parts by weight of carbon, six parts of hydrogen, and sixteen parts of oxygen, forming a total molecular weight of forty-six $(24+6+16=46)$. The molecule of ethylic ether contains forty-eight parts of carbon, ten parts of hydrogen, and sixteen parts of oxygen, giving a molecular weight of seventy-four $(48+10+16=74)$. The molecule of ethylic bromide contains twenty-four parts of carbon, five parts of hydrogen, and eighty parts of bromine, forming a molecular total of one hundred and nine $(24+5+80=109)$. The molecule of chloroform contains twelve parts of carbon, one part of hydrogen, and one hundred and five parts of chlorine, making a total of one hundred and eighteen $(12+1+105=118)$. In this way a table might be constructed which should display the relative molecular energy of each anæsthetic substance, something like the following :

Name.	Formula.	Molecular weight.	Relative weight.
Methyl alcohol	CH_4O	32	1
Methyl ether	C_2H_6O	46	1.5
Ethyl alcohol...................	C_2H_6O	46	1.5
Ethyl ether....................	$C_4H_{10}O$	74	2.3125
Ethyl bromide	$C_2H_5Br.$	109	3.40625
Chloroform....................	$CHCl_3$	118	3.6875

Such a method of comparison, however, would lead to erroneous results, because it makes no account of different degrees of diffusibility, and of chemical affinity which cannot be indicated in this way. The rate of elimination of each substance should also be taken into account. As a matter of fact the physiological and toxicological properties of any given substance depend upon so many facts and relations, in which its atomic constituents take an active part, that it is impossible in the present state of our knowledge to predicate the properties of any substance from a simple inspection of its chemical formula. We may form certain more or less probable hypotheses—conjectures which may assist us in the search for knowledge; but theoretical dogmatism is quite out of place. The only final and satisfactory appeal must still be taken to the court of experimental research.

In the case of alcohol, experiment and observation are not difficult, so far as the grosser physiological and pathological phenomena are concerned. It is when we desire to explore the more intricate relations of the substance with the phenomena of nutrition and excretion that we find ourselves beset with difficulty. This difficulty, however, is largely owing to the fact that the quantity of alcohol that has been thrown into the blood has not been taken sufficiently into the account by different observers. If less than the amount which the tissues can assimilate in a given unit of time be conveyed to the tissues, they will dispose of it without giving any sign of disturbance. There will be no alcohol in the pulmonary, cutaneous, or urinary excretions. In such cases alcohol will only be found free in the blood under the same conditions that permit the discovery of sugar in the blood. It serves as a nutrient very much in the same way that sugar serves to sustain the energy of living protoplasm. If more alcohol than the tissues can assimilate be introduced into the blood, a certain portion of the excess may possibly be transformed into glycogen and be stored up by the cells of the liver; but of this there is no experimental proof. The surplus alcohol will circulate in the blood, and will be eliminated as fast as the excretory glands can manage the quantity thus thrown upon them. According to Perrin and his collaborators, the excess of alcohol tends to accumulate in the nervous tissues. From the nervous tissues of dogs which had been intoxicated with alcohol they recovered alcohol by distillation. From 440 grammes of brains, nerves, etc., deprived of their envelopes and carefully washed, they obtained 3.25 grammes of inflammable alcohol. From the same quantity of the blood, treated in the same manner, they obtained a little less—about three grammes. From the nervous substance of an old toper, who died thirty-two hours after a brandy debauch, they obtained three times as much alcohol as could be extracted from an equal weight of his blood. In the liver, also, these observers found a similar accumulation of alcohol. As might be expected, they found that when alcohol was introduced by the way of the stomach the liver contained more in proportion than the brain. This was reversed when the substance was introduced by direct injection into the veins. We need not, however, infer from these observations that there is any special attraction between the elements of nerve-tissue and alcohol. The brain, like the liver, is an excessively vascular organ, which is at the same time, unlike another vascular organ—the lungs—richly endowed with cellular elements. These are penetrated by every excess of alcohol, and the organ of which they compose so important a part becomes appreciably filled with the substance. The relatively insignificant cellular organization of the lungs and the kidneys cannot contain so large a relative amount. The quantity of alcohol recoverable from such organs is principally dependent upon the volume of the blood which they may chance to contain, and this fluid, as it circulates through lungs and kidneys, is continually losing its foreign impurities. Alcohol filters away in the urine, and in some small quantity is given off through the breath, so that the cells of the lungs and of the kidneys can never become overcharged with the liquid.

That alcohol may serve as a nutrient to the tissues can no longer be considered doubtful. The fact that so large a portion of the ingested substance disappears during its passage through the body is suggestive of this doctrine. Liebig gave to alcohol high rank in the list of alimentary substances, considering it gifted with special value as a "respiratory aliment," for the liberation of heat in the act of oxidation to carbonic anhydride and water. This view of the subject was stoutly contested by observers who had remarked the diminution of eliminated carbonic anhydride under the influence of alcoholic potations. Perrin found ("Dict. Encyc. des Sci. Méd.," t. II, p. 585), by experiment upon himself, that when he compared the amount of carbonic acid gas eliminated during five hours of a day in which he took 670 c.c. of red wine, containing nine per cent. of alcohol, with the amount eliminated during the same number of hours of a day of abstinence, there was a uniform reduction of the gas.

		Use of wine.	Abstinence.
1...		207.500	259.500
2...		226.700	240.300
3...	Weight of CO$_2$ exhaled during	195.900	247.200
4...	the experiment (five hours)	200.800	253.100
5...		210.000	252.700
6...		225.700	247.800

The same experimenter ascertained that the influence of alcohol upon the exhalation of carbonic anhydride is at its maximum about three hours after the ingestion of the liquid. At the expiration of five hours its influence seems to be exhausted. This does not represent the whole time necessary for its total elimination. Dupré found that it could be detected for a longer time in the excretions—from nine to twenty four hours; but he was of the opinion that, inasmuch as there is no increase of alcoholic elimination during the days of an alcoholic diet, the alcohol of each day must be either eliminated or consumed during each day. There is no cumulative process within the tissues. The urine is increased in quantity during an alcoholic regimen, but its composition does not sensibly vary from the normal standard. Nearly all experimenters agree that there is no diminution in the amount of urea that is excreted. For this reason Parkes and others have found it difficult to believe that there can be any real diminution in the exhalation of carbonic acid gas.

In this connection it is worthy of remark that the quantity of alcohol employed by Perrin in his experiments upon himself was quite considerable. He was in the habit of taking at a single dose 670 c.c. of red wine, containing nine per cent. or 60.3 c.c. of absolute alcohol. This amount—nearly two ounces—is very near the amount which Anstie considered a full dietetic allowance for an entire day. It is, therefore, highly probable that in his experiments the paralyzing effect of alcohol was more conspicuous than it would have been had the amount been distributed throughout the day. That the same result was not equally conspicuous in the excretion of urea is probably due to the relatively small amount of urea that is excreted, and to the fact that observation of its discharge cannot be continuous, as in the case of carbonic anhydride eliminated through the lungs. The urine is carried for several hours, perhaps, in the bladder, during which time many variations in the rate of excretion may have occurred, but all are concealed by the admixture of the urine of different periods in the bladder. The formation of carbonic anhydride, is, moreover, a direct effect of oxidation in the tissues, and is therefore more easily disturbed by anything that may interfere with the movement of oxygen in the tissues. But the formation of urea is a more complicated process, which is probably less dependent upon the immediate action of oxygen. The formation of urea might, therefore, go on with comparatively little disturbance while alcohol was retarding all processes of direct oxidation. The experiments of v. Beck and Bauer (*Zeitschrift für Biologie*, X., 1874), and of Rabuteau (*L'Union Méd.*, 1870), indicate, moreover, that the excretion of urea is actually diminished like that of other products of tissue-change.

The capacity of alcohol to replace other alimentary substances is well exhibited by the effects of an alcoholic diet. In certain breweries it is customary to allow the head brewer as much as sixty glasses of beer *per diem*. He lives almost entirely upon this liquid food, consuming very little else of any kind. This, however, is not a fair example of an alcoholic regimen, because in beer the unfermented sugar, and the other nutrient substances besides the alcohol, occupy a position of no inconsiderable importance. But the observations of Anstie have placed beyond question the fact that life can be sustained by a diet consisting almost exclusively of diluted alcohol. In his work on Stimulants and Narcotics (p. 386) he relates the history of an old soldier, eighty-three years of age, who for about twenty years had lived principally upon a bottle of gin each day. This he drank diluted with water, but without sugar. Besides this he was in the habit of eating "one small finger-length of bread, usually toasted," which was "all that he *ever* took from one end of the day to the other." He did not drink tea or coffee, or any other beverage besides his gin and water. He was in the habit of smoking a few pipes of tobacco each day. This case was carefully investigated by Anstie, and was under his immediate case for a year until he died of bronchitis. The author remarks that "the man's appearance was very singular and not easy to describe; it was not that he was very greatly emaciated, but he had a dried-up look which reminded me of that of opium-eaters." A number of similar cases were also collected by Anstie from the experience of his medical friends. "Dr. Slack, of Liverpool, informed Dr. Inman that two female patients of his own, who loathed all ordinary food, had subsisted for months on nothing but alcohol in one shape or another; one of these, who was bed-ridden, appeared actually fatter at the end of three months than she was at first. A surgeon's widow informed Dr. Inman that, after several successive severe illnesses, she had suffered much after her last confinement; at this her appetite had entirely failed her, and she had lived for many weeks on nothing but brandy and water. A surgeon at Wavertree 'attended a young man with hypertrophy and patulous valves of the heart, from September 24, 1855, to April 26, 1860. For the last five years no animal food would remain on his stomach, and farinaceous food he would seldom take. In the first two years brandy was the principal nutriment he subsisted on, as nothing else would remain on the stomach. Subsequently he *lived upon* this same beverage. His allowance first was six ounces of brandy, but it was gradually increased to a pint a day; he kept his flesh and good spirits nearly to the last. During the last two years he was dropsical, and he died at the age of twenty-five.' Mr. Nisbet, of Egremont, communicated to Dr. Inman the case of a man in the middle class of life, who subsisted for seven months entirely on spirit and water; 'he was apparently in good health and good condition.'" The same medical practitioner reports the case of a child affected with marasmus, who subsisted for three months on sweet whiskey and water alone, and recovered ; and that of another child, who lived entirely upon Scotch ale for a fortnight, and then recovered his appetite for common things.   Dr. Inman himself " had a lady patient who was several times on the verge of *delirium tremens*, and he gained an intimate knowledge of her habits from personal observation, from the reports of her husband, of mutual friends occasionally residing in the house with her, of her mother, of her sisters, and of her nurse.   She was about twenty-five years of age, handsome, florid, and *embonpoint*, of very active habits, yet withal of a delicate constitution, being soon knocked up.   This lady had two large and healthy children in succession, whom she successfully nursed.   On each occasion she became much exhausted, the appetite wholly failed, and she was compelled to live solely on bitter ale and brandy and water ; on this regimen she kept up her good looks, her activity, and her nursing, and went on this way for about twelve months ; the nervous system was by this time thoroughly exhausted, yet there was no emaciation, nor was there entire prostration of muscular power."   Among my own patients I was once called upon to treat a young man who was threatened with delirium tremens.   He assured me that for three weeks he had lived on nothing but whiskey and water, taking between forty and fifty glasses of the mixture each day.   He had not lost flesh during this time, but his nervous system was much exhausted, and he could not sleep.   He rapidly recovered, and I never saw him again.

The following table, from Anstie's work on Stimulants and Narcotics, will be found interesting in this connection :

No.	Sex.	Age.	Occupation.	Duration of Intemperate Habits.	Quantity of Alcoholic Liquors taken.	Effects upon Diet.
1	M.	27	Tailor.	12 years.	1 pint of gin per diem and 2 pots of porter.	Eats very little solid food.
2	M.	83	Pensioner.	Many years.	1 bottle of gin per diem for the last 20 years.	Eats one small fragment of bread in the day.
3	M.	49	Hawker.	Many years.	About 1 pint of raw brandy per diem.	Eats no meat, only a little bread and tea.
4	M.	29	Hawker.	10 years.	About 1½ pint of raw gin per diem.	Eats a very fair quantity of food.
5	F.	42	None.	15 years.	About ¼ pint of brandy (with water) per diem.	Eats almost no ordinary food.
6	M.	28	Tavern waiter.	8 years.	4 pots of beer and 1 pint or more of spirits per diem.	Says that he hardly ever touches solid food.
7	M.	46	Tavern waiter.	22 years.	Has lately reached 2 pints of gin and a little beer per diem.	Eats only one small meal a day.
8	F.	64	None.	30 years or more.	Latterly 1 pint of gin per diem.	Eats no food except biscuit; no tea.
9	M.	42	Coal-porter.	24 years.	For some years past 12 pints of beer per day.	Eats pretty well.
10	M.	21	Cabman.	6 years.	For some time past 1 pint of rum per diem.	Eats little solid food.
11	F.	21	None.	4 years.	From ½ a pint to 1½ pint of gin per diem.	Eats hardly any solid food.
12	M.	27	Brewer's drayman.	8 years.	2 gallons of beer per diem, a bottle of whiskey every Saturday.	Eats little solid food.

Observations like these render it impossible to deny the nutritive value of alcohol.   It is not correct to say that alcohol is merely useful as a means of preventing the waste of pre-existing tissue.   No substance can thus for years supply the place of the greater part of ordinary food without being really capable of assimilation by the tissues.   At the same time the history of all such cases indicates the insufficiency of such a diet.   Though the subjects of such a mode of living may preserve their bulk, like Falstaff and the brewer's drayman, they all, at length, exhibit the phenomena of slow starvation. They become sleepless and the prey of hallucinations. Muscular weakness and muscular tremors, irregular action of the heart, nausea, loathing of food, a filthy taste in the mouth, constipated bowels, neuralgia, vertigo—finally, fever and delirium of an asthenic type—all mark the uncompensated process of tissue-waste which is the inevitable result of a restricted diet.

Having thus concluded that alcohol is a substance which can be absorbed and assimilated by the tissues, contributing in moderation to their proper nutrition, but capable, if used in excess, of hindering their normal function and of producing the phenomena of starvation, it now remains for us to examine the nature of the disturbances which result from the presence of an excess of alcohol in the blood and in the tissues. These disturbances involve the functions of sensation, reflex action, and voluntary motion. The motor derangements involve not merely the power of locomotion, but they extend also to the movements of respiration, circulation, secretion, and the distribution of heat. Obviously these disturbances occur in proportion to the amount of alcohol that is taken into the blood. In this respect the effects of alcohol are produced just as the effects of other anæsthetic substances are brought about. The principal difference between the anæsthesia of alcohol and the anæsthesia which follows the inhalation of ether or of other stupefying vapors consists in the length of time that is necessary for its induction. The absorption of an alcoholic liquid from the stomach requires much more time than is needed for the absorption of a sufficient quantity of chloroform vapor through the membranes of the lungs. Alcoholic intoxication, therefore, proceeds at a slower pace than ethereal intoxication. Its several stages are, consequently, extended over a much longer period of time—a circumstance which greatly facilitates the observation of its different phenomena.

The ordinary immediate effect of moderate and repeated doses of well-diluted alcohol is the production of an agreeable sensation of gentle warmth in the stomach. This is soon followed by a feeling of general well-being. Any moderately painful sensation or lack of perfect comfort is relieved. The secretion of saliva and of perspiration is increased, though sometimes the skin and the mouth become dry and hot. This increase of the salivary secretion is a part of the general secretory excitement that is now aroused. The skin becomes suffused with blood, the arteries fill more completely, and, if the dose is considerable in quantity, they may throb violently. The heart beats more rapidly, and with greater vigor at first. Respiration is quickened. The eyes shine, in consequence of the increased activity of the lachrymal glands. The conjunctivæ become injected. The pupils are somewhat contracted. The muscular system everywhere becomes excited. The individual experiences a desire for movement and change of place. If youthful, he feels disposed to run, to dance, to fight. If not inclined to such exercise of the locomotive apparatus, he gives full scope to the muscles of the tongue, and indulges in the most loquacious hilarity. The brain becomes an early participant in the general exaltation of function. The senses are for a little time exalted. Perception becomes more vivid. Ideas flow with the utmost ease. All the intellectual faculties are aroused. The emotions and the passions are also intensified. Tears flow upon the slightest provocation, and they may alternate with the most joyous bursts of laughter. Sometimes—especially after wine—the amative passions are greatly stimulated, hurrying their

16

victim through all the phases of sexual appetite.   The dominant characteristics of the individual make themselves conspicuous.   The restraints of
reason, conscience, prudence, timidity, habit, education and association are
all thrown off, and the patient becomes, at length, actually beside himself.
He is drunk and temporarily insane.   Sometimes, instead of this exhibition of vivacity, the tippler becomes sedate and reserved.   His self-consciousness becomes exalted, and his powers of self-control are actually enlarged.   Instead of becoming sentimental and garrulous, he seems more
thoroughly himself, and can converse or carry on business with greater
appearance of intelligence than ever.   But the final narcosis is the same.
If the ingestion of alcohol is allowed to proceed, the sensitiveness of the
cutaneous nerves decreases.   The power of co-ordination is diminished.
The patient staggers as he walks.   His articulation becomes thick and
confused.   Speech grows less rational, and may be varied with sudden
ejaculatory outbreaks.   All voluntary motion becomes, at length, impossible.   The turgid features lose their power of expression.   Articulation
ceases.   All the senses are abolished.   The patient lies, dead-drunk, in
whatever position he may have fallen.   He is stertorous, comatose, completely anæsthetic.

The amount of alcohol that is necessary to effect such a catastrophe
varies with each individual.   The condition of the patient relative to food,
and the time of day, exercise a very considerable influence upon the action
of alcohol.   As a general rule, a person who takes a certain quantity of
alcoholic drink upon an empty stomach, in the early part of the day, will
experience a more rapid and more considerable result than if the same
amount were taken after a hearty meal.   This, doubtless, is owing to the
fact that absorption of liquids from the empty stomach of a fasting person
is much more speedily accomplished than it can be when the blood and
the tissues are already partially satiated.   The activity of the excretory
organs, also, exercises a profoundly modifying influence upon the degree of
tolerance which may be exhibited by the drinker.   As we sometimes discover great tolerance of poisons, due to the rapidity with which they are
eliminated through the kidneys or through the bowels, so we not unfrequently meet with "hard heads" whose superior sobriety is to be referred
to the vivacity of their kidneys rather than to the solidity of their brains.

The duration of the state of profound intoxication is exceedingly variable : it depends largely upon the quantity of alcohol that was drank before
the access of anæsthesia.   The respiration falls, even below the normal
standard of frequence, though the inspirations are deepened.   The heart
beats with less energy, consequently the pulse is small and rapid.   The
temperature of the body falls.   The surface is bedewed with a cold, clammy
perspiration.   Sometimes there is vomiting and relaxation of the bowels.
At length, a gradual return toward the original standard of function becomes apparent.   The drunkard awakens heavily, then relapses again into
slumber.   Finally he arouses himself to a condition of confused consciousness, with a dull, distressing headache, and general incapacity for elaborate
intellectual activity.   He is slightly feverish, the tongue is coated, the
breath is offensive, there is loss of appetite, nausea, perhaps a certain degree of epigastric tenderness, and a feeling of muscular weakness.   There
is, in fact, a low grade of acute gastric inflammation, which may considerably retard convalescence.

In cases of death from alcoholic poisoning, if a large quantity of alcohol
has been taken at once, as sometimes happens when men drink raw brandy
or whiskey by the bottleful on a wager, the stage of exhilaration is either

greatly shortened or is absent altogether. Children have sometimes been murdered in this way. Sailors and ruffians long deprived of liquor have, in cases of shipwreck or disaster, drank themselves to death as a consequence of gaining access to an unlimited supply of strong drink. Such individuals pass almost immediately into a condition of coma, like that described above. Convulsions are sometimes developed, especially in young children. There may be hemorrhage from the stomach or from the bowels. The temperature sinks astonishingly. The pupils, previously contracted, become widely dilated. The skin becomes cyanotic—in old topers it may even become acutely gangrenous, as sometimes happens during the collapse of cholera. Respiration becomes feeble, intermittent, and finally ceases altogether. The pulse becomes excessively feeble, but usually persists longer than respiration. The heart is the last to die.

Proceeding now to the analysis of these symptoms which characterize the various stages of alcoholic poisoning, from the commencement of exaltation to the termination of life, we shall find that they all depend upon one primitive cause—the paralyzing energy of alcohol when brought in contact with living protoplasm. All forms of protoplasm—vegetable as well as animal—are in like manner affected by this substance. The action of the yeast-fungus is suspended when the fluid in which it vegetates contains twenty per cent. or more of alcohol. The concentrated vapor of alcohol arrests the growth of ordinary plants; it also depresses the vital manifestations of animal tissues, and may even destroy their life, if sufficiently concentrated.

This depressing influence of alcohol is its peculiar and characteristic action upon living tissues. It is a special influence, to be considered separately and apart from its purely physical effect upon the sensitive nerve-elements with which it is brought in contact at the instant of application to the external or internal surfaces of the body. The burning sensation which is experienced when strong alcohol is swallowed or is applied to the delicate cutaneous surfaces near the orifices of the body, is due to the sensory commotion that may be excited by sudden abstraction of water from the nerve-endings, and by their consequent partial coagulation. Such a change cannot be suddenly effected without a great change in the modes and distribution of motion throughout the affected territory. Conveyed by the sensitive nerves to the cerebral sensorium, the effects of such agitation declare themselves in consciousness under the form of pain. We say that the alcohol burns in the mouth or in the stomach. But this primitive physical agitation is soon followed by a diminution of movement in the part, and to the painful sensation succeeds the specific action of alcohol. If largely diluted at first, the mechanico-physical effect may be very trifling, and the specific effects are the only features of the case that become noticeable. The tissues with which alcohol is first brought into relation after its absorption from the stomach exist in the walls of the blood-vessels. It is in the smallest arteries and in the capillaries that this relation is most intimate, and that its effects are most conspicuous. This follows as a necessary consequence of the fact that the smaller the diameter of a tube the greater the relative area of the surface that limits its contents. The smaller vessels—the arterioles—are furnished with a muscular coat which renders them capable of exhibiting considerable variation in their diameter. This muscular coat is also placed under the control of the nervous system in a way which renders it peculiarly adapted to illustrate the effects of any disturbance of the nerves of the body. This vascular nervous apparatus constitutes the well-known vaso-motor nervous mechanism about which so much has been written. ₊A brief review of the present state of knowledge regarding the vaso-motor nerves may be found useful as a means of rendering intelligible the action of alcohol and of other anæsthetics upon the circulation.

In the walls of the smaller blood-vessels, upon the vascular nerves near their terminations, exist a great number of minute collections of nervous matter, apparently identical with the nerve-cells which are discovered in the larger ganglia of the sympathetic nervous system. These microscopical ganglia are found at the crossings of the filaments of the nervous net-work which enmeshes and interpenetrates the wall of the vascular canal. They are thus in communication with each other, very much as the knots in a net are connected together by the cord which forms the knot and the mesh. This net-work of nervous filaments forms at the external surface of the blood-vessel a plexus—called the fundamental plexus—which is connected by appropriate fibres of communication with the central ganglia of the sympathetic. Beneath this plexus, but intimately connected with it, lies the intermediate plexus, constituted essentially like the first, but more immediately in relation with the bundles of muscular fibres in the walls of the vessel. Finally, within the muscular layer itself, lies the third and deepest plexus, called the intramuscular plexus. This is the terminal nervous net-work which connects the muscular apparatus with the nervous system. Various modes of connection between the filaments of the intramuscular plexus and the muscular fibres have been described. Some have thought that the terminal nervous fibrils penetrated the muscular cells and joined themselves to the nucleoli or to the nuclei. Others have believed that these terminal fibrils simply run between the muscle-cells, without becoming attached to their substance. Ranvier has recently (*Comptes Rendus de l'Acad. des Sciences*, p. 1142, 1878) described the mode of termination of the intramuscular nerves of a species of snail (*Helix pomatia*), in which the muscles, though voluntary, are non-striated. In this creature each ultimate nervous fibril terminates in a "motor spot" upon the surface of each muscular cell, forming an exceedingly delicate terminal arborization analogous to that which exists at the nerve-ending upon the surface of the striated muscular fibres of the higher animals. This indicates what may be considered as true of every muscular element, that it is in direct motor continuity with the motor centres of the nervous system. It is, moreover, certain that the ganglia of the vascular plexuses are capable of receiving impulses from the higher ganglia in the sympathetic chain, in the cord, or even in the brain. They appear, also, to have sensitive prolongations which extend to the superficial endothelium lining the canal of the blood-vessel. By virtue of these connections, the ganglia of the vascular plexus may become the seat of reflex actions by which the musculature of the blood-vessel shall be regulated. According to this view, each little ganglion is in communication with at least three sets of nervous conductors: motor fibrils which lead directly from the ganglion to the muscle-cells; sensory fibrils which pass from the lining of the canal of the blood-vessel to the ganglion; and thirdly, a more or less continuous pathway of conduction between the peripheral ganglion and the highest nerve-centres in the brain. Cerebral or spinal disturbances of motor nervous substance may be thus transmitted to the peripheral vaso-motor ganglia, exciting in them a process by which the muscular fibres of the vessels may be either relaxed or thrown into a state of contraction. This may be termed a centrifugal reflex process. Or, the nervous excitement may originate upon the surface of the lining membrane of the vessel. The irritation of the recipient (sensitive) nervous fibril thus aroused will travel in a centripetal direction until the corresponding ganglion is reached. Here may be produced another reflex transformation of motion by which the vascular muscular cells shall be thrown into a condition either of contraction or of relaxation, without the intervention of the central nervous apparatus. This would constitute an ordinary centripetal reflex action, entirely analogous to the usual cerebro-spinal reflex processes.

That the condition of the muscular apparatus throughout the body is dependent upon the integrity and the character of its relations with the nervous system is very well shown by a few familiar experiments. If we examine a living frog while at rest, we shall find all his muscles in a state of persistent, uniform contraction. By this tonic contraction the attitude of the animal is preserved. If now a wire be thrust down the whole length of the cerebro-spinal canal, so as to break up and destroy the brain and the spinal cord, every muscle in the body and limbs of the creature will become instantaneously relaxed, as if their life had ceased. This effect is not the result of any direct injury to the muscular apparatus: it is due to the arrest of that tonic influence which, in the perfect living animal, is continually radiating from the central nervous motor ganglia to the muscles. In like manner the muscular tunic of the arterioles is innervated by its nervous connection with the sympathetic system.

We are now in a position to comprehend the manner in which alcohol affects the circulation of the blood. As soon as it mingles with the blood-current it necessarily comes in contact with the vascular walls. Whether its effect upon the primary reflex arc within the coats of the vessel is in the way of an increase of motion over the arc, can hardly be said to have yet been decided by experiment. Theoretically and analogically, from the fact that the contact of alcohol with the sensitive nerve-endings in direct connection with the cerebro-spinal centres is productive of pain—which ordinarily is referable to an exaggeration of motion—we may infer that the initial effect is an increase of motion. This would imply an increased action of the vascular muscles—a contraction of the muscular coats—a diminished diameter of the vessels—an increased arterial pressure. The subjoined sphygmographic tracing indicates the same thing. This result, however, can only be of very short duration, for to the mechanico-physical effect of the alcohol must almost immediately succeed the chemico-anæsthetic effect of the drug. Each little recipient (sensory) nerve-fibril that is bathed with alcoholic blood becomes rapidly paretic—incapable of sufficiently transmitting impulses to the ganglia of the intramural plexus. By diffusion, also, the alcohol penetrates to the ganglia themselves, and paralyzes each cell, each individual molecule of nervous matter. The muscular fibres in the vascular walls must necessarily follow suit, exactly as if the vaso-motor nerves had been cut or destroyed by the knife of the experimenter. Vascular relaxation everywhere exists, in connection with diminished cardiac vigor, with great consequent diminution of the arterial pressure. The following sphygmographic observations illustrate the alterations thus effected :

EXPERIMENT I.—The following tracing was taken from the radial artery of a healthy young man, aged twenty-one years :

He then swallowed sixteen cubic centimetres (half an ounce) of ninety-eight per cent. alcohol, diluted with eight times as much water. Five minutes afterward, at 10.55 A.M., his pulse yielded the following tracing :

He then drank thirty-two c.c. of alcohol, diluted with one hundred and thirty c.c. of water, and at 11.05 A.M., he felt dizzy. The following tracings were immediately taken :

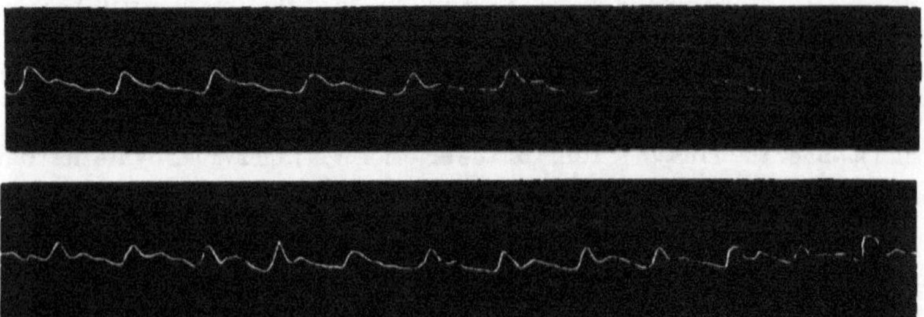

He then drank another potion equal to the preceding, and at 11.12 A.M. the following tracing was obtained.

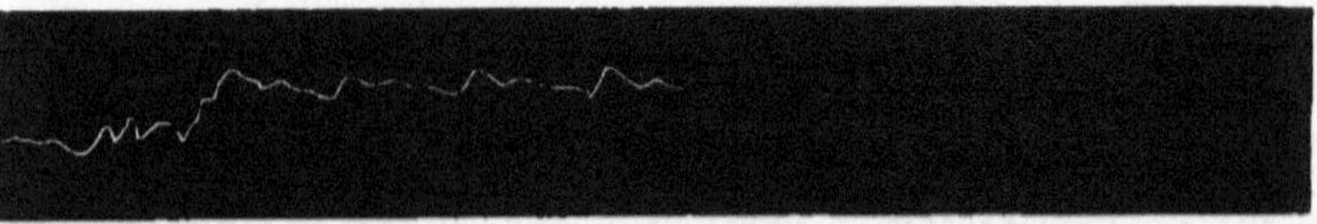

The patient felt numb, and did not experience much pain when pinched. At 11.15 the pulse was thus represented :

and at 11.18 thus :

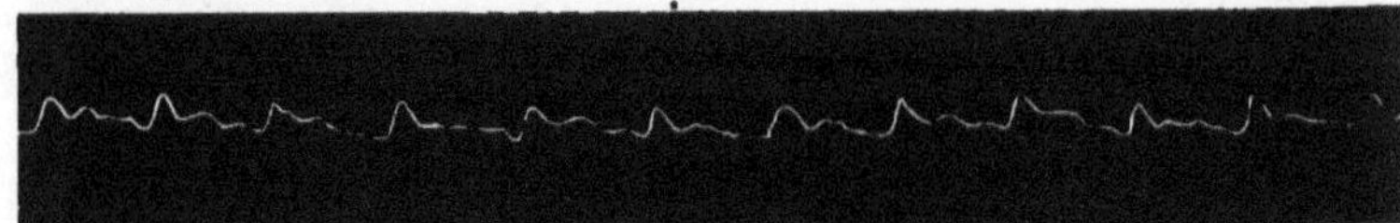

He was now quite drunk. Could not stand. Muscles relaxed. Surface cool and moist. Pupils widely dilated. Utterance thick. He drank forty-eight c.c. of alcohol, diluted with double that quantity of water, and was immediately collapsed. The last tracing was taken at 11.20 A.M.

It was impossible after this to obtain an intelligible tracing, on account of the weakness of the pulse. The patient vomited and soon fell asleep, and slept soundly until 6 P.M., when he awoke feeling "as if he had been on a spree." At 8.30 P.M. his pulse gave the following:

and at 9 A.M. the next day:

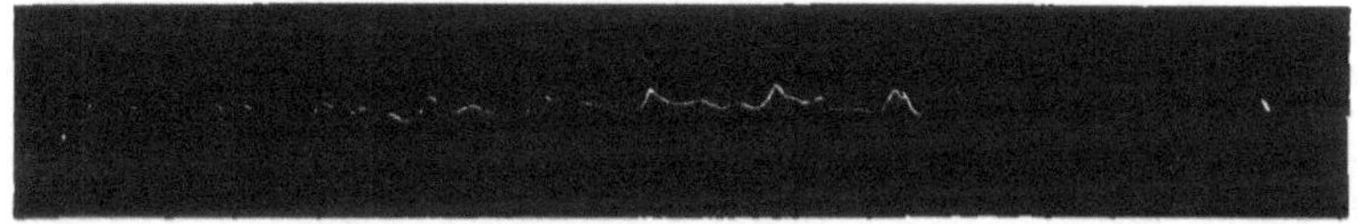

The first consequence of arterial relaxation is an increased flow of blood into the capillary net-works of the body. The heart is the first of the motive mechanisms to feel the advantages of an increased supply of blood. Its nervous ganglia and its muscular tissues are roused to increased activity under the impulse of this more copious irrigation with the nutritive current of the blood. The heart beats at first with greater vigor. By this activity of the central organ a larger supply of blood is forced into the relaxed arteries. A larger supply of blood in like manner is admitted to the medulla oblongata, by which the respiratory processes are stimulated. The general hyperæmia involves the spinal cord, which immediately begins to dispense locomotive force in every direction. Hence the disposition to motion that is so characteristic of the early stages of alcoholic excitement. The brain is also invaded by the rising flood. Its vessels dilate, and the cortical capillaries are crowded with blood. An increased function of the cerebrum is the immediate consequence. All the intellectual functions are increased in vigor. Ideas rise and follow each other with wonderful vivacity and rapidity. The sensory apparatus also shares in the universal exaltation. Sensation is heightened. Perception becomes more vivid. Reflex action is more easily performed. Secretion is stimulated. The salivary glands pour out a larger quantity of saliva. Under the influence of a moderate quantity of alcohol the peptic glands increase their product. The same thing is true of the entire glandular apparatus connected with the alimentary canal. The perspiration is notably increased. This general state of glandular activity may very well be occasioned by the quickened circulation of the blood alone ; but, if the intervention of the nervous system in the act of secretion must be taken into the account, we can refer this glandular excitation to the stimulation of the central origins of the secretory nerves. They must necessarily participate in the general distribution of motion by the nervous motor centres which has been aroused by the increased circulation of the blood. The temperature of the surface of the body is elevated by the increased cutaneous circulation, though the general temperature is not yet materially affected.

Such, then, are the results of alcoholic paresis of the muscular walls of the blood-vessels. So far the consequences in any particular locality do not differ from the effects which would follow any mechanical interruption of the vaso-motor innervation of the part. The vaso-motor paresis after alcohol, however, is universal, involving every portion of the body in a manner which can only be effected by an agent which can act upon all parts at once—that is, an agent which operates through the medium of the blood. If the quantity of alcohol mingled with the blood be relatively small, these effects of increased circulation may be the only noticeable consequences. But ordinarily the secondary effects of alcohol become equally conspicuous with the primary. As it finds its way to the higher nervous mechanisms outside of the walls of the blood-vessels, it begins to reduce their energy, as it has already overcome the nervous ganglia within the vascular walls. The sensory nervous organs yield first; then reflex energy diminishes; the power of muscular co-ordination follows; cerebral sensation and perception diminish; voluntary motion becomes increasingly difficult; secretion—notably that of carbonic anhydride—diminishes; the bodily temperature falls; and all these failing functions grow less and less until complete loss of sensation and voluntary motion is apparent. If the quantity of alcohol that has been ingested surpasses a certain amount, relative to the tissues, the functions of respiration and of circulation cease at length, and the victim is dead.

Death, as a result of acute alcoholic poisoning, is produced by paralysis of the respiratory centres in the medulla oblongata. If an animal be thus poisoned, the heart will yet be found in motion, when the thorax is opened, after the cessation of all respiratory movements. The pulsations of the heart, notwithstanding their persistence, are greatly enfeebled long before the cessation of life. This—like the relaxation of the arterioles—is the direct consequence of the effect of alcohol upon the cardiac structure, both nervous and muscular. It is also in part the cause of the great diminution of arterial pressure throughout the body, and is the principal cause of the accumulation of blood in the venous portion of the circulatory system. To this is due the cyanotic complexion of profound intoxication. As an example of this great diminution of pressure, Binz tells us ("Real-Encyc. der gesammten Heilkunde," vol. i., p. 191) that he has seen the pressure, in the larger arteries of a dog, which normally equals 150—170 mm. of mercury, fall as low as 70 mm. after intoxication with alcohol. To the same author we are indebted for several remarkable illustrations of the manner in which the bodily temperature may be depressed during drunkenness. This depression is particularly exaggerated when a low temperature of the external air co-operates with the depressing influence of alcohol upon the liberation of heat within the body. A drunkard, thirty-four years of age, who had lain in the snow during a part of a night in February, on being carried to a hospital, exhibited a rectal temperature of 24° (75.2° F.). Ten hours later it was only 32.6° (90° F.), and twenty-four hours elapsed before the normal temperature was recovered. This remarkable heat-depressing energy of alcohol, when taken in large doses, explains the mode of action of this substance in fevers with a high temperature. In many of these diseases, it forms a much more convenient and profitable depressor of the temperature than quinine. Binz has given (*loc. cit.*) a very interesting diagram illustrating the effect of alcohol upon the temperature of a dog which was suffering with septic fever produced by inoculation. Two animals were subjected to inoculation. One of them was treated with alcohol, the other was left to the natural course of the disease. The following chart exhibits the temperature-curves of the two animals:

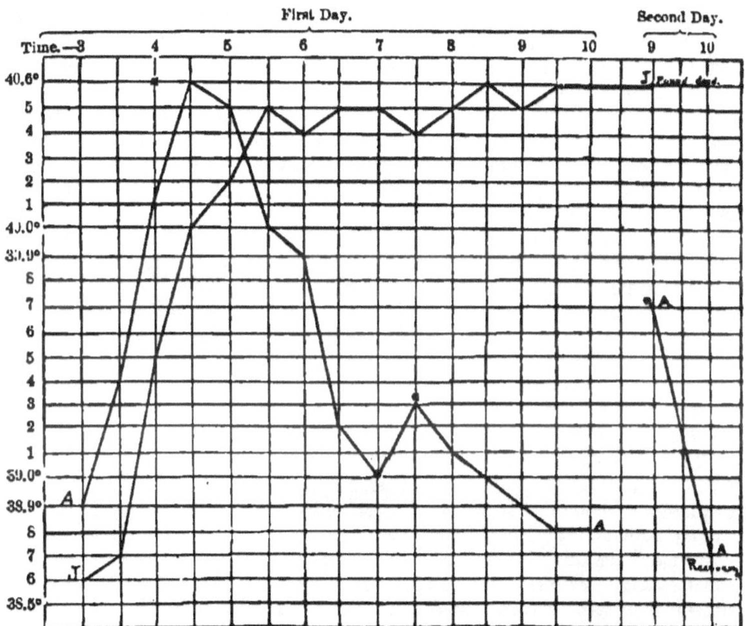

The lines AA and JJ exhibit the course of temperature during the parts of two days in which the animals were under observation. JJ belongs to the animal which was left to die without medication. The stars on the line AA represent the time of administration of alcohol. On each occasion ten cubic centimetres of absolute alcohol, well diluted with water, were introduced through an œsophageal tube into the stomach. The effect upon the temperature was very marked, and resulted in the recovery of the animal. This corresponds with what is so often witnessed in the treatment of fevers. Large doses of quinine may depress the temperature, but it soon rises again. But, if alcohol be given with the quinine, the depression is more durable. The favorable effects of whiskey, or any other alcoholic beverage, at the outset of an intermittent fever, are well known. In order, however, to procure this effect, it is necessary to administer the remedy with a liberal hand. To an ordinary adult the dose should be not less than forty grammes (about three tablespoonfuls) of pure alcohol.

For the purposes of this discussion it is not necessary to enter upon a consideration of the phenomena and course of chronic alcoholism. Certain cerebral symptoms, which are sometimes manifested as a consequence of acute alcoholic poisoning, should not be allowed to pass without notice.

First of these may be noted the convulsions which may occur, especially in the case of children who have received a poisonous dose of the drug. Taylor, in his work on Poisons, relates the following cases : " A boy, aged five years, swallowed a large quantity of brandy. Vomiting speedily followed, and he passed a restless night. In the morning it was observed that he had trembling of the hands, and that he could not hold a cup steadily. Convulsions with cramps ensued. The pulse was slow, the look timid, the pupil dilated, and the face pale. Delirium supervened, and there was difficulty of passing urine, with great thirst. Under treatment the symptoms abated, but there was a return of the trembling toward evening. An opiate was given, and the symptoms disappeared. . . . The smallest quantity known to have proved fatal was in the case of a boy aged seven years, who swallowed two wineglassfuls of brandy (between three and four ounces). Soon afterward he was observed to stagger ; he was sent to bed, and vomited violently. There was then a remission of the symptoms. He got up and sat by the fire ; his head, face and neck were very red, and he was in a profuse perspiration. Half an hour afterward he was found perfectly insensible, *strongly convulsed*, and the skin cold. He died in about thirty hours." Woodman and Tidy, in their work on "Forensic Medicine and Toxicology" (p. 43), have collected several cases of convulsions occurring in children after poisonous doses of alcohol.

Male, aged seven years. Half a pint of gin. *Symptoms.*—Complete insensibility in half an hour ; pupils contracted; no delirium ; injection of conjunctivæ ; *convulsions ;* death. *Result.*—Death in sixty-seven hours and a half. *Post-mortem.*—No particular post-mortem appearances, except that all parts seemed dry ; no odor of the spirit observable.—Dr. Chowne : *Lancet*, p. 231, May 4, 1839.

Male, aged three years. A quartern of rum and about ℥ ij. of gin. *Symptoms.*—Insensibility set in in ten minutes ; no stertor ; pupils immensely contracted ; face flushed (emetics were given) ; after a short time the pupils became dilated ; *convulsions set in*, and death. *Result.*—Death in two hours. *Post-mortem* in eighteen hours. Mucous membrane of the stomach injected. Lungs congested. Left side of heart full. Blood fluid. Brain and membranes intensely congested.—Dr. Rose : *Med. Times and Gaz.*, p. 236, September 8, 1860.

As a result of chronic alcoholism it is not a very uncommon thing to encounter cases of epileptiform convulsions, or of apoplectic seizures. Hemianæsthesia extending to the organs of special sense, and paralysis of motion, together with other symptoms of profound central disease of the nervous centres, may exist in these cases ; but their discussion must be omitted here, as we are only concerned with the phenomena of acute, temporary, alcoholic intoxication. The convulsions which are observed as a result of this intoxication occur almost exclusively in young children, or in susceptible females who have not yet fully emerged from the infantile condition. It appears to be not the result of any direct irritant action of alcohol upon the convulsive centres in the brain, but rather it is the result of an asphyxiated condition of those centres. The blood tends to accumulate in the venous capillaries and in the veins of the body. The respiratory centres and the neighboring convulsive centres receive, therefore, a deficient supply of blood, and convulsions are liable to ensue. They probably would always occur if the appropriate centres were always as sensitive to the withdrawal of oxygenated blood as they are in a large number of young children. The same causes, doubtless, contribute to the changes in the diameter of the pupil which may be noticed during the course of intoxication. During the earlier stages of alcoholic influence, as a direct consequence of the action of alcohol upon the carotid plexus, the control ordinarily exercised by the sympathetic fibres over the iris is diminished. As a consequence of the increased cerebral circulation that is produced by the same process, the energy that is dispensed by the nuclei of origin of the *motor oculi* nerves is considerably increased. This disturbance of equilibrium causes contraction of the pupils. But, as the process of stupefaction becomes intensified, and the brain-substance actually begins to die, the scale is at length turned in the opposite direction, and the slower dissolution of the sympathetic nerve gives it once more the upper hand. The pupil becomes, then, widely dilated, just as it does before death from injuries and compression of the brain. It is a matter of clinical observation that patients in a condition of alcoholic coma are more likely to recover if their pupils are contracted than if they are in a condition of wide dilatation.

In order to arrive at a clear understanding of the manner in which the functions of the cerebro-spinal nervous system are perverted and finally overpowered by alcohol, it is desirable to remember that the elements of the so-called sensory tract are probably more easily disturbed than the elements of the motor tract, so that a coarse impression made upon the body at large acts upon the sensory nerves to produce reflex motion rather than upon the motor nerves to produce direct movement without the intervention of the recipient nervous apparatus. In other words, the motor nuclei which form so large a portion of the anterior gray columns are more easily aroused through the medium of the posterior sensory columns, or by means of impressions which have traversed the higher sensory centres, than by any direct irritation of the motor tract itself.

As a consequence of this arrangement, it is in the sensory territory that we first observe the effects of alcohol. The initial hyperæsthesia—brief and ordinarily overlooked—which is caused by the first rush of blood into the sensory centres as the arterial walls relax under the influence of alcohol, having disappeared, the centres for the reception of sensory impressions begin to lose their susceptibility. The tactile sense and the muscular sense are usually the first to yield. Muscular co-ordination becomes difficult, and, finally, impossible. The patient staggers and falls to the ground. The posterior extremities give way before the anterior, apparently because of the great number and complexity of the muscular co-ordinations that are necessary for the preservation of the upright position, and because the lower segments of the cord, by reason of their peculiar arterial relations, suffer from anæmia more severely than the upper when blood-pressure is diminished. Cutaneous sensibility diminishes at the same time. The sense of pain becomes greatly diminished—even before the cerebro-spinal motor centres give signs of failing energy. This fact is the cause of a diminution of reflex action while voluntary motor power is still in a state of exaltation.

Extending our examination to the brain, we find in that organ a vast complexity of organization. Besides the simple structures devoted to the reception and distribution of ordinary impressions, we discover certain highly organized centres differentiated for the reception of special impressions derived from the organs of special sense. Above these lie the cerebral hemispheres and the cerebellum. In the cortical substance of these organs lie the highest centres of receptivity, and the primary organs of voluntary motor impulse. As a result of the impressions which are received, and the impulses which arise in this region, consciousness is aroused with each agitation of the cellular elements of the gray matter upon the surface of the brain. With each material agitation in this portion of space an idea is projected upon the corresponding field of consciousness. This is the groundwork of thought—the condition of intelligent life. As the structure of the brain increases in complexity and in the multiplicity of its elements, so will the multiplicity and the complexity of ideas be enlarged in the field of consciousness. This origination of ideas does not seem to be the special function of any single portion of the brain. It seems to accompany certain particular modes of motion in the cellular structure of any part of the cerebral cortex. That it does not accompany every molecular motion is indicated by the fact that in deep sleep, or in a condition of complete artificial anæsthesia, the production of ideas is arrested, notwithstanding the persistence of life and all its vegetative functions in the cerebral cell. That the generation of ideas is largely dependent upon the circulation of the blood is proved by the fact that within certain limits an increased rate of circulation increases the activity of the intellect. This, however, is not the only cause of increased cerebral activity. A sudden intellectual stimulus of any kind may arouse the brain; but it is soon followed by an increased afflux of blood to the seat of activity, so that it still remains true that intellectual processes are largely dependent upon the state of the cerebral circulation.

From anatomical study of the brain we learn that certain portions of its cortical substance are more intimately connected than other portions with the external organs of special sense. Other territories, notably the districts bordering the fissure of Rolando, are directly connected with the motor ganglia and the motor apparatus below the cerebrum. Here we have a differentiation of substance analogous to what exists in the gray matter of the cord. The white substance of the brain, like that of the cord, is made up of conducting fibres which serve to connect with each other the different areas of gray matter in the cortex, binding together the different parts of the same convolution, the different convolutions, the opposite hemispheres, the superficial and the basal portions of the gray matter of the brain. Each cell is thus brought into a circle of communication, more or less direct, with every other cell in the body, and is thus rendered liable to impressions derived from a multitude of sources. Ideas may thus arise, in connection with the activity of the cerebral cells, without the intervention of impressions from without the body. Upon the quality of the connection between the cerebral cells and the organs exterior to the brain, and upon the perfection of the connections between the cerebral cells themselves, depends the perfection of the generation of ideas and the completeness of the association of ideas originating under different conditions in different portions of the brain. An impression, transmitted from the eye, for example, to the visual centres in the cortex of the brain, excites at that point the production of the material conditions for the generation of visual ideas. The movements which have thus originated the idea of a visual object are not limited to that single result alone. They are transmitted by the appropriate conductors to other cerebral cells, where, in accordance with the structural peculiarities by which these elements are differentiated, they act as incitements to motion, or as originators of the conditions which produce new ideas in the realm of consciousness. Thus, one idea begets other ideas and associates itself with them to form harmonious thought. By this delicate mechanism any great increase of the cell-functions which at any portion of the brain serve as conditions for the production of ideas must necessarily quicken the production of ideas at other points in the cerebral substance. Ideas are thus produced, recalled, and associated with greater rapidity and vividness. This is the cause of that intellectual exaltation which follows as the immediate result of that first rush of blood to the brain when the arteries relax, and the heart pulsates with temporary increase of vigor, under the paralyzing influence exerted by alcohol upon the arterial coats.

But, as soon as alcohol has thus penetrated the structure of the brain, it begins to manifest upon its cells and its conductors the same depressing influence which it first displayed among the arterial elements. The sensory cells and fibrils suffer first. Impressions of sense become less perfect and less numerous. The conductors which associate the different cells can no longer perform their functions with precision. Like a skein of telephonic wires swayed by the wind, or relaxed by excessive heat, so that they interfere with each other, bringing to the ear a confused jangle of half intelligible sounds, so the precision of the cerebral functions is disturbed, and the field of consciousness is occupied with imperfect and disproportionate ideas, which may, nevertheless, crowd after each other with a rapidity that defies all possibility of attention and logical combination in thought. In the earlier stages of alcoholic excitement, the reflex functions of the cerebrum may share in the general reflex exaltation of the nervous system. In the healthy, natural state of the brain this entire cortical reflex apparatus is under the control of the will. But, when alcohol modifies the delicacy of the apparatus, the intimacy of the connection between the will and the cerebral substance is correspondingly modified until a point is reached where the material forces of the brain become released from the control of the immaterial will-power. This divorce first takes place in the motor regions of the cortex, so that, though a certain degree of sensation and perception may still persist, and an intelligent personality is still active in the field of consciousness, all power of directing the functions of the brain, and of the body through the medium of the brain, is temporarily arrested. In this state of things the individual feels as if possessed by two separate personalities—one, entirely intelligent, calm, and tranquil, occupying the position of a dispassionate spectator of their rational and tempestuous behavior of the other. This is sometimes the condition of the tipsy individual who cannot control his garrulous tongue or restrain his purposeless movements, but who may, nevertheless, be looking down from the sphere of consciousness with the composure of a philosopher engaged in scientific observation of the results of uncontrolled nervous action. Physiologically speaking, this peculiar condition is the result of inharmonious and disproportionate activity in different parts of the brain, producing intense functional exaltation in certain sensory portions of the cortex, with corresponding functional depression in the motor zone of the hemispheres. Psychologically considered, this condition is the result of a modification of the ordinary relation between the material substance of the brain and the immaterial personality which constitutes the conscious, intelligent individual. It is a condition which finds its analogue in certain conditions of trance. It differs from the condition of the "mind-reader's" trance in the fact that, while his nervous system is passively submitted to the control of another intelligence, the brain and the nervous apparatus of the tippler are left free to "flutter in the wind" of physical impressions from without. It differs from the cataleptic trance in the fact that, while all power of bodily motion is abolished in the cataleptic state, the victim of alcoholic intoxication may still be capable of displaying a great amount of involuntary muscular movement. He may even from time to time succeed in regaining momentary control of his physical powers—long enough perhaps to volun-

teer the information that he knows he is acting as if he were very drunk—
a statement which may be entirely unnecessary for the enlightenment of bystanders, but which the subject of the observation feels constrained to utter
as a vindication of the serene sobriety of his inner personality, which remains self-conscious of its complete independence of the physical disorder
of the body.

It is in the stage of cerebral exaltation, after the commencement of the
anæsthetic process, so far as the special senses are concerned, that we
sometimes meet with exhibitions of a *quasi*-clairvoyant state. Dr. J. F. B.
Flagg, in his work on Ether and Chloroform, relates the case of a dentist,
who, after an operation performed on his forehead, under the influence of
ether, "said that, although his eyes were shut, he saw every cut of the
knife. *He saw the shape of the wound upon the forehead ; and, what was better than all, this cutting appeared to him to be done upon somebody else.*" In
this case we have an example under ether of that dual personality which
has just been described as resulting occasionally under the influence of
alcohol upon the brain. The cerebral exaltation thus produced is probably
common to all disturbances of the brain which powerfully affect its circulation. In this state of exaltation one sense may supplement another so that
the patient seems to see with his eyes shut. This is not real seeing, but it
is a case in which the molecular changes in the cortical cells that are connected with the visual tract are now initiated by impulses coming to
them through the less direct pathway of the net-work which connects them
with other still open avenues of sense, such as the tactile sense, or the
sense of hearing, or even the muscular sense. However initiated, the
molecular movements must be accompanied by the projection of ideas into
the field of consciousness—ideas which, though lacking the precision and
the exact conformity with fact which would characterize them under ordinary circumstances of production, may yet present to the mind, especially
when aided by association and memory, a very vivid picture of external
scenes. So far as the mode of origin of such knowledge is concerned, it
must be ranked as an illusion of sense, or, more accurately, an irradiation
of sense. The knowledge of the external world thus acquired cannot compare in precision with that which is derived through the appropriate organs, because it cannot be subjected to comparison and correction by reference to other immediately preceding or succeeding impressions upon the
same organs ; but, nevertheless, it does contribute to the mind a certain
amount of very solid and substantially accurate information. The consequent processes of thought must, therefore, rest upon a basis of facts quite
different from the ideas which form the groundwork of dreams.

Hallucinations are less commonly the result of acute alcoholic poisoning. They occur as the consequence of morbid changes produced by the
chronic use of alcohol. Among the phenomena of delirium tremens they
are always present. It is said that the hallucinations which accompany this
disease are almost invariably of a loathsome or terrifying character. Ob-
scene and filthy figures, disgusting actions, alarming situations, occupy the
mind. It is seldom that anything agreeable serves to diversify the dreams
of alcoholic delirium. This must be referred to the fact that the long use
of alcohol injures that delicate perfection of the brain by means of which
the healthy individual is capable of perceiving and enjoying the higher
qualities of every object. The victim of chronic alcoholism has so long
practised upon himself the production of anæsthesia that all his senses at
last become degraded. Sexual gratification loses all its delicious perfection. Food and drink no longer delight the senses of smell and taste.

The blear-eyed drunkard has become a proverb. Tactile sensibility is singularly perverted. And finally, the higher senses—latest and most difficult of evolution—by which we appreciate beauty and morality, are almost if not wholly abolished. For this reason, the patient who suffers delirium tremens can only derive the ideas which dominate the mental processes of his disease from the lower residue of his sensory apparatus. Whatever objects habit and association have connected with the functions of that portion of his nervous system will now be reproduced by memory as the groundwork of his disorderly and purposeless thought.

For the reasons which have been thus set forth in the preceding pages, it becomes evident that, while alcohol is the great prototype of anæsthetic substances, the slow progress of insensibility under its influence renders it in many respects unfitted for use in the production of artificial anæsthesia. For external use, as a means of benumbing the cutaneous sensibility, it is often exceedingly valuable. The dentist has long employed it, in various degrees of concentration, for the relief of aching teeth. A pledget of lint, saturated with alcohol, may be inserted into the cavity of a decayed tooth with great advantage in many cases. The pain of a superficial burn or scald, which has not been sufficient to destroy the life of the skin, may be completely abolished by the continual application of alcohol. In like manner the distressing uneasiness in the neighborhood of a blistered or otherwise inflamed surface may be alleviated by similar lotions. The progress of a wound or of an ulcerated surface, toward recovery, is rendered less painful and dangerous by alcoholic dressings. This ancient practice of Arnauld de Villeneuve has in late years been revived with great *éclat* as one of the methods of antiseptic surgery.

It would be interesting, did the limits of this discussion permit such an extension of our view, to examine the mode of action by which alcohol produces its antiseptic effects. We would find that it is chiefly by intensification of its anæsthetic effects—by pushing to their last results its power of preventing molecular change in protoplasm. But sufficient evidence of the remarkable energy of alcohol in this particular has been already produced, and we must pass on to the consideration of other anæsthetic substances.

PHENOL—$C_6H_5.OH$.

Carbolic acid, Oxybenzene, Phenic acid, Phenylic alcohol, E.; *Acidum carbolicum, Acidum phenicum crystallisatum,* L.; *Acide phénique, Acide carbolique, Hydrate de phényle,* Fr.; *Carbolsäure, Phenylsäure, Phenylalkohol,* G.

Specific gravity, 1.056 at 46° (114.8° F.); melting-point, 39° (102.2° F.). Boiling-point, 182° (359.6° F.).

The chief source of phenol is coal-tar, from which it may be separated in long, colorless, acicular crystals. It possesses a peculiar, characteristic, not unpleasant odor. It is moderately soluble in water, and forms with it a hydrate, $2C_6H_5O.OH_2$, which crystallizes in large, six-sided prisms; it is extremely soluble in alcohol, ether, acetic acid, carbon disulphide, chloroform, and hydrocarbons of the benzene series. The aqueous solution of phenol does not redden litmus; it coagulates albumen, and on this account, apparently, it is a most valuable antiseptic, preventing fermentation and putrefaction, and therefore preserving animal substances from decomposition. Phenol itself is a powerful caustic, and when applied to the skin at once whitens it; many of the haloid derivatives of phenol exhibit this property to a more pronounced extent (Miller).

Phenol was discovered by Bunge in the year 1834. Its physiological and therapeutical actions were investigated by Le Bœuf (1859), by Lemaire (1863), and by Lister (1867), since which time its use has become universal. The attention of physicians and surgeons has been generally directed to the antiseptic qualities of the substance, while its anæsthetic properties have been less carefully noted. This, however, is not surprising, since it is only as a local anæsthetic that phenol possesses much value, while its antiseptic energy is beyond all possibility of estimation.

Careful observation of the action of phenol upon unicellular plants and animals indicates that its mode of action closely resembles that by which alcohol and other anæsthetic substances produce their specific effects upon living matter. Phenol does not destroy protoplasm, either living or dead. It arrests the movement of its molecules; it may coagulate its proteid constituents; it protects them from change. By virtue of this power it prevents decomposition; it may even preserve alive certain bacterial organisms or their spores, keeping them in a state of inactivity analogous to sleep, until by removal from the carbolized fluid they are set free from its paralyzing action and recover their power of vital manifestation. Its action upon the white blood-corpuscles is the same as its action upon bacteria (Prudden). Its action is then truly anæsthetic, admirably illustrating the fact that anæsthesia is partial antisepsis, while antisepsis is merely anæsthetic paralysis of molecular motion carried to its highest degree. The difference between the lesser action and the greater is shown by the effects of different solutions upon albumen. A five per cent. solution of phenol produces complete coagulation; a three per cent. solution only disturbs the transparency of the albumen; a one per cent. solution produces no perceptible change.

The action of phenol upon the lowest forms of vegetation is analogous to the action of alcohol. In an aqueous solution containing one or two per cent. of carbolic acid the process of fermentation is greatly retarded. In a solution containing five per cent. the process ceases entirely. The action of carbolic acid upon bacteria is largely dependent upon the degree of its dilution with water. Weak solutions (1 : 200) do not destroy the vitality of bacteria, though they may retard their development. For complete destruction of the vitality of these organisms a more concentrated (1 : 25) solution is requisite. A five per cent. solution diffused through the air in the form of spray is, therefore, of very little value as a means of destroying such bacterial spores as may be floating in the atmosphere. For the same reason it becomes possible, as Mr. Lister has recently stated (*Brit. Med. Journ.*, p. 183, February 5, 1881), for micrococci to multiply in the fluid contents of wounds which have been treated antiseptically. These organisms, to which has been given the name granuligera, have been "shown by Mr. Cheyne to occur very frequently in cases treated antiseptically, without any interference with aseptic progress" (*loc. cit.*). Decomposable animal substances require a very intimate contact with the antiseptic in order to prevent the growth and propagation of those organisms which favor putrescence.

The activity of the chemical ferments is also diminished, or destroyed, by the presence of phenol in the solution. If present in quantity varying from one-half to two and one-half per cent., the conversion of starch into sugar by ptyalin, and the transformation of proteids into peptones, is arrested.   That this action is, in solutions of moderate strength, of a paralyzing rather than of a destructive character, is shown by the observations of Van Geuns ("Real-Encyc. der gesammten Heilkunde," vol. ii., p. 670) upon the relation between phenol and emulsion.   He found that the development of hydrocyanic acid from amygdalin was only temporarily hindered by a four per cent. solution of phenol.   By reducing the strength of the solution through the addition of water, the fermentative process was renewed, showing that the ferment had not been destroyed.

Upon the various animal tissues it may also be shown that weak solutions exercise no destructive effect.   But stronger solutions—five per cent. and upward—are very powerful agents for the coagulation of albumen and the arrest of the life of protoplasm.   The effect of phenol upon the nervous apparatus, therefore, depends upon the degree of concentration with which it is applied.   The cutaneous nerves may thus be either irritated, benumbed, or paralyzed.

It is with these local effects of phenol that the student of anæsthetics is chiefly interested.   If the pure crystals, or if a concentrated aqueous or oily solution of the substance be placed upon the skin, a painful sensation immediately follows the application ; the surface is whitened, and soon becomes insensible.   The vitality of the epidermal tissues is destroyed, and after a few days there is exfoliation of the superficial layers.   If the application has been protracted and severe, inflammation will be established. A red zone of congestion surrounds the necrotic area, and the various exudations which characterize the inflammatory process will be displayed. The anæsthetic stage of this process is rapidly developed after the application.   In order to accomplish the production of complete local anæsthesia, it is necessary to paint the surface with liquid phenol or with a very highly concentrated solution of its crystals in water or in ether.   Its solution in oil or in glycerine is less energetic.   Thus applied, a degree of anæsthesia sufficient to effect the painless incision of abscesses, etc., can easily be procured.

As a local application to rheumatic joints it has been employed both externally, and by hypodermic injection.   Its external use for this purpose can scarcely be preferred to the similar use of cantharides.   If employed hypodermically, the quantity of pure phenol should not exceed nine or ten centigrammes (one grain and a half) at once, lest symptoms of poisoning should appear.

The average fatal dose of phenol is said to be not far from twelve grammes ("Real-Encyc.," vol. ii., p. 673).   Smaller doses, however, have been known to produce a fatal result, and a comparatively inconsiderable quantity—half a gramme (six or eight grains)—may occasion disagreeable results.   The toxic phenomena are the same, no matter through what channel the substance may enter the circulation.   It is ordinarily introduced through the stomach ; but its employment in vaginal or rectal injections has sometimes produced symptoms of poisoning.   Severe toxic effects have been known to follow its energetic application to the surfaces of healing wounds.   The susceptibility of children to its effects is such as to interdict its extensive use in their treatment.   Inhalation of its spray during a protracted operation is not without prejudice to certain patients.   It is therefore important to know the symptoms which indicate its action upon the general system.   Apart from the local action of the substance upon the surface to which it may have been applied—skin, mucous membrane, or wound—the general effects are the same, without reference to the manner in which the poison has gained access to the circulation. The symptoms of poisoning are manifested chiefly by the nervous system, and consist of headache, more or less interference with consciousness, giddiness ; finally, insensibility, spasmodic contractions of the muscles of the face, sometimes even reaching the intensity of trismus ; spasmodic and paretic conditions of the muscles of the limbs, culminating in complete resolution.

Thus far the train of symptoms is quite analogous to the consequences of alcoholic or chloroformic anæsthesia. The pulse becomes less frequent, weak, and irregular. Respiration is also considerably disturbed. The temperature of the body falls, the extremities become cold. Clammy perspiration bedews the skin. The countenance becomes pale, or even cyanotic. The pupils are contracted until the near approach of death occasions their dilatation. If the dissolution of the patient is averted, vomiting not unfrequently occurs during convalescence. After death the lungs are usually found gorged with dark, fluid blood. The heart is generally empty.

Such is the course of poisoning by large doses of phenol. Of more frequent occurrence are cases of slow intoxication by the gradual introduction of the poison into the current of the circulation, through the medium of surgical dressings in accordance with the ultra-antiseptic method. As long ago as 1876, Tardieu could give the details of fifteen such cases. In certain instances the patient passes rapidly into a state of collapse after the first application of the carbolized dressings. It must, however, be difficult to speak dogmatically of such cases, for the surgeon can always vindicate his method by referring the moribund condition of his patient to the loss of blood, or to the shock of operation, or to previous exhaustion. But there exist other cases, to which attention has been called (*London Med. Record*, May 15, 1880), that are characterized by a gradual development of the toxic symptoms days or weeks after the immediate effects of operation have disappeared. The patient becomes restless. "His temperature will rise three or four degrees above normal, symptoms apparently of incipient septicæmia will develop themselves, and will in all probability be met by a more vigorous employment of antiseptic methods. The condition of the patient, however, becomes daily worse. Nausea, loss of appetite, giddiness, clonic spasms, great prostration, with coma, and even death, may close, and indeed have too often closed, the scene. In many of these cases there is no room for doubt as to the cause. It has been shown many times that, where recovery has taken place, the improvement in the symptoms has coincided in the most marked manner with the cessation of the use of carbolized dressings. On the other hand, it has been noticed that the symptoms have always become aggravated shortly after the dressings have been applied."

The recognition of phenol-poisoning by the toxicologist is effected by distillation of the contents of the alimentary canal, or other suspected substances, with dilute sulphuric acid. Phenol may thus be separated in oily drops, which respond to the appropriate tests, of which the characteristic odor is the most delicate. Urine containing the substance is often of a greenish or dusky brown color. It is sometimes almost black. This discoloration is caused by the presence of the products of the oxidation of phenol and hydrochinon, and the appearance of hydrochinon under the form of hydrochinon sulphate (Baumann and Preusse : *Archiv. f. Anat. und Phys.*, p. 245, 1879). In testing the urine it is advisable to acidify the liquid with acetic acid, in order to avoid the possibility of developing phenol by the action of sulphuric acid upon substances normally existing in urine. After distillation it may be extracted from the distillate by the action of ether. From its ethereal solution it may then be easily separated by a second distillation.

For the antidotal treatment of phenol-poisoning the administration of saccharated lime has been recommended. This enters into combination with phenol, forming an insoluble and but slightly noxious compound. Sodic sulphate has also been praised on account of its formation of a harmless sulphocarbolate in the alimentary canal. For the general symptoms of carbolic toxæmia symptomatic treatment alone is applicable. Under this head may be enumerated the administration of diffusible stimulants, and the employment of friction, warmth, sinapisms, electricity, and artificial respiration.

CHLORAL HYDRATE—$C_2H_3Cl_3O_2$.

Trichlorethaldehydrol, Chloral hydras, L.; *Hydrate de chloral*, Fr.; *Chloral hydrat*, G.; *Hydrate of chloral*, E.

This substance was discovered, in the year 1832, by the celebrated chemist Justus Liebig. For many years, like chloroform, it was regarded merely as a chemical curiosity, and it was only in the year 1869 that its physiological and therapeutical qualities were discovered by Prof. Liebreich.

Chloral, from which chloral hydrate is derived, is a colorless, oily-looking fluid, with a density of 1.502. It boils at 94.4° (202° F.). The density of its vapor is 5.13. It has a decidedly ethereal odor, and is irritating in its action upon the mucous membranes of the eyes and nose. Its taste is acrid and disagreeable—almost caustic. It dissolves readily in water, alcohol, and ether, entering into combination with these substances. In contact with water it combines energetically with its elements to form a definite *hydrate of chloral*, which crystallizes as its solution evaporates.

Chloral is formed by the prolonged action of dry chlorine gas upon pure anhydrous alcohol. Hence the name chloral, derived from the names of these substances by uniting their first syllables—*chlor* and *al*.

Chloral hydrate occurs in white, crystalline masses, formed of rhomboidal prismatic layers, or in separate crystals which at first sight closely resemble certain salts with an alkaline base. It has a disagreeable taste, and a penetrating, fruity odor like that of the melon. At ordinary temperatures it is slowly volatilized, like camphor. It melts at a temperature between 56° and 58° (133°—136° F.), and boils without decomposition at about 95° (203° F.). It dissolves easily in water; at 15° (60° F.) 100 grammes (about three ounces) of distilled water will dissolve 384.615 grammes (about 5,935 grains). The solution is neutral or only slightly acid, and should give no precipitate with nitrate of silver. Impure chloral hydrate is much less soluble than the pure article. In a state of purity its vapor does not readily fume with vapor of ammonia; but if its crystals are dry, and if the temperature is somewhat elevated, light clouds of white vapor are visible. If the substance contains hydrochloric acid, very abundant fumes are given off as a result of the formation of considerable quantities of ammonium chloride. When the pure hydrate is subjected to the vapor of ammonia it is first changed into ammonium formiate and chloroform; and with an excess of ammonia this is further transformed into ammonium chloride and ammonium formiate.

In the presence of alkaline hydrates chloral is decomposed into an alkaline formiate and chloroform :

$$\underset{\text{Chloral.}}{C_2HCl_3O} \; + \; \underset{\text{Sodium hydrate.}}{NaHO} \; = \; \underset{\text{Sodium formiate.}}{NaCHO_2} \; + \; \underset{\text{Chloroform.}}{CHCl_3}$$

This was the reaction which led Prof. Liebreich to suggest the use of this drug as a means of generating chloroform in the blood and tissues themselves. How this hypothesis conforms with facts we shall presently inquire.

PHYSIOLOGICAL ACTION OF CHLORAL HYDRATE.

The application of the crystallized hydrate, or of its concentrated solution, to the skin, causes considerable irritation, which may even result in vesication and the formation of an eschar. If it be injected into the tissues, it produces a circumscribed inflammation which in the lower animals may sometimes result in actual destruction of the part. If a solution of the drug is swallowed, its local effects depend largely upon the degree of its dilution. Strong solutions produce a reflex secretion of saliva, with acrid, disagreeable taste in the mouth, especially in the region of the palate and fauces. In the stomach chloral hydrate produces a sensation of warmth, accompanied by a certain degree of gastric uneasiness and nausea. Large doses not unfrequently excite vomiting. Small doses excite the sense of taste, but do not particularly disturb the stomach or the salivary glands.

According to Labbée ("Dict. Encyc. des Sci. Méd.," t. XVI., p. 457), if under the skin of a frog be injected a solution containing from 25 milligr. to 5 ctgr. of chloral hydrate, the voluntary movements of the animal soon become enfeebled, and after a little time there is complete muscular resolution ; sensibility also diminishes by degrees ; reflex movement ceases ; the movements of respiration and of circulation become less frequent ; the creature lies without motion, as if it were dead. After a few hours the powers of sensation and of motion are renewed, and life seems as if restored. If a larger quantity be injected, the movements of respiration and of circulation cease, and death takes place.

Upon the rabbit similar effects may be produced. After the hypodermic injection of 1.50 gramme (about twenty-three grains) of chloral hydrate, the muscular apparatus relaxes ; the animal falls asleep ; its sensibility diminishes ; respiration becomes dilatory ; the temperature of the body is lowered. After the expiration of an hour or two these symptoms pass off, and recovery takes place. But if a large quantity, such as three grammes (about fifty grains), be employed, in addition to the above-mentioned symptoms will be added the occurrence of dyspnœa. Respiration becomes irregular and jerky ; anæthesia is more complete ; finally the respiratory movements cease, the heart stands still, the animal is dead.

Dogs present analogous symptoms. After receiving under the skin four grammes (about one drachm) of the hydrate, the voluntary movements of the animal are seriously compromised. He totters around ; his hind legs give way ; he at length lies down and goes to sleep. Cutaneous sensibility becomes less acute ; respiration loses its regularity ; the pulse falls below its ordinary rate. After a time recovery takes place. Sensibility is the first to reappear ; then the special senses and the brain revive.

Voluntary motion is the last thing to be renewed. If the quantity of chloral hydrate be increased to double the original amount, there will be complete anæsthesia, chills, and dyspnœa. Death occurs as the result of cessation of respiration and circulation.

Upon the human subject the effects of the drug do not differ materially from its effects upon the lower animals. After a moderate dose, say from a gramme and a half (23 grains) to four grammes (one drachm), the patient soon falls asleep; the pulse and respiration grow less frequent; the pupils contract; the eyeballs turn in; the muscles relax; all the phenomena of natural sleep are exhibited. If an excessive dose has been administered, death may take place. It is preceded by phenomena of excitement; instead of quiet sleep there is stupor, with muscular agitation, hurried respiration, an irregular, feeble, and intermittent pulse, tumultuous beating of the heart, paleness of the face, depression of temperature, loss of sensibility, and death.

Post-mortem appearances.—In frogs the heart is found relaxed in diastole, and distended with black, uncoagulated blood. The other viscera present their usual appearance. Rabbits exhibit the same condition of the heart. Their lungs are pale and free from blood, enphysematous, and atelectatic. The abdominal viscera and the mesenteric vessels are gorged with blood. Within the cranial cavity the meninges are injected; the sinuses are distended with black blood; the brain presents its natural appearance; the spinal cord is healthy; and the muscles are very dark.

Death following the use of chloral hydrate has not been sufficiently common among human beings to furnish a considerable literature regarding the post-mortem appearances. In the few cases that have been examined, the cardiac ventricles were empty; the right auricle was filled with fluid blood. Crichton-Browne reports the heart dilated; the lungs congested; abdominal viscera distended with blood, the brain anæmic. Other observers have noted a hyperæmic condition of the meninges of the brain. The appearances presented by dogs which have been poisoned with chloral hydrate do not differ from the above.

It is evident from the preceding summary that there is nothing characteristic in the post-mortem appearances after chloral hydrate. They are common to the condition of asphyxia or of syncope. In order to determine the cause of death in a doubtful case, it is necessary to resort to a chemical analysis. Even then the result may not be wholly conclusive, since chloral and chloroform are both to be identified by the chlorine which they contain.

It appears, then, that chloral may act as a poison, as an anæsthetic, and as a simple hypnotic. The effect is closely related to the size of the dose. When administered in moderate quantities its action is purely hypnotic. Cutaneous sensibility is not abolished; the sleeper can be aroused from his slumber; his spontaneous awakening is fresh and agreeable, without any of the unpleasant cerebral sensations which usually follow the awakening from opiates or anæsthetics.

It has been remarked that in certain cases of cerebral congestion chloral hydrate has failed to produce sleep. It is then desirable to administer with the drug other remedies which may serve to relieve the congested state of the vessels in the brain. For this purpose bromide of potassium, quinine, digitalis, etc., have been recommended.

The proper dose to be given as a hypnotic is about one gramme and a half (from twenty to twenty-five grains). This quantity may be repeated at the end of half an hour or an hour, if the first dose is insufficient. In this way the medicine may be safely administered for a number of weeks. Smaller doses have been taken every night for many years without apparent injury, but it is a practice that is liable to abuse. Fortunately, however, it may be thus constantly employed for many years without that necessity for increasing the dose which is so characteristic of the abuse of opiates. I am acquainted with a gentleman, now sixty-nine years of age, who has been in the habit of taking from sixty to seventy centigrammes (ten grains) of chloral hydrate, every night at bed-time, for at least ten years. He has never experienced the need of increasing the dose. Prof. Edward L. Holmes recently treated a lady who for six years has been accustomed to take not less than ten grammes, every evening, without apparent injury.

Chloral hydrate has been employed by surgeons as an anæsthetic, but its effects are not thoroughly satisfactory. When administered to animals it only destroys sensibility if given in poisonous doses. Willieme and Jastrowitz ("Dict. Encyc. des Sci. Méd.," t. XVI., p. 462) claim that even the nasal septum does not become wholly insensible. It is said that intravenous injections of its solution are much more efficient for the production of anæsthesia than simple hypodermic injections. In the physiological laboratory it is not an uncommon thing to employ this method of stupefying the inferior animals. As Claude Bernard has shown, it is necessary in such experiments to make the injection as far as possible from the heart. An injection into the jugular vein is very likely to arrest the action of the heart. Bernard was of the opinion that dogs are less tolerant of the substance than human beings. Three grammes and a half or four grammes (about fifty or sixty grains) were fatal to dogs, whereas the French surgeons, Labbée and Oré, have safely used it in relatively equal doses by injection into the veins of the human subject. With an interval of only three or four minutes Oré injected two doses of nine grammes (about seven scruples) of chloral hydrate into the radial vein of a patient who was suffering with tetanus. For the relief of a case of subacute tetanus, following gangrene of the great toe, Labbée made a similar injection of ten grammes (more than two drachms and a half) of the drug. The patient entered a condition of complete coma, which lasted for two hours; tetanic symptoms then reappeared, and the patient died. In another case Oré repeated his injections as often as the tetanic symptoms were renewed, until the patient had received twenty-eight grammes (nearly an ounce) of the drug. ("Leçons sur les Anesthésiques et sur l'Asphyxie," par M. Claude Bernard.) This audacity, however, has not found many imitators. Other surgeons ("Dict. Encyc. des Sci. Méd.," *loc. cit.*), it is true, have attempted to procure anæsthesia by its internal use, but pain was often experienced in spite of the remedy. Nussbaum employed it in twenty cases of capital operation. Only once did he obtain complete insensibility to pain. In this respect the effects of intravenous injection are much superior, but the evident hazard of the operation must necessarily preclude its admission to the rank of an approved method.

Effects of chloral hydrate upon the blood.—Dr. Richardson showed that chloral shrivels the corpuscles of the blood, and also destroys its power of coagulation. But if a strong solution of chloral hydrate be injected into a human vein, the blood will be coagulated. In the blood of frogs it produces deformity and enlargement of the corpuscle, a hyaline appearance of the hæmoglobine, and coagulation of the serum. Dr. Turnbull reports the presence of amyloid bodies in the blood after poisonous doses of chloral hydrate.

Effects of chloral hydrate upon the heart and the circulation.—According to Labbée (*loc. cit.*) ten centigrammes (one grain and a half) of chloral will arrest the movements of the heart of a frog within fifteen minutes. Three grammes (about forty-five grains), will stop the heart of a rabbit, and six grammes (one drachm and a half) will accomplish the same result in a dog. In the first-mentioned animal the cardiac movements subside gradually, but in the warm-blooded animals the arrest is instantaneous. It is preceded, at the commencement of the process of chloralization, by a brief acceleration of the heart. For a considerable time after the death of other organs the heart continues to pulsate feebly when exposed to the air by removal of the thoracic wall.

In the human subject the result is similar. Large doses produce violent cardiac excitement, or even a sudden arrest of the heart, with paleness of the cutaneous surface, as in ordinary cases of syncope. Small doses produce very slight changes in the action of the heart. It requires a considerable quantity to produce a notable effect. The heart is then accelerated at first, and retarded afterward. Prof. Liebreich expressed the opinion that the drug acts first upon the brain and the spinal cord, and finally produces paralysis of the intracardiac nervous ganglia, thus arresting the action of the heart. He excluded the intervention of the pneumogastric nerves, basing his opinion upon the fact that, after the heart had ceased to beat under the influence of chloral, and was no longer responsive to irritation, if the portion beyond the ganglia were excised it would again contract when touched. He therefore concluded that the paralysis must be of peripheral character. Labbée, however, is of the opinion that chloral acts upon the medullary centres, at first exciting the pneumogastric nerves, and through them arousing tumultuous pulsation of the heart, but finally paralyzing the nerves and producing arrest of movement. No doubt the pneumogastric nerves share in producing a disturbance of the cardiac contractions, but their paralysis alone would not cause cessation of cardiac motion. The paralysis is general, affecting both the medulla and the nerve-ganglia in the heart itself.

After the administration of chloral hydrate the face becomes suffused with blood in consequence of paresis of the vaso-motor nerves of the head. Demarquay and Van Lair have compared the vascularization of the eye and the ear, thus produced in the rabbit, to the effects of section of the sympathetic nerve in the neck. To a similar modification of the peripheral vaso-motor nerves must be assigned the cause of various cutaneous eruptions which follow the use of the drug. These eruptions assume various forms, resembling sometimes the rash of scarlatina, or of measles, or of purpura, or of urticaria. The scarlatiniform eruption is one of the most common. When it appears shortly after the use of chloral, in a child who is suffering with a febrile movement and a sore throat, the counterfeit presentment of scarlet fever is well-nigh perfect.

Effect upon respiration.—When placed under the influence of moderate doses of chloral, the respiration of the lower animals is somewhat retarded. Sometimes the respiratory movements become irregular and jerky. Large doses speedily disturb the rhythm of respiration, and occasion its arrest. Similar results have been observed in the human subject. After poisonous doses the movements of respiration become irregular, feeble and shallow. Sometimes there is actual panting for breath.

These disturbances are evidently produced by the action of chloral upon the respiratory centres in the medulla oblongata, and upon the roots of the nerves in the spinal cord. The concurrent derangement of the circulation doubtless contributes to the production of respiratory disturbance.

Effect upon the production of heat.—Chloral produces a diminution of the temperature of the body. After ordinary doses, dogs and rabbits will exhibit a fall of 2° (3.6° F.). Demarquay has noted, during sleep after chloral in the human subject, a depression of temperature equal to about 1° F. Animals which have been poisoned with chloral hydrate quickly exhibit a temperature falling below 30° (86° F.), and progressively diminishing until death. In fatal cases after taking chloral, no thermometric observations have been recorded for the human subject. Cold sweats and general depression of temperature have alone been mentioned in such instances.

This depressing power of chloral hydrate would naturally lead one to anticipate that the excessive temperature of fevers might be lowered by its use. No such favorable effect, however, has yet been observed. When administered under such circumstances, only a slight fall of temperature has been remarked.

Condition of the pupil of the eye.—Upon the innervation of the iris chloral produces effects that are quite similar to those which have been discussed in the chapter on alcohol. The cause of the contraction which is finally followed, in dangerous cases, by dilatation, lies in the varying rate of progressive paralysis of the cerebral and sympathetic sets of nerves.

Effect upon the muscular apparatus.—The initial effect of chloral hydrate is the induction of muscular debility, diminution of the power of co-ordinating their movements, and final abolition of muscular tonicity. Complete relaxation only follows excessive doses. During ordinary chloralic sleep reflex power is not destroyed, for an animal thus sleeping will respond to a pinch by removal of the limb. So powerful are the effects of large doses that Demarquay has pronounced chloral hydrate to be the most potent agent for the production of muscular relaxation that we possess. In a full-grown man it is necessary to employ seven or eight grammes (about two drachms) in order to effect such complete resolution of the muscles. Under the influence of such enormous doses the sphincters may be relaxed in the same way that has been observed in chloralized animals.

It sometimes happens that, instead of muscular relaxation, the use of chloral hydrate may produce an increase of muscular energy. This has been particularly observed among drunkards and insane persons. It may occur under other conditions, producing muscular rigidity very much like the rigidity that is sometimes observed during the inhalation of chloroform. Dr. Allbutt relates the case of a woman who received a hypnotic dose of chloral during her convalescence from articular rheumatism. The drug produced violent pain in the muscles, accompanied by muscular tremors in the thighs, with spasmodic contraction of the hands, and finally resulted in a degree of opisthotonos which led to the belief that strychnia had been administered by mistake. It was, however, proved that only the purest and best quality of chloral hydrate had been employed. An Italian physician, Giovanni di Ranzoli, has reported the occurrence of convulsions after chloral. They are sometimes observed in frogs after poisonous doses. Richardson has also seen them exhibited by other animals before death. Their precise cause has not been determined, but it seems highly probable that they are induced by causes analogous to those which produce convulsions after poisonous doses of alcohol.

Returning to a consideration of the relaxing effects of chloral upon the muscles, it is not probable that these are due to any direct modification of the contractile elements of the muscular fibres, because there is no loss of electro-muscular contractility, even after poisonous doses.   Aside from a stationary condition of the blood in the muscles, no special alteration of structure has been described, though Richardson mentions some change as having occurred.   If there is any appreciable change, it cannot be of a paralyzing character, for the muscles do not lose their power of contracting when stimulated.   Nor can it be the nerve which is at fault, for if a motor nerve be laid bare in the limb of an animal which has been stupefied with chloral, and if an electrical current be transmitted through the nerve, the muscles with which it is in connection will immediately contract.   The power of conveying irritation is not destroyed.   If then the muscle and the motor nerve remain capable of function, it can only be the spinal cord and the brain that are the principal seats of the paralyzing energy of chloral. This is rendered additionally probable by the well-known effect of the substance upon the excitability of the motor centres in the cortex of the brain.   The fact is this, that chloral, like other hypnotic and anæsthetic substances, diminishes the vital energy of all living matter; but it is in the peculiar and delicate structure of the nervous system that this depression becomes most conspicuous.   The invisible molecular movements of the elements of the nervous centres are registered by muscular movements possessing a degree of amplitude that is almost infinite in comparison with the changes to which they correspond.   The very smallest alteration in the rate or in the character of the motion within a cerebral or a spinal cell may be sufficient to produce changes in the muscular apparatus which shall vary all the way from convulsion to paralysis.

Upon the non-striated muscles of the body small doses of chloral hydrate may produce increased power of contraction.   Large doses, however, arrest their activity.   Liebreich thought that by its use the peristaltic action of the intestinal coats was increased in sleeping rabbits.   This, however, seems to be a secondary effect of the drug through its suppression of the inhibitory energies of the brain and spinal cord.   Besnier and Martineau have collected numerous cases in which threatened abortion during the early months of pregnancy was prevented by its use in large doses.   Other observers have remarked an increased vigor in the uterine contractions of labor after its administration.   But this may have been either the result of the suppression of inhibitory influences of various kinds, or it may have been due to reflex excitement, such as frequently follows a draught of cold water or any other liquid during the course of a lingering labor.   In the earlier stages of confinement a large dose of chloral hydrate will frequently occasion an arrest of pains for a number of hours.

The effect of chloral hydrate upon the nervous system is thus summed up by Labbée (*loc. cit.*) : The spinal cord loses first its excito-motor powers, then its sensory power, and finally its reflex capacity.   The spinal nerves are overcome in an ascending order, from below upward.   In certain rare instances there is an exaggeration of the functions of the nervous centres, producing psychical exaltation, increase of muscular excitability, and general hyperæsthesia.   The cranial contents are very speedily affected by chloral ; in a very short time after its administration the ophthalmic branch of the trigeminal nerve is paralyzed, and the conjunctiva becomes insensible in consequence.   After the special senses have yielded, the brain gives way to the influence of the drug.   Sleep almost invariably comes on without previous intellectual excitement, though occasional exceptions to this rule have been noted.   It is very seldom the case that sleep is disturbed by dreams—it is quiet and refreshing, and the patient wakens without disagreeable after-effects.

Effect upon the secretions.—The glandular organs of the body seem to be aroused by the influence of chloral hydrate. The salivary glands are excited, in a reflex manner, no doubt, as well as by direct action through the blood. Animals froth at the mouth after hypodermic injection of a solution of chloral. Profuse perspiration occurs after poisonous doses, but moderate doses do not visibly increase the cutaneous secretion in the human subject. The action of the kidneys is notably increased. These organs are considerably injected with blood, and Vulpian has even observed the occurrence of hæmaturia in dogs which had received chloral by intravenous injection. After ordinary doses the quantity of the urine is ordinarily augmented, without any other special change in the character of the liquid. It very rarely contains sugar, differing in this respect from urine that has been modified by the action of chloroform upon the system. Neither chloral nor chloroform can be detected in the urine. Bouchut, Tuke, and others, have reported an increase of the specific gravity of the urine, but this is not an ordinary result. Liebreich and Byasson determined the presence of alkaline chlorides, and, occasionally, of sodic formiate.

Antiseptic properties of chloral hydrate. —As long ago as 1869, Dr. Richardson remarked the coagulation and preservation of blood that had been allowed to flow into a solution of chloral. The Italian, Pavesi di Mortare, stated, in the year 1871, that animal and vegetable substances would not putrefy in an atmosphere charged with the vapor of chloral hydrate. Other observers followed in the same channel until the antiseptic properties of the substance were thoroughly established. Solutions of chloral, containing from one to ten per cent. of the substance, are capable of preserving animal substances for weeks together. Dead animals may thus be preserved by intravascular injections of solutions of chloral. If the aqueous solution alone be used, the flesh becomes hardened and friable ; but, if glycerine is added to the liquid, the natural pliability of the tissues will be preserved. The best proportion for such a solution is chloral hydrate one part, water seven parts, the whole to be mixed with an equal volume of glycerine (Personne).

The process of fermentation may be retarded and completely arrested by the addition of from one to four per cent. of chloral hydrate. The germination of microphytes in alkaline organic solutions can in the same way be prevented. Pavesi recommends its use as a parasiticide, and as a substitute for camphor as a means of protection against moths. He is also of the opinion that it will be very serviceable as an antiseptic agent for use in hospitals, ships, and other infected localities. In this respect, however, it may well be questioned whether it would be any more valuable than an equivalent amount of alcohol.

Mode of action.—Prof. Liebreich, in the course of his experiments, finding that chloral was decomposed by the action of alkaline hydrates, with the production of chloroform and a formiate, announced the inference that in the alkaline blood a similar reaction might take place, liberating chloroform among the tissues, and furnishing sodium formiate to be excreted in the urine, unless further reduced by oxidation to water and carbonic anhydrides. According to this hypothesis, the sole cause of the hypnotic energy of chloral resides in the secondary product, chloroform, which may be derived from it. Byasson and Follet believed that the alkaline formiate also contributed to produce the anæsthetic and hypnotic effects that follow the use of chloral hydrate. Their argument may be stated as follows ("Dict. Encyc. des Sci. Méd.," t. XVI., p. 472) : Sodium trichloracetate can, like chloral hydrate, be reduced, in the system, into chloroform and a minute quantity of formic acid. Now, the trichloracetate is far less energetic than chloral hydrate. It produces sleep and anœsthesia, but in a very much less degree. Since the transformation of chloral yields a much larger proportion of formic acid, its superior energy must be due to the difference in favor of the acid, which must, therefore, be considered a hypnotic as well as chloroform. Its effects are produced by deoxidation of the blood, which yields its oxygen to combine with the carbon and hydrogen of the acid, leaving the blood and the tissues minus that amount of oxgyen, and, consequently, in an asphyxiated condition. For these gentlemen, therefore, the condition produced by the action of chloral hydrate is, in part at least, a condition of asphyxia.

The chemists have generally arrayed themselves in favor of the hypothesis of Liebreich. Physiologists like Claude Bernard, and practical physicians, have preferred to look upon chloral as a substance possessed of certain specific qualities by virtue of which it acts primarily as a hypnotic, and secondarily, when given in large doses, as an anæsthetic. Bernard ("Leçons sur les Anesthésiques ") calls attention to the parallel which may be drawn between many of the phenomena caused by opium and many that are produced by chloral hydrate. The peripheral vascular dilatation, the reduction of cardiac energy and arterial pressure, the preservation of sensibility during the sleep that follows the drug—proved by the fact that if the ear or the toe of a dog be smartly pinched, the animal groans, even though he does not wake up—alike follow the use of either substance. Notwithstanding certain minor points of difference—relating chiefly to the degree of susceptibility to certain kinds of noise—the sleep of chloral much more nearly resembles the sleep of morphine than the anæsthesia of chloroform. The observations of Claude Bernard are decidedly in favor of the specific qualities and action of chloral hydrate. He was not able to detect, in the breath of animals to which chloral had been given, any odor of chloroform. The odor of chloral itself was very evident. On the contrary, Dr. Richardson claimed that, after poisonous doses, he did recognize the odor of chloroform in the air that was expired.

Clinical examination of the blood has convinced the majority of chemists that chloroform exists in that liquid after the administration of chloral. To speak more exactly, they have found that under such circumstances the blood contains a volatile body which, when decomposed by passage through a red-hot porcelain tube, yields chlorine. This may be fixed by passage of the gases of decomposition into a solution of nitrate of silver, which retains the chlorine in the form of silver chloride. This seems to be the only chemical test upon which reliance can be placed, but it is an indirect method of arriving at the result. The presence of chloroform is inferred from the resulting chlorine. But chlorine is also a constituent of chloral. When the volatile body is secured by collection of the breath, it may be urged that chloral is not sufficiently volatile to enable it to traverse the pulmonary membranes ; consequently, the chlorine-yielding substance contained in the breath must be chloroform. This conclusion, however, rests upon the rather doubtful hypothesis of the imperviousness of the pulmonary membranes. The experiments of Horand and Peuch ("Dict. Encyc. des Sci. Méd.," t. XVI., p. 475) appear to give a more satisfactory result. They first determined by the usual tests the presence of chlorine in the volatile substance obtained from the blood after chloral. They then undertook to verify the inference that this chlorine was yielded by chloroform rather than by chloral. Into their apparatus, in place of chloralized blood, they introduced a solution of chloral. From this they sought by the aid of an aspirator to withdraw the vapor of chloral, which was then to be passed through a heated tube and tested with nitrate of silver. If chloral were thus given off from the solution, it should be decomposed by heat, and its chlorine should precipitate silver chloride from the argentic solution. Nothing of the kind occurred, and the experimenters, consequently, concluded that the chlorine which was identified in the first experiment must have been yielded by chloroform in the blood. That this chloroform was not produced by decomposition of chloral existing in the blood, during the experiment was further shown by treating the blood, which had yielded the chlorinated vapor, with an alkaline solution. If chloral still existed in the blood, it should be thus decomposed, and should yield an additional quantity of chloroform. No such result followed the experiment, therefore it seemed to be certain that chloral, as such, could not exist in that specimen of blood.

Another experiment, performed by Liebreich, seems to prove the transformation of chloral. A rabbit was subjected to a qualified diet until the urine contained no more chlorides. A solution containing one gramme (15.5 grains) of chloral was then injected under the skin of the animal. The amount of chlorine in the injection was about sixty-six centigrammes (ten grains). The urine was collected and analyzed, with the result of recovering 0.05805 of the chlorine. Evidently a portion of that element had been retained by the tissues; but the portion recovered could only have been derived from the chloral. The experiments of Arloing ("Revue des Sciences Médicales," tome XVII., 2e. fasc., p. 748) show that the irritability of the sensitive plant is suspended by the absorption of chloroform through its roots; but a similar absorption of chloral produces no such effect. This is supposed to be dependent upon the fact that the acid fluids of the plant do not permit the transformation of chloral into chloroform, while the alkaline fluids of animals furnish a vehicle admirably adapted to promote such a change.

Such are some of the considerations which have proved to the satisfaction of many that the action of chloral hydrate consists in nothing more than the slow evolution of chloroform in the body. Many weighty names, however, have rallied in defence of the doctrine that chloral acts as chloral, and produces a specific effect as such. Demarquay, Claude Bernard, and others testify to the odor of chloral hydrate in the breath of animals under its influence. Labbée and Goujon could not discover the odor of chloroform either in the breath or in the blood; but they admit that the odor of the blood overwhelms and nullifies that of chloroform. The symptoms that are produced by chloral hydrate are different from the symptoms produced by chloroform. If slowly introduced into the blood of an animal, chloroform produces excitement, sleeplessness, and finally death—phenomena which should be exhibited after chloral if it is gradually transformed into chloroform. But the results of the administration of chloral hydrate are quite different.

According to Gubler ("Dict. Encyc. des Sci. Méd.," *loc. cit.*), if frogs are immersed in the vapor of anhydrous chloral, they become violently excited, and die very quickly. Similar treatment with vapor of chloroform produces speedy relaxation of the muscles and anæsthesia, from which the animal recovers if the dose is not too large. By these experiments the toxic energy of anhydrous chloral has been estimated at ten times the strength of chloroform. This does not seem consistent with the theory of transformation. The albumen of the blood, moreover, has the power to prevent such transformation in its presence. If chloral be mingled with the albuminous serum of the blood or of a blister, no odor of chloroform can be detected. If then a highly concentrated alkaline solution be added to the mixture, the odor of chloroform is at once perceived. In order, therefore, to effect the transformation of chloral with the production of chloroform, it is necessary to secure conditions which cannot exist in the animal economy. The experiment performed by Lissonde, who allowed the blood of a rabbit to flow into a solution of chloral hydrate without the liberation of any chloroformic odor, or any vapor that by analysis could be made to yield chlorine, serves to support the same view of the subject.

Another fact which seems inconsistent with the chloroform hypothesis has been observed. If, to a patient who has taken chloral hydrate, chloroform be given by inhalation, instead of sleep and anæsthesia, a high state of excitement will be produced. According to the transformation doctrine, the inhalation of chloroform would simply be an addition to the chloroform already liberated in the body. A more profound anæsthesia should be the result, if this were the actual process.

Amid all these conflicting opinions it may be admitted that the results of experiment have not always been as luminous as might be desired ; but yet sufficient has been effected to enable us to form a probable theory of the manner in which chloral hydrate affects the animal organism. The symptoms which in the vast majority of cases follow its use are considerably different from the symptoms which follow the inhalation or the ingestion of chloroform. Now, the symptoms which are produced, let us say in the nervous system, are not the result of the activity of that portion of the drug which may be dissolved in the blood. They result from the presence of the active agent in the cells of the nervous tissues. This active agent which enters the cells must be chloral hydrate, unless that substance is decomposed in the blood before it reaches the tissues. But, if it were thus wholly decomposed, the symptoms should be the symptoms due to chloroform alone. Such is not the fact. Having entered the cells, then, as chloral its primary effect must be a specific effect. That we observe as the hypnotic influence of chloral. But once within the cells, the substance, like alcohol, is subjected to the action of oxygen, and is soon broken up into various constituents. Water, carbonic anhydride, and chlorine are certainly to be counted among these products of metamorphosis. Chloroform and formiates may also be formed. If thus produced, of course the chloroform would produce an effect within the cell ; but it would be a secondary effect, and in considerable degree obscured by the action of the chloral from which it was derived. Its effect would be almost as insignificant as the effects of the water, carbonic anhydride, and sodium or potassium formiate, which are also supposed to be produced at the same time. Every excess of chloroform which cannot be oxidized in the cell itself must necessarily be excreted into the blood. As it cannot be oxidized in the blood, whatever amount of chloroform is thus discharged into the blood must seek to escape by the ordinary channels. The pulmonary tissue affords the readiest avenue of exit from the body ; consequently the breath contains the larger proportion of the chloroform that is formed within the body. Hence the result of analysis of the breath. Whenever the blood becomes in any way overloaded with chloral, this less volatile substance may also (as in cases of poisoning) sufficiently charge the breath to be recognized by its characteristic odor. Ordinarily it is retained in the blood until it has reached the tissues, where it produces its characteristic effects, and is transformed into new substances that are better fitted to undergo elimination from the body. It is as correct to suppose that chloral acts upon nervous tissue in its character of chloral, as to suppose that alcohol acts upon the same tissue as alcohol rather than as carbonic acid or water which are formed in the tissues out of the alcohol which has been subjected to their modifying action.

Accidents produced by chloral hydrate.—Like all other substances that are capable of overwhelming the brain, chloral has produced its share of mortality. In August, 1874, Labbée reported more than twenty fatal cases of chloral-poisoning (" Dict. Encyc. des Sci. Méd.," t. XVI., p. 476). He has recorded among these the names of two English surgeons who died after taking the medicine, and he intimates that Sir James Y. Simpson experienced a similar fate. In every instance where an autopsy has been secured, it has been shown that there were serious degenerations or chronic inflammations of the vital organs, such as the heart, liver, or kidneys. Sometimes, also, there has been a concurrent abuse of opium or of alcohol.

Reference has already been made to certain fugitive eruptions upon the skin, which sometimes appear after the administration of medicinal doses of chloral. When the drug has been thus used for a long time, it may produce cutaneous alterations which are occasionally of a more chronic character. Changes similar to those effected by chronic poisoning with ergot have been observed, such as desquamation of the fingers, ulceration at the margins of the nails, painful hyperæsthesia, enfeeblement of the heart, with frequent pulse, dyspnœa, anasarca, and albuminuria. Disuse of the drug soon effected a cure. Other observers have noted the appearance of rashes like measles, lasting three or four days, or like scarlet fever, with sore throat, fever, and desquamation on the fifth day. Such cases, however, are to be received with a wholesome degree of scepticism. More trustworthy are the reports of eruptions like urticaria or erythema, which follow the use of the drug and disappear shortly after its discontinuance. In feeble and cachectic individuals, such as are found among the insane, a purpuric or even scorbutic condition has been noted as a consequence of the continued use of chloral. Various papular and petechial eruptions, with other trophic alterations of the skin, have been remarked under such circumstances. I have observed a chronic conjunctivitis, with redness of the nose and other cutaneous appearances similar to those which are produced by long-continued abuse of alcohol, resulting from ten-grain doses of chloral hydrate, repeated every night for many years. Anstie has reported similar cases. He insists upon the danger of developing a veritable *chloro-mania*, analogous to ordinary alcoholic mania. There certainly is no little danger of producing by the use of chloral a gradual degeneration of the tissues of the internal organs quite similar to the degenerations that are originated by the abuse of alcohol. It is doubtless by its excessive irritation of the various channels of elimination that are produced the chronic inflammations of the skin, kidneys, and bronchial membranes, which follow its long-continued administration.

Therapeutic employment of chloral hydrate.—As a hypnotic agent chloral doubtless surpasses all others. It has been used in all diseases accompanied by sleeplessness.

In cases of insanity of every type, excepting acute general paresis and specific cerebral lesions, it is of the greatest service. In acute mania, if the patient can be made to sleep, his chances of recovery are considerably increased. Accordingly, it is found advantageous to administer the drug freely until sleep is procured.   It is interesting, in this connection, to re-call the fact that it was among the insane that Liebreich undertook those experiments which established the reputation of chloral hydrate as a hyp-notic.   The drug should be administered in considerable doses, every hour in violent cases, every two or three hours if the symptoms are less extrav-agant, until the patient sleeps.   It has been remarked that small doses serve to excite the patient, while large doses produce sleep.   Two grammes (half a drachm) for an enfeebled patient, and four grammes (one drachm) for a vigorous person, are considered sufficiently moderate quantities.   Many physicians prefer to combine with the dose of chloral an adjuvant quantity of morphine and of potassium bromide.   Morphine is especially useful in cases of a melancholic type ; and in cases of violent and incurable mania, opiates should be preferred to chloral.   As a general rule, however, chloral hydrate should be administered in all forms of insanity that are character-ized by sleepless excitement.   Its constant use should always be avoided, especially among insane patients who are enfeebled and cachectic.   If any organic disease or degeneration of the heart, liver, or kidneys is known to exist, large and frequent doses should be employed with great caution.

As a remedy for the wakefulness and mental derangement of delirium tremens, chloral hydrate is without a rival.   It often succeeds in cases where opiates have failed.   It should be given in considerable quantity—two grammes (half a drachm) every hour until sleep is procured.   In cer-tain cases, however, it fails to produce the desired effect.   Violent excite-ment, collapse, and death itself have been known to follow its use.   In this respect the dangers that attend its employment do not differ from the dangers which accompany all active treatment in this disease.   The chronic diseases of the brain, heart, liver, and kidneys, which are so common as a result of chronic alcoholism, will always render delirium tremens a disor-der that is difficult and dangerous to the patient, whatever be the method of treatment.

Spasmodic and convulsive diseases are particularly benefitted by chloral hydrate.   This is no more than might be anticipated from the great power of effecting muscular relaxation which is manifested by this agent.   Nearly every case of nervo-muscular excitement may be relieved by its action, so far as the muscular symptoms are concerned.   Its effect upon the ulti-mate cause of those symptoms is not so certain.

Puerperal eclampsia, for example, finds the convulsive manifestations of the disease suppressed by large doses of chloral ; but death may yet occur in spite of the suppression of the convulsions.   Less prompt than chloro-form in its action, its good effects are more durable.   The medicine should be given in doses of two to four grammes (half a drachm to a drachm), and it should be repeated until the patient sleeps.   This method may be em-ployed even during labor, and the process of parturition will scarcely be hindered.

Infantile convulsions and the convulsions of Bright's disease may be arrested by the use of chloral in doses appropriate to the age of the patient.

Chloral hydrate has been recommended in chorea.   It appears to be more successful than bromide of potassium, and in a certain proportion of cases does undoubtedly shorten the course of the disease.   It is most valuable in the treatment of patients who are in a condition of perpetual agitation that prevents the possibility of sleep, and scarcely permits the acts of eating or drinking.   The administration of large and frequent doses of alcohol, or of chloral, will almost invariably prove successful as a means of arresting the jactitations of the patient during a time sufficient to procure necessary sleep.   By this means the exhaustion of the patient may be prevented.

In like manner chloral should be employed in tetanus.   Administered in conjunction with alcohol and bromide of potassium, it forms one of the safest and most efficient remedies that has ever been used in the treatment of this disease.   Unfortunately, it seems to address itself almost exclusively to the muscular spasm, so that other remedies which tend to modify inflammatory conditions in the nerve-trunks and in the spinal cord should not be neglected.   The great fatigue which results from tonic muscular spasm may be diminished by keeping the patient continually relaxed with chloral.   Liégeois ("Dict. Encyc. des Sci. Méd.," t. XVI, p. 481) has advised the maintenance of sleep by this method during the whole course of the disease.   One of his patients was thus made to sleep for eight days without interruption.   For this purpose as much as sixteen to twenty grammes (four to five drachms) of the medicine have been administered during a period of twenty-four hours.   Such heroic doses, however, are liable to compromise the act of respiration, and to produce a certain degree of danger from asphyxia.   It was in the treatment of tetanus that Dr. Oré, of Bordeaux, made the experiment of injecting a solution of chloral hydrate into the veins.   In a case of tetanus, excited by the crushing of a finger, each day for three days in succession he injected into the radial vein not less than nine grammes (seven scruples) of chloral dissolved in ten grammes (two drachms and a half) of water.   The patient recovered after an illness of seventeen days.   Cruveilhier and other eminent surgeons in Paris attempted the same method of treatment, but their patients did not recover, and *post-mortem* examination revealed the existence of solid blood-clots in the injected veins.

In cases of hydrophobia, chloral hydrate has yielded no satisfactory results.   The same thing may be said concerning its exhibition in epilepsy and hysteria.   It has been highly recommended as an adjuvant to the bromides in the treatment of epilepsy.   For a certain period of time its use is attended with beneficial results, and the quantity of potassium bromide may be reduced ; but at length, in a large proportion of cases, it ceases to control the disease.

Paralysis agitans and the tremors of disseminated sclerosis are not favorably influenced by chloral hydrate.

Hiccough and other allied reflex movements of a morbid character are easily arrested by the drug.

Nocturnal incontinence of urine and seminal emissions may be ranked in the same category.   They may be often relieved, but are seldom radically cured by chloral hydrate.

Chloral hydrate is exceedingly useful as a means of relieving the irregular reflex contractions and the irritations which often accompany the first and second stage of parturition.   Given in doses of one gramme (fifteen grains) every twenty minutes, until three or four doses have been administered, the patient will often pass into a condition of refreshing sleep, which may continue for several hours.   Uterine pains are not thus abolished—they are made endurable.   Sometimes the patient sleeps in spite of the contractions of the womb ; in other cases she may be aroused by the pain, and again falls asleep as soon as it has ceased.   By this method the vigor of the patient is preserved, and the constant attention of the physician, which is imperative during inhalation of chloroform, is rendered unnecessary.   If any of the greater operations of obstetrics are required, chloroform or ether are more convenient than chloral for the induction of artificial anæsthesia.   The after-pains, which so often torment the mother after confinement, may be greatly relieved, if not altogether abolished, by the administration of chloral.

Whooping-cough is another spasmodic disease in which the paroxysms are greatly mitigated by the action of chloral hydrate.   It is principally useful in non-catarrhal cases, especially after the crisis of the disease has been past.   Against the introductory phenomena and against inflammatory complications it possesses very little power.

Asthma is very slightly benefited by the drug.   By its use sleep may be procured, and for a brief period the paroxysms may be somewhat relieved ; but the effect is transitory, and produces no abiding result.

As a palliative remedy in pulmonary consumption, chloral gives great satisfaction.   By its use in small doses the severity of the cough and the colliquative character of the sweats are greatly diminished.   In this respect it soothes the patient and produces agreeable results similar to the effects of opiates.   It fortunately is superior to opium in the fact that its use does not destroy the appetite and disorder digestion.

All forms of bronchitis may be advantageously treated with chloral hydrate.   This is especially true of those cases of copious bronchial secretion which will not tolerate any sudden arrest of the discharge.   Chloral becomes in all such cases an excellent substitute for the opiates which ordinarily enter into the composition of cough-mixtures.   The effect of the drug upon the air-passages is apparently complex in its character.   It is partly topical, by virtue of the constant process of elimination through the mucous membrane, and partly general as a result of the effect of the medicine upon the central nervous system.

Diseases of the heart should preclude the use of chloral in large doses, especially if there be concurrent disease of the kidneys.   But in small doses it may for a moderate period of time be used with advantage to the patient as a means of procuring sleep, and for the diminution of pulmonary hyperæmia and dyspnœa which may accompany certain cardiac diseases.

For the production of artificial anæsthesia in surgical practice, chloral hydrate has been administered by the mouth and by intravenous injection. The first method is not very successful, since the size of the dose which must be employed is sufficient to render it more dangerous than chloroform. For brief operations, especially on children, where it is only necessary to remove a tooth or open an abscess, chloral may be used.   The patient is put to sleep, and the operation is concluded before he can arouse himself.

Intravenous injection constitutes the most effectual method for the induction of artificial anæsthesia by the aid of chloral.   This method is continually employed in the physiological laboratory, with the most satisfactory results.   The animal becomes profoundly insensible, and continues in this condition for a time sufficiently long to permit the performance of the most difficult and protracted experiments.   Emboldened by this observation, Oré, of Bordeaux, treated a case of tetanus by this method with such a degree of success that in the month of May, 1874 ("Dict. Encyc. des Sci. Méd.," t. XVI., p. 488), he again resorted to it in an operation for the removal of a sequestrum from the astragalus of a young man.   In this case he injected eighteen grammes (four and one-half drachms) of a watery solution, containing thirty-three per cent. of chloral hydrate, into one of the radial veins.   The patient soon passed into a quiet sleep without any disturbance of the respiration or the circulation.   After the conclusion of the operation, a few electrical shocks, along the track of the pneumogastric nerve in the neck, served to awaken the patient, who declared his utter ignorance of all that had occurred during the period of anæsthesia.

Two Belgian surgeons (*loc. cit.*) in like manner operated for the relief of a cancer in the rectum of a man fifty-seven years of age.   In this case eight grammes (two drachms) of chloral, dissolved in twenty-four grammes (six drachms) of water, were thrown into the vein.   Three-quarters of an hour elapsed before the patient became insensible.   Anæsthesia was then perfectly established, and he slept twelve hours without waking.

Notwithstanding these successful attempts, the majority of surgeons have not been favorably inclined toward the method.   One of Oré's patients experienced a severe attack of bronchitis after the injection, which may have been the consequence of excessive irritation of the bronchial mucous membrane during the act of elimination of the drug.   In this connection it is well to remember the fact that Vulpian has reported numerous deaths, and, in two cases out of sixty or seventy experiments, hæmaturia and extensive lesions of the kidneys, occurring among the animals subjected to this treatment in his laboratory.   The experience of Cruveilhier, and of other surgeons, previously noted, indicates a source of grave danger in the formation of intravenous clots, and in the production of phlebitis, to say nothing of the risk of death from the direct action of chloral upon the walls of the heart and upon the nervous centres.   The method possesses all the risks that attend the inhalation of chloroform, and is characterized by many additional inconveniences and dangers.

As a local anæsthetic, chloral hydrate is not very energetic.   Certain observers have recorded its efficacy against the pain which is sometimes experienced in wounds and blistered surfaces.   Applied in substance to the nerve-pulp of a carious tooth, it has relieved the pain of tooth-ache.   Vidal has recommended a two per cent. solution of chloral as a lotion for the relief of pruritus.   Richardson praises its virtues as a local application in neuralgia.   The relief which is thus obtained is due in part to its counter-irritant effect, and in part to its intrinsic anæsthetic properties.   Applied to a surface from which the epidermis has been removed, it produces a local anodyne effect similar to the results which are secured by the endermic use of morphine.

As a topical application for the dressing of ulcers of a venereal origin, or any offensive and indolent sore, a one per cent. solution of chloral hydrate has been highly recommended.   Under its influence the surface of the ulcer cleans itself, and begins to granulate.   Since chloral is not a disinfectant, if the discharge from an ulcerated surface or a chronic abscess becomes offensive, the one per cent. solution should be reinforced with one part in ten of an alcoholic essence of eucalyptus.   Martineau has proposed the following formula :

Solution of chloral hydrate, one per cent............ 1,000
Alcoholic essence of eucalyptus.................... 100

The essence is composed of one part of the essential oil of eucalyptus mixed with one hundred parts of alcohol.

In many other forms of local inflammation such solutions have been used with varying degrees of success.   Its good effects are based upon its qualities as an astringent, caustic, fermenticidal, and anæsthetic substance. Its superiority to alcohol and carbolic acid consists in its greater anæsthetic energy—a property which it shares with chloroform.   Its greater solubility and its inferior volatility render it more convenient than chloroform.

For the relief of severe internal pain chloral hydrate is a very uncertain remedy.   It is usually inferior to opiates for this purpose, but it may be substituted for those preparations when they cannot be tolerated by the patient.   Used in connection with opiates, its effects are often very satisfactory.   In the febrile condition it is of very little value as a means of reducing the temperature of the patient.   In sea-sickness and in cholera-morbus it is at least as useful as chloroform.

The effect of chloral upon the blood has suggested its use as an intravenous injection for the radical cure of hæmorrhoid and other varicose conditions of the veins.   For this purpose equal parts of chloral and of distilled water are thrown into the projecting hemorrhoid with a hypodermic syringe.   The pain is very slight, and recovery soon takes place.   Certain accidents, such as phlebitis, abscess at the site of the injection, and local eschars, have followed the employment of this method of treatment.

For the relief of the pain of uterine cancer, chloral has been used in the form of a vaginal suppository, with considerable success.   One gramme (fifteen grains) of the hydrate should be incorporated with each suppository.

In cases of poisoning with strychnia or with Calabar bean, the resulting convulsions may be arrested by the administration of chloral hydrate. These substances are not by any means antagonistic.   The progressive effect of the poison is merely retarded, and the convulsions are abolished. This, however, is a great advantage, for it gains time for the possible elimination of the poison by the emunctory organs of the patient.   We may not from this conclude that either strychnia or Calabar bean are antidotes to chloral in poisonous doses.

The subject of chloral inebriety has recently been treated by Dr. J. B. Mattison ("Proc. of the Med. Soc. of the County of Kings, N. Y.," vol. iv., No. 3, pp. 65–77).   Attention is called to a form of dyspnœa that is produced by long-continued use of the drug. The following case is quoted from Kirn, as an illustration of this effect of chloral.   A prominent physician "was summoned in consultation to a lady prostrated by long sufferings, who had of late suffered from attacks of extreme dyspnœa, which had increased.   At the same time the face was swollen, the facial muscles paralyzed, and there were also all the signs of cerebral effusion.   Every remedy had failed, and the patient seemed on the brink of the grave.   The physicians, therefore, recommended the discontinuance of a daily dose of forty-five grains of chloral, which had been given as a hypnotic, whereupon all these highly alarming symptoms vanished in an almost magical way, the cerebral disturbance ceased, and the respiration quickly resumed its normal type."

Under the prolonged influence of chloral hydrate the pulse becomes weak, rapid, and irregular; the heart beats feebly, and there is a tendency to syncope.   This enfeeblement of the circulation, together with the impoverished condition of the blood, produces imperfect gastric secretion and digestion, so that the phenomena of partial starvation appear.   "Nausea and vomiting come on; the tongue is covered with a whitish fur; the desire for food is variable, deficient, and in well-marked cases almost extinct, the morbid appetite seeming to feed upon itself; the breath is fetid, or gives off an odor of chloroform or alcohol; jaundice appears, though oftener there is a pallid, anæmic look from blood-vitiation; the bowels are torpid—exceptionally relaxed—and the alvine dejections are hard and peculiarly pale."

As an extreme case of the degree of enfeeblement to which the senses of sight and of hearing are liable, may be mentioned a case reported by Dr. Keyser, of Philadelphia. A gentleman who was in the habit of taking "sixty and eighty grain doses of chloral, suddenly became blind. Ophthalmoscopic examination revealed great retinal anæmia. The drug was discontinued, and in a few days sight was restored."

Certain peculiar pains have been described by Dr. Mattison as consequent upon chronic chloralism. These pains resemble neuralgia and rheumatism, but exhibit points of difference in their location. Unlike neuralgia they are not limited to particular nerve-territories. Unlike rheumatism they avoid the joints, and seem to girdle "the limb or finger just above or below them, without pain or pressure, and unaggravated by movement."

The prognosis in chloral inebriety is variable, and generally unfavorable. "The disease is less frequent than opium and much more infrequent than alcoholic inebriety, . . . while the habitual use of opium admits of its gradual increase without risk, so that enormous doses can be taken with impunity, that of chloral is sometimes the reverse, and serious effects have followed the use of a smaller dose than the patient had for some time been accustomed to taking." The proper treatment in all such cases consists in the withdrawal of the drug, and in the substitution of a tonic and restorative regimen.

BUTYL CHLORAL HYDRATE—$C_4H_5Cl_3O.H_2O$.

Trichlorobutaldehydrol, Chloral butylicum, L.; *Hydrate de chloral butylique,* Fr.; *Butylchloralhydrat,* G.

Butyl chloral hydrate, formerly called croton chloral hydrate, is formed by the combination of water with butyl chloral. It may be easily recrystallized from water, forming thin, dazzling white, shining plates, which pertinaciously retain water and melt at 78° (172.4° F.). It is very volatile in a current of steam. Scarcely soluble in cold water, it dissolves readily in hot water and in alcohol. Its vapor is very irritating to the mucous membranes and the eyes (Watts).

Butyl chloral hydrate produces upon animals effects quite analogous to the effects of chloral. It may be used by intravenous injection, with a completely stupefying effect. The animal sleeps profoundly, and the limbs remain in whatever position they may have been placed. The first effect of the administration of this substance is the production of a brief period of excitement. This is followed by drowsiness, and by a reduction of sensibility about the head. The remainder of the animal becomes gradually involved in this loss of sensibility, and finally all consciousness is lost in sleep. The movements of respiration and circulation become restricted, and there is a remarkable depression of the temperature. Fatal doses destroy life by an arrest of respiration. After death, some degree of vascularity about the cerebro-spinal membranes has been remarked, but in general terms the results of post-mortem observation are negative.

Butyl chloral hydrate may be administered to the human adult in doses of sixty-six centigrammes (ten grains) to two grammes (thirty grains). Its persistent, acrid taste sometimes produces nausea and vomiting. This result may also be caused by the hypodermic administration of the drug. Large doses have been known to excite diarrhœa. In the course of a few minutes after swallowing the drug, the patient begins to feel heavy and drowsy, and the sensibility of the face is diminished. Gradually, other portions of the surface become insensible, and sleep is established after fifteen to thirty minutes, without muscular relaxation or any special disturbance of respiration, circulation, or temperature. After awaking, no particularly disagreeable sensations are experienced, and recovery is rapid.

Butyl chloral hydrate is hypnotic and moderately anæsthetic, though not universally analgesic. Its most pronounced effects in the matter of relief for pain are exhibited in cases of trigeminal neuralgia. For this disease it may be given in doses of thirty to sixty centigrammes (five to ten grains) every half-hour until relief is experienced or sleep is induced. For other diseases it may be used as a substitute for chloral hydrate, under the same general condition that should regulate the employment of that drug. The dose should not exceed one-third or one-half the usual dose of chloral hydrate. It is contra-indicated in irritable conditions of the stomach, and in all cases of enfeebled action of the heart. Combined with equal parts of tincture of camphor, it makes an excellent local anæsthetic. Hypodermic use of butyl chloral hydrate cannot be recommended on account of the irritant effect of the solution. Poisoning by this substance must be combated by the application of warmth sufficient to sustain the bodily temperature, and by artificial respiration. Electricity has been recommended, but it should not be allowed to act upon the heart.

METHYLIC ETHER—C_2H_6O.

Methylic oxide, Methylene hydrate, E.; *Éther méthylique, Oxyde de méthyle*, Fr.; *Methyläther, Holzäther, Formäther*, G.

Specific gravity of vapor, 1.617.
Boiling-point, —21° (—5.8° F.).

Methylic ether is a colorless, inflammable gas, with a peculiar, oppressive, ethereal odor, and a pungent taste. It was discovered by Dumas and Peligot, in the year 1835. It may be prepared by distillation from a mixture of one part of methylic alcohol and four parts of sulphuric acid. The ether, as it is evolved, is accompanied by carbonic acid gas and sulphurous acid gas, with a certain proportion of methyl sulphate $(CH_3)_2SO_4$. These gases may be removed by keeping the gaseous mixture for twenty-four hours in contact with slaked lime or with caustic potash. The methyl sulphate is by this process decomposed into methylic ether and sulphuric acid.

Gaseous methylic ether is dissolved readily in water, one volume of the liquid being sufficient to detain thirty-seven volumes of the gas. It is also dissolved by strong sulphuric acid, and still more readily by methylic alchohol, ethylic alcohol, and ethylic ether. The gas is very inflammable; it burns with a pale, but luminous flame. According to Berthelot it may be liquified at a temperature of —36° (—32.8° F.).

Ethylic ether dissolves one hundred volumes of methylic ether, at 0° (32° F.). This solution was recommended as an anæsthetic by Dr. Richardson, in the year 1867. In the month of May, 1868, he inhaled the gas itself. It produced unconsciousness in seventy seconds, and on awaking he experienced no disagreeable sensations by way of after-effect.

When the vapor is administered to pigeons they fall into a quiet sleep without convulsions. Administered to animals in a sufficient quantity of an ethereal solution, it may produce death by paralysis of the nervous centres. Death is preceded by muscular spasms. The respiration ceases before the action of the heart. The lungs were not engorged, but the pulmonary veins and both sides of the heart were filled with dark, fluid blood. Four to eight grammes (one or two drachms) of the solution are sufficient to produce anæsthesia in the human subject. It has been employed in several cases for the extraction of teeth, without any disagreeable symptoms or unpleasant after-effects. The rapidity with which the gas escapes from its solution, and its decidedly disagreeable odor, render it objectionable as an agent for the production of anæsthesia.

ETHER—$C_4H_{10}O=(C_2H_5)_2O$.

Æther, L.; *Sulphuric ether, Ethylic ether, Ethylic oxide*, E.; *Éther vinique*, Fr.; *Schwefeläther*, G.

Specific gravity, 0.723 at 12.5° (54.5° F.).
Boiling-point, 35.6° (96° F.) at 760 mm.
Vapor density, 2.586.

Pure ether is a colorless, transparent, very mobile liquid, having a peculiar, exhilarating odor, and a sharp, burning taste, with cooling after-taste. It is perfectly neutral to vegetable colors, and refracts light strongly. Cooled to −31° (−23.8° F.), it crystallizes in white, shining laminæ. It is very inflammable, and its vapor, when mixed with air, detonates with great violence on the approach of a burning body. As the vapor of ether has a considerable tension at ordinary temperature, and consequently diffuses quickly to a considerable distance, great danger is incurred in pouring the liquid from one vessel to another in the neighborhood of a gas-light or any burning body. The decantation of any considerable quantity of ether should always be performed in a room where there are no lights burning (Watts).

Ether was discovered in the year 1540, by Valerius Cordius, who gave to the new substance the name of *Oleum vitrioli dulce*. Frobenius changed this name to *ether* in the year 1730.

Ether is usually prepared by heating a mixture of alcohol and sulphuric acid. The best method is that introduced by Boullay, in which the alcohol is supplied in a constant stream, and the formation of ether goes on uninterruptedly. Ordinary ether may be completely freed from water and alcohol, and converted into absolute ether, by placing it in contact with lumps of fused chloride of calcium, which takes up the water and alcohol, and rectifying. Absolute ether should form a clear mixture in all proportions with oil of copaiba; ether containing water or alcohol forms an emulsion with considerable quantities of the oil. Ether mixes in all proportions with alcohol, wood-spirit, chloroform, acetone, and many other liquids, and to a certain extent also with water. When ether is shaken up with water, two layers are formed, the upper consisting of ether containing a little water, and the lower of water which has dissolved one-tenth of ether. Ether dissolves iodine and bromine, and small quantities of sulphur and phosphorus; also chloride of gold, chloride of iron, mercuric chloride, and mercuric nitrate. It dissolves with facility most organic bodies containing a large proportion of hydrogen, such as fats and resins, which are but sparingly dissolved by alcohol, whereas it acts but little on those which are easily soluble in alcohol (Watts).

Pure ether is neutral in its reaction with litmus. If it reddens blue litmus paper it contains either sulphuric, sulphurous, or acetic acid. Of these the sulphur acids may be detected by their reaction with a solution of barium chloride. The addition of a solution of an iron salt gives a dark red color if acetic acid be present. The presence of alcohol as an impurity may be suspected if the specific gravity of the specimen exceeds the standard figure. The addition of a solution of potassic acetate, followed by concentrated sulphuric acid, liberates an odor of acetic ether if alcohol has not been entirely removed from the ether. Contained alcohol will produce a red color with crystals of fuchsine, while pure ether remains colorless. The presence or absence of water may be determined by the behavior of ether with tannic acid. If anhydrous, the tannin preserves its pulverulent appearance; otherwise it is transformed into a syrupy liquid below the supernatant ether. The contamination of ether with fusel-oil may be detected by evaporation of the liquid from filter-paper, when the presence of the oil may be readily detected by the characteristic odor which clings to the paper after the dissipation of the more volatile liquid.

The chemical reactions which effect the liberation of ether from alcohol are thus represented:

Alcohol.   Sulph. acid.   Ethylic hydric sulphate.   Water.

$$C_2H_5.OH \; + \; H_2SO_4 \; = \; C_2H_5HSO_4 \; + \; H_2O.$$

The ethylic hydric sulphate thus formed then enters into a reaction with another portion of alcohol:

Ether.

$$C_2H_5.HSO_4 \; + \; C_2H_5.OH \; = \; C_2H_5.O.C_2H_5 \; + \; H_2SO_4.$$

The resulting molecule of ether is removed by heat in the process of distillation, and the liberated molecule of sulphuric acid again combines with the remaining alcohol to form ethylic hydric sulphate. This cycle of changes should, theoretically, continue indefinitely, or as long as the supply of alcohol is maintained. But, as a matter of fact, the acid is rapidly expended in the processes of oxidation and carbonization of the alcohol, so that one part of acid cannot change more than five parts of alcohol into ether.

The physiological action of ether presents very close resemblance to the actions of alcohol and chloroform. Much more speedy than alcohol, and less profound than chloroform, its effects are manifested by the same general order of symptoms, and they result in the same condition of the nervous centres. It will, therefore, only be necessary to dwell at this point upon the peculiarities which differentiate the action of ether from the action of other anæsthetic agents.

It was long since pointed out by Flourens that ether manifests its most conspicuous effects, first upon the cerebrum, then upon the sensory nerves and spinal centres, then upon the motor centres and motor nerves, and finally upon the medulla oblongata. The fact should not, however, be forgotten that while this order of sequences characterizes the greater phenomena of anæsthesia, it does not sufficiently take into account those more intimate phenomena which result from the universal action of the agent upon all parts of the nervous system, including the vaso-motor centres and conductors. This general result has been discussed under the head of the general physiology of anæsthesia, and need not be again considered in full.

Like alcohol and chloroform—in short, like all other anæsthetic substances—ether, by the first contact between its molecules and the molecules of tissue-protoplasm, produces a liberation of motion in the tissues. The effect of this is manifested in the department of circulation by an increased movement of blood in the capillaries. This signifies increased cardiac activity. Soon this increased activity is transferred to the arterial walls, which contract upon their contents. The more energetic the anæsthetic, the more complete the contractions; but in such case the spasm is proportionately less enduring. When chloroform and similar powerful vapors are inhaled in considerable quantity, their paralyzing effect soon produces relaxation of the vascular canal. The heart beats with less energy, the artery contracts with less vigor, the veins become more capacious, the blood lingers in the capillaries and tends to accumulate in the venous portion of the circulatory apparatus. As a consequence, the vascular pressure in the arteries, which may have exhibited an increase at the outset of inhalation, displays a decided fall. When ether is employed, this diminution of pressure is much less notable than when chloroform is used. Ether depresses the action of the heart, and interferes with the circulation of the blood; but this effect is slight in comparison with the result of chloroform inhalation. The English Chloroform Committee found that sometimes the column of mercury in the manometer attached to an artery marked a higher figure during the inhalation of ether than before the administration of the vapor. This was doubtless due to the excitant effect of the anæsthetic upon the walls of the arterioles and the cardiac tissues. During the inhalation of chloroform it was noticed that, after the brief initial rise of pressure, there was a steady fall of the mercurial column. This phenomenon was often absent, or occurred in less degree during the inhalation of ether. The Committee of the British Medical Association (*Brit. Med. Journ.*, pp. 957 to 972, December 18, 1880) observed that the effect of ether upon the heart "is simply to produce a retardation of the impulses" after artificial respiration for five minutes. This committee also verified all previous observations of the comparatively slight effect of ether upon blood-pressure during normal anæsthesia. Death from ether was usually found to result, in the animals subjected to experiment, from failure of respiration. This failure appears to be the consequence of paralysis of the pulmonary circulation, occasioned partly by direct medullary paralysis and partly by a local action of the anæsthetic upon the structure of the lungs. Experimenting with chloroform, ethidene dichloride, and ether, the committee found that these three substances produced identical changes in the lungs. Their experiments were performed upon frogs which had been anæsthetized. Having opened the thorax so as to expose the lung, anæsthesia was maintained by means of artificial respiration of air charged with a definite quantity of the anæsthetic vapor. The process of circulation through the lung was then observed with the aid of the microscope. By this method it was possible both to study the changes which occurred during the whole course of events, and to compare the effects of different anæsthetics. When placed in an atmosphere of ether, eight and one-half minutes were required in which to overcome reflex action. In an atmosphere of ethidene dichloride, five minutes were consumed in the accomplishment of the same result, while in chloroform vapor only two and one-quarter minutes were requisite. "500 c.c. of ether vapor were given (by artificial respiration) before the circulation in the large vessels of the lung could be stopped (time twelve minutes), whilst the capillary circulation required 175 c.c. (time 110 seconds) before any change could be noticed, and 300 c.c. to make it stop completely"—the pulse in the meanwhile having fallen from 24 to $6\frac{1}{2}$ per minute. "The frog was now made to inhale air. When 150 c.c. had been given, the circulation began to be re-established in the larger vessels, the pulse being nine per minute, and, when the air passed into the lungs, amounted to 200 c.c.; the capillary circulation also returned to what it was before the ether was given artificially. Chloroform vapor was now given for 180 seconds to the same frog, with the following results: in fifteen seconds a marked change was observed in the capillary circulation; in thirty it stopped; and in forty-five, the flow through the large vessels ceased."

The comparative results of these experiments are given by the committee in the following table :

	Chloroform.	Ethidene.	Ether.
1. Time required to produce complete stoppage of pulmonary circulation	75 seconds.	180 seconds.	270 seconds.
2. Amount of anæsthetic vapor employed	50 c.c.	250 c.c.	500 c.c.
3. The quantity of air necessary to re-establish circulation in lung	600 c.c.	250 c.c.	200 c.c.
4. Time occupied in restoring the circulation	720 seconds.	240 seconds.	180 seconds.
5. Heart's impulses before artifical respiration	18	23	24
6. Heart's impulses when circulation has stopped	4	7	$6\frac{1}{2}$

The superior safety of ether is fully indicated by every item in this table. Its inferior energy is shown by the relatively large amount of vapor and of time necessary for the production of the given result—arrest of pulmonary circulation. Its safety is illustrated by the relatively small amount of air and of time necessary for the revival of that circulation. The manner in which circulation is arrested in the lungs was thus described by the committee :

"When anæsthetics are administered in excessive quantities, the first change noticed in the circulation in the lung is a diminution in the rapidity of the flow in the capillaries; and this, notwithstanding that the number of the heart's impulses remain unchanged and the circulation through the larger vessels is unimpaired. Very shortly after this, instead of the flow of blood being constant, it gradually becomes intermittent—first in the capillaries, afterward in the arterioles, and subsequently in the larger vessels. This intermission in the flow of blood is followed by a swinging to-and-fro movement of the corpuscles just previously to the stoppage of the circulation through the capillaries. It must now be observed that the stoppage of the circulation in the lung takes place first in the capillaries, then in the arterioles, and, last of all, in the larger vessels; further, that the sequence in recovery is exactly the reverse. Again, it is to be noticed that the circulation in the foot stops—not previously to, but shortly after, that of the lung; and in its re-establishment never occurs before, but always subsequently to, the restoration of the pulmonary circulation."

The cause of these phenomena in the lung is by the committee attributed in part to impairment of cardiac vigor, substituting an intermittent current for the continuous flow of blood which traverses the lungs under normal conditions.   A certain portion of the effect is, however, to be attributed to a local resistance to circulation developed in the pulmonary tissues by the direct action of the anæsthetic substance, changing the ordinary relationship between the blood-corpuscles and the walls of the capillary vessels.   The retarded evolution of similar phenomena in the web of the foot may be explained by the remoteness of that network from the point of gaseous reception and exchange in the lungs.

The effect of ether upon the pulse is best illustrated by reference to sphygmographic tracings taken from any one of the larger arteries of the body.   The following series was taken from the carotid artery of a healthy dog weighing four and one-half kilogrammes.

The dog was properly confined upon his back, July 10, 1880, the right carotid artery was laid bare in the neck, and the sphygmograph was applied.   The tracings were taken as rapidly as the plates could be conveniently adjusted for that purpose.   Ether was administered upon a cloth, and was urged as vigorously as possible, for the avowed purpose of killing the animal.   Death occurred twelve minutes after the commencement of inhalation.   Respiration ceased before the heart stopped.

1.—Immediately before the commencement of inhalation.

2.—Commencement of inhalation.   Animal attempting to struggle.

3.—Profound anæsthesia.

4.—Slight rallying.   Heart weak and irritable.

5.—Continued anæsthesia.

6.—No change.

7.—Diminishing cardiac vigor.

8.—Rapid failure of the heart.

9.—Progressive failure.

10.—Diminishing arterial elasticity, shown by rounding of the apices of the curves.

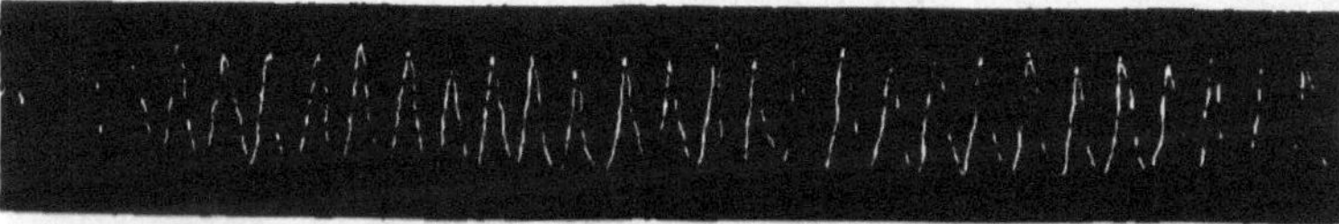

11.—*In articulo mortis.*

12.—Immediately after the final cessation of respiration.

The next series of pulse-curves was taken from the radial artery of a boy, aged eight years, suffering with caries of the hip-joint, for which the operation of resection was performed. The patient breathed the vapor of ether from a towel, and was kept in a condition of insensibility for half an hour.

1.—Immediately before the commencement of inhalation.

2.—Immediately after the commencement of inhalation.

3.—Patient snoring and insensible.

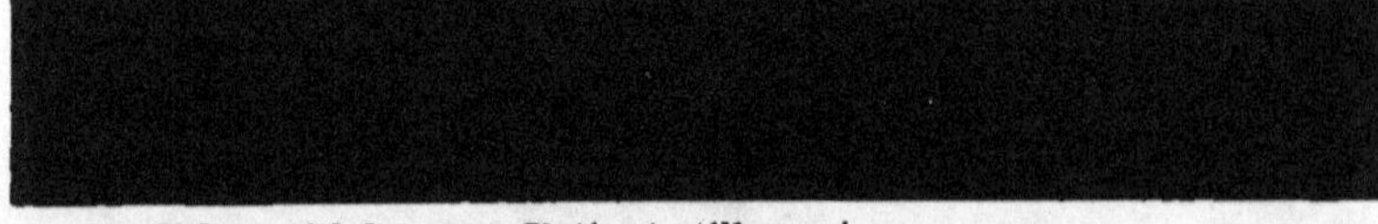

4.—Ether withdrawn. Patient still snoring.

5.—Inhalation renewed. Operation in progress.

6.—Operation still progressing.

7.—Operation concluded. Ether withdrawn.

8.—Still completely insensible.   Exhibits evidence of nausea.

9.—Persistent nausea.

10.—Immediately after vomiting and recovery of consciousness.

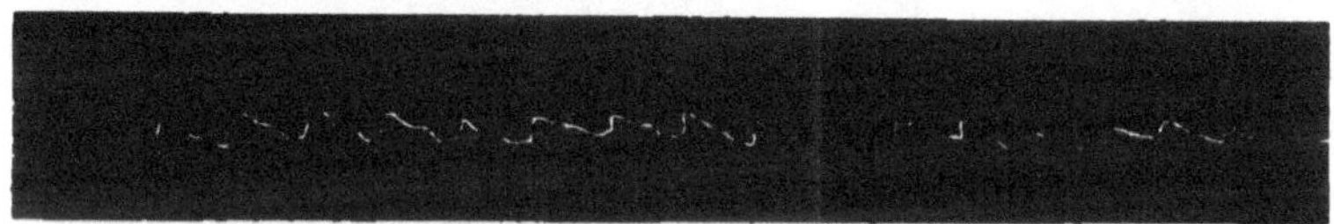

11.—Twenty hours after operation.   Pulse, 130 ; temperature, 100.5° F.

The foregoing series admirably illustrates the contrast between the effects of ether and of chloroform upon the heart and the arterial walls. During the most profound insensibility the ascending branch of the curve maintains its original angle with the perpendicular, showing that the ventricular contractions have lost none of their relative vigor.   The apex of the curve loses none of its natural sharpness, a fact which shows that the succession of movements—contraction of the arterial muscles—is not retarded. The diminished height and length of the curve exhibits the diminished sum of motion liberated during each individual contraction and dilatation of the heart.   The enfeeblement of the circulatory apparatus is further illustrated by the almost total disappearance of the waves of oscillation and recoil when the patient (No. 3) was most profoundly insensible.   The great and speedy improvement in the condition of the organs of circulation is well illustrated by the tracing (No. 4) taken immediately after the readmission of pure air into the lungs, and by the tracing (No. 7) which followed the final withdrawal of the anæsthetic.

Another evidence of the minor degree of depression following the use of ether, as compared with the effect of chloroform, is shown by the redness of the face which so long persists during inhalation of the former agent. Under the influence of chloroform the countenance becomes pale, in consesequence of diminution of the cutaneous circulation.

Respiration is almost invariably disturbed by ether to a degree beyond the corresponding disturbance of the heart.   The initial effect of inhaling an atmosphere well charged with ether vapor is an arrest of inspiration.

The patient feels a sense of suffocation, and snatches at the inhaler, striving to escape from the vapor. The considerable increase of pharyngo-tracheal mucus, which soon follows, frequently excites a cough. Tracheal rattles are frequently audible. The rate and depth of respiration may vary exceedingly, until complete unconsciousness ushers in the stage of deep and regular respirations. When death occurs, respiration almost invariably ceases before the heart is arrested. When death occurs under the influence of chloroform, the reverse may be apparently true. This tendency of chloroform to produce paralysis of the heart is conclusively exhibited by the researches of Schiff, who, in the course of not less than five thousand experiments upon animals, observed great diminution of blood-pressure when chloroform was administered, even though the movements of respiration presented no change. When, on the contrary, ether was employed, there was no special failure of blood-pressure until respiration had been greatly enfeebled and deranged.

The bodily temperature is reduced by the action of ether. Among twenty cases observed by Kappeler the average diminution of temperature was 0.68° C. The minimum fall was 0.3° C.; the maximum was 1.5° C. Among twelve cases uncomplicated by any febrile movement, the average fall was 0.52° C. In thirteen of the nineteen cases, in which the commencement of heat-depression was noted, the mercury began to descend when inhalation had been continued for ten minutes. In five instances fifteen minutes, and in one instance twenty minutes elapsed before any depression was noticed. The shortest time in which the greatest fall was reached was twenty minutes after the commencement of inhalation; the longest time was two hours. It was always remarked that the greatest depression of temperature accompanied the most abundant use of the anæsthetic agent and the most profound anæsthesia. The only cases in which elevation of temperature is observed are presented by patients in whom, for a brief period during the stage of excitement, an increased muscular activity liberates a slight increase of heat.

It is frequently observed that the initial stage of excitement is more protracted during inhalation of ether than when chloroform is used. This, however, depends chiefly upon the amount of vapor with which the respired air is charged. If allowed to evaporate rapidly from a cloth held loosely before the face, much delay and considerable excitement will be thus occasioned. But if the towel be covered with a cone of paper or of leather, or if the inhaling apparatus recommended by Mr. Clover be used, very little delay, and no waste of ether, will be experienced. By this method at least three-fourths of the ether can be saved, and complete anæsthesia can be induced in from two to six minutes. Sufficient saturation of the air which passes into the lungs is all that is needed to cut short the period of excitement.

The condition of the pupils is variable during the progress of etherization. They are not as uniformly and as closely contracted during the period of insensibility as when under the influence of chloroform. There is, consequently, less notable dilatation of the pupils when the patient awakens from the sleep of ether than after chloroform. This is dependent upon the minor degree of paralysis of the oculo-motor nerves, and upon the better condition of the cerebral circulation which is maintained during anæsthesia by ether.

The increase of secretion which is effected by the inhalation of ether is illustrated by the moisture of the skin, which soon becomes apparent, and by the greater discharge of saliva and mucus into the mouth and pharynx.

The increased flow of gastro-intestinal fluids has been already signalized by physiologists.

Vomiting constitutes one of the most disagreeable phenomena in connection with the use of ether. It was observed in twenty-five per cent. of the cases recorded by Kappeler. Children are more liable than adults to this accident. It is very likely to occur if the stomach is distended by a recent repast. It is always advisable, when preparing a patient for operation, to secure an interim of four hours between the last meal and the commencement of inhalation. The food taken at that time should consist of liquids and semi-solids, such as gruel, milk, tea, soft puddings, and well-soaked bread. By this means one of the causes of death from ether—suffocation by the passage of food into the trachea during the act of vomiting—may be almost wholly obviated.

The period of recovery from ether is often marked by distressing symptoms. Vomiting is sometimes very persistent for many hours after the operation. Headache is not uncommon. Great prostration may be usually assigned to excessive loss of blood or to previous disease. Sometimes there is considerable cerebral excitement. The patient may talk wildly, accentuating his remarks with furious gestures and savage grimaces. Hysterical phenomena are not unusual among the gentler sex. But such excitement is generally of brief duration. The patient passes into a state of natural sleep, from which he finally awakes to complete self-control. It may, however, require another day to dissipate all the disagreeable effects of the intoxication. The smell of ether frequently clings to the person for twenty-four hours, or even longer.

Severe and persistent neuralgia sometimes follows the recovery of consciousness after inhalation of ether. Prof. E. L. Holmes states that, when a student, in the city of Boston, his attention was called to this fact by the late Dr. Edward H. Clarke. Since then he has observed three cases in which this was one of the sequelæ. In one instance, a young woman, who had inhaled ether for an operation upon the eye (strabismus), suffered for three months afterward with excessive pain, numbness, and paresis affecting the outer aspect of the left forearm and finger. A middle-aged woman also experienced similar pain in the left arm and shoulder for more than three months. A third female also suffered for a number of weeks in the same way, with severe pain in the shoulder and neck.

The inflammability of ether renders great caution necessary in its employment at night, or in the neighborhood of any incandescent body. It is for this reason that hydrobromic ether, by reason of its comparative incombustibility, has been proposed for operations necessitating the use of the actual cautery. It is recorded that, in several instances, patients and surgeons have been severely burned through neglect of this precaution.

That the inhalation of ether involves a certain amount of danger is true. Death has occasionally followed its use. As already indicated, the principal peril lies on the side of respiration. It sometimes happens that, during the progress of inhalation, the pulse becomes feeble and the countenance grows pale, while respiration assumes an irregular and superficial character. This is a moment of real danger. But, fortunately, the readmission of pure air into the lungs is almost invariably followed by a prompt revival. Such depression very rarely occurs, and it is generally associated with some profoundly exhaustive condition of cachexia. The only instance of this character that ever came under my own observation was the case of a man, twenty-eight years of age, undergoing etherization for the purpose of examination of an encephaloid tumor situated within the rectum. Before the induction of anæsthesia was complete, his muscles became rigid; his face was pale and covered with sweat; the pulse was rapid and almost imperceptible; respiration was exceedingly irregular and superficial. For several seconds death seemed inevitable, but by the aid of artificial respiration he soon revived. In this connection it is worthy of remark that, of the eighteen fatal cases collected by Turnbull, two, and perhaps three, were cancerous patients. Of the thirteen cases recorded by Kappeler, two, and probably three, were also cancerous. My own collection contains four, perhaps five, such cases.

Local application of ether to the surface of the body produces rapid refrigeration, with a sensation of cold, and a diminution of sensibility in the part if evaporation is encouraged. If, on the contrary, the vapor is confined in contact with the skin, considerable burning pain, associated with an erythematous redness of the surface, will be experienced. Applied by means of Richardson's spray-producer, the part may be superficially frozen, so that minor surgical operations may be performed without pain. This method, however, has its disadvantages, which have been discussed under the head of local anæsthesia in general.

Ether may be safely used by hypodermic injection. Thus administered, in doses of two to four cubic centimetres, it is rapidly diffused and operates as a powerful stimulant. Patients may thus be rallied from profound collapse in which the heart-sounds are scarcely audible. This method of procedure is preferable to administration by the mouth in cases of cardiac debility, for the reason that the extreme volatility of the liquid occasions its almost instantaneous conversion into vapor within the stomach. Displacement and compression of the heart thus produced might add to the dangers under which the patient was laboring. Distressing eructations, followed by sensations of suffocation, usually result from the entrance of ether into the stomach. H. C. Wood, for these reasons, recommends its administration in ice-cold water. The hypodermic method, however, avoids all these difficulties, furnishing a stimulant more rapidly diffused than alcohol, and less dangerous than chloroform. This method will be found very useful in all cases of neuralgia associated with great depression, such as angiospastic hemicrania, angina pectoris, gastralgia, renal and hepatic colics, etc. It is exceedingly useful in cholera, and in other diseases which, by reason of frequent vomiting, prevent the administration of restoratives and stimulants by the mouth.

Ether has occasionally been injected into the rectum for the relief of intrapelvic pain of all kinds. Here, again, the rapid vaporization, and the burning sensation excited in the mucous membrane of the intestine, serve to limit its use almost exclusively to the destruction of ascarides.

Theoretically, the use of small doses of ether should facilitate digestion, by exciting the secretions of the alimentary canal; but, as a matter of fact, it has been found that the disagreeable effects of its vaporization in the stomach are more than sufficient to counteract the supposed benefit accruing from its use. The ethers contained in good wine are generally found more beneficial in such cases.

For the relief of toothache, ether is often used with camphor as a local application to carious cavities. Mixed with sweet oil and laudanum, and applied by saturation of a pledget of cotton-wool introduced into the external ear, it is an efficient means of relief in cases of neuralgic earache. Certain cases of deafness dependent upon rheumatic inflammations of the inner ear are said to have been much benefited by the vapor of ether. Hysteri-

cal spasms and contractures may be easily overcome by its use ; and
malingering may sometimes be thus detected.   Whooping-cough has been
arrested by the induction of complete anæsthesia with ether ; and all forms
of spasmodic cough are greatly benefited by its use as an adjuvant to other
remedies.   The local application of its spray by projection against the spine
has been recommended in chorea ; but, thus used, its effects are generally
too evanescent to be of any great value in the treatment of this disease.

CASES OF DEATH CAUSED BY THE INHALATION OF ETHER.

1. A man, forty-five years old, was operated on for cancer of the breast,
after having breathed sulphuric ether, and died during the operation with
evident symptoms of asphyxia.   The ether was inhaled from a Charrière's
apparatus.   "The want of care in administering the ether, which was given
in a manner likely to produce asphyxia, and the insufficient means used for
the restoration of the patient, sufficiently explain the cause of death."
Such is the opinion of the Boston Committee.   Perrin and Lallemand
relate the case with greater completeness ("Traité d'Anesthésie Chirurgi-
cale," p. 250) : The patient, after inhaling the vapor for two or three minutes, became violently excited.   At the same time his respiration was
hurried, and his face was vividly injected with blood.   While endeavoring
to free his mouth from the inhaler, he kept up an indistinct utterance like
that of a drunken person.   At the end of five minutes of such excitement
the skin was still sensitive to the prick of a pin.   He was accordingly made
to inhale as large a quantity of vapor as the apparatus would yield ; and,
at the expiration of ten minutes from the commencement of the inhalation,
the patient was completely insensible.   His breathing was deep and slow,
but not noisy ; his face and the anterior surface of the chest were purple ;
the pupils were dilated and immovable ; the eyeballs were rolled upward
under the upper eyelids.   The inhaler was then removed, and the surgeon
had just made his first incision, when the countenance changed, and the
respiration slackened.   The pulse, then noted for the first time, was full,
soft, and very slow.   Suddenly it ceased to beat, and all was over.
Autopsy, twenty-two hours after death.—The smell of ether pervaded
every portion of the body.   The blood was everywhere fluid, very dark, and
viscous, resembling molasses in the posterior portion of the lungs.   The
anterior portion of the lungs was filled with frothy mucus.   The respiratory mucous membranes exhibited a lively injection ; the spleen was very
soft.—Figuier, Auxerre, France, 1847 ; "Report of the Boston Soc. for
Med. Improvement," October 24, 1861.
2. Male, seventy years ; anæmic.   Gangrenous ulceration of the leg, necessitating amputation.   Ether was inhaled from a jar with an opening large
enough to include the nose and mouth of the patient.   The operation was
completed, but the arteries were not tied when the indications of approaching death were noticed, which shortly occurred, with symptoms of syncope.   There was no hemorrhage.   *Autopsy* negative.—De Oettingen,
Dorpat, Russia, 1847 ; "Report of the Boston Soc.," *loc. cit.*
3. Male, suffering with tetanus.   It was proposed to apply the actual
cautery.   Ether was given by a dentist.   The pulse was good, and there
were no signs of an immediate extinction of life.   In one minute the
patient was under its influence ; in a quarter more he was dead beyond
all efforts to produce artificial respiration or to restore life.   All present

thought he died from inhaling ether.—J. Y. Bassett, Alabama, 1847; "Report of the Boston Soc," *loc. cit.*

4. Female, fifty-three years. Suffering with an osteo-sarcoma of the right upper jaw. She was cachectic and feeble. Ether was given from a sponge placed in a bladder. When anæsthesia was complete, the sponge was removed, and the operation was commenced. After a minute or two respiration suddenly stopped. The pulse could not be felt at the wrist, and the cardiac impulse was doubtful. The face was pale, the eyes were fixed. Artificial respiration and tracheal insufflation produced no effect. The quantity of ether which had been used did not exceed thirty grammes (one ounce). Hemorrhage had been very slight, and no blood had entered the pharynx.—Barrier, Hôtel-Dieu, Lyons, France, September 11, 1852; Perrin: "Traité d'Anesthésie," p. 252.

5. Male, thirty-two years; much addicted to drink. Sustained a compound fracture of the left leg, the tibia protruding an inch. Five days after the accident, delirium tremens appeared. On the second day of the attack the patient's wife was told that he could not live. He was exhausted, bathed in perspiration, and had a feeble and rapid pulse. The delirium was such that the house pupil undertook to etherize him. He made the usual struggle, and had some opisthotonic spasms. The ether had been continued some minutes, when the breathing was noticed to be abdominal, although the pulse was quick and sufficiently strong. Within a quarter or half a minute the pulse suddenly ceased; the lips were not blue, and the head and hands were warm. No efforts to restore life were of any avail. *Autopsy.*—The subarachnoid fluid was more abundant than usual. Brain healthy. Heart soft and flaccid, containing yellow coagula in the right cavities, and a small quantity of fluid blood in the left. No valvular disease. The liver was fatty. The kidneys and other organs were healthy.—Mass. Gen. Hospital, Boston, U. S. A., 1855; *loc. cit.*

6. Female, twenty-seven years, entered the hospital on account of an intense and persistent headache. For four or five weeks she had exhibited a tendency to roll out of bed, invariably to the left side. Inhalation of ether was the only thing that relieved her suffering. It was given in doses of two or three drachms without unfavorable result. Three months after her admission to the hospital, she inhaled ether, as she had previously done. After a few minutes, respiration suddenly ceased, and her countenance became slightly livid, though the pulse continued to beat rapidly and with considerable vigor. Artificial respiration was maintained during seven hours. The pulse remained perceptible for twenty minutes and then stopped. The livid color yielded to a brighter hue for several hours; but, in spite of every effort, the patient could not be revived. *Autopsy.*—The right hemisphere of the brain contained a tumor. The blood was everywhere dark and fluid. The veins of the head contained a considerable quantity of air.—Alonzo Clark, Bellevue Hospital, New York, 1859; *loc. cit.*

7. "A very large, old scrotal hernia had become irreducible. Inhalation of sulphuric ether was resorted to, and, while the patient was under its full influence, the hips being raised, and the head allowed to be forcibly flexed upon the chest, taxis was resorted to. The large mass of intestines very suddenly receded into the abdomen, and just at that moment the patient was noticed to be in a dying condition, from which he could not be recovered."—New York, 1860; *loc. cit.*

Another very similar case, which is probably only another version of the same case, is given (Case No. 23) in the "Report of the Boston Society."

8. Female, forty-eight years; of feeble constitution. Application of a splint for chronic hip-disease. Forty grammes (a little more than an ounce) of ether produced insensibility. Two or three minutes after the inhalation had ceased, respiration became embarrassed, the lips grew pale, and the pulse could not be felt. Lowering the head, and cold aspersion of the face restored the patient, but scarcely had she been carried to her bed, a quarter of an hour after this first syncope, when another attack come on, and in spite of artificial respiration, electricity, etc., she never rallied. *Autopsy.*—The air-passages contained mucosities; the base of the left lung was hyperæmic, the pulmonary tissue itself being impregnated with the odor of ether; the heart was normal, its ventricles empty, its auricles gorged with blood; the nervous centres were healthy, exhaling a slight odor of ether; the spinal cord was compressed by a mass of tuberculous matter, seated in the seventh and eighth dorsal vertebræ. Advanced disease of the hip-joint existed on one side, while on the other, the joint was filled with blood from a recent fracture of the neck of the femur.—Laroyenne, Lyons, France, May 1, 1867; *Med. Times and Gaz.*, p. 633, June 8, 1867.

9. A feeble old man, a drunkard, greatly debilitated by the want of food and shelter, had suffered for several days with a strangulated hernia. After etherization, it was found impossible to return the gut, and herniotomy was decided upon. The patient had been etherized for a considerable length of time, and inhaled badly. Soon after the commencement of the operation, a copious bronchial secretion kept filling his mouth; and, during an effort to expel this a large portion of the bowel was forced out; respiration became labored, the pulse faltered, the mucus could no longer be expelled, and asphyxia was rapidly developed. Electricity, and other restorative measures, were tried in vain, and the patient expired on the table.—Morton and Hewson, Philadelphia Hospital, 1867; *Am. Jour. Med. Sci.*, p. 415, October, 1876.

10. The operation was to be an amputation of the thigh for gunshot wound. An ounce of ether was administered on a small napkin in a bowl, which was placed over the face, and one or two drachms were added every two or three minutes. In about ten minutes anæsthesia was induced, and the ether was withdrawn. Slight sensibility returning, the ether was renewed with the desired effect, and was again suspended. The surgeon then ordered the napkin to be reapplied with a drachm of ether freshly poured upon it. After one or two inspirations the patient ceased to breathe.— Burnham, Lowell, Mass.; *Boston Med. and Surg. Jour.*, December 8, 1870.

11. Male, sixty-eight years, fracture of left femur just below the trochanter. About three weeks after the accident it was decided to apply a plaster-of-Paris splint. Ether was given slowly, and insensibility was complete at the end of about ten minutes. A few turns of the bandage had been made, when respiration became rather frequent and gasping. The pulse, however, was full and regular. The thorax was compressed two or three times, and the breathing again became normal. The anæsthetic was now withdrawn for about five minutes, until the patient began to move, and to exhibit rigidity of the muscles. Ether was again administered, but after a minute or two the pupils dilated and respiration ceased. The heart still continued to beat. Artificial respiration and electricity, though continued during forty minutes, failed to arouse any spontaneous respiratory effort. *Autopsy*, three hours after death.—Blood fluid; brain and membranes normal; a little fluid blood in the heart, base of the aortic valves slightly atheromatous; pleural adhesions over both lungs; lower lobe of right lung œdematous, and in a state of red hepatization; rest of the lung normal,

but somewhat emphysematous; liver small and firm; other organs healthy. Six ounces of ether had been used.—Dunning, Bellevue Hospital, New York, August 20, 1872; *Med. Record*, p. 411, October 1, 1872.

12. Male, fourteen years, strumous, had suffered from repeated attacks of corneitis. Iridectomy was to be performed. Patient was much alarmed by the prospect of an operation. Half an ounce of ether was first given on a sponge in a cone of spongiopilin, closely applied to the mouth and nose. After a few minutes, three drachms more were poured on the sponge. The patient soon began to struggle violently, becoming almost opisthotonic, and his face was intensely flushed. The pulse now became very feeble, and the anæsthetic was discontinued, when, as the pulse improved, the brief operation was performed. Before the eye could be bandaged, the pulse became imperceptible, breathing ceased, and the face grew livid. The tongue was at once drawn out; the calves of the legs were flagellated, and the chest was slapped with a wet towel. This caused the patient to breathe and to cry out lustily, and to kick about upon the table for about a minute; but the pulse did not reappear, and respiration soon stopped again. Artificial respiration and faradization of the phrenic nerve were employed in vain for about three-quarters of an hour. *Autopsy.*—The right cavity of the heart was full of dark fluid blood, the left cavity was nearly empty, the valves were healthy, the muscular substance flaccid; the lungs were hyperæmic, and brightly colored; the brain was normal; all the other organs were healthy.—Royal South Hants Infirmary, October, 1873; *Brit. Med. Journ.,* October 11, 1873.

13. Male, fifty-four years, resection of the jaw on account of caries of the bone. After the patient had been fully etherized, an incision was made over the jaw, and four teeth were extracted. Almost immediately the face became blue, and the patient died, in spite of artificial respiration and electricity. The autopsy gave no information concerning the cause of death.—*Boston Med. and Surg. Journal,* November, 1875.

14. Male, removal of a necrosed portion of the superior maxilla. Two and one-fourth ounces of ether were given. After the patient had become insensible, an incision was carried through the lip, and extended over the upper jaw, when the man became cyanosed, and died. Inversion was performed without effect. Death occurred ten minutes after the commencement of inhalation. *Autopsy.*—No trace of blood in the trachea; the larynx was œdematous; the heart was fatty, and weighed six ounces. All other organs were healthy.—Finnell, New York Homœopathic Hospital; *New York Med. Journ.,* February, 1876.

15. Male, seventy-four years, exceedingly corpulent. Operation for cataract. Ether had previously been given for an iridectomy; on which occasion respiration had been arrested, while the pulse continued good, but pressure on the chest had immediately aroused the breathing again. The patient had a slight bronchial cough, and was asthmatic. On the present occasion Squibb's ether was inhaled from a folded towel in a paper cone, until half a pound had been used, when a violent cough commenced. The face became livid, and respiration ceased. The pulse was also failing. Depression of the head, and artificial respiration immediately restored the patient, and the operation was safely performed. This did not occupy more than two minutes, including the application of the bandage, when it was noticed that the patient had again stopped breathing, and the pulse was very weak. The restorative measures were renewed, and mouth to mouth insufflation was attempted; but at the expiration of about one minute, the sounds of the heart could no longer be heard, and the face was

very darkly discolored. Artificial respiration was continued for an hour and a quarter, without result. No autopsy.—Holmes, Eye and Ear Infirmary, Chicago ; *Chicago Med. Journ.*, p. 411, March 27, 1876.

16. Male, twenty-eight years, railway laborer. Amputation of the femur, for a compound fracture. After the completion of the operation, as the patient was recovering consciousness, he exhibited signs of nausea. Brandy was given him, but this was followed by severe vomiting, and by symptoms of asphyxia. Half-digested food was removed from the mouth without relief, so tracheotomy was performed, and an effort was made to clear out the trachea, but in vain. The patient died of suffocation.—House, Guy's Hospital ; *Brit. Med. Journ.*, September, 1876.

17. Female, adult. Incision of the cervix uteri. Death occurred soon after the commencement of the operation. The autopsy revealed Bright's disease, chronic pleurisy, and obstruction of the pulmonary artery.—Sinclair : *Brit. Med. Journ.*, October, 1876.

18. Female, married. A recurrent tumor of the breast, which had been twice previously extirpated under ether. Ether was administered for the third time, in a conical inhaler. During inhalation the pulse improved in volume and force. About twenty minutes after the operation was commenced, the pulse, which had been failing all that time, became extinct, and the respiration was irregular. Hypodermic injection of brandy, lowering the head, and artificial respiration revived the patient so that she seemed to be conscious, and the operation was completed without ether. After a few minutes she vomited, and died, in spite of every effort to save her.—Robinson, Fayetteville, N. C.; *Virginia Med. Monthly*, April, 1877.

19. Male, sixty-nine years ; much exhausted by a strangulated hernia of three days' duration. Two drachms of ether were administered with Clover's inhaler. He did not take it well, and struggled violently. Air was then admitted freely, but, though respiration continued a short time, the pulse became weaker and finally stopped half a minute before the breathing ceased. The patient had been previously exhausted by vomiting before the operation, and the abdomen was tympanitic. *Autopsy.*—Heart flaccid throughout ; lungs emphysematous ; bronchi filled with muco-purulent matter ; internal incarceration of the intestine.—London Hospital ; *Brit. Med. Journ.*, May 26, 1877.

20. Female, forty-eight years. Cancerous tumor of the left breast. Half an ounce of brandy was given just before the commencement of inhalation. Half an ounce of ether was then poured into the inhaler, which consisted of a bag of muslin covered with a leather case, having a valvular opening at the apex, and another larger one at the lower edge. This was held lightly over the nostrils. She clasped the hand of the surgeon, and almost immediately called out his name in a semi-conscious manner. She then drew two more inspirations, when her face became livid, and the pulse ceased at the wrist. Drawing out the tongue, turning the body on its side, and cold affusions upon the chest, caused several forcible inspirations. These were repeated with diminishing vigor and at greater intervals ; but, in less than fifteen minutes from the commencement of inhalation, all was over. *Autopsy.*—With the exception of a number of small cancerous nodules in the lungs and ovaries, there was nothing to account for the death of the patient.—Geo. M. Lowe, Lincoln, England, November 5, 1877 ; *Brit. Med. Journ.*, p. 692, November 17, 1877.

21. Male, over fifty years ; coal-porter. Strangulated hernia during four days previously. There had been complete obstruction of the bowels and fecal vomiting. About an ounce and a half of ether was given. The

patient came rapidly under its influence without any bad symptoms. During the local examination respiration was regular, and the pulse was good, until about six minutes after the commencement of inhalation, a sudden spasmodic inspiratory sound was heard, as if he were choking. The tongue was immediately drawn forward, but respiration had ceased, though the pulse continued to beat for another half minute. Silvesterism was employed for quarter of an hour, in vain. During the artificial respiration some fecal matter came up into the mouth. *Autopsy.*—Left ventricle contracted, heart healthy ; lungs extremely hyperæmic ; fecal staining of œsophagus and larynx, but no such matters had been drawn into the lungs ; liver healthy ; kidneys slightly granular ; the strangulated portion of the intestine exhibited incipient peritonitis.—London Hospital ; *Brit. Med. Journ.*, May 18, 1878.

22. Male, adult. Injury of the hand, necessitating amputation of the lacerated fingers. The operation was performed under the influence of ether. Shortly afterward, before recovering his consciousness, the patient vomited, and a portion of the vomited matter passed into the trachea, causing suffocation. Tracheotomy was performed, and every effort was made to save the man's life ; but in vain.—Northern Hospital, Liverpool, August 9, 1878 ; *Brit. Med. Journ.*, p. 266, August 17, 1878.

23. Female, forty years ; negress ; five feet six inches tall, weighing two hundred and forty pounds. The dentist was unwilling to use any anæsthetic, but, as she insisted upon taking ether, it was given. The patient was in a state of great nervous apprehension. About one ounce of ether was inhaled, in the sitting posture, from a towel. There was no struggling, and she very quickly became insensible. Ten teeth were then extracted. She soon revived sufficiently to speak, when she spat the blood from her mouth, leaned back in the chair, breathed twice, and then, with a convulsive expiration, ceased to respire. Artificial respiration was continued for an hour. Electricity was also tried. *Autopsy.*—The heart was loaded with fat, but all the other organs were healthy.—L. L. Lewis, dentist, Chicago, U. S. A., 1879.

24. Male, thirty-one years. Empyema. Had twice previously been tapped, when ninety-eight ounces of pus had been withdrawn from the right chest on one occasion and sixty-four ounces on another. The operation was to be repeated June 11, 1880. Ether was inhaled from a sponge. The patient was considerably excited, and grew pale. About three minutes after the commencement of inhalation, respiration became shallow, and the operation was commenced about five minutes afterward. There was an attempt at vomiting, and respiration ceased. The heart continued to beat for two minutes longer. Artificial respiration and electricity did no good. *Autopsy.*—Both lungs were tuberculous ; heart healthy ; right side of the chest contained about three quarts of sero-purulent liquid.—German Hospital, Newark, N. J. ; *Newark Morning Register*, June 16, 1880.

25. Male, sixty-one years. Strangulated inguinal hernia. Had been delirious during the previous night. His pulse was irregular and very feeble ; he had constant vomiting. The pulse became imperceptible, and finally respiration ceased. *Autopsy.*—The heart-substance was slightly fatty, the cavities were nearly empty, no clots ; lungs emphysematous, all the posterior parts engorged with blood.—St. Bartholomew's Hospital, 1880 ; *Brit. Med. Jour.*, p. 103, January 15, 1881.

26. Male, forty-seven years. Suffering from intestinal obstruction, for which lumbar colotomy was undertaken. In the morning he had a severe attack of dyspnœa. The official administrator of anæsthetics objected to

the use of ether, but his advice was not adopted.   At the time of the operation (4 P.M.) the patient was in a state of profound collapse, with a tumid belly, shallow respiration, and feeble pulse.   He vomited frequently, and, after inhaling ether for ten minutes, became livid and never rallied.—Mills, St. Bartholomew's Hospital; *Brit. Med. Jour.*, p. 103, January 15, 1881.

27. I. N. D., male, fifty-nine years ; with a well-defined arcus senilis. An old inguinal hernia had become strangulated the night before.   This had excited constant vomiting, by which the patient was much exhausted. His countenance was haggard, and his abdomen was greatly distended, causing considerable dyspnœa.   Six ounces of ether were administered on a towel, and were taken without excitement.   When the patient had become insensible an attempt to reduce the hernia by taxis was made without success.   The body was then inverted for the purpose of effecting reduction, but this method also failed.   During inversion the countenance became very darkly discolored.   On restoring him to the horizontal position, the distention of the belly seemed to have been considerably increased, and respiration immediately ceased.   Death occurred suddenly, about ten minutes after the commencement of inhalation.   No autopsy.—Buchan and Strong, Chicago, March, 1881.

Of these 27 cases of sudden death from ether, 19 were males, 7 were females, and the sex of one was not recorded.   In 5 cases the ether was administered with an inhaling apparatus of more or less complicated character.   The years of 19 patients, whose age was specified, were : 14, 27, 28, 31, 32, 40, 45, 47, 48, 48, 50, 53, 54, 59, 61, 68, 69, 70, 74. Another was mentioned as a feeble old man.   The great majority of the patients were far advanced in life.   The most formidable danger in connection with the anæsthetic springs from obstructions of the intestinal canal.   Seven deaths occurred during an attempt to relieve strangulation or obstruction of the bowels.   Malignant neoplasms rank next as reducing the power of resistance to ether : in four such cases etherization proved fatal ; and, if the cerebral tumor in the patient of Alonzo Clark was also of this character, the evidence is correspondingly increased.   In tetanus and delirium tremens, ether is probably as dangerous as chloroform.   Each numbers a death from its administration during the profound depression of the disease.   It is evident that any previous condition of exhaustion is to be feared, especially if it be the result of conditions likely to interfere with the function of respiration.

Death, in the majority of deaths from ether, is produced by one of the varieties of asphyxia.   In two instances this was occasioned by the passage of vomited matters into the trachea.   In at least one other case it was the consequence of excessive mucous secretion into the bronchi.   As a general rule, however, it results from direct paralysis of the respiratory centres. The heart often continues to beat for some time after the patient has ceased to breathe.   In this persistence of the movements of the heart consists one of the principal differences between the action of ether and of chloroform. Ether kills by paralysis of respiration, and then only when the respiratory apparatus has been already enfeebled ; while chloroform strikes down the heart at almost the same instant with the respiratory apparatus, even in cases where no apparent defect of vigor has ever been discovered.

Besides the possibility of sudden death from the direct action of ether, another danger attaches to its employment in certain cases.   After the immediately anæsthetic effects have disappeared, the patient may become delirious or comatose, or suddenly asphyxiated, and the case may result fatally a number of hours after the operation. The following series of cases will serve to illustrate this mode of lingering death. In connection with the preceding list, they also place in a very clear light the dangers which attach themselves to the use of ether in aged and feeble persons, especially if suffering from any accidental cause which tends to reduce vitality and to embarrass respiration. For this reason, doubtless, the administration of ether to elderly patients with a tendency to bronchial catarrh must always be attended with hazard, on account of its stimulant effect upon the mucous glands, producing obstruction of the bronchi. It is not yet possible to assert that ether is more dangerous than chloroform to old people ; but certainly it is evident that its risks increase with the age of the subject to a degree which is by no means as conspicuous in the case of the more potent anæsthetic.   .

1. Male, eighty-four years ; feeble. Had suffered an apoplectic attack about ten years previously. Inhaled ether for the extirpation of several cancerous glands in the neck. The operation occupied about twenty minutes, during which ether was given intermittently. Very little blood was sacrificed. After the operation the patient seemed to be in a good condition. Pulse, 80. Countenance somewhat cyanotic. He never fully recovered consciousness, but remained in a dazed and somnolent condition, becoming comatose after the expiration of eight hours. The right arm exhibited signs of paralysis, with convulsive movements of the right side of the face, afterward involving the right arm. The eyeballs were rolled up to the left. Death occurred, in this condition, forty hours after the operation. *Autopsy.*—The residuum of an old clot in the right hemisphere, but no other change in the brain ; the left carotid was patent ; the kidneys were contracted.—Hutchinson : *Brit. Med. Jour.*, March 1, 1873.

2. Male, an old man, weak, but not excessively so. Had undergone an operation which lasted three-quarters of an hour. Five hours afterward he had a violent attack of dyspnœa, and died. Food was found in one of the bronchial tubes. (A similar case had occurred some time previously. A fat woman, while lying on her back, under ether, vomited, and some of the vomitus, getting into the trachea, killed her).—Cabot, Boston, Mass. : *Boston Med. and Surg. Jour.*, May 29, 1873.

3. Male, nineteen years ; a telegraph operator. Had partial anchylosis of the right knee, and posterior spinal curvature with great prominence of the sternum. Tenotomy and forcible extension of the limb were effected under the influence of ether, June 3, 1876. About three ounces were used on a towel. The patient inhaled well and quietly ; there was no vomiting ; the respirations were not labored ; and on removal of the napkin he rapidly recovered consciousness, after having been under the influence of the anæsthetic for about twenty minutes. About fifteen minutes later, at 12.30 P.M., he suddenly exhibited the symptoms of asphyxia ; pulse moderately full, 160 ; respiration nearly ceased ; surface cyanosed, especially in the face and at the tips of the fingers. The tongue was at once depressed, and cold water was dashed on the chest, producing violent respiratory efforts. At 1 P.M. his condition was much the same, with evidences of pulmonary engorgement, the throat being constantly filled with frothy blood-stained mucus. The action of the heart was labored. Eight ounces of blood were taken from the radial artery, and dry cups were applied to the chest. This produced a slight improvement in respiration, and the pulse fell from 160 to 152 ; but at 1.45 the patient was evidently sinking, and he died at 2 P.M. *Autopsy*, twenty-one hours after death.—Abdominal viscera normal ; the

pleural cavities contained a considerable amount of serum, included in the meshes of an old inflammatory network of adhesions; considerable serum escaped from the lungs during their removal; both lungs were moderately crepitant, and pitted deeply on pressure everywhere, yielding on section a great quantity of frothy and bloody serum; there was no solidification or deep congestion of their tissues, every part floating in water; blood fluid; considerable clear serum in the pericardium; heart quite healthy; no foreign substances in the trachea or bronchi.—Morton, Pennsylvania Hospital, June 3, 1876; *Am. Jour. Med. Sci.*, p. 411, October, 1876.

4. Female, thirty-five years. Suffering with contracted knees, for which forcible extension was performed, October 4, 1877. Ether was given, with Ormsby's inhaler, at 12.45 P.M. Very little was used, and anæsthesia was procured without unfavorable phenomena. The operation was completed, and the patient was carried to her bed. After this she roused up, and spoke to the nurse, who noticed nothing unusual about her. At 2.45, about one hour and a half after her return to the ward, she suddenly became cyanotic and pulseless, with *râles* all over the thorax. All attempts to rally her were fruitless, and she died at 4.15 the same afternoon. *Autopsy*, the following day, exhibited some œdema of the membranes of the brain; no thrombosis of the pulmonary artery; heart healthy, containing a little blood in the right auricle; ventricles contracted; lungs pale and œdematous; other organs healthy.—Saundby, General Hospital, Birmingham; *Brit. Med. Jour.*, October 13, 1877.

5. Female, twenty-six years. Fibrous anchylosis of the hip-joint. She had previously taken ether without ill effects, and her viscera were all healthy. She took between two and three ounces of ether, and the operation was safely performed. She did not rally from the anæsthetic, however, and, notwithstanding the use of stimulants, an hour and a half after etherization commenced she died. The autopsy revealed nothing abnormal.—J. R. Levis, Jefferson College Hospital, Philadelphia; *Medical Record*, p. 251, February 26, 1881.

This tendency of ether thus, in certain instances, to produce lingering death, probably belongs, though perhaps in lesser degree, to other anæsthetic agents. The following case of death after chloroform seem to manifest similar characteristics, though easily open to sceptical objection.

Male, twenty months. Had suffered with symptoms of stone in the bladder since birth. Was pale, emaciated, and in the habit of drinking gin and porter in considerable quantity. After treatment for six weeks in the hospital, he presented the appearance of a healthy child. Half a drachm of chloroform was administered on a sponge, and was inhaled for a minute and a half. He then became suddenly comatose, snoring loudly; respiration slow, but regular, as was also the pulse. The chloroform was at once withdrawn, and was not renewed. Scarcely any blood was lost in consequence of the operation. He continued asleep for twenty minutes, and was then roused by applying cold water to the face. He, however, continued pale, depressed, and languid. He rallied slightly toward evening, but still appeared more depressed than he should from the small amount of blood lost. On the evening of the day following the operation there was more reaction. He took nourishment, and slept a good deal through the night. After taking some milk at about six o'clock, he went to sleep again, and was found snoring at seven. He could not be roused, and speedily passed into a state of profound coma. In spite of everything he soon died. *Autopsy.*—The head could not be examined ; all the abdominal viscera were healthy, except the kidneys, which were pale, bloodless, and damaged by interstitial fibrinous deposit, both in the cortical and medullary portions. The incisions of the operation were correctly placed, and with the adjacent tissues were in a healthy condition.—Le Gros Clarke, St. Thomas's Hospital, September 24, 1853 ; *Lancet*, June 20, 1857.

METHYLAL—$CH_2(OCH_3)_2$.

Specific gravity. 0.8551.
Boiling-point, 42° (107.6° F.).
Vapor density, 2.625.

Methylal is a limpid liquid, smelling like acetic acid. It is a product of the oxidation of methylic alcohol. It dissolves in three volumes of water, and is separated therefrom by potash; it is also soluble in alcohol and ether (Watts).

Richardson has expressed the opinion, based upon his experiments, that on account of its very rapid evaporation, and by reason of the less agreeable quality of its effects, methylal must be ranked inferior to chloroform.

ALDEHYDE—C_2H_4O.

Ethaldehyde ; Acetic or *Ethylic Aldehyde.*

Specific gravity, 0.801 at 0° (32° F.).
Boiling-point, 22° (71.6° F.).
Vapor density, 1.532.

Aldehyde is a volatile liquid, produced by the oxidation and destructive distillation of alcohol and other organic compounds. It is a thin, transparent, colorless liquid, having a pungent, suffocating odor. It does not redden litmus, even when it is dissolved in water or alcohol. Very inflammable, it burns with a blue flame. It mixes in all proportions with water, alcohol, and ether. It dissolves sulphur and phosphorus, also iodine, forming a brown solution.

Aldehyde possesses very energetic anæsthetic power. Three to five cubic centimetres (thirty-six to sixty grains) injected in watery solution into the veins of a medium-sized dog produce almost immediate insensibility and arrest of respiration. Small quantities of the vapor accelerate the respiratory movements, while large doses arrest them. The action of the heart is not proportionately disturbed. Death is preceded by dilatation of the pupils. From moderate inhalation of the vapor, recovery is rapid, without vomiting or other disagreeable symptoms. Administered to human beings, anæsthesia is produced in about two minutes ; but the irritation of the air-passages, and the persistent sense of constriction about the chest, with a marked tendency to respiratory arrest, which accompany its use, have marked aldehyde as a disagreeable and dangerous anæsthetic.

ACETONE—C_3H_6O.

Dimethyl Ketone.

Specific gravity, 0.814 at 0°.
Boiling-point, 56.3° (133.3° F.).
Vapor density, 2.0025.

Acetone is a limpid, very mobile liquid, possessing an agreeable odor, and a biting taste like that of peppermint. It is very inflammable, and burns with a white flame, without smoke. It mixes in all proportions with water, alcohol, ether, and many compound ethers. It does not dissolve potash or chloride of calcium. It dissolves many camphors, fats and resins.

Acetone may be prepared by various processes. It may be obtained by passing the vapor of acetic acid through a red-hot tube ; or by heating gum, sugar, tartaric acid, and other vegetable substances in contact with lime. It may be obtained perfectly pure by distillation at a moderate temperature from barium acetate or calcium acetate (Watts).

Acetone was originally used for the relief of chronic pulmonary affections. Sir James Y. Simpson found that inhalation of its vapor produced dyspnœa and irritation of the air passages. Though possessing in some degree soporific qualities, the disadvantages which accompany its use are too considerable to admit of its employment. Administered to frogs by the Committee of the British Medical Association, it produced only a slight degree of anæsthesia.

FORMIC ETHER—$C_3H_6O_2,=C_2H_5CHO_2.$

Ethylic formiate, E. ; *Æther formicus,* L. ; *Éther formique,* Fr. ; *Ameisenäther* G.

Specific gravity, 0.944 at 0° (32° F.).
Boiling-point, 54.9° (130.2° F.).
Vapor density, 2.593.

Formic ether is a thin, transparent, and colorless liquid, having a strong, agreeable odor like that of peach-kernels, and a strongly aromatic taste. It burns with a blue flame, yellow at the edges. It dissolves in nine parts of water at 18° (64.4° F.) ; absorbs moisture quickly from the air, and is slowly decomposed thereby into alcohol and formic acid ; it must, therefore, be kept over calcium chloride.

This ether, isomeric with propionic acid and acetate of methyl, was discovered by Afzelius of Upsal, in 1877. It is obtained by distilling alcohol with strong formic acid, or formiate of sodium and sulphuric acid, and by the decomposition of oxalic ether (Watts).

Byasson, who experimented upon the lower animals with this preparation, supposed that it was decomposed in the blood, by the alkaline constituents of that fluid, into alcohol and alkaline formiates. Inhalation of its vapor lowers the temperature as much as 3.5° (5.4° F.), causes muscular relaxation and anæsthesia, with some degree of asphyxia. Its effects resemble those produced by chloral hydrate rather than the effects of an ether. Upon the human subject the use of six or eight grammes (one drachm and a half to two drachms) only caused drowsiness, without any other sympton.

ACETIC ETHER—$C_4H_8O_2 = C_2H_3C_2H_3O_2$.

Æther aceticus, L. ; *Ethylic acetate, Ethyl acetate*, E. ; *Éther acétique*, Fr. ; *Essigäther*, G.

Specific gravity, 0.91046 at 0° (32° F.).
Boiling-point, 74.3° (165.7 F.).
Vapor density, 3.06.

Acetic ether is a colorless liquid, having a pleasant ethereal odor, a cool aromatic taste, and a neutral reaction. It burns with a yellowish flame, giving off the odor of acetic acid, and leaving that acid in the liquid state. It dissolves in eleven or twelve parts of water at ordinary temperatures, and in all proportions of alcohol and ether. Acetic ether was discovered by Lauragais in 1759. It may be prepared by heating alcohol with acetic acid, or with an acetate and strong sulphuric acid, or by distilling ethyl-sulphate of calcium or potassium with glacial acetic acid (Watts).

Acetic ether has the advantage over sulphuric ether in being less inflammable. The experiments of H. C. Wood indicate that it has the power to produce complete anæsthesia in pigeons and rabbits with less struggling than when sulphuric ether is used. Kappeler has recorded a number of cases in which this variety of ether was administered to man. The experience of Tracy was entirely opposed to its employment, and Sigmund and Bouisson found it less agreeable and efficient than sulphuric ether.

The death of animals which are killed with acetic ether is preceded by diminution of temperature, dilatation of the pupils, arrest of respiration, and cessation of the circulation. The results of post-mortem inspection are purely negative.

NITROUS ETHER—$C_2H_5NO_2$.

Ethylic nitrite, E. ; *Éther nitrique*, Fr. ; *Salpeteräther*, G.

Specific gravity, 0.947.
Boiling-point, 18° (64.4° F.).
Vapor density, 2.627.

This ether was first observed by Rumkel in 1681 ; but its composition was first exactly determined by Dumas and Boullay. The safest method of preparing it consists in the distillation with starch, or sugar, or with copper turnings of equal volumes of alcohol (sp. gr. 0.83) and nitric acid (sp. gr., 1.36). The acid should be gradually added, and as the reaction is liable to become very violent, no external heat should be applied after the process has once commenced. The vapors which are evolved contain hydrocyanic acid ; they should be transmitted through a washing-bottle containing water, then through a long bent tube filled with calcic chloride, and finally should be condensed in a flask cooled with ice (Miller).

Ethylic nitrite is a yellowish liquid, having an agreeable odor like that of apples. It mixes in all proportions with alcohol, but requires forty-eight parts of water for the solution of one part of ether. It is easily decomposed, especially in contact with water, giving off nitric oxide, and often bursting the container (Watts).

A solution of ethylic nitrite in alcohol constitutes the sweet spirits of nitre which are so popular in medical practice.

Ethylic nitrite was tested by the Committee of the British Medical Association. They affirm that it produced "great excitement and convulsions, almost immediately followed by cessation of respiration."

NITRIC ETHER—$C_2H_5NO_3$.

Ethylic nitrate, E.; *Éther azotique*, Fr.; *Æthylnitrat*, G.

Specific gravity, 1.112 at 17° (62.6° F.).
Boiling-point, 85° (185° F.).
Vapor density, 3.094 at 90° (194° F.).

Ethylic nitrate is a colorless liquid, of an agreeable odor, and a taste at first very sweet, but followed by a bitterish after-taste. It is insoluble in water, but mixes in all proportions with alcohol and ether. It burns with a white flame; its vapor, if heated above the boiling-point, explodes violently on the approach of a light (Watts).

Ethylic nitrate may be formed, after the method of Millon, by gently heating together one volume of nitric acid (sp. gr., 1.40) and two volumes of alcohol (sp. gr., 0.842) with a small quantity of nitrate of urea, added to prevent the formation of nitrous acid. The entire quantity of the mixture should not exceed one hundred and fifty cubic centimetres (four to five ounces). The receiver should be changed as soon as the alcohol which first comes over is followed by nitric ether, and the distillation should be stopped as soon as the residue is reduced to one-third of the original mixture. The ether thus obtained is washed with aqueous potash, and afterward with water, then, after contact for two days with calcium chloride, it should be decanted and rectified.

Sir J. Y. Simpson found that the inhalation of the vapor of fifty or sixty drops of this ether was sufficient to produce a very speedy anæsthesia. The subsequent headaches and disagreeable after-effects were of so serious a character as to condemn it as an agent for the induction of anæsthesia.

AMYLIC NITRITE—$C_5H_{11}NO_2$.

Amylum nitrosum, L.; *Amylo-nitrous ether, Nitrite of amyl*, E.; *Azotite d'amyle*, F.; *Amylnitrit*, G.

Specific gravity, 0.877.
Boiling-point, 96° (205° F.).

Amylic nitrite, or nitrite of amyl, was discovered in 1844 by the French chemist, Balard, but was first brought into notice by Guthrie, in 1859. Since then it has been made a subject of investigation by Richardson, 1863–4 and 1870; by Rutherford, Gamgee and Brunton, 1869; H. C. Wood, 1871; Pick, 1873; Ladendorf, 1874; Bourneville, 1875; and also at various times by Hoffmann, Eulenberg and Guttmann, Filehne, Urbantschich, Amezdroz, and others. It is a clear, colorless liquid, which after long standing upon the shelf of the apothecary may acquire a slightly yellow tinge. It has a peculiar, though not disagreeable odor, suggestive of apples and bananas. Its specific gravity is 0.877, and it boils without decomposition at 96° (205° F.). Almost wholly insoluble in water, it dissolves readily in alcohol and ether. If it be added, drop by drop, to caustic potassa heated to fusion, valerianate of potassium will be formed, frequently with the production of flame. It may be considered pure if its physical properties agree with the above, and the boiling-point does not rise above 100° (Maisch).

Amylic nitrite is prepared by heating purified amylic alcohol with an equal quantity of nitric acid.

Dr. B. W. Richardson, in his report to the British Association for the Advancement of Science, stated that amylic nitrite is absorbed by the bodies of animals, however introduced. Its first effect is noted upon the circulatory apparatus—the heart beats violently, the smaller vessels are widely dilated. This powerful excitement of the circulation is succeeded by diminution of the cardiac energy and contraction of the terminal vessels. Frogs exposed to the vapor of amylic nitrite pass into a state of suspended animation from which they very slowly recover after removal of the stupefying agent. In warm-blooded animals the movements of respiration and of circulation may be so reduced by the nitrite of amyl, that they shall pass into a condition closely resembling the state of trance in the human subject. The effects of the substance are most conspicuous upon the motor apparatus of the body—especially upon the vascular motor apparatus. Its effects on the power of sensation are not as early apparent, hence the substance is often considered to be destitute of anæsthetic properties. Consciousness, however, may disappear before death from its use. Its action is directly addressed to the molecular constituents of the body, affecting the movements of oxygen in a manner quite analogous to the action of chloroform or ether. Upon the nervous system its effects are progressive from the periphery toward the centre.

The experiments of Dr. Brunton, led him to the belief that amylic nitrite diminishes the blood-pressure by a local effect upon the walls of the smaller arteries.

H. C. Wood, of Philadelphia, showed that amylic nitrite diminishes motor energy, and reflex excitability. The sensory functions are also depressed, though not abolished until near death. The same thing is true of consciousness. Blood-pressure is diminished by paralysis of the walls of the vessels, and by a directly depressing effect upon the heart itself. The blood itself assumes a peculiar brownish hue throughout the body. The temperature falls—in one case as much as 6.66° (12° F.) without the occurrence of death. Ladendorf found that in man the temperature was elevated by the action of amyl nitrite. Among thirty-four cases under observation, the smallest increase was 0.1° the greatest increase was 1.88° (3.38° F.), and the mean was 0.39° (0.7° F.).

Bourneville found the temperature of rabbits invariably lowered—sometimes as much as 2° (3.6° F.). The cause of this discrepancy between the effects upon man and the lower animals, is undoubtedly due to the smaller relative dose administered to the human subject.

The effects of amylic nitrite, like that of all other similar substances, are generalized throughout the system. Local effects and general effects concur, so that it is sometimes difficult to assign each particular symptom to an exclusive change in either the central or the peripheral nervous system. It is certain, however, that amylic nitrite is a depressing agent, and that the symptoms of excitement which follow its use are secondary consequences of an increased supply of blood to the nervous centres. This subject has been so fully discussed in connection with the general theory of anæsthesia, that it need not be here reviewed.

For purposes of inhalation three or four drops of the liquid may be allowed to evaporate from a handkerchief, placed about one inch from the face. Intense redness of the skin of the face, and even of the neck and upper portion of the body, is almost immediately produced. A sensation of general warmth is now experienced, with a feeling of fulness or dizziness about the head. The heart beats violently, and the rate of the pulse is accelerated. Arterial tension and the normal dicrotism of the pulse are at first greatly diminished, but are increased as the primary effect passes off, as may be discovered by examination of the following sphygmograms, taken from the radial artery of a vigorous young man, 23 years of age, and weighing 160 lbs. :

No. 1.—August 9, 1880.   Normal pulse, 84 per minute.

The vapor of five drops of amyl nitrite was now inhaled from a handkerchief, with the following result :

No. 2.—Four drops more were now added to the original five, and the tracings were taken at intervals of half a minute till the end of the experiment.

No. 3.—Pulse considerably accelerated.   Quality improved.

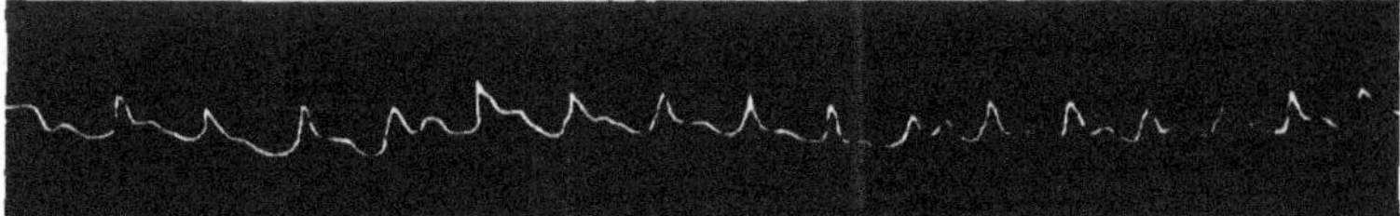

No. 4.—Feels giddy.   Face flushed.   Pulse, 132.

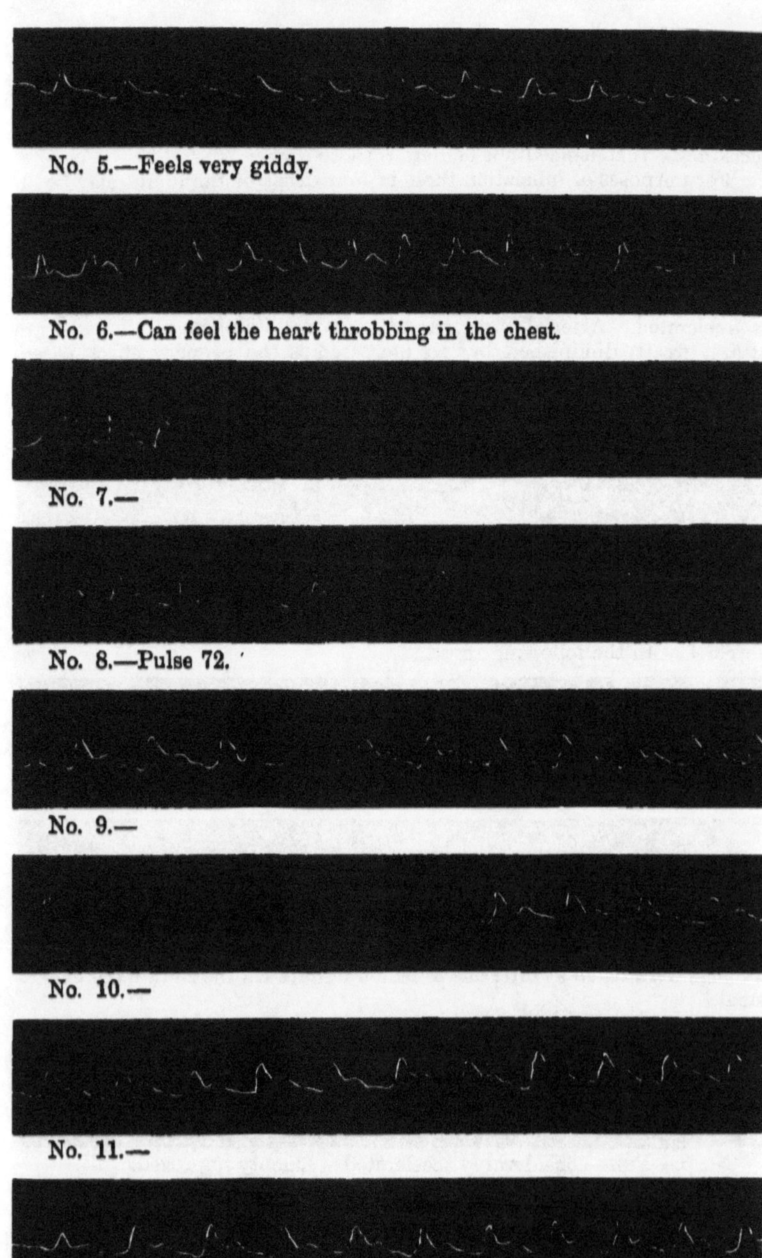

No. 5.—Feels very giddy.

No. 6.—Can feel the heart throbbing in the chest.

No. 7.—

No. 8.—Pulse 72.

No. 9.—

No. 10.—

No. 11.—

No. 12.—The patient feeling perfectly natural again, the experiment was discontinued.

The above tracings indicate a lesser degree of vaso-motor paresis than is produced by chloroform. The sharpness of the graphic cones, and the speedy return of dicrotism, indicate the action of something more than mere elasticity of the vascular walls. Gospey, of Heidelberg (*Med. Record*, February 28, 1880), has shown by his experiments on curarized frogs that amylic nitrite affects both the arterial and the venous system. The dilatation of the vessels amounts to about one-third of the original diameter. The rapidity of the blood-current is at first somewhat accelerated, but it soon falls back to the normal point. In the web of the foot, dilatation is not so marked as in the tongue, and the blood-current, which is at first more rapid, becomes slower, and sometimes ceases altogether. Vessels that have been divided and have ceased to bleed, begin again to discharge blood when amyl is inhaled. The migration of white blood-corpuscles is not affected by the inhalation.

The stimulation of the circulation which thus occurs is not a permanent effect, but is analogous to the early effect of other anæsthetics upon the heart and blood-vessels.

Delicate and susceptible persons may sometimes become unconscious, or may fall into a condition of syncope as a consequence of inhalation of amylic nitrite. It is not an uncommon thing to notice the occurrence of cough and of a prickling, disagreeable sensation in the fauces. The respiration is hurried and somewhat irregular.

I have not found any record of death from the use of amylic nitrite, but there is no reason why it should not produce a fatal result if employed in sufficient quantity. Animals can be killed by its use. Death may be preceded by convulsions. The action of the kidneys may also be increased, and Hoffmann has discovered as much as two per cent. of sugar in the urine of rabbits.

The therapeutical employment of amylic nitrite is indicated in those diseases which are characterized by the existence of a spasmodic or excessively tonic contraction of the arterial muscular coats in any part of the body. For this reason it is exceedingly useful in the angiospastic variety of hemicrania, marked by pallor and coldness of the surfaces of the head and face, with contraction of the retinal arteries. A person in this condition, who is nearly unconscious with agony, may be almost instantaneously relieved by inhalation of the vapor of a few drops of amylic nitrite. Cases of angina pectoris, especially those in which the radial artery on the affected side is notably smaller than the other during the paroxysm, may be relieved in a similar manner. Numerous illustrations of this fact have been published in the medical journals. But the pain of angina pectoris is not always thus suppressed—a fact which becomes perfectly intelligible if we accept the hypothesis of Poincaré, that there are two varieties of the disease, one in which the sympathetic nerves and the vaso-motor apparatus are chiefly involved, and another in which the pneumogastric nerves are principally concerned.

The paroxysm of epilepsy may very often be averted by the timely inhalation of the vapor of amylic nitrite. In lunatic asylums its employment by the attendants may serve to diminish the severity and the frequency of paroxysms among the epileptic insane. The cases in which the drug is most useful belong to the class of cases that are preceded by an *aura* of considerable duration. Immediate inhalation at the commencement of the aura will usually break up the attack. For this purpose such persons may be provided with a small vial containing a pledget of lint that has been moistened with a few drops of the liquid, or he may carry in his pocket a little glass-pearl containing two or three drops, which may be instantly crushed in a handkerchief at the first warning of an imminent attack.

Tetanus, trismus, neonatorum, infantile convulsions, hysterical convulsions, puerperal convulsions, hiccough, whooping-cough, spasmodic asthma, blepharospasm, certain forms of tinnitus aurium, and other diseases of a spasmodic character, have been benefited by the drug. It certainly is a potent agent for the control of the spasmodic phenomena, though by no means always efficacious in the relief of the disease by which they may have been produced.

For the relief of dysmenorrhœa this remedy has been highly recommended by Dr. Mary P. Jacobi. Her method consists in the administration of ordinary doses of belladonna for a week or ten days before the menstrual epoch. The commencement of pain is the signal for inhalation of the nitrite of amyl.

It is also useful in cases of insomnia and melancholia that are dependent upon an anæmic condition of the brain.

Lead colic is frequently relieved at once by its use.

It has been highly recommended as a remedy for sea-sickness, but, like chloroform and other similar agents, it often fails to give relief.

One of the most important of the qualities by which amylic nitrite is entitled to a high position among the *materia medica*, consists in its supposed efficacy as an antidote to chloroform in cases of impending death during the inhalation of the vapor of that anæsthetic. Its powerfully exciting effect upon the heart, and the dilatation of the cerebral vessels that follows its use, serve to counteract the depressing effects of chloroform upon the circulation. Consequently, a few inspirations of its vapor are usually sufficient to arrest the progress of syncope, and the patient is thus resuscitated. If respiration ceases, it can no longer reach the blood through the lungs, and it should be hypodermically injected. Great caution should be exhibited in its use under such circumstances, for the remedy itself is a depressing poison, and the addition of its effects to those of chloroform may very easily become doubly disastrous. In fact, it is not unlikely that in certain fatal cases of chloroform-inhalation, death has been rendered more thoroughly inevitable by the use of amylic nitrite. But in cases where the patient is not actually dead—where respiration continues, and only an extreme pallor and a failure of the pulse indicate danger, the cautious exhibition of this remedy may become very advantageous.

When the condition of the patient during chloroform-poisoning is, therefore, such that artificial respiration and reflex excitants are powerless to renew the phenomena of life, amylic nitrite will prove to be an ineffectual remedy. It will probably act as a positive source of danger, adding its own depressing energies to those of the chloroform that has already been absorbed. But when the dangers present are primarily dependent upon a feeble and insufficient circulation of the blood, judicious administration of the amylic vapor will be very useful. Turnbull has collected several cases that illustrate this proposition in a very interesting manner.

During the last three or four years, a few physicians have experimented with a mixture of amylic nitrite and chloroform, in the hope of thus procuring a greater degree of safety than with chloroform alone. Dr. L. B. Balliet was in the habit of adding sixteen drops of amylic nitrite to each ounce of chloroform. In *The Medical Record*, October 5, 1878, Dr. George E. Sanford has recorded his experience with a similar mixture. He mixes 7 grammes (ʒ ij) of amylic nitrite with 0.453 kilogr. (one pound) of chloroform, and administers its vapor in the usual way. By this method the action of the heart is sustained, and the arteries remain distended with blood. The countenance of the patient becomes flushed, and has none of the deadly paleness often observed during the inhalation of unmingled chloroform vapor.

For brief operations requiring the use of chloroform, the employment of a mixture like the above, if freshly prepared and frequently shaken, may have some advantages over the exhibition of chloroform alone, especially if the circulation is enfeebled. But the very considerable difference between the specific gravities of the two liquids—1.499 and 0.877—must render their permanent mixture quite out of the question. The long continued inhalation of amylic nitrite which would be necessitated by the employment of the mixture in any protracted operation would be likely to exert a more depressing effect than the inhalation of chloroform vapor alone. Such à priori considerations, however, cannot be said to have yet been tested by any sufficient array of experiments.

NITROGEN.—N.

Nitrogenum, L.; *Azote*, Fr.; *Stickstoff*, G.

Specific gravity, 0.9713.

Nitrogen is a colorless, tasteless, odorless gas, which until recently has resisted all attempts at liquefaction. It is neither inflammable nor a supporter of combustion. Its reaction is neither acid nor alkaline. At $0°$ ($32°$ F.) 100 volumes of water dissolve 2.03 volumes of nitrogen. At a higher temperature the quantity diminishes.

Nitrogen exists in the atmosphere, mixed with oxygen, for which it serves as a diluent. Otherwise it appears to be the type of an inert substance. It may be readily inhaled in an undiluted form, with the production of only such consequences as result from the exclusion of oxygen. It thus produces simple, uncomplicated asphyxia. It, therefore, cannot be considered as an anæsthetic substance—the insensibility which follows its inhalation being merely one of the preliminaries of death by asphyxia. Burdon Sanderson, Murray, and Turner (*Brit. Med. Jour.*, June 13, 1868) have, however, experimented with the gas. Its primary effect was an acceleration of the movements of respiration and circulation. Respiration was then retarded and labored, while the pulse became slow and irregular. The pupils, which had been dilated, now became contracted. The countenance was pallid, and there was no appearance of cyanosis. Continued inhalation occasioned a renewed acceleration of the pulse, accompanied by retardation of respiration, and the establishment of a degree of insensibility sufficient for the painless extraction of a tooth.

NITROUS OXIDE—N₂O.

Laughing gas, Protoxide of nitrogen, Nitrogen monoxide, E. ; *Protoxyde d'Azote,* Fr. ; *Stickstoff oxydul,* G.

Specific gravity of gas, 1.527.
Specific gravity of liquid, 0.908.
Boiling-point, —88°.
Freezing-point, —101°.

Nitrous oxide is a transparent, colorless gas, with a faint sweetish smell and taste. According to Bunsen, one hundred volumes of water at 0° (32° F.) dissolve one hundred and thirty volumes of the gas; at 15° (59° F.), seventy-seven volumes; and at 24° (75° F.) only sixty volumes. For this reason it should be collected over warm water. A pressure of fifty atmospheres at 7° (45° F.) reduces it to a colorless liquid, which resumes the gaseous state as soon as pressure is removed. It may be frozen into a transparent solid at about —101° (—150° F.). By mixing liquid nitrous oxide with carbonic disulphide, and exposing the mixture to evaporation *in vacuo,* Natterer obtained a fall of temperature to —140° (—220° F.). The gas is neutral in its reaction, being neither acid nor alkaline (Miller). Like oxygen, it possesses the power of relighting a candle plunged into a jar of the gas, provided the wick is still incandescent. An ignited piece of charcoal, a burning fragment of sulphur, or a bit of phosphorus, will burn with a brilliant flame in the gas, a circumstance which would very naturally lead to the inference that it is an excellent supporter of combustion; but the actual process seems to be a decomposition of the gas by the heat of the ignited substance, surrounding the burning body with an atmosphere of oxygen and nitrogen in which the oxygen exists in about double the quantity of the oxygen in an equal quantity of atmospheric air.

Several methods of procuring the gas are described by chemists. The purified gas is usually stored in an ordinary chemical gas-holder, of a size sufficient to hold one hundred gallons or more. Or it may be led into a condensing apparatus, and liquefied for the purpose of storage in strong metallic cylinders of a portable form. In this state it occupies very little space, and can be kept for an indefinite period of time. It thus forms a more convenient article for use by the dentist than when stored in the gaseous state. By the dental manufacturers it is furnished, with a complete set of conducting tubes and rubber gas-bags of a convenient size. When a quantity of the gas is needed for inhalation, the rubber-bag is attached by a coupling to the orifice of the cylinder, and a turn of the stop-cock relieves the pressure under which the liquid has been preserved. It immediately escapes in the gaseous state into the bag, which is thus easily charged for use. By this method is avoided the loss of gas by solution in the water of a gas-holder, and also the deterioration of the gas which always follows its preservation over a tank of water.

Sir Humphry Davy, during his residence as assistant to Dr. Beddoes in the Pneumatic Institution at Clifton, first observed the anæsthetic properties of nitrous oxide. Its exhilarating effects, however, chiefly engrossed the attention of chemists. Inhalation of the gas, mingled with more or less atmospheric air, formed a favorite method of diversion in the chemical lecture-rooms of the world, but its power of producing complete insensibility to pain was overlooked until Horace Wells, the Hartford dentist, noticed its anæsthetic effects upon those who inhaled it for amusement. Experimenting upon himself, he had one of his own teeth extracted without pain while under the influence of the gas. But his discovery was for a time overlooked during the excitement created by the discovery of the anæsthetic property of ether. It, however, was not forgotten; and by the Colton Association in New York, and by Dr. Thomas, of Philadelphia, its use as a means of destroying the pain of tooth extraction was popularized to an astonishing degree. It has been occasionally employed in brief surgical operations, but its general use is almost monopolized by the members of the dental profession. It still remains *par excellence* the dental anæsthetic.

The history of the manner in which nitrous oxide was reintroduced as an anæsthetic is not without interest. After the death of Horace Wells, January 24, 1848, the use of the gas in dentistry was almost forgotten, until in the month of June, 1863, the peripatetic chemical lecturer, Colton—the same man who had by his experiments inspired Wells with the idea of dental anæsthesia by the aid of nitrous oxide—found himself in New Haven, Conn., but a short distance from the scene of his experience with Wells. Before repeating the administration of the gas, he prefaced his lecture with a narrative of the events which had led to the discovery of the anæsthetic properties of nitrous oxide. In the course of this statement he casually remarked that for many years he had not been able to find a dentist who was willing to make trial of this method for the production of anæsthesia. At the close of his lecture, a dentist, named Smith, accosted Dr. Colton, expressing his willingness to attempt the employment of nitrous oxide in the extraction of teeth, provided the doctor would administer the gas and would assume all responsibility for its use. To this proposition Colton readily consented, and immediately turned to his audience with the announcement that at a given time he would commence the administration of the gas, at the office of Dr. Smith, for the painless extraction of teeth. So successful was the experiment, that in less than three weeks Messrs. Colton and Smith had removed three thousand teeth from the mouths of the citizens of New Haven. Encouraged by this success, Colton proceeded to New York, and, in connection with a number of prominent dentists, there opened an office for the extraction of teeth. This establishment became widely known as the Colton Dental Association, and it was soon imitated in the other principal cities of the United States. On February 4, 1864, the registration of each case was commenced, and this practice has been continued ever since. Dr. Colton states that among all the patients not a single death has occurred, nor any accident of sufficient importance to necessitate the use of a carriage in order to get the sufferer to his home. The following note gives his own personal experience

COLTON DENTAL ASSOCIATION, 19 COOPER INSTITUTE,
NEW YORK, March 14, 188:.

PROF. HENRY M. LYMAN:

DEAR SIR—We commenced the use of the nitrous oxide gas on the 15th of July, 1863, and on the 4th of the following February we began to take the autograph signatures of all our patients on a scroll, numbering them on the margin. The present scroll number is one hundred and twenty-one thousand seven hundred and nine (121,709). We have never had a fatal case, or a case of serious ill effects from the gas.

Very respectfully,   G. Q. COLTON.

The physiological action of nitrous oxide gas has been carefully investigated by Hermann (1864–65); Jolyet and Blanche (*Archiv. de Physiologie*, p. 364, 1873); Goltstein and Zuntz (*Pflüger's Archiv.*, Bd. 17, 1 u. 2, Heft

1878, s. 135); Krishaber (*Bull. de la Soc. Med. de l'Elysée*, 1866); by the Committee of the Odontological Society (*Med. Times*, January 16, 1869); by Dr. Evans, of Paris (*Brit. Med. Jour.*, July 25, 1874); Holden (*Am. Jour. of Med. Sci.*, July, 1870); B. W. Richardson; Drs. J. H. McQuillen, Thomas, and Turnbull, of Philadelphia; R. Amory, of Boston (*N. Y. Med. Jour.*, August, 1870); Paul Bert, of Paris; a Committee of the British Medical Association (*Brit. Med. Jour.*, January 4, 1879); and by numerous other physiologists.

When arterial blood is acted upon outside of the body by the gas, it becomes dark in color. Dr. Turnbull found that the blood-corpuscles did not exhibit any visible change after respiration of the gas. Frogs and rabbits were placed in receivers filled with nitrous oxide until they exhibited its stupefying effect. Their blood, however, exhibited no change in the shape or in the integrity of the red corpuscles. Jolyet and Blanche found that seeds placed under otherwise favorable conditions would not germinate in an atmosphere of nitrous oxide. It was observed that other seeds, which had already sprouted, ceased to grow when placed in such an atmosphere, and again resumed their development when returned into the atmospheric air. The exhalation of carbonic acid gas by living plants was arrested when immersed in nitrous oxide. By these experiments it was proved that the respiration of plants could not be sustained by this gas.

Frogs placed in jars containing nitrous oxide died after two hours' immersion in the gas. Similar animals placed in hydrogen, nitrogen, or carbonic oxide, continued to live for two or three hours before exhibiting signs of stupor and death. Carbonic acid gas proved quickly fatal. A sparrow placed in twenty-five litres of nitrous oxide died in half a minute. Inspiration of the gas proved fatal to a guinea-pig in two minutes and a half. A rabbit died in the same way after breathing the pure gas for two minutes and twenty-four seconds. From these experiments, MM. Jolyet and Blanche concluded that pure nitrous oxide gas is not capable of sustaining animal life. They also concluded that sensibility to pain persisted in the animals upon which they experimented until the establishment of asphyxia. By causing frogs to inhale nitrous oxide and oxygen, in such proportions that the mixture contained about one-fifth of oxygen, no apparent effects were produced. A sparrow was placed under a bell-jar containing air, and another was in like manner placed under a jar which contained nitrous oxide and oxygen, mixed in the same proportion that oxygen and nitrogen occupy in the atmosphere. At the end of an hour and forty minutes both birds exhibited signs of dyspnœa. Half an hour later they were alike panting for breath, and they both died shortly after. The remaining air in the air-filled jar contained eleven per cent. of carbonic acid gas and six per cent. of oxygen. The other jar contained twelve per cent. of carbonic acid gas and five and eight-tenths per cent. of oxygen. Similar experiments with other animals gave similar results, showing that the two mixtures were equally respirable, and that death without previous anæsthesia ensued in each after the exhaustion of a certain quantity of the oxygen.

A series of experiments was then instituted upon a dog, to ascertain the quantity of oxygen in the blood after respiration of different gaseous mixtures. After breathing one hundred cubic centimetres of pure air, the arterial blood contained:

Carbonic acid gas .... 48.8 per cent.
Oxygen .... 21.0   "
Nitrogen .... 2.0   "

The dog was then made to inspire, from a bag, fifty litres of a mixture containing sixty-two per cent. of nitrous oxide gas, twenty-one per cent. of oxygen, and seventeen per cent. of nitrogen. After seven minutes and a half, the animal was still sensitive to contact with the conjunctiva and to pinching the toes. The arterial blood then yielded:

Carbonic acid gas	46.0	per cent.
Oxygen	19.7	"
Nitrous oxide	29.0	"
Nitrogen	0.3	"

After resting for half an hour, the same dog inhaled pure nitrous oxide for one minute and forty-five seconds. This produced dyspnœa, but not anæsthesia. His blood yielded:

Carbonic acid gas	37.0	per cent.
Oxygen	5.2	"
Nitrous oxide	28.1	"
Nitrogen	0.7	"

Another dog treated in the same way became insensible after three minutes. The blood from his arteries then gave:

Carbonic acid gas	36.6	per cent.
Oxygen	3.3	"
Nitrous oxide	34.6	"

A third dog became insensible to electrical excitement of the sciatic nerve at the end of four minutes. In his blood (arterial) was found:

Carbonic acid gas	34.00	per cent.
Oxygen	0.05	"
Nitrous oxide	37.00	"

The experiments of Paul Bert have shown that when the oxygen of the arterial blood falls to two or three per cent., the animal begins to exhibit signs of anæsthesia. Hence it seems that these experiments indicate an absence of oxygen rather than the presence of nitrous oxide as the real cause of such anæthesia as was observed.

This conclusion would leave nitrous oxide in the position of a gas that is destitute of positive qualities. Its stupefying properties would be purely negative and dependent upon its exclusion of oxygen from the blood. That it does actually possess positive energy seems, however, to be indicated by the exhilaration that is produced by inhalation of a certain proportion of the gas. The experiments of Goltstein ("Kappeler: Anæsthetica," p. 194) show that frogs placed in pure nitrous oxide lose their reflex powers in a few minutes, while an immersion in hydrogen is not followed by such a result for several hours. Mammalian animals suffocated with nitrous oxide experience less desire for respiration than if an indifferent gas, like nitrogen, is employed. Convulsions are almost unknown during the use of nitrous oxide, but are almost uniformly present during the asphyxia that is occasioned by other suffocative gases.

The effects that follow the respiration of nitrous oxide differ from the consequences of inhaling a mixture of the gas with atmospheric air. The mixed gases produce a feeling of exhilaration, with humming sounds in the ears, and a subjective sensation of warmth and lightness, as if one could leap and fly into the air.   There is a disposition to irregular and excessive movement, and a diminution of tactile sensibility, together with a loss of sensibility to painful impressions.   The patient laughs and shouts, but does not lose his consciousness.   The pulse is somewhat excited, the eyes are injected, and the pupils dilate.   Very rarely convulsions occur.

When the patient is made to inhale the undiluted gas, the phenomena of exhilaration do not appear until the cessation of inhalation permits a dilution of the gas already in the blood.   Then laughter and some degree of excitement may be manifested.   The early effects of inhalation are often marked by a sensation of dyspnœa.   The pulse becomes rapid and feeble ; the countenance becomes livid ; the lips and mucous membrane assume a ghastly purplish hue.   Unconsciousness speedily supervenes.   The recovery of the patient is exceedingly rapid, even after the appearance of unfavorable symptoms.   The asphyxic phenomena promptly disappear with the admission of pure air to the lungs.

Kappeler states, that while in the majority of cases the respiration of nitrous oxide produces no very disagreeable sensation, it sometimes occasions very distressing feelings of constriction about the thorax.   Agonizing dreams may disturb the serenity of the patient, and a disposition to convulsive shuddering may be observed.   Sexual excitement may be experienced, but vomiting is of rare occurrence.   Giddiness and other disagreeable cerebral phenomena are of short duration after awaking.   Anæsthesia sufficient for the performance of minor operations may be reached after inhalation of pure nitrous oxide for fifty or sixty seconds.   If air be admitted at the same time into the lungs, the period of anæsthesia will be greatly deferred.   The inhalation of pure gas through an inhaling apparatus that is perfectly adapted to the face and mouth is the only proper method.   Reinhalation of the expired gas, or inhalation of gas mixed with the air that has been expired from the lungs, should never be practised.

The effect of nitrous oxide upon the arterial circulation is illustrated by the following sphygmographic tracings.   The first series was taken from the radial artery of a young man in fair health, age twenty-eight years, weight one hundred and fifty-five pounds, who inhaled the gas July 14, 1880, for the extraction of a tooth, in the office of Dr. M. W. Sherwood, an experienced dentist, practising in this city.

No. 1.—Just before inhalation.   Pulse small, contracted.

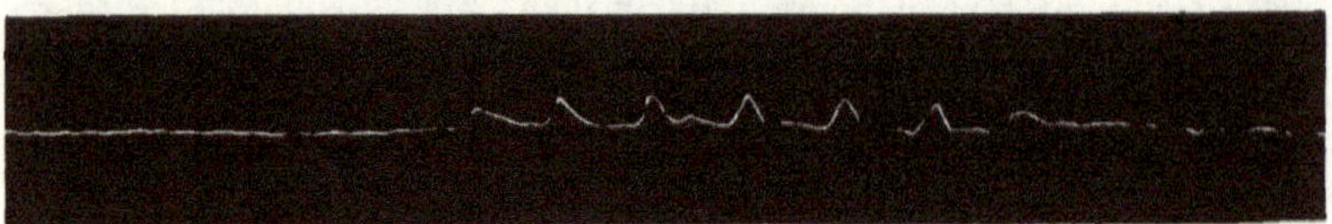

No. 2.—First inspirations of the gas.

No. 3.—Slight exhilaration. Muttered laughter. Anæsthesia commencing.

No. 4.—Complete anæsthesia. Extraction of the tooth.

No. 5.—Inhalation suspended. Consciousness returning. Patient laughing.

No. 6.—Consciousness fully restored.

The second series was taken in the same office from the radial artery of a young man, apparently in good health, July 20, 1880.

No. 1.—Immediately before the commencement of inhalation.

No. 2.—Immediately after the commencement of inhalation.

No. 3.—Inhalation progressing.

No. 4.—Slight exhilaration.

No. 5.—Anæsthesia.

No. 6.—Continued anæsthesia.

No. 7.—Inhalation discontinued.   Extraction of tooth.

No. 8.—Return of consciousness.

The first effect of the inhalation upon the excursions of the arterial wall is very noticeable.   What is lost in frequency of the heart-beat is compensated by the limitation of the height of the arterial wave.   The preservation of the incisures and elevations that mark the waves of recoil is much more perfect than anything that is witnessed during the inhalation of chloroform. In that respect the pulse-curve resembles that of ether rather than the curve of chloroform.   The rapid succession of the different stages of anæsthesia produces great variety in the successive tracings—in this respect presenting a very marked contrast to the majority of anæsthetic sphygmograms, and more nearly approaching the phenomena that are produced by uncomplicated asphyxia.   Krishaber observed that when a rabbit was made to inhale the gas mixed with a variable quantity of air, the pulsations of the heart became at first almost uncountable.   After a brief period the number was one hundred and forty-five per minute.   After another half minute there was a sudden retardation of the action of the heart, immediately followed by an increase of the pulsations to one hundred and seventy-eight.   At the expiration of twenty seconds there was a second period of retardation continuing for twenty seconds, and then another brief acceleration. This alter-nation of rates continued for about three minutes, during which time the aggregate number of beats was increased rather than diminished. Rhythmic irregularity was the most conspicuous peculiarity of the movement of the heart during this stage of inhalation. With the establishment of insensi-bility, the heart beat with diminishing rapidity, and sank to seventy-five or eighty pulsations at the time of its final arrest. The movements of respira-tion seemed to follow suit with the general muscular agitation of the animal ; but as insensibility appeared, respiration fell, and, finally, descending from fifty-five per minute to twenty, was suddenly arrested.

When rabbits were made to breathe pure nitrous oxide through an opening in the trachea, the successive phenomena were developed with such rapidity that it was difficult to follow all their details. Death usually oc-curred after breathing the gas for two or three minutes. The cardiac move-ments were more irregular and tumultuous than they were during the res-piration of the mixed gases. The heart-beats usually ceased suddenly, with very little preliminary retardation.

The movements of respiration were at first considerably accelerated, and they ceased while inspiration was going on at the rate of once every three seconds. General muscular agitation was less violent than during the inha-lation of the mixed gases. Partial insensibility was rapidly developed, but complete anæsthesia was only manifested immediately before the death of the animal.

As a contrast to these phenomena, Krishaber asphyxiated a number of rabbits by ligature of the trachea. The heart continued to beat during the first ten seconds at the rate of one hundred and thirty-two pulsations per minute. The respiratory efforts could not be counted by reason of the struggles of the animal. The cardiac movements were not retarded until the middle of the second minute. Their rhythm exhibited no change, and the force of contraction was scarcely altered during the first four minutes of the experiment. After this the cardiac contractions became irregular. Total cessation of the action of the heart took place in one experiment after seven minutes, in another during the eleventh minute. To the very last moment the subjects of experiment gave signs of sensibility on pinching their skin. After the heart had ceased to beat, it was found impossible to resuscitate the animal by insufflation through an opening in the trachea ; but in one instance a rabbit was revived by artificial respiration after the trachea had been compressed for six minutes, and the heart had ceased to beat. In this case the fortunate result was attributed to the instantaneous commencement of artificial respiration, without waiting to open the trachea for the introduction of a tube. With this exception, it was noted that arti-ficial respiration always failed to restore an animal whose heart had been arrested by any anæsthetic, or by asphyxia. As long as the heart con-tinued to beat, artificial respiration might be successful, but once para-lyzed, the heart could not be revived.

As the result of his experiments, comparing the effects of nitrous oxide gas with the effects produced by inhalation of chloroform vapor, and with the effects of ligation of the trachea, Krishaber concluded that the action of nitrous oxide could be more justly compared with the action of chloro-form than with simple exclusion of oxygen from the blood. Like chloro-form it retards the action of the heart before death, but its effect upon that organ is much more disturbing than the effect of chloroform. The anæs-thesia which it produces is not simulated by any of the phenomena of as-phyxia excepting at the moment of death, and it disappears almost as rapidly as it is induced, if the gas is withdrawn.   The precipitancy with which the symptoms succeed each other, constitute the principal source of danger in the use of nitrous oxide gas.   To such an extent is this true, that his experiments upon animals, together with a consideration of the risks of adding asphyxia to anæsthesia by exclusion of the air from the lungs, inspired Krishaber with the belief that, of the two, chloroform is the safer agent. The experiments of Goltstein—in fact, the experiences of every one who employs nitrous oxide—show that the anæsthetic effect of the gas is prevented or suspended by the admission of a small quantity of oxygen into the lungs.   This anæsthesia is, therefore, associated with the existence of a certain degree of asphyxia.   It is anæsthesia plus asphyxia— hence the chief danger in the use of nitrous oxide.   Inhalation of chloroform vapor involves the simultaneous introduction of such a quantity of oxygen into the lungs that asphyxia rarely occurs under such conditions. The danger lies in the directly poisonous effect of the chloroform itself.

The experiments of Goltstein have shown that the modifications of blood-pressure, and of the movements of the heart which are produced by nitrous oxide, do not materially differ from the effects that are occasioned by ordinary suffocation.   The asphyxia produced by nitrous oxide is characterized by three stages.   During the first stage, respiration is accelerated and becomes more profound.   During the second stage, active aspiratory efforts cease much sooner than during the corresponding stage of suffocation by ligation of the trachea.   In the first class of cases these efforts ceased sixty-five seconds after the inhalation of the gas, while after occlusion of the trachea they continued from one hundred and two to one hundred and eight seconds.

During the second stage of asphyxia, the animal which inhales nitrous oxide is fully insensible, while sensibility persists throughout this stage of simple asphyxia.

The third stage of this latter form of asphyxia is characterized by the appearance of convulsions.   This stage of nitrous oxide asphyxia presents no such phenomena, in consequence of the anæsthetic condition of the convulsive apparatus under the influence of the gas.

These considerations led Professor Paul Bert, of Paris, to imagine that if air, containing free oxygen, in quantity sufficient to sustain life, could be introduced into the blood along with nitrous oxide gas in quantity sufficient to produce anæsthesia, the patient might be kept in a state of insensibility with perfect safety for an indefinite period of time.   In a paper read before the Academy of Sciences, November 11, 1878, he expressed himself as follows:

"The fact that nitrous oxide must be administered in a state of purity, signifies that in order to impregnate the organism with a sufficient quantity of this gas, its tension must be equal to the pressure of a single atmosphere.   Under the normal atmospheric pressure, in order to obtain this result, the gas must form one hundred per cent. of the air that is breathed. But, if we suppose the patient placed in an apparatus where the pressure can be raised to the equivalent of two atmospheres, the necessary tension will be secured by respiration of a gaseous mixture containing fifty per cent of nitrous oxide and fifty per cent. of atmospheric air.   Under these conditions there should be manifested a species of anæsthesia, while, as a consequence of the presence of the normal quantity of oxygen in the blood, all the natural conditions of respiration are maintained.

"My experiments, though hitherto conducted only upon animals, have had precisely this result. They are performed in the following manner: Entering the cylindrical chamber, and increasing the atmospheric pressure by one-fifth, I compel a dog .to breathe a mixture containing five-sixths of nitrous oxide and one-sixth of oxygen—a mixture in which it is evident that the tension of the so-called laughing gas is exactly equal to the tension of an atmosphere. Under these conditions, after a very brief period of excitement, the animal becomes in one or two minutes completely insensible. The cornea or the conjunctiva can then be touched without causing the eye to wink. The pupil is dilated; nerves of sensation may be exposed and irritated, or even a limb may be amputated, without arousing the slightest movement. The degree of muscular resolution is something really extraordinary, and, were it not for the movements of respiration which continue with perfect regularity, the animal would appear as if stricken with death. This condition may persist for half an hour or an hour without the slightest change. During the whole of this time the blood preserves its bright red color and its full proportion of oxygen, the heart continues to beat with its accustomed force and regularity, and the bodily temperature maintains its normal degree. During this entire period, every excitement of a centripetal nerve produces in the phenomena of respiration and circulation all those reflex modifications which may be effected in the healthy animal. In a word, all the so-called phenomena of vegetative life remain intact, while all those functions which are peculiar to animal life are absolutely abolished.

"When, after an indefinite period of time, the bag that contains the gaseous mixture is removed, three or four inspirations of pure air suffice to restore the faculty of sensation, volition, and intelligence to the animal; in proof whereof he sometimes immediately exhibits a disposition to bite. Released from confinement, he hurries away, stepping freely, and immediately displaying his usual joyous vivacity.

"This rapid return to the normal condition, so different from our experience with chloroform, is due to the fact that nitrous oxide does not, like chloroform, contract any chemical combination in the organism, but is merely dissolved in the blood. When no longer contained in the air that is inspired, it rapidly escapes through the lungs, as my analyses of the gases in the blood have shown.

"The absence of danger in connection with the action of nitrous oxide is exhibited by this recital of my experiments. On the one hand, in fact, anæsthesia, while overpowering the sensibility of the spinal cord, always respects these reflex activities of organic life, the suppression of which—so easily effected by chloroform—can alone endanger the vital existence; while, on the other hand, the immediate restoration of the normal condition when pure air is again permitted to enter the lungs, renders the operator always master of the situation."

The only difficulty in the way of using nitrous oxide as indicated above is connected with the question of expense. A large and costly apparatus,—a special chamber, in fact,—in which the operation can be conducted in compressed air, is needful. Such an apparatus has been actually constructed and operated with success by M. Bert. Since the date of the above quoted communication he has also submitted his method to the test of experiment upon the human subject. The attempt was crowned with perfect success. Obviously, however, the expense that attends the installation of this method must necessarily limit its adoption. The increasing popularity of mixed anæsthesia by Clover's method of successive inhalation of nitrous oxide and ether vapor, will also serve to hinder any very general attempt at realization of the suggestions contained in the reports of Prof. Bert's experiments.

We may now justly derive the following conclusions regarding nitrous oxide from the laborious investigations which have been thus detailed :

I. Nitrous oxide gas possesses special anæsthetic properties.

II. If inhaled without dilution it produces asphyxia, as well as anæsthesia, by exclusion of oxygen from the blood.

III. Nitrous oxide does not enter into any chemical combination with the elements of the body, but is simply dissolved in the blood—hence its speedy entrance and departure from the organism.

IV. Nitrous oxide is not decomposed in the blood, consequently it cannot replace oxygen or yield oxygen for the respiration of the tissues.

V. Nitrous oxide produces special effects upon the nervous system. When diluted with air these effects are limited to the manifestation of a peculiar exhilaration. When inhaled without dilution, the gas produces first, excitement, then anæsthesia, and finally, asphyxia. The ultimate phenomena of asphyxia (convulsions, etc.) are suppressed by the anæsthetic energy of the gas.

VI. In order to saturate the system with nitrous oxide sufficiently for the production of anæsthesia, the tension of the gas must equal the pressure of the atmosphere. A mixture of the gas with oxygen or common air will therefore produce complete anæsthesia if it be inhaled under a pressure sufficient to raise the tension of the gas in the mixture to an equivalent of the tension of the undiluted gas under the normal atmospheric pressure. By this method anæsthesia and normal respiration may be indefinitely prolonged with perfect safety.

The first operation on the human subject under the influence of nitrous oxide administered according to the method of Paul Bert, was performed February 13, 1879, by M. Leon Labbé. The operation consisted in the removal of an ingrowing toe-nail from a young woman, twenty years of age. She inhaled, under pressure, a mixture containing eighty-five per cent. of nitrous oxide and fifteen per cent. of oxygen. "I was holding one of the arms of the patient," says Paul Bert, in his description of the scene, "noting the considerable rapidity of the pulse, when suddenly, without any change in the pulse, in the respiration, in the color of the skin, or in the aspect of the countenance, without the occurrence of any rigidity, agitation, or excitement of any kind, about ten or fifteen seconds after the first inspiration of the anæsthetic gas, I felt her arms relax completely. Insensibility and muscular relaxation had taken place ; the cornea could be touched with perfect impunity. The operation was commenced at once, and the dressing followed, without a single movement on the part of the patient who slept in perfect tranquillity. At the expiration of four minutes, just as M. Labbé was finishing the application of the dressing, there were slight muscular contractions in the arm, then in one of the legs. Having completed the operation, the inhaler was removed, and the contractions immediately ceased. For thirty seconds longer she continued to sleep, when, some one having tapped her on the shoulder, she awoke, looked around with an air of astonishment, then sat up, and suddenly cried out that her foot was hurting her. In fact, it pained her so much that she shed a few tears over it. In reply to our questions, she declared that she had felt nothing, and had dreamed of nothing, but she did remember that after the first inhalation of the gas she had experienced a very delightful sensation as if she were going up to heaven, and that she ' could see the blue sky and the stars.' Having said this, she jumped up and went on foot to the conveyance which was to carry her to the hospital, but she complained so much of hunger on the way, that it was necessary to stop and let her have something to eat. She experienced no ill consequence from her adventure."

This experiment, however, was not considered conclusive, by reason of its brevity—four minutes having been frequently equalled under the ordinary conditions of administration of the gas. The experiments were pursued, under the direction of Paul Bert, by a surgeon named Pean, assisted by a number of eminent physicians and surgeons. The operations were at first performed in the æropathic establishment of Dr. Fontaine, whose apparatus for the treatment of patients with compressed air was easily adapted to the new method of producing anæsthesia. Dr. Fontaine, soon contrived a portable apparatus, which was conveyed to the Saint Louis Hospital and the Lariboisière Hospital, where numerous operations have been performed according to the new method since the month of October, 1879. Among these operations, reported by Rottenstein, may be counted three amputations of the breast, four operations upon the bones, six extirpations of different varieties of tumor, a resection of the infra-orbital nerve, and two reductions of shoulder-dislocation of three or four days standing. The duration of anæsthesia varied from four to twenty-six minutes. Complete anæsthesia supervened, without any preliminary excitement, after a period of inhalation that varied from fifteen seconds to two minutes. Consciousness always returned within half a minute or a minute after the cessation of inhalation. There was neither vomiting nor any subsequent disagreeable feeling. In this respect the anæsthesia produced by nitrous oxide is decidedly superior to the effects of ether or of chloroform. Rottenstein, however, records a case in which vomiting occurred after the patient had been kept for thirty minutes under the influence of the gas. The patient had eaten heartily just before inhalation. During certain of the earlier essays with this method, the operators were disturbed by the occurrence of muscular contractions in the limbs. Paul Bert, however, soon discovered that these were caused by an insufficient saturation of the blood with the gas. By a slight increase of the gaseous pressure within the operating-chamber, the tension of the gas was increased, the blood became more thoroughly impregnated, and the contractions disappeared. M. Bert also ascertained the fact, that by thus augmenting the pressure a little beyond the degree that is necessary for the induction of anæsthesia, the blood and the tissues might be supersaturated with the anæsthetic gas, so that anæsthesia might be prolonged beyond the usual time occupied by the elimination of the gas and the recovery of consciousness after the act of inhalation had ceased. This delay of recovery would be exceedingly advantageous to dentists, who might thus gain a little time for their operations about the mouth.

The only impediment in the way of the general adoption of the new method devised by M. Bert, consists in the cumbersome nature of the necessary apparatus. A vivacious Parisian has already conceived the idea of an amphitheatre, seating three hundred students, hermetically sealed, and adapted for the increase of pressure upon its atmospheric contents at the pleasure of the operating surgeon. In such a space, attached to every large hospital, the method of Paul Bert might be employed with no other inconvenience than that of expense. But for the present, the portable receiver devised by Dr. Fontaine, limits the ambition of the practitioners

of the new method. The following description of Dr. Fontaine's apparatus
was published in *L'Union Medicale* for September 18, 1879 :

"This apparatus, mounted on wheels, is painted white inside. It receives light through ten port-holes, of which the four upper serve for the
direct illumination of the operating table. The width of the chamber is

Bert's Pneumatic Chamber for Nitrous Oxide.   (Rottenstein.)

two metres (about six feet and a half), its length is three metres and a
half (eleven feet and a half), its height is two metres and sixty-five hundredths (eight feet). Ten or twelve persons can very easily be accommo-
dated within.

"The receiver in which M. Pean has operated during the last three
months, and into which he was usually accompanied by five or six assistants, had not one-third of the available surface presented by this apparatus. The atmospheric pressure can be regulated at pleasure from within
or from without. In either case a metallic pressure-gauge indicates the
degree of compression.

"By the side of the receiver are placed, upon a little car :

" 1. A double-barrelled brass pump, A, with liquid piston, capable of
yielding from four hundred to six hundred litres of air per minute.

" 2. A refrigerator, B, interposed in the current of compressed air in
order to intercept its heat, and to prevent the temperature of the air
within the receiver from rising more than one or two degrees above that
of the surrounding atmosphere. During the winter this refrigerator may
be replaced by a hot-water bath.

" 3. A sheet-iron container, C, holding three hundred and fifty litres of
the anæsthetic gaseous mixture subjected to a pressure of ten atmospheres
(about three and a half cubic metres at the ordinary pressure of the air).

"Upon the sides of the receiver may be seen two keys, of which the
first operates a stop-cock which communicates with the gas-holder and
with a gas-bag that is placed under the operating table. When the bag is
nearly empty, it is refilled from the store of compressed gas in the gas-
holder. The second key is connected with a whistle for making signals to
the men at the pump."

The same contrivance by which the air within the receiver is compressed, provides for the ventilation of the apartment—air being forced
out at the top of the room by the same pressure that drives it in through
properly graduated apertures near the floor.

It is impossible, at present, to urge any scientific objections against this method of producing anæsthesia. It seems to be theoretically perfect. Waiving all questions of expense, the question for the future to decide has reference to the period during which anæsthesia can be safely maintained by the use of nitrous oxide. In other words, it must be ascertained how long the tissues of the body can safely tolerate the action of nitrous oxide even when guarded by the presence of a sufficient quantity of oxygen. The anæsthetic property of the gas shows that, even if it does not enter into any discoverable chemical combination with protoplasm, it still possesses the power to modify its modes of motion. How far can this modification proceed without danger? Death has been known to result from the inhalation of the gas; and if death itself may not occur, the following case, published by M. Bordier, in the *Journal de Thérapeutique*, December, 1876, indicates the possibility of occasional disagreeable consequences:

"M. X., a young man, sixteen years of age, with a strong constitution, but a very nervous temperament, having never exhibited any previous ill-health worthy of note, went with his mother to the office of a well-known dentist, who was accustomed to administer nitrous oxide, for the purpose of getting rid of a molar tooth which had kept him in horrible agony for several nights.

"The patient was anæsthetized and the operation was performed without difficulty. No unusual phenomena presented themselves. The mother of the young man, not wishing to be a spectator of all the details of the operation, could not say whether her son was cyanosed or was pale during the period of anæsthesia. At all events, the tooth was extracted without pain, and the young man having promptly woke up, went home in a carriage, in complete possession of his faculties, and much pleased with the fortunate result of his visit to the dentist.

"About an hour after reaching home, his mother saw him suddenly burst into tears. She anxiously asked him again and again for an explanation of this outbreak, but could get no other response than a succession of sobs and a torrent of tears—phenomena of which the *nervous* character did not escape her notice, and which she readily referred to the agitation experienced during the morning, as well as to the susceptible temperament of her son. She, therefore, resigned to time and to various maternal caresses the work of soothing this nervous condition, and after the expiration of about half an hour she witnessed the cessation of his tears as, with a sorrowful expression of countenance, her boy laid himself down upon the bed where he had been sitting, and went to sleep.

"This, it seems, was the anticipated end of the crisis, for which she had hoped. She merely watched him as he slept, until, at the expiration of three hours she tried to wake him, but without success, though she called and shook him energetically upon his bed.

"Full of alarm she sent for me. I found the young man lying on his back, with his clothes on, and soundly asleep. His face was highly colored, especially so when his ordinary paleness was taken into consideration. The sclerotics were injected, and the pupils were contracted to a point, although the room was very dimly lighted. His forehead was very warm.

"Neither my presence, nor my voice, nor pinching, nor rapping the jaws together, nor the most energetic shaking by the arm, could rouse the patient. A light placed before his eyes, while I held the eyelids apart, seemed after a time to disturb him slightly, so that he turned his head away and uttered a sort of groan. Placed by main force in the sitting position upon his bed, he immediately tumbled over, and was fast asleep again.

"It was only after repeated efforts on the part of his mother, his brothers, and myself, that we could get from him a sort of look of astonishment at seeing us around him, and a *Good day, sir!* of which the final syllables were not fairly articulated, for he was again asleep.

"His skin was warm and moist. His pulse—counted several times—was one hundred and twenty per minute. Respiration was retarded—*forgotten,* one might call it—for a certain time. It then became sighing, full, and deep. Anæsthesia appeared to be, if not complete, at least very decidedly marked.

"Feeling, I must confess, very little anxiety, notwithstanding the character of the symptoms, because I knew that, ordinarily, disturbances of this nature, occasioned by inhalation of nitrous oxide, pass off without treatment, I still considered it best to do something on account of the acceleration of the pulse. The condition of encephalic congestion, the contraction of the pupils, and the injection of the conjunctivæ, suggested the use of sulphate of quinia.

"Several powders of this drug happened to be in the house. A very strong infusion of black coffee was prepared; fifty centigrammes (eight grains) of the sulphate of quinia were stirred in; and the patient was with great effort roused sufficiently to open his mouth and to swallow the contents of the cup, which he did without giving any sign of consciousness of the bitterness of its taste.

"One second later he was again asleep.

"I advised the elevation of his head with cushions; the cooling of his forehead with cold compresses, frequently renewed; and the application of a mustard poultice on the calf of each leg.

"The young patient called at my house the next morning, and declared that he had no recollection of anything that had taken place after his return home the day before. He woke up about an hour after my visit, and after sitting up pretty late, had gone to bed and slept as usual.

"His pupils were greatly dilated; but there has been no abiding consequence of his experience."

It can hardly be possible that in this case the symptoms were due to any direct effect of nitrous oxide. It is more than probable that the phenomena were of a nature akin to certain manifestations of hysteria, and that they were simply the result of the complex series of irritations to which an extraordinarily excitable nervous system had been subjected. Still it is well to know that such an incident may occur after the administration of nitrous oxide.

The various unpleasant phenomena that may accompany the inhalation of the gas—such as rigidity of the muscles, excessive excitement, irregular respiration and circulation, cyanosis, etc., are caused by improper methods of inhalation. Muscular rigidity and excitement are due to the admission of air with the gas. When inhaled in the ordinary way, the gas must not be diluted if anæsthesia is desired. But if the undiluted gas be thus inhaled for more than three minutes, the patient may exhibit alarming symptoms of asphyxia. Its use—except when employed according to the method of Paul Bert—must therefore be restricted to very brief operations. It is true that Carnochan and Morton have reported a number of capital operations performed upon patients who were for a considerable time kept in a condition of insensibility by the administration of nitrous oxide. J. Marion Sims thus kept a patient insensible for sixteen minutes while he removed a tumor of the breast, and in another case he occupied twenty minutes in the removal of an abdominal tumor. A surgeon in Quebec, named Blanchet, also used the gas in an operation that lasted twenty-five minutes. But in all these cases the inhalation of the gas was intermittent. Continuous respiration for a lengthened period is only possible when the gas is administered according to the method of Bert.

The mode of administration has been sufficiently considered in the chapter devoted to the general subject of inhalers and inhalation. The principal thing to be considered while giving the gas is the exclusion of air. The easiest method consists in the use of a pipe which is placed between the teeth, so that the patient shall inspire through that channel alone. Since this requires artificial means for closing the nostrils, and inasmuch as many people object to the use of a pipe which has been used by other patients, it is desirable to employ an inhaling-mask whenever it is possible. It is difficult, however, to make such an apparatus fit air-tight upon the face, especially if the patient be a man with a beard. The great variety of inhalers that are now provided for the surgeon, makes it, however, a comparatively easy thing to overcome the difficulties that may be originated by any individual case.

DEATH FROM INHALATION OF NITROUS OXIDE GAS.

1. "A death has just occurred in a dentist's chair from the administration of nitrous oxide ; it was that of a fine young woman, in perfect health, who was induced to have this anæsthetic rather than chloroform."—Kidd : *Med. Times and Gaz.*, p. 301, March 12, 1864.

2. A merchant, named Sears, inhaled nitrous oxide for the painless extraction of a tooth, and died. He was in the last stage of consumption, and death was ascribed to that cause.—*Dental Cosmos*, p. 456, 1864.

3. A young girl, seventeen years of age, apparently in robust health, inhaled nitrous oxide gas, which was administered at the same time to a number of persons by a travelling dentist. She did not take enough to produce insensibility ; but she was taken ill the next day, and died on the following. Her death was attributed to the inhalation, but no evidence exists to substantiate such an opinion.—Swanton Falls, Vt. ; *Dental Cosmos*, p. 456, 1864.

4. Male, about twenty-three years of age, inhaled nitrous oxide in the office of a dentist to have a tooth extracted. A cork was placed between the teeth to keep the mouth open. As the tooth was extracted it slipped from the forceps and, with the cork, was drawn into the pharynx. The tooth was subsequently thrown up from the stomach, but the cork—which does not seem to have been missed—entered the larynx, where it caused suffocation and death in an hour. The autopsy revealed its presence in the larynx, showing that nitrous oxide was only the indirect cause of death—Philadelphia, January 24, 1869 ; *Med. and Surg. Reporter*, February 2, 1867.

5. A female patient (America) died in the office of a dentist, immediately after the extraction of a tooth. An ineffectual attempt to produce anæsthesia with nitrous oxide had preceded the extraction. It is doubtful whether this had any effect as a cause of the fatal result.—*Dental Cosmos*, p. 452, August, 1872.

6. A patient died in the office of a dentist, under the influence of nitrous oxide, two or three days before the great fire which destroyed the most

important part of the city. As a consequence of the confusion produced by that event, the fact of this death became known to very few persons, and was soon forgotten.—Chicago, October, 1871.

7. Female, thirty-years, in good health. Had not eaten for several hours preceding inhalation. A large upper molar tooth was to be extracted. The gas was supplied from one of the iron cylinders in which it had been compressed. Gas from the same source had been administered to other patients without accident. At the beginning of inhalation the pulse became rapid and less full, whereupon, the patient being quite sensible, the inhaler was taken away, and the extraction was attempted, but was abandoned on account of pain. The patient washed her mouth, and again began to inhale the gas, without any unfavorable symptoms. As soon as she was insensible the inhalation was stopped, and the tooth was extracted. The dentist was obliged to split the fangs, and to take them out separately. Immediately after this, the face became livid and turgescent. A physician was hastily summoned, who arrived in time to find the lady still alive. She was sitting in a chair, in a half-reclining position, before an open window. Her face was livid and swollen, and she appeared to be quite unconscious. She breathed two or three times, and a few moments after her pulse ceased to beat. It was estimated that six gallons of gas had passed through her lungs.—Exeter, England, January 22, 1873 ; *Lancet*, Am. Ed., p. 270, 1873.

8. Male, fifty-three years, a surgeon in good practice, died under the influence of nitrous oxide gas, administered for the purpose of having a tooth extracted. Being unnerved and excited, partly from the suffering he had undergone, and partly from the want of proper food, which the condition of his mouth had prevented him from taking, he insisted on the inhalation being pushed until he should snore, and—for, at any rate, part of the time—held the mouth-piece in his own hand, and inspired very vigorously. The first attempt at extraction was made before he was fully insensible, and was abandoned until more of the gas had been given. Two teeth were then removed. Symptoms of syncope ensued after the operation, and the dentist sent for medical assistance. On the arrival of a surgeon, Mr. Harrison was pronounced to be dead. *Autopsy.*—There was some fat about the heart ; the cavities on the right side were distended with blood, while those on the left side were empty. The lungs were gorged with dark blood. All the other organs were healthy.—Manchester, England, March 27, 1877 ; *Med. Record*, p. 384, June 16, 1877.

CARBONIC OXIDE—CO.

Carbonei oxidum, L. ; *Oxyde de carbone*, Fr. ; *Kohlenoxyd*, G.

Specific gravity, 0.967.

Carbonic oxide is a transparent, colorless, almost odorless gas. It is inflammable, burning in the air with a blue flame as it is oxidized to carbonic anhydride. It is neutral in its reaction with litmus-paper, and does not combine with either acids or bases. It is slightly soluble in water— one hundred volumes of water dissolving 3.28 volumes of the gas at 0° (32° F.) and 2.43 volumes at 15° (59° F.).

Carbonic oxide may be produced by various chemical processes. It is ordinarily encountered as a product of the imperfect combustion of coal. When the supply of air is deficient, carbonic anhydride is reduced in the fire-place, or brazier, to carbonic oxide : $CO_2 + C = 2CO$.

This reduction takes place within the mass of coals upon the grate, and as the heated carbonic oxide escapes into the air above the grate it is oxidized by the oxygen which it meets in abundance, and burns with the characteristic lambent blue flame that usually appears above the coals when the fire-place has been recently replenished.

The presence of this gas in very small quantity in the air of a house is sufficient to exert a very deleterious effect upon the health of those who breathe the air that is thus vitiated. Leblanc ("Leçons sur l'Asphyxie," par Claude Bernard, Paris, 1875) has shown that the presence of one-tenth of one per cent. of carbonic oxide in the air is sufficient to destroy a bird, and two or three-tenths of one per cent. will kill a dog. It is the presence of this gas which renders the fumes of the braziers used by plasterers in the winter season so injurious to the workmen who are employed indoors, in house-plastering, during cold weather. In certain parts of the world, the fumes of burning charcoal are employed for purposes of suicide. They owe a large measure of their deadly qualities to the presence of carbonic oxide.

Inhalation of this gas produces insensibility, and, if continued for any length of time, it destroys life by asphyxia. It is not, however, a genuine anæsthetic, unless all lethal substances which induce insensibility before death may be so classified. It is rather a poison, which occasions asphyxia as a result of its toxic effects upon the blood. Bernard has shown that it manifests an especial affinity for the hæmoglobin of the red globules, expelling the oxygen which they naturally contain, and unfitting them for a renewal of their supply. Blood that has become impregnated with carbonic oxide can no longer change from an arterial color to a venous. It remains of a brilliant vermilion hue on both sides of the heart, and throughout the circulatory passages. All those phenomena which depend upon the successive changes of arterial blood into venous and of venous blood into arterial are completely arrested, and life is soon extinguished. That this result is the consequence of cutting off the supply of oxygen from the tissues, is proved by the character of the phenomena which precede death, and by the fact that chemical analysis shows that death is immediately subsequent to the exhaustion of the oxygen in the blood. That this is not the result of a mere mechanical exclusion of oxygen from the blood, is proved by the fact that asphyxia may be thus produced notwithstanding the continued presence of an abundance of oxygen in the air that is respired. In this respect the toxic asphyxia that is produced by the directly poisonous effect of carbonic oxide upon the red globules of the blood, is different from the asphyxia that results from respiration of hydrogen or nitrogen, which are inert gases, and which destroy life simply by exclusion of oxygen. Carbonic oxide thus exhibits a certain analogy with nitrous oxide, but it is much more deadly in its effects, owing to the persistence with which it attaches itself to the hæmoglobin of the red corpuscles of the blood. While, therefore, it is slightly anæsthetic, it is powerfully asphyxic, and can never be used for the production of surgical anæsthesia.

CARBONIC ACID GAS—CO_2.

Carbonic anhydride, E. ; *Acidum carbonicum,* L. ; *Acid carbonique,* Fr. ;
Kohlensaüre, G.

Specific gravity of the gas, 1.529.
Specific gravity of the liquid at 0° (32° F.) and under pressure of 38.5 at-
mospheres, 0.83.
Boiling-point, 78° (109° F.).

Carbonic acid, or, more correctly, carbonic anhydride, under ordinary
atmospheric pressure is a colorless, transparent gas, with a slightly acid
taste and smell.   If generated under great pressure it condenses to a liquid
as clear and colorless as water.   When a stream of the liquefied gas is
allowed to escape suddenly, it freezes into a snow-white solid.

Carbonic acid gas is not inflammable, nor will it support combustion.
At ordinary temperatures water will dissolve about its own volume of the
gas.   This quantity may be increased by pressure and by a reduction of
temperature.   Liquid carbonic anhydride does not mix readily with water
or with the fixed oils ; but it is dissolved in all proportions by alcohol,
ether, oil of turpentine, naphtha, and carbonic disulphide (Miller).

This gas is found in nature, abundantly dissolved in the effervescing
waters of certain mineral springs.   In certain regions it issues in the gaseous
form from fissures in the earth.   The celebrated Grotto del Cane is thus
filled with the gas.   The Valley of the Upas Tree is supposed to have owed
its fatality to the presence of carbonic acid gas in its hollows.

The effects of carbonic acid vary somewhat according to the degree of
its concentration.   The undiluted gas causes spasm of the glottis, and does
not enter the lungs.   When injected under the skin of an animal, the gas
produces no injurious effects.   Bernard injected a litre of the gas under the
skin of a rabbit.   After a short time the gas was absorbed, and the creature
seemed to be as well as ever.   Bernard also injected this substance into
the veins without harming the animal.   He also caused the subject of his
experiment to breathe air with one lung and carbonic anhydride with the
other, thus causing the absorption of twelve litres of the gas without injury.
But he found that if all the air of respiration contained carbonic acid to the
amount of ten per cent., normal respiration became impossible.   The animals die from asphyxia if compelled to breathe a mixture of eleven to fourteen parts of carbonic acid with one hundred parts of oxygen (Bert).

The contact of carbonic acid, such as takes place when aërated waters
are swallowed, produces a pungent, prickling sensation in the fauces.
Eructations of the gas produce this sensation in the posterior nares in a
very emphatic manner.   Effervescent wines and beers are more exhilarating than still wines, etc., which contain an equal proportion of alcohol.

The local application of the gas to the cutaneous surfaces of the body
is said to cause redness and prickling where the skin is very thin.   The
functions of the skin are considerably hindered, and animals whose cutaneous respiration is active may be greatly endangered by immersion of their
bodies in the gas.   The sensibility of the surface becomes diminished, and
inflammatory action is retarded.   Carbonated applications, such as yeast
poultices externally, and koumis internally, are. therefore, beneficial in cases
of superficial irritation and inflammation.

Diluted with oxygen, or with the air, carbonic anhydride may be inhaled by man. If it exceed three or four per cent. of the amount that is breathed, disturbance of the nervous system begins to appear. Giddiness, a sense of dyspnœa, muscular weakness, most conspicuous in the legs, increased cardiac movement, succeeded by enfeeblement of the pulse, are the principal symptoms that are caused by respiration of very dilute gas. If the proportion of the gas be increased, respiration becomes more laborious, slow, and shallow. The head aches, the ears ring, the patient falls down in a state of insensibility, the pupils become dilated, and death soon follows. After death the blood is nearly black, and the distinction between arterial and venous blood is abolished. The lungs are engorged with blood, and if death has been preceded by dyspnœa, numerous sub-pleural ecchymoses are visible. The right side of the heart is generally filled with black blood, and the cerebral sinuses and large vessels are similarly occupied. Gradual asphyxia does not produce such marked changes in the distribution of the blood.

Death by carbonic acid is the result of asphyxia. When immersed in undiluted gas, asphyxia is caused by the absence of oxygen from the air of inspiration, and by the retention of carbonic anhydride in the blood. When asphyxia results from inhalation of the diluted gas, death is occasioned by the accumulation of carbonic anhydride in the blood as a consequence of the physical impossibility of its escape into an atmosphere that already contains an excess of the gas.

Carbonic acid is not very powerfully anæsthetic in its effect upon the nervous system. Insensibility is induced before death, but it does not appear until a dangerous degree of asphyxia has developed. Unlike the insensibility that is produced by the action of carbonic oxide, it is speedily removed by filling the lungs with pure air. Poisoning with carbonic oxide may be cured by removal into a normal atmosphere, but the process of recovery is very slow in comparison with the rate of revival after asphyxiation with carbonic acid.

This gas has been proposed as an anæsthetic, and Ozanam has actually employed a mixture of seventy-five parts of the anhydride with twenty-five parts of atmospheric air in an operation upon a young man for the evacuation of an abscess. Latterly, some of the English experimenters have advised the employment of forms of inhaling apparatus which virtually serve to produce partial asphyxia as well as artificial anæsthesia. Such economy of anæsthetics cannot be too strongly condemned.

CARBONIC DISULPHIDE—CS_2.

Bisulphide of carbon, Sulpho-carbonic acid, Disulphide of carbon, E. ; *Carbonei bisulphidum,* L. ; *Sulfure de carbone,* Fr. ; *Schwefelkohlenstoff,* G.

Specific gravity, 1.269 at 15° (59° F.).
Boiling-point, 47.7° (117.8° F.).

Carbonic disulphide is a colorless, mobile liquid, having an agreeable odor when pure, and a pungent aromatic taste. It is often contaminated with impurities which give it an offensive smell, like rotten cabbage. It is quite inflammable, burning with a bluish flame, and depositing free sulphur in a finely divided condition. It is almost insoluble in water, though imparting to that liquid its peculiar taste and smell. It mixes readily with alcohol, ether, and the ethereal and fatty oils. Phosphorus, sulphur, bromine, iodine, caoutchouc, the solid fats, and various other substances, are dissolved by it. It possesses a highly refractive power over light, which renders it useful in the construction of prisms when great dispersive effects are desired. It should contain neither free acid nor sulphur, hence it should not redden blue litmus paper, or blacken a solution of lead acctate.

Hermann found that frogs were affected by this substance in a manner closely resembling the action of chloroform. Upon the higher animals its effects do not materially differ from the effects of other anæsthetic agents. Respiration is at first accelerated and then arrested—a process which is delayed by section of the pneumogastric nerves, indicating an irritation of the pulmonary branches of those nerves, succeeded by a paralysis of their central nuclei. In like manner a brief increase of intra-arterial blood-pressure is followed by its progressive diminution.

Thaulow, Simpson, Miller, Serre, and others, have employed carbon disulphide as an anæsthetic in surgery. Insensibility was readily induced, but was very transitory. It, however, was followed by headache, vomiting, giddiness, and a feeling of great depression.

As an external application for the relief of neuralgia it has been used with some degree of success ; but the disagreeable odor that characterizes most specimens of the article has alone proved sufficient to banish it from the materia medica. The poisonous effects of chronic inhalation of the vapor of carbonic disulphide have been observed on a large scale by Delpech and Poincaré, in manufacturing establishments where it is employed as a solvent for caoutchouc. Its inhalation under such circumstances causes general nervous prostration and cerebral exhaustion.

PUFF-BALL.

Lycoperdon proteus.

The following account is condensed from "The National Dispensatory :" This curious fungus grows upon the roots of fir-trees in the southern United States of America, and also in China. In the South it is known as *Indian bread*, or *tuckahoe*. It is an irregularly globular body, varying from a few inches to a foot or more in diameter, and from a few ounces to several pounds in weight. It is externally of an ashy black, and has a rugose surface ; internally it is whitish, fissured, more or less spongy, but firm, of a somewhat farinaceous appearance, sometimes quite compact, and breaks into irregular masses. It is without odor, and has an insipid taste.

The tuckahoe is generically allied to the common puff-ball (*Lycoperdon bovista*, Lin.) and to the truffle (*Lycoperdon tuber*, Lin.). It is said •to have been used as food by the Indians.

In the year 1853 the attention of Dr. B. W. Richardson having been directed to the fact that the smoke of the common puff-ball had been used by country people for the stupefaction of bees, in order to secure their honey without sacrificing their lives, he conceived the idea that it might be employed as a surgical anæsthetic. He accordingly experimented upon dogs, cats, and rabbits, and in one case he removed a tumor from a dog without discovering any signs of pain during the operation. When a moderate quantity of the smoke was gradually inhaled, anæsthesia appeared and disappeared slowly. The animal exhibited all the symptoms of intoxication, accompanied by convulsions and sometimes by vomiting. Life ceased by degrees ; after the induction of complete insensibility a dog might inhale the fumes for twenty minutes or even half an hour before death occurred. Respiration always ceased before the action of the heart. Examined after death, the lungs were pale ; there was no appearance of congestion in any organ ; the blood retained its red color, but did not coagulate quickly ; cadaveric rigidity set in within two or three hours. During recovery from protracted anæsthesia, the animal would sometimes be quite conscious, although insensible to pain. Herapath made experiments which proved that the gas which is the active agent in producing the preceding phenomena is carbonic oxide. His conclusion, confirmed by Snow, was accepted by Dr. Richardson.

ANÆSTHESIA BY RAPID RESPIRATION.

Dr. W. G. A. Bonwill, a dentist of Philadelphia, and Dr. A. Hewson, of the same city, have written several papers during the past five years, calling attention to a form of insensibility to pain induced by rapid respiration. The subject was recently discussed by the Philadelphia County Medical Society (*Medical Record*, August 21, 1880). According to the experience of Drs. Bonwill and Benjamin Lee, the best method of producing this variety of analgesia is by causing the patient to lie upon the side, with a handkerchief over the eyes in order to avoid distraction of the attention. He is then instructed to breathe about one hundred times a minute, expelling the air by a succession of puffing expirations. After from two to five minutes of this exercise, there is developed a degree of insensibility to pain which may persist for half a minute. The face may at first be somewhat flushed by the effort. According to Dr. Hewson, it afterward becomes pale or somewhat cyanotic. The movements of the heart are accelerated, and the force of the pulse is diminished. Consciousness and the sense of touch are not abolished. After the establishment of this condition a smaller quantity than usual of the ordinary anæsthetic agents is required to produce complete insensibility.

In the production of analgesia by this method, we have an illustration of one of the phenomena of apnœa. When the blood of any animal is overcharged with oxygen by artificial respiration, the irritability of the respiratory centres in the medulla oblongata ceases until an oxygen equilibrium is restored. During this time, if left to itself, the animal does not breathe—the recipient nervous matter in the medulla oblongata is anæsthetized by the surplus oxygen, and no longer responds to the peripheral impulses which ordinarily contribute to the maintenance of respiration. In like manner the receptivity and conductibility of that portion of the nervous matter which is concerned in the transmission of painful impressions is overpowered by the excess of oxygen in the blood. It is probable that all forms of nervous matter share in the anæsthetic effect, but it is in those portions which are related to the sensation and perception of pain that the results of apnœa are most conspicuous.

The condition thus developed by rapid expiration cannot, however, be fully likened to the apnœa that may be induced by artificial respiration in one of the lower animals. Forcible expiration hinders the evacuation of the venous system by its opposition to the return of blood into the thorax. A rapid "puffing" respiration might, therefore, be performed in such a manner as to cause an accumulation of blood in the veins, thus occasioning the incipient phenomena of asphyxia. The more forcible the expiratory efforts, the greater the predominance of the symptoms of venous turgescence. It is, moreover, not impossible that in these cases a condition of hypnotic insensibility to pain may be developed as a result of the concentration of attention upon the act of respiration. That this hypothesis is not without foundation, seems probable from a case related by Dr. Blackford, who, having undertaken the induction of analgesia by this method in the person of an hysterical young woman, found it very difficult to get her to stop after she had once commenced rapid respiration. Had the idea of hypnotism crossed the mind of the doctor, he might possibly have found it an easier matter to control his patient.

ANÆSTHESIA BY ELECTRICITY.

A few years before the reintroduction of nitrous oxide gas by Dr. Colton, the dentists were still experimenting in various ways, seeking for an anæsthetic which should be as potent as chloroform, as safe as ether, and as transitory in its effect as the act of evulsion itself. An American dentist, named J. B. Francis, conceived the idea of employing a current of electricity for this purpose. He accordingly contrived an apparatus by means of which the tooth was grasped with an insulated forceps which formed the negative electrode of an electro-magnetic machine, while the positive electrode was placed in the hand of the patient. As soon as the forceps was applied to the tooth, it was traversed by a current of electricity, and this occasioned complete insensibility to the shock of evulsion.

Numerous experiments with this apparatus were performed in America and Europe. Opinions were considerably divided—some being confident that the true dental anæsthetic had been discovered ; while the majority finally ranged themselves with the President of the London College of Dentists, Mr. Peter Matthews, who declared that, after a long and careful investigation of the subject, he was satisfied that electricity is not an anæsthetic agent. He related (*Med. Times and Gaz.*, p. 412, October 16, 1858) with great precision the details of various cases of extraction of teeth in which he had employed galvanism ; but he explained that, although the result was in some instances modified, he could not admit that in any instance had the pain of extraction been abolished. In certain peculiar cases, where the elastic tissue which connects the tooth with its socket is inflamed and painful, the application of electricity adds to the pain of extraction. Whatever good effect is secured by this method is the result of a diversion of pain rather than a genuine induction of anæsthesia.

INDEX.